Ripp Black
A K A
Rhonda Scudoen

MW01530386

To Spell the
Awakening

Ripp Black

Copyright © 2018 Ripp Black.

All rights reserved. No part of this book may be used or reproduced by
any means, graphic, electronic, or mechanical, including photocopying,
recording, taping or by any information storage retrieval system
without the written permission of the author except in the case of
brief quotations embodied in critical articles and reviews.

This is a work of fiction. All of the characters, names, incidents,
organizations, and dialogue in this novel are either the products
of the author's imagination or are used fictitiously.

LifeRich Publishing is a registered trademark of
The Reader's Digest Association, Inc.

LifeRich Publishing books may be ordered through booksellers or by contacting:

LifeRich Publishing
1663 Liberty Drive
Bloomington, IN 47403
www.liferichpublishing.com
1 (888) 238-8637

Because of the dynamic nature of the Internet, any web addresses or
links contained in this book may have changed since publication and
may no longer be valid. The views expressed in this work are solely those
of the author and do not necessarily reflect the views of the publisher,
and the publisher hereby disclaims any responsibility for them.

Any people depicted in stock imagery provided by Getty Images are
models, and such images are being used for illustrative purposes only.
Certain stock imagery © Getty Images.

ISBN: 978-1-4897-1739-9 (sc)
ISBN: 978-1-4897-1740-5 (hc)
ISBN: 978-1-4897-1741-2 (e)

Library of Congress Control Number: 2018905757

Print information available on the last page.

LifeRich Publishing rev. date: 08/20/2018

To my husband and my children who never fail to believe in me; to each of my family members and friends who have encouraged me, and who needled and cajoled me to follow my writing efforts with seeking publication; to the two critique groups who provided encouragement and guidance; to my late friend Judy for her eternal support; to Danie, Laura, Sharon, and Dirk, who took the time to offer their invaluable critique; to Sue for her wonderful cover art; and to David and Julie for their photographic skills - I love you all!

The circle turns, dance all the way.

Though once returned
we cannot stay.

Ever round and begin again,

Moving on, there is no end.

Prologue

Something bad was coming. The foreboding pricked like tiny needles in the blackest corners of her mind—the corners her Aunt Sidra said might someday give rise to the Sight. Dust stirred from the dirt floor as Caer squirmed, shifting from her knees to her bottom and then back again with a heavy sigh. She didn't want such an attribute as the Sight. Not unless it manifests as fully as it did for her aunt. Awareness of dark things to come without being able to name them... Caer's lower lip shoved forward in a pout. The Sight was most frightening when it warned without showing the threat. Unless she saw the bad things, she had no way to avoid them; no way to prepare if she couldn't avoid. If the Sight was to be hers, she wanted to know the details, as Sidra did. Her pout settled to a frown. Sidra knew everything.

Rising, Caer turned enough to peer over the stone bench, her knees smudging the words scrawled on the floor. She afforded them a brief downward glance, one brow cocked. Incomplete--the words to the spell she was to memorize. They simply would not stay in her head. Not with the prickling unease chasing them out. Not with her focus persistently drawn to her aunt, who stood like a granite slab before the low fire in the pit at the room's heart. Sidra saw what was coming. She refused to speak of it, though, other than to say there would be a disturbance in the village tonight. Trouble is what her aunt meant. A lot of trouble.

The room's single electric light flickered, the distant grinding hum indicating the powering down of the massive generators located just outside of Lillith II's domed colony. Soon the light would go out altogether, the generators settling to their limited night-time task of scrubbing and circulating the air. For the colonists the night's warmth came from the residual heat accumulated beneath the dome during the generators' daytime functioning and from the small cooking fires inside their homes. Normally Caer liked this time of the evening. No eyes peering at them with a mix of curiosity and suspicion. No whispers behind their backs. Evening was the time dedicated to Caer's study of herbs, medicinal preparations, and minor healing spells, Sidra at her side encouraging and guiding her. It was also the time she and her aunt could share their meal along with their laughter over events of the day.

Caer sucked a slow breath, her fingers fidgeting with her delicate silver chain necklace. This evening was different. Dinner was not cooking. And her lesson was nothing more than a foolish enchantment to set the room's shadows to dancing. What purpose was there in that, aside from keeping her out of her aunt's way?

For several long minutes, she studied Sidra. Waited for her to move. The woman remained utterly motionless, staring into the embers of the smoldering fire. Her prolonged silence coupled with the severity of her expression was as troubling as Caer's prickles. It set her to twisting her necklace around a finger so tightly that it hurt. Wincing, she sagged back down to her haunches, glaring at the offended digit as if it were somehow responsible for the foreboding that nagged at her; somehow responsible for her aunt's peculiar behavior. If Sidra would just stop whatever it was she was doing and say something. For the fleetest of moments, Caer thought to break the silence by calling out. Her mouth clamped shut against the urge. It was never wise to distract Sidra. Not when she worked with magic. Especially when the spell exuded such power.

Across the room, the electric light blinked out, leaving only the fire for illumination. Caer slipped from her knees, settling to one hip as she tried to focus on other matters. Picking up a fistful of dirt, she watched it sift between her fingers. It wasn't like this on the massive perimeter ship where she'd lived with her parents. The ship had plenty of light. Plenty of warmth, too. Everything clean and shiny. Caer shivered, and not just from the growing night time chill. Truth was, as much as she loved her aunt, she missed the perimeter ship. Missed the people, including the aliens. Missed her parents most of all.

Venting a soul-deep whimper, she glanced back over her shoulder toward the pit. The fire remained low, allowing for deepening shadows around the circumference of the room. Sidra made no move to stoke it, despite the fact they had more than an ample supply of the imported pellets. Instead, the woman remained as she had been, as unmoving as the massive cliffs surrounding their dome, tension radiating from her. The feel of it, along with the charge of the building magic, reinforced Caer's awareness of the uneasiness that troubled her mind, its dark brooding now raising fine bumps along her flesh. Once more she rose to her knees, this time scooting to the bench and propping her folded arms on it as she glowered at her aunt. Shadows played across Sidra's slender, stooped frame, the glow from the sparking embers highlighting her aged and deeply tanned features and affording the white of her long pants and tunic a faintly yellow cast. The woman's long sleeves and loose pant legs fluttered slightly in the air currents, wisps of smoke curling around her before lifting to disappear through the soot-stained opening in the center of their hut's metal roof.

Gradually, the sound of Sidra's whispered chant drifted out from the background hissing and crackle of the fire. Caer struggled to understand the words. Success raised an even greater chill. She knew this incantation. Well, she didn't exactly know it. It was one of many in her aunt's Book of Secrets. Not that Caer was supposed to be privy to that. Sidra rarely brought the book out, and then only to share some simple healing spell. Caer discovered its hiding place, though, when a stone at the base of the wall in their small sleeping room worked loose. Since then, she removed it whenever the opportunity arose. She loved pouring through the crisp pages, careful not to tear them, taking in the smell of the paper and ink, wondering when her aunt had time to write in it. So many spells, most so complex she couldn't begin to guess their purpose. Naturally, she took exceeding care to replace the tome exactly as she'd found it before Sidra returned from her errand of the day.

Of all the book's spells, charms, and enchantments, as well as its recipes for all manner of herbal remedies, the piece of magic Caer found most intriguing was the one Sidra now whispered, though it was among those whose purpose eluded her. Its tremendous power, however, did not. Merely reading the words caused Caer's nerves to twitch and set every hair on her body to stand on end. Now, with the enchantment softly murmured in the confines of their hut, the very air felt on the verge of igniting.

Licking a fingertip, Caer began tracing the opening words on the bench. Abred. Gwynfyd. Ceugant. These were common enough. Struggle. Purity. Infinity. They prefaced many magical endeavors, helping clear the mind, allowing greater focus. She continued her tracing. 'May my summons find and fill you. Know my need as I call out to you. Hear me and... The damp letters suddenly shimmered, glowing thin and fiery. Caer jerked her hand from the bench, shoving it behind her back as she shot a nervous glance at her aunt in time to see the flames within the pit flare briefly, sparking from yellow to crimson and causing the room's shadows to lurch.

Caer's sense of foreboding redoubled, searing sharp stabs through her mind. Her tucked hand shot back to her necklace, grasping it in a white-knuckled clutch. It wasn't that she was afraid. She repeated that thought. Repeated it again as the shadows lengthened and darkened, renewing the icy bite that ate along her bones. Not afraid of the spell. Not afraid of what was coming. Sidra wouldn't let anything bad happen. Not here. Their hut was protected. Shielded by magic. Caer's hands shifted to her pant legs, twisting them back and forth between her fingers, leaving smears of dust on the dark brown weaver's cloth. Alright. Maybe she was a little scared.

The sudden crackle of charged air drew a small squeak from her, even as it shot the flames high once more, glowing angry bright and flooding the room with heat. Swallowing a more pronounced whimper, Caer stood and edged her way to the end of the bench; slipped around it; moved closer to her aunt. All the while, her hands gripped and released, gripped and released her pant legs. Again, the flames fell briefly back, only to erupt once more, their hungry tongues lapping near the ceiling. So great was their heat and brilliance that it staggered Caer backward, her pants snagging on the bench's rough edges as she dropped onto it, her eyes snapping shut.

When she blinked them open again, she discovered her aunt's stance was no longer stooped, though the woman maintained a tense vigilance as a form began to take shape within the dancing blaze. The quiet with which her aunt regarded the dark shape eased Caer's fright a little, her frown giving way to a concentrated, brow-furrowing study of the emerging figure. In another blinding flash, Sidra's spell discharged the last of its energy. And there he was, draped in a long black cloak, and standing smack in the middle of the once again smoldering fire pit, as solid and real as Sidra. He had to be a 'he' because he was positively the tallest person Caer had ever encountered. Pale, slender hands drew the hood of his cloak back, allowing fitful firelight to play across his features. Caer sucked in, gaping. Yellow-white hair framed the slight angularity of a strikingly chiseled and clean-shaven face, the whole of which was set off by the bluest eyes she had ever seen.

"Sidra," the strange man acknowledged, stepping from the diminished flames. The toss of the front edges of his cloak back over his shoulders revealed his burnished bronze shirt and brown trousers, both of which shown with a faint metallic luster. Even his snug, knee-high boots held a gloss, despite the fine layer of ash across their toes. "You wish my assistance," he stated, his tone hard-edged as he offered a low bow.

"Stoirm," Sidra replied with an equal edge, her posture now perfectly erect.

Caer chewed at her upper lip, a hand swiping a dirty smudge across her nose as she regarded their visitor. Should she dislike this man? She didn't want to. Her heart said, "friend". But here he was, manifesting from the fire just as some sort of trouble brewed within their village. Was he the cause of it, then? If so, Sidra would surely scold him severely and send him away.

The stranger cast her a brief glance, though in it Caer sensed a familiarity quite at odds with his question. "This is the child?"

"You know it is," Sidra returned. "You are aware of what is about to transpire, here?"

"I know you and the child are in grave danger. I am prepared to take you both from this place immediately."

"If I wished to leave, I'd have done so of my own accord, already."

"So you persist in saying whenever I offer you escape."

"I stand by my oath," Sidra declared in a tone that suggested she'd repeated those words, as well. "As firmly as you stand by yours." She hesitated for barely a heartbeat, her eyes skimming toward Caer. "My only sorrow is that I shall not see her grown to womanhood."

"Then it is the child I take."

Caer popped from the bench, stretching to stand as tall as she could. No one was taking her away. Not from the only person she had left in the whole of the universe. She was no 'child' to be carried off just because some trouble or other was about to disturb their village. Whatever was coming, she was staying right where she was. Right where she belonged. With her aunt! Her lips parted to declare as much, her pronouncement abruptly stifled by Sidra's piercing gray gaze and her telepathed warning for Caer to hold her tongue.

The man turned his scrutiny to Caer, his stern expression relaxing. "You are quite brave, little one. But this is no place for you."

So captivating was the sudden gentleness of his words that Caer's full attention was once more on this man with the striking features. Topaz, she decided. His eyes were the color of topaz. Most remarkable, though, were his ears. No human she had ever seen had ears that curled delicately into a point at their tops. A few aliens had such ears.

Her face wrinkled as she tried to remember the stories. There was a name for people like this man. The Alainn, she thought. Yes! That's what her mother called them. The Alainn. It meant The Beautiful. Of course, Caer had never really believed the stories her mother told. Of all the alien races who'd peopled or visited the perimeter ship, none had ever resembled her mother's description of the Alainn. Not the way this man did. In truth, few aliens looked anything like humans. Most had odd colors and textures to their skins and not the right number of arms or legs.

Sidra extended a hand, motioning Caer forward. "Come, dear."

Stoirm cocked a brow at her as she approached. "She is so young. Seven? Eight, perhaps? I seem to have lost my grasp of human years. I thought her older."

"Family trait," Sidra huffed. "You can't have forgotten how small our firstborn females are."

Caer stopped part way to her aunt's side, her arms folded as she stamped a foot. "Don't talk about me like I'm not here. I am nearly twelve. I'm old enough to be included."

Stoirm's chuckle rippled softly. "Are you indeed? You are certainly old enough to speak your mind."

As Caer opened her mouth, Sidra looked about to warn her to silence again. Stoirm waved her off. "The girl is correct. This discussion concerns her. She should be included." Nodding toward the bench, he offered, "Come sit with me for a moment, child."

"My name is Caer!" she rumbled back. "And I will sit with you only if you introduce yourself."

Caer heard her aunt's low moan. "I have addressed him, already. You know his name."

"Yes. But he hasn't been properly introduced to me. I'm not to talk to strangers. You always tell me that."

The man bowed. "My name is Stoirm. Storm, if you prefer. It

means the same." He waited for Caer to move past and seat herself on the bench before he straightened.

Caer breathed out slowly, patting the bench to indicate that she granted him permission to join her. "Storm. So, are you the cause of the trouble that's coming? And why do you keep looking at me like you know me? And if you do know me, why did you ask if...." The next rolled off her tongue in the most distasteful manner possible. "...if I was 'the child'?"

"Ah," Stoirm exhaled, his face serious, though his eyes glinted his amusement. "Because I have made your acquaintance once before. You were scarcely toddling at the time. I'm not surprised you have no memory of the occasion." His amusement dissolved, grave solemnity now infecting his eyes as well as his face. "Tell me, Caer. Have you learned of your family lineage?"

Caer darted a questioning glance to her aunt. "What does he mean?"

"She has been taught the family's beginnings and understands how we differ from the Tanai. She also understands that our secret must be kept."

The beginning of the Witches. Yes. She knew the stories. Their origin lay in a past so distant Caer could scarcely imagine it, and from ordinary Tanai—humans who possessed no ability with magic. From the Tanai, a family emerged with the first whisper of the gifts. Over time, their gifts grew in number and in strength. Witches, they were named. The Tanai, the 'Shallow' ones, feared them, hunting and murdering them for centuries. Now Witches kept their secrets so well-guarded that most Tanai no longer believed in such things.

Stoirm turned Caer's face to his, and for several long seconds stared deep into her eyes, making her fidgety. It was like he was looking straight into her thoughts. She didn't like such scrutiny. Her mother had done that often enough, as did Sidra. Her thoughts were hers. No one else had any right to them. Setting her jaw, she shoved her fists to her hips and glared back at the man, screwing her face to look every bit as severe. Maybe she could look into his thoughts. Stoirm, however, gave no sign that he noticed. Maddening how adults could leave her feeling so insignificant, and she couldn't get back at them!

"She will keep the secret," he said at last. "There is a little more that she should know, though."

They were talking around her again. Caer gave a disgruntled growl, assuming an even sterner glower. "Know what more?"

Stoirm grinned. He thought her funny. The knowledge further rankled her, prompting another low rumble.

Leaning toward her conspiratorially, he whispered, "I am your... distant, shall we say. Your distant uncle."

Caer drew back from him, her ire lost in the revelation. "You?" Turning, she accosted her aunt with, "What is a 'distant' uncle? I mean, he must live very far away, but...." Waggling an accusatory finger, she added, "You never told me I had any uncles!" Turning back, she stretched to reach for Stoirm's nearest ear, running a finger up to its point. "And I didn't know I had any relatives with such... such wonderful ears! Are the stories true, then? Did my great, great, great...." She stopped long enough to count on her fingers, then shrugged and went on. "...grandmother really marry an Alainn? Do I have other relatives like you? Why don't my ears look like yours?"

Stoirm nodded. "The stories are true, though it's unlikely you shall ever meet others of your Alainn relatives. They distanced themselves from humans many an age ago." Rising, he gave her nearest ear a gentle flick. "And these are perfect just as they are." His gaze shifted to Caer's necklace, lingering but half a heartbeat. Offering his hand, he jerked his head in Sidra's direction. "Shall we?"

Caer accepted his hand, the two of them returning to where her aunt stood.

Stoirm's features again hardened, his scrutiny now set on Sidra. "You realize what is at stake if you refuse to leave with me. You must be aware that Croi Breag is on the move, once more. She is searching." His head tilted ever so slightly toward Caer. "She will stop at nothing until she has either captured and rejoined both pieces of the key or has found her sisters."

Sidra's eyes narrowed. "There has been no legitimate sighting of that one since..."

Stoirm cut her off with a snarl. "We have had sightings, and worse. Her violent tendencies have not lessened, and her strength has grown. Surely you see the need for you and the child to come away from here. We can ill afford to lose either of you."

The discolored circles beneath Sidra's eyes and the returned slump to her shoulders suggested the weight of her fatigue. "I know all too well the ways of The Dark Heart. My gift, however, has shown me that I remain here."

Stoirm's jaw twitched. "Then I must content myself with taking the girl."

Caer jerked her hand free of Stoirm's, her face drained of warmth, her eyes wide. "No! I'm not going anywhere with you. Not unless Aunt Sidra comes, too."

"There!" Stoirm snorted. "Will you not do as is necessary for her sake?"

For a long moment, Sidra's pained expression remained, her gaze fixed on Caer. At last, turning again to Stoirm, she sighed, "I've given you my answer."

"You will be lost to us forever. You know that."

"There is a chance that I may survive."

The dire urgency of Caer's persistent foreboding seared anew across her nerves, twisting her stomach. Grasping for her aunt's age darkened and wrinkled hands, Caer clutched them desperately. She couldn't lose Sidra. She wouldn't! They did important things together, growing and harvesting herbs and preparing medicines for the people of Lillith II. The colonists would not allow anything to happen to them, despite their whisperings and odd stares. This 'distant' uncle of hers would see. Whatever trouble might come, the colonists would protect them.

With a grating rumble, Stoirm dismissed Sidra and reached for Caer. She dodged him, slipping behind her aunt.

"I don't think you can pry her from me at this moment," Sidra moaned. "She has a will of her own. Another family trait, I fear. And I have seen that she also remains."

Stoirm's glare bore down on Sidra. "So. If I'm not to take either of you from this foul place, just what is it that you wish of me?"

Sidra squared her shoulders, meeting Stoirm's frigid stare with hardened calm. "She will agree to leave once tonight's events are played out. Arrangements have been made for her to be taken immediately to Heshton. See to a guardian for her. Yours is the only judgement I trust in this matter."

Caer opened her mouth to object. Her words, however, were lost to a sudden flood of vertigo as a vision of roiling smoke and flame erupted. In that briefest of moments, her first true brush with full Sight stilled her heart and froze her breath in her lungs. A glimpse only, but it was a glimpse of terror she wished she had never witnessed.

The spell is cast and calls me to sleep.
Hiding the secret the spell holds deep.
Those who remember yet do they weep,
For the loss of the hidden bound in my keep.

1

Emptiness. Thick. Dark. Suffocating. Muffled words intruded; gradually clarified. Someone repeating her name. Shadowed light broke through. The impression of a face flicked briefly. Was clouded out. Reappeared.

Blinking, forehead knotting so tightly an ache crept along the creases, Caer at last willed the world into focus. Though the effort made her head ring, she managed to recognize Jenna Randon's steady brown-eyed gaze studying her from across the small table. Jenna's quick smile highlighted the sweetly rounded face beneath the spiked blond hair. "There you are. Welcome back."

Sounds and smells assaulted Caer--music and laughter, clanking glasses, and scuffling feet, the thick smoke from the too-sweet hybern leaf mingled with stale beer and strong liquor. For several moments, she struggled to recall where she was. Only when her fuzzy vision cleared did she recognize the interior of the High Fancies Club. Teetering from the jolt of vertigo brought on by her head movement, she grabbed the edges of the chair's seat. She was sitting. Why was she sitting? She seemed to recall dancing.

"You passed out, dear," Jenna provided.

"I..." Caer's tongue made a brief foray across her dry lips. "What?"

"Passed out." Jenna gestured toward the dance floor at the center of the club, where a cluster of six humans and two humanoid,

1

chameleon-skinned Zandaks were attempting to move in cadence with the music. The taller, thinner of the Zandaks, Lyrra, was flushing between dark gray and dark blue as she moved through the shadows cast by the cheap wall-mounted lights.

Caer sucked on her lower lip as she watched her fellow dancers. Each appeared to struggle with her newest offering of step sequences. The music had changed from when she was out there, but the same rhythm carried in the medley of tunes sounding from the ceiling. One, two, three, four, five, six, seven. One, two, three. One, two, three. So simple. So clear.

She realized she was staring at the dancers when Lyrra smiled and waved. Caer's face warmed, her gaze turning to a hesitant scan of the rest of her surroundings. The crowd was larger, now, than when she and her friends arrived. It must be evening, already. The warmth of her face renewed as she wondered how many of those now filling the room had witnessed her little fainting episode.

A dark russet-skinned Renthorian two tables down caught her eye. He was one of the largest Caer had ever seen. The broad triangular head and the coarse, shaggy hair of the same russet hue as his skin produced a particularly brutish look, even for his kind. Noting he had her attention, he gestured with two of his six arms. One swept toward the dancers, the other jerked a clawed hand toward his fleshy face, his yellow eyes squinting in a feigned swoon. The drinks he held in the two gesticulating hands slopped about, adding to his mirth as he burst into what she could only assume was raucous laughter, though it sounded more like the crushing of massive wooden barrels. Across the table from him, the smaller, brown, reptilian-skinned Caspian rocked back and forth, his narrow, oblong head swaying in sync with his short barking snorts.

Caer's face flushed even hotter.

"Don't mind them," Jenna consoled. "They're drunk."

Caer scarcely heard her friend. The music drummed out all else, the world clouding again as flashes of imagery gripped her. Flames.

Dense, dark smoke. Something more. Something.... Cold terror brought a sharp inhalation.

"Hey! Don't you go blacking out on me again!"

The vision promptly dissolved, leaving Caer to blink at her friend once more, her body trembling from the lingering sense of horror. Jenna's smile was gone, her gaze penetrating. "What's happening inside that head of yours?"

Before Caer could squeeze a response past her tightened throat, Brandon Jase's gravelly, "You wanted these?" startled her so severely she nearly toppled from her chair. One hand pressed to her pounding chest, she shot a glare at him as he strode around her to thud a couple of glasses down in front of Jenna. "You sure you want to drink two of these poisons?"

"Took your time," Jenna snipped, though she grabbed the front of Brandon's shirt and tugged him down far enough to plant a serious kiss on his mouth. "And these aren't both for me, silly. Here." Scooting one of the drinks to Caer, she grinned, "This should bring you back to life."

"Or kill her," Brandon harrumphed, straightening. For a moment he remained standing, his silent study of Caer adding to her unease. At last pulling a chair from a neighboring table, he plopped down between the two women, his arms folded across his thick chest. Sweaty brown hair fringed his forehead, accenting the scowl that seemed permanently affixed to his countenance. "Wanna tell me what happened out there?"

Caer managed a shrug, her hands trying to still her jittery knees. "Fainted. Apparently."

"You know our silly little marsh puff," Jenna put in. "Spends way too much time working. Weeks on end locked away in her apartment or her office cubicle at the university, going through libraries of articles and research material, taking notes, fussing with this or that theory concerning some vague ancient Earth culture. Today she gets the urge to exercise. Can't do anything simple, though, like taking a quiet stroll around the campus. Oh no. Thinks she has to dance.

Worse, she dives right into one of the most intricate dances in her repertoire. Little wonder the exertion got to her."

Even though she refused to meet them, Caer could feel Brandon's dubious gray eyes watching her. "I didn't buy that line when you fed it to the others, Jen. I don't buy it, now."

Jenna smiled and batted her eyes. "Nonbeliever!" Rocking forward, she pecked a kiss on his cheek. "You picked up Caer's latest step sequences pretty well. Can't say the same for most of the others out there. Why don't you go on back? I'm sure at least one of those ladies would appreciate your assistance."

Caer ventured a sideward glance in time to catch Brandon's curled lip and had to swallow a tenuous giggle. As much as Bran enjoyed her dances, he wanted only Jen for a partner.

"Oh, go on," Jen persisted. "Be a sport. The other ladies don't bite. We have some girl talk to do, here."

"Girl talk!" Brandon's glance darted between Jen and Caer. "Sharing secrets, more like." Pushing to his feet, he stalked away, muttering, "Just make sure your 'girl talk' isn't about me."

Jen waited for Brandon to make his way to the dance floor before gesturing to the glass in front of Caer. "Drink up, dearie. You need it."

Caer responded with a reluctant sigh, downing the liquid in a single gulp. Instantly, she was bent over, sputtering and coughing. Part of the drink singed her nasal passages and throat, while more ran down her chin. Fumbling a napkin from the sticky table, she wiped at the dribbles, choking, "What the!"

"Cantorian gin. Couldn't afford the real stuff from Earth. This is passable enough, though. So long as you don't try to breathe it. At least you're getting your color back."

Gasping, Caer wheezed, "The color is...is from being...roasted from the inside out! That...wasn't nice!"

Jen leaned back in her chair, shaking her head. "Neither was scaring us."

Caer tried to fix her friend through tearing eyes. Wiping them with the back of her sleeve, she strangled, "Scaring you?"

"Out there." Jenna nodded toward the dancers again. "You froze and went positively ashen. Looked like...like... I don't know. Like you'd seen your own death or something. And then you crumpled to a lump on the floor. I don't think anyone besides Bran and I noticed your expression, thank heavens. Otherwise, you might have caused a stampede of idiots running from the universe only knows what. Bran carried you back here." Leaning forward, Jen whispered, "So, what did happen out there?"

Caer's hesitation gave way to a shrug. "I had a dream. I think." Shoving the empty glass aside, she thumped her forearms on the tabletop, leaning wearily against them. "A dream. A vision. I must have fallen asleep."

"Fallen asleep while dancing? So, you've gone narcoleptic?" Getting no reply, Jen scooted around to the chair Brandon had vacated. "Come on, dearie. Truth. It was the same dream that always haunts you, wasn't it? All smoke and fire and such?"

Annoyed, Caer waved off her friend's questions with a curt. "I don't remember."

"It was! So, what was burning? What keeps scaring the eternal twilight out you?"

"I told you before. I never recall anything more than flames and...and..."

"Stark terror," Jen finished for her. Leaning back, she sipped at her drink for several uncomfortably silent seconds. "You know," she said at last. "Bran thinks you possess some sort of psychic ability. Thinks you're one of those...'individuals' who can do weird stuff. Like seeing into the future."

The statement raised the hairs along Caer's flesh. "Don't be ridiculous. There's no such thing. What in the universe have you been telling him to give him such an idiotic notion?"

"Nothing, dearie. He based his conclusion solely on his own observations."

"Observations?" Caer glared across the room to where Brandon was patiently demonstrating the steps for a couple of the dancers. "What's he been doing? Following me?"

"More like trailing behind you when you cross the campus between classes. Says that sometimes you veer off from your usual route to take a more meandering path."

"I like to vary the scenery."

Jen pursed her lips, staring into her drink. "He says..."

"What? He says what?"

Jen regarded her obliquely. "Says every time you do, something ugly takes place somewhere along your usual route. Like when that group of drunken students gathered on the grounds right where you normally walk. You know the time. When the idiots confronted some off-worlders and stirred up quite the fight. That was when Bran inserted himself between the two groups to try and break them up and was stabbed several times for his efforts. You missed the whole business because only moments before, you abruptly back-stepped a pace or two and headed another direction. That's what Bran said, anyway. And then there was the time he narrowly escaped the crash of one of the university's utility vehicles when some fool tried to override its guidance system as a prank. You took a sudden turn off-path that time, too. The pod missed him because he paused to see which direction you were going. He thinks that...that somehow you know what's about to happen and change course to avoid the trouble. He thinks you're afraid others will figure out what you're capable of, so you keep mostly to yourself."

"Well, you can tell Brandon that he's suffering from an over-sized imagination. Unexpected stuff happens. Sometimes people get hurt. My decision to take a different route a couple of times was nothing more than dumb luck."

"Brandon? Overly imaginative?" Jen snorted a short laugh. "Hardly! Nor was it merely a couple of times, Caer. And that doesn't even count that business in the library archives your first year here, when that sinkhole opened beneath the foundation, causing both a collapse and a gas explosion. Without your forewarning, you and Bran might have been blown apart...or fallen to your deaths...or...or been crushed in the rubble."

Caer rubbed her arms, the newly raised flesh running from her fingertips all the way up the back of her neck. "We've been through that a hundred times. I must have heard the cracking and reacted. As for my limited social outings, it's certainly not because I'm trying to hide some ridiculously insane ability. I stay in my apartment or my office because I need to finish my thesis. Simple as that. When my application to Sion finally goes through, I want to be able to leave here with my completed thesis in hand. Besides, if I had some ability to foretell the future, I'd be able to figure out why my transfer applications continually go missing, wouldn't I?"

"So... We aren't going to wake up tomorrow to find that something terrible happened at the university that would have wiped you out had you stayed on campus?"

Caer tossed her hands up in exasperation. "You are unbelievable! I told you when I called and asked you and Bran to meet me here this afternoon why I needed to get away. I simply couldn't stand another minute of listening to those damned compu-lectures."

A grin played at the corners of Jen's mouth. "Couldn't stand another minute in the offices without Dr. Jorn present, you mean." She took another moment to sip at her drink, obviously enjoying Caer's red face. "Fine," she chuckled. "Have it your way. I can't argue with the mind-dulling effect of those bloody computerized holographic lectures. And maybe you did pass out from exhaustion out there. Still." Her expression sobered. "The look on your face, Caer, coupled with the dream you say you had. You saw something that terrified you. What if Bran is right? What if these visions are warnings?"

"They are nightmares. Nothing more," Caer muttered. "Nightmares scare everyone."

"Only this one hit you while you were awake and active."

Reaching irritably for her drink, Caer remembered that she'd emptied it. Furthermore, the table had quite the collection of drained glasses. "Aiyee," she groaned. "Tell me I didn't finish off all those by myself."

"Certainly not. Bran and I helped."

"Doesn't matter," Caer huffed, gesturing at the table. "Here's why I passed out. Way too many rum fizzies."

"Actually," Jen giggled. "There were a few brandy shots as well."

"And you topped that off by trying to poison me with that last drink?"

"I was not trying to poison you! Not my fault you tried to inhale the gin." Jen paused for a moment, sipping her drink again. "Know what I think?"

"No. But I'm sure I'm about to find out."

"I think this little fainting spell and all your scary dreams may be symptoms of your subconscious telling you how stupid it is for you to transfer to Earth. What you need is a long holiday so that you can contemplate just how good life is here. I'm sure if you told Dr. Jorn, he'd grant you some time off to reconsider."

Caer glowered at her friend. "I am not telling Dr. Jorn anything of the sort."

Jenna straightened, her eyes glinting with mischief. "I'll tell him for you!"

"You will not! I'll tell Brandon that you have a crush on the professor if you even look like you're going to talk to him."

"No news, there, dearie. Every female and a good many of the males on Ahira have a crush on Dr. Hugh Jorn. Bran thinks it's ridiculous, of course. But then, I don't suppose Dr. Jorn is his type."

"But you think he's yours," Caer accused.

Grin broadening, Jen needled, "Just like you think he's your type. I've seen the way you watch him when you think he's not looking. I'm surprised you manage to work on your thesis at all when he's around. As it is, you tend to go all dreamy-eyed and swoony every time you pass him in the halls."

Caer's face went hot again. Droplets splatted out between her fingers as she slapped the table with her open palm. "I do not!"

"Do too. Don't worry, dearie. Dr. Jorn takes no more notice of you than he does any of the rest of us. Consider, though. There will be zero chance of you ever gaining his attention if you transfer."

Caer's jaw jutted forward, her sticky hand swiping across her pant leg as she sought for some snappy comeback. None came to mind. Instead, the slight change in music drew her attention back to the dance floor. Same rhythm as before. Only the melody had changed again. Brandon and Lyrra were now partnered and had joined three other couples to make a square set, dancing one of the simpler jig-time pattern dances that Caer had previously taught them. Bran handled both the steps and the figures with reasonable ease. Sadly, the only thing Lyrra and at least two of the others were executing was any hope that their movements could be construed as a dance. Caer marveled at their seeming inability to find the rhythm. Especially with such a distinct beat to follow. One, two, three, four, five, six, seven. One, two, three. One, two, three. So obvious. So compelling. So...

"Hey!"

Caer jumped, banging her knees on the underside of the table.

"I told you not to go fainting on me again. Not twice in the same day," Jenna commanded. "Maybe you are narcoleptic. Wouldn't surprise me, given the hours you keep. Time to send you home, I think. That way, should you decide to fall on your face unconscious again, you can jolly well do so into your own bed. Or at least on your own floor." Tugging her sleeve up, she tapped the communicator on her gold wristband. "Send public pod to High Fancies Club at 231 NE, sector 7. Passenger is Caer DaDhrga. Destination is student housing complex, sector 4, quarters 109."

"Pod 628 responding. Arrival at High Fancies Club in approximately five minutes," whined back at her.

Jenna tapped her communicator again, waving in Brandon's direction and then pointing at the speakers. He nodded and excused himself from the dance floor, drawing another dancer in to take his place. A few moments later, the music changed to something contemporary and annoyingly raucous. Reappearing, Bran strode across the room and flipped a small disc to the table. "Your music chip. You leaving?"

"Yes, she is," Jenna confirmed, snatching the disc and tucking it into the breast pocket on Caer's jumpsuit. "She's going straight home and to bed. Isn't that right?"

Caer considered arguing but dismissed the effort as a waste of energy.

"And stop thinking of going to Earth," Jen added. "Maybe you can get through the night without incurring more bad dreams."

"Earth is not the cause of my nightmares."

"It would be if it were me looking to transfer. The very idea of venturing to that den of insanity is enough to scare any rational person right out of their shoes and cause their brains to puddle."

"I'm not asking you to go with me."

"Good thing, too. I love ya, honey, but not enough to follow you to that crazy place."

"Well," Caer sniffed. "Can you two at least agree to go with me to breakfast tomorrow?"

Jen nodded. "Just you and me, though."

Caer looked up at Brandon. "Not you?"

A frown darkened his features. "I'm leaving in the morning. Going home for a visit."

"Home?" Caer exchanged a perplexed glance with Jen. Brandon rarely spoke of his home. When he did, he was quite emphatic about never going back.

Noting the exchange, Bran surrendered, "I recently became an uncle. Sis wants me to come and meet the little guy. So..."

Caer didn't know how to react. The news should be exciting, but Bran's continued frown indicated otherwise. "Congratulations," she ventured. "That's fantastic news!"

Brushing the matter off, Brandon extended a hand. "Come on. We'll walk you out. Want to make sure you at least get as far as the pod. After that, you're on your own for the night."

2

Caer slipped into the pod with a huff, grateful to be out of the vehicle's backdraft; even more so to be away from Bran and Jen. Their escort to the landing pad was unnecessary, even considering the fuzziness of her brain. Moreover, it was embarrassing. She hated all the eyes that followed them as they left the club, Brandon on one side of her, Jen on the other. Shooting a glance back toward the edge of the lighted pad, she noted that both were still watching her. They'd better not decide to escort her all the way home! Thankfully, Jen merely waved and blew her a kiss, then took Bran's hand and led him back inside the club.

The weight of Caer's relieved sigh blended with the mild grinding sound of the pod door as it closed. A minor ache in her knees and ankles provided forewarning that her joints were beginning to stiffen. Slumping back against the cracked upholstery of the seat, she muttered at her discomfort. Too much dancing on the heels of too many days of sitting on her backside stewing over her thesis. She'd be lucky if she could pry herself out of the pod by the time she got home. Maybe she could just have it tip on its side and let her roll out.

"Is the passenger ready?"

"Oh. Yes, of course." Turning her gaze upward, she stared into the silver-blue retinal scanner mounted just above the door.

"Identity verified for passenger Caer DaDhrga," the pod intoned. "Destination student housing, sector 4, unit 109."

"Correct."

"Departing."

A vague wash of unease prompted Caer's glance from the window as the pod jerked into its gradual ascent. Within the darkness beyond the lighted landing, three deeper shadows moved. Two slunk toward the alley between the club and its neighboring building, the other stalked predator-like toward the light. Aliens, all, judging from their shape and size. Caer guessed one of the twosome to be Renthorian-- possibly the one who'd laughed at her earlier. The second she couldn't begin to determine. Its greater mass and hunched lope matched nothing she knew.

The third, solitary figure, hesitated at the edge of the lesser shadows that bordered the well-lit landing pad. Only when it lumbered out did Caer recognize the creature as human. The features were barely discernable--fleshy face, eyes either lost in the folds or squinting against the dust. Even so, she had little doubt of the gender. Standing with his feet braced, his face upturned, the man seemed to sniff the air as he watched her lifting transport. Caer marveled at his stupidity, trundling forward to stand in the hot backdraft that swirled dust and debris around him. Not that he was likely to be blown off his feet. A fusion bomb might do nothing more than simply rock a person of such monumental girth.

The needling unease grew as she continued to stare down at him. Perhaps this was supposed to have been his ride, too. The thought sent pin pricks along her arms. Courtesy, of course, dictated she direct the pod to return for him. Her mouth opened, the raised hair at the back of her neck cutting her short. No. She was already on her way. The man would just have to wait for another vehicle. His fault for not meeting the pod at the scheduled time. Still, she could not take her eyes from him until distance, at last, obscured him. Rubbing her arms, Caer attempted to settle again, closing her eyes against the subtle mix of foreboding, the growing ache in her joints, a creeping headache, and the occasional flash of lights from other passing vehicles. Too much dancing. Too much alcohol. Too little sleep.

"Message for Caer DaDhrga."

Her brow knotted, though her eyes remained closed. Who would be trying to contact her, now? For that matter, who, besides Jen and Bran, even knew where to find her? "Deliver."

"Dr. Hugh Jorn requests a meeting with you."

One eyebrow edged up a tick. "Dr. Jorn is off world and not expected back until the middle of next week. Tell Jenna Randon that I'm not in the mood for any of her pranks. She insisted I go straight home, and that's precisely what I intend to do."

"No Jenna Randon associated with the message."

Caer straightened, her eyes opening with a renewed cock of her brow. Even assuming Dr. Jorn had returned, why would he want to meet with her at this hour? And why would he not send his message via her communicator? A glance at the thin silver band on her wrist brought a grimace. She'd turned her communicator off when she left the university campus earlier in the day. A tap of it produced a double beep as Dr. Jorn's name scrolled across its tiny face. The first day in ages that she took some time away from her studies, and he had to catch her at it. Worse... Her gaze dropped to her wrinkled, sweaty, and liquor splotched jumpsuit as her hands reached to her hair, poking at the strands that had worked loose from the bun on top of her head. She was a mess.

"Why does he want to meet?"

"No purpose stated."

Lips pinched, Caer considered. She could respond with a statement saying she is unavailable. Could request a delay until morning. She hesitated. Jorn rarely asked to meet with her. Aside from a few group sessions he periodically arranged, it was up to each student to determine when they needed his counsel and to establish a time to sit down with him to discuss their course or thesis work. Perhaps she'd failed to complete some critical assignment. Her weary mind could think of nothing she'd overlooked, though.

"The destination?" she asked at last.

"Coordinates are for the office of Dr. Hugh Jorn."

Not the student offices. A private meeting, then. Caer's mind churned in her continued attempt to sort out what she might have missed or done wrong. Another scan of the state of her attire added to her growing dismay. "Is there time for me to go home and freshen up?"

"Message requests to meet at 2100."

"Time now?"

"2043."

For another long moment, Caer grappled with which was the greater sin--putting off the one individual in whose good graces she needed to remain if she wished for her transfer ever to go through, or accepting his request and arriving as is. "Fine," she huffed. "May as well face whatever is on his mind now and get it over with. I assume you have the destination coordinates keyed."

"Destination request accepted?"

"Yes. Accepted."

"Acceptance forwarded."

Slouching back in her seat once more, Caer scowled at the darkness outside, feeling more than seeing the pod's shift in the angle of forward motion. Breathing in her anxiety, she let it out in a long, soft moan, closing her eyes once more. She should never have taken the afternoon off.

The smell of fresh damp earth rich with overtones of vegetation. A swirl of green in the darkness. Drumming. Footfalls striking out a familiar rhythm. The closeness of others. Flickering warmth upon her face. Warmth turns to heat. Heat erupts in fiery tendrils dancing skyward. Within them emerges a face, the features contorted in agony, eyes full of terror as they fix on her. "I did not know! Not this way! Child! You must away!"

Shadowy images ring a great fire. As one and with rhythmic stride, they dance, advancing and retreating from the flames, warmth waxing and waning with the motion. Still comes the drumming. The circle moves round. Flames explode!

Cold brushed Caer's cheek as she jerked awake. Blinking, she pushed away from the window frame and glanced around, impressions of torrid heat clinging to her foggy mind, despite the chill lurking on her face and deep in her soul. Dreams. Always the dreams.

Bolting upright, she swore, "Hell and damnation! How long have I been asleep?" A check of her wrist communicator indicated the time as 2059, while a glance at the lights rolling by below told her that she had not yet reached the university grounds.

"How much longer to Dr. Jorn's office?"

"Seven minutes fourteen seconds."

Caer's stomach knotted. Bad enough that she'd been out of touch all day. Bad enough that she reeked of the club and looked like…like…she could only imagine! Worse, she was going to be late. Nervously, her fingers jabbed strands of hair at her ever-loosening bun. Why was it that the one man she wanted most in the universe to impress seemed always to be the one for whom she always fell so miserably short?

3

Jorn thudded onto his chair with an irritated grunt, comforted only slightly by the dense shadows shrouding his office. What he wouldn't give for a good century of complete solitude. No students. No travel. No Family. Rocking forward, he set his elbows on his desktop and lowered his head to his hands, his palms pressed against his eyes. The stuff of nightmares, the Family. A mere handful of days confined in a conference room with two of the most annoying of the clan would sour a saint's disposition. And he was no damned saint. Nor had the delay at Ahira's docking station upon his return improved his foul disposition. The authorities might at least have the good grace to offer some explanation regarding their two-hour lockdown. Characteristically, security lacked such grace.

"Lights up four," he grumbled, massaging his temples as he straightened.

The gradual brightening triggered a query from the room com. "Messages received. Do you wish to hear them?"

"Anything urgent in nature?"

"Social calls only."

Jorn groaned. "I'll deal with them later. Please hold all further calls until tomorrow."

"Holding calls."

Leaning back, he swiveled the chair around to gaze out the expansive wall of windows serving as a backdrop to the room. The university buildings on this side of the campus were, for the most

16

part, empty and darkened at this hour. In the distance, the lights from the student housing complex appeared as a yellow glow that reflected off the high ceiling of Ahira's dome. Only the lights from the two security towers marking the eastern perimeter of the university grounds shone more brightly. Caer would be arriving through that point. Quite a challenge, tracking her down. He should have expected as much. No doubt, she took the day to celebrate the news.

His jaw tensed, his snarl rumbling through the silence as his features screwed into a scowl. Pulling a tiny computer chip from his shirt pocket, Jorn flipped it end over end between his fingers several times before tossing it to his desk. The chip contained documentation of Caer's records along with the completed and signed transfer papers she so greatly desired. Earth. No sane person should set foot on that fucked up rock, least of all Caer. In signing her transfer papers, he had consigned a Tanai to the wolves.

The creases of his scowl deepened. Tanai. Such were the initial indications. The notion thrilled him, as it seemed to provide proof of his long-held theory. The first of the family of witches arose from ordinary humans. If it happened once, all those ages ago, it could certainly happen again. Naturally, he brought the girl to the attention of Gwynlyn Berring and Aifa Eliz. It's what he did for the Family--assess for the strength of magic of each young Witch, or in this case, suspected Tanai, who arrived at Ahira. In return, the Family left him alone.

Jorn's assessment of Caer's magic agitated and intrigued both Gwynlyn Berring and Aifa Eliz. Such strength made the girl either a tremendous threat or a prized asset. No surprise that Eliz wanted Caer under her supervision, intent on learning everything possible of the girl's background and potential gifts in order to turn them to 'the cause'.

Jorn's slow, deep breath exhaled in a huff. For all her attributes, Eliz would have no more success digging around in Caer's past than he. The girl's sketchy background records revealed very little. Born on a Perimeter Ship, lived for a time with an aunt on some remote colony, started secondary schooling on Heshton, transferred from Heshton to Ahira four years ago. No names were given for her parents or her aunt. No suggestion as to her family lineage. For Witches, lineage was a most crucial factor. Genealogical information accompanied the packet of documentation shipped to the university prior to the arrival of every Uair Amhain. The documentation also included a list of the young Witch's gifts as witnessed by a reputable Family member. Caer came with no such documentation. Nothing to identify her as Witch. Even the meticulously kept Family genealogical archives failed to list her. Moreover, she appeared to be oblivious of her magic. Tanai seemed the only explanation.

Jorn shook his head. Yet, so much power emanated from her. The very feel of it hummed in tremendous and undisciplined bursts along his nerves, at once familiar and unknown. Admittedly, it intrigued as well as confounded him when he first encountered it those four years ago. He sensed it even before Caer walked into the campus commons for the meet and greet of new students. Its source was easy enough to confirm. Every step in his approach to Caer increased the itch of his flesh and the buzz in his mind. Even recognizing the likely magnitude of her magic, their introductory handshake proved quite the literal shock. His arm still jerked at the memory. Not only did the contact nearly jolt him senseless, it staggered Caer back several paces, her expression both startled and curious. A quickly enhanced and maintained shielding spell had thus far prevented any further such jolts.

Rubbing his right arm, Jorn considered for the thousandth time the improbability of so much potential contained in a Tanai. None but Witches possessed of several lifetimes acquired the amount of raw power wrapped up in Caer. But there she was. No suggestion of the Witch's fire in her eyes to indicate multiples of lifetimes lived; unheralded by Family; undocumented within the archives; her magic seemingly unknown to her and completely undisciplined. No Witch would ever permit their child to remain so ignorant or so isolated. Hence his conclusion of Tanai, despite the strength of Caer's magic.

Still, doubt remained. He should never have brought the girl to the attention of Berring or Eliz. Doing so, he'd set the girl on a dangerous path. His, the fault. His, the responsibility for her safety. But how to teach Caer all she needed to know without her dismissing him as a complete mental case? His sabotage of her transfer applications failed to gain him sufficient time to resolve the issue. When Berring discovered his interference, she immediately alerted Eliz. Jorn shuddered. Aifa Eliz' fury was a horror to witness. The woman's subsequent dictate that he deliver Caer's latest application straight into her hands, and further, that Berring accompany him to guarantee he didn't 'lose' the file along the way, was not to be challenged. He was lucky the Witch didn't bring hell's conflagrations down on him when they met.

His growl again rumbled through the silence. Hell, sadly, was what Caer would suffer under the woman should her gifts prove useless, or should Caer become uncooperative or a threat to it. He needed a means by which he could open Caer's mind to her potential and to possibilities beyond her imagining. Time, however, was fast running out, as were his options.

Running a weary hand through his hair, he vented a resigned sigh, recognizing that he would do whatever necessary to grant some degree of protection to this girl with the easy smile and shimmering laughter. The mere thought of the sound, like the bright chiming of hand bells, brought it dancing through Jorn's mind. Fitting laughter for a pixie. It was how he saw her. Diminutive. Hair a little darker in color than honey, with warm cinnamon overtones. Delicate features that shown with the softness of flower petals. Eyes as green as an ancient Earth forest. Jorn inhaled, the scent of jasmine lifting to his senses. Caer always smelled faintly of jasmine. Standing anywhere near her was a heady thing.

His jaw shot forward, his fists clamping on the arms of his chair. "Don't even go there, old man. One major catastrophe was quite enough."

4

Caer scurried along the brightly lit corridor, her hands either working to poke loose strands of hair back into its bun or tugging at and smoothing her rumpled jumpsuit. Head and eyes lowered, she scuttled past the occasional professor or fellow student, keeping her distance, hoping to go unnoticed. The odor of alcohol mixed with the weed smoked by some of the patrons of the club was sure to raise eyebrows, should anyone catch a whiff. A soft groan escaped. She doubted Jorn would miss it. And she was late. Why was she always such a disaster when it came to meeting with him?

A couple of turns, at last, led her to the proper wing. As she approached Jorn's office, she slowed her pace, her stomach knotting. Perhaps this was the greater sin, after all—showing up in such a state. An unexpected hiccup brought her to a complete halt. Oh please! Not now! Bad enough that she reeked of the club. The last thing she needed was to sound like one of its resident drunks. Inhaling, she held her breath, mentally ticking off a slow count to twenty. When it seemed a full plague of hiccups was not forthcoming, she exhaled and took the last few steps forward. Bad as the idea was, she was here. She may as well get on with it.

The security cam above the opaque glass door whirred as it focused on her. "Welcome, Caer DaDhrga." The door slid open with a subtle whoosh, allowing the soft glow of the room to temper the glare of the hall lighting.

Hesitating in the open doorway, Caer stared across the room

at the man behind the desk, surprised to find him attired in a somewhat rumpled, smoky blue shirt rather than his usual crisp white with its accompanying thin gray tie. She'd never seen him without a white shirt and tie, before, much less with the top two buttons undone and his sleeves rolled up. She liked this new look. The gray-blue accented Jorn's light complexion and smooth, clean-shaven features. Curiously, his thick brown hair, usually impeccably neat, also appeared disheveled. The overall combination provided a softening of his usually serious demeanor.

Flutters rolled through Caer's insides, and she forced her gaze to her feet. The man was too young and too gorgeous to be a tenured professor. It was no wonder he had a bevy of students enrolled in his classes and all but stalking him down the hallways. She attributed the current lack of doters hanging around his office to his early return from his trip.

Dr. Jorn's, "Good evening. Please. Come in," startled Caer from her musings. Another step forward and the door slipped shut behind her.

"I'm...I'm sorry I'm late, sir," she managed, her eyes darting to the wall of windows behind him. Easier to study the night's darkness than to meet his gaze. Merely thinking about the unusual amber color of his eyes or the fact that they tended to lure her into their depths, brought an unwelcome warmth to her cheeks. She hated blushing in his presence. She did it far too often. Such a stupid and childish reaction.

"No need to apologize," he was saying. "I just arrived moments ago, myself. Some security fiasco at the shuttle terminal."

His reassurance prompted a more direct glance his way. "Please," he repeated, gesturing toward the single high-backed chair across the desk from him. "No need to stand. Sit down. Make yourself comfortable."

Caer obeyed mechanically, sitting forward, as she always did when in his office. The chair was deep enough to leave her feet dangling if she sat all the way back. And that made her feel every bit as childish as her propensity for blushing.

"I must confess, sir, I...I didn't receive your request to meet until a short time ago. If I'd left my communicator on this afternoon, I'd have gotten your message earlier and would have gone home to clean up before coming." Why did she always offer explanations when he requested none?

"I wasn't surprised when my communiqué finally caught up to you leaving the High Fancies," Jorn nodded. "I've seen you there on occasion. That's quite a repertoire of dances you have. Seems you've pursued your study of ancient Earth cultures far more extensively than most."

Heat again edged up Caer's face. He'd seen her at the club? When? She'd never noticed him. Maybe her ability to lose herself in the music and motion was a good thing. She'd probably have stumbled all over herself and broken a leg, had she spotted him among the patrons.

Swallowing, she managed, "You wanted to see me about something, sir?"

"I was rather hoping you would permit me to share in your celebration."

Caer's mouth opened, then shut again. Oh dear. What did he think she'd been celebrating? Today wasn't a holiday, at least that she could recall. Nor was it her birthday. As if Dr. Jorn had any reason to know or care.

Rising, Jorn brushed past her, headed toward the massive cabinet filling one corner of his office. "You won't deny me the honor, I hope." Stopping before it, he stated, "Bar."

Caer stifled a stunned inhale as the cabinet's double doors swung open. She'd always assumed it held antique books, like the two large, glass-fronted cases that flanked it. Instead, the open doors revealed upper shelves filled with rows of goblets and glasses of varying shapes and sizes. Below the glassware were shelves and racks holding an assortment of bottles, including a number of wines. At the bottom was a small, glass-fronted refrigeration unit containing several more bottles.

Jorn selected a pair of exquisite goblets, setting them on a narrow shelf mounted to the inside of one of the cabinet's doors. "I believe," he began, pulling a tinted bottle from the refrigerated section and untwisting the base of the wire cage covering the bottle's mouth. The cork shot straight up as it popped. Jorn caught it with one hand as he poured with the other. "That the occasion calls for champagne."

Replacing the cork, Jorn left the bottle on the door's shelf and returned to Caer, holding the crystal ware aloft for the light to catch and play off the riot of bubbles. "This particular label comes from one of the oldest and finest of the vineyard colonies," he added, extending a goblet to her on his way back to his chair.

Caer accepted with both hands, cupping them above the long stem to cradle the delicate glass, afraid she might somehow chip or drop it. "This...this is really unnecessary, sir. It...it must have cost you dearly." Damn! She'd not meant to speak that last thought.

Jorn shrugged as he sat, leaning back in his chair with a hint of his familiar one-sided grin. "Hardly likely to break the bank. And your celebration deserves more than the cheap stuff served at the club."

Wincing, Caer lowered the goblet to her lap, her hands continuing to cradle it. She still had no idea what he thought the occasion might be. Well, no point in pounding round the pod to sort it out. Mustering her courage, she confessed, "Actually, sir, I wasn't celebrating anything. I...I just felt the need to, uhm...run away for a while. I'm sorry, sir. I should have stayed on campus."

"Don't be ridiculous," Jorn snorted. "If anyone deserves to take some time off, you do. I thought, however...." Tapping at his drink, he considered for a moment. "You've not spoken to Dr. Berring, today?"

"No, sir. She's off-world. She left the same day you did, and..."

Jorn's face creased in a sour frown. "Yes, I'm aware of her departure. We attended the same meeting. It concluded yesterday, so

I headed back. Berring had another matter requiring her attention. She had, however, intended to contact you early this morning, Ahira time. I thought your day away from campus was in celebration of her news.

"My communicator was on all morning, sir. I had no word from her. Nor was there any this evening when I turned it back on."

Jorn's frown deepened. "That's not like Berring. What she says she'll do, she does."

"Something more pressing than chatting with a student must have come up." Venturing an anxious glance at Jorn's expression, Caer urged, "So, uhm...would you mind telling me what this is all about?"

The professor's suddenly intense scrutiny set one of Caer's hands to fumbling with her necklace. "I need not tell you," he said at last, "about the department's concern over your disappearing applications to study Earth-side."

Caer's unchecked huff was a deeper admission of her frustration than she'd intended. "Lost in the system, I guess. Though why the computers should take such an interest in eating so many of mine I can't imagine."

"Indeed. Dr. Berring was also concerned about this...odd disappearance of your transfer requests and was determined to remedy the situation. Dr. Eliz of Sion University was in route to a transfer station to return to Earth following another meeting. Berring and I joined her aboard the lay-over station, where I delivered your latest application into Dr. Eliz' hands." He raised his goblet in a toast. "Congratulations. You have been officially accepted to Sion University, Earth."

Caer's inhale held for a long moment as a grin stole across her lips. Accepted. "Earth," she repeated. "I'm going."

"You're going."

A squeal of 'Yes!' erupted as she popped from her chair, the drink in her hand sloshing over her fingers and triggering yet another uncomfortably warm flush.

Jorn cocked a brow, his half-smile again teasing a corner of his mouth. "There was little doubt the news would please you. Rejoicing with champagne, however, is better done by drinking it than by bathing in it."

Caer was certain she had gone bright crimson from the top of her head all the way to her toes. Wiping her hands, one at a time, on her already stained jumpsuit, she stammered, "S...sir. I...I can't begin to tell you how...how...." Where were the words when she wanted them?

Settling back down on the edge of the chair, she clung to the goblet as though to release it would be to release the moment. If she let go, she might find this instant was nothing more than some disjointed fragment from one of her strange dreams. The cold glass in her hands certainly felt real enough, though. Lifting it to return Jorn's toast, she downed a deep swig to try and chase away her lingering doubts. It proved as regrettable an act as her earlier episode with the gin. Heat shot through Caer, sucking the breath from her lungs in a rush, requiring several hammering heartbeats before she could draw another.

Jorn rose and was about to round his desk to come to her aid when she waved him back, choking, "I'm...I'm fine. Just not used to anything like...like this." His dubious glance prompted, "I'm an...an idiot when...when...when it comes to alcohol, I'm afraid."

Sitting again with a bemused chuckle, Jorn offered, "That could be said of a lot of us."

"Yes. Well. When it comes to my studies..." Caer collected another deep breath before continuing. "I assure you, I'm not such an idiot. I won't disappoint you, sir. I promise."

"I have no doubt." For several seconds, Jorn sat contemplating the bubbles in his glass. "Tell me," he ventured at last. "Have you ever been to Earth before?"

"No, sir." Caer had read everything she could find regarding the planet, though. So much life there! Despite the devastation from the Great Wars of a thousand years ago, it remained home to a population unmatched on any colony. It was said Earth even boasted a handful of lush gardens--remnants of the world's once abundant flora and fauna. Plus, Earth had oceans! While there were any number of worlds made of ice, Caer knew of none among the colonized ones containing such vast stores of liquid water.

"Were I you, Caer, I would be cautious of any expectations. You may well have second thoughts upon your arrival."

"Oh no!" she declared. "I'm sure I will never have second thoughts. Earth is where I must go. I've been drawn to her since... since I can't remember when. I promised I would..."

A flash of excruciating pain and the stench of something burning swept her. The sensations vanished as quickly as they'd appeared, though they left Caer shaking. It had to be the alcohol. Champagne on top of all the rest! She was indeed an idiot! Her hand inched her goblet toward the desk but failed to set it down.

"Promised you would...?" Jorn pressed.

Shaking herself, Caer struggled to find her previous train of thought. "I, uh, promised myself to see Earth first hand, some day." True enough. She'd sworn it repeatedly; had done so since she couldn't remember when. A dark suspicion, however, clung to the back of her mind. Her words also carried some other, deeper meaning—a meaning that hung just beyond her conscious grasp The thought might have troubled her, were it not for the rare full smile Jorn granted her. Caer's insides fluttered anew.

"I'm pleased to bring your promise to fruition, then. Arrangements have been made for you to leave within the month."

The statement brought Caer up short. So soon? No. Not possible. The quarter here had only just begun. She would need to complete it, first. And there was the matter of her thesis. She intended to finish it while still under Dr. Jorn's guidance.

"This will allow you to begin at the start of a quarter at Sion when you arrive," Jorn was saying. "I've already signed the waivers for your classes here. Dr. Eliz has a copy of your thesis, to date. You will find new insights on Earth for completing it."

26

Caer blinked, still speechless. Unthinkingly, she downed another gulp from her goblet, her head spinning as much from this newest revelation as from the addition of more alcohol. It wasn't supposed to happen quite like this. She expected to have enough time to prepare; time to relish the anticipation of a new adventure; time to share it with her friends; time to pack; time for...

"Even...even if I...if I left tomorrow," she posited, "I wouldn't reach Earth soon enough to th...start a full quarter. Not...not without going through a matter transfer thtation." Caer bit at her tongue, aware that her ability to enunciate was slipping away.

Tomorrow would indeed be rushing things," Jorn agreed. "Within the month, however, is manageable. We've contacted a transfer station and are awaiting their confirmation of scheduling. No sense in wasting a year or more of your time by sending you the long way. Personally, I find the jump drives of the transport ships more unsettling than mat-trans, anyway."

Caer emptied the remainder of her champagne in a futile attempt to steady her nerves. She had traveled by way of matter transfer only once before and couldn't have disagreed with Jorn more. Jump drives left her edgy. Mat trans... She didn't even want to think about how that left her feeling.

"Looks like you could use another drink," Jorn observed.

Though she knew she should decline, Caer mumbled, "Yes, thir. Thank you."

Retrieving her empty glass, Jorn made his way back to the cabinet. "I would like to make a request if I might."

"A request?"

"A simple one," he said, refilling both goblets. "I would prefer you dispense with the 'doctor' and the 'sir'. Technically, you are no longer my student. Hence, the formality is likewise no longer necessary."

Not his student. She'd been so single-mindedly focused regarding her desire to transfer Earth-side she hadn't fully considered this aspect, though Jen had attempted to point it out. The fact now tumbled in a growing hollowing in her stomach. Here she was, preparing to leave on the adventure of her life, and...and chances were, she would never see him again. She really wanted to see Dr. Jorn again. Somehow. Somewhere.

"Would you..." Inhaling, Caer worked to form her words as clearly as possible. "Would you mind, thir if...if I kept in touch with you?" Ugh. Now she was beginning to sound like some of the ninnies in the infatuation squad that plagued Jorn's existence--and a drunken one at that. Caer chewed at the corner of her mouth, struggling to control her miscreant tongue along with her increasingly murky wits. "To send you some of my papers. You always manage to...uhm...open my eyes to things I hadn't fully understood before."

Jorn gave a dismissive harrumph as he set Caer's drink on the corner of his desk and returned to his chair. "You will find more than an ample number of professors at Sion who are far better equipped to help you than I. Perhaps you might consider keeping in touch as a friend, though."

A friend? Friend was good. Friend was very good! "Of course, th...sir! I would be delighted!"

"Settled. Friends it is. Now, try saying 'Hugh'...or Jorn if you must. But without the Dr., and without any sirs."

"I'll try, sir. Uh...Jorn."

"That will have to do, for now, I suppose," he chuckled. A brief pause accompanied his skimming glance to the computer disc on his desk. "Do you mind if I ask you another question?"

"No. Of course not."

"Your student records," he said, tapping the disc, "indicate you were a perimeter child."

Caer nodded, finding the motion more than a little unpleasant. "I was for a time."

"Was it difficult?"

Scrunching her nose, she puzzled over the question. "How do you mean?"

"I would have thought it a confining life for a child. The isolation aboard a ship so far removed from any major colonies or population centers."

Caer's fingers sought reflexively for her necklace, worrying it as she tried to think. Her head was fuzzing over, making it hard to track the present, never mind attempting to recall something from so long ago. Jumbles of hazy memories flitted through. The living quarters she'd shared with her parents, the lab where both had worked, corridors bustling with humans and a grand assortment of aliens, the large dining hall where personnel and their families shared meals. Each carried with it a cozy warmth.

"I don't remember life seeming difficult or confining. A ship can be all the world you need when you're little. It's always filled with fath…fascinating people."

Jorn rocked back, his amusement twitching his half smile again. "Fascinating, you say?"

Caer's face warmed as she concentrated again on speaking her words clearly. "People are, you know. Fascinating. Surely you think so. Otherwise, why would you be in a field like Social Anthropology?"

"Interesting question. I'll let you know when I have an answer to that one." Sipping briefly, he persisted. "So, you enjoyed a happy childhood among fascinating people."

"Well, yeth." It was most troublesome, having to focus on distant memories while also trying to keep her comments from sounding as stewed as her brain felt. Worse, the effort was beginning to intensify Caer's headache. Still, she was loath to give up on any conversation with Dr. Jorn that ventured beyond academia. With a fleeting inhale, she continued with as much of her mind on enunciation as her pickled brain cells could spare. "I spent my early childhood aboard the ship. I left when I was eight. Mother sent me to Lillith II to live with her sister. Aunt Sidra was a physician for one of the colony's thsmaller mining communities."

She was beginning to hate 's'es as much as she hated the chair beneath her. It was getting increasingly difficult to sit up straight without scooting back for support; which would, of course, leave her feet dangling.

"Sidra?" Jorn's brow shot up. "Sidra Eirene?"

"Why, yes. Did you know her?"

"I know of her. Brilliant woman. I've read many of her works. She did some remarkable studies regarding the evolution of cultures within newly established colonies. It was a great loss to the entire academic community when she died. Plague, I believe I read."

Caer gave a tightly confined nod. "You know, I still miss her." It wasn't difficult to envision her aunt's beloved face or to recall the gentle touch of Sidra's hand on her shoulder, despite Caer's current addled state. Those memories were lovingly forged forever in her mind, though others hovered just beyond her grasp. The circumstances of her aunt's death, for instance. She knew Sidra died of plague only because she'd been told as much. She'd contracted the disease, as well. Or so it was said. Memories of her time in the hospital were not ones she cared to retrieve. "I...." The words stuck in her throat for a moment. "I was one of the...of the lucky ones. I was sent to Heshton for treatment. Aunt Sidra..."

Jorn's sobering expression took on pained regret. "I am sorry, Caer. I should not have pried into your childhood. It appears, however, that you've inherited your aunt's interest in cultural history and evolution. I know she would be proud of you."

"Thank you, thir."

"There you are with the sir, again," Jorn sniffed. "We need to work on that." Once more he flashed a full smile. It lit up his entire countenance, soothing the ghosts back into submission and warming Caer to her core. Aware she was staring at him, she dropped her attention to the goblet in her hands. Empty again. When did that happen?

"Perhaps it would help if I shared something about myself. It's what friends do. Not that my life offers much of interest. Still..." Setting aside his drink and resting his folded arms on the desk, Jorn asked, "Is there anything you would like to know?"

Caer sucked on her upper lip. Oh my! Where could she possibly begin? There were so many things she'd love to ask. Before she could sort through the myriad questions swimming around in her head, one leaped of its own accord from her mouth. "Why aren't you married?" Having uttered the words, she felt the heat rising in her face yet again and sank with a grimace as far back into the chair as possible.

Jorn straightened, breaking into a rolling peal of laughter. "He who invites personal questions had best be prepared to answer them, though I'm not sure I have one for that particular query. How to put this?" His fingers tapped on the desktop as he took a moment to consider. "I was married, once. It was a long time ago." He paused before adding, "The lady deserved much better than she got."

Ouch! Despite rumors of his being a lady's man, Caer had never actually seen him with anyone; never pictured him as being attached to any particular woman. Wishful thinking on her part, of course. Staring at her lap, she fidgeted with her necklace again, fearing a glimpse of his expression would confirm the remorse she'd detected in his voice. He obviously still had feelings for his ex.

"Anything else you care to ask?"

She was dying to say, 'Oh yes! Tell me everything about yourself!' Remarkably, she restrained her tongue. Better to wait until she could converse without sounding like such an imbecile. At least she hoped there would be another opportunity to talk with him.

"It's getting late," she observed. "I th...should be going. Thank you, Dr. Jorn. For the news. I'm thrilled. Really!" Depositing the empty goblet on the desk, she fumbled to tap the face of her wrist communicator. "I'll ju...ust...call for...for a pod to take me home."

Jorn looked injured. "Back to the 'Dr.', are we? Apparently, my friendship skills need a lot of work."

"Oh no! Not at all, thir!"

He cocked a brow. "No? Well, it appears they require some fine tuning, at least." Standing, he addressed the com system. "Call my pod, please." Then to Caer, "No need to wait for public transport. My vehicle is in the reserved lot."

His? Jorn had a pod? No one Caer knew could afford such a luxury.

Jorn rounded his desk, rolling his sleeves down and buttoning them. "Do you know you often wear your thoughts on your face?"

Mortified, Caer stuttered, "I...I do?"

"Afraid so," he grinned. "And to answer your face, yes, I own a pod." His half-smile once more lifted one corner of his mouth as he extended a hand. "Now, please allow me to escort you back to your apartment. It's the least I can do for having filled you with champagne."

Though she was certain she was blushing like fury again, Caer accepted, permitting Jorn to draw her to her feet. Dizziness washed over her, leaving her teetering. Jorn shook his head, his free hand gripping her arm to steady her.

"There. You see? Inebriated and the fault is mine. What sort of friend would permit you to travel alone on public transport when you can hardly stand?"

"I'm fine. I ju...uthst...stood too fast." She'd have winced under his skeptical eye, but her wincing muscles seemed to have nodded off.

"Pod waiting," the com announced.

With elegant grace, Jorn folded Caer's hand in the crook of his arm, the gesture flowing as though it were second nature to him. "Your chariot awaits," he smiled.

5

Caer giggled at Jorn's unexpected and antiquated chivalry. The humor quickly faded, however, when his office, and then the hallway, shifted and swayed, the floor seeming to undulate beneath her feet as they walked. Nor was there anything giggle-able about the wave of nausea that rolled her stomach and rose at the back of her throat. She swallowed against the bile, chewing at her lip as she applied whispered refrains of, "My ...my head i...ith cl...ear. I will...I will not be...be th...sick. M...y head iths....cl...ear. I...will not...be thsick. My head...is...clear. I will...not be sick."

Much to her surprise, the floor began to steady, her thoughts and enunciation clarifying. So, too, the queasiness abated. Willing herself sober had never occurred to her before. It was a trick worth remembering. Assuming the loss of the fog in her head wasn't a delusion, and further assuming she could remember anything come morning.

Her lips twitched to a mortified grimace as she realized she was leaning against the professor. So much so that her head rested against his arm. What if someone saw them like this? Their...position... might be misconstrued. Dr. Jorn could lose his job if anyone thought they were...involved.

Caer's abrupt straightening returned a surge of vertigo. Beside her, Jorn shifted to take more of her weight again, patting her hand where it still lay, tucked in the crook of his arm. "Tired of my proximity?" he asked.

"No. Of course not. I...."

"Or are you afraid to be seen in my company?"

Flushing, she muttered, "Shouldn't that be the other way around? Won't it...uhm...cause trouble for you? I mean..."

His bemused harrumph preceded, "It's kind of you to worry on my account, but wholly unnecessary." Nodding toward a metal door a couple of paces away, he added, "Ah. Here we are." Only after guaranteeing she was reasonably stable on her feet did he release her hand, stepping forward to await the retinal scan from the device adjacent to the door frame. Gliding sideways along its track, the door opened to the chill of the night.

Caer held back. She'd expected to take the elevator to the roof. Instead of going to his pod, however, Jorn had directed the vehicle to meet them at one of the small exterior landings reserved for the university shuttles that whisked staff and VIPs across the campus. Being neither staff nor VIP, Caer had never ventured onto any of the overhangs clinging like warts to the sides of the buildings. She'd have been happy to leave it that way.

Plucking up her courage, she urged her feet to follow Jorn out onto the four-meter square of concrete, attempting to fix her gaze on the lights from the distant security tower rather than glancing down. It was a futile attempt, her knees going wobbly as she glimpsed the ground several stories below.

Jorn was instantly at her side, his firm grip on her elbow. "I'm sorry, Caer. I didn't realize you were afraid of heights."

"It's not the...the heights," she squeaked. "It's the falling."

"Yes. Well." He drew her closer. "I won't let that happen. Let's just get you aboard."

Nodding, Caer shuffled forward as a wash of hot air swept her. Mouth agape, she stumbled to another halt, eyeing the pod that settled to a hover before them. What, exactly, she had expected of a vehicle owned by Dr. Hugh Jorn she couldn't say. Something round, perhaps, and boldly colored. A few such transports often skimmed across the dome's upper reaches, their shockingly intense hues marking the ostentatious balls as the privately-owned vehicles of the extravagantly wealthy.

Before her, however, was something far more impressive. Sleek, elongated, its hue such a perfect satin black, its charcoal gray windows so darkly tinted, that, were it not for the belt of strobing blue-white running lights, it would be difficult to pick it out against the night's backdrop.

"Mind your step," Jorn warned, urging her across the narrow chasm between the docking bay and the vehicle.

Caer shot a brief downward glance at the gap before climbing quickly inside, relieved to have solid containment around her. Jorn settled across from her, the door slipping shut, its lock clicking into place. "You alright?"

"Fine," she breathed. "Just being stupid. I mean, it's not like pods can't fall from the sky. But..." She took a moment, inhaling again and letting it out slowly. "Standing on the edge of anything more than a couple of meters high turns me to jelly. Has ever since the ground opened up at my feet and the entire section of the university's library collapsed." Blanching, Caer clamped her lips together. She hadn't spoken of the incident more than a couple of times since it happened four years ago. She hated talking about it.

"I knew you were at the library that day. In the archives?"

The subtle sense of the vehicle's upward lift provided Caer the opportunity to change the topic. "The coordinates for my apartment are..."

"No need," Jorn interposed. "The destination is set."

Caer blinked, her mouth still half-formed around her address. He knew where she lived?

"I keyed your name into my communicator as we walked. The pod's computer pulled the coordinates from the public records."

Her mouth closed before she could exhale a ridiculously deflated, "Oh."

For several long seconds, she remained perched on the edge of the seat. Grateful when Jorn made no attempt to return the discussion to the matter of the library's collapse, Caer shifted her position, surprised to find the seat's back adjusting forward and down to accommodate her small stature. It stopped when her back was properly supported and her feet were resting on the floor, at which point it molded neatly around her to conform to her contours. The comfort was at once startling and superb and prompted a closer scrutiny of the rest of the interior. Soft light suffused the space, giving the dark blue velvet of the upholstery a sophisticated richness, and granting a shimmer to the silver-gray carpet and the brushed pewter framing the windows. The source of the lighting, Caer discovered, was the myriad pinpricks that covered the ceiling.

"I had it designed to represent the heavens as seen from my home on a midsummer's eve," Jorn provided.

His home. "Earth's night sky?" Caer knew the rumors of Jorn having been Earth-born, though she never quite believed them.

"Seems the gossip mongers have been spreading the word. Yes. Earth's night sky."

Awed silence wrapped her, Caer's hands lingering on the softness of the upholstery while her eyes delighted in the subtle twinkling overhead. She rarely gave the cosmos any thought. The Perimeter Ship where she was born and the transports aboard which she traveled from one world to another when the need arose offered a most limited view, as did the spacesuits she'd had occasion to don now and then. And the various domes beneath which she had lived blurred the heavens. Seeing the universe fully open above her was not within her realm of experience. For that matter, it seemed unlikely for Jorn to have experienced it, either. The people of Earth had, for centuries, lived beneath massive domes, just as the colonists did. Perhaps their domes were clearer, though. "This is...."

"Soothing."

Enchanting, she would have said. Elegant. Exquisitely romantic. She couldn't help but wonder, and with no small degree of anguish, just how many women Jorn had taken for a glide above the skittering mundane-ness of life below, the twinkling heavens as a canopy. What a way to woo a lady!

Jorn snorted. "I make it a habit not to apply the use of this little jewel for anything so devious."

Judging from the heat rushing Caer's face, she was quite sure she had gone crimson once more.

"You need to learn not to wear your thoughts so openly," Jorn chuckled. "It's apt to get you into trouble."

Caer's gaze hastened to her lap. A serious study in front of a mirror was in order, and in the very near future. For now, however, she determined it would be best to remain as expressionless as possible. Relaxing her face, she attempted to empty all thoughts from her head. Not a possibility, given that every question imaginable kept popping up regarding Dr. Jorn. How did he come by such wealth? Why had he never let on? Why wouldn't he use this remarkable vehicle to woo women—or men, if that was his preference? Beneath the rush of questions, a vague undercurrent of foreboding slipped into some dark crevice at the back of her mind.

Squirming, Caer glanced out the window. No flames sputtered from the engine. Nor was there any indication of some other dire circumstance. A small shake of her head accompanied her silent chastising for acting as though Jen's mention of foresight might be real. Jorn certainly appeared unconcerned. His eyes were closed, his head resting against the back of his seat.

Caer used the opportunity to regard him more thoroughly. Fatigue lined his face, dark shadows hollowing the areas around his eyes. How could she have failed to notice before? Her shoulders sagged, "I did that to him," slipping out in a soft murmur.

Jorn opened his eyes. "You say something?"

"Uhm. No. Only that...well...I'm...sorry, sir."

"Oh dear," he sighed. "There we are with that 'sir' again. Too well an established habit, I suppose. Still, I hope you will shake it one day. As for your apology, what awful thing have you done that would require one?"

Bracing herself with a deep breath, Caer blurted all in a rush, "For being such a marsh puff as to go off from my studies today and then show up in your office late and rather drunk or rather quite drunk and all a mess and for taking up so much of your time tonight." Her face now insufferably hot, Caer inhaled again, let it out, licked her lips. "Here you are, sir, just getting back from who-knows-where, all on my account. And here I am, prolonging your day." Twisting and untwisting her necklace, she dropped her gaze to another unhappy scan of her lap. "I even managed to make you feel obligated to see me home."

"Don't be ridiculous. No one makes me feel obligated to do anything I don't wish to do. Furthermore, if there are apologies to be handed out, it's I who owe one to you. I knew when you walked into my office that you were...in your cups, as was once the turn of phrase. Still, I encouraged more drink on you. Pretty shameful on my part."

"I could have declined."

"In your state? Not likely."

Caer considered pressing the matter, at last brushing it off with a small huff. Better to keep quiet and just enjoy the moment. She was, after all, alone and in complete privacy with the man of her dreams. She stifled a threatening giggle. If Jen could see her, now! Catching a glimpse of Jorn's amused expression, she turned to face the window, praying her features had not broadcast those last thoughts!

Her embarrassed unease clung to her for less than a heartbeat, replaced by a dark foreboding rising from the deep crevice where it had earlier taken hold. With it came a rush of blackness so thick Caer feared no light would ever again penetrate it. No light. No sound. Only blackness. Sharp palpitations slammed her heart against her ribs, ice prickling every millimeter of her flesh. Then came the shock of stabbing pain, like a thin blade, thrust deep into the base of her skull. Thunderous drumming erupted from her temples, scorching every nerve with agony.

"Caer?"

The shroud of black rippled at the distant echo of Jorn's voice.

"Caer?"

The voice strengthened, Jorn's face swimming within the darkness. The feel of his fingers brushed her forehead before pressing lightly against her temples. The pain eased. The frantic hammering of her heart slowed. The soft light of the pod returned. Jorn rocked back, his curious scrutiny almost as unsettling as the vision.

"Are you all right?"

It took several long seconds before Caer could stop shaking enough to manage a bewildered nod.

"Want to tell me what happened?"

She swallowed. Swallowed again. "I...I don't know. It was...." Her words fell off as she was caught by the subtle glow deep within Jorn's eyes. It ignited the amber of his irises to a delicate smolder that reflected back again into the depths. She'd glimpsed that glow before, or at least had noted the hint of it. So fascinating. So mesmerizing. All else faded. There was only the amber of his eyes, drawing her in. Like looking into the reflection of a mirror within a mirror within a mirror. How easy it would be to get lost in the layers of his gaze.

"You're certain you're all right?" she heard him press.

She nodded; realized she'd slumped forward; straightened. And then it came again—the rushing wall of impenetrable blackness, the panicked pounding of her heart, the blade to the back of her skull, the pain exploding through her temples and scorching her nerves. Her outcry died in a white-hot searing that sliced across her throat. The world erupted in red. In blood. It was everywhere. Her blood. Spraying. Her hands groped for the wound, fingers frantically seeking along the ragged gash across her throat. The gash that burned molten hot. The gash from which her life was gushing away. Blood coated her hands, spilled down onto her clothing. So much blood! So much!

"Caer!"

Jorn's anxious call rang through her head, his grip tightening on her shoulders, both shaking her and preventing her from doubling over at the churning in her stomach and the frenzied race of her heart.

"Vision dispel!" rolled through her mind.

Within seconds the excruciating agony was gone. For several more, Caer could do no more than hang limply in Jorn's grip, gasping. At last, she pulled back, drawing her shaking hands up to stare at them; turning them this way and that. Empty, bare hands. They revealed no gore. Reaching to her throat, she found no indication of any injury. She was whole, with not a trace of blood.

Caer forced a ragged breath. Hallucinations. Why was she stricken with hallucinations? Surely not from whatever alcohol remained in her system. No amount of drinking had ever caused a reaction like this before.

Jorn leaned forward, taking her hands. "You must be coming down with something. You're freezing." He set to rubbing them vigorously as he declared, "Temperature up four degrees."

"Cccold," Caer admitted, only vaguely aware of the warm breeze that fluttered the loose strands of her hair. "Pppoor ccccirculllllation." The dismissive smile she attempted proved little more than a quiver of her mouth.

Jorn gestured toward the window. "We'll have you home, soon. I suggest you go straight to bed."

Caer found no other words to utter as she stared out to where the regularly spaced lights delineated the student housing complex. Maybe she was already home. Already in bed. Dreaming. Not her usual nightmare. Something worse.

6

The pod closed on the housing quarters, skirting the buildings until it reached the appropriate sector. "Unit 109," intoned the com, the vehicle descending to hover only centimeters above the ground and mere paces from Caer's door.

Jorn slid out first, extending his hand. "I'll see you in." It was less an offer than a dictate. Unwilling to argue, Caer nodded, accepting his waiting hand and slipping out to stand next to him.

Don't go!

The rumble of the warning through her skull sucked the last bit of warmth from her. In its place came a sweep of terror so great as to buckle her knees. Gripping her necklace with one hand and Jorn's arm with the other, Caer willed her legs to stiffen. She'd had quite enough of this. First the visions in the pod. Now a bloody voice in her head. She wanted no more hallucinations!

"Pod secure and wait," Jorn commanded, wrapping an arm around her waist.

Don't go in!

The alarm now twitched through every part of her, causing Caer to stumble, and setting such a thunderous syncopation to her heart beat that she feared her ribs might crumble.

"Take your time," Jorn encouraged. "Or, perhaps we should return to my pod. Maybe there's a friend you could stay with tonight."

"No." Her refusal was barely audible. She tried to shake her head to emphasize her resolve as she reached an unsteady palm toward the keypad in the center of her door. If she could just get inside.

Blood. Enormous splatters of it...rivers of it running...

Caer jerked away, the abruptness of the motion coupled with the rush of nausea nearly dumping her over on top of Jorn.

Righting them both, he shifted her around to face him squarely. "Let me take you somewhere else," he repeated. "Just tell me where you'd like to go."

Caer set her jaw against the chattering of her teeth. No hallucination was going to get the better of her! Turning again to the door, she shoved her hand to the keypad.

The door swung in on the darkened apartment as a wave of putrid air wafted out. Caer gagged, fighting the urge to turn instantly away. She refused to flee. Not without substantive reason. Still, her voice squeaked at her attempt to call the lights up.

Jorn provided the command. The room slowly brightened, allowing them to move in far enough for the door to shut behind them.

Caer's breath remained thin and ragged as she cast furtively about, not knowing what she was looking for; knowing only that the warning still wailed within her, declaring that something was seriously amiss. It was stupid. This was her home. Her sanctuary. There was nothing to be found here but what ought to be. The pervasive stench was no more than a backed-up sewer line, though she admitted that she'd never smelled anything quite so...so... Any appropriate words failed her.

Again, she scanned the living area, this time taking in every little detail. Clean dishes stood undisturbed on the kitchenette side of the counter, just where she'd left them. Her collection of ethnic dolls from various colonies rested in their proper places on the wall shelves of the tiny living room. Her text and music chips remained on top of her desk, their haphazard arrangement her own. So, too, the small sofa along the front wall and the antique high-backed rocking chair that stood askew of her desk were both undisturbed.

The reek, she realized at last, seemed to be coming from her bedroom. Or from the bathroom beyond, more like. Jorn left her clinging to the rocking chair, stating, "Wait here," as he headed for the partially closed door that separated the bedroom from the living area.

Unwilling to be left alone, Caer stumbled after him.

He'd scarcely pushed the door to when he turned on his heels, grasping Caer's shoulders and spinning her away. "Don't come any further. We need to...."

She couldn't help herself. Completing the spin, Caer peered past him. There, in her bedroom she could see the ghastly splatters. The streaks running of red, just as the 'hallucinations' had shown her. It was everywhere--on her walls; on the small chest of drawers; on the bed. Her eyes were drawn downward to the dark pools soaking the carpet and the body that lay sprawled upon it, the limbs twisted in horrific angles. Caer lurched past Jorn just far enough to support herself against the door frame as her stomach gave up its contents. When the heaving at last subsided, dizziness took her. Swaying, the hazing views of sliding walls gave way to emptiness.

7

Jorn nearly missed grabbing Caer as she crumpled. Juggling her into his arms, he studied her for a long moment before glancing back at the carnage.

"I'm a fool," he muttered. "Should have insisted you go elsewhere the moment I sensed the teleportation spell. Give me a chance to come back and investigate without you." Crossing the room, he laid Caer on the sofa, working a silent charm to prevent her coming around too soon. He needed time to order his thoughts.

The girl knew nothing of magic. He'd stake his soul on it. Yet someone with magic had been here. The remnants of the teleportation spell used to gain entry...and to leave again...hung heavily in the air. Turning, he regarded the two security cams located high on the wall in opposing corners of the room. Neither showed the pinprick of green light at their base to indicate they were functional. His glimpse of the cam in Caer's bedroom suggested a similar 'malfunction'. No surprise. The culprit would not want their magical capabilities caught by the cameras, never mind not wanting to be identified as the murderer.

Jorn attempted to identify the specific enchantment used to take out the cameras. If he knew the charm, he might guess the identity of the one who cast it. But it was lost in the more powerful residual of the teleportation. Nor could he identify the 'signature' clinging to the spell. Something about it did not feel right, though. It was too…murky…almost muddled. Like the one who cast it was clumsy with magic.

One thing was certain. Without the interior cams to prove their innocence, he and Caer were likely to become prime suspects. Not much he could do about that, for the moment. Still, the longer he delayed in reporting their grizzly find, the worse it would look for them.

"Emergency!" he barked to the air.

"Nature of?" returned quickly enough, though the male voice sounded bored.

"Homicide."

"Re..repeat, please?"

"Murder."

Batting at the stench, Jorn strode back toward the bedroom. He wanted a closer look at the scene, and security was unlikely to grant it, once they arrived.

"Uhhhhh. One moment, please." A short pause from the com prefaced, "You are in unit 109? The residence of a Ms. Caer DaDhrga?"

Pushing the bedroom door fully open, Jorn huffed grimly. "That is correct."

"It appears that the security cams have failed, sir."

"Is that so? Take my word for it. There is a corpse here. Kindly contact the authorities, if you would."

"Yes. Of course. I'm sending the alarm, now. Just….just…stay where you are, sir. I'm sure they will want to talk with you. Oh. And…and don't disturb anything."

Jorn cocked a less than amused brow. "You have my word." He waited for the subtle click of the com to tell him that the channel had closed. After several seconds, he concluded that the line would remain open. Whether it was protocol to keep 'ears' on untoward situations when 'eyes' failed, or whether it was the result of the curiosity of the young man at the other end, made little difference.

Either way, it necessitated cautious silence on his part, if he wished to investigate.

Again, he batted at the air. He knew this smell, though like the signature in the magic, the source evaded him. Eyes stinging from it, Jorn edged into the room, moving with considerable care around the blood that soaked the carpet until he could squat close enough to check out the body. The legs were grotesquely bent in unnatural angles; the torso so twisted that the stomach and hips lay front-side down while the deeply gashed female breasts were exposed through the shredded clothing, front-side up. The rest remained hidden beneath the corner of the bed.

Standing, Jorn shifted for a glimpse around the bed's end. Near the wall, in a darkening pool, he spotted the severed head. Thickly tangled and blood-clumped tresses concealed the face, making it impossible to note the woman's features. He could only guess from the trim hips and breasts that she was young. Caer's age, perhaps. According to the student housing records, Caer lived alone. So, who the hell was this? Whomever the victim, she was similar enough in age and size to have been mistaken for Caer. Whatever her business, here, she'd paid for it dearly.

In the distance, the sound of wailing sirens echoed. Delicately retracing his steps, Jorn worked his way back to the doorway, sagging against the frame to await security, his arms folded across his chest as he stared across at the still unconscious girl on the sofa. Prescient. He'd suspected as much, though he had been unable to collect anything more than anecdotal evidence...until now. So powerful were Caer's visions just before they arrived, and so unprotected, that she had unwittingly broadcast them straight into his head. Even with that, he'd avoided drawing any conclusions. Not until he recognized the patterns of blood splattered across the wall above the bed as identical to those of the visions did he know for sure. Hell of a way to get proof of her gift. Running a hand wearily over his hair, he whispered, "Who are you? And why does someone from the Family want you dead?"

8

The aroma of freshly brewing coffee drew Jorn from his slump on the sofa. Groaning, he rocked forward, rubbing his face with his hands before shooting a sidelong glance in the direction of his bedroom. He thought he'd heard Caer stirring. Silence greeted him.

Shoving to his feet, he plodded across the room, past his dining table, past the island upon which his antique coffee pot now gurgled its final gurgle of the cycle, and around to the cabinets in search of a mug. After filling it, he stood for several moments, staring at the dark liquid and the rising steam. The question of Caer--who she is and why someone would go to such lengths to kill her--had plagued him all night.

Trudging back to the table, he pulled out the nearest chair, settling on it and sipping coffee as he tried to sharpen his sleep-deprived thoughts. Gifted with at least some degree of the Sight. Many a Witch possessed minor abilities with premonition. Few rose to such a level as he'd witnessed through Caer, though. He sipped again. Family was involved. Nemhain's line. Nemhain. Croi Breag. The Dark Heart. Didn't matter which name he applied, the woman was one bitch of a witch. She was behind this, somehow. His bones ached with the certainty of it. But why?

Jorn closed his eyes and massaged his temples. Not that Nemhain necessarily needed a reason. She killed for the love of it, as did her closest kin. Not in centuries, however, had any of them dared to venture into one of the strongholds for her sisters' lines. Why now? And what did Caer have to do with it?

"Pod arriving," announced the com.

Jorn scowled, his eyes snapping open. "View," he stated, turning to face the middle of the living area. A holographic image shimmered faintly, then shifted into focus in time to reveal a dark, unmarked pod gliding to a hover at the approach to his upper story apartment. A woman with short-cropped brown hair and dressed in the official brown of a security officer disembarked from the vehicle and strode the narrow landing to his door.

"Damnation!" Rising, he barked, "Com-link open," then demanded, "State your identity and business," before the individual had a chance to reach for the com button next to his door.

"Sgt. Sakin to see Ms. Caer DaDhrga."

Sakin. He recognized the name before he recognized the woman. She was one of the officers involved in the interrogation last night. The sergeant stood almost at attention as she waited. Only her shifting of a large bundle tucked under her arm indicated her impatience.

"I hope you will understand my asking, sergeant. What is it you bring?"

With a perturbed cock of her brow, she offered the bundle up for the com to scan. "Personal items for Ms. DaDhrga. Per your request, Dr. Jorn."

"Cleared," droned the com, though Jorn didn't need the confirmation. The truth of the sergeant's words carried readily in her clipped tone.

He was about to suggest that she leave the package at the door when Caer meekly poked her head out from the bedroom. Seeing the holograph, she stepped nervously through to stand at the edge of the living quarters. Half hidden behind long hair still wet from the shower, she utterly swam in the too-large jumpsuit her friend Jenna Randon had provided. Jorn bit back his moan. Caer had called Ms. Randon from the security station. Randon met them here shortly after he and Caer arrived, bringing clean clothes and toiletries. Took him half the night to convince Ms. Randon that Caer was better off staying here than going home with her, after which he feared Randon would never leave.

Returning his attention to Caer, he noted her anguish as she blinked in uneasy expectation at the holographic image before turning to meet his gaze. While the night's terror still lingered in the depths of her green eyes, she appeared reasonably composed. A vast improvement from her previous state. Dealing with a hysterical woman was not among Jorn's strong suites. He knew only two ways of handling them. Either sedate them or spell them to sleep. A little of each seemed in order, last night.

"I'm sorry, Caer. I didn't anticipate security sending anyone out so soon. Are you up to talking with the sergeant?"

She gave a tentative shrug. "Would it make any difference if my answer is 'no'?"

"Probably not." Still, he hesitated, sensing that her hysterics lay only slightly beneath the surface. "Allow entry," he said at last. The holograph shimmered out, and the door slipped open.

Pointedly ignoring Jorn, the officer nodded her acknowledgment of Caer, moving down the two steps of the entry and across the room to her. "Ms. DaDhrga, I'm Sgt. Sakin."

"Yes," Caer murmured. "I remember you."

Sakin extended the bundle. "Dr. Jorn requested that I collect a few things from your quarters this morning. I'm sure you are aware that you'll not be allowed back into your apartment until our investigation is completed."

"Yes. Of course. Thank you." Caer fidgeted with the package momentarily, then moved away from the sergeant's prolonged scrutiny. Setting the bundle on the end table next to the sofa, Caer darted a helpless glance across at Jorn.

Sakin turned as well, following the line of Caer's gaze, her expression suspicious. To Caer she directed, "If you would like to change clothes, I suggest you do so, now. Then gather whatever items are yours so that we can be on our way."

Caer frowned. "We...on our way?"

"We need to get you to a place of safety."

Jorn hastily strode the length of the room to stand between the sergeant and Caer. "We went through this last night. She is safe enough, here."

Sakin's features hardened. "That may have seemed acceptable last night, but it seems rather less so this morning. I must advise you that we are currently unable to finish checking your alibis from yesterday, doctor. Ms. DaDhrga's have been verified. You, however, remain a person of interest, sir."

"That's not possible." Disturbingly, the look Caer shot him appeared far less resolute than the tone of her proclamation. "He was with me."

"Indeed," the sergeant agreed. "The cams in Dr. Jorn's office and those outside of your apartment indicate as much. Still, there is a window of time regarding his supposed trip off-world that remains unconfirmed. We are awaiting the opportunity to view the vids from the shuttle he claims to have taken back to Ahira. That particular vehicle, however, is currently in a dead zone off-world. It may take a few days to reach an area open to communication. We will request their security vids the moment that occurs. In the meantime, we are also attempting to contact Drs. Berring and Eliz to confirm his having met with them. Thus far, we have been unable to locate either of them."

That last bit of news stunned Jorn. He'd expected both women to be back in their respective offices by now.

"Of course, he was off-world," Caer sniffed. "He met with Drs. Berring and Eliz to make arrangements for me to transfer to Earth to study." This time, a glimmer of doubt reflected in Caer's tone as well as her expression.

Needing to put all uncertainty to rest, Jorn set upon the sergeant with, "Check the vids at the shuttle station. I shouldn't be that hard to spot. I spent a good two hours pacing the same four meters of lobby floor during their security lock-down."

Sakin glowered. "The lock-down at the station was brought about by a breach in the security system. The entire network went offline just about the time you said your shuttle docked. Took out every scanning device and every camera. Curious coincidence, don't you think?"

"No more a coincidence for my timing than for that of the hundreds of others caught at the station."

"Yet you are the only one to 'encounter' a murder victim."

Jorn's glare was his only response.

"Until we can get to the bottom of the matter, protective custody is the wisest option for Ms. DaDhrga. Wouldn't you agree, sir?"

"Protective cus..." Caer blinked at the sergeant. "What makes you think I need protection?"

Sakin huffed her impatience. "It seems only reasonable. The incident took place in your apartment, did it not? And at a time you stated that you are usually home."

Jorn stifled a snarl. He agreed with the sergeant's conclusion regarding the target, just not with her assertion that Tanai security could be of any use, either in protecting Caer or in learning the truth about the murder.

Caer fidgeted with her necklace, her eyes downcast. "Dr. Jorn, thank you for your hospitality. I know the sergeant is wrong about me being the target as well as about you being a suspect, but maybe I should go with her. I don't want to impose on your..."

"It's no imposition, Caer. I welcome the company." Not altogether honest, though the words didn't rankle as much as he'd expected. In truth, he preferred his privacy. Just not at the expense of leaving Caer vulnerable to another assault. Forming the suggestion, he carefully nudged it into Caer's thoughts. *You are safe here. You must stay.* Aloud, he said, "The choice is yours, of course. But my offer stands."

Caer's eyes narrowed as her fingers stilled. For a moment, Jorn feared he'd not been cautious enough. Though her brow remained tucked in a confused frown, she murmured, "I will...I will stay here. If Dr. Jorn meant me any harm, he's had ample opportunity to follow through."

The sergeant's glower deepened. "I can't force you to come with me. But I urge you to reconsider."

Caer fingers continued to fuss with her necklace. "I don't know what's going on, sergeant. I don't know who the victim is, or how such a thing could happen in my apartment. But," Her eyes flicked to Jorn, her hands, at last, relaxing at her sides. "But I know I am perfectly safe right where I am."

Sakin remained unconvinced. Still, she appeared to recognize she'd lost this round, grudgingly declaring, "I hope your trust in him is well-founded, Ms. DaDhrga. As for the victim, we have identified her as one of the housing's janitorial personnel: a woman by the name of..."

"Mirra."

The name came so softly that Jorn wasn't sure he'd heard it, or if, rather, he'd simply detected it in Caer's thoughts.

"Yes," Sakin acknowledged. "That is the name we were given."

Caer went suddenly ashen. "The security cams. Do...do they show what happened?"

"The cams show the woman letting herself into your apartment and going about her chores clearly enough. However..." Sakin's glare shifted back to Jorn. "They apparently malfunctioned immediately there after. Not unlike that of the cams at the shuttle station yesterday evening. We've been unable to retrieve any further information from any of them."

Caer persisted. "The cams in my living room. They captured some glimpse of...of..."

"The entire system inside your apartment was knocked out. Aside from your departure early yesterday morning and this Mirra's arrival in the evening, no one else was recorded going in or out. We only know of your arrival with Dr. Jorn from the outside cameras."

While Sakin's persistent suspicion galled him, Jorn refused to waste an enchantment just to put her at ease. It was Caer's trust he needed, not the sergeant's.

"There is another matter that came to light when we spoke to the housing facilitator," Sakin continued gruffly. "We were informed that yesterday was not this Mirra's scheduled day for cleaning your apartment."

Caer blanched. "No. That would be today. She asked if she could change for this week. Said she wanted to spend some time with her mother. It's..." Tears glistened at the corners of Caer's eyes. "It's Mirra's mother's birthday...today."

"So, you did know that she would be in your quarters yesterday evening."

"I had forgotten. I..."

"Did you mention to anyone else this change in the schedule?"

"No. There was no reason to."

"Mm." The sergeant cocked her head. "Perhaps you begin to understand why we feel that you were most likely the intended victim."

Caer squared her shoulders as much as her trembling would permit. "Then it's all the more reason for me to stay with someone I know. Someone I trust."

The sergeant looked about to argue again but dropped the matter. "Very well. Should you think of anything else that might be helpful to our investigation, or anyone who has access to the security code for your apartment..."

"I told you a thousand times last night that the student housing department and their janitorial staff are the only ones here who know it."

Sakin's brow shot up. "The only ones here? There is someone else, though?"

Caer's face flushed. "Well, yes. Just Adrian."

Pulling a small keypad from her pocket, the officer began punching in the name. "And Adrian's surname?"

Caer hesitated. "Starn," she said at last. "Adrian Starn. He is a close friend."

"Why didn't you mention him before?"

"I just didn't think to," Care returned indignantly. "I had rather a lot spinning around in my head last night. Besides, Adrian lives on Bester III, not here on Ahira."

Creases cut across Sakin's brow, the edge to her tone sharpening. "The matter transfer station?"

"What!" Caer snapped with a stomp of her foot. "Do you think he just mat-transed straight into my quarters and murdered Mirra? Matter transfer requires a receiving unit, you know. Have you any idea how huge those things are? Ahira itself doesn't even possess one, never mind trying to fit such a behemoth into one tiny apartment. Besides, what possible reason could Adrian have for killing someone he'd never even met?"

The sergeant eyed Caer the way an exasperated parent might regard an obtuse adolescent.

Caer could only sputter several times before she managed to blurt out, "He's my friend!"

"Please, Ms. DaDhrga. You needn't shout at me. I'm merely doing my job." Pocketing the keypad, the officer moved up the steps to the landing, pausing long enough to regard Jorn one last time.

He dismissed her with a crisp, "Good day, Sergeant."

Sakin called icily over her shoulder as she departed, "If you should have second thoughts regarding our offer of protection, Ms. DaDhrga, we can send someone to pick you up at any time."

"Secure," Jorn commanded sharply, the door whooshing shut behind the sergeant, the lock snapping into place.

Caer stared at the empty entry, thick tears trailing down her cheeks, her voice dulled to a coarse whisper. "I'm so sorry, Mirra. So sorry. But you must have been the one the murderer was after. It couldn't have been me. I'm no one. Just a student. I don't even own anything worth taking."

9

Caer snapped awake with a cry, the image of Mirra's mangled and bloody body hovering within a ghosting of other grotesque corpses, many of which Caer feared she might know if their faces turned toward her. Dismissing the vision required several shuddering breaths. Only then did she realize she was back in Jorn's bedroom, clothed in her own jumpsuit. She'd fallen asleep. She'd hardly finished changing out of Jenna's clothes and into hers when the urge overtook her. Pushing up, she swung her feet around, listening as she slipped from the bed. Sounds of clattering greeted her from the room on the other side of the closed door. A quick scan of the room swept past Jenna's jumpsuit where it lay draped over the end of the bed and settled briefly on the empty mug left on the bedside table. The tea would help to calm her, Jorn had said. More like knock her out. At least until the dreams came, these more disturbing than the usual ones. All she ever recalled of those that so often plagued her was the impression of flames, scorching pain, and terror. This set she remembered vividly. Mirra's and the other tortured bodies. So very many of them. All broken. All twisted. All dark with the gore of their own blood.

Shuddering again, Caer forced her morose scrutiny to her reflection in the mirror above the small dresser. How pale she looked, the dark, hunter green of her jumpsuit casting her as a specter within it. Her eyes were hollowed, with heavy shadows underscoring them. Her hair was a disaster of tangled strands. How easily she could be taken for one of those ghostly corpses from her dreams. She needed to set herself in order. Locating her hair brush in the bundle Sgt. Sakin had delivered, she collected the pins she'd removed from her hair before taking a shower this morning, then set to brushing, twisting and pinning the length of her thick mane back in its usual tidy bun.

That accomplished, she returned to sit on the edge of the bed, uncertain whether to venture into the other room where she might disturb Dr. Jorn at whatever he was doing. A glance at her wrist for a check of the time informed her that her communicator was missing. She could ask the time of the room's com system. But that would alert Jorn that she was up and about. Her imposition on his good graces was most assuredly wearing very thin by now.

Her stomach rumbled as she noted the wafting of rich and spicy aromas on the room's gently circulating air. The rumbling repeated. When was it that she last ate? Probably yesterday afternoon with the two nutrient bars she'd devoured before leaving the university grounds for the club. After that, it was all alcohol…and tea.

The smells continued to waft, stirring more rumblings and prompting a faint dizziness. If she didn't eat something soon, she was likely to start gnawing on the furniture. Bracing herself with a deliberate breath, Caer rose, smoothed the front of her jumpsuit, and made tentatively for the door, opening it just enough to peer out. Jorn stood in his kitchen, his back to her as she edged her way into the living room, her bare feet padding silently on the dense pile of the carpet.

For several long seconds, she stood there taking in the incredible spaciousness of the man's accommodations. She'd been too preoccupied to pay them much heed, before. The fact that the rooms were sparsely furnished added to their sense of grand scale. A sofa, one end table, and two chairs were all that occupied the living room, and those were shoved off to the front corner opposite the steps to the entryway. The lush, azure blue velvet of the upholstery provided a dramatic counterpoint to the furniture's polished ebony wood.

An island separated the living area from the kitchen--a commonality with most apartments. This island, however, was twice the size of Caer's. Plus, there was additional space for a dining table on the nearer side of it. Caer chewed at her lip as she regarded the lovely ebony table with its six matching chairs upholstered in exquisite silver brocade. Even the soft silver-gray marble on all the counter tops was beautifully striking, rendering the entire space an elegance the likes of which she'd only ever seen in pictures. So much wealth, and she never knew. In truth, she doubted that very many people did.

Jorn's rattling finally ceased as he turned and acknowledged her with a nod. "I wondered how long it would take for the smell of dinner to lure you out." Granting her a bemused scrutiny, he added, "Found something more suitable to wear, I see." His quick glance at her bare feet prompted, "I assume you found your shoes on the bathroom counter. It's apt to take them a good while to dry, I'm afraid. Seems your friend Ms. Randon got a little over zealous with scrubbing them last night after she peeled you out of your clothes and tucked you in bed. I sent your clothing to be cleaned, by the way. Oh. You will find your wrist communicator in the drawer of the nightstand. I found it on the floor next to the bed."

Predictably, Caer felt her face warming. "Uhm... Thank you...for that...and for asking the sergeant to collect some of my things. And... well...everything." Staring at her toes, she mumbled, "I really must let you get back to your own life, though. I will just call for a pod."

"And go where?"

"Jen's, maybe."

Jorn shook his head. "There is no need for you to go anywhere, Caer. Certainly not before you sample my efforts at dinner. You'll insult me if you don't stay that long."

Caer's fingers plucked absently at her pant legs as she watched Jorn return to his preparations. He must have taken advantage of her napping to shower and clean up. The hint of dark circles still rimmed his amber eyes, but otherwise, he appeared well scrubbed and freshly shaved. She liked that he retained a more casual air, keeping the top two buttons of his crisp shirt undone, and his sleeves rolled up to his elbows.

The realization that he'd turned once more and was watching her, a faint half smile curling one corner of his mouth, sent her gaze to her feet again, while her hand searched out any strands of hair that may have escaped her bun. There were none.

"I hope you're hungry," he said. "Dinner's nearly ready. Please. Come. Sit down."

Caer hesitated. She didn't want to insult the man, though she wasn't entirely certain he had been truthful on that score. Finally, she padded her way past the elegant dining table, settling on the island's nearest barstool. Jorn, in the meantime, had dropped out of sight and was clanking around in the cabinet, leaving her to stare at his amazing assortment of kitchen appliances. Most people had perhaps one or two small items in their confined kitchenettes, preferring to leave any serious cooking to the staff of their respective apartment complex's kitchens. The residents either ate in the community dining halls with their neighbors or had meals sent up to them.

Before her, however, and flanked by cabinets that matched the ebony in Jorn's other furnishings, were a magnificent refrigeration unit, a cooking surface with enough burners for at least half a dozen pots, and the largest oven she'd ever seen. There were also a dozen or more small appliances tucked in the space beneath the upper cabinets. Curiously, all of them looked like they'd been taken straight out of some ancient 21st-century museum catalog.

The lid on one of the two pots currently occupying burners rattled as the contents began to boil enthusiastically.

"I...I hope you're not going to all of this trouble on my account."

"Only in some small part," muffled back at her from below. "I enjoy doing this."

"You...you do it often? Cooking? I mean, why go to so much bother?"

Jorn reached two crystal goblets up, depositing them on the

island top before rising seconds later with a bottle in hand. "Like I said, I like cooking. Do it every chance I get."

Caer's incredulous stare took in the antiquated appliances once more. "It must be quite a challenge, using those things."

"You can't improve on perfection," Jorn returned, opening a couple of drawers and rummaging through them. "I don't care how many 'upgrades' are added to contemporary cooking devices, they never function half so well as these. Besides," he noted, making a broad gesture. "I have something of an affinity for old things. The challenge was finding and getting all of this delivered here, having them modified for the building's power cells, and then acquiring the permits to install it all." Triumph on his face, Jorn withdrew a small corkscrew from one of the drawers. "I don't know what the fool of a building manager thought I intended to do with this stuff if I wasn't going to be allowed to use them."

"Why would you want to? I wouldn't even know where to begin."

"It's the satisfaction of preparing a meal the way I want it, I guess." Popping the cork from the wine bottle, Jorn offered, "Can I interest you in a glass with dinner?"

Caer blanched. "You think I should after last night, and after... after whatever it was you slipped into my tea?"

Jorn's response was more than a little taken aback. "You knew?"

She shrugged. "What's not to know? It isn't likely that my foolish hysterics would have evaporated so quickly, or that I'd have so suddenly dropped off to sleep, either last night or this afternoon, if you hadn't done something of the sort."

"Under the circumstances, Caer, I'd hardly classify your hysterics as foolish. Still, I'm sorry. I had no right."

"No right to what? Give us both a little peace? I'm grateful." Now she was the one who wasn't being completely honest.

Jorn's chuckle accompanied his half-smile ticking to a lopsided grin. Caer would have liked it better if he'd offered one of those rare and glorious full smiles. The thought instantly set her to a pointed scrutiny of the basket of warm bread and the bowl of apples in front of her, hoping mightily that her face was nowhere near as red as it felt, or that he hadn't read her thoughts on her countenance, again. Jorn, however, had returned his attention to the pots, draining water from one into the sink before adding the contents of the second to it and delicately mixing the combination with a couple of long-handled forks."

"I suppose you're going to tell me that you always eat like this as well."

"Often enough," he agreed, pulling a couple of plates from one of the upper cabinets. Filling each with a sauce-covered pasta, he set one in front of Caer and the other on his side of the island, tugging a barstool over from the island's corner with the toe of his shoe. "You don't have to drink this if you'd prefer not to," he said, filling a goblet with a red wine and setting it next to her plate. Again, he rummaged in one of the drawers, this time retrieving a pair of forks and handing one across to her. Taking a seat, he encouraged, "Go ahead. Eat."

Caer's delighted nod with the first mouthful prompted a wider grin from Jorn. "It's an old recipe. Been around for generations. My mother passed it along to me."

Caer's hand paused, fork partway to her mouth. "Your mother."

"You needn't look so stunned. I do have one, you know."

Her face went warm again, damn it! "I guess I just hadn't given much thought to your having a family somewhere." Just like she'd not given any thought to the possibility that he might once have been married.

"Believe me,' he snorted. "I do."

"Are they very far away?"

"Not far enough. Some are on Old Earth. The rest are scattered." He took a moment to savor a few bites. "Not bad," he admitted. "Mother always has known her way around a good meat sauce. What of your parents? Are they still on a Perimeter Ship?"

"No. They died in a lab explosion just a few months after I went to live with my Aunt Sidra."

There was a leaden pause before, "I'm sorry, Caer."

"No need to be. It was a long time ago."

The meal continued in uncomfortable silence for a long while before Caer finally broke it with a timid, "You said you were Earth-born."

"Guilty."

"I can't imagine why you ever left."

"When you see her, you'll know why." Rising and taking up his wine, Jorn strolled quietly around to stand in the middle of his living room, his back to her. At length, he asked, "Do you believe in magic, Caer?"

That was certainly an odd question. "Magic? How do you mean?"

"The hocus-pocus sort. You know. Someone mumbles a few words and something completely inexplicable and totally unexpected happens."

"I might buy the unexpected part, but not the inexplicable. Why?"

"Mmm. Thought as much. Humor me for a moment, will you? Pretend that you believe." Addressing the air, Jorn stated, "Setting. Old Earth. Seascape. Night." The room lights flickered and dimmed.

Caer gave a small gasp as everything shimmered briefly, each object within the room shifting, changing. The familiar forms of sofa, chairs, dining table—all took on the manifestations of boulders or rock outcroppings of varying sizes and shapes. Beneath her, though the softness of the carpeted floor remained, its appearance was that of sand, white and glistening in the moonlight. Moonlight! Caer bit back another gasp as, overhead, a magnificent full, blue-white orb shone, the faint glimmer of distant stars scattered through the depth of blackness surrounding it.

Slowly, her eyes widening, Caer took in the full scope of her surroundings. Nothing was as it had been. Where the island stood, there now sprawled an enormous uprooted stump of some ancient tree, Caer's plate and goblet seemingly perched on it. Instead of walls, there now stretched an unimaginable expanse of rugged beach with rolling and frothing surf.

"Once upon a time," Jorn murmured, "the cradle of humankind held tremendous beauty."

Caer slipped from the stool that now resembled a boulder. Taking a couple of uncertain steps past Jorn, she managed a hoarse, "I don't believe in magic. But I never believed in the abilities of the Dream Painters, either." She turned full circle, gaping in dazzled amazement. "Not until now. I've heard about such works, of course. But I thought them greatly exaggerated. Never did I believe I would actually see one."

"This one is my favorite."

Favorite! Surely, he didn't mean that he owned more than one! Caer cast an awestruck scan between him and the breath-taking setting.

"You once told me you wish to study human culture at its place of origin. There is no hope of understanding our earliest stirrings of thought or the structure of ancient beliefs unless you have some understanding of the Earth of those distant times. It's a reality you can't possibly experience, now. This..." Jorn gave a sweeping gesture. "This is a mere reflection of what once existed."

Downing the last of his wine, he called, "Shift. Old growth oak forest. Daylight." Everything shimmered again, resolving in a dense stand of towering trees, some with immense and burly trunks of gray, others with long, slender, silvered trunks—all draped in tatters of moss. A breeze brushed Caer's cheek, stirring the boughs and rustling the heavily lobed leaves. Here and there a few of them dropped to join the littering of yellow and brown on the forest floor. The heady aroma of damp soil and dense vegetation filled Caer's senses as a dappling of sunshine gently filtered through the canopy to touch her face. Somewhere in the deepest recesses of her imaginings, she felt she'd once known such a place.

"Shift. Seascape. Night." The room glistened in its return to the first of the images. "There are others," Jorn said, setting his glass aside on the dining table turned stone outcropping. "But in these two I find the greatest sense of serenity."

Caer could only stare in undiminished wonder as she tried to soak in the panoramic view. Above them, the moon appeared to trace its way slowly across the heavens. In all the colonies she'd visited, all the planets and moons she'd seen from onboard the Perimeter Ship and various shuttles, never had she experienced anything like this. Always, she'd viewed the universe through the dull translucence of shielding domes, or through the confines of survival suits or ship's portals. Here, with the heavens open above her and the ocean's horizon stretching out to meet it, there was a sense of both magic and mystery unlike anything she'd ever known. Here, the colossal moon felt close enough to touch, the surrounding stars a set of icy jewels to be collected by the outstretched hand. "Is it truly this magnificent?"

"Was," he corrected. "Far more so than the meager impression represented by this painting. Think how our earliest ancestors, possessing no science to explain their world, must have felt, surrounded by a vast richness of life set within such a remarkable cosmos."

"No wonder the moon was such a powerful image for them."

"Very powerful. As was all of nature."

The nearness of Jorn's voice startled Caer. Turning, she found him standing scarcely a hand span away. Her heart thumped furiously at the heat of his proximity. His hands reached for and plucked the pins from her hair. When it tumbled loose over her shoulders, his smile was the one that most dazzled her; that made her dizzy and stole her breath away all at once.

"You would have been right at home in that time and place, I think."

"I..."

"Sshhh. Just stand there and let an old fool enjoy looking at you." Caer complied, not knowing how else to respond. "Green suits you, you know. And your hair. You should leave it down." His brow furrowed as he stepped even closer. "I had no idea it would be so difficult to send you away." His fingers played, for a time, with the tendrils of hair that hung at her temples. At last, he took her shoulders and pulled her gently to him.

Perhaps she should have been embarrassed at her eagerness for his embrace. Perhaps she shouldn't have met his kisses with such relish. But when a girl's most glorious fantasy becomes a solid reality, and a whole multi-verse of new possibilities opens before her, what's she to do?

10

Caer rocked on the bed, her arms wrapped around her raised knees. A thin line of light filtered in beneath the door. What the hell happened out there? Jorn's embrace was so unexpected, his kisses full of such heat. Equally unexpected was his pull away from her, his expression suddenly guarded as he suggested she should return to the bedroom. Said she needed her sleep and he had work to do.

Her lower lip jutted into a pout. Perhaps the wine coupled with whatever sympathy he felt for her current predicament played into his actions. She didn't believe he'd had that much wine, though. And she didn't want his sympathy. She wanted to trust the passion she thought was there. Apparently, she was mistaken about the passion. Angry tears misted her eyes, and her jaw tensed. What a fool to let him play her like that! Were the hour not so late, she'd call for a pod to take her to Jen's.

For a short while, she listened to him pacing in the other room. Then it was quiet, with only the occasional murmur of "scan" breaking the stillness. That and the flickering light beneath the door suggested that Jorn was busy with some computer file or other. Making up for the day's worth of university matters, no doubt. He certainly never made it in to his office. Caer wondered what Jenna made of the fact that she and Jorn were both missing from the university. What was she going to tell her friend?

Plopping back on the bed, Caer closed her eyes, shoving the thought aside in favor of recalling the warmth of Jorn's arms; the hot and hungry pressure of his lips against hers. Those were not wine-induced kisses. She would know if it were otherwise. Wouldn't she? Maybe Jorn was afraid he'd embarrassed her or thought he'd expected too much of her. Maybe he didn't want to love her. Maybe the sting of his divorce left him unwilling to chance another relationship.

Caer sat up. What if she slipped back out there. Let him know... What, exactly? That she was madly in love with him; had been from the moment of their first meeting? How many other women thrust themselves at him, feeling as she did? Her feelings might not even be love. How could she know for certain?

Maybe. What if. Caer wanted specifics, not qualifiers. Even if she couldn't settle on any regarding her own feelings, the man at least owed her an explanation for his coming on to her, and then suddenly rejecting her. Dropping back, she rolled to her side to watch the seepage of light as it blinked out. With an irritated grab for the blankets, she tossed them over her head, twisting around to hug the pillow. For a long time, she lay there, lost in the profusion of questions that haunted her. Had she done or said something to offend him? Had she surprised him by responding so quickly and eagerly? Did he feel the passion insinuated in his kisses? Would he come to her, now that he'd apparently finished his work? If he did, was it out of lust? Was that all her own reaction was? In the end, she fell into a fitful slumber. Unwelcome visions of blood and fire and death wrapped around and smothered the sweetness of Jorn's embrace; blotted out the heat of his kisses; concealed the romance of the Dream Paintings, of the moonlight. Together, they sent her, lost and wandering, in a dark and twisted forest.

The smell of fresh, damp earth, rich with overtones of vegetation. A swirl of green in the darkness. Motion and sound blurred together as one. Drumming. Footfalls striking out a familiar rhythm. The closeness of others. Flickering warmth upon her face. Fingers of fire dance skyward. A face in the flames.

No, child! You must away!

Her hand reaches for...

66

One, two, three, four, five, six, seven. One, two, three. One, two, three. The circle moves. In its midst, a blazing geyser erupts. Red! Fire! Blood!

Drumming. Wailing. Blood gushing from the very air; pouring over her; pooling beneath her feet, thick and sticky. Like the drumming, the blood does not stop. It deepens, rising to her calves...to her knees...to her thighs. A face glistens within it. A sweet face. An achingly familiar face. Sorrowful eyes regard her, then widen in horror. Flames billow, devouring the face; boiling away the blood; searing her with agony.

Peace. For a moment. At a great distance below lies the whole of Ahira in crystalline clarity. A flash. Sparks. A great explosion. Massive chunks of debris shoot skyward from the crumbling of the great dome complex. Dark smoke engulfs twisted metal and masses of concrete, as a roiling blaze eats through. From the depths of the flames extends a great arm, covered in long, matted hair. Protruding, razor-sharp claws reach for her.

11

The sheer panic of Caer's scream brought Jorn instantly awake. It took another few seconds for his brain to make all the appropriate connections and send him flying into the bedroom, expecting to find gore-smeared mayhem in progress. There was nothing. Only Caer thrashing in the throes of some nightmare. Taking her shoulders, he pulled her up, shaking her gently, calling her name. The screams subsided—slowly—replaced by violent trembling.

"Emergency?" queried the com for at least the third or fourth time.

"No emergency. Lights up minimum." Jorn wrapped his arms around her, holding her close. Her skin was ice-dry to the touch. Rocking her, he waited for the trembling to die away. At length, she managed a ragged sigh and pushed back, ashen, her eyes downcast.

"Was it something I said?" he asked, hoping to tease out at least a glimmer of a smile. Getting no response, he took her chin and turned her face to his. Terror still danced in the depths of her green eyes.

"It's all right, Caer. There is nothing here to harm you." Drawing her close again, he leaned back against the bed's headboard. "Must have been some dream! About last night, I presume."

She could only shake her head.

What else could be stalking her subconscious? "Would you like to tell me about it?"

Her voice scraped out a hoarsely whispered, "No."

"As you wish."

Gradually, she relaxed, her head resting against Jorn's bare chest, her breath coming more regularly. Just as he thought she might drop off to sleep once more, she tensed, and, with a muffled cry, jerked suddenly away from him. Wild-eyed, she stared past him, as though witnessing in the empty ether, an act of unspeakable horror. Again, her breath came in a series of terrorized gasps.

"Look at me, Caer. Breathe deeply, slowly, and look at me."

Jorn pressed his fingers lightly against her temples, his gaze locked on hers. "Return to the dream. See it for me." His words pushed delicately past her resistance. "What is it that haunts you? See for me but remain separate from the dream. Observe without fear."

A vision gradually formed, filled with a sense of motion, as of dancing. Then came fire and blood and roiling clouds of smoke. At the center hovered the faint impression of a single post or pillar that seemed almost alive with its writhing. Flames lapped at it. And from it, a voice screamed, "No, child! You must away!" Heavier flames overtook it. And then...a moment of settling and shifting. In that moment, Jorn recognized the whole of the Ahiran complex sprawled far below him—the curve of the translucent master dome that housed the university; the shuttle docking bays and station at the master dome's northern periphery; the clusters of smaller residential and business domes; the interconnecting series of tubes. All of it snaked across only a fraction of the vast emptiness that was this world.

Sparks ignited. Jorn saw them begin at the shuttle station. Flicking like tiny lightning flashes, they moved quickly across the shuttle station's inner circumference before shooting into the master dome, then splintering into the tubes and lesser domes. Each spark, each flash, crackled in his ears. Together, they built at last to a rolling rumble that shook the entire complex. And then came the rending series of splits that traversed the full curve of the master dome, fracturing it and extending along the tubes. The blast that followed ruptured domes and tubes alike exploding fireballs the size of buildings outward from the shattering colony.

Huge shards of debris hurtled outwards on tongues of flame and wind. Dust and ash and smoke billowed in the dense air below, revealing through the thick haze the blazing remains. And from them, as though rising from the brimstone of hell, a great, clawed hand stretched out.

Jorn dispelled the vision with a flicking wave of his hand. For several long seconds, he sat staring at the young woman whose glazed eyes remained locked on his. At last finding his voice, he whispered, "Listen to me, Caer. It was a dream, and now it is forgotten. Do you understand?"

She nodded.

"Good. Sleep, now. Forgetfulness is your balm. Upon waking, you will have no memory, either of the dream's content or my presence in your mind."

Slowly withdrawing from the bed, he eased Caer down, tucking the blankets around her. His temples ached. Massaging them, he considered. Another premonition. This one was of a magnitude even greater than the one from last night. It gave him little choice but to accept it as a grave portent.

No accident, this. Someone had to go to a great deal of trouble to lay so many charges within the massive complex. And that would take time, depending on how many saboteurs were at work. Perhaps the work had already begun. If they'd started with the shuttle station, it would explain why security had been breached and the cams knocked out.

Wearily, Jorn sank back against the wall. The level of violence within the premonition was a sure indication that Nemhain's line was behind the pending disaster, just as they had undoubtedly been behind the murder in Caer's apartment. Why should they care so much about eliminating this one girl? Why seek her with such vehemence as to destroy an entire world? Or was there something more they were after?

It was a mystery he would have to resolve later. The more urgent need was to get Caer away from Ahira as quickly as possible. Most of the people here were going to die—a fact that could not be helped. There was simply no way to evacuate the whole of the population, particularly when he had no more reason to offer than a young woman's nightmare; a nightmare she could no longer recall, thanks to the enchantment he'd placed within her mind.

"I'm none too keen on setting you on your journey," he muttered. "Even less so knowing that I'm about to acquire passage for you through the mat-trans station where this Adrian Starn is posted. My search of the records this evening has produced information on the man that is full of more holes than your sketchy background. You've declared, however, that you have known him for many years. That he's a friend. I dare say you could use one, right now." Running a hand through his hair, Jorn sighed. "I hope your confidence in him is warranted, Caer. May your prescience warn you well away from him, should he prove to be a threat."

For a handful of minutes, he continued to study Caer's face, brushing her cheek with the backs of his fingers. Finally, straightening and extending his hands over her, Jorn pronounced somberly, "Abred. Though I am human, impure, now do I call to thee. Draw to me, ye spirits of earth and air. Draw to me, ye spirits of fire and water. Gwynfyd. I call to you, ye elements of purity. Ceugant. I call thee through infinity. Draw to me. From the ancients of old, the graces bestowed such powers to unfold. Draw through time and space the strength to form this spell. Find through me the power to bind. Round this woman no evil shall come. Unto her, no harm may fall." White energy surged from his fingertips, briefly encapsulating Caer.

Lowering his arms, Jorn fell heavily back against the wall, the throb in his temples redoubled. Too long, he'd remained complacent. His strength and skills had suffered for it. "I can do no better than this, for now. May it be enough."

Again he straightened to stand over her, his fingers once more brushing her cheek. "I should never have allowed you to know that I

71

care for you. It was a stupid mistake. Perhaps someday. But it cannot be now." Leaning, he kissed her gently on the forehead. "Once you reach Earth, you will be in the best possible keeping I know. May my spell protect you, at least until then. If the fates are with me, I will follow after you."

12

Tucked at the edge of her seat, her cheek planted against the portal, Caer shivered at the vast, bleak space beyond the shuttle. Somewhere, Earth awaited her. Mysterious. Intriguing. The ancient world beckoned, as it always did. Yet her journey was tainted, now. She never said goodbye to Jenna. Would probably never see her or Brandon again, except by way of vid contacts. The weight of missing them slumped her back in her seat with a deep sigh. As soon as she reached the mat-trans station she would send her deepest apologies to Jen, along with an explanation for her sudden departure. Assuming she could sort out what to say.

A more ragged sigh escaped, despite her attempt to bite it back. She'd likely never see Dr. Jorn, again, either. Maybe he wanted it that way. He'd certainly rid himself of her quickly enough. Had gone into hyper-drive, following her nightmare. Caer didn't remember anything about the stupid dream; only that she woke screaming. Afterward, she fell asleep in Jorn's arms, then awakened again to him urging her to shower quickly and gather her few belongings. The next thing she knew, they were on their way to the shuttle station. He said a change of scenery would do her good. Her change of scenery would do him good, more like.

Caer's sullen frown became a full pout. Three days on this shuttle, a grand adventure ahead of her, and all she could do was stew over missing her friends and...and fretting about Dr. Jorn's last impressions of her. One minute he was asking to be her friend, another, she was lost in his embraces and kisses, and another he was shoving her onto a shuttle. Well, maybe not shoving, exactly.

Closing her eyes, Caer's mind drifted back to that evening in Jorn's apartment, his arms folding her to him, the warmth of his body tight against hers, his kisses searing her lips. She wanted those moments back. Would even settle for the little she remembered after waking from her nightmare--how he nestled her against him until her trembling and her tears ceased and she settled into a quiet slumber. Then there was the shuttle station. Though Jorn was resolute in getting her boarded, his eyes suggested a deep sorrow. She hoped it was sorrow for her leaving.

An abrupt round of thunderous snores from the adjacent seat shattered her wistful thoughts. Shooting an uneasy glance toward the man, Caer rubbed her arms at the chill that came over her. A woman initially occupied that seat. The woman, however, became suddenly ill, and had to be escorted from the vessel. Scarcely minutes before the shuttle's engines fired for departure, this guy turned up.

Caer's lip curled. Of all the individuals waiting to fill last minute vacancies, why did it have to be this guy? It wasn't the man's tremendous bulk that bothered her, though she admitted she didn't appreciate his massive rotund-ness spilling over the armrest onto her side when he could as easily shift to let it spill toward the aisle. No. It was more the manner of his solicitous attempts at conversation that put her off. That and the coldness of his eyes and the shameless leer with which he persistently regarded her when he was awake. He reminded her of some great, predatory beast. If she could scrunch into the crevice between her seat and the shuttle's hull, she would gladly spend the entire trip huddled there.

Instead, she edged closer to the portal once more. Seconds later, her murmur of relief at the glint of light reflecting from a distant metallic speck breathed out more loudly than she'd intended. Caer avoided the temptation to glance at her neighbor again, taking his continuing snores as a good sign. Rather, she kept her eyes trained on that distant shimmer, the shuttle creeping ever closer to it, until, at long last, the enormous wheel loomed before her. The Bestor III Mat-trans Station.

Despite her eagerness to be on her way, Caer made no motion to pull her pack from beneath her seat. Disembarking would be a while, yet. Still, it felt good to have this much of her journey behind her. And, given the two-day lay-over before she was scheduled for mat trans, she would have a fair amount of time to spend with Adrian. She wondered if he would be in his quarters when she arrived, or if he was working.

Ayee! Adrian! Caer's head thumped against the portal in dismay. She'd sent no word to him of her coming. Hadn't even thought of it until now. Not that she expected he would care. The last several times she'd spoken to him he suggested it was time for her to visit him again. Arriving unannounced, however, was likely not what he had in mind. Well, best to make the most of the situation. It might even pick up her spirits a bit, surprising him.

A scowl worried her brow. What if Ahira's security had contacted him already? Oh, she really hoped not! Better for her to broach the subject of the murder in her apartment without mention of the ridiculous suspicions Sgt. Sakin held regarding him. Better yet if she could avoid mentioning the incident altogether. Adrian would not take any part of the news well.

"Almost there, I see."

Caer cringed. Oh, fine! The great snoring mound was awake. "Yes," she muttered. The sense of the man's gaze on her sent a shudder down her spine.

"Cold?"

"No."

"I would be happy to loan you my jacket."

The condescending quality of the man's voice grated along Caer's nerves. "No. Thanks," she managed through clenched teeth as she attempted a polite smile. "I'm fine." His perpetual leer made her feel like prey, again. Fortunately, the beginning roll of the shuttle provided the opportunity to avert her gaze. Unfortunately, it also set a wave of nausea in motion.

The man chuckled. "First space docking?"

Why couldn't he just leave her alone? "No. They always leave me feeling turned inside-out."

Reaching across to Caer's lap, he gave her hand a patronizing pat that sent an unexpected jolt through her. Worse, his unwelcome touch lingered. "Yes. I understand that happens to some," he acknowledged. "You know, if you don't watch, it won't bother you as much."

She preferred watching the rotation to looking at him. Both visuals kept her stomach churning. At least the vast station beyond the shuttle's hull wasn't ogling her. When the man's fingers finally lifted, Caer took the opportunity to quickly sit on her hands, relieved that the roll of the vessel had at last ceased. A few minutes later, the craft eased into position at its appointed docking bay with barely a bump.

Another shudder took her at the parting leer the man cast as he pried his bulk from his seat and forced his way into the crowd filling the aisle. Retrieving her pack, Caer took her time to check its straps, making sure they were buckled and tight. Only when the man was well ahead of her did she shoulder it and edge into the press of passengers, human and otherwise, making their way slowly toward the hatch.

Passengers disembarking from other flights mixed with them as they shuffled along the confined corridor running the length of the docking spoke, everyone pushing and bumping toward the large public sector at the center of the station. Overhead, the com system hissed with a barely intelligible, "Urgent message for passengers of shuttle 713 arriving from Ahira. Please meet in the public gathering room on deck C of the hub. Thank you."

Caer gave a disgruntled huff. She was in no mood to sit through some stupid public announcement, particularly if it meant coming back into contact with the guy she'd just escaped. Her flesh suddenly prickled with the sense that he was breathing down the back of her neck. Venturing a quick glimpse over her shoulder, she discovered him some three or four meters behind her. How he'd gotten there without her noticing was a mystery. However he'd managed it, he was watching her in that ugly, predatory manner of his. Damn! She picked up her pace, pushing hard against those in front of her.

The bottlenecked corridor finally opened out to a series of security posts that marked the entry to the station's core. Caer dared another uneasy glance back, waiting to see which post the man would make for before picking a line as far removed from his as she could manage. Happily, her line moved more quickly than his. Offering voice verification and a retinal scan, she slipped through the gate, holding back again to scan the milling passengers who'd also cleared. At last, she spotted the familiar great hulk just passing through his gate and heading toward the lifts to C deck.

Caer set out at a quick trot across the large, circular hub, weaving her way through the throng, making for the nearest checkpoint to the private sector before noticing the series of guards ringing the hub's outer perimeter. Rarely had she seen so many. The station always maintained an unobtrusive, plain-clothed contingent, of course. But these were fully uniformed, armed, and highly visible. The nearest stood at attention next to the security panel at the checkpoint she needed to clear, his constant scan of the area settling on her as she approached. Caer fidgeted with her necklace, uncertain whether to address him or simply speak to the panel.

The guard resolved the dilemma by stepping forward, blocking her way. "State your name and business, Miss."

"Caer DaDhrga. I wish to visit Adrian Starn. The security panel's voice recognition will bring my name up and show that I have clearance."

"First Officer Starn, huh?" The guard withdrew a small, keyed communicator from his shirt pocket and coded something into it. The screen lit up.

"There," she said, peering around his arm. "I told you. I already cleared security at the checkpoint entering the hub." Her brow wrinkled as she noticed the red 'DEC' next to her name. "What's that mean?"

The guard frowned, eyeing her suspiciously while mumbling, "Clear." Holding the now blank screen up to face her, he added, "Not all of the checkpoints have received the current updates. So, state your full name, please. And look squarely into the device."

Another voice and retinal scan? Security really was tight. She'd have to find out from Adrian what was afoot. "Caer Rowan DaDhrga," she complied.

The guard turned the screen back for his own viewing. "Well, you certainly appear to be whom you say." Scratching his head, he offered a shrug. "Must have been an input error. There's been a lot of that with all these last-minute updates." Nodding toward her pack, he asked, "What are you carrying?"

Caer held it up. "Clothing and personal items."

The guard used his device to scan it, watching the information scroll across the screen. "Your pack is cleared. Any other luggage?"

'No."

"I'm sending your request for a visit directly to first Officer Starn," he said, his fingers quickly keying the message into the communicator.

"I was rather hoping to surprise him."

"Yes. Well. Under the circumstances, I'm afraid I can't permit you access to the private sector without his personal approv..."

The guard jumped, grabbing at his ear. "Please, sir!" he huffed. "I can hear you without your shouting!" Taking a deep breath, he stated with more decorum, "Yes, sir. I know. That's what the system told me, as well, sir. But the voice and retinal scans indicate otherwise."

With an indignant harrumph, the guard stood back a pace and eyed Caer up and down. "Petite young lady. Sort of cinnamon-colored hair, green eyes..." He grinned. "Actually, sir, she looks pretty lively to me." Sobering instantly, he snapped, "Yes, sir." Granting

Caer a curt nod, he muttered, "Acceptance confirmed. If it's a surprise visit you wish, you certainly have it."

Caer puzzled over the guard's behavior all the way from the hub, down the moving walkway that ran the length of the private sector spoke, and around the rim to Adrian's quarters. The end of her shuttle trip was fast becoming as disconcerting as the start of it had been. Nor did the request for yet another voice and retinal scan at Adrian's door do anything to lessen her grumbling irritation. Cleared--again--the door opened to the familiar thin and tinny greeting of, "Welcome, Caer DaDhrga."

She'd hardly stepped across the threshold, however, when the station's alarm blared a series of short, high- pitched wails. The apartment's metal door slammed shut, sealing her within. For a long moment, she stood with her heart thrashing against her ribs, waiting for her eyes to adjust to the blackness that enveloped her. The siren sound from the corridor outside was muffled to near oppressive silence, here, and minutes later faded altogether. Then came the crackle of the room's com.

"All security personnel report to your duty quadrants. All guests are to remain within the quarters of your hosts. If you have been caught in one of the corridors, please move quickly to the hub. All currently off-boarded travelers are to remain in or return to the hub. Those who are currently aboard a docked shuttle are to return to your seats and remain there until security issues an all-clear. We apologize for this inconvenience and request your patience as we identify the source of a recent security breach. You will be allowed to resume your travels as soon as this matter is resolved."

Caer's hands pressed to her chest as she drew a shaky breath, letting it out in a slow, equally shaky exhale. "You'd think security had better things to do than scaring people out of their wits," she muttered. "And likely for no more reason than some idiot getting in a hurry and jumping a checkpoint post." Shooting a glance in the direction she knew one the apartment's security cams to be, she added, "Resolve the matter indeed! It's not like you guys don't have eyes everywhere to know precisely what's going on."

The cam, its green light barely visible in the dark shadows between the wall and ceiling, offered no comment. Not that she'd expected any. Nobody cared about one lone visitor quaking in her shoes while some lowly security officer was busy making excuses for having blinked at just the wrong time, thus missing the checkpoint jumper. "Lights up full," she snipped. The room brightened, though it did nothing to lighten her mood. Instead, a chill raised the hair on her arms, causing her to hesitate, still just inside the door. Something wasn't right.

"Oh, for pity's sake, Caer!" she erupted. She was the thing that wasn't right--showing up so unexpectedly. She should be thankful Adrian accepted her visit. For all she knew, she might have come at a time when he had some other lady friend in residence. He did, after all, have other lady friends.

Rubbing her arms, Caer cast about for any indication of another 'guest'. Nothing was obvious, at least from where she stood. The counter in Adrian's small kitchenette bore nothing more than his favorite mug. A customary pile of computer chips topped the desk in his living area. And the little grouping of sofa and couple of conform chairs, along with their flanking end tables, occupied the same area in the center of the room where they always stood. Though Adrian was definitely a man of habit, surely having a woman in residence would result in additional dishes on the counter, or at least one of the pieces of furniture adjusted differently. In truth, the absence of such evidence was almost disappointing. Caer could do with a bit of company, about now.

As if sensing her need, the unmistakable music of Adrian's voice lilted from the com system. "Caer?"

"Adrian! When..."

"I'm sorry I can't greet you in person, love. I'm more than anxious to see you. As you can guess, however, something has come up that requires my attention. You know your way around. Make yourself at home. I will join you as soon as I can."

And then it was silent again. He'd not even hung around sufficiently for her to ask how long he thought 'as soon as possible' might be. Agitation sucked Caer's lower lip in. First, she couldn't surprise him. Now she had to wait to see him. And with security in some state of hyper-vigilance, she couldn't even leave the confines of his quarters to meander about.

"Make myself at home," she grumbled, scuffling a brief circuit of the room before heading to the sofa, undecided as to whether she should just sit and wait, or go freshen up a little. She was still mid-dither when the hair on the back of her neck rose again, charging every fiber of her body with a disconcerting and painful tingle. Spinning, she stared hard at the open doorway to Adrian's bedroom, her hands clutching at the renewed hammering of her heart, the image of her own bloodied room filling her head.

"No," she insisted, swallowing hard. It's absurd to even think such a thing could happen again. It couldn't.

Air stirred ever so slightly behind her. With a jerk, she spun once again, this time to stare into the far corner of the living room. The air seemed to ripple, just at the edge of her vision. She tried to fix on it, waiting. Another ripple? No. No. She was wrong. There was nothing more in that corner than the usual shadows created by the room's lighting.

With a long, ragged sigh, she mumbled, "Now whose hyper-vigilant...and paranoid, as well? You're losing it, Caer DaDhrga." Her stomach rumbled. "This is what comes of fatigue and the failure to eat for too many hours. You should have had some lunch on the shuttle. The brain is the first to go when you fail to eat properly. Want proof? Just listen to you talking to yourself."

A small flip of her hand indicated her effort to dismiss her lingering tension. What she needed was a distraction. "Music list," she called. A partial display of Adrian's extensive catalogue flickered to light against the wall. Naturally, it had to be the wall nearest the doorway to his bedroom. Still edgy, Caer slipped close enough to lean around the doorframe for a peak in. The room was as tidy as ever, Adrian's bed neatly made, his closed locker topped with the same picture of her that she'd given him years ago. "Told you so," she sniffed, straightening. "So, put your silliness out of your head."

Stepping back, she returned her attention to the music list. "So. For my distraction. Traditional ethnic pieces from ancient Earth." The wall shimmered as the list jumped to a series of category headings—each the name of some country that no longer existed, or the name of the tribes or societies that once peopled said country. Caer's choice was a toss-up between her two favorite categories--Macedonian and Celtic. "Celtic," she decided. Again, the wall shimmered, another list skimming into view. Chewing at the side of her lip, Caer tried to remember the names of some of the liveliest dances. Shrugging, she settled with, "Apply the list of my last selections."

The sound of bagpipes, penny whistles, and a type of hand drum Adrian called a bodhran instantly filled the room with a frolicking reel. It was exactly what she wanted! Contentedly, she set her feet into the easy rise and fall of the rhythm pattern, gliding around Adrian's living room, through the open-ended kitchenette, and around to slip delicately through the space that separated the sofa and one of the chairs. Wheeling, she continued the dance, retracing her route.

A flash of thick, grizzled hair and yellowed fangs shot through her mind, bringing her to a stumbling halt. Then came the crackle of putrid air. Though something deep within her screamed for her to run, her feet refused the command. Instead, a macabre sense of curiosity edged her slowly around.

Drumming. Footfalls striking out a familiar rhythm. Hands held. Bodies moving as one. Forward and back. The dance moves Deosil, one, two, three, four, five, six, seven. One, two, three. One, two, three. Widdershins. One, two, three, four, five, six, seven. One, two, three. One, two, three. Heat. Fingers of fire dance skyward. A face in the flames. There is something she must take. Reaching out, her hand closes on...

Angry red tongues of flame coil around her. Searing pain eating at flesh. Eyes stare down on her glowing with a turquoise heat, grim and scowling. Agony gnaws through to her very bones. She opens her mouth but can voice no cry. The grim eyes soften. Cool arms encompass her.

Drumming. The circle moves round.

"Caer!" The melodic voice called to her from heavy darkness. Wrapped around it was the sound of bagpipes and drums.

"Caer! Look at me!"

Urgency rippled through the rhythm of the droning pipes. Emerging light set Caer's head to pounding in time with the cadence of the percussion. Tears streaked her cheeks as the light brightened. Wiping her face with a shaky hand, Caer slowly focused. Blue-gray eyes stared anxiously at her from above. One of those eyes was bloodshot and ringed with a swelling of dark purple.

"Adrian?" It was a weak and squeaky attempt, but somehow, Caer managed to get his name out.

"By the grace and power!" he breathed, relaxing a little, his hand running through the thick matt of his disheveled black hair.

"What ha...?" A brief motion to sit brought an abrupt and intense agony to Caer's skull, along with a shooting pain down the length of her left arm. Adrian's hands to her shoulders, he gently forced her to lie back.

"Stay still." The musicality of his voice rang with a mix of worry and relief. "By all the heavens, Caer, I thought you were dead!" He fiddled for a moment, adjusting the pillow for her, taking care not to move her much.

Pillow. Caer reached to touch it, realizing she was stretched out on Adrian's sofa. What was she doing here? It was to Adrian she expected to address the question. But when she looked up again, an unfamiliar face peered down, frowning mightily.

"Look into this," the man said.

Something flashed and Caer blinked.

"Mmm. Very good. Can you move the fingers of your left hand for me?"

Caer wiggled her fingers.

"Any numbness in them?"

That one took a moment's thought. No. Aside from being painfully cold, they seemed to be fine, though her upper arm ached like fury. Caer managed a small shake of her head.

"I believe she will be all right," the man concluded. "The antidote worked remarkably well." He eyed her again before retreating just beyond her line of sight. "She should, however, be taken the medical bay for further observation."

Caer's reaction was an instantaneous, "No!" Thankfully, the hammering in her head had eased enough for her to make another attempt at rising. She must have been even hungrier than she'd thought, to have passed out like that. Must have banged her head and arm on the way down, too. It certainly didn't warrant going to any medical bay, though. "I'm fine."

Adrian returned to hover over her once more. "Are you certain?"

Caer kept her eyes on her lap as she shifted slowly around to let her legs dangle over the sofa's edge. Eased, the pain might be. But she didn't think her head was entirely ready to look all the way up at his towering frame. Instead, she offered a tentative nod.

"Nothing personal, Ian," Adrian said. "She doesn't like med units. I will keep a close watch on her, here, if that's acceptable."

Caer could glimpse the doctor, now, standing next to the end table near one of Adrian's conform chairs. "Very well. But keep her still." Turning to go, he added, "I hope you will forgive me if I don't stick around with all that racket in the background. What is that infernal noise?"

Humor played in Adrian's reply. "It's her favorite music."

Scowling, the doctor made his way to the door. "Is that what you call it? Odd taste your friend has."

"Yes. Well, I like her all the same."

The doctor's mouth twitched in what appeared to be a quickly stifled grin. "Indeed. Well, buzz me if you need me for anything further."

13

Caer sat cross-legged in the middle of the sofa wishing Adrian would say something. He shut down the music when the doctor departed, the silence making her as fidgety as his pacing. Between periodic glances at him, she fussed with the pins that had fallen from her hair. She couldn't recall when they came loose, only that she found most of them scattered on the sofa and floor. In truth, she remembered very little since she stepped inside Adrian's quarters. The more she tried to muddle through the murk in her brain, the hazier it became. Worse, every attempt brought on an ache in the back of her skull, which in turn invited a flush of queasiness. Even looking around triggered the ache and nausea. Adding to her misery, her left arm throbbed hot pain from her neck all the way out to her fingertips.

Shifting slightly, she flexed her left hand, the small motion intensifying the burning in her arm. Biting back a cry, she allowed her hand to fall back on the pillow that currently occupied her lap, her right hand dropping the few pins she held onto the sofa next to her. For several long minutes, her focus was held by the throb. As it finally subsided, her right hand sought out one of the pillow's corners and began plucking at it while she ventured a slow, hesitant scan of the far side of the room. Whatever she'd injured her head and arm on was over there, though she couldn't identify any piece of furniture that might have done the damage.

Adrian's footfalls at last fell silent. Caer knew he was staring at her, which only contributed to her agitated pillow fussing. Nor did it help when he strode across and repositioned his conform chair squarely across from her.

"Hi," she muttered through a weak smile without raising her head.

"Hi?"

"Uhm..." She braved the queasiness, pushing the long tangles of her hair from her face to venture a tentative peek at her friend, who was now sitting and tapping his fingers on his thighs as he eyed her. Licking her lips, she tacked on, "Well, I sort of didn't say it before, did I?"

"I think your presence rather spoke it for you."

Her fidgeting paused, then resumed, her gaze studying her lap to avoid watching Adrian watch her. His unrelenting scrutiny was as unsettling as her fractious memory.

"I'm sorry," she managed.

"For what, precisely?"

"Not very thoughtful of me, failing to tell you I was on my way. Only, the trip came up so unexpectedly. Well, not exactly unexpectedly. I mean, I applied for this transfer dozens of times, and they kept getting lost. Only this last one was hand delivered, and my application was accepted, and they want me there by the beginning of the new semester, and the arrangements came about so quickly that I didn't have time to do anything, really. And I didn't eat much on the way here. So, fatigue and hunger got to me, I guess, and I fainted and..."

Adrian reached across and rested his hand on her knee. "You're babbling, love."

"I..." She took a deep breath, looking him full in the face. Even from beneath his dark and swollen eyelid, the intensity of Adrian's troubled gaze sent a shiver through her. "Why do you keep staring at me like that?"

Folding his arms, Adrian leaned back in his chair, shaking his head. "Lady, you have caused me no end of grief and scared me out of a millennium of lifetimes."

"I didn't faint on purpose. Honest."

"Faint!" Adrian huffed. "Didn't you hear what Ian told you?"

"Who? The doctor? About what?"

Exasperation prompted another huff. "Never mind," he grumbled. "There's a multitude of far more pressing questions. And security will be back soon to do their share of asking. They've already posted guards at the door."

"Security?" Caer moaned. "Again?"

"Again!" Adrian's uninjured eye narrowed, a canyon of a crease pinching his brow. "Caer, are you in some sort of trouble?"

Her pillow plucking became pillow punching. Now she'd done it! Of course, there had been some trouble, though she wasn't in it, exactly. What explanation could she offer, though, that would not dig her into a very deep hole? "Uhm..."

"All right," he said, venting a weary sigh. "Let's try this approach. Start with what you remember from the moment you arrived in my quarters."

His quarters. He wasn't interested in the murder in her apartment. Maybe he didn't know about it, yet. Good. All she needed to do was recount this afternoon's events--if her brain would just get a handle on them.

"I, uh...I remember I let myself in...and I, uh...I got your message." She tried to fix him with a serious frown but was none too sure of her success. "It's morbidly quiet in here when I'm alone. I really hate that. So, I called up your music for a bit of company, and..."

"And?" he prompted.

"And... I don't know." She closed her eyes, trying to think past the fuzzy dance of imagery. Something dark flashed to the fore and she jumped, her eyes snapping wide open, fear tinging the edge of her awareness. "There was a flicker...of light, I think. In the corner."

"Which corner?"

She nodded to the one furthest from the door, her pulse

quickening as the shadows in her mind tried to weave themselves into a form. "That one."

"Then what?"

"I thought...I thought my eyes were playing tricks on me, because when I looked again, there were just the shadows. So, I...I...." Her words strangled off as memory crept back--memory of the dark and brooding malevolence looming from the darkness; of the beastly form reaching for her, closing its massive claw in a crushing grip of her arm; of the agonizing heat stabbing her flesh beneath that grip; the searing pain flooding into her veins, scorching her nerves. Heat... the shimmering air...the grip...the terrifyingly familiar stench...the sense of the beast dragging her away.

Screaming, Caer swung wildly, fighting, pushing, trying to break free.

"Caer!"

The sharpness of Adrian's tone snapped the vision from her mind, revealing the nearness of his anxious face as he knelt directly in front of her. A glint of glowing turquoise sparked in his eyes, vanishing as quickly as it appeared. Breathless and trembling, Caer realized that Adrian's hands were closed securely over her fists.

Gently, he released them. "Take it easy, love," he murmured, moving to sit beside her. "The beast is gone."

Reaching a shaky hand to touch her bandaged arm, she darted a glance around, certain that the creature must still be lurking. "It did this to my arm? Why? Where did it go? Will it come back?"

Adrian shrugged. "I don't know where it went, Caer. You were lucky, though. It only managed to scratch you a little. Those talons could easily take a person's head off. Even short of decapitation, the creature might have killed you. Its talons also harbor a very nasty toxin. Were it not for Ian's quick thinking in providing the appropriate antidote..."

Caer ran her tongue slowly over her lips, trying to regain some small degree of composure. "Adrian, what was that thing? How did it get in here?"

"I was rather hoping you might provide some insight on those scores. When I arrived, I found you on the floor, that beast crouched over you. The only thing I recall after calling out the alarm and charging the creature is finding a couple of the security officers standing over me. By then, the beast was gone."

Caer slumped back, stunned. Adrian had tried to protect her, and that…that thing had attacked him. Why hadn't she realized? Mustering a faint nod toward his face, she ventured a quivering, "Your eye. Is that what happened to your eye?"

Adrian's brief touch of the swollen bruise brought a flinch. "I assume so. I certainly didn't start out the day with it."

"Oh, Adrian! It might have killed you!"

A disgruntled smile flicked across his lips. "Seems to be an echo in here. I could swear I said something of the sort about you. This is the second time in less than a week that I thought I'd lost you, Caer."

Second time. So, he had heard about the mayhem in her apartment. Apparently, news of the event had mixed things up. He thought she was the murdered victim. Her pant leg now became the object of her anxious and suddenly guilty plucking. He thought her dead, and she'd made no effort to contact him.

Adrian wrapped an arm around her, careful to avoid the bandage. "I know you are tired and hurting, Caer, but I need for you to think. Can you tell me anything about the incident on Ahira? Maybe it has some connection to the security breach and what followed, here."

Caer let him pull her close, reassured by his proximity. Adrian was her best friend. Well, perhaps he shared the position with Jen, though she would never confess as much to him. He always watched over her. Was always here for her.

"I…I don't know where to begin," she sighed. "When did they contact you? How much do you already know?"

"Word came within hours. When a complex the size of Ahira blows, and rumors of sabotage are attached to it, well, security was immediately tightened everywhere in the quadrant."

Caer's tenuous hold on the moment vanished in a dizzying

white void as the feeling of a great weight crushed the breath from her. Gradually, the emptiness gave way to a kaleidoscope of swirling impressions. Fireballs. Roiling dust and smoke. Shards of debris rocketed into space. "Ahira." she choked.

Adrian hesitated. "You didn't know?" He groaned, "You didn't report to C deck like the passengers from your shuttle were directed, did you?"

She gave only the slightest shake of her head, her whisper pleading, "Tell me."

"Ahira suffered a series of explosions, Caer. Massive ones."

"The domes." She swallowed. It was a dream. She saw it in a dream. In the nightmare that night when Jorn comforted her; before he rushed her from Ahira. The press of the vision surged back to her awareness in all its fury. The rasp of her voice was all but lost in the crashing pulse behind her eardrums. "And...and...survivors?" But she already knew the answer.

14

Adrian rocked forward; stood and stretched, wincing; sat again. Even his conform chair couldn't ease his aches. He was out of his mind, charging a bloody Coran'ian. Lucky for him, the creature failed to anticipate his sudden teleportation into his quarters. Failed to anticipate, as well, his instantaneous call of alarm, or his charge. Instead of a sweeping slice from the Coran'ian's talons, thereby separating Adrian's head from his shoulders and sending his soul in search of a new host, the beast's wildly swung backhand sent him sailing across the room. He recalled, vaguely, casting his kill spell just before he slammed into the wall; recalled telepathing Ian as he watched the Coran'ian's suddenly lifeless hulk disappear. He remembered nothing after that until the pain of a broken collarbone, several cracked ribs, and the mother of a black eye brought him back to consciousness.

For several hours, security swarmed his quarters seeking for the assailant, or for any suggestion of how the station's security measures had been breached. Telling the Tanai officers that an alien had entered via teleportation, of course, was out of the question. They'd have him in med bay under examination for brain damage. As for the Coran'ian's exit, whether the beast's disappearance resulted from his kill spell blasting it back along the thread of its original teleportation, or from its master yanking the creature back, he couldn't say. At this point, it hardly mattered. The Coran'ian was gone, leaving security with nothing for their efforts. In the end, they gave up their search, here, contenting themselves with standing guard outside his door.

A small whimper drew Adrian's attention to Caer as she tossed in uneasy slumber on his sofa. She had repeatedly rejected his offer of the sedative Ian left for her. Only when he slipped the medication into the soup brought in for her was he able to quiet her distraught ramblings and periodic outbursts of wracking sobs. Her slumber, fitful as it may be, at least granted him time to deal with his injuries. Sadly, the number of Tanai officers who witnessed many of his bruises, including his seriously swollen eye, meant those had to be left to heal in their own time. The broken bones, however, could be dealt with.

Easing back, Adrian closed his eyes and drew a slow breath, concentrating. In silence he sang the words of healing, working the magic slowly, deliberately. When, at last, relief washed through him, he straightened slightly, testing. The pain in his shoulder and chest were gone, leaving only the annoying discomfort of the remaining bruises, the throb in his temples from his damaged eye, and the irritation of his vision trying to compensate for the fact that the eye was nearly swollen shut.

"Hell of a day," he grumbled, cocking his head to study Caer again; reflecting on her earlier question regarding what he already knew about the occurrence on Ahira. Apparently, her query alluded to some incident prior to the colony's annihilation. Caer's genuine shock and wracking grief at the loss of her friends indicated her ignorance of that disaster. "Make that a hell of a week," he amended. "Whatever is going on, Love, it seems centered squarely on you. What happened to send you away from Ahira barely in time to escape its eradication? Why did you not tell me of your leaving? I thought you dead when the news first came. Took me hours to finally sense otherwise. You lived, I knew. Yet I could not touch your waking mind to find you."

For a long while, he sat, drumming his fingers on the arms of his chair, wishing he possessed the rare gift of a Dream Reader.

Such an attribute permitted one to see into another's subconscious mind. His telepathic gift limited him to reading only conscious thoughts. Caer's ignorance of any need to shield them, much less how to accomplish that specific feat, served him well. The clarity with which her thoughts were broadcast marked her as Tanai to any passing Witch. Hence, they were quick to shut her out. Witches bore little patience for the mental ramblings of the 'Shallow'. Caer's ignorance further served him by allowing him to know her comings and goings; to know her intentions in time to prepare arguments against them. Not that such preparations generally did him much good. Still, his ability to read her conscious thoughts meant she kept no secrets from him. Until now.

Adrian's finger drumming ceased, his lips thinning to an agitated pinch as he considered the presence of a foreign magic. He'd not detected it, at first, the magic used to teleport the Coran'ian along with its stench overwhelming his senses. Only with the beast gone and his head cleared from the blow he'd taken did he recognize the spell by the vague static itch that rippled along his nerves. At least a portion of its purpose was clear. Someone had wrapped Caer in a cocoon of protection. Whether the magic held any other significance was impossible to tell.

Growling under his breath, Adrian muttered, "Someone knew you were in danger. I should have known. My prescience failed me. Because of this spell? Who did the casting? What do they know about you? Without the ability to touch your thoughts, I've no way of learning the truth of what has been happening."

His sudden sense of impotence deepened the crevice running the length of his forehead, setting his injured eye to an irritating twitch. "Still!" he snapped. The twitching calmed, but not before aggravating the throbbing ache in his temples. Lips still drawn tight in concentration, Adrian attempted to take in the full measure of the enchantment surrounding Caer. The only way he would know if his guardianship had failed, or whether it was simply blocked, would be to eliminate this spell. It was strongly woven, though. And without knowledge of its source or the full extent of its purpose, he dared not tamper with it.

"She is mine to protect," he snarled. "If I can no longer do it properly, I'll not leave her to the mercy of some unknown."

Once again, he closed his eyes, turning his focus inward, banishing all the questions and uncertainties that plagued him. Calm, he sought. An empty mind. The emptiness was hard won. Once gained, however, seeking the familiar image with which to fill it was not. White-gold hair framing the thin, fair face; eyes the color of and as clear as Earth's once pristine mountain lakes; prominent cheekbones; resolute mouth.

"Stoirm." Adrian breathed the name, his whisper lifting it in melodious softness, directing it outward...on and on. Again, he beckoned, stretching the thin strands of his will to reach far beyond the boundaries of humanity's expanding realm.

Faintly, at first, and then with growing strength, Adrian's ancient name whispered back to him. "Amhranai Fearalite."

"Stoirm," he pressed, this time with greater force. The chill of a biting wind touched his face, and he detected the smell of dust. Slowly, a hazed and rocky landscape filled his head.

"I am here, Lord Amhranai. I would say that it is good to speak with you. I would do so at length, save I am on urgent business at present."

"I beg your forgiveness for my intrusion," Adrian returned. "But there is news you must hear and a desperate request that I would not make of you had I any other choice."

A disorienting sweep of motion washed over Adrian as a blur of brown and gray terrain shifted and moved. When the wind, at last, ceased its sting on his cheek and the morphing landscape finally resolved, he saw a place of dark stone, as of a sheltering overhang or cave. With it came the clarifying image of the Alainn.

"Your words carry much turmoil, Amhranai. What troubles you?"

"The magic of my oath has failed me and has placed Caer at great risk."

An edge filled Stoirm's, "How so?"

"A beast's attack within my own quarters here on Bestor III very nearly claimed her life. I had no forewarning. I could not protect her."

"The child lives, though? She is safe?"

"Yes. For now."

"How is it that any creature might slip past the shielding spells you've woven to guard your door?"

"There is no explanation other than my own arrogance. I had not considered the possibility that Madadh Mire would attempt a strike on Bestor III, much less that he would strike in the heart of my quarters. I neither believed him capable of magic strong enough to shatter my protections, nor of possessing sufficient strength to control and teleport another...a Coran'ian at that. I have woefully underestimated the strength he has gained during his long silence."

There seemed more resignation than surprise in Stoirm's response. "You are certain this is Madadh's doing?"

"You think I could mistake his magic for any other? I knew it the moment he breached Bestor's secured inner sectors. His is the signature embedded in the magic that broke through security, just as his signature permeates the magic that mangled my shielding spells. Moreover, he teleported the Coran'ian, delivering the beast straight into my living chamber. Delivered it straight to Caer. The beast wounded her before I could get to her, Stoirm. A mere scratch, but one capable of injecting its venom. Had Ian not responded so quickly to my call, had he not brought the antidote..." Adrian hesitated, taking a ragged breath. "My oath would be broken; Caer dead."

Stoirm remained silent for several long seconds, his brow a chasm as he considered. "The Coran'ian was sent to kill you, Amhranai. Perhaps that is why your gift gave no forewarning."

"It should make no difference, and you know it. The prescience that makes my guardianship possible should still foresee any potential for danger to Caer, whether it was intended for her of for someone else."

Stoirm's image suddenly clouded, his voice muffling as he turned part of his attention to the growing sounds of commotion from just beyond his shelter. There followed an indistinguishable barking, as of orders being shouted. The sounds of other voices faded but did not disappear entirely as Stoirm addressed Adrian once more, the Alainn's words broken by his divided attention. "I...again, my fr... The crea... se... for you." At last the verbal contact clarified, though Stoirm's image remained a haze, the Allain's focus obviously still split.

"Finding Caer where it expected to find you likely confused the creature, else the child would have died the moment it saw her. Your prescience foresaw this and..."

Adrian cut him off with a sharp, "Madadh did not send the beast for me, Stoirm. He delivered his assassin to Caer."

Stoirm's image snapped back into focus; his full attention suddenly returned to Adrian. "How do you know this?"

"I saw it in the Mad Dog's mind!" Adrian growled back. Then, sucking a long breath, he attempted to condense the whole of the day's events. "I, too, believed that he came for me when first I sensed his presence. I left the helm immediately and made my way to a locked storage room. My intent was to draw Madadh away from as many others as possible; to seal us in a place where we could battle unseen and without collateral damage. But he refused to come to me, teleporting, instead, randomly through the quadrants; destroying cams before any could register his image and identify him to security; leaving the corpses of any he encountered in his wake.

"I had no idea where he would go next until he emerged in the corridor just outside my quarters. He did not linger there for more time than was necessary to complete his final act. He was teleporting away even as he was delivering the beast within; just as I was teleporting to try and intercept him. In that moment, when we faced one another in the corridor, I caught a glimpse of his mind. It's Caer he pursues, Stoirm. And I was unable to protect her as I should."

Stoirm scowled. "It's your demise that Madadh seeks, my friend. He seeks it always."

"And he came damned close to achieving that, as well," Adrian rumbled. "No doubt he would take my elimination as a major bonus. But I was not his prey, this time." Stiffening, Adrian added with growing agitation, "I must find him, Stoirm. I must know where, how, and what he has learned of Caer. And I must rid us of him, once and for all. Madadh and his spies. Yet I dare not leave Caer alone. I need to place her in the care of your people. She will be safe in your world. The Alainn can hide her while I take care of the Dog and his spies, and while I try to sort out what has gone wrong with the magic of my oath."

Stoirm's features hardened. "Send her back to Ahira, Amhranai. Surely, there is no failure in your guardianship. The magic simply foresaw that you would arrive in time to save her without any need for action on its part." He turned again, preparing to step back out in the winds. "You can keep watch over her as you have always done."

"I cannot send her back, even if I felt it was safe to do so. Ahira is no more."

Stoirm came to a brisk halt. "How? When?"

"Three days back. Sabotage, say the authorities. At Madadh's hands, I'm guessing. I had no forewarning of that either. How Caer managed to escape I can't say. I knew she was alive. Were it otherwise..." The thought trailed off. It was not a possibility Adrian cared to dwell upon. "There is something else," he continued. "I am unable to touch her waking mind...to know her thoughts. Some spell prevents it, the signature of its maker unknown to me. It is possible that this same magic may be responsible for blocking that of my guardianship. I cannot penetrate it. Nor do I dare attempt to dismantle it.

"I need to find the source of this magic; to destroy the Witch, if necessary. Until then, I cannot guarantee my ability to keep Caer safe. Madadh will send another assassin, or come for her himself, once he's recovered from this failed attempt. That he knows something of her means Nemhain does, as well. The bastard isn't capable of keeping secrets from the bitch. He may wish Caer dead merely for his own amusement. But I'm betting the order for Caer's demise comes from Nemhain, which suggests that she suspects Caer's importance. Madadh's failure will not set well with the Dark Heart. Caer must be given a level of protection that I can no longer guarantee."

He hesitated, running a hand over his face. "You must let me send her to you...to your people."

Stoirm gave a single, firm shake of his head. "She cannot come here. Nemhain Croi Breag has betrayed us. She has given over knowledge of our realm to others of her clan. Many have already infiltrated our border colonies. Some have managed to break through to our home world. They strike without warning and leave none alive. I am with a party pursuing one of their bands, even as we speak."

Adrian's sharp intake stuck in his throat, nearly choking him. Nemhain's grievous sins were as multitudinous as they were horrendous. But giving away the secret of the Alainn's worlds, allowing attacks on the Alainn people--this was not an act he'd ever have expected of her. It was Stoirm, after all, who rescued Nemhain and her two sisters as children; kept them safe from those who'd murdered their parents. Stoirm risked much, taking the three human girls back to his home. Yet the Alainn took in the children, nurtured them, raised them, instructed them in their gifts. In return, each of the sisters swore a blood oath never to breathe a word of the location of the Alainn's home world or its colonies.

"It appears," Stoirm declared with a cold edge, "that Nemhain Croi Breag believes the time is near. She knows that my people will stand with her sisters in the coming battle. Moreover, our spies warn us that her warriors have come, not just to destroy us, but in search of Dana and Roisin. Croi Breag believes they are here. A false belief, yet one she holds, nonetheless. Caer will not be safe in our keeping."

"But if the magic of my guardianship remains silent," Adrian persisted.

"Do not doubt your gifts, my friend. Magic does not fail, though we who wield it may sometimes fail to understand its limitations and adjust accordingly."

Adrian blanched. His own failure to understand the limits of his gifts brought him to a near grievous end only once. He'd believed that the prescience at the core of his guardianship could stretch infinitely into the future, and would therefore give him warning in ample time for his return to his ward, no matter where he roamed. He discovered his error when he ventured too far from Caer, nearly outstripping the 'distance' in time foreseen by the time required for the multiples of teleportation jumps necessary to return to her. He arrived with barely seconds to discern the nature of the threat to Caer; conjured the spell to slow the collapse of the crumbling library wing almost too late. Caer's subconscious sense of danger and her instinctive reaction were as much responsible for her survival as his belated spell. Had she not reacted so quickly, his actions would likely not have held the wing long enough for her to escape. Caer's corpse would have been buried in the rubble.

The incident still haunted him. Never again did he place himself at a greater distance than two teleportation jumps could cover to return him to her.

"This is different, Stoirm. This was not for any failure to recognize the limitation of my gift. An attempt was made on Caer's life right under my nose, and I had no warning!"

Stoirm remained equally adamant. "The magic foresaw that you would arrive and get word to the good doctor in time." With another shake of his head, the Allain declared, "There is no choice but for you to stand by your oath, Amhranai. Lash the child to your side if you think that will help. She is yours to guard."

"She won't allow me to keep her that close, and you know it!" he shot back. Sinking back in his chair, he muttered, "Perhaps I was wrong to bury her memories so deeply; to keep her ignorant of her past...of who she is. With that knowledge, she may have chosen other paths than the one she is on. In her continued ignorance, and with Ahira gone, she will undoubtedly insist on taking her studies to Earth."

Adrian's urgency intensified. "If it is as you say...if Nemhain believes that the time is near, then perhaps it is time for you to return to us. Perform the Awakening, Stoirm. Allow Caer a chance to know who she is, what she carries, and why. Allow her to fight."

There was a fleeting, anguished flush to Stoirm's face and the faintest suggestion of a slump to his erect frame. "It is not within my power to bring about the Awakening. Nor must the spells that have sealed her past within her subconscious be undone. They are all that prevent others from learning the secret the child holds. For now, Caer must remain ignorant. I will join you, though. Soon. Be prepared to bring me through when I call to you. In the meantime, my friend, trust your oath. Your magic will not fail. Of this much I am certain.

The contact vanished abruptly. Adrian shrugged deeper in his chair, stunned. Always, he had believed it was Stoirm who was entrusted with the secret of the Awakening. If not the Alainn, then who?

Once more he fixed his gaze on the girl lying on his sofa. His faith in the magic of his guardianship was not so unwavering as Stoirm's. It seemed, however, the responsibility for Caer remained his. Summoning his ragged reserves, he set about weaving new shielding spells around his private quarters; adding them to those he'd earlier reconstructed; building more layers. For nearly an hour he sang, quietly calling up and interlocking enchantment upon enchantment, binding them with tremendous care and fine detail, the magic inherent in the music of his voice enhancing and strengthening each layer. Only when he was satisfied that not even Nemhain's magic could breach his barrier without considerable time and effort, did he cease, giving in to the relief of sleep.

15

Caer completed yet another circuit of the room, her stomped frustration muffled by the soft carpeting.

"I'll not let you leave, yet," Adrian growled. "And will you please light somewhere? You're going to wear your legs off at the knees, not to mention wear my floor down to bare metal."

Smugly satisfied at knowing she annoyed him as much as he aggravated her, Caer made two more spiteful circuits. Getting no further remark from him, however, she finally aimed her steps for the sofa. Plopping irritably in its middle, she tucked her legs beneath her and diligently set to a study of her lap.

"Did you hear me?"

"Of course, I heard you," she sniffed. "You've only said it a million times over the last three weeks." She refused to meet Adrian's gaze. Didn't need to. She could feel his glower as he drummed on the arms of his chair. Instead, she focused on knuckling her fist into the pillow at her side.

Adrian's tense voice rumbled again, its inherent music discordant. "Until the authorities have found and taken into custody whoever is responsible for these attacks, I don't want you out of my sight."

Caer shuddered. Since her arrival, she'd hardly been out of his sight. She couldn't so much as cough without Adrian hovering over her. Even their lovemaking failed to bring her comfort, his touches feeling overbearing and possessive. She could almost take the all-pervasive station security over Adrian's smothering. Whether by his command or from some higher authority, a full contingent of guards stood along the corridor outside his door, and at least two of them followed her every time she set foot outside of his quarters without him. On top of that... She shot a wary glance at the nearest cam.

Adrian gestured in the direction of her glance, the delicate musicality returning to his voice and skimming the edge from his tone. "Those? Is that what's bothering you?"

She shrugged. Better, perhaps, for him to believe the cams responsible for her agitation than to bluntly confess she'd had just about enough of him.

"They've always been there, Love. They certainly won't be lacking on Earth. Their constant watch has never bothered you before."

Yes, the bloody things were always there. They were everywhere--on the Perimeter Ships, in every building and thoroughfare in nearly every colony, in every shuttle and mat-trans station. Caer punched the pillow again. At least Lillith II only posted them in the public spaces, not in their private homes. Adrian was right, though. She'd never given the damned things much thought before. It just seemed different, now. Different since she discovered just how truly invasive they were, her every move watched by half of Bestor's security detail.

Barely able to contain her exasperation, Caer forced it to an indignant grumble. "Between you and your constant vigil and the always staring eyes of those things, it's making me crazy."

"Better a little crazy than dead."

Her pillow punching turned to full-scale hammering. "How better?"

Rising, Adrian moved to stand before her, lifting the pillow from under her fist and tossing it to the floor. "Look, Love, there are just too many unanswered questions."

"You think I don't know that?"

Beside her, the sofa sagged, alerting her to the fact that Adrian now sat next to her. She still refused to look at him. He had a maddening way of playing on her guilt and grief, coaxing information from her. He knew about the murder in her apartment--got that out of her several days ago. Somehow, she kept the mention of it brief and sketchy, knowing Adrian would be furious. As expected, he erupted over the fact that she failed to contact him immediately.

She omitted the fact that the Ahiran police had cast their suspicions his way. Nor did she mention her nightmare regarding the explosion on Ahira. Sharing the scarcely remembered fragments of her ever-recurring dream with him was one thing. In fact, he and Jen were the only ones with whom she felt secure enough to speak of the strangeness of those disturbing bits and pieces. But the nightmare from that last night on Ahira...

Her lower lip pinched into a pout, a thin whisper inside her head nagging at her, telling her the nightmare in Jorn's apartment was nothing. In all honesty, she remembered none of its specifics, now. Perhaps the dream had nothing to do with Ahira's demise. Perhaps her over-active imagination had simply filled in some horrific imagery as Adrian told her of the catastrophe. The stress and the depth of her grief were obviously wreaking havoc in her head.

"I hope your silence is an indication that you are reconsidering."

Caer shook her head, still refusing to look at him. What could she say to make him understand? She needed to move on, wanted the distraction of her studies. "No, Adrian. My mind is made up."

The air all but crackled as he snapped, "You saw the vids the other day. Security told you the news of the others, this morning."

The vids. Caer tensed, reaching for the pillow, wanting something to pound again. Instead of the pillow, her fingers brushed Adrian's leg. She'd have hammered it, but thought better of the notion, her hand retreating to her necklace, twisting it back and forth. Yes. She saw the vids. The recordings from the day she arrived showed everything--the shuttle's docking and her disembarking; her odd maneuvering to pass through to a particular checkpoint into the hub; her sojourn across the hub and her discourse with the guard at the checkpoint to the private sector; her long trek out to the rim and along the curl of corridor; her entrance into Adrian's quarters; her mindless meandering and that silly jig around the room. The whole of security knew everything about her every movement.

A shudder prompted a darting glance at the room's far corner. No. Not everything. Though all the other cams in Adrian's quarters continued working without error, the one that should have captured the intruder malfunctioned mere seconds before the beast appeared. Only the periphery cams caught any part of the assault. They chronicled Caer's scream well enough; picked up Adrian seconds after he arrived in the room, bellowing for security, then charging something out of sight. They also recorded the force with which the unidentified assailant hurled Adrian backward into the wall.

Caer's chain fidgeting increased as she sucked on her lower lip. Adrian came to her aid, always watched out for her. She rewarded him by giving him grief over the fact that he cared enough to want to protect her. But she wasn't a child. She had a life. Adrian needed to let her live it. She wished, now, that Jorn had routed her through one of the other mat-trans stations. Why had he picked this one, anyway?

And if she'd gone through another mat-trans station, then what? If she hadn't been here, that creature might not have been distracted enough for Adrian to call out the alarm. It might have killed him. Without him, she would be entirely alone. She drew a shaky breath. Yet, what if that thing hadn't come for him? What if it came for her? There was the murder in her apartment, after all, and the destruction of the whole of Ahira. What if Sgt. Sakin was right? What if she really was the target? Would the creature have followed her, regardless of which station she set out for? If she'd gone to another station, she might be dead, now. But why?

Increasing dismay vented in her edgy huff. Adrian was right. There were too many unanswered questions. How could it be a coincidence that just the right cams on Ahira and here malfunctioned at the most opportune moment for the assailant? And how did the assailant...or assailants...manage to get into and out of her apartment or Adrian's quarters through locked doors?

She twitched an anxious sideways glance at her friend, whose silence by no means meant that he was no longer observing her. The malfunction of the cam in her bedroom or the fact that the murderer came and went without any indication of how they'd done so was another bit she'd failed to mention. She wanted to add nothing else to fan the flames of Adrian's over-zealous hovering. This morning's news accomplished enough of that, already. Attacks, it seemed, had been carried out on other individuals, each of them students or staff from Ahira's university who happened to be away from the colony at the time of the devastation. Upon hearing the report, Caer feared Adrian might resort to locking her in a trunk on rollers so he could keep her 'safely confined' and constantly with him.

Guilt dulled her indignation. She possessed only a scratch to show from her attacker. Adrian suffered more. How he walked away without any broken bones was beyond her. Other victims of the attacks were even less fortunate. Dr. Berring, for instance. The reports indicated the assault on Berring took place at the station where she and Dr. Eliz had met with Dr. Jorn. Took place within a day or so of Jorn's return to Ahira. While the authorities stated Berring would survive, she'd sustained injuries serious enough to put her in ICU for several days. Others had not survived the attacks at all. How many? How many had died, and who? Thus far, Adrian refused to say if security possessed a list of their names.

Hugging herself, Caer tried to quiet her persistent bout of trembling. Brandon was among those who were away from Ahira. Did he make it to the Andromedin colony safely? Did he know about Ahira and...and Jenna?

"Caer, are you listening to me?"

She granted a small nod.

"I thought I'd lost you before. I can't stand the idea of going through that again."

Raising her head, she settled a reluctant gaze on him. His eyes pleaded with her, his features drawn into an expression of profound grief tinged with the faintest glimmer of hope--as if he saw in her something long missed; something both treasured and feared.

"Caer, why can't you see reason? I can keep you safe, here."

It was that tone of possessiveness again that needled at her, churning her anger and resentment. Occasional lovers they might be, but neither of them had ever laid any permanent claim on the other. She wanted no such claim placed on her, now. Not by Adrian. She closed her eyes, knowing it would be Jorn's face filling her mind. Jorn's face, not Adrian's. Grief mixed with her guilt, shooting it through with the pangs of knowing she could never again experience the sound of Jorn's voice, or the wonderfully odd tick of his half smile, or the mesmerizing depths of his amber gaze. "I can't stay," she murmured.

"Just until...."

"Until when?" Turning, she cocked her head at him. "What happens if the one...or ones...responsible for all of this are never found? I can't stay locked away forever." Her hands still trembled, but she reached for his anyway. She wanted Adrian's blessing for her endeavors; wanted his support. He was all she had left in the whole of the universe. "I love you, Adrian. You know I do. You are my dearest and truest and oldest friend. But I can't stay here."

The tightening knot in her throat made it difficult to swallow, near impossible to speak. At last, she squeaked, "I owe it to Dr. Jorn. For everything he did to help me get this far...with my studies." It was more than that. More than the thwarted infatuation with a man now dead; more, even, than her need to distance herself from Adrian's stifling watchfulness. An inexplicable urgency crept along her desire to leave Bestor III.

Adrian stood, staring down at her in silence for several piercing minutes. "I see," he said, turning away. "It's Dr. Jorn I have to thank for putting all these foolish notions of Earth in your head."

Caer swung her legs out from under her and slowly pushed to her feet, glaring at him in a fury of disbelief. "Adrian Starn! How dare you lay that on him! It is my idea to go to Earth, and mine alone. You, of all people, should know that. I've talked about it for as long as I've known you."

The harshness of her retort faded as a shadowy, skittering thought found voice before she realized she was speaking aloud. "There is something I'm supposed to do, Adrian. I'm not sure what it is, but I know lies on Earth." Instantly biting her lip, Caer cast a startled and confused glance up at him noting how his features shifted to something quite unreadable, his sharp blue eyes boring into her. His towering frame and that penetrating gaze left her feeling frightfully small. Small and smothered. She couldn't think under his scrutiny. Instead, his stare prompted ghostly whisperings--subtle voices nudging just at the edges of her awareness.

16

Adrian ushered Caer into the lift, adjusting one of the straps of her small backpack across his shoulder as he followed. Light as the pack was, it still might suffice for knocking her in the head. If it didn't knock her out so he could carry her back to his quarters, it might at least knock some sense into her.

"Down three," he rumbled, the words morosely discordant, even to his ears. Caer took no notice. Her thick silence made the soft swoosh as the lift doors closed and the subtle hum of their descent seem a roaring gale by comparison. At least her thoughts were open to him again, the enchantment that had encompassed her having dissipated a few days prior. As a result, he'd relaxed his orders to have a guard with her every moment he was unavailable. While it wasn't enough to convince her to stay, it was sufficient to reassure him that his prescience regarding her safety had also returned. Twice, he'd detected her inattentive stumbles before they occurred. No real threat, of course, but reassuring.

Having his abilities restored was a mixed blessing, though, as Caer's thoughts flitted constantly through events, beginning with her meeting in Jorn's office and ending with the attack on her, here. Worrisome as they were, he dared not press her concerning the details she'd conveniently left unsaid to him. Nor could he find a means of soothing away the suffocation she felt under his watch. In the end, he acquiesced to her demand to leave.

For the moment, Caer's thoughts churned with apprehension,

though she refused to speak of that, as well. He accepted credit for her anxieties; held no regrets. His stories of various mat-trans mishaps always played on her nerves. Tales of individuals arriving at their destinations with missing appendages, or with body parts misassembled; tales of those who arrived as a gelatinous puddle, or who never arrived at all. No one ever knew what happened to those missing souls. In truth, such occurrences were exceedingly rare, and Caer knew it. Still, his tales found fertile ground in her imagination. For years, his tactic kept her to travels at distances easily handled by a couple of shuttle jumps, well within his limitation of two teleportation jumps to reach her.

Playing on her fears was no longer enough, though. The more he tried to use them to keep her here, the more resentful and determined she became. Fighting against her resentment and resolve strained both he and Caer near to their breaking points. His exasperation finally vented in one long and heavy groan. Protect her at all costs. Do not stand in the way of the path fate has laid for her. Those were the directives set by his guardianship. The distance between Earth and Bestor III hovered at the very edge of his limitation, requiring two very taxing jumps. Mat-trans was useless for his needs. It could only deliver him to one of Earth's receiving stations, not directly to Caer. Only teleportation could get him to her in a matter of seconds.

The slight shudder and jolt as the lift settled to a stop tugged Adrian from his brooding considerations. Caer jerked from her thoughts, as well, and edged past him to the doors as they opened, the tinny sound of her tread against the metal floor doing little to hide the flutter of her tremulous sigh. She hesitated in the corridor, turning a nervous scrutiny to the grand curve that stretched out in both directions. Grudgingly, Adrian gestured toward a chamber several doors down along the curve to their left. Therein lay one of the smaller mat-trans units--one dedicated to moving individuals or small groups rather than the more lucrative freight shipments. Moreover, from this unit, he could most easily monitor every detail of Caer's departure.

The air in the room buzzed faintly and smelled of ozone as they entered, the sound and aroma the consequence of the energy being drawn to power up the system. The procedure also cast an eerie, pale blue haze over the raised, circular transport platform occupying the center of the room. It was a simple arrangement, really, belying the massive amount of equipment tucked away in the bowels of the station--equipment sufficient for the operation of seven mat-trans units in all, making Bestor III the largest station in this quadrant of the Draco Dwarf galaxy.

Lieutenant Gavin Macstrum sat at the console, the young man dressed in the sharp, royal blue uniform depicting his rank. Adrian was grateful to have him at the controls, as Macstrum was the best mat-trans operator to be found. He was also one of Adrian's most trusted officers. The Lieutenant's eyes flicked across the panel of icons displayed on the console's screen, the controls responding with faint clicks and flickers to the slightest change of his visual focus.

Adrian nearly tripped over Caer when she shuffled to a halt a few meters from the platform, her uneasiness palpable as she tried not to stare at its blue haze. Completing his delicate manipulation of the controls, Lieutenant Macstrum looked around to acknowledge is next 'passenger'. The sight of Adrian, however, brought him instantly to his feet, his hand snapping sharply to his cap.

"Sir!"

Adrian motioned him back to the console. "At ease, Gavin. I'm not on duty. I'm just here to see my lady on her way."

Relaxing his stance, Gavin returned to his seat. "Yes, sir. Good Day, Ms. DaDhrga."

Caer's thin reply came with an equally thin smile. "Hello, Lieutenant. It's good to see you again. Missed you in the dining hall last night."

Gavin grinned. "Dined in with a friend. Nice to know that somebody notices me, though. I seem to be invisible to most travelers."

"I'm sure it has nothing to do with you," Caer returned softly, her anxious gaze still fixed on the platform.

"I understand you are headed for Earth."

Her nod was barely distinguishable from her trembling. "Yes. To Sion University. To complete my studies."

Gavin's thoughts carried to Adrian in a knot of surprise and concern, though his face remained pleasantly passive. "Sion! Sir, you..."

"Can do nothing to stop her, or I'd have done so."

The Lieutenant cocked a curious brow at him before addressing Caer again. "Well, good luck to you. With your courses."

Caer's smile firmed a little as she took the final steps toward the platform. "Thanks."

Adrian followed her, extending his hand for her support. She took it only long enough to step up, though if she thought she could hide her shaking with the brevity of the contact, she was mistaken. Still unwilling to give in, Adrian ventured one final plea. "Caer, are you sure you want to do this? Earth isn't going anywhere. We can always reschedule your trip for later."

Her sigh was as heavy as the crestfallen look on her face. "I don't want to go through this all over again. We've been through it a million times, already."

And he would argue the case a million more; would argue until the worlds collided; would even propose marriage to her, if he thought he stood the slightest chance of convincing her to stay. Silently, he swore a barrage of expletives at the piece of oath that prevented any real intervention. Protect her, he must. Stop her from following her path, however...forbidden. And judging from the statement that ended one of their last confrontations--that there was something she needed to accomplish on Earth--her path was clear, even if she failed to understand what her words meant or what she was to do. Resigned, he slung her pack from his shoulder, dropping it at her feet.

Caer stared at it briefly, then turned her eyes up to his, her gaze begging his forgiveness; begging for his blessing in this venture. So much like her distant grandmother. Her childlike stature, the innocent sweetness on her face, the earthen green of her eyes, the glint of smoldering red in her hair. Each featured jarred him with the pain of its familiarity. So much like Roisin. Right down to her unwavering will.

Adrian's fists clenched at his sides. Caer, however, was not her grandmother. She lacked Roisin's lifetimes of experience. A woman Caer might be in the Tanai count of years, but in the span of a Witch's existence, she was yet a babe, ill prepared for where her journey would take her. She didn't even possess a full accounting of her own short existence. Damn the oath! This was not what Adrian believed he was taking on when he accepted the guardianship. How could he fulfill his oath to protect while allowing her unsuspecting march toward catastrophe?

For a fleeting second, he considered pulling her into his arms, praying that by proposing to her while her fears were high, she might falter and accept. She might have done so at one time. But now... Now she grieved for another man. The weight of it clung to every thought she had of Ahira. She would not marry anyone. Not while her grief was so raw.

Caer's fingers reached to brush the remaining bruises around his eye, her lips pinched thin. Adrian winced, though not from pain. He'd tried this ploy, as well, hoping to play on Caer's grand capacity for sympathy. As with her fears, he'd played it too long. His last effort failed. He knew, even as he attempted it again, that it would work no better this time.

"You try too hard," she murmured with a faint chuckle. "Thank you."

Frowning, he swallowed the harshness that threatened to edge into his words. "For?"

"For caring about me so much. For risking yourself to save me."

Adrian simply looked at her. What was left for him to say? With a strained calm, he managed, "Where will you be staying?"

"I'm not sure. The message I received from Sion said that someone by the name of Emer Kyot would be my contact. She's already arranged housing for me. I just need to check in with her when I arrive. She will tell me to which of the student halls I've been assigned. I will let you know as soon as I'm settled."

"Promise?"

"Promise." Taking his hands, she gave them a slight squeeze. "You worry too much, Adrian. You know that. Everything is going to be just fine. After all, what could possibly go wrong? Here I am, in your company until the moment of transfer. I will arrive at a station that is undoubtedly filled with security personnel, whom I am equally convinced you've already instructed to dote on me like I was an unescorted five-year-old. The authorities will direct me to Sion's shuttle. I will ask for Emer Kyot at the administration building. And I will then take a pod straight to the appropriate dorm. I can't possibly be any safer."

Her voice held utter composure, despite her continued trembling. Ironic that she should be the one offering reassurances. Her defiant will and sheer determination, so much like Roisin's, was cause enough for Adrian to smile. Leaning, he kissed her gently on the lips. "Yes. Well. Just make sure that you keep your promise. Let me know which dorm and what room number as soon as you arrive." Backing away, he declared, "Ready, Gavin." His eyes locked on hers. "Stay safe."

"I will. Oh!" she called out above the rising equipment whine, her words coming in a rush. "I almost forgot! Here's something that should make you laugh. I had a dream a couple of weeks or so ago. You were talking to some gorgeous man with pointy ears. If you know who he might be, send him to my dreams again!"

Adrian gave a sharp gasp. She saw Stoirm. That should not have been possible! "Gavin!"

"It's too late, my lord."

With a brilliant flash of light, the equipment whine ended in an abrupt snap. Caer was gone.

17

Disorientation, dizziness, nausea--each vied for momentary top billing. Then, as abruptly as they'd occurred, they were gone. Gone, too, was every other sensation--just like Caer's singular previous mat-trans experience, a fact she hardly found encouraging. Rather, the vast emptiness that swallowed her would most certainly raise an anxiety-ridden chill, were there something to note the reaction. There was nothing. Only consciousness.

Unfortunately, Caer's consciousness included an imagination overflowing with an accumulation of fears garnered during her first mat-trans trip, each greatly augmented with Adrian's stories. That the mishaps were quite rare made no difference. The thought of being lost in this void for all eternity...or of emerging with her body parts scrambled...or worse still, emerging as...how did Adrian describe it? As pudding of person? Caer was certain her heart would be thrashing mercilessly inside her rib cage about now, if they possessed any substance. Oh, to have that rib cage again! To feel her heart slamming would be a great mercy! This emptiness with only her thoughts for company threatened her sanity.

"You are frightened."

The thought came as scarcely a whisper, prompting a subtle shift in Caer's awareness. For a moment, she was uncertain she'd 'heard' the voice; wasn't sure hearing could be said to apply in the current situation. The urge to look around annoyed Caer. There was, after all, nothing to see in this state--except the visions of her imaginings...and apparently, the sound of them, as well.

"I am real," the whisper declared. Accompanying the proclamation came the growing sense of a presence. But where? Was this some other 'traveler' whose molecules were floating about like hers--someone streaming through the universe on their way to their own far-flung destination? Had their...essences...somehow overlapped, allowing them to communicate?

"Who are you?"

"My name is of no consequence. Just know that I can help." The murmur oozed a disturbing sweetness. *"Come to me. Let me guide you to safety. All I ask in return is that you bring me news. Tell me if you are the one. There is a strangeness about you. A power that is at once familiar and unfamiliar. Are you the Finder? Finder of the Key, perhaps? Finder of one of the Sleepers? Join with me. Help me unbind the spell. Help me find Slievgall'ion."*

Almost before the whisper completed, a faint rumble undercut it, racing to a deafening roar that lifted like the surge of a great wave, sweeping Caer's essence away from the sugary invocation.

"Not yours to take!" rolled thunderously around her with a dark richness of tone and a vague musicality. Searing white flashed everywhere at once. *"Not yours to have!"*

"Mine!" The sweetness thinned to a whine, gripping Caer with a horrifying strength. The sense of the alien presence pulled at her, clouding her sense of identity, merging it with a will terrifying in its hatred and its savagery. *"Mine! I take whom I wish!"*

Blood and death colored the decree, driving deep into Caer's soul a far greater terror than she had ever known. Desperately, she struggled to separate from the alien pull, her mortified defiance splitting into myriad echoes of *"no!"*--each magnified by the still rolling thunder.

Like the snapping of a too-taut chain, the will that gripped her broke, slamming her into an icy and impenetrable darkness filled with a flood of commingled smells--metal, machine oil, perfume, sweat--their thickness choking her. Burning cold and stabbing pain enveloped her, while the deafening scream of sirens and bells and yelling voices assaulted her.

"Come..." The command no longer held its power, sounding distant and feeble as it faded against the nearer cacophony.

"Somebody catch her!"

Multiple hands grabbed her arms and shoulders; holding tight; supporting her. The darkness lifted. Caer's eyes snapped shut against the shock of blinding light, waiting...waiting... Cautiously, she blinked them open, attempting to focus on the spinning room.

"Get a chair!" barked a voice. "Somebody find the doctor and get a tech crew in here! NOW! And shut that equipment down until we can get it checked out!"

A chair was thrust beneath her, the clutching hands slowly releasing her.

"Ms. DaDhrga. Ms. DaDhrga!"

The voice was very near. With a renewed flicker of terror, Caer jerked away, the reaction shifting her to the edge of the chair. Hands grabbed her once more; preventing her from slipping off; settling her firmly back to its center.

"Ms. DaDhrga!" No hint of sweetness, no menacing pull accompanied the words. Only anxiety. "Ms. DaDhrga, can you hear me?"

Caer blinked again as a face swam into hazy focus. Large gray eyes--a woman's eyes--stared at her from a face contorted by fretful concern.

Licking her lips, Caer rasped, "Yes?" The unexpectedly loud and grating sound of her own voice startled her.

"Are you alright?"

"All right?" she repeated, holding her words to a mumble lest the sound explode in her ears again. The question recalled the alarming image of 'pudding of person'. Caer's stomach lurched. Was she all right? Her hands moved in fearful assessment of her extremities.

Legs...arms...torso... Still blinking at the woman nervously, she stammered, "Everything is...is where it should be?"

The heavy scent of Gray-eyes' perfume once again assaulted Caer as the woman straightened, frowning. "Excuse me?" Understanding at last registered on the woman's face. "Yes. Yes, of course. You are properly intact. Do you know where you are?"

"Uhm..." A jumble of fragmented thoughts tumbled around in Caer's head. She was sure someone had put whatever gray matter was left inside her skull through a land skimmer's propeller. What was the question again? Where was she?

"Earth," she managed with only the smallest degree of conviction. "At least I think that's supposed to be my destination."

"Very good. Indeed. Though we were afraid we had lost the impulse signal for a moment." Gray-eyes looked Caer over once more. "Are you certain you are all right?"

"Uh...yes. I think so."

"Right. Well, you just sit here for a while. The station doctor will be along momentarily. Just a precaution, mind you. But I must insist."

If the woman's hovering was an indication that she expected some objection, she could think again. Sitting still was precisely what Caer intended to do, at least until she could screw her head securely back down. With no protest forthcoming, Gray-eyes nodded, moving away to quietly discuss matters with a small knot of people.

Caer made little attempt to watch them. Much better to focus on her lap, since the room continued to spin. Vaguely, she noted that every fiber of her body ached. Far more notable, however, were the bizarre impressions that remained swimming in her mind. Someone pulling her away, wanting her help to find... What had the voice said? The word seemed disquietingly familiar. A sleeve gallon? What in all the universe was a sleeve gallon? Probably nothing. Only nonsense from her wildly rampant imagination. No doubt, the scrambling of her molecules had seriously addled her brain. That sealed it! No more mat-trans travel--ever! From here on out, she would travel the long way to her destinations, or she wouldn't go at all.

The swish of a door opening and closing preceded, "Is this the young lady?" The booming voice came from somewhere off to Caer's right.

"Yes, doctor."

Hesitantly, Caer raised her eyes as a large man with a barrel chest and sparse, gray-speckled brown hair stepped into her field of vision.

"Ms. DaDhrga?"

Caer ventured a small nod and started to rise.

The man hastily waved her back. "No, no. Stay seated, please." Squatting in front of her, he stared directly into her eyes. "I understand you experienced a rough trip."

She responded with a shaky smile and a tentative shrug. "Trip was a little...uhm...off-putting. Don't care much for the bumpy landing, either. I don't suppose you've seen any spare brain cells hanging around. I think some of them failed to find their way home."

The doctor snorted. "At least you didn't misplace your sense of humor." Pulling a small, metal disc from his pocket, he placed it against her forehead, adding, "Just relax." After observing the face of the disc for several seconds, he at last gave another quick check of her eyes.

"You appear none the worse for your bumpy landing," he smiled. "Still, mat-trans does tend to come with a few unsettling side effects. Headaches, some nausea, fatigue. Maybe even some periods of disorientation. Might last for a few days."

Caer sighed. "Somehow it figures."

"Pardon?"

"Nothing. I'm just grumbling."

"Would you like for me to give you something to take for it?"

She blinked at him. "For the grumbling?"

The doctor's laugh filled the small room. "Don't know that I have anything for that. I'm certain I could find something for the headaches and nausea, though."

"Oh." Caer's face flushed warmly. "Uhm...no. I can manage. Thanks." She wished she was as certain as she'd attempted to sound.

The doctor stepped back, still eyeing her. "It would be no problem to keep you in the med unit overnight for observation."

Caer stiffened. "No. Really. I'm ready to go."

Shrugging, the doctor took Caer's backpack from the floor near her feet and offered his hand. "Very well."

Teetering precariously, Caer managed to stand only by clasping the man's hand more tightly than she'd intended.

"Here," he said, hooking the pack's strap over one shoulder. Taking her by the hand, he slipped his other arm around her, providing additional support. "If you insist on leaving, let me at least help you as far as your escort. Perhaps you'll have your Earth legs by the time we reach the hall."

Escort? Caer didn't recall anyone from Sion mentioning anything about an escort. An indignant huff slipped out. This was undoubtedly Adrian's doing. When was he going to get it through his very thick skull that she wasn't a child?

18

The doctor took his time guiding Caer through a corridor of twists and turns, offering a monolog to which she was paying little attention. It made her head hurt to concentrate. Embarrassed as she was at appearing helpless in the eyes of a stranger, she privately admitted her gratitude that the doctor maintained such a firm grip on her arm and kept his pace tailored to her own wobbly steps. She was equally grateful to be relieved of the necessity of reading the signs that marked the way. Each attempt to do so only increased the throbbing in her temples.

At last, a set of sliding double doors opened to a wide waiting area where a series of benches lined the walls. The sole occupant, a tall, slender woman dressed in a simple black jumpsuit, promptly rose and strode toward them. Caer's breath caught, first at the woman's uncommon grace as she moved, and second by her striking beauty. Midnight eyes so dark that the pupils were all but lost, elegantly fine features, and soft waves of shoulder-length hair that shone blue-black against the woman's pale complexion, created a stunningly ethereal appearance.

"Emer," the doctor smiled. "They didn't tell me you were this young lady's escort. How nice to see you again, my dear."

"And you, Donal," the woman returned. "You and Ginger need to come out for a visit one of these days soon. It's been far too long."

"We would be delighted." He gave Caer's hand a pat. "Thought

I should deliver your guest to you in person. Her journey appears to have been less than optimal."

The woman regarded Caer with concern. "Ms. DaDhrga?" she asked, extending a hand. "My name is Emer Kyot."

Caer withdrew from the doctor's support, hoping to keep her unsteady knees in check. Fine thing it would be, to fall on her face right in front of the doctor and a member of Sion's staff.

"I'm pleased to make your acquaintance," she managed. Her acceptance of the woman's hand, however, instantly shot a jolt of needled tingling from her fingertips all the way to her shoulder, jerking both women back in momentary surprise, and nearly depositing Caer to the floor on her backside. Only the doctor's quick reaction, supporting her once more, kept her on her feet.

The curiosity that darted across Ms. Kyot's face was quickly replaced by an apologetic sigh. "Sorry about that. The equipment here can raise some pretty disconcerting static charges."

Caer flexed her fingers as she eased away from the doctor once more. Thanks to her numerous visits to Adrian, she was familiar with the static that built up in the mat-trans chambers and some of the equipment rooms that stood in close proximity. The charge that just staggered her, however, was far more intense than anything she'd experienced on Bestor. Apparently, Earthers were rather lax in shielding their stations' outer chambers.

"It's quite all right," she said, mustering a faint smile. "Thank you for coming to meet me. It's very kind of you, though it wasn't necessary. I don't wish to be a bother."

"No bother at all. When Dr. Berring requested that someone meet you, I was pleased to do the honors. I enjoy getting acquainted with new students before they're overwhelmed with settling in. Besides, the trip gave me the perfect excuse to escape my office for a while."

"Dr. Berring," Caer murmured. "Is she here, then? I hope she's all right. I heard about the attack."

Ms. Kyot's brow drew down in a tense frown. "She was taken

to the primary colony on New Holland where she is recovering, thankfully. Her plan is to head Earth-side as soon as she gets a doctor's release." Appraising Caer, once more, she added, "The question is, are you alright? You look a little green."

Caer flushed, the warmth embarrassing her further, thus igniting a hotter flush. "I'm fine. Really. The trip just reminded me why I hate mat-trans travel."

The woman's frown dissipated in a sympathetic nod. "Matter transfer is my least favorite method of journeying, as well. There's no hurry for us to leave if you'd like to sit here for a few minutes. Get your bearings."

"I'm good. Honest."

Ms. Kyot gave her a final scrutiny, then gestured toward the far end of the corridor. "Very well. My pod is this way. We'll take the stroll nice and easy."

A quick glance down the corridor left Caer trying to guess its length from the distance between the doorways and benches lining the walls. The arithmetic proved beyond her capacity, for the moment, leaving her to conclude that it seemed a hell of a long way. "Right," she acknowledged. Reaching for her pack, she offered a miniscule nod of thanks to the doctor.

"Just a moment," he said, pulling a compu-pad from his shirt pocket and keying a code as he spoke. "Ms. DaDhrga may find, later, that she has need of something to offset the after effects of her bumpy arrival." He turned the device to Ms. Kyot. "If you'll enter your pod's code, I'll send the prescription to you, and you can arrange for its delivery from whatever pharmaceutical suits you."

Ms. Kyot tapped in the code and voiced the conceal command to secure its privacy. "Thank you, Donal. I'll arrange a pick-up on the way home."

In a single, fluid motion, the woman flicked Caer's pack from her grasp. "Here. Let me carry that for you. You'll find it much easier to regain your equilibrium if you're not toting around extra weight. "She hefted the pack with mild surprise. "No matter how slight that extra weight may be," she added, slipping one strap across her shoulder. "Believe me, I know." Cocking a brow, she sighed, "I'm guessing your light travel isn't entirely by design. I'm so very sorry for your losses. If there is anything you require, let me know and I will see to it in the morning." Setting out at a leisurely pace, she asked, "So. Have you ever been to Earth before, Ms. DaDhrga?"

"No. This is my first time."

"Mm. I'm sorry your trip proved problematic. A 'bumpy' arrival, I believe Donal said."

Caer's face warmed again. "It was nothing, really."

"When bells and sirens go off all over this end of the compound, it's hardly nothing. And since you were the only arrival in the past hour, the alarms were obviously connected with your 'landing'. You needn't be embarrassed that it left you more than a little shaken. Happens to a lot of us, even when everything goes smoothly."

Somehow, Caer couldn't imagine Ms. Kyot as anything other than the perfect picture of composure, no matter how many of her atoms had been jostled and juggled.

"You'll feel much better once you've had a nice hot bath and a good night's sleep," the woman continued. "In the meantime, you can nap, if you like, on the way home."

Home. How odd, thinking of Sion University that way, though she would have a good three or four years to get used to the idea, Caer supposed. "How far is it to the university?"

Ms. Kyot cast her a sidelong glance. "Actually, we've arranged off-campus housing for you. Ms. Cowl was to have informed you."

Caer's perplexed draw of her brow triggered a renewed twinge at her temples. "Uhm...No. Her message didn't say anything about that."

An agitated huff preceded Ms. Kyot's response. "Seems I need to have a word with that woman. I don't know what she has against the arrangement. She's been bucking it ever since Dr. Jorn made the request."

Jorn. Caer stumbled, her insides suddenly a gaping hollow. He'd requested special arrangements for her? When had he done that? He certainly hadn't said anything to her about it. Eyes fixed on the floor as she moved on, she ventured, "I, uh...I don't suppose he mentioned why he wanted me off campus."

"It wasn't so much that he wanted you off campus," Ms. Kyot replied. "He just didn't think housing you in a dorm would provide you with a 'clearer understanding of our earliest beginnings'."

The woman captured Jorn's diction and inflection perfectly in those last few words, prompting a small chuckle from Caer. "He did say I needed something of the sort. What did he do? Ask you to put me up in one of the ancient digs?"

Ms. Kyot grinned. "We figured he was speaking more in terms of something that approximates the environment Earth once knew. There is precious little of anything like that, now. Earth boasts a good many agricultural and livestock domes, of course. Though they hardly offer the feel of the ancient open prairies or farmlands. There are also a few sad little parks in some of the larger metropolitan domes that offer a vague hint of the various woodland and wetland flora that was once abundant." She chuckled again at Caer's growing look of alarm. "Don't worry. You won't be sleeping with livestock, nor in the middle of a park."

"So...he had you recreate the Garden of Eden for my coming?"

Ms. Kyot's laugh bubbled with genuine delight, the formality easing from her tone. "He told me that I would like you! No. He didn't ask us to recreate anything. The solution was simple enough. Your housing is the closest thing to the Garden of Eden that I know of. At least, it's been so for me."

Caer was relieved when they reached the exit at the end of the corridor more quickly than she'd anticipated. She took the pause as Ms. Kyot addressed the com system to lean as inconspicuously as possible against the wall, wishing her legs didn't feel so utterly boneless.

"Pod, Kyot 0-4," Kyot declared. Turning to Caer, she explained, "We've arranged for you to stay with Auntie and me."

Caer straightened, taken aback. "Oh! I...I wouldn't want to impose myself into your private living quarters!"

"He said you might say that. Believe me, my dear, it's no imposition at all. Auntie and I welcome your stay with us. Anyway, try it for a while, won't you? If you find the arrangement unsatisfactory, we will move you into one of the dorms on campus."

Caer was still struggling with the magnitude of the invitation, overwhelmed that these people would so willingly open their home to a total stranger. "I...I don't know what to say."

"Say, 'of course I will'." Receiving only Caer's continued stare, Ms. Kyot mouthed, "Of course I will," again, this time motioning for Caer to repeat it.

With a hesitant shrug, Caer relinquished. "Of course I will. Thank you, Ms. Kyot."

"There. That wasn't so hard. And please. The name is Emer. Ms. Kyot conjures up images of an antiquated spinster."

"Emer," Caer corrected, still trying to wrap her mind around this newest turn of events. "Uhm. I'm Caer. Just call me Caer."

19

Drumming. Hands held. Bodies moving as one--forward and back. The dance moves Deosil. One, two, three, four, five, six, seven. One, two, three. One, two, three. Widdershins. One, two, three, four, five, six, seven. One, two, three. One, two, three.

A face in the fire--a woman writhing. There is something that must be taken; something that must be found. Reaching out... A white-hot jolt as fingers touch. **Child! You must away! I call upon the guardian! Protect her!**

Hungry red tongues of flame coil around. Searing pain gnawing at flesh.

Eyes stare down, glowing with a turquoise heat, grim and scowling. Agony gnaws through to her very bones. She opens her mouth but can voice no cry. The grim eyes soften. Cool arms enfold her.

Caer fumbled for the arms that wrapped her with such strength, such reassurance. They protected her; cooled her burning flesh. But the arms were gone. Slowly, the feel of velvet against her hands registered in her consciousness. Velvet. On the seats of a pod. Jorn's pod.

The sudden, weighty ache in her chest prompted a soft whimper as she struggled to wake. Jorn was gone. Like the arms. Like the flames of her dreams. All that remained were confusing memories, some shaping themselves with Adrian's countenance, others with Jorn's. Caer slid her hands gently over the velvet seat, the act giving prominence to her memories of Dr. Hugh Jorn. The man with whom she thought, perhaps, she'd fallen in love. She fought against the rush of emotions, pushing them back to the darkness. She couldn't be in love. Not with a man who didn't love her. Not with a dead man.

"Feeling better?"

Caer started, then blinked uncertainly at the person seated across from her. Hovering in front of the woman was a holographic image of a partially buried building. The woman regarded her through the translucent image with intense dark eyes, her expression a mix of concern and curiosity.

"Uhm..." Gradually, awareness of the day's events sifted into place, allowing the woman's name to lift to the fore. Ms. Kyot. Emer Kyot.

Realizing she was slumped against the pod's door, Caer straightened, poking disconcertedly at several stray strands of hair in a futile attempt to marshal them back inside her bun. "Uh. Yes. Thanks," was mumbled through an unsuccessfully stifled yawn. "Sorry. I didn't mean to doze off."

"I'd have been surprised if you hadn't," Emer smiled. "It's been a very wearing day for you, I'm sure. Excuse me for just a minute while I finish up this little bit of record keeping."

Eyeing the holograph, Emer dictated, "Site 362. Excavation ongoing. Verify dates of building with marble façade and the most recently unearthed artifacts. Send report to Dr. Eliz. Close file." The image evaporated, leaving Emer to settle back. "You do look better. I was afraid you might still be pretty miserable, considering your restlessness."

Caer winced, wondering just how restless she'd been. Nothing so extreme as talking, or flailing about, she hoped. "I was dreaming, I guess."

"And I'm guessing it wasn't particularly pleasant. Want to talk about it? They say that telling a dream can help put it to rest."

Caer sighed. "Nothing to tell, really. I've never been any good at recalling mine." In truth, she did remember something more than the impression of fire and fear, this time. There was a woman she was sure she should have known. She could almost picture the face... Almost. And there was the feeling she'd been looking for something. It made no sense, of course. Just more of the snarled mush that so frequently plagued her sleep.

Emer shrugged. "Should you remember something and want to talk about it, I make a pretty good listener."

"Thanks," Caer repeated. "But whatever the dream involved, I doubt there's any retrieving it, now. Once I'm awake, they're gone." Another yawn escaped. Just as she started an expansive stretch, the pod banked sharply. Gripping the edge of her seat to keep from sliding, Caer again noted the velvet beneath her fingers. A quick glance around the pod's interior reminded her so much of Jorn's. This one was every bit as richly cushioned, and, like Jorn's, carried a primary color theme. Where his had been in varying shades of blues and silver-gray, however, Emer's was heavy on burgundy and deep rose tones. It exuded wealth, making Caer wonder if all Earthers were rich.

"We're nearing New Hope," Emer said, gesturing toward the windows. "So, we will be returning to the transit tunnels soon. If you want a peek at the way Earth looks outside of the great domes, best look now."

The thought of traveling outside of the domes stunned Caer. In the colonies, venturing beyond the domes and their interconnecting transit tubes was not an option unless you were a highly skilled technician or construction worker. And those went outside only when sent on a mission to repair some external portion of the dome's shell or the equipment that produced and scoured the oxygen. Leaning nearer the window, Caer peered out and down.

She couldn't say what her expectations might have been, but the ghastly yellow-gray haze hanging over everything was not it. Nor was the vast expanse of broken and crumbled buildings that rose like specters in the murk. Most were barely recognizable as anything more than twisted girders, mangled concrete, or great shards of grime-encrusted glass. The sprawl of what must surely have been a once grand city stretched out over multiples of rising and falling hills, with the lowlands footing them partially submerged in a thick muck of greenish-brown that oozed outward in slicks and swirls, feeding at last into what Caer could only assume were the waters of a vast ocean. She knew about Earth's oceans; had seen pictures and holographs...and Jorn's Dream Painting. In those, she easily imagined an abundance of life, despite what the history texts claimed. Here..

Sickened at the reality, Caer turned away, glancing instead, out the window on the opposite side of the pod where the hills rolled on, disappearing in the shrouded distance. Nearer at hand on that side, a solitary structure caught her eye. Standing amid the ruins that dotted the undulating foreground with overlapping shadows, this lone tower lurked ominously over the jagged and tumbled landscape. Scooting across the seat for a better look, she could only frown at the odd visage. The tall, spindly framework climbed from the tangle of decaying debris and oily, sulfurous fog, like the ghost of a last-standing sentinel. Consisting of a tripod of rusted legs, it tapered upwards, flaring out in six thin arms to support a large saucer. A pointed spire topped the precarious construct. Thin, jaundiced clouds played around the spire and in and out of the saucer's two encircling rows of dark and shattered windows.

Caer's gaze traced the length of the peculiar framework back to its base, where fog made a slow slither through the legs and surrounding debris. "What is that thing, and how is it standing when nothing else seems to be?"

"Magic holds it up."

"Yeah. Right," Caer snorted. Jorn had referenced magic, once, as well. Apparently, Earthers enjoyed labeling certain marvels with the tag.

Grinning, Emer offered a shrug. "No? Ah well. Facts, then. According to the information in Sion's archives, the structure was created in the twentieth century, the saucer you see near the top serving as a rotating restaurant and observation deck. Apparently, it was designed to impress people with its 'futuristic' lines and its grandiose panoramas. Many believed it worthy of preserving. Even established a museum in what had been the restaurant. Nor was this the only local building they maintained, though it's certainly the most distinct."

"They've maintained that spindly tripod for this long? Why?"

"Not maintained any longer," Emer corrected. "The group is defunct, now. Has been for nearly fifty years. Let me answer your question this way, though. Why did you come here? What is it you intend to do with whatever artifacts you find?"

Shrugging, Caer replied, "To learn from them, of course."

"And then what? Bury them again? Let the world of decay take them back? Or do you hope to find a means of preserving them for others to behold and to learn from?"

"I would want to save them for others, of course," she acknowledged, cocking her head in consideration. "But you said the group is now defunct. Why did they give up on this structure if they thought it worth preserving in the first place?"

"Oh, it wasn't just this building. It was every site the preservationists maintained in this entire region. The end, sadly, was brought about by the last series of earthquakes to hit the area."

"Earthquakes?"

Emer nodded. "Surely, your studies have mentioned such things. They rattle anything from isolated regions to the whole length of the coastline periodically. The ones that shut down the local preservation projects, however, proved to be among the strongest ever recorded. They killed something just shy of a hundred of the people who were working the various sites. No one's come forward to fund the effort, since." Grinning again, she added, "Don't worry. Quakes like those are exceedingly rare. And all contemporary structures are seismically quite sound. Humankind can learn to do things properly when the stakes are high enough. It was only the ancient buildings outside of the domes that suffered in that last big shake. While severely rattled, everything else remained standing."

Caer's attention returned to the ruins below, wondering how much of it was the result of the quake, and how much had crumbled long before that time. Twisting to peer out of the window behind her, she watched the towering tripod slowly fade into the yellow fog, wondering, as well, what view had stretched out beneath and around that strange building's observation deck. Was it one of a solid mass of buildings and streets, or had it included hills and mountains?

Drawing a slow breath, she straightened around. Whatever the view had been, there was nothing but sorrow, here, now. If anything lived out there, it could only be a few toxic strains of algae and lichen. She knew it would be so. The history texts had drilled that much into her skull. Moreover, Adrian frequently harped on and on about the devastation. Even Jorn had seen fit to warn her. Seeing it first hand, however, experiencing the vastness of it, settled a demoralizing sense of loss over her. Emptiness, she understood. Every world she'd been on was cold and barren beyond the domes where technology made life possible. They had always been so. Not here, though. Species beyond count had once arisen and flourished, here, covering the entire world with life forms the like of which would never again be seen. A subtle whisper within Caer whimpered its pained anguish over the magnitude of the loss, slumping her back, her eyes misting.

"Hard to look at," Emer acknowledged. "Though most off-worlders are more awed than dismayed."

"How can anyone not be moved to grief by this?"

A brief silence prefaced the suggestion of weary resignation in Emer's voice. "Most people do not mourn the loss of something they never knew. While children are taught Earth's history, it seems more a myth and legend to them than fact. Very few people ever venture beyond the security of the domes and the transit tunnels. They have no idea what lies outside, much less what it was like before the dramatic shift in Earth's climate and the resulting Great Wars. They are oblivious to the toxic waters of what was once known as the Salish Sea; oblivious to the islands that dot it; oblivious to the ocean beyond. They stick to the confines of the dome in which they were born, traveling, perhaps, to its nearest neighbors by way of the tunnels. Only a handful of diplomats, archeologists, or the very wealthy with a modicum of curiosity ever travel further afield."

So, it was not so different from the colonies, after all. Caer could hardly blame the inhabitants. What would be the point of coming out here, unless on some scientific excursion? She wondered at the hardships she would endure, should she participate in such a venture. Closing her eyes, Jorn's glorious Dream Paintings shone in her mind, once more. It was not the contrast between their beauty and the devastation below that pained her, however. Rather, it was the reminder that she would never see Jorn, or any of her friends again. These people still had a planet, at least. They had their friends and families and... Her throat tightened, her stomach knotting as tears seeped from beneath her closed lids.

"I'm sorry," Emer offered softly. "I hadn't considered that watching the landscape move by might trigger the after effects of your mat-trans journey. Just keep your eyes closed for a while. We'll be back in the tunnels, soon. I'll direct 04 to a pharmaceutical where we can get that prescription filled for you."

Caer found it simpler to remain silent, leaving Emer to her assumptions. She had no words to explain the weight of grief that threatened to crush her.

"0-4."

"Yes?"

The deep, rich, masculine voice brought Caer's eyes open once more.

"How far are we from the nearest entry point?" Emer asked of the air.

"Approaching entrance to tunnel system, now."

"Good. We need to make a brief stop in New Haven."

The pod decelerated and descended, banking slightly to aim for one of the many hills. A few minutes later, it slipped smoothly through a gaping hole in the hill's side, the jaundiced light from the fading day blinking out. Inside the pod, the ceiling lights rose automatically to a faint glow. The change in motion and lighting triggered a new roll of nausea. She clenched her teeth against it.

"Requested interim destination?" queried the enticing voice.

"We need to fill a prescription for our guest."

Swallowing, Caer waved a hand. "No, no. It's all right. I'll be fine."

"Fine if you wish to retain your current shade of green for a few more hours," Emer sniffed. "0-4, the prescription has been keyed in under Dr. Donal Sandon's file. Send it to the nearest pharmaceutical and arrange for pick-up."

"Prescription sent. Pick up arranged at Pharmaceutical 1374, southeast quadrant."

There was another subtle change in the pod's motion as they slowed further and nosed slightly downward. After a short time, 0-4 leveled off and sped up.

"Exit in seventeen minutes. Will emerge New Hope, Southeast."

The sensuousness of the com's voice would have set Caer to giggling, had she not been fighting the ongoing pitch of her stomach and the ache of her heart. "That's quite an auditory system," she managed at last.

Emer beamed. "You like it? I programmed it myself. Perhaps someday I will figure out how to add seductive, flashy eyes to it. I considered giving it a name rather than the usual alphanumeric address. But I decided 0-4 pretty well said it."

"Yes, Emer?" the pod responded.

"Sorry. Just discussing you."

"I trust it's good."

Emer leaned forward, whispering, "Oh for a body to match the voice!"

Caer's appreciative snicker won out over her distress.

The tunnel they traversed quickly widened, the lighting increasing as well. Caer tried to determine the source of the light, concluding, finally, that it emanated from the walls. It filtered in, now, through 0-4's encircling tinted windows. Tentatively, Caer set her attention to what lay outside, curiosity further overriding her queasiness. The tunnel was enormous, with at least five or six lanes of traffic all speeding along in the same direction. Below, she could see an equal number of lanes with vehicles moving along in the reverse direction. Faster pods from each level shifted in lanes between the primary upper and lower ones before cautiously merging back into the appropriate stream. Never had she seen such gargantuan transit tubes, nor so much traffic.

0-4 conducted some remarkable maneuvering, working its way to an outside flight lane before exiting into a smaller side passage. There was less traffic here, allowing their pod to glide effortlessly into the flow. Abruptly, a larger vehicle appeared from somewhere behind them, pulling alongside and matching their speed. The windows of the flanking pod were as heavily tinted as 0-4's, making it impossible to see who was inside. Its mere presence, however, sent a chill through Caer, raising the hair on the back of her neck.

Emer's pod shuddered. Caer felt the tug, as though something was attempting to pull their vehicle from its lane. As 0-4 corrected, reestablishing the distance between the two pods, another tug lurched them sideways, their exterior almost scraping against that of their neighbor. Again, they shifted back to their lane.

"0-4, shielding," Emer commanded, the unmistakable static of an energy field immediately encompassing them. Emer stared at the pacing vehicle, her jaw set, an intense scowl creasing her features. "That should keep us safe. 0-4, can you spot an ID on our friends, here?"

"It appears to be an unregistered pod."

The vehicle continued to pace them for several more minutes, then hastily sped off, zipping into an exit passage ahead. Emer turned to face the pod's front, silently watching the other vehicle disappear.

Caer was about to question the incident when 0-4 announced,

"Entering airspace, New Hope, quadrant 24 southeast." Decelerating, they moved into the same exit tunnel the unidentified pod had taken, the transit tube now rising at a ridiculously steep angle. Their ascent continued until the transit tube connected to a portal near the top of a dome.

Caer gaped, dumbstruck, as they emerged high above the city. A real Earth city! The scale was beyond anything she'd ever imagined. The far curve of the enclosure was only barely discernable, even from this height. The whole of at least five Ahiran complexes could easily have nestled inside the confines of this single construct, and still have room to spare.

0-4 gently dropped a short distance below the general traffic flow. After a slight adjustment in direction, they headed toward a grouping of tall, concrete buildings. Caer fidgeted with her necklace, an uneasy prickling creeping along her nerves, raising the hair on the back of her neck again, even as a sudden flash of bright light ignited to the east of them. Squinting, she stared hard at what she thought to be the point of origin. The light came again, this time as a series of flashes in quick succession.

"What's that?"

Emer turned to look, as well. "What's what?"

Caer pointed and heard Emer suck in, declaring, "Trouble is what that is. 0-4, head for and circle the building at two o'clock--the old Stafford warehouse. Just maintain a safe distance."

The pod altered direction once more, aiming for the designated structure. Several more flashes shot up from the shadows at the north end of the flat warehouse roof, striking a small pod that hovered unsteadily above it, smoke pouring from its sides. Another series of flashes bathed the disabled vehicle's underbelly in flame. The stricken pod lifted slightly, listed to one side, and then dropped with a grinding crunch onto the rooftop.

"Damn!" Emer breathed. "0-4, contact the authorities. A pod is down on building... What's the bloody number for that warehouse?"

"Building 1436 East," 0-4 provided.

"Right. Let security know that immediate assistance is required."

"Message sent. Do you wish for me to continue on, now?"

Nerves still prickling, Caer prayed Emer's answer would be an unequivocal 'yes,' though she couldn't keep from pressing her nose to the window, her eyes riveted on the unfolding scene below.

"Not yet. Continue to circle until help arrives."

A small knot of people rushed from the shadows created by a taller neighboring building, their destination the downed pod. Caer held her breath, hoping they would reach the burning debris in time to rescue those aboard the disabled vehicle. A startled cry broke from her when she realized a rescue was not in the offing. Instead, the rushing group beset the two individuals as they crawled from the flames.

"Look there," Emer hissed. "Just next to the roof's north wall. Isn't that the pod that messed with us just a few minutes ago? Where the hell is security?"

Caer, however, failed to search out the pod, her attention, snagged by the dark figure that stalked out from the shadows. The man's enormous size and the manner of his predatory gate evoked an eerie familiarity, sending a shiver through her. Stopping, he turned, lifting his gaze to track 0-4's circling pattern. For an instant, Caer had the disquieting sense that he was looking directly at her. Her breath froze as the flames from the downed and burning pod threw enough light across the man's face for recognition to hit. Here stood the same man who'd occupied the seat next to her on the shuttle from Ahira.

Still marking 0-4's path, the man raised a hand and leveled a weapon at them.

Emer shouted, "0-4, climb!"

The sudden upward thrust threw Caer back into the seat, leaving her stomach in her shoes. From beneath them came the sounds of several explosive bursts. Light flared all around, the percussion of the blast rocking the pod.

"Authorities responding," 0-4 stated calmly, settling to a hover above the weapon's range.

Caer dared another look from the window. Other pods were quickly closing on the warehouse, lights flashing. The attackers broke and ran--all save the man who had just fired on them. He was nowhere to be seen.

Several officers poured out from the landing security pods, most giving chase after those who now fled. Three, however, darted toward the injured victims. Caer's thoughts raced between her profound hope that help had arrived in time to save them, and her utter horror at having recognized one of the assailants.

"Alright, 0-4," Emer stated quietly. "Let's get out of here."

Caer pried herself from the window, the man's face still etched in her mind. "What...what do you think that was all about?"

Emer's brow cocked as she regarded Caer for several seconds. "Robbery, I would guess," she said at last.

Robbery. Caer took a long breath to steady the tremor in her voice, her fingers closing anxiously around her necklace. "You stayed there, even after alerting the authorities. What would you have done if security hadn't arrived when they did?"

Emer sighed. "Gone in firing, I suppose. I couldn't very well go off and leave the victims."

"Firing," Caer repeated dully. "This pod is armed?"

"Of course, it's armed. As am I."

"Approaching pharmaceutical," 0-4 declared.

"Good. Let's get our friend's prescription and go home."

20

Caer's gratitude for the medication's quick relief was tempered by the fact that it also had her nodding off again. Accompanying each moment of drowsing came dark visions of the man from the shuttle trip to Bestor III, his repugnant features either leering predatorily at her or regarding her with contempt. Though the dreams showed nothing beyond his countenance, she knew that he held a deadly weapon; that he aimed it directly at her. Each time he fired, she jerked awake with a gasp, only to nod off again, repeating the cycle.

At last, a gentle stir of fresh, crisp air brushed Caer's face, carrying with it an unfamiliar, yet pleasant, sweetness. The menacing phantoms diminished and faded as Caer breathed it in. Blinking awake, she noted the ghostly pale light that filtered through the pod's windows. She noted, as well, that the pod's power cells were quiet, and that the seat across from her was empty.

"We're home," Emer announced from just outside the pod's open door. Her hands-on-hips stance suggested she'd likely repeated the proclamation more than once. "If you prefer, of course, you can stay out here all night. Personally, I'm looking forward to the comfort of a bed." Reaching for Caer's pack, she hooked it over a shoulder and gestured with a wink. "I suspect you would, too. Come on, sleepyhead."

Caer scooted to the door, a sudden chill stopping her at the edge of the seat to take in the small landing pad. A soft glow lit the area, the illumination emanating from the full length of four tall corner posts that marked the pad's boundaries. A short distance from Emer's pod sat another, glinting in the pale shadows. The vehicle appeared identical to Emer's, save for its color. Where the exterior of Emer's was a deep, metallic blue, the other shone as a burnished russet. Apparently, there were others on Earth who could afford the luxury of their own pod.

A continued scrutiny of the area had Caer wondering briefly at the lack of benches at the pad's edges. Perhaps this was strictly a private pad, rather than one that accommodated public transport. She made a mental note to acquaint herself with the pick-up locations and the schedule for the public vehicles first thing in the morning.

Caer's chill increased as she slipped out onto the tarmac. Rubbing her arms, she darted a glance around, aware that her unease was due, at least in part, to a charge that ran along her nerves. The landing pad must be in the proximity of one of the heavy generators that provide air filtration for this particular dome. The surrounding darkness, however, precluded the ability to spot the dome's wall.

Her arm rubbing became more vigorous. No, she decided, sucking on her lip. She remembered well the ever-present sensation of mild tingling created by the massive equipment just outside of the dome where she and her Aunt Sidra had shared a home. This was different. No faint tingle, this. More like sharp needle pricks--the sort that raise flesh. Like... Like... The flashes hit her, freezing her where she stood--flashes of the grisly corpse on her bedroom floor; of the creature in Adrian's quarters; of...of the figure standing in the shadows outside the club on Ahira; of the man who'd fired on Emer's pod. This was much like the charge that chased along her flesh in each of those instances.

Already half way across the tarmac, Emer stopped when she realized that Caer failed to follow. "Something wrong, dear?" she called back.

"Uhm..." Chewing anxiously at the corner of her mouth, Caer made a slow turn, peering into the near shadows that edged the landing area...finding nothing. Paranoid. Recent events were making her paranoid. Embarrassed, she shook her head, muttering, "No. No, of course not. I just...uh...feel sort of..." How insane would it sound if she said something as ridiculous as 'unwholesomely tingly'? "Rattled," she finished with a self-conscious cough.

Emer moved on with a harrumph. "I shouldn't wonder. Given what you've been through, recently, I'm surprised you're not edgier."

Caer ventured several more glances at the surrounding shadows as she trotted after the woman. The lack of anything menacing reinforced her conclusion of paranoia and left her pondering Emer's comment. Just how much did the woman know about recent events? According to Adrian, security on every colony and on Earth was alerted within hours of Ahira's demise. But how quickly would such news go public? Word of the murder in her apartment, of course, was unlikely to have spread. As for the security lockdown on Bestor III. Adrian said information regarding that little episode had also gone out to every security detail, though it was unlikely to be announced publicly.

"Oops!" Caer jerked up just shy of running the woman over, surprised that Emer had stopped. "Sorry," she mumbled. "Guess I should spend more time watching where I'm going."

Emer shrugged it off amicably. "You have a lot on your mind, I expect." Nodding toward a path that began near one of the four corner posts, she suggested, "You might want to watch yourself here, though." Caer took in the path's stone steps with a weary sigh. From where she stood, she could see that it switch-backed up through the darkening shadows of a steep slope, the only light above the top of the post coming from the glow of the steps, themselves. "We have a little climb ahead of us," Emer said. "Take it at your own pace. While the colonies do their best to simulate Earth gravity, they tend to fall short of the mark. You will find that you weigh rather more here than you did, either on Ahira or on Bestor III." Eyeing Caer with amusement, she sniffed, "Not that there is that much of you to start with. Still, this may be more of a challenge than it looks."

Caer's already lagging energy plummeted as her gaze tracked the glowing stone stair to the top of the bluff. Fine time for someone to warn her of the gravity issue, now!

Despite Emer's moderate but steady pace, it took no time for Caer to fall well behind. Jenna's nagging about how much time Caer spent at her studies drifted to mind. Too much time sitting and not enough time living, was Jen's oft-repeated reproach. Thoughts of her friend left a knot in Caer's throat and a hollow in her stomach. Jen would never again tease her about her work ethic. Never again needle her about her various infatuations, or complain about the difficulty of this or that dance. Would never again return from one of her many off-world excursions, grinning like a Franzian lizard as she presented Caer with another little doll attired in the customary clothing of whatever colony Jen had just visited.

Caer tried to swallow. Her precious collection of dolls was gone, now. Just as Jen was...and Jorn...and....and perhaps everyone else she'd known on Ahira. Quietly blinking back her tears, she trudged the final long switchback to the wide, level platform that marked the halfway point.

Leaning against the railing, Emer gazed out at the darkness as she waited. "We'll take a few minutes, here, to catch our breath," she offered. "I tried to convince Auntie some time ago to install a lift from the pad to the top. But she prefers it this way. Says the climb is good for us."

Caer used the back of her sleeve to wipe quickly at her eyes, softly clearing her throat in an attempt to make both her breathing and her strangled voice sound normal. "I don't mind. We can go on whenever you wish."

Emer gave a bemused huff. "Glad you enjoy the workout. I'll take the respite, though, if you don't mind."

Caer's face warmed. The respite was for her sake, and she knew it. Joining Emer at the railing, she glanced down, all the more chagrined at her weak knees and breathlessness. The tarmac couldn't be more than ten or twelve meters below. In an attempt to hide her gasping, Caer turned to eye the remaining face of the bluff, wishing profoundly for that lift. Surely, there were Earthers who lacked the stamina for this little climb. So, why would Emer ask her aunt to install one when it should be a project for the community to undertake?

"As long as we're just standing here," Emer began, glancing across at Caer. "There's something I should mention."

Caer cocked her head at the woman. "What? Like a full-fledged mountain beyond this little warm-up?"

"Don't worry," Emer laughed. "No mountain. Though I'm sure I could find one for you if you really wish it. Of course, with the mountains lying outside of the domes, you will have a great deal of protective gear to haul along with you."

"I think I'll save that expedition for some other day, thanks."

Emer laughed again. "Just don't make any mountaineering plans for tomorrow, or you'll miss your visitors."

"Visitors?" Who, besides Adrian, could possibly know where she was, or even care? She fought back a moan. Oh, please don't let Emer tell her that Adrian was here!

"Tomorrow afternoon," Emer nodded. "That's what I wanted to mention. Dr. Eliz wishes to meet with you before she has to leave to check on some dig sites."

Caer stifled another moan. That was almost as bad. It was said that Dr. Eliz was a tough, dour woman who demanded perfection from everyone around her. Perfection was not one of Caer's strong suits, even on a good day. She would prefer to have a few days to at least get past the brain-addling aspect of her journey.

"That's...uhm...kind of her. But she doesn't need to make a special trek on my account. I'm sure there will be plenty of opportunities on campus for us to meet."

"Eliz expects to be gone for several days, and she's been most anxious to make the acquaintance of the student for whom Hugh has given such high accolades."

Hugh. Dr. Jorn. The ache that abruptly devoured her insides sucked away any reply she might have made. Dropping her gaze, she stared back down at the landing pad, thankful for the night shadows as she blinked back another misting of tears. How long would it take before the mere mention of Jorn's name would cease to echo through the emptiness of her soul?

"Brenna Cowl will be coming out, as well," Emer continued. "Brenna is, as I'm sure you know, the Student Facilities Coordinator."

Caer pursed her lips. Yes. Brenna Cowl had spoken to her briefly a couple of times. The woman had been quite stingy with the information she'd given Caer about Sion, about upcoming classes... and about her housing. According to Emer, Ms. Cowl didn't approve of the arrangements Jorn made. Perhaps justifiably so. It must seem an unwarranted privilege when most new students were required to live in the dorms for the first four semesters.

"Brenna doesn't generally venture too far from the university," Emer was saying. "I'm only guessing, here, but I suspect her intention for this little trip is to divest herself of a pest."

"A... Excuse me?" Caer turned a perplexed scrutiny to her companion. "A what?"

"A friend of yours, or so he claims. Said his name is Brandon Jase."

"Brandon!" Caer's stunned relief threatened to sink her to her knees. Bran's alive!

On the move, again, Emer continued talking. Caer scuttled to catch up to her. "Your 'friend' showed up a little over a week ago, and has been asking about you ever since. Pretty much took up residence in Brenna's office every day, pestering her half to death about any word of your arrival. I think she's eager to unload him on you."

Bless Bran! He always did have a way of annoying people. Caer could scarcely wait to see him, though. No doubt he suffered from the same overwhelming emptiness she felt. They needed each other.

The two women continued their climb in silence for several minutes before Emer glanced back over her shoulder. "There is one more thing I should probably tell you before you simply stumble across it. You will find some boxes stacked in the closet of your room. They're yours."

"Mine?"

Caer detected a slight catch to Emer's voice as she explained. "Hugh had your belongings sent out from Ahira the same day you left for Bestor III. I figured...under the circumstances...perhaps you didn't know."

"My things," Caer repeated, tripping on a step at the surprise. How? She thought her apartment still sealed off for the investigation when she left.

Emer climbed the last step, disappearing from sight, her delicate sigh drifting back from the darkness above. "Hugh always was full of surprises."

"My things," Caer muttered dully. She owned nothing of value--save for her sentimental attachments to a few items. Yet Jorn had taken the extraordinary measure of sending her 'boxes' of her things. Why would he do that?

Stumbling with exhaustion and emotionally wrenched by this last revelation, Caer cleared the final rise...and halted, mouth agape. Laid out across the gently rounded hilltop and illuminated by hundreds of small ground lights, stretched the remainder of the stone pathway surrounded by a sea of garden flowers. So startling was the sight, that it temporarily swept every sorrow, every anxiety from her head. Never before had she seen anything like this, not even in the supposedly wide-ranging botanical gardens of Heshton. Her memory of those paled shamefully, next to this. Here, the whole of the broad hilltop undulated with an unimaginable assortment of blossoms, most night-closed, while others fluttered their open petals delicately in the slight stir of circulating air. Their colors were muted by the heavy shadows, but their fragrance filled her, rich and intoxicating.

The sea of flowers gave way only where the path crested the hill, some three hundred meters or so from where she stood. There, at the path's end, and squarely centered on the hilltop, stood a single large building. The grand two-story structure appeared to be constructed of stone below and white plaster with dark wooden crossbeams above. It put Caer in mind of the textbook holographs of structures from Earth's early European history. Tudor, she believed the style was called. She doubted, however, that any of the early Medieval-inspired buildings could come close to this in scale.

Emer's pleasant, "Well, hello Merri," tugged Caer from her enchanted reverie to find the woman kneeling on the path a short distance ahead. A large black cat arched contentedly beneath Emer's extended fingers. "Out for an evening stroll, are you?" Mewing, the cat accepted Emer's head and chin scratches for several seconds before turning its luminous green eyes purposefully toward the newcomer.

Caer had not seen such animals since living with her aunt. She loved the cats her Aunt Sidra kept. Seeing this one eyeing her with curiosity prompted a broad grin. Moving forward a few steps, she squatted, slowly extending her open hand. The cat approached, unconcerned, and licked her fingers. "Yours?" she asked Emer as she stroked the thick, glossy fur.

Emer rose, shaking her head. "Aunt Del's. Or, perhaps Aunt Del belongs to Merripen. Sometimes it's hard to tell."

"Merripen. Nice name."

Emer chuckled. "Yes, well, it's supposed to be a boy's name, though Merri, here, is female. Auntie chose the name because it means both life and death. She figured it was appropriate for an animal that required nine deaths to bring about its end."

Caer was familiar with the ancient folklore. Her aunt often mentioned it when one of her cats survived the constant teasing and worse from the colony's children. Sidra, however, had always explained it as the animal's having nine lives rather than requiring nine deaths to end it. She rather preferred Sidra's slant. The cat mewed again, moving from beneath Caer's hand to purr against her legs.

"Consider yourself one of the rare chosen, Caer. Merri doesn't normally take to strangers."

"I'm honored!" Caer gave the animal a final stroke as it completed its circuit of her. Then, standing, she gestured expansively. "This is absolutely amazing! I've never seen a park like this. Does the whole community have access to it?"

Emer frowned for a moment, obviously confused. "Community?" Understanding finally glinted in her dark eyes. "Oh. No. This dome is our own. The nearest community is New Hope, where we picked up your prescription." Turning to head toward the building, she added, "The house and grounds have been in our family for generations. The gardens, however, are strictly Aunt Del's pet projects."

Caer's wide-eyed stare returned to the structure at the crest of the hill. "That's a house?" Just how big was Emer's family, anyway? All that had been mentioned, thus far, was herself and a single aunt. Caer found it all the more unnerving to think that she was about to step, not just into Emer and her aunt's home, but that of a large, extended family. How did the rest of the members feel about a stranger's imposition into their private lives?

"I'll give you the grand tour in the morning," Emer called back. "Right now, I think a nice, warm meal and a decent night's sleep would do us both some good."

21

Fedel'ma rounded the top of the stairs, the fullness of her skirted pants fluttering around her long legs as her stride carried her across the broad landing to the library's double doors. Hesitating, she shot a glance to her left where the corridor ran the length of the house's north wing. The door to the nearer suite on the opposite side of the hall stood slightly ajar, the light from the bedroom casting a small puddle of brighter illumination in the hallway's dim glow. She heard, however, no sound of stirring from within. Their guest had cried herself into oblivion, earlier. Hopefully, she remained asleep.

Setting her shoulder to the doors, Fedel'ma pushed them open only enough to pass between them. Then with her back to them, she closed them as quietly as possible, not daring to utter a sound until she heard the dull thud of their contact. "Lock," she murmured, listening for the subtle click.

For a long while, she remained with her back braced against the doors, her mind crowded with an ever-growing number of ill-defined concerns and wild conjectures. Her observations of the girl answered none of her questions. Instead, they posed a great many more. Worse... Pressing a hand to her breast, Fedel'ma tried to bury the ancient sorrow ushered to the fore by the girl's arrival.

"Trouble," she rumbled, at last, raising her eyes to skim the darkness. "You sent me a bundle of trouble."

The silence that greeted her as reply came weighted with the smell of paper dust, leather book bindings, and furniture polish. The lack of ozone in the air, along with the absence of any suggestion of a static buzz, added to her bleak mood. Hugh had not come. Not through this port, nor through the kitchen or her gardens. These were the only locations she permitted teleportation by anyone other than Emer or herself. When Hugh chose to turn up—whichever location he used—she would sense his arrival.

'Don't expect my return right away,' he'd said. Still, at least four weeks had elapsed since the catastrophe on Ahira--more than ample time for her son's transmigration and return. She shuddered. That, of course, assumed the survival of his soul. Stiffening, she dismissed any possibility of his soul's death or banishment. Hugh survived. She would accept nothing less. The girl was here. He'd not be far behind.

Again, she cast her gaze about the room, hoping for the charged magic to announce her son's arrival; watching for him to emerge stretched out on the settee a few paces in, or parked on one of the two well-cushioned chairs that flanked the round reading table across to her right. Her lips twitched to an irritated pucker. More likely, he would shimmer to substance, lounging in her chair with his feet propped puckishly on her antique mahogany desk, the tall windows that spanned the exterior wall serving as his dramatic backdrop.

Fedel'ma skimmed the dark room again, waiting. Her wait yielded nothing. Long, empty moments of nothing.

"Fine!" she huffed, pushing away and striking out with her long stride, making her way with no need of calling up the lights. "Dump your little puzzle on me, then. Trouble thrice over, that's what this child is. Just like you. Disappearing and leaving me to unravel whatever mess you dump in my lap."

Stopping at the side of her desk, Fedel'ma glared into the blackness of night that lay beyond the diamond cut, leaded glass panes of the windows. The view from this side of the house did not include her gardens with their dotting of lights. Before her lay only the thickness of a domed night, clouds apparently shrouding the moon above, thereby preventing even its muted glow from filtering through.

"And what, pray tell, do you expect me to do with this little puzzle?" she muttered. Not that she needed to ask. Hugh made his expectations quite clear.

Turning, she yanked her desk chair out, its wooden moan punctuating her agitation as she sank onto it, her fingers pulling loose the tie that held her thick white hair in its long braid. For several seconds of restlessness, she sat, finger-combing through the plaits until her hair fell in smooth, dense waves over the front of her shoulders. Mouth pinched, she admitted that, had she half a brain, she'd cease this ridiculous vigil and go to bed. Her prolonged mental connection with Merripen after all, left them both exhausted and out of sorts. Merri, no doubt, was already tucked somewhere in the spaces beneath the house, settled in deep sleep. Bed, however, held no appeal for Fedel'ma. Not so long as her son insisted on maintaining his impudent silence.

"Enough of this!" she barked to the air, her short sleeves flapping as she thumped her folded arms onto the polished desktop. "Wherever you've gone, Hugh MacFaolan, whatever you are up to, you can damn well trot your bones home this instant! Take care of this little bundle of trouble yourself, if you think she's worthy of a personal bodyguard!"

She expected no reply, yet was gallingly dismayed when her expectations bore out. Even if her son's mind happened to be open to her railing at this particular moment—which she found highly unlikely—Hugh complied with her dictates only when it suited him. And the simple fact of the matter was that it generally suited him not to suit her.

"Fine!" she repeated, her voice grating. "Keep your distance. Refuse to talk to me. Your objection to being anywhere around me, however, does not give you the right to do what you've done! No right. At the very least, you should have had the decency to warn Emer. Haven't you put her through enough?"

Though her reserves were already strained, Fedel'ma straightened, determined to accomplish one more objective before retiring for what remained of the night. Once again, she must make up for her son's selfish, insensitive actions. Drawing a slow, deep breath, she focused her mind...reaching out...seeking for the feel of her niece's presence...delicately prodding with, *"Emer, dear."*

Getting no response, she pressed again, and several more times besides. *"Emer, we need to talk."* Precisely what she intended to say... how she might present the situation...eluded her. She would think of something, though.

At last, her niece's bleary reply came as a thin, sleep-fogged, *"Who...?"*

"What do you think?" Fedel'ma urged.

"Wha..."

The sense of her niece's fuzzy yawn promptly spawned a duplicate from Fedel'ma. "You can sleep later, you old fool!" she growled to the darkness, working to keep her mind focused on the issue at hand.

"Let me sleep, now, Del. And watch who you're calling an old fool!" Emer shot back with a disgruntled harrumph.

Fedel'ma blanched. *"I'm sorry, dear. The reference was meant for me, not for you."*

The haze of, *"Yes, well,"* drifted with the tinge of Emer's lingering annoyance. *"You just aren't content unless you're pestering someone, are you? Where were you, earlier, anyway?"*

"Watching," Fedel'ma responded curtly.

"Judging from the hostility infusing your manner," Emer snipped back, *"I'm guessing you played your spy game a little too long. Serves you right. You deserve to be miserable for putting Merri up to such mischief. Think how agitated she must be, now. What would it hurt for you to observe in person? Why didn't you enjoy some of your own soup while getting acquainted with our guest, and save Merri the wear of your presence in her head?"*

Fedel'ma exhaled with a snort. *"Observations are more easily accomplished when the observer is unobserved. But never mind that. Just answer my question, if you would."*

"Which was..." Another yawn insinuated itself before Emer managed a weary, *"Oh yes. What do I think? I assume you are referring to my impressions of Ms. DaDhrga. Much as I hate to break the news to you, Auntie, Hugh is right. The girl does, indeed, possess the most astonishing degree of magic. And she appears to be as oblivious as he claimed. Thankfully, I took Hugh's advice and employed a hefty spell to act as a buffer before finding myself in her company. Otherwise, the jolt from our handshake would likely have thrown me across the station lobby. I'm surprised that the Tanai in the mat-trans chamber weren't knocked for a loop. But then, I'm always surprised by the dullness of their senses."* Amusement played across Emer's next thought. *"I trust you followed Hugh's recommendation, as well."*

Fedel'ma frowned, suspecting her niece was very much aware that she had not. Del readily accepted that this Ms. DaDhrga might possess some degree of magic, even that the level might be somewhat notable, despite the child's being Tanai. She never gave any credence, however, to her son's tales of its magnitude, and even less to his claim that precautions were necessary, lest its strength 'set her on her ass'.

She resented her son's choice of phrase, the more so because of its accuracy. The abrupt and sharply increased charge of energy that filled the dome when the girl arrived, even before the last of the access tunnel's three security gates had closed, was so great that the impact had, in fact, tossed Fedel'ma backward a good two meters, dropping her squarely onto her backside in the middle of her freshly irrigated herbs. Several palpitating heartbeats were required before she could gain control of her senses sufficiently to conjure the necessary buffer. Even now, the persistent and unfamiliar ripples through the normal patterns of magic remained an irritation.

"You know, Del," Emer offered with an ill-concealed giggle. *"Hugh has long proclaimed the possibility of a Tanai turning up with more than the rare flicker of promise...magically speaking. Looks like he is right about that, as well."*

"I'm glad to see that you're enjoying yourself at my expense," Fedel'ma returned. *"What else can you tell me?"*

"Ooooh, Auntie, I don't think you really want to hear what I have to say about your perpetual refusal to take Hugh seriously."

"Don't be impertinent! What else can you tell me about the girl?"

"What else do you want? I was too tired to try and work my way through so much potential in order to determine the specific nature of our guest's attributes. I'll tackle that issue later, assuming you allow me some sleep."

Fedel'ma shook her head. *"You wouldn't be so exhausted if you didn't waste so much time digging around in the muck and debris of ancient sites, including that partially submerged mess south of here. Why you insist on adding protections to any of those crumbling structures is beyond me. They've served no purpose for many an age."*

"Don't play dumb. I don't need to explain my reasons again."

"As I told you before," Fedel'ma rumbled. *"Wherever the pieces of the key are hidden, they are not among those rotting relics."*

This time it was Emer's annoyance that flared. *"And you are certain of this, how?"*

"I'm not," Del confessed, struggling to keep her aggravation under control. *"Think about it, though. To the best of our knowledge, neither of the sisters was ever in this part of the world. Moreover, structures decay over time, unless they are magically protected. They would not hide the key any place that will eventually fall to ruin. And protecting the hiding place with a spell of preservation would immediately draw attention. The key, however, isn't our concern, at this moment."*

"And our current concern is?"

Fedel'ma heaved a frustrated sigh. *"Have you detected nothing more with regards to Ms. DaDhrga? Nothing of consequence?"*

Emer failed to respond for several seconds, a sense of her mounting suspicion filling the silence. *"What, precisely, are you digging after, Del?"*

"Just...just tell me how the girl...seems...to you."

"You mean like suffering from an abundance of anxiety and confusion? That much I can tell you for a certainty. Small wonder, given the recent run of events in her life. And today didn't help much."

Fedel'ma groaned, certain she would regret the asking. *"How do you mean?"*

"Let's just say," Emer began guardedly. *"Let's just say that the day presented a couple of...curious...episodes."*

"Those being?" Another few seconds elapsed before Fedel'ma detected her niece's resigned sigh.

"The first, if you must know, was some sort of mishap at the mat-trans station. I was not informed of the precise nature of the problem. The station personnel tried to brush it off as nothing serious. They were certainly quick to shut down the entire system, though. I sent a query to Donal a short while ago to see if he might have some insight regarding the matter. He said he heard only that there'd been a temporary interference with the impulse signal during Caer's arrival. Said the techies are still trying to locate the source. Whatever the issue, Caer was left rattled, but otherwise unharmed, thankfully."

"Dicey business," Fedel'ma acknowledged. *"Leaving your molecules for machines to scatter and reassemble. Too much potential for too many screw-ups. I'll trust my trips to my own magic, thank you very much."* She ignored her niece's attempt to point out the profound difficulty and danger of completing a series of teleportations by magic; especially when the series equaled the distance Ms. DaDhrga had just traveled. Instead, Fedel'ma pressed, *"And the other incident you mentioned?"*

"An unregistered pod tried to lock in on O-4 in the tunnel just outside of New Hope. Made a couple of failed attempts to pull us out of our flight lane before leaving in rather a hurry. Initially, I wrote it off as malicious mischief."

"Initially?"

Emer's renewed sigh carried across with, *"The incident was followed with another, a short time later. Inside the New Hope dome. Turned out to be instigated by the occupants of the same pod from the* tunnel. *Caer noticed the flares from their weapons out over the old Stafford warehouse.*"

"*You know better than to go meandering about in New Hope,*" Fedel'ma protested. "*That dome houses nothing but thieves and worse.*"

"*Not true! Plenty of good people live and work there. Besides, Donal wrote a prescription to help Caer with the lingering effects from her journey, and New Hope seemed the only reasonable place to get it filled. Not my fault that we encountered a commotion that wanted investigating.*"

"*Wanted investi... So, you flew straight toward trouble?*" Fedel'ma ran a hand across her face. "*And you're sure the perpetrators of this 'incident' were the same people from the tunnel?*"

"*No doubt of it. O-4 identified the vehicle from its heat signature. By the time we arrived, those bastards were already attacking victims from the pod they'd downed.*"

"*So, you called the authorities and left the scene, did you?*"

"*Yes. No. I mean... I directed O-4 to get word to security. But I couldn't very well just fly off. What if those people needed help before anyone else could get to them?*"

"*Why must you jump to rescue everyone in need? Damn it, girl! You'd fly into a black hole if you thought there was someone within who needed help!*"

"*Would not!*" Emer sniffed. "*At least, not into a bloody black hole.*"

Fedel'ma tapped her fingers irritably on her desk. "*Since this wasn't a black hole, I suppose you decided that security was too slow in responding and charged in, weapons blazing.*"

"*I did not! Security got there and we left. Only...*"

Fedel'ma shook her head, waiting.

"*Only, just before security arrived, one of the assailants took note of us. Tried to blow us out of air space. As you can see, he didn't succeed. We came away completely unscathed.*" Emer's proclamation was followed by a pronounced hesitation before she added, "*Caer recognized the guy, though. The one who fired on us.*"

Fedel'ma fought the urge to erupt. Emer was too much her

mother's daughter. Ranting at her mother never served to stifle the woman's insane belief that she had to help any and every person in need. And where had it gotten her? Dead. Permanently. *"I don't suppose Ms. DaDhrga gave you the name of this 'guy',"* she grumbled.

"No. She didn't say anything at all. I got the impression that she doesn't know who he is. She's seen him somewhere before, though. I felt her shock when she glimpsed his face. The sight of him had her both confused and more than a little frightened."

"At least one of you has the wits to show some fear," Fedel'ma snapped.

"Just stop, Del. O-4 is a mobile fortress armed with everything I could work into his weight limitations. We were never in any danger."

"Did it never occurred to you that the assailants could well be among the butchers hunting down every Ahiran that escaped the colony's demise? Somehow, I don't think your little fortress stands much of a chance against the likes of them."

"I'm not an imbecile, Del. Of course, it occurred to me. Answer me this, though. If those bastards are part of the assassination squad, why were they so public in their attack in New Hope? All the other murders were handled far more surreptitiously. Bloodied and mangled bodies were found, but never with any witnesses. Also, the pod they attacked in New Hope bore a local license. There's nothing to suggest that anyone on that vehicle was from Ahira." Emer paused, picking up with, *"In case you're wondering, though, the possibility of their being connected to Ahira in some manner occurred to Caer, as well."*

"She said as much?"

"No," Emer confessed. *"Not exactly."*

Fedel'ma was genuinely surprised. *"Reading minds uninvited, now? A bit out of character for you."*

"Of course I didn't get into her head. Like every Tanai, however, Caer is utterly ignorant of both the need to guard her thoughts and the means by which to do so. Bits and pieces of them come across quite clearly."

"And did they tell you anything else?"

"No. They didn't. You're still fishing for something specific, Del. Will you please just spit out whatever is eating at you? Maybe then you'll leave me alone and let me go back to sleep."

"I just need to learn more about this child that Hugh expects us to protect."

"She's not a child, Del."

"When you're as old as I am, my dear, anyone younger than a thousand years is scarcely out of diapers. Ergo, Ms. DaDhrga is still virtually an embryo."

"Yes. Well. I'd keep that to myself if I were you. The sentiment isn't likely to be appreciated. And don't try to sidestep the point."

"Which is?"

"What are you trying to get at? This is about Hugh, isn't it? So, what's he done, this time?"

Fedel'ma sank back in her chair, her anger and grief at last pouring into, "I trust you saw the chain Ms. DaDhrga wears."

"I did," Emer sighed. "Is that what this is all about? You think Hugh gave Shannon's chain to Caer? Well, he didn't. He mentioned to me some time ago that Caer wore it. Said she told him the necklace was a gift from her mother."

Fedel'ma stiffened. Hugh might at least have mentioned that fact to her. Instead, he left his own mother to discover the necklace through the eyes of her cat! Nor was that the whole of it.

"The chain isn't all the child possesses," Fedel'ma retorted. "Hugh gave her Shannon's charm, as well. The girl found it when she opened some of the boxes he shipped to her."

Emer's stunned, "Oh," was a more exquisite statement of her pain than any lengthy proclamation might express, as was the long and heavily guarded emptiness that followed. "He must have his reasons," came at last.

The fullness of Fedel'ma's pent up sorrow and fury now frothed into an explosion. "Reason has nothing to do with it! My son is an idiot! He had no right to give that charm to this stranger!"

"You give him entirely too little credit, Del."

"And you give him far too much!"

"Hugh's actions are often for the best," Emer persisted. *"Whether you choose to admit the fact or not. Just look how long he's served our cause by sending Eliz the most gifted of his students."*

"He doesn't serve the cause. He serves only himself. As long as he does what Eliz asks of him, she stays out of his hair." Del snorted. She would never understand how her niece could forgive him; how she could continue to offer Hugh the benefit of the doubt in every circumstance.

"He had good reason, Del. Even for that. He will explain when he's ready."

"And when will that be? He's had centuries to make himself ready."

Fedel'ma lowered her head to her hands. She'd not intended to leave her pains from the past so exposed. For several uneasy seconds, there was no further exchange.

"Why didn't he leave?" Emer sent at last, desperation creeping into her words. *"Why didn't he teleport away from Ahira? Hugh had to know what was coming. Otherwise, why such urgency in getting Caer off-world. Once he had her safely away, why didn't he leave? I've tried to reach out to him, Del. But he doesn't answer. You do think he's all right, don't you?"*

"Of course he's all right. He isn't about to give up aggravating me."

"Del?"

"What?"

"I'm sorry."

"For what, dear?"

"For doubting that he'll return. That's always been your specialty--doubting him. Deep down...deep down, I know he'll be back." Again, there was silence. Finally, Emer prodded, *"Hugh's absence and the matter of the necklace aren't the real reasons for your upset, are they? It's that he likes this young Tanai, isn't it?"*

There was little point in denying the fact. Emer would detect the lie.

"Did you honestly think I wasn't aware?" Emer asked. *"It's been*

obvious for a good while. He couldn't hide something like that from me. For what it's worth, now that I've met Caer, I confess that I like her, too."

"You like everyone. That hardly counts for anything."

"Not everyone," Emer replied, a glimmer of her familiar humor returning. *"I will admit, however, to liking far more people than you do. Even Merri likes Caer. You couldn't miss picking up on that. Surely, your familiar's assessment counts for something. If it helps any, I believe Caer is as thunderstruck with Hugh as he is with her. That counts for a lot, as well. At least in my book."*

There was another brief hesitation, followed by, *"You aren't the only one with a million questions regarding her, Auntie. Believe me, I have just as many. I trust, however, that there is time to figure them out. Hugh would never have allowed himself to be blown to bits if he didn't think we had time. Right? So...so let's just wait for him. Then we can tackle all the questions together. In the meantime, be nice to our guest. She's hurting a lot. Lost nearly everyone she knew when Ahira was destroyed. She believes she lost Hugh, as well."*

"Yes, well. Nothing we can do about that, is there?"

"Del... Thanks."

"For?"

"For telling me about Shannon's charm. It's all right. Truly."

Fedel'ma stared at her hands as they lay on her lap. It wasn't all right. Emer would make it so, though. Eventually.

There was nothing more from her niece, leaving Fedel'ma to settle into weary and brooding aloneness. How long she sat there, how long she spent avoiding looking at the desk's lap drawer, she couldn't begin to guess. Minutes? Hours? At last, she reached for the drawer, sliding it open and withdrawing a small, well-worn bronze frame. Set behind the yellowed and scratched glass was a faded photograph of a young girl of fifteen, whose laughing blue eyes and broad grin gave testament to her bright-spirited nature. This was the last picture ever taken of Shannon before Fedel'ma's daughter disappeared.

Fedel'ma clutched at her chest as she struggled with the ancient ache. Sagging back, she tenderly traced the young girl's rounded face and long, dark braids with her finger. The delicate silver chain bearing the beautiful charm could be seen adorning Shannon's slender neck. She wore the necklace without fail from the moment Del and her husband gave it to her on her fifth birthday. She was still wearing it the day she left.

One day, a good many decades afterward, the charm from Shannon's necklace had simply appeared on the kitchen table. Fedel'ma discovered it when she went down to breakfast. Initially, she feared its appearance an indication of her daughter's death--until she found the note. The writing was distinctly Shannon's. Much to Fedel'ma's anguish, however, the graceful script was not addressed to her, but to Hugh. Still, she'd opened and read it.

The note included Shannon's love for both her mother and her brother, as well as for Emer. Included, too, were her apologies for breaking their hearts with her leaving. She missed them. She'd made a commitment, though. And for that, she was not sorry. She was well, and happy; content in the knowledge that her abilities were of such value in her new home. She added that there was something she needed to ask of Hugh. Said that she wished for him to have her charm; asked that he keep it safe until he could present it to the right person. He would know who she was.

Fedel'ma believed her daughter meant the charm as a wedding gift for the woman Hugh was about to make his bride. That he had not bestowed the beautiful piece on Emer gnawed at Fedel'ma, still. Perhaps his failure reflected his continued resentment at Shannon's having defied him; of her leaving without his consent or blessing. Whatever his reason, he tucked the charm away and never spoke of it again.

Now, this Tanai wore Shannon's necklace. Though Fedel'ma saw the chain only through Merri's eyes when the girl first stooped to pet the cat, she had no difficulty discerning the faint shimmer of green that wrapped the delicate silver. Hugh had undoubtedly detected the cast, as well. The sheen was Shannon's enchantment, worked immediately upon receiving the gift; her way of granting the necklace 'most favored' status among her belongings. Bad enough that this...this Tania had somehow come into possession of the chain. That Hugh gave her the charm, as well, was unforgivable. He had no right!

Fedel'ma's lips pinched tightly, her hands going again to her chest, the ache almost unbearable. The truth was, she could lay blame on her son no longer. There was no denying the rest of what she'd witnessed through Merri's eyes. She saw Ms. DaDhrga standing before the mirror; saw the child's tearful reflection after she'd attached the charm to the chain and fastened it around her neck; witnessed the bright flash of green. In that instant, Shannon's face had shimmered just above the charm. Not the face of Del's five-year-old daughter, nor even that of the fifteen-year-old who'd believed so strongly in her oath and her gifts that she walked away from her home and her family. Instead, she beheld the face of Shannon as a woman, her smile filled with vibrancy and contentment, despite the faint lines that spoke of her hard work. Her daughter was happy. Moreover, Shannon's enchantment upon her necklace--an enchantment that had held for all these long ages--was, in the end, released by the magic required to reveal the image to Ms. DaDhrga. This was Shannon's indication that she gave her approval to this stranger; that she willingly relinquished her treasure to this child.

Fedel'ma's acceptance of the truth was excruciating. It burned through the very depths of her soul and rushed her with wrenching tremors. For the truth, at last, shattered her final sliver of hope. Her daughter had given over the last tie to her family. She was never coming home.

22

Caer plopped down in the broad patch of shade, her lips pinched as she mopped her face with the backs of her sleeves. Funny. The distance from the house seemed much shorter when she noticed this spot from the bedroom window this morning. "Either I am woefully out of shape, or I can't seem to adjust to Earth's gravity," she declared. "Thank goodness for this...what did Emer call it? An oak tree, I think." The subtle stir of circulating air fluttered the loose strands of hair at the sides of her face. Brushing them back, she inhaled with a faint smile. "Smells wonderful down here, doesn't it?" Nodding toward the hillside down which they'd traversed, she added, "I've never seen such an assortment of flowers! They must like this warmth. Emer says Fedel'ma uses the dome's climate control sparingly. Prefers to allow the temperatures in here to fluctuate with the day and the seasons outside. I had no idea Earth's autumn could get this warm. Thought the season was supposed to be the lead-in to winter."

Getting no response, she darted an exasperated glance at Brandon, noting that he remained at the edge of the shade, his shoulders as slumped, his countenance as dark and brooding as when he first arrived this afternoon. She was losing patience with her friend's sullen silence.

"Come, sit down," she coaxed, tugging off her shoes and socks. "Don't know about you, but I need a rest before tackling the climb back to the house." Her nose wrinkled the minute her bare feet met the grass. "Wow! Emer said I should try this--wiggling my toes in the vegetation. I thought it would be soft. It's not. It's kinda prickly. Still," she grinned. "It's nice. You should try it."

To Caer's surprise, Brandon shuffled over, selecting a spot that allowed him to sit with his back braced against the tree's enormous trunk. He said nothing, though, turning his gaze to the ground, his left hand rubbing absently at the sling that cradled his right arm. Caer wanted desperately to ask him about his injury. Or, more appropriately, his injuries. His hands and face bore the signs of burns, though they appeared to be healing well, suggesting he'd received prompt and excellent medical care. She'd refrained from bringing up the matter while the others were around. Even now, she was reluctant to do so. Better for him to offer explanations in his own time. Again, she gestured at the gardens, continuing her hand sweep to include the entirety of their surroundings. "Amazing, isn't it?"

Brandon cocked a brow at her. "Very...interesting people you've fallen in with."

His unexpected reply startled her. Moreover, his accusing tone struck her as offensive. "I don't know what you mean by 'fallen in with', Bran. I'm staying with them for a while. That's all."

He fell silent once more, reaching for a stick near his feet and poking at the ground with it. When he spoke again, the edge to his voice rumbled slightly. "You knew these women before coming to Earth, did you?"

"No. Why?"

"How is it, then, that you came by such...exclusive accommodations?"

Caer sucked at her lip, biting back the stab of guilt and grief. Here she sat, lounging in luxury, while so many had perished. "Dr. Jorn," she stated flatly. "He made the arrangements when my application to transfer went through."

"Dr. Jorn," Bran repeated. "And where is he?"

"Dead," she murmured through a deep sigh. "Like everyone else on Ahira."

Brandon flinched, his features softening a little.

Merripen chose that moment to poke her head out from the edge of the flowers that bordered the patch of grass where they sat. A cluster of blue, bell-shaped blossoms caught between the points of her ears and dangled just above her large, green eyes, prompting a half-hearted grin from Caer. Merripen lost her headdress, the flowers left swaying on their stalks, when the cat dropped to a crouch, surveying Caer's bare ankles.

Pulling her legs toward her, Caer warned, "Don't even think about it!"

Merri held the crouch a couple of seconds longer before turning it into a long, elegant stretch. Then, with a soft mew, she trotted out of the flowers and across to rub against Caer. In return, Caer offered a scratch to the animal's head, using the moment to steal another glance at Brandon. The cat nudged past her fingers, circling her once before leaping onto her lap and settling with contented purrs.

Brandon took little notice, his attention again on the landscape, skimming from the distant hills to the slope that led back up toward the house. From where they sat, the contour of the upper rise hid the building from view.

"A far cry from the madness...out there," he huffed, gesturing nebulously. "You are the luckiest person I know, Caer DaDhrga."

Caer stiffened at the accusation that crept back into her friend's tone. "I don't feel all that lucky, Brandon Jase. I lost my best friend. I miss Jen, too, you know. I miss her a lot! Jenna's gone. Dr. Jorn is gone. So many friends...my home...everything. All of it gone. I would trade this in a heartbeat to have it all back."

With a leaden exhale, Bran lifted his hand to his face. "I thought," he choked from behind it.

Caer waited. When he failed to continue, she prompted, "What? You thought what?"

"I...I hoped Jen might be here with you." Lowering his hand, he dropped his dull gaze to his feet. "But I knew. The moment I saw you...saw the flash of pity and sorrow in your eyes. I knew she was...lost."

The comment hollowed Caer's insides. "I would never leave her behind, Bran. Not if I thought for a second that she was in any danger." For several long and painful heart beats both fell mute.

"It was a stupid hope."

Caer shook her head. "Hope is never stupid. Sometimes it's the only thing that can get us through."

"Is that what you're doing, here? Hoping? For what, Caer? That your life moves on? Looks to me like you are already doing so."

"Excuse me?"

"You are where you wanted to be, are you not? Here. On Earth. You can continue with your studies, here. You can lose yourself in classes and papers and....and in this." He swept his hand around to indicate the whole of the estate."

His disdain triggered Caer's eruption. "You think this makes my life easier? You think my being here...in this...this place... suddenly makes everything wonderful? What would you know of life's difficulties, Brandon Jase? So, you were estranged from your family. You chose to leave them. I had no choice. My parents died when I was very young. Lost my only aunt just before my twelfth birthday. I have no more family. No home. I spent what seemed an eternity in a hospital on Hillel, recovering from the plague that claimed my aunt's life. Thankfully, I don't remember much about that horrible time. What I do remember is meeting Adrian, though the circumstances are a little murky. He came to see me several times after our first meeting. When he learned that I had nowhere to go once the hospital was ready to release me, he arranged for me to stay in his home.

Working on Bestor III kept him away for all but the occasional holiday or vacation. So the caretakers of his property looked after me. They are a pleasant and courteous couple, but never really connected with me. I couldn't connect with the other children in school, either. I didn't know how. So, my studies became my sole focus. Only when

I transferred to Ahira...when I met Jenna...did I discover that life could mean something more than solitude. Jen found her way in. Made me laugh. Cried with me. Teased me. Helped me to see others not as obstacles to my studies, but as potential friends. Now she's gone. And..." Caer swallowed, biting back the pain that threatened to overwhelm her at the thought of losing Jorn, as well.

"What do you want from me, Bran? I can't bring anyone back from the dead. And thinking about them hurts too much. So...yes. Though I only just arrived last night, this place does provide a little bit of comfort. Would you condemn me for that?"

Brandon sucked a deep breath, letting it out with a shake of his head. "Hardly. It's just..."

"Just what?"

"I'm trying to understand. You don't know these people, Caer. Okay. So, Dr. Jorn knew them. Why would you trust his judgment so much that you would stay with complete strangers?"

Caer stifled a growl. "You sound just like Adrian. And why shouldn't I trust Dr. Jorn's judgment?"

Brandon sat staring at his knees his weary groan prefacing, "Jen sent a message to me just before the shuttle I was on hit a communications dead zone. Told me that your transfer went through; that you left the day after I did. Said you were on your way to a mat-trans station. I'm just trying to understand how it is that your trip came about so quickly. No requirement to complete the quarter. One day your transfer is approved, the next you are gone... And now, you're here."

"Dr. Jorn wanted me arrive in time to start Sion's new quarter."

"Dr. Jorn, again," Bran snorted. "Leaving within a few hours of receiving your transfer? Booking a shuttle normally takes days. Your abrupt exit and settling here was all Dr. Jorn?"

Caer's aggravated huff disrupted Merri's purring. The cat raised its head, studying her with ears twitching before nestling back to lick its paws. "You talked to Adrian, didn't you?" Caer snapped. "He's put you up to this."

"I wouldn't know this Adrian from a Renthorian slug," Bran retorted. "And unless he knows how to raise the dead, I don't give a damn about him. I'm just trying to figure out how and why you managed to end up...so well situated; why, considering the current set of circumstances, you would trust strangers, regardless of Dr. Jorn's recommendation."

"They are good people, Bran. Honest."

Bran began poking at the ground with the stick, again. "And that based on less than twenty-four hours in their presence. Your reaction to Brenna this afternoon proved far less positive."

"Who?"

"Ms. Cowl. You don't like her. Why?"

Caer cringed. Admittedly, Cowl fell far from the top of her list of favorite people. The woman's failure to provide complete information about which classes would be open when she arrived, her failure to even mention the housing arrangements, didn't sit well. Worse, there was the matter of Cowl's grand entrance on Bran's arm, striding into the sitting room with an air of superiority, this afternoon--showering him with smiles, completely monopolizing their conversation. Neither she nor Bran could have gotten a word in, even had Bran been inclined to do so. When Dr. Eliz and Dr. Berring joined them a few minutes later, Cowl ushered Bran to a small settee, cozying next to him. She seemed obsessed with flirting with him the entire time Dr. Eliz and Caer talked.

"That's ridiculous. I don't dislike her. I just..."

Brandon waved off her protest. "I can read you pretty well, Caer. You're very good at hiding overt reactions. Not so much with the subtle ones. Like the tension that creased the corners of your eyes and mouth, the moment Brenna and I arrived." Laying the stick aside, he asked quietly, "Do something for me, will you?"

"You're not going to insist that I take myself immediately to one of Sion's dorms, are you?"

"No. Yes. No. I don't know," Brandon admitted gruffly. "Doesn't matter. You will do as you please, in any event."

"So, what is it that you want from me?"

"Just this. Take your time. Think it through carefully and tell me precisely how you...you feel in the presence of these women."

"What?"

"Emer and Fe...Fe...Fedel'ma. How do they make you...feel? You can add Brenna, Dr. Eliz, and Dr. Berring to that, as well. Like I said, take your time, but be absolutely honest."

"Why?"

"Just humor me, please."

Caer had no idea where he might be going with this, but if it made him happy, why not? "Where do you want me to start?"

"With whomever you wish. Just be certain before you answer."

Caer nodded, putting the strangeness of his request aside while she considered. Seemed straightforward enough with respect to Emer. The woman's unpretentious nature and quirky sense of humor had Caer at ease almost from the start.

Fedel'ma...Del, as she preferred to be called...was a little more difficult. While Caer was certain that the woman scrutinized her every word, she'd enjoyed their light prattle over breakfast this morning. They chatted about this and that, all with Del gently coaxing out details of Caer's life. It reminded her of how her Aunt Sidra used the same technique, particularly when wanting to tease out information concerning the various not-Sidra-sanctioned excursions Caer had been wont to take now and again. Only rarely did said escapades draw a rebuke from her aunt. More often, they prompted an amused glint to Sidra's eyes, though she never allowed her amusement to go so far as full-on acceptance of those unsanctioned ventures.

Also like Sidra, Del and Emer both smiled often. Caer found it somehow reassuring. Nor did she mind sharing bits and pieces of her life. Curiously, Del had also taken an interest in her necklace, remarking on its simple beauty. The chain, Caer explained, was a gift from her mother--given to her shortly before the lab accident that killed both her parents. All she could bring herself to say about the charm, however, was that it was a recent gift from a friend. Thankfully, Del didn't pursue the matter further.

A fascinating pair, these two women. Similar with respect to their tall, slender frames and the fact that they shared the same fluid elegance of motion. Likewise, they shared a profound sense of confidence that showed in their poise and the directness of their eye contact. That's where the similarities ended, though. Where Emer was porcelain pale, Fedel'ma's coloring spoke of long hours working in her gardens beneath the glare of sunlight, diffused though it was by the great dome. Emer's shoulder-length hair and her eyes held the darkness of a starless universe. Del, on the other hand, had intense blue eyes. And her hair, white as starlight, was worn pulled back in a thick braid that hung all the way to her waist. Emer positively sparkled with energy, her laughter coming as readily as her smiles. Fedel'ma was more subdued. Caer sensed a remarkable closeness between the two women. As close as she had once been with her aunt, perhaps.

How could she explain any of this to Bran, though? Bran, by his own admission, had a very strained relationship with his family. "I'm not sure what to tell you," she said at last. "I quite like Emer. She's sweet and she makes me laugh. I like Fedel'ma, too. She's more reserved than her niece. But she's very gracious and welcoming. I enjoy being in their company."

Bran's scowl betrayed a less than approving assessment of her comments, but he pressed only with, "What about the others?"

The others. Dr. Gwynlyn Berring's presence this afternoon surprised Caer, and not just because Emer said last night that the woman was not Earth-side, yet. Berring must have arrived late in the night or very early this morning. Why the woman chose to travel in her condition, though, baffled Caer. The ugly puckering of numerous sutures crisscrossed much of her face and neck. Heavy bandages covered both her arms and, judging from the thickness beneath her shirt, her torso, as well. The woman who had once moved with amazing quickness and agility now needed a cane just to get up and down from a chair. Walking was halting and obviously painful for her.

The change Caer saw in Brandon was bad enough. Battered and bent as he appeared, the strength at his core remained. It shone in his eyes now and again; was detectable in his current round of inquiries, strange as they were. He just needed time to see it. With Dr. Berring, though, the change was far more disturbing--more than just the severity of her injuries. Her body seemed to have crumpled in on itself, as though her spirit was completely shattered, leaving nothing within to support her fragile frame. Brandon would recover. Berring? Perhaps not.

"What can I say about Dr. Berring," she sighed. "The woman always seemed a bit...I don't know. Distracted? On the few occasions that I met with her, her focus never seemed to be on my thesis, but elsewhere. She was politely pleasant, of course. Just preoccupied. I never gave her much thought beyond that. Now I just feel very sorry for her."

Again, Brandon offered only silence as he waited for her to continue. Still looking for some explanation regarding her aversion to Ms. Cowl, no doubt. Privately, Caer confessed to a profound dislike of the woman. Her aloofness and her willful refusal to share appropriate information still rankled, as did Cowl's behavior around Bran this afternoon. Emer seemed as surprised and disgusted by it as Caer. Was the display of affection all for show? Who was Cowl trying to impress with it? More to the point, why had Brandon put up with the act if Cowl had previously been in such a hurry to be rid of him? The woman was attractive. Caer would give her that. Delicate, rounded features, short, curly blond hair, bright blue eyes. Appearance wise, Cowl bore a vague resemblance to Jenna, right down to the similarity in their names.

Acknowledgment of the fact instantly flushed Caer with revulsion. Surely, Bran wasn't so shallow as to let mere resemblance turn his head. It was difficult to keep the edge from her voice. "I'm not sure what I think of Ms. Cowl. Until this afternoon, my only contact with her was by way of holo-calls. Hard to form much of an impression from those. I don't really know what to make of her from this afternoon, either, except that she made me...uncomfortable, I guess."

Eager to leave the subject of Cowl, Caer took a deep breath and moved on to Dr. Eliz, regretting the shift of attention almost immediately. Aifa Eliz. Now there was an unpleasant woman! The very presence of Eliz seemed to super-charge the air with the surge of a dozen lightning bolts. The sense of it left Caer's flesh itching mercilessly. Worse, the woman's gaze threatened to bore holes straight through her. Oddly, Caer remembered nothing specific about Eliz' appearance--not the color of her hair or eyes, or whether her face was long or round...nothing.

"Dr. Eliz," she breathed. "That woman makes me want to duck and run. I think my hair actually stood on end when she walked in. Shaking her hand was like...like grabbing a high voltage power circuit and not being able to let go." A fleeting thought of a couple of other jolting handshakes flashed to mind. Neither her first encounter with Dr. Jorn, nor with Emer had triggered such an urgent desire to flee, though.

"No doubt," she muttered, hoping to dismiss the matter before Bran latched onto it as something significant. "No doubt an accumulation of static electricity in the air accounts for the sensation. It does tend to build up inside domes. Still, when Eliz looked at me, I thought she would sear a hole straight into my soul and out the other side."

It took a minute for Caer to shake free of the lingering impression, admitting, "I've never been so relieved to see someone leave." Dropping her gaze, she added a sheepish, "In truth, I was happy to see all three of the women go. Eliz, Berring and Cowl. I'm just glad you agreed to Fedel'ma's offer to take you back to your hotel later. I feared you might leave with them...and without ever saying a word to me."

Brandon's jaw tensed. "Afraid I would leave with Brenna, you mean."

Caer opened her mouth to protest, but the words failed to come.

Huffing wearily, he grumbled, "I just hope my trust in your judgment proves to be well placed. Maybe I'll even survive long enough to see my hotel room again."

"What's that supposed to mean?"

"Listen to me, Caer," he said, his voice raspy as he leaned toward her. "You have an uncanny knack for knowing things about people; sensing things before..."

"Oh, please, Bran. Don't start on that nonsense again."

"No. Hear me out. I don't know how you do it, but you do it over and over again. Do you have any idea how many times you steered Jen and me away from some particular individual or some group for no apparent reason, only to learn from the news, later, that those in question committed some crime or other just after our vacating the area?"

Caer gave him a sarcastic smile. She never listened to news broadcasts. She didn't like the stories that filled the headlines-- stories of anguish and misfortune. "Did you get all that just from following me?"

"Jen told you I've been watching you, didn't she?" he grunted, settling back to lean against the tree again. "Took me a while before I realized the significance of what you were doing. That you possessed some sense of who to stay clear of. Over the course of the past four years, though, it's happened a lot—your changing routes just in time to avoid some calamity."

"Okay. So, maybe I had a few fortuitous hunches. So what? Maybe I read people like you say you do with me."

"Maybe. But I don't think so. Besides, some of the instances I witnessed had nothing to do with people. At least not directly."

"Such as?"

"Like the collapse of the north wing of the main library. Remember? It happened your first quarter at Ahira."

Caer shuddered as the memory peeled grudgingly out of some hidden cubicle in her mind. "I was happy not recalling that little episode, thank you very much."

"Dr. Berring had..."

"Had asked us to look for something in the archives, I think," she finished for him. "Yeah, that much I remember. Can't think what she sent us to find, though."

"Doesn't matter. You do remember how you came charging out of the back room, though, don't you? Grabbed my arm and screamed for me to run. We only just made it out of the door before a section of the upper floors came crashing down. When the investigation revealed that the structure had been sabotaged, I almost believed you had something to do with it, considering the timing of our escape."

"Bran! I could never!"

"I figured that out...in time."

"I must have heard a warning crack or something. That's all."

"So you've said before." Running a hand through his hair, he muttered, "But I doubt it. And don't give me this 'coincidence' crap. The number of times your 'hunches' have worked to yours or our benefit have been far too many to be shrugged off like that."

He fell silent for another long while before picking up with, "Whatever it is that's behind this ability of yours, I've come to believe in it." Drawing a deep breath, he let it out slowly. "I also believe in this...this sensation I get when I'm anywhere near you. Near a number of others, for that matter. At least...at least I believe in it, now."

"What sensation? What are you talking about?"

Brandon rubbed his injured arm, looking ever more distraught. "I can't explain it, Caer, any more than you seem able to explain how you do what you do. Certain people just give off...an energy or something. It makes all of my nerves prickle like they've gone to sleep and are just coming round again.

Growing up on Andromeda, I encountered maybe a dozen people that...well, that did that to me. There were significantly more of them on Ahira. Dr. Jorn and Dr. Berring, for instance, along with a good many of the students in Jorn's classes. And then there's...well... you. Since coming to Earth, I've encountered even more people, especially at Sion University. Dr. Eliz does it. So do most of the people who go in and out of her office. I know. I spent enough time in the outer lobby, recently."

He flicked a glance in the direction of the house. "Those two women you're staying with. They do it, too. Not Brenna, though. She's like most people. But..."

"But?"

"Nothing," he sniffed. "If it turns out to be something, I'll let you know." Glancing at the ground, he sighed, "I realize I haven't been acting like it, Caer. But I am thankful you survived. Honest. It's just that..."

"You thought I was somehow forewarned and brought Jen with me."

He raised his head, turning his troubled gray eyes to her. "Stupid as it is, I almost believed it."

Caer withered under his tortured stare. "I would have dragged Jen with me, kicking and screaming if necessary, had I the abilities you seem to think I possess." Reaching for her necklace, her hand cupped around the unfamiliar charm, twisting it back and forth as she remembered the disturbing visions that occurred just before finding Mirra's decapitated body; remembered the nightmare that night in Jorn's apartment--the one in which she'd seen Ahira blown to the heavens. What if Bran was right? What if she could see into the future? Fat lot of good it did her if she couldn't recall such visions long enough to understand or act on them. She quickly dismissed the notion as preposterous. Alcohol and stress explained those visions. Brains did stuff like that--creating bizarre scenarios from emotional upheaval. "Honest, Bran. I had no clue what was about to happen on Ahira."

"Yet you escaped at just at the right time."

Caer met his gaze. "Not my doing. And besides, you escaped at just the right time, too, you know."

"Not the same thing. My trip was planned beforehand." His gaze settled to his shoes once more. "I wish, now, I'd never left for Andromeda."

"Then you'd have died with everyone else. What purpose would that have served? I'm glad I didn't lose you, too. And I'm grateful that you came looking for me, regardless of your reasons."

Brandon cocked his head, a chasm creasing his brow. "Well, do me another favor," he said nodding toward her wrist. "If you brought your communicator with you, put it on and keep it on. If you don't have it with you, then I'll buy one for you."

"I will pick up a new one, first chance I have," she returned with a shrug. "The mat-trans screwed up my old one."

"Just do it soon. Okay? I..I might want to talk to you...without having to go through someone else's com-link." Hesitating, he fixed her with an uneasy stare. "I don't know what's going on, Caer, but it's something big and very ugly. And I'm sure it has to do with some of these people."

"Which people?"

"The ones that make me...make me..."

Caer shifted her position to sit back, drawing her knees in tight to hug them. "That make you feel odd? You mean like me? Believe me, Ban, I have no more idea what's happening than you do."

"I believe you. Still, I think you're connected with it somehow. Why else would someone be murdered in your apartment on Ahira? Why else would you be attacked on Bestor. And..."

"How did you hear about those?"

He tilted his head, his lips curling with a guilty frown. "Jen filled me in on the business in your apartment...in her message. I got the other information out of Brenna when your expected arrival Earth-side continued to be delayed. Everyone here thinks the assailant on Bestor III was looking for your friend...this Adrian fellow. Personally..." His eyes narrowed as he peered at her. "I think the culprit may have found the person he was looking for, even if he didn't succeed in killing you."

Caer shuddered, both from the news that the attack on Bestor had gotten out, and from Bran's conclusion. "Say you're right," she grumbled, "I'm not the only one who's been attacked. I'm told that anyone who's had recent dealings with Ahira is being hunted down. Even Dr. Berring was attacked. And...and you, from the looks of things." She gestured at his sling. "Want to tell me about it?"

There was no answer for a good while. Caer waited, afraid to press him. At length, his voice so low she had to strain to hear, he said, "An old friend of mine spotted me when I first arrived at the Andromeda complex. He told me that some men had been through a day or so earlier, asking after my whereabouts. Said they'd been directed to Mede."

"Your sister."

He nodded. "She and Traxton have..." His voice cut off. Several seconds elapsed before he continued. "Had...a small agricultural dome about 160 kilometers south of the township enclosure. When I got there, I found three men holding Mede and Traxton and their baby captive, waiting for me. They called me...sensitive, or... or something like that. Said they wanted information; wanted the names of people I had detected with my ability; asked if any of them had warned me to leave Ahira. I didn't understand. Mede seemed to, though, and begged me to tell them nothing."

There was another long hesitation. "When we were little," he murmured, "Mede and I, we made a game of identifying people who... We never understood why a few people made us feel so odd. Mede asked Father about it once. He threatened to lock her in the storage shed for a month if she ever mentioned it again. After he died, Mede started contacting me about old papers and computer chips she found buried in a metal box in a corner of the barn. She was beginning to piece things together and needed to see me in person." He paused, running a shaky hand over his face. "Even then, I wouldn't have gone back, had it not been for the birth of..." A long, ragged breath was followed by, "She's dead, Caer. Mede. Traxton. Their baby. All dead. If I'd stayed on Ahira, maybe they would still be alive." Tears streamed down his face. "They were the only family I had. Now they're gone. And Jenna is gone. And..."

Caer was numb. Scooting to settle next to her friend, she wrapped an arm around him, perhaps as much for her own sake as for his. She wasn't sure. Even Merripen joined them, the cat's mewing sounding anxious as she snuggled in with the two humans.

"I fought with them," Bran managed. "The ones who'd taken my family hostage. I tried to free Mede and Trax and... But I couldn't do it. The thugs were too strong. I tried not to tell them anything, like Mede said. They made me do it, though. They got into my head, somehow, and...they found out about you...and the others like you. I..." He pulled away, his defeated gaze riveted on the ground. "Then they made me watch. They lit the fires and made me watch. Mede, Traxton, little Saichel." His voice choked so badly that Caer barely made out his last words. "They burned them alive. And they left me there to burn with them. I..."

Caer's hands flew to her necklace as she fell back from him, her cry frozen in her throat.

Flames! Everywhere, bright hot tongues licking with ravenous aggression. Within the searing heat and dancing orange brilliance, blackened bodies writhe. Screams rip the air.

23

"Caer! What are you seeing?"

Brandon's sudden grip of her arms jolted Caer. His demanding tone as he repeated her name and the urgent shaking she received, forced the flames into submission, the image of blackened corpses fading with them. Yet the landscape remained, hovering in Caer's mind as a bleak and barren slope littered with blasted boulders and shattered stone. Fingers curled tightly around her necklace, she shuddered at the creep of profound longing and intense dread that vied within her. She knew this place—once a place of comfort; of sanctuary. How often she'd trod the shaded paths beneath its dense forests. How she'd danced upon the hill's broad brow at a time when forests had given way to grasses, airy sunshine, and brisk breezes. How she'd fled its summit in terror, chased by the fiery tongues of hell and the screams of the dying. She remembered.

A feeble inhale accompanied another shudder. Impossible. How could she remember anything about a place where she'd never set foot? This was illusion. It was her mind running mad. With a vigorous shake of her head, she tried to clear the image. Tried to bring back the luxurious gardens through which she had, but moments ago, strolled. The bleak landscape refused to dissipate.

Brandon barked her name yet again. "Caer! Don't shut me out like this! Tell me what you're seeing!"

"A hill." Her automatic reply choked as she watched the suggestion of smoke and flame rising again at the periphery of her vision. "Fire. Burning." As she spoke, the flames scorched her face. She cried out.

"There's no fire, Caer. None. Not anywhere around us. Is there going to be? Do we need to leave?"

For the span of half a breath, the cold gray of Brandon's intense gaze broke through. So, too, did the vague realization that he'd slipped his injured arm from its sling, allowing his vise-like two-handed grip of her arms. Twisting, Caer attempted to break free. She needed air. Needed the perfume and the color of Del's gardens to fill her...to shove the nightmare back into the depths.

Brandon persisted, his clamp on her holding fast. "Do we need to leave?" he demanded. "Where is the fire going to be? Do we need to warn others?"

Caer drew a slow, ragged breath, fighting the urge to see the illusion more clearly. To try and understand it. As the vision drew her, the flames died back, leaving only the ruins of the hillside to fill her mind. "No," she murmured. "No fire. Not now. The hill is far away. The flames long extinguished. It's an ancient place. Curses were sworn on its slopes. Oaths were spoken. Many ages ago. Ash, bones, blasted stone. That's what lies there, now." The words tasted strange on her tongue--like they belonged to someone else. It was through her lips that they passed, though, and as they did so, her necklace warmed and began to pulse within her clenched fingers.

At first, the pulse matched that of her own anxious heart. Each beat, however, brought a slow and subtle shift, until the cadence took on the familiar rhythm of a dance. One, two, three, four, five, six, seven. One, two, three. One, two, three. The rhythm repeated... again...and again...and...

With each recurrence, the hill gained greater clarity. A thin wash of pale light fluttered in and out, skipping across the rugged and muddy terrain that appeared to slope upwards. Low and flattened earthen mounds dotted the hillside, with clusters of broken and crumbling stone blocks...or perhaps slabs...scattered around them. Some of the blocks...slabs...stood upright. Some leaned precariously.

Others lay toppled, their jagged edges pointing toward the heavens. Beyond them, just where the slope crested, rose a much greater mound, the rounded top mimicking the curve of the hill's broad crest. Black as the deepest shadows, this greater mound stood in silent watch beneath a dark and turbulent sky.

The visage was as haunting as it was desolate. It beckoned to Caer. She wanted to respond. Needed to respond. Needed to set her feet upon that ground. Needed to kneel before the great construct that stood in black silhouette against a moving sky. So strong was her need that it ached within her, intensifying the pounding rhythm that thrummed across her nerves. One, two, three, four, five, six, seven. One, two, three. One, two, three. It commanded her to rise... commanded her to move...to...

Caer's alarmed scream shattered the air as the earth dropped suddenly away. At the same instant, emptiness as obsidian as dark matter opened all around, swallowing her. She knew Brandon was with her only because his clutch on her arms tightened, his sharp gasp sounding as a staccato caught within her cry. Snug against her ankles, Merripen pressed in a tensed arch, the animal's hiss underscoring her panic.

The black void lasted the full length of Caer's ragged scream. As she gasped a breath, a sizzled pop of air pressure and an electrified charge prefaced the slam of the ground under her feet, cold and hard...and wet. Shivering, she chewed fretfully at her lip, her senses overwhelmed with the smell of damp earth, the feel of mist on her face, the ooze of cold mud between her toes, the sharp jab of a rock beneath her heel. The pain of it registered sufficiently for her to sidestep, her foot suddenly sliding in the thick muck. Only Brandon's squeezing hold on her kept her from falling. Slowly, his ashen face swam into focus, as did the gray world around them. At first, she could make out little but the swirl of dense shadows. Then came the dim outline of scattered boulders and stone shards littering the rugged slope. Merripen bolted, springing away into the mist, the animal's yeowl trailing through the chill air. Caer resisted the urge to dart after the cat, forcing her eyes shut. Illusion. She was standing in the shaded grass on the clearing below Fedel'ma's magnificent gardens with Bran's painful grip trying to shake some sense into her.

The vision, however, refused to dispel when she blinked her eyes open again. Night and mist still encompassed her, the cold and dampness gnawing at her bones, her feet and ankles aching at the chill mud. Scarcely a meter upslope of where she and Brandon stood rose a series of stone slabs, their towering presence casting darker shadows through the murk. A biting breeze whistled faintly around and through the standing and toppled stones alike, and skittered in a rattling rustle through the sparse stands of tall grasses and the occasional low scrub that dotted the ground. The muted browns of the vegetation swayed and twitched an eerie dance set against the gray gloom.

Brandon at last released Caer's arms, his shallow breath expelled with, "What the!"

Without his support, Caer's knees failed to support her. Wobbling, she dropped, her backside and hands hitting the ground simultaneously, splatting in the cold muck. For a painfully jarring moment, she could do no more than sit there, trying to settle the thready, terrified patter of her heart...trying to make herself breathe. This isn't real. Not real.

"What the hell, Caer!" Brandon wheezed. "What did you just do? Where in all the bloody universe are we?"

Swallowing, Caer lifted her trembling hands, blinking at the sludge that dripped from them. Touching a finger to her tongue, she promptly spat the bitter grit. "Not real,' she persisted, breathing out, darting a glance downslope. The mists deepened, there, merging with the dense and creeping fog. Nearer, the thick, moist air swirled in gusting eddies, setting the grasses and brush to a momentarily livelier nod and bob.

The hand Brandon extended to Caer was every bit as cold and shaky as her own. "Are you seeing this?" he muttered, drawing her to her feet.

"Yeah," she squeaked. "If you're seeing..." Gesturing with a tremulous jerk of her chin, she managed, "...this."

"No gardens?" Bran pressed. "No tree? No mansion? No..."

"Yeah," Caer squeaked again. Clinging to Bran's arm with one hand, she clutched her necklace with the other, gripping the trinity knot so tightly that each of its triple loops dug into her palm and fingers. Their bite would surely wake her.

It didn't.

"D...d...dream Painting," she stammered, her brain scrambling for the most reasonable explanation it could conjure. "Has to be."

"Generated from what, Caer?" Bran asked, his voice so tight it cracked. "Dream paintings require holographic projectors. Where are they? Did you see any in the gardens or on the tree? From what I'm told, Dream Paintings are visual only, not tactile. You feel how wet the air is? Does the stuff we're standing in feel like grass to you?"

Caer blinked at the mud on her hands and wriggled her toes to verify the squish of it underfoot. She also noted, with growing discomfort, the chill dampness on her backside. "No," she murmured. "But...but maybe Del didn't realize we were out here and turned on the irrigation system."

"And that would turn the grass to this mire in such short order?"

Still hoping to confirm that they'd never left the beautiful estate, Caer bent and reached for one of the scraggly scrubs, praying to find nothing but emptiness, or perhaps a handful of the blue flowers Merripen had stalked through. Instead, a woody twig broke away in her hand, thorns digging across her palm. Straightening with a start, she promptly dropped the stick, staring at the fine line of blood welting along the length of the scratch.

"So." Bran snorted, eyeing Caer's hand. "I repeat. Where the hell are we?"

Caer pressed her stinging palm against her pant leg, biting at her lip to keep its quiver from revealing the depth of her anxiety. The landscape was much too much like the vision of moments ago--the pale light flicking intermittently across the shadowy slope, the standing stones, the.... "A Dream Painting," she insisted, adding a barely audible, "or...or inside my head."

Haltingly, she ventured a step or two, darting nervous glances through the thick mists below before daring to face what lay above. Her heart tripped over several beats as her eyes skimmed the slope, coming to rest on the massive earthen and stone mound, prominent on the hill's summit. Accompanying her palpitations came a rush of vertigo that nearly set her on her backside again. For, even in the darkness, clouds could be seen racing high above the great mound. As she stared, they parted--only for a second or two--just enough to reveal the thick crescent of a blue-white moon.

Caer stumbled, grabbing for Brandon once more, her eyes snapping shut as she clutched his arm.

"What?" he rasped, pulling free of her grasp. "What else do you see?"

Scarcely daring another glimpse, she pointed. "U....p. L...look up. If this...if this is real, then...then we are not inside a dome."

"Don't be ridiculous. We'd be dead by now if we were..." Bran's assertion cut short as he gaped at the sky.

The weight of their combined silence hung over them for uncounted and near breathless moments before giving way to a muffle of distant voices, the irritated strains of an argument rising through the saturated air. The quarrel, it seemed, issued from the dense fog somewhere downslope. At first, Caer was relieved, expecting Emer and Fedel'ma to climb from the darkness in search of her. They would explain this. They would assure her that this was, indeed, nothing more than a Dream Painting; that the equipment was somehow camouflaged in the garden's vegetation.

Brandon gave her no time to consider further. Lunging for cover behind the standing stones, he yanked her after him.

"You're imagining things," came the husky, deriding tone of a man.

Renewed dread swept Caer, setting off alarm signals through every nerve. The voice obviously belonged to neither Emer nor

Del. It was, however, disconcertingly...terrifyingly familiar. Peering around the edge of the slab, she waited, watching for the quarrelers to emerge from the soupy lower slope.

"You're an incompetent fool!" a woman snarled in reply. "If you two weren't so preoccupied with drowning yourselves in drink, you'd have felt the teleportation."

"So. Where is this intruder?" asked a second male voice, this one high pitched and only vaguely challenging.

"Not just an intruder, idiot. Someone has turned up with the key. The whole of it. You're drunker than I thought if you can't sense its throb." A momentary pause followed before the woman indicated, "Up there!"

Seconds later, a single individual climbed from the murk, tendrils of mist clinging to her as she made her way upslope. At least, Caer assumed it to be a woman. The wrap of the long, richly purple cloak suggested a slim frame beneath, and the individual's tread was smooth and graceful, despite the rugged tilt of the ground. Caer's assumption was confirmed when the woman raised her head and lowered her hood. Long strands of dark, moisture frizzled hair fell across her shoulders to frame her pale and somewhat angular face. Her well-defined features might have been quite lovely, were it not for the shock of the woman's eyes. For, within them roiled an unnatural glow of flaming emerald. Behind Caer, Brandon sucked in sharply.

Stopping just a few meters up from where she'd emerged, the woman stood erect, her thin lips pursed, the ends of her cloak flapping wetly around her ankles in the increasingly stiff breeze as her burning gaze skimmed the stretch of slope still before her. Fear of being caught by the woman's scan chased Caer back from the edge of the stone, her heart pounding.

Brandon, too, withdrew, his face pinched, the hand of his injured arm clenching and unclenching at his side. His nervous gesture indicated his desire for Caer to move further back into the shadows, even as he leaned across her for another glimpse downslope. Caer, however, was equally drawn to the edge, worried that the strange woman might, at this very instant, be creeping up on them. The woman, however, remained as she was, though she continued to scrutinize the hillside. Behind her, two other figures gradually emerged from the gloom. Both were wrapped in cloaks of purple much like the woman's, though theirs were faded and frayed. One man appeared quite thin, the other exceedingly rotund. Their stooped bearing and the way each clutched their wraps tightly around themselves hinted at their ill humor over slogging around in the cold and wet. Even when they reached the woman, halting on either side of her, they remained hunched within their wraps, reluctantly pushing their hoods back to better study the hillside. As with the woman, fire burned within their eyes. Unlike the brilliant green of their female companion's, however, theirs smoldered a deep brown, as rich soil might look if it could burn.

With considerable effort, Caer broke her gaze free of those strange eyes, noting that the skinny man who now stood to the woman's right resembled her in both height and in the paleness of complexion. Even the man's dark, shoulder-length hair frizzed in much the same manner. His angular features, however, were far less attractive, elongating his face to the point of gauntness.

The man to the woman's left, on the other hand, lacked the height of the other two, rising to slightly less than the woman's shoulders. Or perhaps he was more hunched against the elements. There was no question of his girth, however. He easily made more than the breadth of his two companions combined. Struggling to avoid fixing on his eyes, Caer at last took note of his face. Instantly, her hands clasped tight against her mouth as she swallowed her gasp. This! This was the one whose voice she'd recognized! The broodingly dim light could no more conceal his repugnant features than the folds and billows of his cloak could hide his massive width. Here stood the man who'd occupied the seat next to her on the shuttle... the very same bastard who'd fired on Emer's pod in New Hope.

"Over there," the woman gestured. "Behind the remains of that cairn."

The men took a couple of steps forward, their wraps falling back from their hands. The one who resembled the woman called out, "Show yourself. Let us see who has come to visit Great Granny's gravesite."

Caer's every fiber screamed that she should snatch Bran's hand and run as though the hounds of hell were on their heels. Her trembling body, however, failed to oblige. Bran pushed her further into the shadows, his sharp nod intimating that she should stay there. Instead, she forced a cautious lean toward the edge of the stone once more, catching the unified and stunned gape from the threesome below as Bran stepped out.

"You! How did you get here?" the woman spat. Turning, she set a seething glare on the prodigious man to her left. "Your stooges were supposed to eliminate him right along with the rest of his family."

"They told me they'd succeeded," the older man boomed back.

Caer shot a glance at Brandon. For several breathless seconds, he simply stared down at the trio, his face ghastly, his jaw rigid in its forward thrust.

"Why?" he choked. "We never did anything to you. I don't even know who you are."

"Oh, but we know you," the woman affirmed, venom in her tone. "Your kind has always made for troublesome meddlers."

Brandon's face erupted in fury, his muscles tensed in preparation for a launched attack. Caer grabbed his pant leg, halting his forward progression and nearly tripping him. Grabbing for his hand, she pulled up to stand at his side.

"Ah!" The woman nodded, her brow cocked with interest. "I knew this man could not be the one. Not even my soppy aunts would have allowed it to be in the hands of a Sensitive."

Brandon shoved Caer behind him, his glower radiating his resentment and outrage. "I'm assuming you're referring to me. Allow what to be in my hands?"

"Nothing that concerns you," the woman jeered. "Just a little thing. A key. Your lady friend can't deny she has it. Give it up, and perhaps I'll let you both live."

Caer responded to Brandon's questioning glower with a timorous shrug. "I don't know what that woman's talking about. I don't have any key. I don't even own anything that would require one."

"That's the girl," proclaimed the repugnant man. "The one I told you about. I knew she possessed at least part of it."

Caer shrank against Brandon as the man turned his attention wholly on her, his glowing eyes skimming her up and down with the same ugly leer that had been such a loathsome part of his countenance during the shuttle flight from Ahira.

"A very curious little puzzle of a cherub you are," he grinned. "I'd been warned that you held extraordinary potential. Wouldn't have believed it if I hadn't sought you out, myself. Most interesting, the way you managed to avoid me almost every time I got close to you. Still, I wasn't thoroughly convinced of your prescience until you cleverly arranged for that Tanai to be in your apartment in your stead. Very well played, my dear. My agent, naturally, was more than a little out of sorts when he realized he had the wrong girl. Not a very pleasant outcome for her, I'm afraid."

Caer's color washed out of her with the sense of her frantic heart sliding to the churning liquid of her stomach. "I...I didn't...I..."

"You can't deny your gift," the man asserted. "Not to me. I've observed you for far too long. If the episode in your apartment wasn't sufficient confirmation of your attribute, your attempt to escape just before we blew Ahira certainly was. Very cunning of you to take the shuttle rather than simply teleport away. We might have detected your teleportation and destroyed you before its completion. Your timing and your choice of transport, however, proved most fortuitous for me. I had only just placed the last of the charges at the station when you passed within a meter of me on your way to the boarding gate. That's when I sensed it. Took a bit of hasty work to delay the timers for our explosive charges while also managing to sicken the shuttle passenger whose seat was next to you. Still, I couldn't afford killing you just yet. Not if my suspicions were correct."

Caer's pulse throbbed with such force through the whole of her body that she rocked with it, her breath coming in short shocks. This man had stalked her! And he'd been involved, both with Mirra's death and the annihilation of an entire world. He'd just admitted as much.

"Why?" was all that strangled out.

The man shrugged. "Why kill the Ahirans? Why not? They've long been a thorn in our side. It's well past time to be rid of them."

Caer's head reeled. Such cold, matter-of-factness over such vile murder! Her repulsion doubled at the ugly wash of relief that accompanied her mortification. All those people...they hadn't died merely because someone wanted her dead. Still, someone wanted something from her. Why? What had she ever done? What was this key they thought she possessed? He could have ambushed her for it, there at the shuttle station; could have taken her by surprise and lugged her off to some dark corner to search her for it. He'd have been disappointed. She swallowed. And she'd likely be dead, now, like everyone else.

"You know of Caer's...abilities," Brandon rumbled. "Said you'd been told of her. By whom? How long have you been...observing her?"

The man's leer expanded into a foul grin. "Ah yes. The guilty conscience speaks up. Not to worry, my friend. We have observed the girl since well before the encounter you and your family experienced with a few of our agents, recently. Not that we didn't learn a few other useful pieces of information from that...visit."

Brandon again looked ready to launch. That he held his ground, Caer could only assume, was for her sake. He'd not leave her standing alone and unprotected. Silently, she thanked him with all her heart.

The gaunt man's dubious expression remained as he, also, continued to regard her. "For supposedly possessing some great gift of prescience, your attribute appears to have fallen short of warning you away from here." Turning a look of disgust on the other man, he huffed, "I think you grossly overestimated her abilities."

The former waived him off. "No gift is perfect, Ailill. You, of all people, know the truth of that."

The statement prompted a sudden tensed and guttural snarl from the one called Ailill. Again, he was waived off. "This girl is young. And apparently woefully uneducated in the use of her abilities. A unique Tanai, I've been told. Unique, indeed!" The man's great rolls of flesh rippled beneath his cloak in his mirth. "Let's just put that assumption to rest, shall we? Tanai are neither unique nor gifted, at least with anything more than the most rudimentary of parlor magic. For what it's worth, I'm putting my money on this girl being Uair Amhain. The key would no more have been left in the hands of some ordinary Tanai to be passed down their line, than in the hands of a Sensitive."

An intensely growing lust reflected in the glow of the man's eyes as he returned his attention more directly to her, though whether the lust was for her or for this key he sought, Caer couldn't tell.

"As I said," he went on. "I suspected you possessed one of the pieces when you passed me near the boarding gate. Confirmed it the moment I laid my hand on yours, there on that shuttle."

Memory of the instance sent an icy tremor through Caer.

"Ahhh." The man's loathsome grin broadened. "I see my touch made as much of an impact on you as it did on me." For half a second he said nothing more, taking her measure in a manner that made her skin crawl. "It's a curious little treasure you hold. Tell me, my dear. Where did you come by the first piece? Did someone on Ahira give it to you? And the second. Obtained on Bestor III, perhaps? Or did you know where to find it once you arrived Earthside? Who was it that joined the two pieces for you?"

"I told you," Caer insisted, trying to force the quake from her voice. "I don't have any key."

"Just figure out where she's keeping the bloody thing and take it from her," Ailill growled.

The woman shook her head, agitation knitting fine lines through her fair features. "Have you learned nothing over the centuries? We dare not take it by force." Sweeping a distasteful glance at the repugnant bulk of a man, she acknowledged ruefully, "Seems that the failed attempt of your beast to kill this girl has proven providential. Had your plan succeeded, whatever piece she possessed at that time would have vanished before we knew how close we'd come to it. We don't even know what form the pieces have taken. And from the sounds of things, neither does she."

"What form?" Bran's tone was incredulous. "You don't know what this bloody key looks like? So, what makes you think she has it?"

"Weren't you listening?" the older man huffed. The mounded folds of his cloak shifted as he edged forward another step. "I don't have to touch her, now, to know of its presence. Its energy throbs with her very pulse." Rubbing his hand down the front of his cloak, his malicious gaze skimmed over Caer yet again. "Perhaps a thorough examination will reveal what it is on her person that so keenly reflects the fretful rhythm of her heart. Once we know that, we can begin a few...persuasive techniques to convince her to simply give it to us."

Brandon grabbed Caer's arm, shoving her behind the cluster of standing stones. "I'm warning you. Stay away from her."

"You're warning me?" the man laughed. With deliberate slowness, as if to draw full attention to the tiny, translucent sparks beginning to flick across his huge hands, he raised and aimed his palms directly at Bran. "Don't be stupid, boy. You don't stand a chance." When Brandon refused to move, the man feigned a resigned sigh. "Have it your..."

His words twisted into a screech of profanity, his great bulk staggering ponderously backward as the air erupted in highly charged and sparking blue-white veins of brilliant light. With a deep rumble of thunder and an explosion of spraying mud and rock shards, two men snapped into existence midway between Brandon and the trio below. The newcomers stood shoulder-to-shoulder, each draped in long, midnight-dark cloaks that accented their extraordinary height. The nearer man turned, pushing the hood of his cloak back, the length of his white-gold hair catching and whipping in the increasingly gusty winds.

A disturbing rush of déjà vu staggered Caer against the side of the stone slab. This was madness--the stuff or her dreams become real! Only in her dreams had she encountered such a man. No human nor any race of alien she could name bore such an elegant resemblance to finely sculpted marble. Turning to acknowledge her, the internal heat that ignited the depths of the man's deep topaz eyes further staggered her, Caer's sharp intake of breath catching midway to her lungs.

The man's glance and nod lasted but half a heartbeat before he fixed his attention on the threesome below. Only then, did his companion move from his mute watch of the trio, his black cloak snapping around his long legs as he adjusted the angle of his stance. Angrily, he tossed back his hood, leveling a grim scowl on Caer, his eyes like molten turquoise.

With lungs already starved of oxygen, she fell back a pace, choking, "Adri...?"

Before she could complete his name, the hillside rocked with a second explosion of charged and distorted air, once again spraying rock and earth about. Fedel'ma and Emer abruptly emerged a scant few meters in front of Adrian and his companion. Unlike the others, the women were not wrapped in long, hooded cloaks, but stood with the light fabrics of their shirts and pants fluttering in the blustery dampness. Their tensed postures and raised palms clearly indicated their wariness as each made a quick, nervous assessment of the situation, their eyes also ignited from deep within--Fedel'ma's burning with the heat of flaming sapphire, while Emer's shone a scorching indigo.

Caer darted an anxious glance at Brandon. Perhaps there was something about this place that caused eyes to reflect light in some peculiar manner. With his back to her, however, she had no way of catching his gaze. Nor was there anything available with which she might check her own.

The unknown woman's low growl quickly snapped Caer's attention back to the threats from below. Standing motionless, the woman's gaze was that of a deadly beast sizing up her prey as it shifted between the newly arrived men. The intensity of that predatory scrutiny increased significantly as it settled on Adrian. The woman's mouth opened, though whether to speak or snap or snarl was lost in her wail of outrage as a third blast of charged air, complete with the veins of blue-white light and spray of earth, rock, and mud, popped one more individual into being. Delivered but a few paces to one side of Emer and Fedel'ma, the lone man darted his glance first toward Caer, his eyes like flaming amber.

Caer sagged back against the standing stones, sucking for a shallow breath. How did these people suddenly appear from nowhere? And what was this place doing to everyone's eyes? Straightening, she edged forward, shooting a hasty glimpse around and up at Bran's face. A dance of fear, confusion, and fury flicked within his constantly skimming gaze, but they remained gray, with no hint of any fiery glow.

"Just who in the infernal universe are you people!" Brandon bellowed.

"Name's Dylan," declared the most recent arrival. The man's voice was unexpectedly calm, despite the cold scrutiny he passed from Adrian and his companion, then down to the malevolent trio. Jerking his head toward Fedel'ma and Emer, he added, "I'm with them."

Both women flashed stunned stares his way. Their expressions, however, turned quickly to recognition and relief.

Adrian did his own rapid assessment of those gathered. "Caer!" he barked. "Come to me. We're leaving."

She reacted instantly, taking several steps toward him before she realized she'd moved. Against her every instinct, but with a surge of resentment, Caer rooted her feet in place, swiping a hand toward Bran and then Fedel'ma and Emer. "Not without my friends."

"Your...!" Adrian's sputter shifted his expression from anger to disbelief as he turned to track the slow, stalking movements of the threesome below.

The leer, Caer noted, no longer occupied the nameless brute's face. Malevolence now contorted his features. The one called Ailill edged closer to the woman, his countenance pinched and twitching. So close was he that he nearly ran her over when she came to a stop. The woman gave him a shove. "Go bury yourself under a rock, coward! And stay out of my way!"

Ailill stumbled back a few steps. Still, he continued to shadow her. The woman ignored him, her burning study fixed on Adrian. "It really is you," she hissed. "I thought you dead and banished long ago, though Mother seemed to believe otherwise. I doubt she will be pleased to know she was right."

"Nice to see you, too, Maura," Adrian growled.

A smile of sickly sweetness curled her lips as she turned her gaze to Adrian's companion. "Of course, Mother doesn't know everything, does she? I don't believe she's aware that you've returned. I'm sure she will be more than pleased to learn of your presence, should I happen to mention it. But then..."

With a singeing electrical charge and a pop of air pressure, Maura vanished, the hollow echo of her voice trailing off with, "I don't always tell her everything I know." As quickly as she disappeared, she reappeared with another charge and pop, now a short distance to one side of where she'd been, her new position providing her an unobstructed sight line to Caer. "Kill them!" she cried. "Leave the girl to me!" Fine streams of lightning streaked from her palms as she raised her hands.

Brandon instantly drove sideways into Caer, sending her sprawling. Fedel'ma and Emer blinked out with that now all-too-familiar pop and charge, reemerging side-by-side directly in front of where Caer had fallen. Maura's attack, instead, struck Brandon squarely, lifting him from his feet in screaming agony and holding him there.

The whole of the hillside erupted in brilliant light, sizzling and crackling with a fiery confluence of mercurial streams from multiple directions at once. It was impossible to tell whose blast was responsible for first taking Ailill and then the older man to the ground. There was no mistaking Adrian's strike of Maura, though. The force of its casting staggered him backward and left him struggling for his footing, even as its impact tossed the woman into the air, dumping her like a rag doll in a twist of brambles several meters further downslope.

Caer gaped, horrified, as the force that had engulfed Brandon suddenly released, dropping him with a resounding splunk into the mud. Scrambling to her feet, she shoved past Fedel'ma, sick with fear at the terrible convulsing that wracked her friend's body. Dropping down beside him, she cast about wildly, her screams of, "Help him! Somebody help!" lost in the crashing discharges of electrified air.

Quickly regaining his footing, and with his hands sweeping in an arc as he spun, Adrian relocated his target in the thicket below. Maura drug herself painfully to her feet, her face twitching in a tortured grimace of bloody abhorrence.

"You can't always win!" she shrieked. Her hands thrust skyward as an unintelligible flow of words rushed from her lips. Instantly, the winds roared to a full gale, the already tumultuous clouds high overhead thickening in their race to blot out the occasional tatters of moonlight. Then came the rains, slicing in a near sideways wall. Gushing water quickly cut trenches underfoot, the rush sweeping ever-expanding rivers of mud and crumbled rock downhill.

Bracing against the raging torrent, his cloak flailing out behind him, Adrian fought to take aim at the now barely visible silhouette of the woman who'd whipped the elements down on them. "Get Caer out of here!" he roared against the wind's howl.

"I have to hold these two!" returned from another, closer bellow.

Caer hunkered against Brandon's severely thrashing body,

squinting against the deluge at the tall, fair man who'd accompanied Adrian into this mayhem. Barely ten meters from her, he held one palm aimed at Ailill, the other at the nameless hulk. Having gained their own footing, both now stood frozen within some invisible force. Ailill's face was contorted with fear, his hands only partially raised. The other man seethed with contempt and outrage, his palms aimed squarely at Caer, though he seemed unable to take any further action. Caer's heart thundered agonizingly within her ribs. If Adrian's companion released whatever hold he had on the man, she was certain she would meet the same fate as her convulsing friend.

The one called Dylan blinked out from where he'd fallen when dodging a blast Maura succeeded in getting off before being struck again by one of Adrian's attacks. Promptly reappearing between Fedel'ma and Emer, he gestured for them to encircle Caer and Brandon. Rising over the gale's now deafening howl, Fedel'ma commanded, "Merripen! Come!"

Black fur streaked from the shadows through the continuing deluge as the air ignited. In the next heartbeat, a sharp, needling surge of electricity slammed Caer. Her eyes clamped shut, her arms wrapped desperately around Brandon's torso as obsidian emptiness once again embraced them.

24

The charge expelled with a momentary slicing of icy wind and a rough thump that landed Caer on a carpeted floor, the jar tumbling her from her haunches to her backside. Beside her lay Brandon, still violently convulsing.

"Hold him!" Emer barked, dropping to her knees near his head.

Caer tossed herself across Bran's torso. Pinning him, however, proved more than she could manage. The man calling himself Dylan quickly moved into place, grasping Brandon's legs while Caer concentrated on his arms. Together, they managed to prevent the thrashing man from knocking Emer senseless as she splayed her fingers across his face, her thumb and little finger as near his temples as the stretch of her hand allowed.

"Still the nerves. To me the pain," she commanded.

The sudden slackness beneath Caer was nearly as disconcerting as Bran's fierce flailing had been. Uncertain what to do next, she rolled aside, turning to address Emer in time to see the woman slump from her knees. Dylan bounded to Emer's side, supporting her. For several worrisome moments, she sat with her eyes closed, her features and her slender frame twitching with agony. At last, with a single shudder, her body relaxed, her eyes fluttering open, the smolder of indigo still burning behind their midnight blue.

Too exhausted and still too anxious about Brandon to give any more thought to that strange glow, Caer sagged where she sat, lips pinched as she eyed her friend. He lay quite still, now, his face grayer than his dull and empty stare. "Will...will he be alright?"

"He'll be fine," Emer rasped. "The assault wasn't meant to kill, only to incapacitate. He may need a little time to recover, and he'll likely ache for a good while. But he should be none the worse for wear."

"What about you?" Dylan asked, assisting Emer to her feet.

"Fine. Grand," she replied.

"Of course you are," Fedel'ma put in with a huff. Whether she'd emerged...materialized...whatever it was they did...elsewhere in the mansion, or whether she'd left the room as soon as they arrived, Caer couldn't say. All she knew was that the woman now strode through the library's double doors, a large towel draped around her shoulders and a bundle of blankets in her arms. She tossed one each to Emer and Dylan, then tossed the other two to the floor in front of Caer. From beneath her towel, Fedel'ma's clothes left a trail of muddy droplets as she continued across the room to the chair behind the massive desk.

Settling, she shot a contemplative glance back at Caer. "Snuggle up in the blanket, dear. And mind that Mr. Jase, stays warm." Caer obliged, laying one blanket across Brandon and tucking it beneath him before taking the other in hand.

Dylan scarcely took note of Del, his dubious contemplation remaining on Emer. Wincing under his scrutiny, she withdrew from his support. "Been a long time since I've done anything like that," she muttered, tugging her blanket around her shoulders as she headed for the nearest of the two armchairs that flanked a reading table. Plopping down with her legs dangling over one of the chair's arms, Emer busied herself drying her hair with one edge of her blanket. "Seems I'm a little out of practice."

Dylan gave a disgruntled harrumph before turning to Caer and extending a hand. Through all the previous mayhem, she'd paid little attention to him. Now that she regarded him, his appearance came as something of a surprise. He looked to be only a little older than herself. A mass of damp curls draped his forehead, their darkness complimenting his rich olive complexion. It was his return gaze, however, that startled her most. For it bore the underlying remnants of burning amber within the rich brown of his eyes. Amber. Like Jorn's, though she couldn't recall the professor's eyes ever ignited as this man's had been.

Rubbing her arms, she declined his offer of assistance. That momentary reminder of Jorn rushed her with a wave of grief, leaving her with little trust that her legs would support her, should she attempt to rise. Instead, she shifted her position, leaning to brush wet hair from Bran's face; wishing his eyes would lose their dullness; wishing they would reflect some indication of mental activity. "I'll...I'll just stay here," she murmured.

Dylan nodded, strolling off in Del's direction. "As you wish."

For what seemed an eternity, no one ventured to speak. Withdrawing into her wrap, Caer attempted to ignore both her grief and the mounting tension in the room. If Bran would just move...say something...let her know he was alright... Waiting in the silence, her fingers plucked uneasily at the soggy, cream-colored carpet, a million questions crowding her brain. She fought the urge to blurt any of them out. She wasn't entirely sure she wanted to know the answers. Perhaps she would wake in a while; find herself nestled in bed, the recent events nothing more than a very bad dream. She would shake it off and forget it.

Brandon's snarl snapped her attention around to find him working his way, first to sit, and then shifting into a crouch. Slumped, shaking, his eyes darted from the muddy stains on the carpet where he'd lain to a fearsome assessment of Fedel'ma, Emer, and Dylan.

"We're not your enemies, Mr. Jase," Fedel'ma offered. "Otherwise, we'd not have bothered to go looking for you."

Her chair protested with a squeak as she tilted it back to turn an agitated scowl on Dylan. Water dripped from his gray shirt and dark trousers onto the corner of the desk where he sat. "Hope you intend to take care of any damage your filthy posterior is doing to my furniture," she grumbled. "For pity's sake, use that damned blanket and dry off."

Dylan granted her a curt nod, his dark curls still trickling small streams down his face. "Nice to see you again, too, Mother," he said, applying the blanket to dry his face and hair, though he made no effort to dry his clothes or mop the corner of the desk.

Warily, Brandon pushed to his feet, Caer rising with him. When her fingers inadvertently brushed his arm, he jerked away, the sudden hostility that swept his features stinging her. Reflexively, she drew her wrap tighter around her.

"What in eternal madness happened out there?" he demanded, one hand waving toward the windows. "What kind of weapon does that bitch have?"

Getting no response, he swore beneath his breath. "Who are you people? And what is this key those bastards want?"

"Key?" Emer straightened. "Not *the* key."

"Just what other key would the likes of that little group have in mind?" Del sniffed.

Emer's stunned gape shot to Caer and then to Brandon. "Why? What did they say? Surely they don't think that one of you..."

Del nodded toward Caer. "Our guest, here, brought part of it with her. A gift from her mother, I recall her saying this morning. Though when and how it fell into the possession of her family I'd very much like to know. As for the second piece..." She waved a hand irritably in Dylan's direction. "Talk to H...my son. He gave that one to her."

Dylan cocked a brow. "You recognized it for what it was?"

"Guessed, initially, based on the strangeness of the currents in the magic when the boxes you sent arrived, and increased with Ms. DaDhrga's arrival." Del's eyes narrowed, her glower so profound Caer feared it might cause the woman's son to vanish in a flare of briefly combusted air.

"Am I to understand," she continued, "that you knew in whose hands the first piece resided? Don't tell me that's the reason behind your foolishly giving the second to Ms. DaDhrga."

Caer's mouth worked several times, her head shaking vigorously. Finally, she managed, "If you're saying I have this key thing, I don't! Your son gave me nothing! I've never met him before. Never even seen him before...before...his popping into existence on that...that hill."

Dylan rose, the hint of a half-smile ticking up a corner of his mouth. The subtle expression was another eerie reminder of Jorn, the thought casting a chill over Caer. "Forgive me," he said. "Name's Dylan."

"Yeah," Caer mumbled. "That much you mentioned already."

"So I did." He considered briefly, then added, "Truth is, while you don't know me, I do know you. Well...know of you, anyway."

Caer squirmed at the suggestion of familiarity. "How?"

"Through a...mutual friend."

"Names don't answer my question," Brandon growled. "I ask again, who are you people? Who were those...those...people on that hill? And...and how in all the eternal hells of the universe did we get there?"

Dylan shrugged. "Let's just say that the woman, Maura, along with her goons are...members of a very powerful family. A family that possesses abilities the likes of which I doubt you could even begin to imagine."

Brandon gritted his teeth, his response a guttural rumble. "After what I've been through, I can imagine quite a lot." Pointing an accusing finger at Fedel'ma, he pressed, "Were you the one who sent Caer and me off to that place? How'd you do it?"

"I'm sure neither Mother nor Em sent you anywhere," Dylan returned. "Just be thankful they were able to sort out where you'd gone and went after you. Otherwise, you would likely be dead by now, and Ms. DaDhrga taken captive."

Casting one more suspicious glance between Dylan and the two women, Brandon turned on his heel and headed for the door, snapping "Come on, Caer. We're not going to get any straight answers from these people. I don't know what they're up to, but they're crazy, the lot of them! And they're dangerous! We're out of here!"

Caer held her ground, staring bleakly at her friend's back. There was a time when she might have followed Bran's dictate, fleeing and never looking back. She couldn't deny that these three could easily be as dangerous as that other trio. The forces in play on that hillside was proof enough of that. Still, Del, Emer, and Dylan had just saved their lives. Caer's lips pinched. Adrian and his companion had helped in that. Which begged a whole host of questions.

"I'm not going, Bran."

Brandon spun back, his brow-raised expression one of incredulity. "Are you out of your mind?"

"You heard what that creep on the hill said. He admitted to the destruction of Ahira. Admitted responsibility for the slaughter of your..." Caer's voice trailed off. Swallowing, she continued weakly. "I know I don't have whatever it is that they want. But for so long as they think I do, they will try to get it from me. I have no way of fighting them, Bran. And neither do you. If we stay here..." Darting a sidelong glance at the two women, she concluded, "Maybe we have a chance of staying alive. Maybe we can get to the bottom of this."

"Yeah. Six feet to the bottom. In a bloody box!"

"Please, Bran. Stay here with me. You know those people will be looking for you, too."

"I'll take my chances." Spinning once more, he stomped out of the room.

"And just how do you expect to leave?" Del called after him.

"In a pod," snarled back.

"I doubt your communicator is functional after the attack you took. Even if it is, calling for a pod will do you no good. I'm not about to allow anyone entry to the estate right now."

Storming back into the room, Brandon bellowed, "Well, I'm not staying here! I'll walk out if I have to."

"Clever trick, that," Dell huffed. "Go ahead. Hike across the hills and valleys to the nearest section of the dome's wall. I doubt, however, that you have the skills to scale the traction-less concave surface to reach the access tunnel near the top."

"Then mat-trans me out of here the way you sent us off to that other place and brought us back."

Del leaned forward, her shoulders drooping as she braced her elbows on the desktop. "First, Mr. Jase, you're an imbecile if you think there is a mat-trans unit here. Most are constructed in space, the rest contained within their own remote domes for a reason. Any seepage of energy from the surges of their activation, should they suffer any ruptures, would destroy life for miles around. Second, we sent you nowhere. It's as much a mystery to us how you got to that hill as it appears to be to you. If you insist on leaving, then I will take you."

"I'm not going anywhere with you, lady!"

"Fine," Del snorted. "Then you stay here."

"You should trust Caer on this," Emer offered. "You truly are safer here."

"Safe! Nowhere is safe so long as the likes of you are running around. If Caer wants to stay, that's her death wish. I have other business to attend before I die."

A sick hollow opened in the depths of Caer's stomach. She suspected what 'business' he had in mind, making him the one with the death wish. Looking for vengeance for the murder of his family and Jenna was nothing short of suicidal. "Bran..."

Del waved her to silence. "I told you earlier today, Mr. Jase, that I would deliver you back to your hotel. I stand by my word. I'll even help you pack your bags and provide you safe transport to the nearest mat-trans station, where I strongly recommend you arrange for jumps that will take you to the furthest outlying colony."

Brandon glared at her, his voice ice-edged. "Why should I trust you to deliver me anywhere?"

"Because you've no other choice."

25

Caer tried to will her muscles to relax as the hot water cascaded over her head and shoulders. Her mind, however, insisted on reliving everything that happened on that bloody hillside…and since. The fresh memories left her tense and edgy. Just what sort of key could be worth killing over? Why would those people think she had it? Why would they want Bran and his entire family exterminated? How, in the name of all things sacred in the universe, did everyone keep popping in and out of existence? And what sort of weapons did they possess that allowed them to shoot lightning from the palms of their hands?

She shivered, despite the water's heat. Too many questions. No one telling her anything that made sense. Bran was right. They were dangerous, the lot of them! At least Emer and Fedel'ma, for whatever reason, seemed genuinely interested in her well-being… and Bran's. He should have stayed. She should have tried harder to convince him.

Slumping against the shower wall, Caer fidgeted anxiously with her necklace, wondering where Bran was, right now. Was Fedel'ma still with him, or had she delivered him to his hotel already? He wasn't safe, alone. Her lips pinched. And just what made her believe she was any safer, here, among these strangers? What if the world once again opened its maw and swallowed her, spitting her out in some other hell? Would they make another attempt to rescue her?

Or were they responsible for delivering her and Bran to that hill in the first place? Bran thought so. They denied it.

Emer promised that the world wouldn't swallow her again. So long as she remained inside the house, it couldn't happen. Something about the house being better protected than the gardens. Caer didn't know what that meant, and wasn't sure she wanted to know. What she did want was to learn how Emer and her aunt and this Dylan fellow…and for that matter, how Adrian and his companion, were able to find her. Fury flushed through her. Adrian! Whatever abilities these people possessed, he possessed, as well. And he never told her! How could he not tell her? This was not the Adrian she thought she knew. What other secrets had he kept from her all these years?

Shuddering, she forced her rage to the back of her mind as she shut off the water and stepped out of the cubicle to dry. Without the hiss of the shower, though, the suite she'd been given was too quiet. In the silence, every minor creak of a floorboard, every subtle moan of the old house, screamed at her, making her jump. Eager for the presence of the others, she donned a pair of loose trousers, a pullover sweater, and her shoes and socks, then headed for the hallway. Emer had suggested they meet in the parlor after cleaning up.

Scurrying along the empty hallway and past the darkened library, Caer crossed the broad landing and wound her way down the grand stairs, wondering which of the at least three parlors Emer meant. Could she remember how to find any of them? Sitting rooms, parlors, libraries, atriums. Impressions from her morning's tour of the mansion…a tour that seemed to have taken place a full age ago, now…slid together in a mental maze. Thankfully, the soft light spilling through an arched doorway near the bottom of the steps suggested this to be the correct room, as did the sounds of someone moving about.

Though grateful for the company, Caer was also dismayed to find only Dylan present. The man's vague familiarity troubled her. He knew her through a mutual friend, he said. What mutual friend?

She didn't recall anyone ever speaking of him. She'd certainly never met him before. So, why did his presence make her feel otherwise?

Hanging back, she waited in the shadows of the hall as he coaxed a small blaze to life in the fireplace. The light of it shimmered off the silvered blue of his fresh shirt and highlighted his dark complexion. She would never guess him to be Fedel'ma's son. They bore no physical resemblance to one another. Instead, Dylan reminded her disconcertingly of Dr. Jorn. Not that the two men looked anything alike, either. This man stood at least a head taller than Jorn, his coloring darker, his black hair much curlier. It was something about their eyes. Amber. The color was far more noticeable in Jorn's eyes, whereas in Dylan's the strange color carried a wash of dark brown overlay. Still, the amber was there…flicking out now and again. There on that hill, the color had ignited in a golden-red glow.

"Come sit down," Emer directed, nudging past her, the slim lines and dark blue of the woman's jumpsuit accenting the grace of her movements. Caer trailed in behind her. While Emer settled on one of the two settees, Caer scanned the three upholstered rosewood armchairs and the accompanying low rosewood table that occupied the center of the room, opting for an overstuffed chair that shared a corner with a lamp. Perching on the chair's edge, she noted the darkness beyond the leaded glass windows flanking the fireplace. Evening? Night? When she and Bran fell through that dark hole in the universe, it was afternoon, here, yet they emerged in a place of deep night. Their return brought them back to…what? Her answer came with the large clock in one corner of the room chiming eight times. How could four hours have passed since the time they were… elsewhere? Had that awful battle really taken that long?

"Feeling better?"

Caer jerked with a start, snapping her gaze across to Emer as the woman adjusted her position, tucking one leg beneath her.

"Apparently not," Emer sighed. "Relax, dear. I told you. You're safe here. A shame your friend refused our hospitality. Del will look after him, though. At least as far as his hotel. If he has any sense, he will take her advice and leave as quickly as possible."

"He won't," Caer moaned, scooting back on the seat only so far as to keep her legs from dangling. "Not unless he has to track those barbarians across the universe. He wants vengeance."

Dylan placed the grate in front of a now fair-sized blaze and turned. "For today's little incident?"

"Little!" Caer snorted.

Dylan gave an apologetic shrug. "Bad turn of phrase. You're right. It was no minor happenstance."

Only slightly mollified, Caer confirmed, "And yes. At least in part, for today." Rubbing her arms to try and still the shivering that took her, she asked, "Wouldn't you want vengeance if you were swallowed up and spit out in a hell where the demons claimed responsibility for the murder of your family and the woman you loved?"

Dylan's brow cocked with interest. "His family and lady love were all on Ahira, then."

"Jenna was."

"Jenna being his girlfriend, I take it. And his family?"

Caer dropped her gaze and poked at the doilies on each of the chair's arms. "The Andromeda colony. Bran left Ahira just before I did. To visit them."

Emer tapped her fingers on her lap, considering. "You said the people on the hill also murdered his family. Was that while he was visiting them, or after? And what brought him to Earth?"

Caer tried to blink back the sudden misting of tears. "Me. He came looking for me and..." With a half-choked breath, she managed, "And Jenna. He thought...he hoped...that she was with me."

Dylan found his way to the second settee, choosing to stand behind it, leaning with his arms braced on its back. "My understanding is that you just received your transfer from Ahira to Sion a day or so before you left. I didn't realize anyone else was transferring here from Ahira."

"No one else was, so far as I'm aware. Bran hoped...wanted..." Again, Caer fussed with the doilies. "Bran is my friend. Jenna my best friend. She contacted him when he was on his way to Andromeda, telling him about my transfer. That's how he knew to look for me here, after..."

The others waited patiently, Emer finally asking, "After what, dear?"

Caer stared blankly at her hands for several seconds. "Bran told me that...that when he arrived at the colony, some men were waiting for him. At his sister's place. They seemed to think he had some...some information they wanted." She swallowed, fighting the growing constriction in her throat, her eyes still downcast to avoid Dylan's penetrating scrutiny. "They tortured him, and...and killed his sister. Killed her husband and their new baby, as well. Burned them alive. They had the same fate in mind for Bran, I think, because they left him there. Unconscious. With the flames consuming everything."

Emer filled in softly, "But he escaped. Did he say how?"

Caer shook her head. "I don't know when he learned of Ahira, either. Couldn't have been too long after that, though. That's why he came here looking for me, hoping to find Jenna with me. But Jenna had no interest in coming here. Bran knows that. I guess...I guess in his grief, he just wished so hard for the impossible that he convinced himself it was possible."

For a time, silence hung over the room. At last, Emer broke it. "Your friend, Mr. Jase. Did he know the men who killed his family?"

"No. At least, he said he didn't. And I believe him." Plucking at the doilies again, Caer drew a shaky breath, exhaling slowly. "When that woman...Maura...saw Bran, she seemed surprised. Said he was supposed to be dead. Said that one of the men with her was supposed to have seen to it."

Bracing herself, Caer flashed a guilty glance at Emer. "I recognized him. The man who was supposed to see to Bran's death. He admitted responsibility for what happened on Ahira, as well. I don't know who he is, mind you. Only that he turned up on the shuttle I took when I left Ahira for Bestor III. He sat next to me. He was...was also the same man who fired on O-4."

Emer went expressionless as Dylan responded with a sharp glare in her direction, mouthing, "We need to talk."

Caer's fingers twisted one of the doilies into a tight knot. "Why should those people want to murder Bran and his family...or everyone on Ahira?"

"Violence is part of their nature," Dylan confessed, setting off in a pace. "Especially when it comes to Tanai. Curious, though. Since the initial mass murder on Ahira, they've been strangely cautious, attacking each of their other victims when they were alone; taking no interest, so far as we can tell, in their families. Mr. Jase's family appears to be the exception. I can't help but wonder why that would be the case."

"All I know," Caer returned weakly, "is that Bran said the men wanted information."

Dylan's pacing ceased. "Did he say what sort of information?"

It was hard to remember her conversation with Bran precisely. So much had happened since then. "Something...something about giving them names. Of people..." She flicked a nervous glance between Dylan and Emer. "People like you, I think. They called him...sensitive. At least, I think that's what he said. As if that explained their belief that he would know anything."

The tension in the room shot up as Emer, and Dylan repeated, almost in unison, "A Sensitive?"

Stiffening, Caer nodded. "Yes. I guess so. Why? What does that mean? And what is this other thing you mentioned? Tan...tan...?"

"Tanai," Dylan replied, resuming his pacing. "Means 'shallow'. It refers to most humans. People who don't possess any..." He gave her a measuring scan. "...Any unusual skills, shall we say."

"Like popping in and out of places in the blink of an eye, you mean? Or...or shooting lightning bolts from your hands...or freezing Bran while suspending him in the air?"

Dylan nodded. "Like that, and more. Since the beginning of

time, those who lack our capabilities have labeled us Witches, called our gifts magic. Their fear of us forced us to keep our talents hidden. Secrecy is a vow we take very seriously."

"Witches. Magic." There was a time, not so long ago, Caer would have dismissed the very idea. Everything she'd witnessed on this day, however, declared some degree of truth to the notion. "And 'Sensitives'?" she ventured. "What are they?"

"Like the Tanai, they lack our abilities. They do, however, possess a skill that, many ages ago, made their rare kind a great threat to us. They can identify us. For many ages, a few of them did so for hire, bringing about the slaughter of hundreds of thousands of good people. We believed that Maura's clan had hunted them to extinction long ago. Even the suspicion that Mr. Jase and his family might carry the trait, however, would be sufficient cause for Maura and others of her clan to want them exterminated."

Caer's head swam. Bran tried to tell her that he sensed something...odd about...about certain people, herself included. It was nonsense. It had to be. "It's not real. Witches. Magic. Sensitives. They don't exist."

"So, tell me," Dylan prompted, coming to a halt again. "What was it you witnessed today?"

"I...don't know. Hallucinations."

"Perhaps..." Dylan ventured wearily. "Perhaps another demonstration is in order."

"Demonstrate," Caer agreed, her thin voice lacking the challenge she'd hoped to make. "Take me back to that hill. Show me how you do that."

"I think not," Dylan returned. "While Maura and her stooges are likely out looking for you and your friend, rumors have been circulating that worse than their little trio prowls those hallowed grounds. No. A little less dramatic conjuring will have to suffice."

Something thick and warm suddenly draped across Caer's shoulders. With a startled yelp, she shot to her feet, instinctively yanking at the thing and throwing it to the floor. Cautiously, she poked at it with the toe of her shoe, realizing that it was a shawl. Fedel'ma's, if she remembered correctly. She saw the woman come in from the gardens wearing it before breakfast, this morning. The last she recalled, it was hanging on a peg near the kitchen door.

Dylan's grimace indicated his dismay at her reaction. "I'm sorry. It was not my intention to frighten you. You've been shivering all evening. I thought only to provide you with a little warmth."

Caer stooped, gingerly retrieving the garment and holding it at arm's length. "How did...?"

"Objects are fairly easy to move."

Shaking the shawl at him, she stammered, "If...if this is...n't some sort of...of sleight of hand, some...hallucinogen that you've... you've slipped me...if you can do this...then..." Her anxious gaze shot to Emer. "Then you must be the ones responsible for sending us to that hill, just like Bran thought."

"We didn't," Emer objected, looking genuinely insulted. "You heard Dylan. That hill isn't safe."

"Maybe you thought you could get rid of us."

"And then we show up to save you?"

"Okay. Okay. Then...then explain to me how...how we got there. Where was 'there'? And...and...how did...how did you know where to find us?"

Emer's mouth torqued with indecision. Dylan, however, stated flatly, "She has a right to at least some explanation. The place is known as Slieve na Calliagh. Hill of the Witch. Whether you choose to believe us or not, we honestly have no idea how you ended up there."

"Obviously, Mr. Jase lacks the ability to teleport," Emer interjected. "Which leaves us with either Maura reaching through our shielding and taking you--something I desperately pray is not the case--or you did it yourself. Inadvertently, I should hope, as I really like you and would hate to have my feelings prove erroneously placed."

A stinging charge jolted the air. "That's enough!" roared from a distortion that whipped into existence just above the rosewood table in front of the three armchairs. Emer shot to her feet, darting for the table and yanking it away from the intensifying ripples. "Not on this, you don't! This belonged to my mother!"

Dylan joined her, his palms aimed at the disturbance. Caer clung to the shawl, her sharp inhale catching in her lungs. She knew the musicality of that bellow. The distortion focused with an outward gust of electrified wind, sending her chair's doilies fluttering to the floor several paces away. Adrian and the man who'd accompanied him at the Hill of the Witch stood, now, where the table had been only seconds before, both men still wearing their cloaks. The shawl dropped from Caer's fingers. People really needed to stop popping into existence like that!

"Who in damnation are you, and how did you get through?" Emer hissed.

Adrian granted her an irritated nod of acknowledgment, his eyes glowing like molten turquoise, just as they had done on that hillside. "Not easily, if it's any consolation to you. Caer, you need to come with us."

Caer shook with outrage. "I'm not some...some child to be commanded about! I'm not going anywhere with you until you start explaining things, Adrian Starn! You never told me any of this! That you could do...do the things I saw you do, today! What other secrets have you kept from me?"

"There isn't time for explanations or for arguing," he growled, starting for her.

She darted away, turning back to glare at him, her fists stuffed to her hips. "If you think I'm blinking in and out of places even one more time, you can think again! I'm staying right where I am until somebody offers some explanations that make sense."

"You will know everything you need to when it's time," Adrian snapped, moving toward her again. "Right now, your safety takes precedence."

Dylan sprang between Caer and Adrian, amber flashing

bright-hot in his eyes. "Who the hell do you think you are, breaking our barriers and barging uninvited into a private home?"

Adrian regarded him with icy contempt. "Her guardian. And now I've had the opportunity to identify the signature of your workings, I will thank you not to meddle with protective spells where they are not needed. We are responsible for Caer, not you."

"We?" Caer's eyes narrowed as she studied Adrian's companion. The burning blue light of the man's gaze shown from beneath his hood. Nor could the shadows hide his elegant features or the long strands of white-gold hair that framed his face.

Recognition struck her with the force of a mat-trans slamming, buckling her knees and dumping her jarringly onto the arm of the settee she'd backed up against. "Stoirm! Your name is Stoirm! You were there," she rasped. "You were in Aunt Sidra's house. You came to take us away. But Sidra wouldn't go."

Stoirm pulled his hood back, his stern countenance revealing a flash of anguish as he nodded.

More wisps of memory rose, hazy as dense smoke, offering only vague impressions. "You left us. You came to save us from..." Something horrendous had taken place all those long, dark years ago. Her mind recoiled before she could grasp it.

"But your aunt refused my help."

"So...so you just left us?" Caer's words came thin and tremulous. "You didn't even stay to...to..."

"This is not the time for dredging up old memories," Adrian barked. His glance flicked to her necklace. "Caer, it is imperative that you leave with us. Now."

Caer noted the track of his eyes, her hand promptly grasping the chain and charm. It pulsed, warm within her clutch. Why was it doing that--again? It shouldn't be doing that at all!

Adrian vanished, reappearing less than a hair's breadth from her side. "We're going," he declared, taking her by the elbow and pulling her roughly to her feet.

She jerked away, seething. "I told you! I'm not going anywhere!

You lied to me, Adrian Starn! You've kept secrets from me! Am I like you? Do I have powers you've never told me about? I'll have answers to my questions, whether you wish it or not. If you won't provide them here and now, then just...just leave me alone! I'll find them some other way!"

For a moment, she thought he would explode in fury. The rage on Adrian's face, however, drained to a sorrow that seemed to bore through to his soul. "I can't force you, Caer," he groaned. Turning to Stoirm, he beseeched, "Is there nothing you can say to convince her?"

"What little she has remembered leaves her trusting me no more than you, right now, Amhranai. Her conviction is firm. You cannot break your oath by forcing her to a path against her will. To do so would serve no one. Either explain now, or let her remain here without knowing the truth."

A hard scowl etched a furrow across Caer's brow. What truth? And what oath had Adrian sworn? Somewhere in the dark fog at the back of consciousness slithered the suggestion that it was connected to another oath--one that she had sworn. But... The moment was gone, the impression evaporated.

Adrian cast an agonized and grudging nod to his companion, the lilt of his voice breaking beneath the strain of his resignation. "I cannot tell her. Not yet." Fixing Caer with a tortured gaze, he rumbled, "If you must have it so, then this is where we will leave you. For now."

Turning on Dylan, he charged a heated, "Understand this. Wherever she goes, I will know it. Should you attempt to surround her with another spell, I will know that, as well. It is for me to protect her. Block my ability again and you're dead. Do anything that places her in harm's way, and I will guarantee that your death is neither quick nor painless. Nor will I allow your soul's return."

"And you," he growled, flicking his broiling scrutiny back to Caer. "Stop seeking for answers to things that are best left alone."

With that, the air rippled and distorted once more, Adrian and Stoirm vanishing in another rush of charged air.

26

Caer's breath came in agitated spasms. They needed to stop! Her nerves couldn't take much more of their sudden appearing and disappearing! And Adrian! How dare he blink into existence in the middle of a private home, declaring her to be his responsibility and threatening anyone who got in his way! She was no one's responsibility but her own! Caer clenched her fists, glaring at the empty space left in his wake. Who appointed him her watchdog, anyway?

Her fists stopped clenching and started shaking, her fury muddled in a wash of frustration and near panic. She sent him away! First, she refused to go with him on that hill. Now she'd refused to leave Fedel'ma's and Emer's estate. She'd refused to go with Bran, too. What was she doing? Adrian and Bran were right. These people were strangers. Why did she choose to stay with them?

Her hand went to her necklace, her fingers cautiously lifting the chain enough to see the charm, its stone a swirl of deep reds. "All of the madness for this?" she choked. "All because of this necklace?" It was the only thing that came close to fitting what Fedel'ma said-- that Caer told her part of the sought-after key was given her by her mother. But Fedel'ma also claimed the second part came from her son. Not true. Jorn sent the charm to her. Caer's fingers clamped around the bedeviled jewelry, her intention to yank it free and throw it as far from her as she could. If this is what everyone wants, then let them have it!

An urgent thrumming attacked the back of her skull, freezing her motion just as the chain jerked against her neck. Locked in her grasp, the necklace grew hot, its pulse increasing to a frantic tempo. The more she tried to cast it aside, the more painful the thrumming grew. From somewhere in the depths of her soul and rising through the pain in her skull, lifted a whisper. The words were too distant, too hushed to be discernible, yet she recognized their essence. They formed an oath, sworn in a high-pitched voice...a child's voice... Her voice. The truth of it jarred through her. Her promise. What had she sworn?

Unclenching her fingers, she stared at the charm that still pulsed hot against her trembling palm. A pledge. Her solemn word. An oath given as a child. An oath connected to...to this? Certainty jarred her again, robbing her of her breath.

"Ms. DaDhrga."

Caer felt a light pressure on her shoulder and jerked away, spinning to come face to face with Dylan.

He nodded toward the chair behind her. "You look like you need to sit down."

His suggestion barely registered, the shift of her gaze dismissing him as she fixed her attention on the spot where Adrian and his companion had emerged and then disappeared. His companion. Stoirm. She remembered the man turning up in the hut she shared with her aunt. Turning up and...and then abandoning them. He should have stayed...should have... What? The rest of the events of that night lay in a black abyss in the back of her mind.

Caer tried to calm herself; tried to sort through her riotous thoughts. One thing was certain. Adrian and Stoirm knew one another. For how long? Was Adrian aware of Stoirm's brief visit to Sidra's hut? What else did he know? Why had he never told her anything? Not about his abilities. Not about knowing Stoirm. Nothing. So, by what right did he show up here making demands of her? Demanding that she leave; demanding that she stop seeking answers. She'd have those answers! If Adrian refused to provide them, then she'd dredge them from the depths of her subconscious.

Pinching her eyes shut, she struggled to concentrate. Too many fragments of memory tangled themselves in her mind-- her mother's anxious-sweet face as she removed the delicate silver chain she'd always worn, fastening it around Caer's neck and carefully tucking it into her shirt; Sidra's calm smile following Stoirm's visit, her aunt's eyes reflecting a mix of pride and sorrow, resignation and hope; her own terror at...at... White-hot pain exploded in Caer's temples as she fought to draw forward those ghostly images. The harder she tried to grasp them the more intense the agony grew. At last, gasping for breath, her vision swimming in a sea of nausea, she relinquished the effort.

Again, she felt the pressure of Dylan's hands on her shoulders, steadying her. Several seconds passed before the pain subsided and the world cleared enough for her to see the grave concern etched in the man's features.

"It's been a tough day," he said, gently nudging her backward until her legs met the chair and she dropped onto it.

"You." She swallowed. "Fedel'ma said you gave the key to me. Or...or part of it." Glancing down, she reached for but came short of touching the silver chain with its trinity knot set with the red stone. "But you didn't. Dr. Jorn sent the charm to me. Why would she think it came from you?"

"Jorn was...a good friend," Dylan stated, turning and making his way back to the fireplace. His back to her, he added, "When Jorn requested the charm from me, I obliged. According to my mother's logic, since the charm is now in your possession, she would say that, in effect, it came from me."

A ring of half-truth clung to his statement. Caer took Emer's quiet huff as confirmation that he was leaving something out. "The note," she persisted. "I received a note, as well. Jorn said the charm belonged to his sister."

"True," Dylan acknowledged. "The piece was too great a

reminder of the sister he lost, though, so I held it in safe keeping for him."

"Did you know?"

Dylan turned and leaned against the mantle, regarding her. "Know what?"

"That this thing was more than a simple adornment? Did Jorn know? Were either of you aware that others were willing to kill for it?"

"I suspected what the completed necklace might be, but suspected only. Until I saw you on Slieve na Calliagh."

"Did Jorn also suspect? If he did, why would he give something so deadly to me?"

Dylan shrugged. "I'm afraid Mr. Starn may be correct."

Caer pursed her lips, glowering. "How do you know Adrian? And what is he right about."

"I'm not acquainted with your friend. This is the first I've encountered him. Hard to miss his name, though, when you rather shouted it couple of times."

Blanching, Caer exhaled an agitated, "Fine. That still doesn't tell me what Adrian is right about."

"There are some answers you shouldn't go looking for."

"And why would that be?"

Dylan eyed her, then shrugged. "I suggest you ask your friend, Mr. Starn."

Anger warbled in Caer's voice. "You heard him! He isn't going to tell me anything! Here I am, carrying this bloody...key around, and I don't even know what it's a key to. What does it open? Where did it come from? And why the hell do I have it?"

Dylan stood mute for several long seconds before turning to the fireplace to remove the grate and poke at the pellets fueling the flame. "I have no answers to give you, Ms. DaDhrga. If you think Mr. Starn will continue refusing to provide them, perhaps you should try asking his friend."

"Stoirm," Caer snorted, disgusted. "Why would he tell me anything? I don't know him."

Emer repeated the name, straightening. "Stoirm. You're sure that's what he's called."

"It's the name he gave when I first met him."

Emer's brow cocked. "I thought you said you don't know him."

"I only met him once." Or maybe twice? Hadn't he said something about meeting her prior to that night in her aunt's hut? Everything was such a jumble in her head. "I was only about twelve at the time. Never met him again, after that."

"He's human?" Emer pressed.

"I don't think so. Hard to tell with his hood and his hair in the way, but I seem to recall something about his ears being pointed. I don't remember what he said he was, though."

"Alainn," Emer breathed. "I knew it!"

Dylan shook his head. "You're not going to start with that old fairy tale, are you?"

"Not a fairy tale," Emer sniffed. "You've seen the archives. The Alainn exist. Or at least did at one time. You saw the man. Have you ever seen a human so fair? They say there's never been a race, human or alien, as beautiful as the Alainn. They spawned fantastic tales of fairies and the like."

"Beauty is not the same to every person's eye," Dylan scoffed. "And personally, he's not my type."

Emer dismissed him with a flip of her hand, returning her attention to Caer. "You accused him of abandoning you. When? What were the circumstances?"

Caer doubled her fists, hammering them onto the tops of the chair's arms. "Enough with the questions! My turn to do the asking!"

"Please, Caer," Emer persisted. "When did you meet him?"

"Like I told you," she steamed. "I was maybe twelve at the time, and living with my..."

Caer's words were cut short by a nerve-shattering yowl, sending her heart to her throat. She and Emer were both instantly on their feet as Merripen hurtled into the room, charging past Caer and disappearing under the settee where Emer had been sitting.

"What in the... Merri?" Emer dropped to her knees, extending a hand, palm up. "Here, Sweet. Come, Kitty." The cat refused to budge.

"Urgent call for Ms. Kyot," piped from the com system.

"I'm here," Emer returned, standing to address the caller. "What's urgent?"

A moment of white noise filled the air before the holograph shimmered in midair where Adrian and Stoirm had previously stood. Ms. Cowl stared out, her face drawn and desperate. "Emer?"

"Yes, Brenna. What can I do for you?"

Barely containing the tremor in her voice, Cowl whimpered, "There...have been a...couple of ...of accidents."

Emer's brow shot up. "What sort of accidents?"

Cowl swallowed. "The first happened late this afternoon. A collapse at the dig site where Doctors Berring and Eliz had gone." She hesitated, her eyes refusing to lock on the camera responsible for sending her image. Shuddering, she proceeded. "Dr. Eliz was killed. Dr. Berring survived but is in bad shape. I contacted Fedel'ma on my way back from the hospital. Your aunt had just dropped off Mr. Jase and came straight here to the university. I met with her just a short while ago." Another, longer hesitation preceded, "When she left she said she had a couple of things to do before heading to the hospital to check on Berring. Only..."

Emer tensed. "Only what?"

"Her pod exploded...just after lifting from the landing strip outside our building. There...there was nothing anyone could do."

Emer's pale complexion washed to transparency.

"I'll be right there!" Dylan barked, already halfway to the door.

Cowl's anxious gaze swept the image she was receiving, apparently only now aware that Emer wasn't alone. "No! No. There's nothing can be done. Nothing identifiable left."

Silence weighted the room, broken at last by Emer's choked,

"Thank you." She left Cowl to end the contact. The holograph flickered out.

Numb, Caer stared at the once again empty space, her necklace pulsing warmly with the same fretful flutter as her heart, Cowl's words running through her head. An accident, she said. Or was this, perhaps, connected to the annihilation of Ahira and the attack on Bestor and...and all the rest? Falling back on the chair, tears welled up and overflowed.

Dylan glanced between the two distraught women before going to Emer, ushering her back down on the settee and settling beside her.

"I...I am so sorry." Caer could barely strangle the words out. "This is my fault. All because I have something those...those...people want."

"Don't be ridiculous," Dylan offered softly.

"But if I had never come here...if..."

"You hold no blame in this Ms. DaDhrga. Believe me."

She couldn't believe. Death's shadow had merged with her own, treading every step she took with her. "I'll just...I'll just go upstairs and...and..." Rising, she stumbled from the room. Behind her, she heard Dylan say, "Try and get some rest. We will talk tomorrow."

Guilt carried her aimlessly away from them. Her meandering delivered her, first, to the kitchen, where she walked in circles for a long while. Jenna's face...Jorn's...Fedel'ma's...Mirra's and a thousand others all hung in a visage dripping with blood. Would Bran be next? Oh, please let him change his mind and go far, far away! Maybe he could be safe.

Eventually, Caer's circling broke, her feet wandering back to the hall. The door to the parlor where Dylan and Emer remained was closed, now, light seeping along the edge of the carpet. Muffled sounds of conversation filtered out as she passed. Her steps took her to the stairs, her mind fighting against the ever-increasing swirl of questions as she wound her way up. In the darkness of her room, she stripped from her clothes, donning the light chemise that served as her nightgown. Eyes pinched tight against the renewed flood of tears, she collapsed in bed, the rhythm of the charm's delicate throb pulsing just below the hollow of her throat, echoing that of her mournful heart. For a long while, she refused to touch the necklace. At last, she lay her fingers across the charm, wondering when its pulsing would cease; wondering why this awful thing had come to her.

Struggling against the pain of guilt and grief, she fought through the ache in her temples, searching her mind for the phantoms that shrouded her memories. Did her mother know the significance of the chain? What promise had Caer given that could possibly tie her to any of this? With each effort to push deeper into her past, the agony beat her back. At last, her mind tattered and exhausted, she fell into a fitful sleep.

Drumming. Hands held. Bodies moving as one--forward and back. The dance moves Deocil. One, two, three, four, five, six, seven. One, two, three. One, two, three. Widdershins. One, two, three, four, five, six, seven. One, two, three. One, two, three.

A face in the fire--a woman writhing. Something must be taken from her; something must be found. Reaching out... A white-hot jolt as fingers touch.

Child! You must away! I call upon the guardian! Protect her!

Angry red tongues of flame coil around. Searing pain eats at flesh. Eyes stare down, glowing with a turquoise heat, grim and scowling. Agony gnaws through to her very bones. She opens her mouth but can voice no cry. Grim eyes soften. Cool arms enfold her.

Caer jerked awake. Adrian. They were his eyes. She remembered. There was a great fire on Lillith II. A fire that threatened to devour her. Adrian came. Sidra called for a guardian and Adrian came.

Her flesh raised as other shrouded images clustered beneath the fragments that had just been revealed. She sensed their shadows. Closing her eyes again, she forced the chill and mounting anxieties aside; tried to retrieve the dark visions. Why was there fire? Why had Sidra called out? And why was it that Adrian was the one to respond?

The vision from the nightmare refused to return as anything more than gossamer strips of rippling grays. Again, she tried, her effort snapped short as a surge of energy lit the room, sending hot needle stings chasing along her nerves. Shooting upright, eyes wide, she saw it--the dark and malevolent presence emerging from the electrified rippling of shadows near her.

27

Remorse clamped iron-fisted around Dylan's chest as he took in Emer's slumped, trembling frame and despairing stare. She would shed no tears, though. Those were exhausted long ago. His, the blame for that. Tentatively, he draped his arm around her, fully expecting to be shoved away. Instead, Emer curled quietly against him. For a long while, neither of them moved, the sounds of Caer's restless meandering the only imposition on their silence.

Emer stirred, finally, murmuring, "Del's not gone." The statement sounded more a plea for reassurance than a proclamation of conviction.

Dylan did what he could to keep his doubts from his voice. "Of course not. Her demise leaves the estate in my hands. She isn't about to stand for that."

The faintest hint of amusement glinted briefly in Emer's eyes as she flicked a glance at him. "What makes you think she won't leave everything to me?"

"Ah," Dylan chuckled. "So the two of you worked out a new will, then."

"Don't be an idiot!" Emer snorted. "The terms of her will were established at the Council when you were born. You know that. The estate can only come to me if you are both eliminated."

"My back needs watching, does it?"

Emer struck his arm with a half-hearted punch.

"Seriously," he huffed. "Mother hasn't hung around for more than three thousand years just to be taken out by some little explosion."

"Like mother like son?" Emer's mild amusement dissipated. "There's never any guarantee, though," she sighed. "This might be the time that she can't return. Did you ever consider that, after all these years, Del's soul might be too worn out or weak to transmigrate? Or...or what if she met with a banishing spell?"

Dylan cocked his head. "You're kidding, right? Mother is too damned bullheaded to allow her soul to weaken, much less let a little thing like a banishing spell get through her shielding. She'll turn up soon enough, if for no other reason than to annoy the hell out of me."

The glimmer of amusement returned, this time ticking the ghosting of a smile at the corners of Em's mouth. "You two are impossible."

"Yes. Well." Dylan shrugged. "You've known that for centuries, haven't you?"

"Mmm." Emer's voice lowered slightly as her eyes dropped to a study of her knees. "Nemhain is behind all of this, isn't she? Those of her line aren't just running amuck on their own, anymore. Del always said that the Dark Heart would eventually come out of hiding. I thought...I hoped that the longer Nemhain's absence lasted, the greater the possibility the old hag had met her proper end. Del was right, though." Following a long pause, she ventured, "But why now? Because of the key? How did Nemhain learn it was whole, again? And how did she discover the identity of the bearer?"

Dylan withdrew his arm from her shoulders and rocked forward, resting his elbows on his knees, his chin on his doubled fists. "We don't know that Nemhain is aware of the key's status. Her interest in Caer may be for other reasons. Perhaps someone from her clan had a chance encounter with Caer, recently. We may be a rare breed, you and I, but we are not the only Witches capable of noting the amount of magical energy emanating from her. Given that Caer is not listed in the Family Archives, said individual might conclude as I did--that Caer is Tanai. Nemhain would not take kindly to the idea of the rise of an entirely new line of Witches. It would account for the fact that someone tried to murder Caer before she left Ahira and again at the mat-trans station."

"You honestly think the attempt had nothing to do with the key?"

"Any Witch who values their soul would be insane to attempt the assassination of a person thought to be carrying one or both pieces of the key. Whichever piece the victim carried would vanish before the perpetrator could identify its form. No one within Nemhain's line would risk bringing her wrath upon them by such an action."

Emer gave a reluctant nod. "Seems obvious that the ones we encountered on Slieve na Calliagh hadn't worked out the key's form, at least." Her lips pursed as she regarded Dylan obliquely. "But you knew."

"Not at first. Took me a while before I realized that not all the energy emanating from Caer was hers. Something lay beneath her power. When I finally caught a glimpse of the chain she wore--Shannon's chain--a few things started to make sense." Noting Emer's knotted brow, he admitted, "Yes, I recognized the chain as Shannon's. Caer kept it tucked inside her jumpsuit when she was on campus, hence the delay in my discovering it. My opportunity came when I saw her dancing at the High Fancies Club, one evening. The shirt she wore was open at the neck, revealing the glint of her fine silver necklace. I was almost certain merely from that glimpse but decided closer investigation might provide confirmation. The next day I asked her to my office to discuss her progress on her thesis, getting close to her under the pretext of reading some of her work over her shoulder. There was no question of the faint signature of Shannon's magic imprinted on the chain."

He fell silent for several minutes, staring across the room into the now low tongues of red and orange that curled and hissed within the fireplace. "I can't say what made me consider, at that moment, the possibility that the chain was part of the key, but when I did, everything seemed to fit. Shannon must have allowed Dana, or perhaps Roisin, to imbue the pieces of her little treasure with the powers of the key before sending them back separately. The charm came to me. The chain was sent elsewhere, though it remains a mystery how it came into Caer's mother's hands." He shook his head. "I'm a fool for sending the charm to Caer. That she attached it to the chain is no surprise. What I didn't anticipate was her ending up on the slopes of Slieve na Calliagh, much less that the necklace would throb like a bloody beacon, there. Little wonder Maura detected its presence, if not its form."

Emer frowned. "Why such a flare on the hill?"

"Perhaps Slieve na Calliagh, itself, caused the surge."

Emer's blank gaze prompted, "Consider, Em. That hill is the nexus for the veins of magic that extend outward into the world. Perhaps the key was reacting to the strength of the forces there. Even on the hill, though there appears to be a limit to the distance over which the magic of the key's making and breaking can be detected. As strong as the throbbing was, I wasn't aware of it until seconds before I joined you and Mother. And as soon as we returned to the estate, the magic dropped back to a level that is only faintly discernible. I doubt Maura or Nemhain are capable of locating it, here."

Emer's jaw tightened. "Perhaps not. But Maura has successfully identified Caer, now. Shouldn't be long before she passes that little tidbit along to her mother."

"Maybe not. The morons on the hill were unable to take either Caer or the key. Nemhain will not be pleased with their allowing her treasure to slip away. The hunt is on, of course, at least with regards to Maura. Whether she can trace the magic of our teleportation back to the estate, I can't say. I did what I could to confuse the path. Still, we will need to take Caer elsewhere, soon."

Emer considered in silence, briefly. "If you suspected the significance of Shannon's chain and charm, why didn't you keep the charm safely hidden?"

"I expected you and Mother would figure out what Caer

possessed. I thought she and the key would be far better protected in yours and Mother's keeping."

Emer jerked her head up, her eyes narrowing. "You didn't expect to survive Ahira, did you? You knew Ahira was about to be blown apart. How? I've not known you to possess any foresight."

"Let's just say that the warning came from a nightmare, the impact of which left me seriously concerned about my prospects."

For several seconds Emer's scrutiny remained on him. He was certain she grasped that the nightmare was not his. She declined to pursue that aspect, though, choosing instead to press, "If you were so worried, why didn't you leave with Caer?"

Dylan pushed to his feet. "There was no reasonable way to do so," he muttered, his weary stroll carrying him first to the windows, then to the fireplace to stoke the fire with more pellets. "As it was, a great deal of fast talking and a very large bribe were required to obtain a shuttle seat for Caer on such short notice. And before you ask, teleporting out would not have been wise. How long do you think it would take for the authorities to come after me as a suspect in Ahira's destruction, had I unexpectedly turned up Earth-side with no rational explanation for how I managed to get here so quickly, and without any record of a shuttle trip to one of the mat-trans stations?" He'd never mentioned to Em that he was already a suspect for the murder in Caer's apartment. This hardly seemed a good time to add that information. "Luckily, Eliz filed a record of Caer's acceptance to Sion immediately after our meeting, providing me a verifiable reason for her departure. Better, however, for 'Hugh Jorn' to go up in smoke, wiping out any possibility of drawing suspicion my way. I don't need Security dogging my every step."

Emer's scowl followed him. "Well, you damn well took your sweet time in getting back to us."

"I needed to guarantee that my new vessel would not be recognized, either by Earthers or by any surviving Ahiran refugees who might find their way here. I acquired this dearly departed fellow's body in one of the more remote colonies, then had to wait until I'd recovered sufficient strength to accomplish the triple jump necessary for teleporting back from such a distance."

"You could at least have sent word. You had Del and me nearly beside ourselves with grief." Emer dismissed his attempted comment with an agitated flip of her hand. "So. Did your recovery time allow you any new insights regarding the current situation? If Maura and her ugly squad only figured out the identity of the key's bearer on Slieve na Calliagh and aren't likely to tell Nemhain right away, why has the Dark Heart slithered out of the darkness now?"

"Jase may be the reason."

"Jase? Why?"

"Sensitive. Remember? Nemhain has always taken a personal interest in searching out and seeing to the elimination of Sensitives. Someone from her line obviously learned of Mr. Jase and his family. News that Sensitives were yet running about would not be taken lightly."

"Yet, she sent her goons after Caer, first."

Dylan massaged his temples. "I'm only guessing, here, but I suspect the assassins discovered Caer after arriving on Ahira in pursuit of Jase. Getting close to him also put them close to her. Close enough for a sufficiently gifted Witch to note Caer's tremendous potential. With all indications suggesting her to be Tanai, eliminating her became their priority."

"You don't suppose..." Emer fixed Dylan with a darkly contemplative stare. "You don't suppose Jase was the one to tell Nemhain's hit squad about her? Maybe they hunted him for the purpose of using him."

"Oh, they undoubtedly planned to play with him for their amusement. As for any serious plan to use him, to what end? I seriously doubt Jase can distinguish between a Witch and some poor Tanai whose only claim to magic is some flimsy ability to scoot a thimble a centimeter or two along a tabletop. He couldn't single Caer out as someone with any significant potential. Nemhain had to learn of her through some other source."

Emer chewed the edge of her lip. "You don't really believe it, do you? That Caer's Tanai."

"I did at first," he acknowledged, turning to lean against the fireplace surround. "And, unfortunately, I did a very thorough job of convincing both Berring and Eliz. If Nemhain's spies infiltrated either woman's staff and accessed whatever records they keep, or worse, learned of her directly from one of them..." He waived off Emer's starting protest. "I don't believe either of them would give over such information willingly, Em. That doesn't rule out Nemhain's ability get what she wants from people. Their conviction that Caer is Tanai, alone, would be proof enough for the Dark Heart to order her assassination." He sighed. "And no. I no longer believe Caer is Tanai."

For several minutes, Emer sat glumly studying her hands, at last submitting, "All right. Let's say Nemhain suspected Jase to be a Sensitive and learned of Caer while her assassins sought him out. That's only two people. Why take out an entire colony?"

"You're too young, Em. Maybe you don't remember the centuries before Nemhain's sisters split the key, hid the pieces, and then went into hiding; the time before Nemhain finally disappeared. She's always been prone to untold violence with little regard for who she slaughtered. Death and destruction. They're part of the Dark Heart's nature." Fatigue burdened Dylan's sigh. Hell of a day, expending the energy to teleport from such a distance, only to be faced with another, albeit shorter trip halfway around Earth to do battle on Slieve na Calliagh.

In his silence, Emer twisted strands of her hair between her fingers, her face creased in thought. "Poor Mr. Jase. Here he is, caught up in a bloody feud he had nothing to do with, and me thinking he might be the one to bring Nemhain's hounds after Caer."

Dylan flinched at the soft-around-the-edges quality Emer's tone had taken on. He could guess what was coming.

"I think we need to protect him as well as Caer, even if he doesn't want our help."

"Of course you do," he groaned.

Emer leaned forward, jabbing a finger in his direction. "You're not as hard-assed as you want everyone to believe. Your better qualities were always more obvious on Ahira than when you're here. Your mother and I seem to draw out your coarser edges." Before Dylan could object, she added, "By the way, you really haven't picked up some minor gift in prescience, have you?"

The question caught Dylan off guard. "Of course not. Why would you ask? If I had even the glimmer of that attribute, your gift would tell you so."

"Maybe," she sniffed. "You're pretty good at hiding things from me, though."

"Such as?"

"Such as how you managed to know when to send Caer away from Ahira."

Dylan scowled, wondering why Em would come full circle back to this issue. "It was Caer's nightmare that warned me," he replied, an edge to his voice. He preferred not to get into the specifics. Em, however, would continue to pester him until he explained. "Not that she was aware of doing so. I'm convinced she has no clue regarding any of her gifts, including her prescience. It's another reason I sent her to you and Mother. I am aware of the strength of magic that resides in Caer, but I lack the ability to identify her specific attributes. I figured you and Mother could sort her out."

Emer wrinkled her nose disconcertedly. "Yes. I detected the prescience about her. But what's this business about her nightmare?"

"She had one. I drew it out to see what had terrorized her slumber. Since there was nothing either of us could do to alter such an impending event, I saw no point in alarming her with memory of the dream. So, I spelled it into submission."

Emer sank back, eyeing him. Instead of pressing him for details regarding his presence as Caer slept, however, she said, "Clueless about her gifts. Very strange. I have the same impression, though. Confirmation came when I had O-4 take that detour to the warehouse. Caer seemed not to recognize her mounting fears as a sign of forewarning. But I knew them for what they were."

"What warehouse?"

"What really bothers me, however," she continued, ignoring his question, her face creasing with anxiety. "is that I can't seem to get a good read on this girl to ascertain what other gifts she may have. Maybe I'm losing my ability to identify the specific nature of Witches' attributes."

"I've never heard of such a thing, Em. Witches don't just lose their gifts. An attribute may temporarily weaken due to fatigue, but..."

Still ignoring him, she mumbled, "It's like...like...like Caer's abilities are wrapped in several layers of wet blanket. Only this fragment of prescience flickered to the surface."

"So long as we're on the topic," Dylan broached. "How did you know to leave your message for me in the library this afternoon? So far as I'm aware, foresight is not one of your gifts, either."

Emer cast him a puzzled glance. "Say what?"

"This afternoon," he repeated. "You certainly imprinted your message with a vengeance, telling me where to find you and your need of my assistance. The imprinting slammed me almost before I completed my teleportation back to the estate. How did you know I was about to turn up?"

Shifting slightly, she cast a sheepish glance at the floor. "I thought I felt the faint resonance of your returning just prior to our leaving. I imprinted the message in the library because that seemed the most predictable place for you to arrive."

"Predictable," he grumbled. "Have to do something about that." An annoyed huff prefaced, "Must have been Mother, then, who was close enough to Caer and Jase to be whisked off with them and alert you."

"Actually, Merripen alerted us. Del set the cat to shadow Caer from the moment the poor girl first arrived. Merri's immediate fright response when she was teleported along with Caer and Jase raised the alarm. Del's connection with Merri allowed her to see where they were and... Oh my. Merri!"

Scooting from the settee, Emer knelt to search the shadows beneath. "I forgot she was down here. Poor kitty. I'm guessing she sensed what happened to Del this evening. The two have always had a really strong connection." She held out her hand and called softly. "Merripen. Come, Sweet. Come out." The cat remained firmly rooted in the shadows.

Dylan stiffened, awareness of a familiar presence at last registering. "No."

"What?"

"She wouldn't."

Emer straightened, staring at him. "Who wouldn't what?"

"Mother is here, Em. I'm so accustomed to the sense of her presence, here, that I wasn't paying attention to what should be a lack of it until... She's here. I'm an imbecile not to have noticed the moment Merri darted in." Crossing to the settee, Dylan squatted, reaching under and hauling the cat out by the scruff of its neck.

"Dylan! Don't be so rough! I'm sure Merri must be suffering from a terrible shock!"

"More than you can imagine, I'll wager." Holding the cat up, he peered into its eyes. "Mother, tell me you're not in there."

Emer snatched Merripen from Dylan, cradling and stroking the trembling lump of fur. "Are you out of your mind? We don't transmigrate into animals. Too risky, both the getting in and the getting out. If Del needs to return before she can find an appropriate, freshly deceased human vessel..." A shudder produced a pronounced tremor to Emer's voice. "She knows...knows I would allow her to merge with me."

"You're either crazy or a saint," Dylan jeered. "There is no way in the universe I would want Mother sharing my head."

"I'm sure she wouldn't like doing so any more than you! Doesn't matter. She'll find a body soon enough. You'll see. She knows we need her." Glowering mightily, Emer plopped back down on the settee and turned the jittery cat to face her, stating with somewhat less conviction, "She wouldn't do anything as stupid as merging with Merri."

The faintest whisper touched their minds. *"Stupid, am I? Just give me a few more seconds. I'm having trouble getting...getting the telepathy to work properly. Cats don't think the way we do."*

Emer inhaled so sharply it whistled. Holding the cat at arm's length, she managed an anguished and breathy, "No!"

"Yes," came back, a little stronger than the initial whisper. *"You can sense Dylan's return but not mine, huh? And what does he mean, calling me bullheaded?"*

Dylan suddenly erupted in peals of laughter.

Emer glared at him. "Dylan Hugh Jordan MacFaolan! This isn't funny!"

"No? No? Mother has become far more familiar with her familiar than I suspect she ever wished to be." His laughter rolled again.

Emer opened her mouth, but whatever deriding remark she intended to make was promptly swallowed. So, too, was Dylan's mirth as a faint charge raised his flesh. Judging from the fact that Emer was rubbing her arms, she appeared to share the reaction. She exchanged a disturbed glance with him as he struggled to pinpoint the source of the charge. It was too hazy to be emanating from within the room, though it was most certainly coming from somewhere in the house. The strength of the intrusion suddenly redoubled, giving the telltale charge of a teleportation spell. With it came a malevolence Dylan wished he had not recognized. In that same instant, Caer's terrorized scream echoed through the halls above.

28

The explosion of electrified air from Dylan's abrupt teleportation slammed him into the room he knew had been given over to Caer. The force of it also slammed him against a large chest, the impact driving his breath from his lungs, prompting a rasped series of expletives. Damn his mother for her habit of constantly rearranging the furniture in every room!

The air still crackled from his overdriven and flawed entrance when the pop of pressure of a second charge snapped Emer into existence a few paces from him. Gasping, her hands flew to cover her nose and mouth. "By all the...! What is that smell?"

"Coran'ian," Dylan snarled, regaining his breath. Hands raised, palms turned outward in readiness to counter the attack he expected, he set his gaze to a swift sweep of the area. With no attack forthcoming, he turned his attention briefly to Caer, who sat slumped on the bed, pallid and shaking but alive. Relieved, he made a more extensive scan. The beast was close. The charge along Dylan's nerves told him so. But where?

Tracing the line of Caer's terrorized stare, he edged cautiously around the end of the bed. There, in front of the closet, sat the hunched form of the massive creature, crumpled and twitching, the faint remnants of a remarkably powerful stun spell hanging in the confines of the room.

Dylan had no time to consider how Caer could cast a spell so powerful as to knock a Coran'ian senseless, nor could he take proper aim for a kill spell. Without warning, the creature shifted and lunged at him, crushing him windless to the floor, the blast meant for the Coran'ian's skull gouging a smoldering score across the closet doors. Frantically, Dylan snatched at the thick, snarled hair, the creature's reek a suffocating cloud engulfing him, the pain of raking claws tearing across his right shoulder blade. A flash of light and a scorch of energy seared the air mere centimeters from his face, throwing the Coran'ian sideways. Dylan instantly rolled away, the smell of burning fur and flesh adding to the putrid air. Another blast brought a deafening howl that grew to an agonized crescendo as the beast vanished in a bloodied shockwave of expelled magic.

Dylan shot a glance across to Emer, who stood wide-eyed, her palms still poised. He couldn't recall the last time she'd used a kill spell. It wasn't in her nature. Thankfully, Em's reaction had been instantaneous, her aim true. A mere fraction off and she might well have fried him along with the beast.

Pushing slowly to his knees, he muttered, "Thanks, Em. I owe you--again."

"Yeah," she warbled faintly, her hands falling limp at her sides. "Maybe...maybe I should keep score."

"You'd be denying Mother one of her primary joys," he managed through a wash of vertigo. Steeling himself with a long, deliberate breath, he added, "How's Caer?"

Caer hesitantly scooted to the edge of the bed, her eyes as wild as Emer's, her voice no steadier. "I'm...I'm fine. I..."

A disturbance at the periphery of Dylan's vision made him jump, sending a slash of molten pain through his right shoulder and impressing on him the urgent fact that he'd not escaped the fray unscathed. Another attack might well be his end. Palms again aimed, he made a cautious turn, spotting Merripen as the cat slunk from the shadows near the wall.

"You're late," he rasped. "And no help at all." Struggling to his feet, agony again sliced along his shoulder, this time blazing down his back and the length of his arm. Through clenched teeth he declared, "Your 'death', Mother dear, has left the shielding here too compromised to repair quickly. We need to get Caer out."

His mother sent a sadly resigned, *"Agreed."*

"Are you all right?" Emer asked.

Thankfully, Dylan found her question directed at Caer. He couldn't afford to let her know he was injured. She'd insist on fussing over him, and they had no time for that.

Still trembling from head to toe, Caer managed, "Uh...yeah. Just..." Swallowing, she eyed the blood spatters where the Coran'ian had been. "That...that thing went for my necklace. The moment he grabbed it, we both went flying."

Dylan bit back another burst of expletives. Maura and company had figured it out, then--the manifestation of the key. But why would they try to take it? They knew the thing would be protected; knew that any attempt to take it by force would not go well for the assailant. Were they merely testing their hypothesis regarding the key's form, or were they testing the strength of its protections?

The pain in his shoulder intensified, the heat of it boiling down the full length of his right side, leaving his knees rubbery beneath him. The act of remaining lucid and keeping his agony from his voice was almost more than he could manage. "They'll send another beast or three. The sooner we're out of here, the better."

Emer shook her head. "Where are we to go? If Del's shielding spells failed to keep that monster out, where can we possibly be safe?"

"Dylan is right. The spells failed because of my brief death."

"My place will be safe. Em, can you grab Mother?"

Emer scooped Merripen into her arms. "I'm not going to be much help with the teleporting. You've never bothered to share the secret of finding your hideaway."

Dylan locked his knees, trying to fight his precarious sway. "Wouldn't be much of a hideaway if people knew how to find it. Just...stand close. Caer, you as well."

Caer hesitated but a heartbeat, looking dazed and confused as she eyed the cat. She required no further urging, however, collecting herself from the bed and sidling in as close to him on one side as Emer did on the other. Willing himself to remain upright, he called his sanctuary to his mind. So familiar was it that every aspect of the image clarified practically of its own accord. No sooner did he feel the brush of the women next to him than the room blinked out and the other space, dark and cold, gained a slightly lurching reality.

Satisfied that they'd arrived, Dylan sank to his knees on the hard stone floor, throbbing heat eating from his shoulder to his fingertips and all the way down his back to his leg. His misting gaze searched out Emer as she set the cat to the floor and began moving about in the darkness. The Family's gift of shadow sight allowed her to find her way with reasonable ease.

"What?" Caer mumbled, her voice tinged with doubt. "No big blast for our arrival?"

Dylan knew she remained near him. It pained him too much, though, to turn and look for her.

Emer chuckled. "Apparently, Dylan didn't need to show off for you, this time. It's about time he demonstrated his subtler side."

Her meandering carried her to the center of the great hall where she stood with fists jammed to her hips, the glow of her eyes searching. "Oh, please. Don't tell me you never updated this place!" At last, with a triumphant, "Ah ha!" she marched to the nearest of a series of small niches set in the walls. With a point of her finger, the wick of a lamp sparked to a flickering glow. "Leave it to you," she huffed, "to always do things the hard way. I can't believe you never bothered to install fuel cells here. Must be some testosterone thing, this stupid notion of cloistering yourself away periodically with no amenities."

"Emer..." Fear tinged Caer's tone. Dylan felt her drop down beside him; felt her hands supporting him.

"Emer, he's hurt."

"What?"

"It's nothing," he forced. "Just...I need a chair."

Emer's startled expression told him she detected the lie in his words. Spinning around, she cast anxiously about. "Where the bloody inferno are the chairs?"

Unable to comment further, much less track her, Dylan could do no more than wait. Though it felt an eternity, he supposed only a matter of seconds elapsed before Emer appeared at his side. "We need to get him to the dais," she said. His teeth clamped into his lip so hard that he tasted blood as she and Caer hoisted him up by the armpits. It was a serious struggle to make his feet move, especially since their destination seemed a universe away.

Between them, the two women managed to mostly drag him the length of the great hall and up the two steps. There, they carefully settled him on the large wooden table that occupied the center of the dais. Staying seated on it, however, provided another major issue. Somewhere along the trek across the hall, shaking took Dylan, further intensifying the pain and robbing him of any sense of balance. Served him right for being an idiot. Of course, the shielding spells protecting the estate were weakened by the death of his mother's body. If Starn could break through before they were weakened, Maura would certainly be capable of tracing Caer's whereabouts and teleporting her beast through afterward.

"Dull witted," he muttered.

From somewhere near at hand, he heard Em's momentary swearing, followed by the sound of heavy scraping. Through his misted sight, Dylan noted that she was working her way to the back of the table upon which he now teetered, apparently thumping into the bench that ran its length. Her hold on him never faltered, though, even as she shoved the bench out of the way with her legs. Remarkable woman, Emer. Always there when he needed her. He should have been there for her. Should have... He tried to fix her in his now swimming vision. "I'm sorry, Em." His mouth was so cottony, he wasn't sure his muttering sounded anything like the words he'd intended.

"Sorry for what? For being the dull-witted imbecile you just fessed to? For always being such an obnoxious pain in the ass?" She eased him onto his side. "I forgive you."

Ripping his shirt free of his back, Emer sucked in sharply, her breath hissing between her teeth. He could feel her trembling as she carefully replaced the torn fabric across his shoulder. Her voice almost as tremulous as the hands that pressed the shirt against him, she commanded, "Spell of healing to begin. Poison slow, blood to flow, damage cease therein." She'd scarcely finished when she demanded, "Herbs. Do you have any?"

Sweat ran from Dylan's face. Em's spell may be slowing the poison, but the effort to concentrate long enough to formulate a response was still excruciating. "Kitchen," he forced. "Just...just don't let Mother rearrange anything while she's here."

Constricted as it was, Emer's tight chuckle was worth the pained effort of his comment.

"Yeah, like you have anything to rearrange," she returned. "Now shut up and lie still. Caer, over here, please. I need for you to put pressure on this."

Caer's quick, barefooted patter tracked her progress as she rounded the table. Her small hands replaced Emer's, again pressing the cold dampness of his shirt against his shoulder blade. Renewed flushes of heat and agony set stars dancing in his head. His sharp moan brought Caer's squeaked, "I'm sorry!", though, like Emer, her hands didn't flinch.

"Just keep the pressure on," Emer called. I need to find a few things. I'll be right back."

Dylan closed his eyes, no longer willing to fight for consciousness. Em would take care of him. She always made things right.

29

Caer braced against the table, praying for steady hands as she pressed the bloodied cloth against as large a swath of Dylan's wounds as their span allowed. Just how deeply the claw marks ran she couldn't tell. Emer had been too quick to replace his tattered shirt over them. Judging from Emer's expression, though, the wounds were bad. Closing her eyes, Caer murmured, "Please. Find what you need and call for help quickly. We can't let him die. No more deaths."

The feel of warm blood oozing between her fingers brought her eyes open again. A tiny rivulet of sticky red also seeped from beneath her palms, pooling on the table and dripping to the floor. Where her chemise touched the table's edge, a damp, dark stain wicked up the front, adhering the flimsy garment to her abdomen.

Caer stared at the man stretched out on the table. He was losing too much blood. His pulse was rapid and thin, his breathing labored. Leaning slightly, she noted the ghastly paleness of his face. This man...Dylan...he didn't even know her, yet he risked his life to protect her. Twice. First on that hill, then at the estate. All in the span of a single day. And his reward?

Her breath rattled as she struggled to calm her thoughts. There had to be something more she could do for him. Something...

Words. Words held tremendous power when infused with the proper will. Her Aunt Sidra told her that once...long ago...in another place. It seemed an eternity since her childhood, yet that statement rose clearly in her mind. Words have power. Speak the right ones. Fill them with purpose. Will them to action.

"Let him live," Caer whispered. adjusting her hands, trying to cover more of Dylan's wounds. "Let him live." But she felt no power in her words. He could die and she could do nothing more than wait and pray Emer returned immediately. Tears stung her eyes as she turned her gaze away. If she didn't watch, perhaps death wouldn't take him.

Blinking past the tears, she forced her attention to other things. Like the dozen oil lamps set within the wall niches that ran the length of the hall on both sides. She'd watched Emer's silhouette moving about in the darkness. Saw the sparks ignite from her fingertips to light the first two lamps. The rest flicked to life as Emer scurried past them moments ago.

Caer continued her survey of the room. The enormous cavity flickered in the wan light, the dance of irregular shadows giving vague definition to the long, broad hall, while dark and darker patterns played off the peeling, white-washed plaster of the walls and jigged fitfully along the dusty floor. At last, her gaze came to rest on the massive stone fireplace. Stretching floor to ceiling, it stood centered on the long wall to her left, its darkened maw large enough to swallow her whole. If mere words or wishes could accomplish the feat, she would quickly have it blazing with heat and light. Her wishes, of course, had no effect. The hearth remained cold and dark.

Flanking it, she noted, were two high, arched and shuttered windows, thin bands of pale light seeping in through the narrow wooden slats. Beneath the furthest window stood a rectangular table like the one on which Dylan lay. The space beneath the nearer one held a box, the contents of which she couldn't make out. A solitary, matching window was situated midway along the wall to her right. The light seeping between the slats of its shutters was somewhat more intense, the striping of its light and shadow slowly creeping further out along the floor. Beneath this single window, a smaller table held lonely vigil, dust stirring in the faint illumination that fell to it. Caer wished mightily that the shutters of each window could be thrown back to cast aside the sense of desperation that threatened to drown her in this bleak place.

Dismally, she peered at last into the twisting jitter of shadows that teased down the center of the hall's length. Only emptiness lay there. No tables. No benches. In the far corner of the right wall, the outline of a closed door could be distinguished. An exit, perhaps, though Emer hadn't gone that way. She'd disappeared through the only other apparent exit from the hall--a yawning abyss of an archway slightly left of center on the back wall. Clanging noises rang in hollow echoes from the black fissure.

The noises at last ceased and Emer emerged, striding toward the large table beneath the furthest window. A bulk of cloth was draped over her shoulder, and her arms were filled with bowls and spoons.

"At least he's not a complete barbarian," she grumbled aloud. "He's upgraded the plumbing. And it even works." Laying her accumulated items out on the table, Emer quickly headed back to the abyss. Caer stared after her. What was she doing?

When Emer returned the second time, she wore a full-length smock over her jumpsuit. Pausing before the fireplace, she mumbled something Caer couldn't make out. Instantly, a large black cauldron appeared at her feet, sloshing with water. Bracing a shoulder against the edge of the hearth, Emer swung out a long metal rod and hoisted the caldron's handle over it, then repositioned the hanging cauldron over the fireplace's empty interior.

For the next few minutes, the woman set about collecting several handfuls of pellets from the box beneath the nearer window, carefully spreading a level bed of them beneath the enormous pot. Finally, wiping her hands on the sides of her smock, she extended a palm toward her handiwork. "From air unite, spark for light, heat to burn." A burst of blue flame flashed from her hand, setting the pellets ablaze.

"I suppose," she muttered, "that a fuel cell to heat this place, provide hot water, and a decent source of light really was too much to expect of him. I will never understand why he likes it this way."

Returning to the table that held her supplies, Emer hauled it away from the wall far enough to allow clearance all the way around, stopping briefly to lean a hand against its top. "Damn," she moaned. "This is too much all at once. It's been far too long since I've needed to call up so many spells in such quick succession. Centuries of quiet, and now this!" Shooting a glare at the cat as it stalked the shadows at the room's periphery, she snorted, "And you're no help at all!"

With a frustrated shake of her head, she proceeded to the back side of the table where she could view Caer and Dylan. "How's he doing?" she asked, reaching into various pockets down the front of the smock to withdraw several pouches and a small jar.

Caer ventured a hasty glance. Dylan's face had gone from pale to gray. At least he was still breathing. "He's alive," she managed, unable to choke out, 'just barely'.

"He'll stay that way if he knows what's good for him!"

"Have you called someone? Are medics on the...?"

"The Tanai can't help him," Emer returned. "Even if they could find this place." Fixing her attention on the items she'd laid out, she set to work, her shoulder-length black hair framing her intense features and accenting the distinct indigo glow of her eyes.

Somewhere in the buried recesses of Caer's consciousness, something stirred. A memory, perhaps. She tried to concentrate on it. The glow of the eyes. It had significance. The knowledge was there. She just had to find a way to access it. Later, though. When she possessed the time and energy to devote to it. In the meantime, she prayed the amber would once again ignite within Dylan's eyes. Surely, the glow would be verification that death was turning its back on him.

Emer's voice drifted softly to the dais once more, her words rising and falling in the unmistakable cadence of a chant, though they were spoken too quietly for Caer to discern. As the chant continued, pungent aromas wafted through the musty air. Nostalgic smells. Calendula. Chamomile. Perhaps skullcap. And...

Her small hands worked methodically, cutting the flower heads from the calendula. Sidra smiled down at her. "When you are done with those, child, the comfrey needs harvesting."

A sudden ache of homesickness swept Caer. So often she'd dealt with such herbs, working at her aunt's side in their little garden. This much she remembered clearly. Sidra spent most of her physician's pay to obtain the special soils, seeds, and seedlings--all imported from distant worlds. Together, she and her aunt tended the plants with such care, the soils smelling so rich, especially when damp. And the herbs each held their own distinct perfumes. Caer longed for the security of Sidra's calm presence, longed for all those hours spent helping with the planting, the tending, and the harvesting.

There is much to do before daybreak. Bark and leaf of white oak and ash; leaf, twig, and berry of belladonna. The night is not right for the gathering of the black willow bark. Still, there is much to be found that might help. Must help. I am the eldest. She is my responsibility. I will not lose my little sister. How could Nemhain have done this?

"You all right?"

Emer's unexpected proximity made Caer jump. "Uh...Yes. I just...I, uh..." Blinking, she tried to recall the vision that had just vanished, leaving a rush of profound sorrow, anguish, and rage. Instead, her attention was caught by the pile of cloth strips and the two large bowls Emer had placed near Dylan's shoulder. One bowl was filled with clear, steaming water, the other with a brew of steeping herbs.

Gently lifting Caer's hands from Dylan's wounds, Emer peeled away the torn pieces of blood-soaked shirt, revealing the deep and jagged gashes where the Coran'ian's claws had raked along his right shoulder blade, exposing the bone. A red streak ran down his back, disappearing beneath the remaining tatters of his shirt. Another extended halfway along the back of his right arm. Caer's heart lurched to her stomach.

Emer's tense murmur of, "Blood poisoning," confirmed Caer's fear.

Wiping her shaking hands on her chemise, Caer shook her head, denying what her eyes told her. "It can't be. It's not possible for it to happen so quickly."

"Nothing is impossible where magic is concerned," Emer muttered. Closing her eyes, she extended her hands just above the damaged shoulder, palms down, her lips moving silently. It seemed an eternity that she remained thus. Finally, she dropped her hands to her sides, her eyes opening at the sound of Caer's stunned inhale. The bleeding of Dylan's wounds had lessened, his dark blood turning a bit brighter, the ugly red streaks running down his back and his arm slowly diminishing.

Recognizing the need to do something more than gape, Caer set to soaking and wringing excess hot water from some of the rags. When she'd accumulated a fair pile, she began bathing the wounds, discarding bloodied ones to the floor and replacing them with fresh. Emer shuddered slightly, then gave a faint smile, nodding her appreciation for Caer's assistance. With a slow, weary breath, the woman began soaking strips of cloth in the tea-colored brew, stirring the smell of clove, thyme, and southernwood into the already heady mix of aromas.

Caer took up several more cloths, placing them in the hot water to soak, gingerly retrieving and wringing one at a time to continue her part in cleansing the wounds. Her words scarcely a whisper, she ventured, "Magic allowed poisoning to set in so quickly?"

"Magic coupled with the venom from that beast. Yes."

"And your magic stopped it?"

"That is my hope."

"The...Coran'ian." Caer breathed out a long exhale. "I don't know anything about such creatures. I never even heard of them before...before..."

Emer nodded. "I've never encountered such a beast before, either. At least not up close, though I've seen the damage they can do. A Coran'ian's venom would be trouble enough in its own right. It kills slowly, painfully. The damage inflicted here acted much more quickly, as the beast's toxins have been magically enhanced."

"I can't," Caer murmured.

"Can't what?"

"Magic." Caer cast a sidelong glance at Emer, her furrowed brow beginning to produce a headache. "I can't get my...my brain around it. How can I accept the impossible? First, I'm expected to believe that everything I saw you...saw Fedel'ma and...and..." She nodded toward Dylan. "And him...and Adrian and Stoirm..." Licking her lips, she sucked in and expelled a shorter breath. "What I saw all of you do was magic. I'll admit, I have no better explanation for any of it. But...but now you're telling me that creatures like...like that beast...are capable of such feats, as well."

Emer shrugged. "Until your friend Stoirm showed up, I believed humans were the only species to hold such powers. The ancient stories, of course, spoke of Stoirm's kind, the Alainn, having equal or even greater gifts than we. But we've believed for centuries that the Alainn no longer exist. Some believe they never did."

"You mean Stoirm is the only one left of his kind?"

"I don't know. Perhaps we will have an opportunity to ask him. Those who persist in believing in them say the Alainn removed themselves to regions well beyond our colonies, choosing to have nothing to do with us. Not that I would blame them. We humans are not always known for playing nicely with our neighbors. Whether there are other Alainn still existent or not, Stoirm seems proof enough that at least some of them possessed magical capabilities. How creatures like the Coran'ian came to possess magic, however, I can't begin to imagine. The beasts are barely sentient. How can they hold the necessary incantations in their minds?"

Sighing, Emer gestured to the cloths she'd been stirring in the herbal brew. "Try using some of these, now," she suggested, moving away and heading back to the table laden with other bowls and bottles and such.

By the time Caer had exhausted the herb-steeped rags, Emer returned carrying a smaller bowl. This one contained a viscous yellow substance that emitted a whole new array of potent smells, none of which Caer recognized. Emer spread a thick layer of the ointment over Dylan's deep wounds, then covered them with several more cloth strips from the clear water. That done, she motioned for Caer's assistance. Between them, they rolled Dylan sufficiently to wipe down the bloodied table before binding clean, dry lengths of cloth over the damp ones on Dylan's back, tying them around his shoulder and across his chest.

Exhaustion overtaking her, Caer slumped onto the bench Emer had earlier kicked aside, her gaze dully following Emer as the woman used the last of the soaking cloths to clean the blood from the floor. She should help. Instead, Caer remained sitting, watching Emer until the woman headed for whatever room lay at the back of the hall. For a long while after, Caer sat staring at the man on the table, her shaking hands absently rubbing her arms, though whether to rid herself of the chill that hung about the hall or to ease her bone-aching fatigue she couldn't say. Gradually, Dylan's color improved, his breath coming more easily. He would be all right. He would. The man was strong. She'd sensed it the moment he appeared on that hill. It was the same sort of strength she'd felt in the presence of Jorn. Her frown shifted to a faint cock of a brow. Maybe the two were related. It might explain why Jorn had apparently spoken to Dylan about her; why Dylan reminded her so much of Jorn.

The weight of her guilt and sorrow in combination with her weariness, at last, overwhelmed her, tears flooding her eyes and running streams down her face. "Don't die," she whispered. "You mustn't. I can't take another death on my account." If she could just understand what was so important about her necklace...why the chain and charm should both fall into her hands.

I take up this task freely, though it leads me through darkness and danger. I believe in the sanctity of Slievgall'ion. I trust in and pledge my life to Dana and Roisin. To this cause, I commit myself. I so swear it.

Caer's breath caught, ghosted whispers of ancient stories muddling in her head. The names. Dana. Roisin. Sisters. There was a third. Nemhain. Long ago, her mother sang the songs of their myth to her. She could almost hear her mother's voice, soft and sweet, weaving the refrains through flowing rhythms. The lyrics. She struggled to concentrate, but the words were lost to her. Still...they had something to do with a key. And there was something about a dance. Always, a dance was involved.

Emer's return startled Caer from her thoughts.

"Sorry," Emer mumbled, settling next to her. "So much for you to digest. It's no wonder you're jumpy. Thanks for your help, by the way. Here." Handing a couple of fresh, warmly wet rags over, she added, "Thought you might like to clean up a little. I'll heat up enough water for a proper bath later."

Caer gave her face, arms, and hands a couple of nominal swipes before gesturing toward Dylan. "He'll be all right, won't he?"

Emer didn't answer right away. When she did, her voice strained beneath the burden of her fatigue and concern. "I hope so. I can't imagine how he managed to teleport us here, especially with the Coran'ian's magic hastening the effects of its venom. I can only pray that I was able to slow their progression with my earlier spell sufficiently, and that I prepared and applied the correct herbs and healing enchantments in time. We'll know more by morning."

Glancing toward the nearest window, Emer corrected, "By nightfall." Groaning, she rose and shuffled to each of the windows in turn, swinging the shutters in to allow the cool light to fill the hall. With it came a crisp, salty breeze. Emer inhaled a few long, slow breaths. At last, she nodded toward a door Caer had not previously noticed at the back of the dais. "If memory serves, there should be several small, private rooms back there."

"I thought," Caer managed through a yawn. "...you said you haven't been here before."

Emer frowned. "I believe what I said was that I didn't know how to get here. I've been here twice, counting now. And I still don't know how to find the place. The usual paths for teleporting don't work, here. Dylan has blocked them. Only he knows the coordinates and the spell to get past his shielding. Anyway, I'm going to seek out one of those rooms in the back. A nice, quiet, dark one. Maybe I'll get lucky and find a bed. I'll sleep on the floor, though, if that's all there is. I suggest you get some sleep, as well."

Alone in the dark was the last place Caer wished to be. Better to remain where there was a little warmth from the fireplace, the reassuring spread of light, and another person--albeit an unconscious one. "Thanks, but I think I'll stay here. Keep an eye on...on Dylan."

"Suit yourself." Emer cast a slightly dismayed scrutiny over Caer. "I'd forgotten you were so ill dressed for this damp place. I'll send a blanket out for you. Settle yourself by the fire with it. That should keep you warm enough." Her sunken gaze strayed one more time to Dylan. "Better send one out for him, too."

30

Shivering woke her to a subtle thrum hanging in the air. It throbbed along her nerves, underscoring the Gordian knot of bloodied imagery left over from her dreams. Always, there was smoke. Always, there was fire...and dancing. This time, shadowy visions of battles and chants and spells came wrapped in the smoke and flames. So, too, came the faces--those of her parents and her aunt. Each face lifeless; each with pale lips repeating something she couldn't quite make out.

A stronger shudder dislodged the phantoms, leaving a suddenly sharp awareness of the cold and the continuing thrum. The latter, it seemed, had troubled her subconscious for... Caer couldn't guess how long. Nor, after a startled glance at her surroundings, could she recall where she was.

Grasping the edges of the blanket that wrapped her, she struggled to sit, her breath fogging in the chill air. Stabs of pain shot through her lower back as she straightened, her still sluggish brain noting the stone floor that had served as her bed. The floor. Yes. She remembered, now. They'd come to Dylan's... Another brisk glance around failed to name what sort of place this happened to be. Not a home, exactly, though Emer said there were private rooms in the back, some of which might have beds.

A grumbled harrumph attached to Caer's irritation. She'd opted to remain out here for the sake of the fire and the light and the presence of another person, even if he was comatose. At least there was currently adequate light. As for any warmth from the fire, the blaze Emer had set in the enormous fireplace had long since diminished, leaving little more than smoldering embers.

Caer gave only brief consideration to collecting more pellets. She had nothing with which to ignite them. Even the lamps in the wall niches no longer burned. Lips pursed, Caer studied her fingers. Fat chance of her ever sparking flames from them. Snuggling her blanket more tightly around her shoulders, she pushed to her feet, hoping for some sign that Emer was up and about. The man lying on the table in the center of the dais remained her only company. Daring a lengthier scrutiny of him, Caer feared there might be the flush of fever on his cheek. At least he was still alive, though in the drafty chill he might succumb to the cold.

Her barefoot steps carried her quickly across the frigid floor and onto the dais where she reached a tentative hand to Dylan's face. Feverish, yes, but his breathing was unlabored as he slept. Aside from adjusting his blanket, there was nothing more she could do for him. Nothing she dared attempt, anyway. Her memories of all the times she spent helping her aunt were too murky to trust for mixing or applying fresh herbal remedies, even if she knew where to find proper ingredients.

Instead, Caer left Dylan as he was and headed to the nearest of the two huge windows flanking the fireplace. She remembered vaguely, Emer opening them, allowing the biting draft to breathe into the hall along with the wan light that suggested early morning. The light was more intense, now. Hard to tell, though, whether it was mid-day or early evening, or even if it was the same day.

Suggestions of salt and damp earth carried on the brisk breeze, stirring the dust on the floor and fluttering the cobwebs draping the high ceiling's corners. Moving to stand directly in a pool of light from the nearest window, Caer closed her eyes, taking several moments to luxuriate in the delicate kiss of warmth on her cheeks. Another bite of chill air tossed her hair about her face and brought her eyes open once more. The intense blue of the dome's upper reaches stared back at her. Such a rich and bright hue; one unfamiliar to Caer. She could recall nothing like it in other domes. Though translucent, the thickness of the materials used in the construction of the protective enclosures muted the natural light, washing out the color of whatever atmosphere lay beyond them. Perhaps a new material had been invented and employed in making Earth's domes.

Rising on tiptoe, she tried to see what other buildings might be close at hand, hoping for some indication of whether they were in an industrial, business, or residential area. But the window's sill was too high, and she too short to glimpse anything. Moreover, she heard no sounds of a bustling metropolis or of overhead traffic. Only the subtle and persistent thrum and the occasional soft snore from Dylan carried in the stillness.

Her brow knotted as white wisps appeared and drifted lazily across the intense field of blue. Stepping back, she shot a glance at the window's twin on the other side of the fireplace. Shortly after the wisps disappeared from the nearer window, they reappeared at the second, continuing their leisurely journey until they were out of sight entirely. Clouds?

Caer's mind stumbled over the notion, even as she recalled the night on that hill, where the sky seemed open to the heavens. A dream painting, surely. There was nowhere on Earth, nor, so far as she knew, on any human colony, where life existed outside of the confines of the great, human constructed enclosures.

"In time, we shall breathe the pristine air once more. In time, we shall open the way to Slievgall'ion, and all shall be renewed."

"What?" Caer glanced around, expecting to see Emer standing on the dais, though the voice didn't sound like hers. There was only Dylan. And he remained asleep. Turning, her brow deepening its furrows, Caer studied the lingering shadows around the room's edges and corners, finding no one.

"Slievgall'ion shall be the redemption for all."

The gently murmured words seemed at once to surround Caer and run through her. She held her breath, straining to listen, to identify the location of the speaker, calling out, "What is Slievgall'ion? What does it redeem?"

"The promise. The hope." The murmur now seemed bound within her own skull. *"So much pain and suffering. So many lost. Murdered. Murdered..."*

Caer fought the shiver that raised the hair on her arms. "Who?" she demanded. "Who was murdered?"

The vision hit her with the impact of an explosion, staggering her back several more paces and dropping the blanket from her hands. The faces. Her mother. Her father. Sidra. Mirra. Jen. Jorn. And others. So many others. "No!" choked from her lungs. "An accident. My parents died in a lab accident. Sidra died from... Ice traced down her spine as she recalled the words on the lips of her parents and her aunt in many of her nightmares. "Murder," they cried; had repeated over and over. That was what she had been unable to make out from the visions that clung to her upon waking moments ago.

The soft plodding of footfalls spun Caer around as Emer trudged out from the rooms behind the dais, dark circles rimming her eyes. Stopping a pace or two out from the doorway, she gave herself over to an enormous yawn.

"I think I could sleep for a hundred years," she muttered, stretching. A glance down at her jumpsuit prompted a disgusted, "Ugh! I believe I have as much of Dylan's blood on me as he has in him." With a nod in Caer's direction, she added, "You, too. I'll have to do something about that, once I'm fully awake. So..." She stretched again and headed toward the table where Dylan lay. "How is our patient?"

"Fine," Caer returned distractedly, her eyes again searching the shadows. As her gaze came back around to Emer, she corrected, "I...I mean...he's improving. I think." Truth was, she'd paid him little heed since turning her attention to the windows.

"Ah yes," Emer agreed, bending over him. "He does look better."

One more scan of the great hall assured Caer that no one else was around. Stooping to retrieve her blanket, she ventured, "What... what were you saying when you came in, just now?"

"That I could sleep for..."

"Before that."

"Nothing that I recall."

"You're sure? I mean, I thought I heard someone say something."

"Well, not me, dear. Maybe Dylan was talking in his sleep."

"It sounded like a woman's voice," Caer persisted.

Emer cocked her head, her narrowed eyes skimming the shadows. "I don't suppose you've seen...uhm...Merripen."

"No. Not since you wandered off to the back. Why?"

There was a brief hesitation as Emer passed a curious scrutiny over Caer. "No reason," she offered with a shrug, scuffling down the steps and making her way to the fireplace. "Just thought the cat might have passed through." Her huffed annoyance at the fading embers prefaced her retrieval of more pellets from the nearby box. Once spread to her satisfaction, she coaxed the fire back to life with the point of a finger. "I wonder if there's anything edible in the kitchen. I didn't have an opportunity to look, before. Something that doesn't have to be cooked would be nice. I really hate having to cook without a decent stove."

Caer couldn't help pressing again with, "You're sure you didn't say something about...about..." She bit her lip barely in time to stop from blurting out 'murder', inserting instead, "...clean air...or some such?"

Emer cast her a more curious assessment. "Look, dear. You're obviously still exhausted. And I dare say, you've had nothing worthwhile to eat in at least twenty-four hours. Easy to imagine things in that state." Indicating the area behind the dais with a short toss of her head, she added, "I was right about the rooms back there, and the beds. There's also an honest to goodness bathroom about halfway down the hall. No hot water, mind you. But there is plumbing, complete with a flush toilet." She grinned, thumbing toward Dylan. "It seems his predilection for 'roughing it' has at least some limits. Why don't you go clean up a little and get some real sleep? I'll heat up some water for a bath once I figure out what's to eat."

Caer fidgeted with her necklace, still being in no humor to wander off alone. Not with voices mysteriously speaking to her from nowhere. "If it's all the same to you, I prefer to stay here where I have some company. Even if part of that company is...well...not exactly responsive."

"I'm responsive enough," rasped from the dais.

Startled, Caer whirled around to find Dylan cautiously sitting up.

"No one can harm you, here, Caer. I promise." His voice was breathy as he shifted his position. Instantly, his left hand clutched at his right shoulder, his sharp intake hissing between his teeth. "Remind me," he managed, "...to conjure some body armor the...the next time I'm foolish enough to wrestle with a Coran'ian."

Emer flew to his side, snapping, "You lie back down this instant!"

"I'm...fine, Em." His feeble attempt to waive her off was shoved aside.

"You are not!"

His scowl was met with her glare. "If you aren't comfortable where you are, then I'll help you to one of the beds."

Dylan pushed her away, rising unsteadily to his feet, his declaration carrying only a little more forcefully. "I'm fine. Your skills are excellent. I knew I could count on you to save my ass."

"Saved the rest of you, as well," Emer harrumphed, still trying to push him back down. "But you're going to undo all my hard work if you don't take it easy for a while."

Finally relenting, Dylan sat back on the table. The flush in his face had brightened a little, and he was sweating. His eyes, however, were clear, and they focused on Caer. "As I was saying..." He took a moment to let his breathing settle, finishing with, "You needn't worry. You're safe, here. No one can find this place. No one. Unless I will it so."

"You said I was safe at Fedel'ma's, too," she sniffed. "But that proved otherwise. That...that beast managed to get right into the house. Right to me." The same sort of creature had breached Bestor's tight security, and Caer suspected a Coran'ian was also responsible for passing unseen through the security at Ahira's student housing complex, murdering poor Mirra. "If that woman and those men from that hill have employed creatures who can get through to Fedel'ma's estate, what's to stop them getting through, here?"

Darting an uneasy glance toward the windows, she grumbled, "And where, precisely, is 'here'?"

Dylan's weak half smile preceded, "My manor house. A bit rustic, I confess."

"Rustic!" Emer snorted. "Try crudely primitive!"

"A matter of perspective," he returned. "As for our whereabouts, suffice it to say that we are well hidden. Now, where's..."

Merripen padded out from the back rooms with a slightly drunken gait.

"Oh. There you are," Dylan finished.

In an awkward bound, the cat went from the floor to the bench to the table, making an irritated mew as it struggled for balance, then sat, eyeing Dylan.

"You needn't worry, either, Mother. I've been superbly thorough with the spells concealing my little retreat. They won't unravel easily. I would have to be dead and banished for a couple of centuries before the shielding here will yield."

Caer's lips pulled thin. Mother? She seemed to recall Dylan referring to the cat that way, last night, as well. Emer had good reason to be concerned about him. The man was obviously delusional.

"I'm not delusional."

Caer's face warmed. "No. Of course not. I just..." Her thoughts abruptly snagged. "I didn't say you were. I only..."

Emer moved away from Dylan with a heavy sigh, plunking onto the bench. "You couldn't let it pass, could you? You should at least have given Caer time to gather her wits."

Dylan passed a glance from Emer to Caer, blanching. "Oh. Yes. Had I been thinking clearly..."

Emer's brow cocked. "There. You see? You should have given yourself time to collect your wits before opening your mouth." Sighing heavily, she gestured for Caer to join her on the bench. "You had better come and sit down, dear. There are a few...things we should probably clear up for you."

31

Emer wasn't serious. Fedel'ma couldn't possibly be in the cat. Caer twisted and untwisted her necklace, avoiding Merripen's intelligent and steady gaze. Of course, there was intelligence. She'd recognized years ago, with her aunt's cats, just how smart the little creatures were. Swallowing, she, at last, raised her head to meet Merri's scrutiny. The startling depth and intensity of purpose in those luminescent green eyes quickly returned her to a fidgety study of her knees.

How could this be happening? For Del to survive an explosion that left nothing identifiable of her body...for whatever it was that remained of the woman to take up residence in...inside...

"It's the soul," Emer offered softly. "The soul survives death. Or, at least it does so for most Witches."

Caer wasn't sure she believed in souls. Yet the notion stirred a growing turmoil in her skull, lifting veiled impressions of a song. It came as a thin thread, at first, the song...the story...its melody rising on her mother's sweet voice. A tale of three sisters. Dana. Roisin. Nemhain.

The lyrics came in a rush of clarity, weaving through her head in mournful meter, laying out how the young sisters witnessed the brutal slaying of their parents; how they stood together against the same shouted accusations of treachery and dark witchcraft that had been flung at their mother and father. Their family brought no harm to anyone, yet they were accused and convicted in the chaos of the maddened masses. Their parents slaughtered, the sisters were dragged to a single great pyre, beaten, tied, and set ablaze. As their bodies burned within the inferno for evils they'd never committed, their voices joined together to call upon a powerful spell. In unified breath, they swore their souls and those of their descendants would not rest; swore that they would live again to seek out their accusers and any others who thought to murder their kind. And the sisters were reborn. As they grew, they were again accused; again threatened; were saved by a fairy creature who whisked them away.

Their spell, the lyrics proclaimed, also extended to the souls of their descendants, who possess the ability to acquire new flesh when death claims the old; learning ways of doing so without the need for rebirth. Always, through every lifetime, their kind is feared. Always their deaths come by brutal means.

Drumming. Hands held. Bodies moving as one. Forward and back. The dance moves Deocil--one, two, three, four, five, six, seven. One, two, three. One, two, three. Widdershins--one two, three, four, five, six, seven. One, two, three. One, two, three. Heat. Smoke.

A face in the fire. A woman writhing. Something must be taken from her; something that must be found.

Rough hands grip her shoulders, holding her back. **It is done!** *The declaration echoes, vile, malicious.*

Fire erupts, heat scorching, even from a distance. Fingers dig into her shoulders as she struggles.

Her beloved aunt's scream rises through the billowing flames and acrid smoke.

Freedom from the grip. Running. Yellow-red closes around. Searing pain eats at flesh. Something glows that is not fire--something locked within her aunt's body. Anguish and terror fill her. She must do this. Her small voice cries out, wavering, yet full of resolve. **To me! I shall protect you!**

She reaches out. A white-hot jolt as fingers touch.

No! I did not know! You are too young! You do not understand what you have done!

Shivering. Knife-sharp cold mingles with devouring molten agony.

Child! You must away! I call upon the guardian! Protect her!

Angry red tongues of flame coil around. In the midst of hell shimmers a tall, dark figure. His eyes stare down at her, glowing with a turquoise heat, grim and scowling. Pain gnaws through to her very bones. She opens her mouth but can voice no scream. The grim eyes soften. Cool arms encompass her.

Caer struggled for air, drowning in panic, tattered shadows of flame still clinging to her. This! This was her recurring nightmare. This was the whole of it--the terror and the torture. This was memory. The people of their village took Sidra from her. Like the verses out of the ancient song, they took her, bound her, and...

Flames flick hungrily upward, eating, burning, consuming.

"There is no fire, Caer." Such was the power of the statement that the vision diminished, the heat abating.

"No fire." Dylan's voice was calm, firm. "You are safe."

Caer's heart drummed like a frenzied bodhran, red still lapping at the edges of her mind while the remnants of pain twitched her nerves.

"You are safe," he pressed.

Emer's voice choked, "Did you see?"

"Of course, I saw." The weight of the universe hung in Dylan's acknowledgment.

"She went into the fire! She tried to save her aunt! Dylan, she was only a child!"

"Hush!"

Sidra's cries still trembled through Caer's head, mingling with more distant voices--those of disembodied souls from other burnings, from other deaths. Souls released and returned, murdered again, released again, returned again…and again… Casting a wild-eyed glance around, she expected to see a host of specters filling the hall. It was the continued scrutiny of the cat, however, that captured her frantically darting gaze, the feline/human eyes watching her from the animal's perch on the table.

The gentleness of Merripen's mew and the solidity of the animal's form gave a momentary purchase for Caer's struggling mind. Forcing a deliberate breath, she tried to steady the shaking of her hands and the tremor in her voice as she rasped, "The returning. Transmigration. I knew. I had forgotten." How long ago had she forgotten? She must have known of it when Sidra died, or she'd not have tried to call her aunt's soul to her. But did she know at the time of her parents' deaths? Was it possible that none of them were truly gone? If they'd returned, could she find them? Would she know them if she did? Would they know her? Had they, like Fedel'ma, come back as animals? Was that why they'd never reached out to her?

With a feeble gesture toward Merripen, she managed, "When souls come back…do they always…"

"Rarely," Dylan huffed, his tone markedly agitated. "As in almost never."

The cat made a peculiar stretch, as though having difficulty sorting out the command of its muscles. Rising to all fours, its study of Caer did not waiver. *"Not,"* brushed a whisper in her mind. *"Not one's first choice."* The sound carried the suggestion of Fedel'ma's deep tones. *"One does what one must, though. I thought that, once you were told of my merging with Merri, you would believe. I did not anticipate the information calling up other images for you. I am sorry, child. Perhaps it was too soon for us to speak of this matter."*

The insinuation of Fedel'ma's words in her head spat another memory jarringly into place. "T..t…telepathy," Caer stammered. She and Sidra had often used the technique for conversing across the garden. It allowed them privacy when neighbors wandered by, giving them the freedom to discuss the magical properties of certain plants.

Telepathy and magical properties. Transmigration of the soul. How could she have forgotten any of it?

Falling more than leaping from the table, Merripen staggered for a moment before ambling along the bench to sit next to Caer. *"I thank my ancestors for the gift. Without telepathy, I would be completely useless in this state. Regrettably, after that hasty teleportation away from my estate, it took a while for me to work through Merri's addled wits sufficiently to draw upon the gift. As has been pointed out, Merri would not have been my first choice. But there was no time."*

Dylan pushed briefly away from the table, flicking the cat a derisive sneer before resignedly propping his backside against the table's edge once more. "Perhaps you should have made time."

"The need for haste outweighed all else," Fedel'ma rumbled. *"You think I enjoy trying to function like this? Very confusing for both Merri and myself, I can assure you."* The cat's brow lifted in such an un-cat-like manner that Caer stiffened, blinking twice before believing what she saw.

"You'd have preferred, perhaps," Del hissed, *"that I joined with you?"*

Dylan bristled. "Hardly!"

"Didn't think so."

"Tell me, Mother. Just what did haste gain you? Your shield around the estate had already failed enough to allow a breach."

Merripen shifted to an ungainly arch of its back with another hiss. *"I wasn't in any condition to recognize that little fact, now was I?"*

Oh, for the..." Emer groaned, standing and reaching around Caer to snatch the cat in her arms. "I'm going to send each of you to your rooms without dinner if you don't stop this infantile bickering." Stalking angrily away from the dais, she set Merri down just below the steps. "None of your little disagreements or perceived slights matter, right now." She paused, looking back with a mix of worry and curiosity. "What does matter is Caer. There's a lot more going on, here, than her merely possessing the key. How many other surprises are buried in her head, I wonder."

"More than is good for her, I'm sure," Dylan returned.

Caer squirmed, her fingers closing around her necklace. They had no idea how much more was buried in the black holes of her mind. Nor did she. More than she wanted them to know, she was sure. These were her memories to recover. If she called back the images that were now revealed, perhaps they would lead her to the rest. She needed to see...to understand everything. Perhaps armed with her memories, she could find her parents and her aunt.

The pieces from her nightmare were recalled easily enough. The attempt to press deeper, however, brought immediate vice-like pressure inside her skull, and a sickening churning in her stomach. Why? Why should some things lift ghost-like from the abyss only to offer more questions, while their answers refused to be touched? She needed to unravel the secrets. They were a part of her life and she would know them!

The more she persisted, the greater the agony grew, until all hope of either seeing or understanding was lost in the searing torment and the cacophony of screams and cries from a host of specters that battered her.

"Stop!" The command edged through the discord. "No more!"

The screams dulled, though the agony in her head remained. Still, grasping at the minor reprieve, Caer fought to concentrate. If she could just push through...

The suggestion of a cadence impinged on her awareness, faint and distant. As it strengthened, it brought forth the undertone of a chant. Though the words were indiscernible, their soft repetition gradually lessened the throbbing in Caer's head and quieted her stomach. She listened intently, thinking it to be yet another memory rising. Instead, the rhythm and the chant carried a slow, numbing drowsiness that she scarcely noticed until she felt her eyelids droop. Instinctively, she snapped straight, fighting to stay awake. No sleep. Not now. There was too much she needed to discover. More bloodshed would surely come unless she could find a way to stop it. The way had to be somewhere in the darkest depths of her subconscious.

The cadence with its chant strengthened, and again she struggled, pressing it back...pressing it...

32

Dylan sank onto a large, stuffed chair, his head buzzing from the abruptness of Emer's teleportation. Caer was delivered more delicately to the bed in front of him, with Emer shimmering into existence next to it, her hand quickly bracing against the wall for support.

"That," she breathed, "should not have been so difficult. The distance from the hall to this room isn't all that great."

"I'm surprised you attempted such an act," Dylan returned. "You look as exhausted as I feel. Why teleport us back here? We were fine, remaining in the great hall."

Straightening, Emer brushed her hair behind her ears and surveyed the gloomy quarters. "What? And leave Caer to lay on the cold stone floor, again, while you pass out from your exertion and end up on the floor, as well? You're both better off, here. The effort just winded me, is all." Taking a moment to catch her breath, she admitted, "I'm just glad you were able to stop her from probing around for more memories."

"And that shouldn't have been so difficult," he grumbled. "Not even accounting for Caer's resistance to my efforts."

"Oh really. Here you are, half dead, and you're surprised that the girl was able to cause you some trouble."

"I'm not half dead."

Emer aimed a finger at the lamp in the room's single wall niche, watching the flame catch and flutter, muttering a harrumph. "I was being charitable. You look at least two-thirds dead."

Dylan glowered. "Thanks for the positive assessment."

"You're welcome."

Watching Em close her eyes in concentration, Dylan demanded, "Now what are you up to?"

A pile of blankets appeared on the end of the bed. "Found these last night," she said, tossing a couple of them to him. Turning her attention to Caer, she gently removed the girl's chemise. "It's all your blood, you know," she accused, shaking the filthy garment at him before teleporting it off to who-knew-where. "I'm surprised you have any left." Taking up at least three of the blankets, Emer tucked each one carefully around her patient.

"Stop, Em."

"Stop what?"

"Just stop," he said. "Caer will be fine. As will I. So, stop what you're doing and sit down before you fall on your face."

She ignored him, adding, "Found a number of other things, as well. There's so much...stuff...here. All that furniture stacked in a couple of the rooms back here. Why apply magic to protect everything in this place from decaying with age if you aren't going to pull it all out and make the manor house a little more comfortable?"

Dylan managed a tentative shrug. "I'm the only one who comes here. It's comfortable enough for me. So, why bother?"

"Your choice, you know. Always coming here alone," Emer returned. Flicking him a dismissive glance, she headed toward the door. "Besides, you're not the only one here, now." Pausing in the doorway, she set a fist to her hip, giving him a challenging glare. "I trust you won't mind sleeping while sitting up. I would deliver you to the only other room with a bed already set up, but I don't think it would be a good idea to leave Caer alone. She seemed quite worried about that prospect. Can't say that I blame her, given everything that's happened, recently."

"If you expect me to sleep, you needn't have lit the lamp."

"And risk the poor girl waking to your ugly face peering at her in the darkness? Now, if you'll excuse me..."

"Just where do you think you're going?"

"To do a little interior decorating with some of the items I found."

Before Dylan could protest further, she was gone. For a short time, he could hear her roaming from room to room, poking about. In the end, her footfalls faded in the direction of the great hall. Shifting slightly, he shook out one of two blankets Em had tossed him, drawing it around his shirtless shoulders, glad for the little warmth it offered. The other blanket he opened across his lap as he settled back, his feet propped on the crossbar of the bed's footboard. From its niche, the lamp sputtered, the continuing flicker adding a headache to his other pains and his exhaustion. Unfortunately, he lacked the energy to douse it, either by magic or by physically getting up and crossing the room.

In truth, his first order of business should be to go in search of some clean clothes and to haul a bucket of pellets back from the box in the great hall. A blaze in the chamber's small fireplace would take the chill from the room. The crisp air was adding to the ache in his throbbing shoulder. Moving from the chair, however, seemed an overwhelmingly impossible feat, at the moment. His lip curled. Here he was, falling apart and utterly useless, while Emer flitted about.

His mother was as useless as he, wherever the woman in her cat suit happened to be. Prowling the kitchen, no doubt. A mirthless half smile accompanied his snort. Not one of her brighter moves, transmigrating into that bloody cat. The animal wobbled about like a drunkard, compliments, no doubt, of his mother's constant badgering to direct it hither and thither, whether Merripen wished to comply or not. Well, that was her predicament, he decided, resting his head against the chair's high back and closing his eyes. She got herself into the mess. She could get herself out of it.

Though fatigue as heavy as a hundred sleepless nights weighted his eyelids, guilt prevented Dylan's doing more than doze now and again. Emer was likely running herself ragged, and he was incapable of stopping her. He might, at least, use his time to try and sort through the puzzle of Caer DaDhrga.

Adrian Starn's admonition to her rose to mind. 'This is not the time for you to know certain things.' Memories were being kept from her. Dylan understood, now, how it was done. A spell guarded them--a most formidable piece of magic. The working was difficult to detect, at first, lacking, as it was, in any hint of a signature to identify its maker. As a result, it blended almost seamlessly into the feel of Caer's inherent magic. Not even his prying into Caer's nightmare back on Ahira had revealed its presence. Only in this last little venture, as he fought to stop her agonizing struggle to draw memories out, had he gone deeply enough into her mind to brush against this curious magic.

The responsible party possessed tremendous skill, weaving the spell cautiously, its intricacies finely tuned to deliver increasing pain with every attempt Caer made to delve past it. Worse, the more she struggled to break through, the more it assailed her sanity. Whether doing so was the spellbinder's intent, he couldn't guess. It served as a warning, however. Any attempt he made to breach the magic might well result in the same consequences for her.

Lowering his feet to the floor, he sagged forward, messaging his aching shoulder. He knew Caer well enough to know that she would keep digging, searching for memories that might explain who she is, what gifts she may possess...how it is that she came to hold the key. His jaw squared. If he could touch her dreams, though... Dreams often carried fragments of memory. If he could see them, perhaps he could piece them together without pressing directly...and dangerously...into her subconscious.

"Don't even think about it!"

Dylan's startled jerk stabbed hot agony from his shoulder all the way down his right side. Wincing a slight turn, he leveled a glare on Emer. Merripen padded awkwardly just ahead of her, the cat heading for the shadows of the nearest wall.

Em dismissed his ire with, "I wasn't eaves dropping on your thoughts. Not my fault if you've become as lax as Caer about leaving them unguarded. She, at least, has an excuse. You... Serious injury and lack of sleep can cause all sorts of unfortunate outcomes, you know. Including broadcasting your considerations." Hovering over him for a moment, she added, "You still look awful. So, stop fussing on about other people's minds and rest your own."

"I am resting. Just like you should be."

"That Coran'ian didn't dump its venom in my blood stream," Emer sniffed. "I didn't come back here to scold or argue with you, though."

"So. Something I can do for you, then?"

"More like there's something I can do for you. Thought you might like this." She handed him a fresh pair of pants, a shirt, and another blanket. "Found the clothes while I was rummaging around. At least they weren't full of dust like all the blankets and furniture were. Hire yourself a housekeeper, for pity sake!"

She stood watching, obviously waiting for him to request assistance as he struggled one-handedly from his blood-stained pants and donned the clean pair. He refused to accommodate her, even when his effort to ease into the fresh shirt triggered a whole new round of misery. Finished, he sat panting, aware that his pain was etched across his face.

Em's brow cocked at his stubbornness. Shaking her head, she held out a hand, quickly grasping the handle as a steaming mug appeared. "Broth. Not the best. I'm guessing your supply of dried soup stock is eons beyond old. Still, it's better than nothing." Nodding toward the empty fireplace at the end of the room, she offered, "Shall I lay a fire for you?"

"I'll tend to it. Later."

"Don't be such a royal ass. It will take me no time at all to..."

"I'm fully capable of setting a fire," he snapped. He didn't need the feline hiss from his mother to make him immediately regret his tone. The look of agitation that pinched Emer's lips and ignited the midnight glow of her eyes was deserved; his slow-to-come attempt at an apology, however, was lost to the clank of a bucket of pellets that materialized next to the hearth.

"Fine. I've provided the pellets. You can do the rest," Emer declared, plopping down on the edge of the bed. "Maybe, when every last bit of your energy is gone, you'll learn that there is no great indignity in admitting you need time to recover. Especially under the current circumstances. The magic used to enhance that Coran'ian's venom was the strongest I've ever encountered. You're lucky that creature didn't dispatch your body and leave your soul incapable of seeking new accommodations for a very long while. Then where would Caer be, with Del wearing a Merripen suit and you missing in action?"

Dylan was forced to admit, albeit in guarded silence, that learning of the magically enhanced venom came as something of a relief. Perhaps he wasn't as decrepit as he felt.

"She would be in very good hands. I'm sorry, Em. You're right. I owe you--again. You eliminated the beast and saved this current chunk of soul-harboring flesh."

Emer grinned. "Yes, I did."

He couldn't help but grin back at her. "Finally learning to pat yourself on the back, are you?"

"I suppose if I don't do it occasionally, I can't expect anyone else to."

"Now who's being an ass? I've always told you how skilled you are. You've a strength about you that's hard to match. Except by me, of course."

"Time certainly hasn't taught you humility."

Dylan flinched. "No. You were the one to do that."

Emer's grin faded. "That was never my intention. I just..."

"I know." Reaching with his left hand, he took hold of hers. "The lesson was justly deserved, though. I've told you a thousand times, you bear no fault in our parting. The failings were mine and mine alone. I truly am sorry, Em. I never meant to hurt you."

Emer gave his hand a brief squeeze. "How many times do I have to tell you that you're forgiven? Neither of us meant for things to turn out as they did. The simple fact is, while we make a great team, we aren't a good match matrimonially. We both knew that from the start, I think."

They fell silent for several minutes before Emer withdrew her hand and asked, "How old do you think she was?"

The unexpected question brought a sharp pang to Dylan's heart. How old? No one ever said, at least not to him. And he never had the courage to inquire. He should never have left Em. Not when he did.

"Caer," Emer murmured, her eyes downcast. "I was speaking of Caer. How old do you think she was when she tried to save her aunt? I'm guessing not much more than ten or eleven. I can't imagine so young a child, one with no previous lifetimes of experience to draw on, finding the strength and courage to go into the flames as she did. And then to try and call her aunt's soul to her, despite the agony of her burning flesh. She must have loved her aunt very much. I don't suppose it's possible that Sidra survived. That her soul did, in the end, find new life in a different vessel."

Dylan made no response. He thought it unlikely, though.

Emer seemed to detect his doubt. Shivering took her. "I wonder if Sidra knew what was to happen that night. Do you think that's why she called a guardian to Caer? Odd, isn't it?"

Dylan cocked his head. "What is?"

"You said some time ago that you found no record of Sidra, nor of Caer or her parents in the Family genealogies. Yet they were Witches. Had to be for Sidra to know about guardians; to possess the ability to call for one. If Sidra was Witch, then at least one of Caer's parents was, as well. It certainly confirms that Caer isn't Tanai. So, why aren't they in the records? I didn't think it possible for any of us to hide our lineage from the Chroniclers. Their gift is said to be too great for any Witch to be concealed from them."

For several seconds she sat there, a look of intense pondering creasing her brow. "And," she said, at last. "And there's the matter of this Mr. Starn. A guardian. At least that much appears to be true of him. There's no question of the powerful magic bound up in the man. Surely, he's listed in the archives."

Dylan shook his head. "I checked every possible entry and cross-reference when Caer first mentioned him as a friend. There is nothing."

"Mm. I was afraid you would say that." Plucking at the bedcovers, Emer's gaze absently tracked Merripen as the cat slumped past the door for a second circuit of the room. With an agitated sigh, she noted, "For all the power in that man's spell casting, it doesn't..."

"Feel right," Dylan finished. He was well aware of the strangeness of Starn's magic. "It was the same with the spells cast by the obese man who stood with Maura on Slieve na Calliagh."

Emer nodded, chewing at her lip. "No discernable signature in his magic, either. Their spells had no....'fingerprint' identifying them. Had I not seen the sparks and the force of their work, I'd have no idea that either man had done anything. How can they do that--hide their signature like that?"

Dylan understood no more than Emer, not that he expected she anticipated any answer. He did, however, have a gnawing suspicion that Starn was the one responsible for concealing Caer's memories from her.

"Too many questions," Emer mumbled. Her eyes narrowed as she fixed Dylan with a stern glare. "Don't you dare do anything so foolish as looking for answers in Caer's dreams, though. The poor girl doesn't need you mucking about in her head. It's unethical. If you want to use up what's left of your reserves, then focus your energy on your own recovery."

"I don't do 'foolish'," Dylan retorted.

Sarcasm dripped from Em's, "Of course not." Pushing to her feet, she looked about to leave before turning another curious scrutiny to Caer. The slight cock of her head suggested there was something more on her mind. Returning her attention to Dylan, she gestured at the mug in his hand. "Drink that before it gets any colder. I'm not bringing you another for a while. I need to go back to the estate."

Surprised, Dylan raised a glower to her. "No."

"Why not?"

"It's too dangerous. Maura's goons may well be there. They'll turn the place upside down looking for Caer and the key."

"I'm perfectly capable of taking care of myself," she insisted. "You just stated that I have a strength that's hard to match." Sarcasm crept back into her tone. "Except by you, of course."

Dylan snorted. "Yeah. And look where mine got me."

"Someone needs to go back to get word on Gwynlyn," Emer pressed. "I'm really worried about her. I'm convinced that the collapse at the dig site was no accident. I need to talk to her."

"Then I'll allow you exit to go straight to the hospital."

Emer rolled her eyes and gestured at her jumpsuit. "Looking like this? They'll throw me on a gurney and haul me off to emergency. And once they figure out that the blood isn't mine, what do I tell them?"

"Give me a couple hours of sleep, then. You can wear one of my shirts until I can go for some fresh clothes and anything else you want. Then I'll go with you to talk to Gwyn."

"Don't be stupid. You aren't going to be up to anything more than the simplest of tasks for at least another couple of days. Messing around with any more magic is out of the question for you. Doctor's orders! Besides, I just might have a few other reasons for wanting to return to the estate."

"Such as?"

Emer's jaw set as her fists went to her hips. "Such as none of your business. I will use the utmost caution, and will leave the instant there's the slightest hint of trouble."

Merripen loped once around Dylan's ankles, then sat, licking ineffectually at its paws and making awkward swipes at its face while Fedel'ma's voice complained in his head. *I need to return, as well. I'm of no use to anyone like this. All Merri wants to do is hunt mice and bathe. I have no appetite for her gourmet fare, or for licking myself. And I'm tired of trying to reach with hands that don't exist, or stand upright on legs that aren't built for it."*

His mother's dilemma might have been amusing, were it not for the fact that she would have to kill her beloved cat in order to free her soul for transmigration to another host. She knew that. Going into the cat in the first place was confirmation of just how urgently she must have felt the need to get back to them. Much as it pained him to admit it, he was grateful for such a sacrifice on his mother's part. Had she not taken up residence in the cat, she'd likely not have been able to return to the estate before he delivered their little group to his sanctuary. His mother would be left outside, with no way of finding them. Annoying as she was, he needed his mother's experience and knowledge to help them get through this mess. She was also correct. Stuck in her cat was not an optimal situation for providing much help.

His mother should return to the estate, he concluded. Emer, on the other hand, had not a single good reason to leave. It might take his mother a little longer than anyone liked, dispensing with Merri's body and inhabiting a more practical one. But once that task was accomplished, she could grab whatever items Emer wanted or needed. Moreover, she could check on Gwyn. The hospital morgue, after all, would be an ideal place to find a freshly discarded human shell

Emer's lips pressed tight as she watched him consider. She'd picked up on his thoughts, again. That meant trouble. Em would try to use his own reasoning against him, and would argue until she wore him down, which, sadly, would take very little time.

"Very well," he growled. "Just tread carefully."

The effort to concentrate long enough to telepath the proper spell and coordinates necessary for the women to leave and return, again, proved more difficult than Dylan expected. Damn Emer for being right about the state of his strength and stamina. Slouching deeper in his chair, he drew several long, ragged breaths, hoping Em and his mother had received the information. He doubted he could accomplish a second clear sending. And he would not speak the spell or the coordinates aloud. Caer might pick up on them, even in her sleep. Given her inability to shield her thoughts, she could easily pass that information on to others.

"Got it?"

Emer gave his shoulder a delicate and grateful pat. "Got it."

Merripen nodded. Very disturbing, seeing a cat wobble assent like that.

"If you need me," he began.

Emer chuckled, eyeing him up and down. "Right."

Dylan caught her by the wrist before she stepped away. "I warn you. Both of you. Do not share that spell or those coordinates with anyone. Not even Gwyn. They are booby-trapped to prevent their combination being used by anyone not of my choosing. Understand?"

Emer nodded, unperturbed. "Understood. Now," she admonished, slipping easily from his grip. "You get some sleep. Understand?"

33

Pain smashed across Emer's shins as she banged hard against something. "Damn it!" There shouldn't be a single obstacle in her path. The confusion of deep shadows baffled her.

"Lights up full."

Nothing happened. Rubbing her shins, she waited for the Witches' gift of shadow sight to lift the veil of darkness. Gradually, the varying dense grays of the room clarified. Her stomach plummeted. Gaping scars in the wallboard stared at her from where each of the library's bookshelves had been ripped away. Their shattered fragments were strewn everywhere, with Del's vast collection of priceless books shredded and tossed about. Jagged pieces of what once had been the room's chairs and table also lay scattered through the jumble. Her stomach took a deeper plunge as she spotted the remains of Del's beautiful antique desk dumped in the center of the room, the jagged edge of one of the battered desk drawers the object she had thwacked against when she materialized.

Her continued assessment of the room sent a chill chasing down her spine. While her cursory mental scan for unwelcome guests just prior to her arrival had detected no one, she couldn't help worry that the perpetrators might yet be skulking about elsewhere on the estate. Breath held, she stretched her senses, delicately probing for any indication of other living presences; praying her 'damn it' hadn't alerted anyone to her arrival. Still, she sensed nothing. Not within the house, not the gardens, not...

The abrupt tingle of her nerves and the sudden appearance of something scuttling along the debris of Del's desk sent Emer lurching backward with a frightened yelp. Only after several thundering heartbeats did she recognize the black form and detect the sense of her aunt's presence mingled with that of the cat.

"By all the powers, Del! Give warning, will you?"

The cat seemed as startled as Emer, yowling and hissing as it scrambled for footing on a teetering piece of the desk. When Merri at last found sufficient purchase, Del rumbled, *"You knew I was coming."*

"Yes, well..." Emer swallowed, waiting for her heart to simmer to a more reasonable pace. "For a moment, I feared you might be one of the bastards who executed this bit of inferior decorating. Do you think they were looking for the key?"

"What else?" seethed in Del's response, the heat of her outage growing as Merripen turned slowly, taking in the devastation. The library served as sacred territory for Del. Such desecration would not be forgiven.

"We can be grateful we were gone before they turned up," Emer offered meekly. "And that Caer still wore what they sought."

"I doubt the child has a choice in the matter. You saw how she tried and failed to remove the necklace when she first realized the murders were for the sake of obtaining it. The bloody thing has chosen her to carry it. It will not be easily parted from her. I suspect Maura and her minions know that. Their rampage, here, was likely borne of their fury when they found Caer missing from the estate."

The cat edged off the unstable desk fragment and padded in something resembling a slow, nervous waddle among the debris, ears laid back and fur bristling as it poked a nose here and there.

"You think the ancient stories had it right, then? That with the key rejoined, it can only be removed from the carrier by the hand of Dana or Roisin?" Emer's brow knitted. "Or by death?"

"That's what the stories say."

"Then we need to keep Caer far away from here. Whoever did this may come back."

Del/Merri gave another hissing evaluation of the shambles that lay about the room as the cat made its way through the debris with a gait that now resembled a seriously intoxicated swagger. Stopping in the doorway, Merri turned back to Emer, the luminescence of its eyes emphasized by a deep, internal glow. With the initial period necessary for the bonding of a soul to a new host complete, the magic that lit Del's eyes now shimmered within Merri's. Emer shuddered at the thought of the action necessary for parting the two.

"It would be best if we don't tarry," Del sent. *"Do whatever you came to do, dear. And then get back to Dylan's manor house. I'll join you as soon as I can."*

"Where are you going?"

"To the hospital morgue. I can't accomplish anything useful until I am properly human, again." Regret and sorrow hung in Del's words. *"I will try to connect with Gwyn telepathically while I'm there. If she's conscious, she'll respond. If not, there isn't much point in going to see her."*

Emer frowned. "You sure you don't want me to go with you? It'll just take a few minutes for me to collect some clothes for Caer and me and find a couple of other things. I could be there for Merri. To help with..."

"Better that you return and let Dylan know what's happened, here."

Emer nodded, uncertain whether she was relieved or remorseful. "Very well. I'll just..." The cat staggered into the heavier shadows of the hallway and vanished. "...wade through all of this on my own, then," Emer finished with a sigh. She was about to pick her way to the door when she paused, glancing down at the shards and splinters at her feet. She could do nothing about Merri's impending sacrifice and the grief it would bring her aunt, but she might be able to provide Del with one tiny sliver of cheer.

Dropping down, Emer set to a cautious and methodic search through the remains of the desk. At last, she found what she sought, withdrawing a small photo in a broken antique frame. Brushing away the remnants of shattered glass, she lifted the picture of Del's daughter free of the frame. Herein lay one small glimmer of hope for Del. Shannon was out there--somewhere. She had to be. Transmigration would carry her through untold numbers of lifetimes. "I miss you Shan. I could use another intelligent head to help me deal with your mother and your brother."

Tucking the photo into the breast pocket of her jumpsuit, Emer rose and made her way across the jumble to the door. She had clothes to collect. And her own little treasure to find. She needed nothing for Dylan. He possessed quite a store of apparel at the manor house. As for Del, the size and shape of her new host would dictate her needs regarding clothing. She could locate what she required; quietly lift it from a shop, if necessary.

Emer's thoughts came up short as she reached the doorway, her stomach taking yet another sickening plunge. There didn't appear to be a single piece of artwork or light fixture left hanging on the walls for the entire length of the corridor, in either direction. Worse, every wallboard had been slashed and splintered. Even the ceiling bore heavy gashes. Emer's fists clenched. How much more of their home had been turned to rubble?

Though she knew the need for haste, Emer couldn't avoid peering into each of the rooms she passed as she worked her way toward her own suite. Everywhere lay shambles. What possible need had these bastards for such destruction?

Reaching her suite, Emer's insides twisted anew. The door hung precariously from a sole, dangling hinge, the room as battered and shredded as elsewhere. The sight spilled hot tears down her cheeks. Dylan had his manor house as his sacred space. The library filled that purpose for Del. This... Emer's gaze skimmed across the disaster that lay before her. Since the death of her mother, this quiet suite had been her refuge; the more so when Dylan disappeared, only to return months afterward, without explanation as to why he'd left her alone just when...

279

Her abrupt inhale choked her. What of her treasure? Her heart hammered out the depth of her sudden anxiety. Stumbling across the threshold, she tried to make sense of each of the pieces of furniture. At last, she focused on the heap that roughly marked where her bed had been. Undeterred by the cuts and abrasions her fingers suffered, she dug furiously through the shards of wood and shreds of fabric. Please let her most cherished possession still be here! It held no significance to anyone else, even if they found it. Well, maybe to Dylan...if he knew of it. But to no one else.

Relief swept her as she spotted the decorative curl of wood that formed what had been the centerpiece of her bed's headboard. Lifting it with trembling hands, her bloodied index finger traced the swirls of the carved pattern as she murmured, "Life's love reveal." The wood warmed to her touch, and with a soft kiss to it, a small section slid silently aside. Within lay a tiny, satin-wrapped item. Pulling it free, Emer unfolded it. A tiny gold ring--a baby's ring-- glistened as it fell to her open palm.

Clutching it firmly to her breast, she used her free hand to dig out a length of finely braided piping that had been part of the trim on her pillows. Several minutes were required to one-handedly pluck loose the threads holding it to the remaining shreds of pillow casing. At last, she strung the piping through the ring and draped it around her neck, knotting the ends. Then, lovingly, she tucked her treasure inside her jumpsuit.

Certain of its safety, Emer turned to the matter of clothing, concerned that every garment may have ended up in shreds. Considerable rummaging through the tangle of textile and furniture pieces at last produced a couple of intact jumpsuits and a few undergarments, along with a few toiletries. Once more, Emer worked her way out and down the corridor, mincing through the destruction, past the library to the suite they'd given Caer. Here, the destruction proved even greater. The interior plaster and wallboard were so severely slashed and shredded that little remained of it. The ceiling likewise suffered gash marks, periodically raining bits of plaster dust down on her. As everywhere, everything lay in pieces, from the furniture to the carpet and the floorboards. Dismayed beyond words, Emer struggled through the room, retrieving a single jumpsuit, a couple of under garments, and a piece of torn sheet. Laying her clothing along with Caer's on the sheet, she began tying up the corners, hoping the bundle would guarantee she dropped nothing. So intent was she on the task that she practically jumped out of her skin when, "Urgent call," blared from her wrist communicator.

"What?" she barked, straightening so fast it set her head spinning.

The cold fury of a man's voice demanded, "Where's Caer?"

Emer's heart fell to her shoes. Adrian Starn. The unique musicality of that voice, despite its current discordant edge, was unmistakable. For the flash of an instant, she considered that he might be the one responsible for all of this. He had, after all, threatened them should any of them get in the way of his protecting Caer. She quickly dismissed the thought. The faint stench of the vile creatures like the one that wounded Dylan still clung to their handiwork throughout the ravaged rooms. Not that Starn couldn't be aligned with Nemhain's kin and creatures.

"Mr. Starn," she managed, struggling to settle her tone to some semblance of cool reserve. "Caer isn't here, at the moment. I will be glad to give her a message for you."

"If I didn't know she wasn't there, I would not ask where she was. I'm teleporting to you. You can answer my question to my face."

Emer's hands clenched. "I, uh...I don't think that's a very good idea, Mr. Starn. We're in the middle of some, uh, redecorating. Everything's in a...a bit of a muddle. You wouldn't want to turn up right in the middle of a piece of furniture or something." Her warning sounded lame, even to her. The man had already turned up here without needing to know the lay of things.

"I'll meet you in the gardens." The icy statement bit through her, the charge of his almost instantaneous arrival shearing across her every fiber. Pushy bastard. Who did he think he was, anyway?

A quick swipe of a sweaty palm on her jumpsuit thrust to mind the fact that she still wore her heavily bloodstained clothes. She dared not meet him looking like this and risk his thinking the worst--thinking she had done something horrendous to Caer. Addressing her communicator once more, she muttered, "Just give me a couple of minutes. I...I need to wash some of the paint and dust from my hands. Just...just wait for me near the back porch."

Her 'couple of minutes' felt more like an eon as she pulled one of her jumpsuits from the bundle and made a hasty change. Retrieving the photo from the pocket of her discarded attire, she laid it atop the remaining items on the sheet and retied its corners. The span of time felt even greater as she finally set out to negotiate the utter chaos through the rest of the house.

When she, at last, reached the kitchen, she stopped long enough to set her bundle beside the door and steady her breathing. Then, with crisply erect posture, she swept out on the porch, casting about for her visitor with as much affected calm as she could manage.

Scarcely three paces from the door, she stopped again, her shoulders slumping as she realized the gardens were as dark as the interior of the house. The dome's entire electrical grid must be down. Even the circulation system was quiet. No wonder the air hung so heavy and still. With not a single whir or stir of air, and with the sense of another's proximity, the stifling oppression that weighed upon her in the confines of the house now threatened to squeeze the last bit of breath from her lungs.

Straightening once more, she glanced about, agitated and unnerved at the lack of signature in Starn's presence. Turning, she found him looming in the deeper shadows at the far corner of the porch, arms folded, black hair tousled, turquoise heat smoldering in the depths of his eyes.

Forcing a smile, she offered, "Good evening. Sorry about the lack of light. We seem to be suffering from a minor, uh, mishap. The unintended consequence of one of our, uh, renovation projects gone awry."

"I need the light no more than you. I granted you the courtesy of announcing myself before I arrived. Now grant me the courtesy of telling me where Caer is."

"She's, uhm, away for a little while. Didn't want to trouble her with the, uh, work being done around here, you know."

Starn's eyes narrowed. "You're lying. I warned you about trying to keep her from me."

Ordinary men flexed or displayed their muscles when they wished to intimidate others. This man flexed his power. The thick, threatening sense of it singing in his voice and the feel of it pressing in all around her were almost enough to drop Emer to her knees. Infuriated and resentful, she squared her shoulders. "Seems to me you also boasted that you would always know where she is. Find her yourself."

Starn's lips curled in an angry snarl, the heat in his eyes glinting dangerously, the continued swell of his power nearly suffocating. Even at her best, Emer recognized she could not take on this man. And she was far from her best, right now. Bracing with locked knees, she waited for the man to smash her to the ground.

Helpless as she felt, her lips refused to lock. "Just where were you, last night, anyway?" she demanded. "Apparently, you were too busy bullying someone else to pay proper attention to your 'duty' to Caer. You're falling short of your proclaimed responsibility to protect her. We were the ones who managed to accomplish that. We saved her life. And she *is* safe, mind you."

The turquoise flame of his gaze and the stranglehold of his power choked off any further comment, binding her speechless before him for several terrorized seconds.

"Truth," he stated, at last, his hold on her easing. "She is unharmed. Now, tell me where she is and I will relieve you of the necessity to keep her safe."

"I...I can't," she choked.

Starn's eyes narrowed again. "Can't?"

"Urgent call," snapped from Emer's wrist communicator once more. Her hand flew to her chest, holding tight over her rapidly thudding heart. "Oh, for the love of now what?" all came with a single exhale.

"Ms. Kyot."

Brandon Jase's voice boomed over her communicator, the sound of it shaken and highly agitated.

"Let me talk to Caer. Now!"

Emer licked her lips. "Uhm, Mr. Jase...we aren't really in a position to welcome company, right now. Perhaps..."

"I'll just bet you're not." Hostility rang through his response. "I'm coming in."

No. Not him, too. Jase may not be capable of teleporting, but the fact did her little good. With the power grid down, she couldn't seal the dome's entry point. Short of expending a tremendous amount of energy on a spell to hold him off, she had no way of stopping him. She shot a furtive glance at Starn. No way would she waste that kind of energy on a Tanai with him still looming over her!

Emer threw her hands up. What could she do? "Oh, why not? Come ahead. I'll meet you in the garden. Let's just throw a party, shall we?"

Starn's glower deepened, his tone demanding. "Who is that?"

"A friend of Caer's," she shot back. "His name is Brandon Jase." She couldn't tell from Starn's expression whether the name meant anything to him. "Brandon Jase," she repeated. "As Caer's 'guardian', surely you know all of her friends."

"I know who he is. What does he want?"

Emer bristled. "You heard him. He wants to see Caer. Not bloody likely, is it, since she's not here? But I can't stop him from coming through, can I? You're welcome to do so, if you wish. Just don't hurt him."

"Get rid of him."

"Get rid of him! Get rid of him! I don't want him here any more than I want you!" Startled by the abruptness of the act, she stood, blinking at the spot from which Starn had just vanished. Only the sense of another's presence told her that he remained near--somewhere in the denser shadows at the side of the house. "You're not far enough away to suit me!" she yelled at him.

"It's as far as I'm getting," growled back.

Calm, she thought. Just be calm. Forcing several deep breaths, she stomped off along the garden path leading to the stairs that switch-backed down to the landing pad. With a little luck, Jase would accept some explanation about Caer's absence--gone shopping or some such--and leave. In the meantime, she could at least take pleasure in knowing that his arrival annoyed the hell out of the great and mighty and very bossy Mr. Adrian Starn!

Several minutes passed before the small, Sion University pod cleared the access tunnel. Several more elapsed before Brandon made it to the top of the stairs and found his way along the dark path to where Emer waited.

The man was some sight! Hands stuffed rigidly in his pants pockets, he stared out from a haggard face, his gaze darting about. The smell and the stain of blood covered his clothes. Emer took a step back, strengthening her personal shielding spell. Thank the heavens he didn't possess any magic. His demeanor suggested deadly intent.

"Mr. Jase," Emer acknowledged with a curt nod. "What brings you here, tonight?"

Brandon froze only a couple of meters from her, blinking into the darkness like cornered prey before he saw her. "Where are the lights?" he demanded. "Bring up the lights."

"I'm sorry," Emer managed evenly. "The power grid has malfunctioned. The whole dome is out. I'd offer to take you inside, but this is probably the brightest spot available, right now."

Jase swallowed, glancing nervously in the direction of the blackened silhouette of the house. "Then call Caer out here."

"She isn't here. Is there something I can do for you?"

He swallowed again. "Then, it's true. You *have* done something with her."

"Excuse me. What?"

Jase's hands twitched in his pockets. "Release Caer. She's coming with me."

"Caer is free to come and go as she chooses, of course." Not exactly true. "Like I said. She isn't here. She's gone out for a little while."

Jase's face pinched with doubt for only a heartbeat before shifting to hostile resolve. "I don't believe you. She told me. She told me all about you."

Emer's brow creased. "Caer told you all about me?"

"You people. All of you. You witches. That's what you call yourselves, isn't it? She told me everything."

"What are you talking about? What has Caer told you?"

"Not Caer."

Emer took a measured breath. She'd had all the chaos and confusion she could handle for one night. "Who, then? Who's been telling you what?"

Jase hesitated, his eyes flicking back and forth between Emer and the ghostly shadow of the distant house.

"Look, Mr. Jase. I'm not interested in guessing games. Either spit out what you want or leave."

The man's hands twitched within his pockets again, his gaze snapping back to Emer. "Bring Caer here. Do whatever it is that you people do with all that appearing-disappearing stuff."

"I can't. She's..."

"Do it or I'll blow you and me and this entire dome to pieces!"

"You! Blow us up?" Emer gaped at him. Suddenly, it seemed quite clear. Sucking in through clenched teeth, she hissed, "You. You were the one who blew up Del's pod!"

"What?"

All of Emer's pent up tension erupted in fury. "You were the last person to be in the pod with her! You were the one who set the bomb! My poor aunt's body is nothing more than red mist, thanks to you!"

"No! You're lying!" His denial came in shallow, shaky gasps. "She's alive! She left me at the hotel. I didn't do anything to her!"

Emer opened her mouth. Closed it again. The man spoke truth. But, if he didn't murder Del, why was he here making threats to her? And just whom had he been talking to?

Though the use of such tactics appalled Emer, she had few other choices, under the circumstances. Cautiously, she made a gentle nudge within Jase's mind, hoping to uncover some core piece of thought...some glimpse of...

"Get out of my head!"

Stunned by the immediacy of Jase's outburst, Emer instantly withdrew her mental probe, remembering too late that the man was a Sensitive. If he could sense the presence of power within people, it stood to reason that he would also be able to detect their infiltration into his own skull. At least he'd not blown her up over the intrusion. Perhaps he was bluffing. The intent of his threat felt genuine, but something didn't fit. If he did possess a bomb, could she cast a rigor spell on him before he triggered the bloody thing?

Del! Where are you when I need you?

And why wasn't Starn doing something? This would be a damn good time for him to demonstrate his bloody magical prowess.

"Look," she said, struggling to keep the worried warble from her voice. "I honestly have no idea what this is all about. Please, Mr... Please, Brandon. Caer is fine. She's just not here. Now, tell me who you've been talking to, and what they've been telling you."

"Brenna." The name sounded almost a sob.

Emer's brow shot up. "Brenna? Brenna Cowl?" What could that Tanai possibly know about Witches? True, the woman had worked under Dr. Aifa Eliz for the past few years. But Aifa would never break honor and risk a banishing by mentioning the Family to a Tanai without the consent of a majority of the Counsel. "Just what is it that's she's told you?"

"She said Caer is being held as your hostage; that you want to take something from her--the thing those people on that hill wanted. Said this thing...this key, or whatever it is, can give the holder horrible powers."

Emer darted a glance at Brandon's hands as they continued to twitch in his pockets, her mind racing for something to appease the man. "In the first place," she offered, working to keep her voice soothing. "We've done no such thing to Caer. In the second place, the key holds no such ability. And thirdly, I don't know how Ms. Cowl could speculate about such things, but I think maybe we should sit down and talk with her. Let's just give her a call and ask her to meet us some..."

"She's dead."

Emer's mouth froze around her unfinished words, her eyes slowly settling on the blood that covered the front of Brandon's clothing. "What?"

Brandon followed the track of her gaze with a hesitant glance down at his shirt. "No!" he groaned. "Not me! I didn't kill her! I swear it! Brenna called me a few hours ago. Asked me to go see her at once. She even sent her pod for me. But when I got there, she was...she was..." He swallowed several ragged breaths. "She died in my arms."

His gaze came up again, fixing on Emer, his words rattling in a raspy wheeze. "You killed her. You people. To shut her up."

"I assure you, we did nothing of the sort!"

The air suddenly tingled with the feel of another teleportation. This one, at least, Emer recognized. Del had returned, at last. Even so, the distant sound of the kitchen door banging open caused her to jump. Brandon did, as well. Emer's glance shot to his pockets once more, fearing a blast. None came. Bluffing. Surely.

Several long, silent moments ticked by, Emer watching Brandon's hands as he waited, watching the newcomer approach. He would likely be even more agitated when he discovered it wasn't Caer. Glancing up to judge the degree of his agitation, Emer found stark terror scrawled across his face. She dared not turn, fearing that even the slightest movement on her part might startle him further.

You wanted me? Del whispered in her head. Once close enough, she called audibly, "Emer, you didn't tell me you had company."

Emer dared a hasty glance around, her heart plummeting to her stomach. The woman approaching carried a lighted candle in one hand and...and cradled a cat in her arm. Merripen! A very much not-dead Merripen. How...? Worse, Emer recognized Del's new accommodations.

Spinning back to Brandon, she watched his mouth work, though no sound came from him, while Del's voice again fluttered in her head. *"What's the matter, dear? Why is Mr. Jase back here? And why does he look like he's just seen a ghost?"*

"Because he has!" Emer shot back. *"Very bad choice, Del. You just turned up wearing the body of the woman who died in his arms only a little while ago."*

"What?"

"Why, in all the universe, did you pick Brenna Cowl's body?"

The polite smile Del wore slipped away. *"Damn! I knew she looked familiar. But you're last sending sounded urgent, so I simply grabbed the freshest corpse in the morgue."*

Brandon backed away. "No. You're dead. This is some trick. Some witch's trick." His pitch went higher, his words chasing in a rant. "You people murdered my sister and her family! You destroyed Jen and all of Ahira! You...you killed Brenna! She died! I saw it! And you're holding Caer as hostage. Tell me where she is! Tell me or I'll..."

Brandon's lips froze mid threat, his body abruptly rigid. Starn stepped from the shadows. "You'll do nothing."

Emer exhaled a long, shaky sigh. "I was beginning to think you were going to let Mr. Jase blow us up."

Starn approached Brandon and reached a hand into one of the man's pockets. "Not with this." He withdrew a small, antiquated handgun and tossed it to her. "Couldn't do much of anything with the chamber empty."

Emer shook her head. He had been bluffing! Had she kept her head, she'd have known as much. Turning the gun over in her hands, she eyed it suspiciously. "This looks like a museum piece. Just how did he get it?"

Growling, Starn asserted, "You can puzzle that out later, assuming you survive that long. My only interest is Caer. I will give you ladies until the count of ten to produce her. Believe me, I need no bomb, nor any gun, to free your souls. And where I'll be sending them, you'll find it very difficult to make your way back for some time to come."

Del brushed past Emer, striding indignantly up to the towering man and shoving her candle toward his face. Even in the statuesque body Del previously occupied, standing on tiptoe would not allow an eyeball to eyeball confrontational stare-down. In her new host, rising to her toes placed her eyes only about chin level with the man. The fact didn't sway her. "Don't you dare threaten us!" She emphasized her words by blowing out the candle, the smoke wafting into Starn's eyes.

He never so much as blinked. "I will dare far more if I don't get some results. I expect to see Caer standing here immediately."

"What makes you think she wants to show up for you?"

Emer tried to wave her aunt silent, her heavy sigh coming across as a groan. Why couldn't this guy read the truth in her words? Delivering Caer was an impossibility. "I told you," she grumbled. "We can't do that. It isn't in our power. So, if you intend to destroy us, get on with it. Poor Mr. Jase, here, looks like he would almost welcome the release."

"Urgent call for Ms. Kyot," blared from her communicator.

Emer blinked in disbelief. "This isn't happening!"

Starn looked almost as dumbfounded and thrice as irritated. "So answer it!"

Glaring at him, she raised the confounded thing, snapping, "What!"

"Ms. Kyot. This is Sgt. Ave Chapman. I am sorry to disturb you so late in the evening. We tried to reach you at home, but..."

Emer rolled her eyes, glancing up at the house. "Yes. Well...I needed to run a few errands. What can I do for you?"

"We are looking for a Mr. Brandon Jase. Have you seen him?"

"Uhm…" Emer leveled her narrowed eyes on Starn, daring him to counter her. "No. Not since a couple of nights ago. Why?"

"One of Dr. Eliz' staff has been murdered. A Brenna Cowl. Her body was found a few hours ago. The suspect got away, but we believe him to be Mr. Jase. A witness saw him running from her apartment covered in blood. Saw him take the victim's university pod. We believe he may also be responsible for removing the victim's body from the hospital morgue a short time ago."

"That's…" Emer shot a sarcastic glance at Del. "That's horrible."

"We received a bulletin moments ago indicating that Mr. Jase may be heading toward your place. We believe he is armed. I suggest you stay away from the estate until we can apprehend him. Officers are on their way, now."

"Yes, of course. Thank you, Sgt." Emer stared at the now silent communicator, seething. "Leave it to the Tanai to be late in their warnings, and to get everything all wrong! Well, that's it! I've had enough of this!" Yanking the wrist band free of her arm, she threw the communicator as far from her as she could.

Fixing Starn with a rebellious glare, she stuffed both fists on her hips. "You want to find Caer. Del and I know where she is. Go ahead. Destroy us, if you wish. I can guarantee you'll get no help from Dylan in finding her. In the meantime, the authorities are about to show up here. As soon as they realize the power grid is down, they will assume Mr. Jase did it. Since they believe Del is dead and I'm elsewhere, they won't hesitate to blast anything that moves. I think you'll agree that it is in the best interest for all of us to vacate before they get here. Otherwise, it's the end for poor Mr. Jase, and you will be forced to postpone your search for Caer until you, Del and I can locate new bodies. But then, you'd have to find us again, wouldn't you?"

She turned to Brandon. The terror in his eyes told her that he remained fully aware of everything going on around him. "Mr. Jase, odd as this may be, I believe you are innocent, at least of Brenna's and Del's deaths. You'll forgive me, however, if I don't ask Mr.

Starn to release you just yet. Much as I believe in your innocence, I don't necessarily trust you to stay that way. You did, after all, come charging in, here, threatening me. What we need is to get you out of harm's way. Then we can talk. Maybe."

A crease worried its way across Emer's brow. Oooooooh, Dylan is not going to like this! Swallowing, she turned again to Starn. "I can't bring Caer to you, but I can take you to her. Just promise me..." She looked from him to Brandon and back again. "Both of you. Promise me that you will behave yourselves. I'm going to be in a multiverse of trouble for this, as it is."

"You're not thinking of... You can't," Del protested. "You heard what Dylan said about booby trapping the spell and the coordinates."

"He said not to give them to anyone. He didn't say that someone else couldn't be brought back with us when we used them."

34

Dark phantoms lurked. They whispered ominously, skimming the edges of Caer's sleep. Part of her wanted to reach for them; wanted to grasp their form and significance. Another part wanted only to be left to a peaceful slumber. A sharp, reverberating clatter, however, prevented her pursuit of either, dragging her grudgingly toward waking.

"They must not fight!"

Groaning, Caer rolled to her back with a mumbled, "hmm?" A bleary-eyed blink into the dimly lit room captured a subtle, twisted dance of shadows. She closed her eyes again, snuggling deeper beneath the blankets, trying to rid herself of the vague sense that someone had been in her head; someone fighting her, pushing her disturbing night visions back to the depths where she could not see them.

"They must not fight!"

Blinking again, Caer tried to focus through eyes that struggled to remain open. A lamp flickered in a wall niche, casting the fidget of shadows. Their jiggery dance caught the edges of the small table standing against a wall, while the darkened mouth of an empty fireplace yawned from another. Beyond that, the room appeared to be empty. Empty and silent.

"Stop them!"

The command bolted Caer upright, her hands instantly yanking the blankets to her chin as both the biting chill of the air and the fact that she was wearing not a stitch impressed themselves on her.

"Who's there? Where are you?" she demanded. "And where is my chemise? I need some clothes!"

A hazy vision of a large wardrobe shimmered to mind. The image clarified slowly, the wardrobe's open doors revealing several pairs of men's trousers and a number of shirts, all hanging neatly within. Caer shook her head, making another quick scan of her surroundings, finding it devoid of wardrobes of any size or shape.

"I need some clothes this instant!" she shouted. The space above the end of the bed distorted briefly, and then...there they were--a pair of the trousers and a silvery blue shirt, much like those in the wardrobe she'd imagined. Her brow knotted, her lips curling in a puzzled frown.

"*Stop them!*" came again, even more urgently than before.

"Stop who? Whoever you are, come out of hiding and explain yourself!"

Again, there was no response. Praying that there were no prying eyes in the darkened hallway beyond, Caer slipped from the bed, donning the trousers, then pulling them off and tossing them aside when her slender hips could not hold them up. Trembling from the cold, she pulled on the shirt, thankful that it extended below her knees. Her icy fingers fumbled to stuff buttons through buttonholes, and the shirt tails flapped at her calves as she minced her way across the frigid floor, nearly tripping over a fallen chair and a couple of blankets that lay there in a heap. The source of the clatter that awakened her? Skirting the chair, she hesitated at the door, peering into the dark and empty corridor. If someone had been in the room with her, they'd apparently left in a hurry.

Faint light seeped around a corner at the far end of the hall. Caer could only speculate that it emanated from the great hall. Perhaps the voice she'd heard was there, as well. That being the case, it probably hadn't been speaking specifically to her.

"*They must not fight!*"

The declaration hit her, now, with such strength and urgency that, whether meant for her or not, it propelled Caer out into the middle of the hall and hastened her toward the light, listening for sounds of commotion as she padded on. There was nothing. No more words, no sound of anyone moving about. Yet foreboding filled her, slowing her pace to a cautious tread. Halting just shy of the pool of light spilling around the corner, Caer's hands curled tightly within the draped sleeves. What was it that she was about to intrude upon?

Bracing herself with a slow, deep breath, she stole a glance around the corner's edge, relieved to see that the light did, indeed, come from the great hall. The door, still a short distance from her, stood open, Dylan at its threshold, his hands on the doorframe in a white-knuckled grip. Uttering a low growl, he abruptly stormed out of sight. For a half a breath, Caer considered turning around and running back to bed. She'd seen how these people fight. If there was going to be another such incident, it was likely to be much healthier for her if she stayed well out of the way.

That's when she noticed it--the disturbing buzz in her ears and the prickles chasing along her nerves. Both had skulked about her senses most subtly for the past several minutes, she realized. She'd just been too drowsy or too preoccupied to pay them any heed. Now that she was aware of them, she recognized them as the sensations that always preceded someone popping into existence from the heavens only knew where.

Keeping to the shadows, she slipped quietly to the door, poking her head around. Dylan now stood at the edge of the dais. His solid, spread-legged stance braced him in agitated waiting, his open shirt front revealing his tensed breathing beneath the thick wrapping of bandages as his focus fixed on the intensifying shimmer of light in the middle of the hall.

"Please," Caer whispered with a moan. "Let it not be another of those beasts!"

At last, the shimmer clarified, dropping the needling of her flesh back to a minor itch, and the buzz to a muted annoyance. Emer emerged first, a cloth bundle tucked under an arm. Caer stifled a gasp as a very rigid Brandon materialized next, Brenna Cowl close behind him, the short curls of the woman's blond hair cork-screwing in disheveled coils. The person emerging behind her barely registered as Caer's gaze caught on a wretched and wildly wriggling Merripen held firmly in Cowl's arms. What was that woman doing here, and why did she have...

A stunned squeak escaped, despite Caer's attempt to stifle it. Jerking back into the shadows, she tried to understand what she'd just sensed. It wasn't Brenna Cowl out there. It was Fedel'ma...inside Cowl...not inside the cat! She couldn't say how she knew this to be true, yet her certainty was beyond question. Sucking a shaky breath, she considered. If Del was now in Cowl's body...where was Cowl?

"Dylan... Let me..."

The tremulous sound of Emer's voice strangled to a pained cry as a bright burst of blue-white light lit up the small space where Caer huddled. The resounding boom that accompanied it shook the entire building, knocking thick dust into the air. Caer batted at it, struggling not to choke as she dared another glimpse into the hall. Emer, she saw, had dropped to her knees. Slumping forward, the woman's elbow struck the floor, knocking her bundle free to scoot along the stonework.

Still poised on the top of the dais, Dylan maintained one arm extended, his palm aimed directly at his cousin, the other aimed elsewhere. Though he was obviously laboring from the exertion of the spell he'd just cast, his thunderous tone suggested he might yet strike again. "I trusted you."

Blinking through her tears, Emer glared up at him. "Like I trusted you!"

Dylan's face flushed crimson. "Is that what this is? Some sort of payback?"

Emer started to rise, then slumped back, her voice thin and sorrowful. "No. Of course not. I didn't mean that. I just..."

"Your argument is with me," Adrian boomed, shoving past

Cowl...or Fedel'ma...or whoever the woman was, to halt squarely in front of Emer. Glowering at Dylan, he proclaimed, "I gave Ms. Kyot no choice. I've come for Caer."

Caer cringed back to the shadows once more, her mind reeling. Adrian. He was the one who'd come through just after the woman who'd once been Cowl. What was he doing here? Chewing at her lip, she again peered around the door's edge.

Dylan lowered his aim from Emer for a fraction of a heartbeat before raising it once more, now standing with both hands pointed at the man he clearly deemed an unwelcome intruder. "My previous strike was just a warning. Now I am giving you no choice. You are leaving. Without Caer."

Adrian raised a hand in mutual threat. "I want no battle with you."

"I'm sure you don't."

Caer passed a terrified glance between the two. This was the battle someone tried to warn her against. Adrian and Dylan were the ones who mustn't fight! But how could she possibly stop them? Already, a tremendous surge of power was building around each man, the charge of it rushing along Caer's flesh. A pinched squeal cracked at the back of her throat as the gravity of what they might do to one another became crystal clear. Before she realized where her feet were taking her, she found herself halfway across the dais, her strong, clear, "Stop!" surprising her so completely that she could follow it with nothing more.

Though both men shot startled glances her way, neither moved from his challenging stance. "Caer," Adrian bellowed, the discord of his tone sharp and commanding. "You're coming with me. I'm not settling for 'no', this time."

"Don't," Dylan snarled, his eyes never leaving his opponent.

Emer pushed to her feet, nursing her elbow and wincing as she hobbled out from behind Adrian to impose herself between the two men. "You heard her. Stop it."

"Move," Dylan commanded.

Emer held her ground, glaring. "No."

"You don't know who this man is. There is no record of him, anywhere in the archives. For all we know, he may be of Nemhain's line."

"Why should I believe that you aren't of the Dark Heart's line?" Adrian spat in return.

Emer stomped her foot, her anger smoldering in her dark eyes. "I said stop it! It appears both of you are after the same thing-- protecting Caer. Neither of you can accomplish that if you eliminate each other."

An ugly undercurrent flowed through Adrian's, "She wouldn't need so much protection had he not enticed her to Earth and given her the second part of the key. And he hasn't the power to eliminate me."

"I enticed her nowhere," Dylan contested. His lip peeled back in a sneer as he added, "And you'd be surprised what I have the power to do."

Blue-white light began to spike around each man's extended hand. Caer wanted to shrink away from them but feared they would surely murder one another if she didn't do something. Choking to find her voice once more, she managed a sufficiently demanding repetition of, "Stop it!" adding a mimic of Emer's stomped foot with as much bravado as she could muster. Pushing past Dylan, she tromped down the steps and across to stand at Emer's side, her determined glower set on the imposing countenance of Adrian Starn.

"No one is to blame for my coming to Earth but me! No one enticed me here. I came because it's what I wanted. You know better than anyone how hard I've worked to get my transfer to Sion accepted. I don't know what you have against these people, Adrian, but if they wanted to harm me, they've had ample opportunity to do so. Instead, they saved my life."

Spinning back to face Dylan, her eyes narrowed. "As for you, I don't know what you have against Adrian. But I can tell you, he has been my friend longer than any other person I've ever known. So, I would appreciate it if the both of you stopped this insanity, especially since it seems to center on me. I will not be used to fuel some feud."

Dylan's challenging stance did not change, though he, at last, lowered his arms. Turning, Caer stuffed her sleeve-tangled fists to her hips, eyeing Adrian. "Well?"

Dismay etched a path across his features, dampening the harsh lines of his fury. Still, his arm never wavered. "You have to come with me, Caer." He jerked a nod toward Dylan. "It isn't safe for you to be anywhere near him."

"Isn't safe!" Growling her frustration, she erupted with, "Adrian, you truly are insane! The man helped you save Bran and me from... from whatshername on that bloody hill. And he saved me from a Coran'ian that broke into Del's estate. That thing nearly killed him. How can you possibly think he's any sort of threat to me?"

A long and uneasy silence hung over Adrian before he finally lowered his hand. "He's a Dream Reader." The words carried a mix of distaste, distrust, and grudging respect. "A master, if I'm any judge. And he's lied to you."

"A..." Caer glanced back at Dylan. She should know what that meant. Why didn't she know what that meant? The question was quickly shunted aside in favor of her outrage at Adrian's hypocrisy. Squaring herself in front of him again, she stretched as tall as she could while shaking an accusing finger at his nose. "What do you mean, he's lied to me? Tell me, Adrian Starn! Tell me straight to my face that you haven't been lying to me for as long as I've known you! You never told me you had these...these powers. And...and you know why my memories keep skittering out of my reach. You've known all along. Don't tell me that you haven't! Yet you won't tell me why! You've lied to me, making believe...letting me believe...that I'm someone I'm not! I'm like you, aren't I?" She gestured broadly around her. "Like them! And you never said! Never let me learn what I might be capable of!"

Furious as she was with him, she couldn't help but cast an

aggrieved scowl at Dylan, as well. "So. Tell me, sir. Just what have you lied to me about?"

Dylan's troubled gaze caught and held hers, drawing her into their incredible depths. It was like looking into mirrors within mirrors, their glow going back and back and back. Eyes in which she could easily get lost. At last, she sensed a presence she'd felt all along, but had rejected as part of her guilt and sorrow.

The shock left her breathless and dizzy. "I...know you," strangled from her. "You're...you're Dr. Jorn."

He had, indeed, lied! How could he do that to her? How could he send her off as he did, allowing her to think he'd been blown to pieces? How could he stand there, now, feigning to be a stranger, offering no explanation...no apology for her anguish or her grief?

Dylan turned away, striding to the center of the dais to lean against the table. With a weary flick of his hand, the long bench behind it vanished, reappearing near the fire. "You look like you need to sit down," he said quietly. "You might want to take Mr. Jase with you. He isn't looking too well."

Caer blinked, her ire and sense of betrayal somewhat offset by the realization that she'd completely forgotten about Brandon. Why didn't he look well?

Brandon remained where he'd first emerged, still just as unmoving and mute, though terror was clear in his eyes.

"What have you done to him?" she fired at Adrian and the two women. "Whoever is responsible, unfreeze him this instant!"

With an almost imperceptible tilt of his head, Adrian released the spell. Merripen yowled and leapt from Cowl's...Del's...arms as the woman swung around to support Bran before he collapsed. His leaning weight teetered them both, threatening to take the woman down beneath him. Caer took a step toward them but not before Bran gained his balance, jerking free of the offered support and backing away.

"What the eternal depths of hell is going on?" he rasped. "Someone tell me what's going on!"

Cowl/Del straightened with an indignant huff as she brushed herself off. "You don't want to know." Tramping past Emer and Caer, she muttered, "Just leave the old woman to hold up the nasty young man and let her get dumped on her face for her efforts. That's all right."

"Unless you want me to reinstate my spell," Adrian warned, "the best thing for you, Mr. Jase, is to find a quiet corner and stay out of the way."

"Not until someone..."

Adrian rounded on him. "I was polite the first time. I didn't use a spell like Maura's. Saved you a lot of pain and convulsions. I won't be so polite a second time. Consider yourself lucky that I opted to save your skin at the estate. Don't make me regret it."

"Saved?" Caer finally took note of Brandon's clothes, the dark stains at last registering as blood. "Bran!"

Adrian grasped her arm, preventing her from dashing to her friend.

"Let go of me! He's hurt! I..."

"He's fine."

Brandon shot Adrian a venomous look as he retreated to a strip of wall near the fireplace, sinking to the floor in hostile silence.

"But the blood..." Caer persisted.

"Isn't his," harrumphed from Cowl/Del as she settled on the lowest of the dais steps. "Belongs to the previous inhabitant of the slab of flesh I currently occupy, if I understand correctly. I knew there was something familiar about the corpse. Should have done more looking around. There had to be someone in that morgue that I didn't know, never mind someone whose soulless husk needed less mending. Someone closer to my previous size and shape would have been nice, as well. I wouldn't be sitting here with pant legs rolled up and a shirt bagging to my thighs, now would I?"

"From...from Cowl? The blood came from Cowl?" Caer gaped at Brandon. "Why?"

"I didn't kill her!"

Emer retrieved her bundle and limped her way to join her aunt. "Much as I believe you, Mr. Jase, the police think otherwise." Plopping down on the steps next to Del, she turned a smoldering glare to Dylan. "It was either bring the poor man here, or let him die. Tell me. What would you have me do?"

"And him?" Dylan growled, nodding toward Adrian. "Why bring him?"

"I told you," Adrian hissed. "Ms. Kyot had no blame in that." Still gripping Caer's arm, he added, "It's time to get you out of here. We'll take your friend Jase, as well, if it will make you happier. Dream Reader, open the way before I..."

"No!" chorused from Dylan, Caer, and Brandon, as Caer yanked free of Adrian's grasp.

Brandon flashed a scathing look at the group. "I've had enough of all of you. Just let me go back to my hotel, and leave me alone!"

"Not wise," Del huffed. "Emer is right. The police are looking for you. They apparently believe you've already committed one murder. Once they get a look at the state of my estate and realize that Emer is missing, they'll undoubtedly be convinced you've added another. Even if you should be lucky enough to avoid them for a while--highly improbable--it's even less likely that you'll be able to hide from Nemhain's baboons. She will certainly have Maura on the hunt for both you and Caer. And believe me, the things either of those two can do to you make being taken down by the police worthy of eager anticipation. From my perspective, your only choice, for now, is to throw your lot in with us. You might accidentally live a little longer. We, at least, don't have any reason to want you dead...thus far."

Brandon's face twitched with a broiling mix of rage and fear, mouth half formed around whatever he was about to say. Caer cut him off, begging, "Please, Bran. Stay. You trusted me before. Trust me now. It's not safe for either of us to leave."

"That may be true for Jase," Adrian thundered. "But I'm telling you, you are no safer here than out there."

Caer's jaw set. "You're wrong, Adrian. And I think you know

it. I'm sure Dylan…Jorn…whoever! I think he will allow you to go, though."

Adrian ran a weary hand over his face, muttering, "Bull headed fool of a… You used to listen to me."

Caer continued to glare at him. "You used to be less dictatorial. This is where I'm supposed to be, Adrian." She shot hesitant glances between Dylan…or Jorn…Emer, and…Fedel'ma/Cowl, trying to shake free from the disorientation brought on by the disturbing thought of wearing someone else's body. "I can't say that I trust these people. But knowing that you've lied to me, too…knowing that you've done so since the beginning…" Shaking her head, she asked, "How can you expect me to trust you, either? I don't know who you are, any more than I know who they are." Her small frame slumped. "I don't even know who I am. Why would you do that to me?"

"To protect you. Like I'm trying to do, now."

"I don't need your protection. I don't want it, if it means never learning who…or what I am."

"My place is at your side, Caer. I've sworn it. If you stay, then so must I. Especially now. You've started remembering things. Things that should not be returning to you. The more you know about yourself, the more your life is at risk. My guess is that the Dream Reader has found a way to weaken the suppression of certain pieces of your past. But there are memories, Caer, that he must not disturb."

Caer moaned. "Dream Reader. What, pray tell, is a Dream Reader?"

"More to the point," Emer interjected as she regarded Adrian with narrowed eyes. "How did you know that to be one of Dylan's gifts?"

Adrian likewise studied Emer as though weighing whether to answer. Shrugging, he relented. "Ever since Caer's arrival on Ahira, one particular piece of her past has increasingly merged with her dreams. Took me long enough to make the connection between the man she called Dr. Jorn and the emergence of those bits of memory.

Once I did, the meddling of a Dream Reader seemed the only reasonable explanation."

Caer's fists closed inside their draping of sleeves, her anger rising again. "That doesn't help me one little bit! I ask again. What the hell is a Dream Reader?"

Adrian's disgust curled his lip. "He gets into your head. Sees your dreams. Disentangles memories and facts from fantasy. He learns all there is to know about you without your knowledge or consent."

"But he didn't. He..." She spun to face Dylan with a sharp sucking of breath. He did get into her head. It was him. Last night. He wove chants through her mind; used them to draw sleep over her. Not once, though, had he tampered with her dreams, as Adrian suggested. Her face screwed with confusion. Rather, he did his best to keep her dreams hidden from her.

"You're wrong, again," she murmured. "He forced me to sleep without awareness of my..."

Adrian cut her off, turning a dubious eye to Dylan. "You stopped her?"

"I tried." Exhaustion and pain were evident in Dylan's slouch. "I managed to work the spell of sleep, but she fought me every step of the way. I don't know that I was entirely successful in keeping the dark elements from her subconscious submerged. She's as damnably stubborn as the rest of the women in the Family."

Adrian squared on Caer, his intimidating height looming over her "Well?"

"Well?" she sniffed.

"Did he succeed?"

Some nerve he had, prying information from her while accusing others of doing the same. Her resentment, however, failed to stop her tongue from retorting with a hostile, "Maybe!" Caving beneath his stare, she admitted, "Yes...Well, sort of. There were a few bits of nightmare that niggled at me. I don't remember them anymore now than I ever do, though. Just hints and snatches that..."

Gripping her arm once more, Adrian roughly escorted her to the bench and sat her down with a thud. "Listen to me, Caer. You have to leave what's hidden alone."

She met his glare evenly. "Why should I? I have a right to know my own mind. A right to know who I am." Reaching absently for her necklace, she leveled a belligerent glare on Adrian, daring him to interfere, then snapped her attention inward, declaring, "I can't know who I am or where I'm going if I don't know who I was or where I've been. I demand to know!"

35

Anticipation of the agony that seared her temples and exploded through her head did nothing to stifle Caer's cry. Her body swayed from the impact, the room reeling around her. Hands steadied her. She didn't know whose. Didn't care. She wanted her memories; would find them. Fighting the pain and the scream that sought release, she pressed for hints...for glimpses of any image that might shed more light on who she was, on why she should be the one to whom this accursed key fell.

The visions came as a flood, daring her to focus. Her mother's face became her anchor. Caer fixed on it, forcing the rush of other images aside. Her mother's face first. As it clarified, her gaze fell to the fine silver chain gracing her neck. Beautiful. Brightly polished. Precious. Infant hands...her hands...reached for the necklace. Even at so young an age, foresight told her the necklace was destined to be hers. Yet, her mother did not yield it.

Barely turned five and the explosion that would take the lives of her parents loomed in her prescience. Caer warned them. Long before their deaths, she foresaw the explosion and warned them. At first, they appeared to heed her warning, accepting her demand that they take her and leave the Perimeter Ship. Their journey took them to a secret place where her parents established shielding spells, the strength of which hummed their tension along Caer's nerves. There, her mother removed the beautiful necklace that had never before been parted from her, fastening it around Caer's neck and tucking it into her shirt.

Instinctively, Caer understood the responsibility and the risks inherent in accepting the chain. So, too, she understood that the choice was hers--keep it, or return it to her mother's hands. Her foresight gave no hint of what would happen, should she refuse the gift, but a heavy foreboding darkened that choice. She accepted. Not with words, but with her small hand to her chest, delicately patting the chain where it lay beneath her shirt. Her mother recited the oath to her--the promise to carry the chain, keeping it safe from other hands. Caer repeated the pledge, word for word, without hesitation.

Despite her wailing protestations, her parents returned with her, then, to the Perimeter Ship. Yet their homecoming was uneventful, the year that followed filled with quiet joys. The foreboding that had prompted her acceptance of the chain and its attendant responsibility was forgotten. Even her premonition of her parents' deaths slipped from her conscious mind--until the vision came again, this time far more clearly and with a greater sense of urgency. The horror awakened her, screaming.

She could not dissuade her parents from their tasks the next day. Rather, they took her with them. How strong were her father's arms as he carried her; how warm her mother's tears as she took Caer from him, hugging her, speaking soothing words inside her head, telling her she must be brave. Her mother held her close, kissing her so tenderly...

With the first thunder of the explosion, Caer cried out. The flash of heat and her glimpse of the flames, however, lasted less than the intake of a single breath before all dissolved in the shimmer of teleportation. At that very instant, her mother had sent her away. When the shimmering ceased, Sidra's arms embraced her. Heaving sobs wracked Caer as Sidra chanted softly, weaving gentle spells. Gradually, the magic cloaked and calmed her, forging a barrier around her gift of foresight. No more prescience. No memory that such a gift had made itself known to her. Even the memory of her parents grew hazy, the specifics of their deaths...of their sending their child away...shrouded.

Sidra's garden kept Caer content. That and her studies. Sidra taught her to work the fine filaments of magic, looping them here to move a broom from its resting place in the corner and swish it along the floor; weaving them there to make the fire for cooking their evening's meal. So many warps and weaves to make, each with its own significance, its own impact on her little world; each with its own toll in energy expended for setting the magic in motion. The best spells, the ones most worthy of the energy required, were those used to enhance the medicines for the people of their community-- the miners and their families.

Caer was curious about the people. She tried to understand their ways, was sorry for them because they lacked the gifts that could make their lives easier. They couldn't weave the magic. Sidra said the common people, the Tanai, didn't understand her any more than she did them. She forbade Caer from talking to them about her abilities. They feared what they couldn't understand, Sidra said. And fear let in terrible things.

The mayor, the only one among the Tanai whom Sidra ever called friend, must have understood the least; must have feared the most. For, what he did was the most terrible. He came for Sidra, allowing harsh men to take her away from their little home. He took Caer, as well. Shoved her along the street to the square where she found her aunt bound to a post atop a great pyre. Flames already ate along the chemical-laced tinder, licking their way toward Sidra, while the black smoke billowed toward the high curve of Lillith's dome to be vented to the outside world. The mayor...the man whom they'd called friend...held Caer. Made her watch as the fire ignited in Sidra's clothes.

Wrenching away from the man, dodging others, Caer ran. She would free her aunt! She would! Together, they would leave these horrible people.

Running hard, darting and weaving through grabbing hands,

she rushed headlong into the flames, scrabbling up the crumbling slope of the pyre through the heat and the pain. But she couldn't free her aunt. Neither could she escape. She could only sob against the torture of the flames and against the death that would surely claim them both. That's when Sidra's cry rang out above the shouted chants of 'witch' and 'burn'. Her aunt called for another--a guardian. He came. Adrian. His eyes glowed like fiery turquoise as he shimmered into existence in the blaze. Seeing Sidra draw her last breath, he wrapped Caer in cool darkness and took her from that hell.

She awoke to Healers all around. They hovered day and night, tending to her. Stoirm was there, too. Each day he sat with her, calmed her when no one else could. Slowly, her burns healed. Even their scarring gradually vanished. But her soul continued to cry, the myriad hateful voices of that night rising from deep inside to haunt her dreams.

When Adrian returned to the Healer's abode, she barely remembered him. Like Stoirm, though, he sat with her, the music of his songs quietly nestling deep within her to work his magic. Her memories dimmed and shifted. Some faded entirely from her mind. Others were carefully altered. The voices that had haunted her in the darkness were driven deeper. They remained--always in the depths, rarely rising again to darken her dreams, until...until she arrived on Ahira. Though she never remembered more from them than the sense of fire and pain, she knew her nightmares were growing darker, menacing her sleep with increasing frequency.

Now... Now she sought for those nightmares, prying them from the depths. The voices long suppressed rose with the memories. Memories of other flames, other tortured souls. So many fires! So much agony! Yet, there was something more. It shimmered in her mind like the faintest glow of the furthest star. Another barrier, however, blocked her way. Unyielding and invisible, it prevented her chasing along the faint strand of light that led into the darkest abyss.

She refused to back away; insisted on learning what still lay hidden. Her struggle to force past the resistance delivered a new searing through her skull, far greater than any previous attempt to seek her memories had produced. Like a burning knife, it sliced through her mind, threatening to ignite her soul...threatening to destroy her.

"Caer! Don't!"

No stopping. She had to see what lay just out of reach. She pressed again, the torture, at last, releasing her scream as, far below, the place where the darkest knowledge lay hidden trembled and tore open.

Drums. Laughter.

"Caer!"

Fire. Exploding agony. Blood running. Voices screaming. A curse raised to the heavens.

"Stop her! Dream Reader!"

A droning chant carries within the screams, its cadence faint. Unsteadily, it grows...fades...

A face almost like her own. Tears glimmer beneath closed eyelids. Darkness closing in. Cold like death. A black too deep to penetrate.

The chanting cadence grows once again; erupts; clings to her; jerks her away from the blackness.

With a shuddering gasp, Caer's awareness plunged back into the light of the great hall. Thunder roared in her head, creating a throbbing pain so severe that her stomach gave up what little it held.

"Dylan!" Emer snapped. "You should have brought her back more gently."

His retort was equally heated. "There wasn't time."

Several tortured seconds elapsed before the sickening spin in Caer's head subsided enough for her to see Adrian standing over her, his hands gripping her shoulders to prevent her falling from the bench. To one side of him stood Dylan and Emer. Each of their faces twisted with shock and grief. She'd have been outraged at their drawing her back from the brink of understanding, except that she had no energy left for such vehemence. A crushing weight, not only from the lingering pain but also from deep sorrow, bore down on her.

Emer pushed Adrian aside, kneeling in front of Caer, a bucket materializing at her side, a damp cloth in her hands. Mute and trembling, Caer submitted to Emer's gentle ministrations, the woman washing her face, sleeves, hands, and lap, rinsing the cloth repeatedly in the bucket.

"Don't do that again!" Adrian's command rang sharply, jarring through Caer's head. "For sake of your sanity, Caer, I relinquished the memories that both your aunt and I hid from you. Whatever lies beneath I possess no skill to open. Those memories must remain where they are." He reached for her chin, forcing her to look up at him. "Listen to me! If you don't wish to destroy yourself, you'll wait until the time is right for you to know what lies there. Understand?"

She didn't. She nodded anyway. A very tiny nod, the faint motion all she could summon past the continuing throb in her temples and the grief of her losses. Her parents, Sidra...all murdered. Worse, each of their deaths had been accompanied by a banishing. The power of such dark magic had scorched her mind. They were forever lost. Their souls would never again return.

"When...when were you going to tell me?" limped as a weak whisper from Caer's lips. "You were going to tell me. Weren't you?"

Adrian stared down at her, his features no longer harsh, the gentle musicality once again filling his voice. "When I thought you ready."

"And...and Stoirm?" she murmured.

Adrian hesitated, his face ashen. His reply, when it came, was barely audible. "What about him?"

"He was there with me after...after you took me from Lillith. He knew me. Knew me even before that time, didn't he? He said so. Is he? My uncle? He said he was my distant uncle." If it was true, he was the only family she had left. Caer longed for his presence; wanted him to wrap her again in the same soothing quiet she remembered when he stayed with her in the Healers' abode.

"Stoirm." Del edged around the bench from behind Caer, her attention on Adrian. "That's at least twice, now, that the man with you at Slieve na Calliagh has been referred to by that name. Lord Stoirm from the ancient stories? That Stoirm?"

Adrian acknowledged with a slow nod.

"Distant uncle, indeed! He's distant uncle to us all!" Leaning closer to Caer, she asked, "You saw the Alainn? Spoke to him?"

Emer rose from her knees, dropping the cloth into the bucket, her gaze shifting between Adrian and her aunt. "He and Starn came to the estate after you left. I..."

"Here! Earth-side?" Elation spread across Del's face. "And me thinking he died centuries ago. That could change everything! With his help..."

Adrian strode past Emer, his head bent as he moved well away from the others. "Do not look for assistance from that quarter."

Del's surprised scrutiny followed him. "Why not? The ancient stories say he was with the sisters in the beginning; that he stood with the two in the breaking and hiding of the key. Surely, he will want to see their efforts succeed."

"Lord Stoirm is gravely injured. Wounded protecting me. When we left Caer at your estate, our teleportation was interrupted and redirected back to Slieve na Calliagh. We could not break the hold."

"No one," Dylan declared, "holds the power to redirect a teleportation by someone actively fighting the interfering spell. Not over such a distance."

"Nemhain achieved the act." Anguish was thick in Adrian's tone. "Her strength has been growing for centuries. Still, I never believed her capable of such a feat. Not until she snared Stoirm and me. The attack that followed was brutal. Stoirm took the worst of it. I doubt he will last more than a day or two."

Caer's soul tumbled into deeper despair, hot tears spilling down her cheeks.

Del straightened, her face--Cowl's face--setting in firm resolve. "He's still alive."

"He was barely so when I left him."

"The type of wounds he sustained?"

"From Coran'ian and worse. Nemhain has used her magic to greatly unhance a multitude of alien beasts. She's given particular attention to those who possess venom. And it seems many of them now lay in wait at Slieve na Calliagh. Nemhain must have summoned them to the hill after we took Caer from Maura."

Dylan stiffened. "I didn't expect Maura to broach her failure to take Caer and the key with her mother."

"I doubt it was she who did," Adrian sighed. "Not that it matters who did the telling. Nemhain knows, now, that the key is whole and who holds it. Took little time for her to trace Caer back to your estate. Whether in the attack on Stoirm and me the Dark Heart expected her beasts to retake Caer, or simply to kill off those who protect her I can't say with any certainty. The beasts held nothing back, though. Neither Stoirm nor I would have survived, had Nemhain not realized who her beasts had ensnared. I used the moment of her distraction, when she called the creatures off Stoirm, to remove us to a place she cannot follow." Adrian shook his bowed head. "Too late, I fear. My best Healers are with Stoirm even now, but his wounds are proving beyond their skill."

Caer made to rise, the motion making her stomach lurch and shooting knives of pain through her skull. "I...I need to see him."

Emer's hand held her in place. "You need to sit still and be quiet. You're in no condition to do anything, after what you just put yourself through."

"Can you bring him here?" Del's question brought a stunned snap of Adrian's attention to her.

"He goes nowhere! He's in the hands of those who love him."

Del's jaw set. "But who can't help him. Emer just might."

"What?" Emer gasped. "Del, I can't! I barely..."

"Your skills are tremendous," Del persisted. "And you've something else going for you, here."

"Like what?"

Del folded her arms across her breast. "Like us. Our combined powers. Can't you feel it? There was already a fair undercurrent of mingled energies with just the four of us locked in, here. Now that Mr. Starn has...uhm...well...joined us, the whole of the manor house throbs. It could drive me to distraction, all that buzzing in my ears and zinging along my nerves. Still, the confines set by Dylan's shielding now contain within them a seriously potent combination. It might just work to reinforce your gift. I say, bring Lord Stoirm here."

"I assure you," Adrian objected. "My Healers are the best in the Family. If they can do nothing for him..."

Del cocked a brow at him. "Not *the* best, I'll wager."

Emer flushed, raising her hands in protest. "Del!"

Adrian turned a barely hopeful scrutiny to Emer. "Assuming you are not grossly overstating Mr. Kyot's abilities, or the possibility that the combination of our powers might somehow enhance them--it would be better to take all of you to him."

"And chance being caught by Nemhain?" Dylan's fists doubled. "Caer goes nowhere."

Del spun on her son. "Lord Stoirm is dying and you say you will not help him?"

"I say no to Caer's going. You can do as you please. Risk yourselves, if you wish. You'll not be coming back, though." His eyes narrowed as he shot a hostile glare at Adrian. "I'll not leave this place vulnerable to treachery at the hands of people I don't know, I don't care who you think this Stoirm is."

His mother's fury exploded. "You're no son of mine if you insinuate that Lord Stoirm would ever fall in league with..."

Adrian silenced her with a glance before leveling his own heated glower on Dylan. "We have always stood against Croi Breag, Stoirm and I. Do you read the truth of my words?"

Dylan frowned but nodded.

"And still you do not trust us."

"Nor you me, I'm guessing."

Caer could sit quietly no longer. If there was hope for the Alainn, even the remotest glimmer, she had to break this impasse. "I trust Adrian and Stoirm," she managed, forcing her unsteady knees to support her as she stood. "With my very soul."

Gripping Emer's arm to avoid dropping back onto the bench, she offered, "I will make this deal, Dylan...Jorn...whoever you are. I will stand by my statement to remain here, if you will allow Adrian to bring Stoirm. Please!"

Adrian shook his head. "I'm not leaving without you."

"Even if I promise to make no more attempts at looking into my own head? Even if bringing Stoirm here may be his only chance?"

Never had Caer seen Adrian looking so worn and haggard. *"You said it before, Adrian. And I know it to be truth."* Her sending was clumsy and slightly broken. All the years of disuse because Adrian kept knowledge of her abilities from her reignited her belligerence. *"You can't force me to go with you if it isn't my will, no matter your threats. Like it or not, somehow, I know I'm supposed to remain where I am. At least for now. If I'm truly Witch, as my memories...and my ability to communicate with you in this manner seem to imply...if I possess even the tiniest flicker of energy to add to what stirs within these walls, it might be just that last bit necessary to aid Emer in this task. Bring Stoirm. Let her try to help. Let all of us try to help."*

Adrian's stunned expression told Caer he'd 'heard' her. Slowly, he turned away, addressing Dylan. "For whatever it's worth, Dream Reader, I believe your shielding hides your sanctuary from the Dark Heart as thoroughly as they hid the place from me." His countenance darkened as he submitted. "I will trust Caer to your protection if you will trust me. Allow me to bring Stoirm and the Healers who are caring for him."

Dylan's eyes flicked toward Caer for but a second. "Very well," he conceded dully. "Take Mother. She can get you out and back again. I'll trust you that far. Because Caer asked it. As for your

Healers..." He shrugged as he turned and headed for the door at the back of the dais. "Bring them if you wish. But no others. If Mother is right about anything, it's that Emer is the one who might work your miracle."

36

Caer pattered barefoot from the bath chamber to the great hall, the ache of cold running from her toes to the top of her head. Foolishness! A manor house completely plumbed for running water, but lacking any provision for heating either water or the building! Her lips pinched tight at her constant shivering. What extra trouble could it possibly be to add a fuel cell? But no. Here, warming the house was done via a fireplace in every room, and a hot bath required heating buckets of water and hauling them to the massive tub. It was an expenditure of time that might prevent her returning to the hall before Adrian and Del returned with Stoirm. So, instead, she opted for a cold shower in one of the bath chamber's small cubicles.

Ridiculous to have to make such a choice! At least Emer's trek back to the estate had provided one of Caer's own jumpsuits. She also now wore two of Dyl...Jor... She threw her hands up in exasperation. Whatever name he chose to go by, she wore two of his shirts over her jumpsuit. She'd discovered the man's cache of clothes while assisting Emer in setting up a room for their expected patient. One of the bed-less rooms they'd raided for the contents of a large wardrobe held not only a fair stash of blankets but clothing, as well.

Caer's lips pinched, recalling her reaction to seeing the wardrobe and its contents. She was sure it was the same one she'd imagined when she awoke just prior to Adrian's turning up. How the shirt and pants had been drawn from it to her remained a mystery. Still, she was most grateful for discovering the wardrobe's actual existence.

Her current extra layers of shirts were most welcome. Unfortunately, she still lacked shoes and socks. She worried that she might never be able to thaw her poor feet from traipsing around on the cold stone!

Caer's grumbled thoughts stopped short as she came to a halt in the open doorway leading to the dais and great hall. A fog of steam rose from puddles splotching the floor of both.

"Compliments of that Dylan fellow," Brandon stated, the hint of slight inebriation in his words. Caer spotted him standing next to the long table at the center of the dais. "He dumped a ton of hot water on everything," Bran continued. "Buckets of it kept appearing and emptying." Batting at the air, his nose wrinkled at the astringent aroma. "Used some sort of disinfectant, as well. At least the smell has faded some."

Caer's gaze fell to the fare that covered the table--fresh breads, cheeses, sliced meats, fruit.

"Oh." Bran gestured at the food. "And all of this. He also provided all of this...out of thin air. It's real enough." Grabbing a thick slab of bread, he took several bites before adding. "Didn't know how hungry I was until all of this appeared."

"So, where is Dyl...Jor...?" Damn! She couldn't keep stumbling over how to refer to him! Nor could she bring herself to think of him as the man she knew on Ahira. So...Dylan, then. "Where is... Dylan...now?"

Brandon shrugged. "Don't know. Not in the manor house, I think."

That much, Caer knew. The telltale charge of the man's first teleported departure came while she was helping Emer set up one of the empty rooms in the back as an infirmary. She noted the charge of his return while she was shivering in the shower; that of his second departure only moments ago.

"You'd better come and eat something," Bran suggested. Nodding toward the kegs on the other end of the table, he added, "You could probably use a drink, as well. The one on the right holds wine. The other has ale." Taking a moment to regard the empty mug on the table in front of him, he picked it up and headed for the cask he'd indicated as holding the ale.

Caer declined, the odor of disinfectant, her jittery nerves, and the ache of the cold all combining to leave her stomach in such turmoil that she dared not attempt to put anything in it. Sweeping past Bran, she descended the dais steps, the damp floor pleasantly warm from their cleansing. Bran made no motion to follow, content with refilling his mug. Caer didn't begrudge him a chance to drown himself in drink. Lost the love of his life. Lost his family. Beaten near to death. Brenna Cowl apparently died in his arms. Suspected of Cowl's murder, and probably Emer's as well. And now he was stuck here.

She ventured a quick backward glance at him. At least he looked almost himself, again. At some point, he must have taken time to bathe. Perhaps while she and Emer were setting up the room. The trousers and shirt he wore were fresh. Dylan's, she guessed, though, given their fit of Brandon's taller, broad-chested build, they must have come from one of the man's previous lives. Dylan's current...'vessel' would be lost in them. Caer chewed at her lip as she shuffled to the far end of the hall, wondering just how many lives these people were capable of living.

The question dropped from her mind as she paused, waiting for some indication of the teleportation that would return Adrian and company to the manor house. Sensing nothing, she turned and headed back toward the dais. Two more trips triggered a grumble from Brandon.

"For the sake of my sanity, Caer, sit down!"

She cast an irritable frown his way, watching him grab a handful of grapes to go with his drink before he left the dais. In the spot near the fireplace that had seemingly become his preferred roost lay a pile of blankets onto which he plopped. She offered no response, though, as she carried on with her pacing.

"Caer," Brandon sighed. "Will you please light somewhere?"

She couldn't. Her nervous energy forbade it.

"At least stop long enough to eat something."

"Not hungry," she muttered.

"Here," he muttered, a testy edge returning to his voice as he pushed to his feet again. Pulling one of the blankets from the top of his pile, he thrust it in her direction. "You're shivering. At least take this and stand by the fire for a while." When she failed to go to him, he trudged across and tossed it around her shoulders, then returned to his spot, thudding back down with a grunt.

Caer's fingers absently closed on the wrap without her missing a step.

After watching her make several more laps, Brandon groaned, "Light, for pity sake! You're going to wear a canyon beneath you if you keep this up. It certainly isn't going to bring the others back any sooner."

The jerk of her head flipped her wet braid around to smack her in the face. "They should have come back, already. It's been way too long."

"Not more than an hour, I'm guessing," Bran huffed. "Perhaps they're taking the scenic route."

Caer stopped long enough to turn an icy glare on him. "Don't be cute! What if Adrian and Del arrived at…at wherever…to…to find that…that…"

A familiar charge to the air and a static sizzle ran along her nerves. Spinning on her heels, Caer fixed her attention on the shimmer at the center of the hall. Fedel'ma's presence was the first she sensed, followed instantly by her awareness of Adrian, and perhaps one or two others whom she couldn't name. The faint impression of those emerging with a litter borne between Adrian and another man gave her heart. Stoirm lived!

A heated flurry of voices scorched the air, even before the cluster of individuals finished materializing. Del's face screwed in heavy concentration as she solidified. Next to her was a man who's angrily barking tirade snapped to a conclusion before Caer could discern his words. Her breath sucked in at her recognition of him. This was the doctor from Bestor III. She remembered trying very hard not to meet the man's stern gaze when he bent over her; only glimpsed his white-flecked red hair as he was leaving Adrian's quarters. But there was no mistaking the deep baritone that rumbled with his vehemence. Ian. She believed that was the name by which Adrian had addressed him.

Del turned, her face now matching the man's hostile glare. "Know everything, do you?" she thundered, poking a finger in his chest. "We'll just see about that!"

Standing next to the man, was a tiny woman. Caer caught herself staring. She'd encountered humans of every race and ethnicity, but rarely one whose skin was so dark and beautiful an onyx. The woman's short-cropped, silvery white hair stood in spiked disarray, framing her furious countenance and her piercing brown eyes that flashed their underlying glow as she held her ground beneath Adrian's towering frame. "You have no right!" Though hushed, her voice held tremendous power. "He should have been allowed to die in peace and among those who love him!"

"You think I love him any less than the rest of you?" Adrian snapped back.

The woman's ire diminished slightly, her features reflecting her deep sorrow. "No. Of course not. But moving him...submitting him to more pain..." The woman's voice trailed off as she turned her eyes to the man on the litter that now rested on the floor.

Caer gasped, her fingers releasing the blanket from her shoulders as she beheld the state of the Alainn, all hope draining from her. He looked like death incarnate. The near luminescence that had once graced his alabaster face was now a dull, sickly ashen gray, his exquisite features marred by a cross-hatching of blackening gashes. Wrapping his bare torso from shoulder to waist and down the length of both arms were heavily blood-soaked bandages.

Caer could scarcely force the words past her choked breath. "Back there," she squeaked, waiving a trembling hand toward the door at the back of the dais. "Around the corner, the fifth door on the left."

Adrian bent to the litter. With a snarl, Ian took up the other end. Between them, they gently lifted Stoirm and bore him in the direction Caer indicated. She hurried to fall in beside the gravely injured Alainn, reaching tentatively for his hand. There was no warmth in the touch. No warmth. No movement. Nor could she detect so much as an eye flutter from him. Only the faintest rasp of breathing indicated the life that yet maintained a tenuous hold.

The diminutive, onyx-skinned woman kept pace on the other side of the litter, her grief-stricken gaze never leaving Stoirm's face. Caer suddenly realized she knew this woman, as well. With only a bit of prodding the memory rose. Blath...Blath Trathnona. That was her name. Blath Trathnona of the Healers. She was among those who'd gathered at Caer's bedside so long ago, following Adrian's rescue of her from the flames that had claimed her aunt.

Caer's brow creased as she dared a peek back at Ian. He, too, had been there. She remembered, now. The man often barked orders to the others. Never at Blath, though. This woman bore a quiet confidence and patient dignity that stood apart from the rest. Though each Healer had doubted, Blath alone never faltered in her resolve to mend the body of the small child in their care. When the other Healers proclaimed Caer to be too young, too inexperienced to keep her body alive long enough for the healing to take hold, Blath remained undeterred. Slowly, with the Healer woman's constant encouragement, Caer learned to assist, doing what she could to mend her body from the inside. Never once did Blath give up on her. Yet, here was the same woman, bearing no hope for Stoirm, her anguish and agony etched in her desolate features.

Emer's shocked reaction when the group reached the room seemed in full accord with Blath's assessment. As Stoirm was lifted from the litter to the bed, Emer's pale complexion bled to ghostly white. There was no need of her speaking. Her hopelessness was reflected in her pained and defeated gaze.

Blath regarded Emer for only a fraction of a heartbeat before rounding on Adrian. "You see? I told you! This woman..." She swept her hand toward Emer. "Even if we assume that this woman does, indeed, possess some ability with Healing, she recognizes the truth. He is lost to us. Better to have left my lord surrounded by his friends and his family."

Del edged purposefully in between Adrian and Blath, her eyes intent on the Healer woman. "Hope may be in very small measure, at the moment. So long as Lord Stoirm breathes, however, I will not abandon that hope. Will you let my niece do what is in her power to do, or will you waste what is left of that sliver of hope with more discord?"

Blath returned Del's gaze with a flare of the fire within her eyes. Del neither flinched nor looked away. At last, sinking onto the chair at the end of the bed, Blath nodded, her dispirited glance flicking back to Emer. "So long as you bring him no more pain, do what you will."

Caer thought for a moment that Emer would take up Blath's side of the argument, but Del moved quickly to her niece's side, coaxing, "As I said, do what is in your power to do, dear. I can ask no more of you than that, can I?"

Drawing a deep and steadying breath, Emer set her jaw and turned to her work.

"Focus on the toxins," Del encouraged. "If you can neutralize those..."

"I know my task," Emer murmured. "Now be still!"

Hours, she spent, chanting, applying her herbs, calling upon her spells. Caer ached to help, but there was no place for her. Even Adrian and Del were forced back from the bedside when Blath and Ian crowded next to Stoirm's side, the subtle rhythms of their hushed voices adding to the electric charge of Emer's magic. Adrian hung at the end of the small table where bowls of water and herbs and vials of ointments and salves had been gathered. Del lingered on the other side of the room, her anxious gaze on Emer as much as on Stoirm.

Caer kept her own vigil from just inside the doorway, vaguely aware that Dylan had returned to the manor house and now observed from just behind her. As Emer worked, the refrain of a meager incantation crept from the shadows of Caer's mind, floating to the fore like a wisp of fluff. At first, she was reluctant to give it voice, afraid she might not remember the whole of it, or that it might interfere with Emer's efforts. Only when Del spoke in her head, encouraging her to make whatever contribution she could, did the words come rushing to her with such clarity that they flowed like a sweet, thin liquid over her tongue.

"Abred. Gwynfyd. Ceugant," she whispered. Though the chant came readily enough, its meaning remained unclear. Still, these were the right words--the words that prefaced so many of her aunt's spells. And so, she repeated them; expanded them. "Abred. Struggle," came at last. "Let this man fight to hold life. Gwynfyd. Purity. Let his body be cleansed of all that is poisonous. Ceugant. Infinity. May his infinite soul know strength beyond measure." Again, she repeated the chant, holding fast in her mind an image of Stoirm as she remembered him from her aunt's hearth fire. And again...and again, the chant.

She was foolish to believe her own minor efforts should have any real impact. Still, the urge to do something was too great to ignore. Over and over, she recited the words, keeping the image of Stoirm firm in her mind. Always, Emer's spells wove themselves in and out of the surrounding murmur of conjoined chants, filling the shadowed room with a dizzying tension, the ever-present aroma of the herbs and medicinal preparations hanging thick on the air.

The process took far longer than cleansing and caring for Dylan's wounds. At last, Stoirm's face flushed with faint color, his shallow breathing deepening, coming more regularly with each inhale. When Emer was done, the small room was ignited with the sense of hope that the Alainn would live.

Overwhelming relief gave way to Caer's weary and silent sobs, the more so when she recognized the toll the effort had taken on

Emer. The woman had barely completed the murmur of her last spell when she simply collapsed. Adrian's Healers immediately turned their full attention to her, Del leading them to another room with a freshly prepared bed. There, they made Emer comfortable with blankets and pillows and incantations for recuperative slumber.

37

Caer hugged her bent knees, the bench at her back, the warmth of the fire on her face. The frequent rattling of the closed shutters echoed around her, the winds that troubled them wafting an icy, wet draft through their slats. Perhaps that was what extinguished the lamps in the wall niches. Thankfully, the light from the fire provided sufficient illumination for her to make her way down the dais steps moments ago. Not that she couldn't see through even the deepest darkness. She need only to wait for her eyes to adjust--something she had always regarded as a peculiar ability. Now... She shook her head. Perhaps not so peculiar, after all. In any event, she was grateful to be sitting in at least some degree of comfort, the reassurance of light and heat from the fire a salve for her nerves.

The shutters banged again, leaving her to wonder at the winds. Or rather, at the fact that there was no great dome to keep the winds out. She was unaccustomed to such soggy, blustering places. Oh sure, her Aunt Sidra's little hut got quite chilly when the dome's power was drawn down at night. The chill, however, was nothing like the damp bite that hung in the air, here. At least someone took the time to stoke the fire earlier. Enough so to keep the flames burning for a good while.

Another draft whistled around the hall. Caer tugged her blanket and extra shirts closer, tucking her toes further beneath the draped blanket. For a long while, she stared at the flames and sparking embers. If only sleep would take her, as it had everyone else. Adrian and Blath were each camped on a spot of floor in the room where Stoirm lay sleeping. Ian was on a chair near Emer's bed. His deep, rumbling snores could be heard, even from here. Fedel'ma was also in the room with Emer, buried beneath several covers in one of the corners. The strain of Emer's ordeal left Del looking almost as drawn and drained as her niece.

Brandon was the only one left to share the hall with Caer. Perched atop a pile of blankets, his back propped against the wall, his head drooped to his chest, he'd not so much as twitched when she returned from the back. She might believe he never left his little piece of the floor, except she caught a glimpse of him watching from the corridor just before she offered up her own quiet chants, hoping to assist Emer in some small way. How long Bran remained, she couldn't say. He was gone by the time Ian carried Emer from Stoirm's bedside.

Caer's lips pursed as she realized Dylan's whereabouts were currently unaccounted for. He was present when Emer began weaving her healing spells for Stoirm, hanging just behind where Caer stood. He remained there through Emer's hours of toil; was the first to her when she collapsed; had yielded grudgingly to the Healers, agitation glowering through his frown as Ian carried Emer from the room. Caer sensed a teleportation moments later and recognized Dylan's signature. She snorted. Signature. She was beginning to sound like these people. Still, she had to acknowledge that there was something identifiable in the magic of each person. Well. Almost each of them. It was the lack of any identifier that suggested the use of magic to be either Adrian's or Stoirm's working. Why did their magic not carry any...signature?

Another draft whistled through the room. Shivering, Caer began rocking back and forth to ward off the bite that even the fire could not quell, her thoughts returning to the missing Dylan. Jorn. She huffed an agitated sigh. He died once when Ahira was blown apart. Might have died again, saving her from the beast that attacked her at the estate, were it not for Emer. How many such deaths could a

Witch endure before they were no longer capable of transmigrating? Tears welled up. How many more deaths would he...or any of the others... suffer because of her? By what curse had the key come to her? She had no skills. If she possessed magic, she had no clue what her gifts might be. Had even less idea how to apply magic in battle. She wished...

Sniffing, she swiped at the onset of angry tears with the backs of her sleeves. Wished what? That the cursed thing had fallen to some other poor fool because she lacked the courage or the fortitude to carry out her childhood promise? Her rocking ceased, her fingers closing around the trinity knot with its jeweled heart of deepest red, warm and pulsing. "No," quivered from her lips. She couldn't wish that. Not on anyone. She understood when she accepted the chain. Had foreseen that it would lead her into great danger. That bit of memory, at least, stood clearly in her mind, now. Clear, too, was the memory of the dark foreboding at the thought of rejecting her mother's necklace. She was meant to carry this thing. Why? What was so important about this key that it was worthy of so much bloodshed?

"You still awake?"

The voice startled Caer. Jerking around, she relaxed at the sight of the woman now carrying Fedel'ma's soul, acknowledging her with a shrug and a thinly mumbled, "More or less."

The woman paused, her face drawn, dark circles underscoring her eyes as she cast a scrutiny to the table that had, at some point since the return of Adrian with Stoirm and the others, been removed from the dais to a position perhaps a couple of meters from the steps. "I assume my son is responsible for this," she harrumphed, noting the fresh breads, cheeses, sliced meats, and the variety of fruit. "At least he had the good sense to scrub the surface first."

Caer gestured to the few remaining sudsy puddles dotting the stone floor. "Seems he scrubbed the entire hall. At least this area is dry, thanks to the fire."

Fedel'ma made her way down and across to the table with a

leaden gait, pausing long enough to consider the array, one hand smoothing her rumpled pants before she finger-combed through her short, blond curls. The actions, however, were as ineffectual as they appeared to be absent-minded. Her pants remained rumpled, her curls cork-screwing at unruly angles.

Caer cocked her head in squinting reassessment of the woman's face. Something was different. More than just the hollowing and lack-luster effects of fatigue. The woman's features appeared to have subtly shifted. Somehow, she looked rather less like Brenna Cowl and more...well...more Fedel'ma-esque. Realizing she was staring, Caer dropped her gaze. Her exhaustion was to blame for such delusional nonsense. That, or her utter loss of sanity. Perhaps this entire episode, from Mirra's death to now, was nothing more than the product of a demented mind.

Del at last snatched an apple, then set out to join Caer on the floor. "There's nothing wrong with your sanity, dear. The features change."

Caer cringed. She hated that people could read her thoughts. And they needn't tell her that she wore said thoughts written across her face. She knew better, now.

Del bit into the apple, continuing to talk around her chewing. "With each new host, our soul tries to return us to our original appearance. It's like the soul remembers, and wants to reset everything. The change is always a compromise, though. Newly acquired bodies rarely accommodate themselves to any significant alterations. Sometimes the compromise is a pleasant improvement. Sometimes not."

Caer shuddered. "It happens every time you...you...you take a...a different corpse?"

"Host, dear," Del corrected. "Every time we take on a new host. And yes, unless we make a conscious effort to stop the shifting. A conscious effort managed by means of a complex set of spells, mind you. Not worth the expenditure of energy, in my opinion."

The vision of a face and body trying to re-form in the image of the soul's original vessel sent a shudder through Caer. What complex spells had Jorn used to stop such changes when taking on his new 'host' and naming himself Dylan?

"Ah. My son."

"Please stop doing that! Stay out of my head."

"Not in it, dear. I can't help it if you broadcast everything that's on your mind. We need to teach you how control that. Anyway, the way you see Dylan, now, is likely as close to his original form as he's going to get in this current host. His size and build are about right, as are the curls. The amber in his eyes is always the same. The overlaying eye color, dark hair and complexion are different, though. Originally, he had hazel eyes, red locks and fair skin. Not that these current attributes hurt his looks any." She finished off her apple and tossed the core into the fire, a faint smile twitching the corners of her mouth. "He always was quite the handsome fellow, if I do say so, myself. If you ever tell him I said so, however, I will flatly deny it."

"Well." Caer murmured, studying her knees. "I'm not one to deny his good looks, whether as Dr. Jorn or as Dylan. The two look nothing alike, though."

"No. It was as Jorn that he was hiding from himself. Ridiculous, really, believing that a change in one's appearance can conceal, or perhaps change, who you are within your very core. Still, he's been doing that for a long time. In truth, I'm surprised that he's allowed the shifting to take place, this time."

"Why would he want to hide from himself?"

Del did not answer for several long seconds. When she did, it was with a disgruntled, "Guilt. At least, that's my guess."

Caer opened her mouth, then shut it again. It was none of her business what the man did to suffer so weighty a guilt. Instead, she ventured, "Quite remarkable, isn't it?"

"What is, dear?"

"What Emer did for him. Preventing him from dying again...so soon after... And now, what she's done for Stoirm." Glancing toward the back rooms, she asked anxiously, "Emer will be all right, won't she? She'll not need to go looking for another...'host', will she?"

"She'll be fine. She needs to rest, but shouldn't be too much the worse for wear, so long as no one expects any more magic from her for a while." Remorse crept into Del's voice, her dull stare dropping to her lap. "I had no right to ask that she push her abilities that far."

Caer recalled how Del cried out in fear when Emer collapsed. She recalled Dylan's instant reaction, as well, rushing to his cousin. Dylan's reaction. Jorn's reaction. Caer bit at her lip, straightening. "It was her," she whispered.

"Excuse me?"

"Emer. She was...was Jorn's...Dylan's wife."

Del cocked a brow. "What makes you say so?"

"Something he said to me, once." She licked her lips. "When he was Dr. Jorn. I asked him why he wasn't married."

"Cheeky question." There was no rebuke in the comment; only mild amusement.

Flushing, Caer went on. "He said he had been married...once. That she was a wonderful woman." There was suddenly a gaping hollow in the pit of her stomach. How stupidly naïve, to think, even for a second, that the man she knew as Dr. Hugh Jorn might fall for her. "He still loves Emer."

Del pushed to her feet with a grunted harrumph. "He has a funny way of showing it." Heading back to the table, she added, "He's always loved her. Always will, I imagine. But not in the way you're thinking."

"They were married, though?"

"Yes."

"I thought that was prohibited. I mean, aren't they cousins?"

Del gave another harrumph. "Kinships are funny things," she said, plucking some grapes from a platter. "At least for us. Gets a bit complicated when you start figuring in multiples of lifetimes lived in a succession of different hosts. While Emer is my sister's child, she is several lifetimes younger than Dylan. Their souls will forever hold the distinction of cousin, but in strictly biological terms, their current hosts are quite unrelated."

It was a difficult set of implications to grasp. What was it like, Caer wondered, having your body die and your soul survive? The thought of moving into someone else's discarded corps sent another shudder through her. Dismissing the notion, she instead, pursued another. "Am I really? Related to Stoirm, I mean." Was it possible that she might be kin to everyone here? Everyone except poor Bran, that is. She suddenly felt her friend's gaze on her and shifted around to meet it. How long had he been sitting there, listening?

Bran stretched out his legs, his face darkly contemplative as he muttered, "Why all the fuss?"

Seeming to notice his presence for the first time, Del returned his query with her own. "Why all what fuss?"

"You said that this Alainn...this Stoirm person...is related to you. Caer said he's her uncle. And you went so far as to say he is uncle to all of you."

Del nodded.

"If he's one of you, then why all the fuss to save him? Or to save your son? If they died, won't they just come back again, wearing..." His face scrunched in disgust. "Wearing someone else's skin?"

"Death is always cause for a fuss, Mr. Jase. Even for us. Only when it comes on the quiet tiptoe of old age, when the body is too weak to contain the soul any longer--which for Witches, can take more than a fair number of centuries---only then is the parting of the soul from its physical vessel a gentle thing."

Scratching at her nose, she confessed, "Unfortunately, in the case of those of us who stand against Nemhain and her ilk, such deaths are rare. Our bodies are far more likely to meet a most violent end. And with a violent death comes a terrible rending of the two--body and soul. It is not a pleasant experience. Nor are we guaranteed a returning when a body is lost. The unrelenting wear of life weakens all souls, eventually. For some sooner than for others. Worse..." This time it was Del who shuddered. "Worse, souls can be banished."

Brandon's brow lifted. "Banished. How? To where?"

"By means of a powerful curse cast at the moment death separates the soul from its physical form. Judging from the screams of those who've met such an end, the curse is even more tortuous than the horrific rending that separates soul from host in the first place."

"And those souls never return?"

"We've yet to find any among us--not a single returned soul who's ever suffered the banishing. Believe me, we've searched."

"So." Bran took a deep breath. "Where do banished souls go?"

"That, sir, is the question of the ages, isn't it? Where souls go. We can answer that no more than the Tanai can. Not for souls who are banished, nor for those who are worn beyond their capacity to return. Nor..." She exhaled with a shrug. "...for the souls of dead Tanai."

Rubbing her arms, Del rounded the end of the table where the two casks stood. Taking up a glass, she filled it with wine from the one dripping a purple stain to the floor, downing half of it before she spoke again. "As for Lord Stoirm, family, he is, being half-brother to the three sisters. Tar On Tine was his father as well as theirs. We, the family of Witches, are descendants of at least one of Tar On Tine's and Samhradh's daughters. Where the sisters are half human, half Alainn, however, Lord Stoirm is wholly Alainn.

They're an exceedingly long-lived people, the Alainn. Legend says that Lord Stoirm's father was well beyond six thousand years old when he first came to Earth." She paused for another drink. "Long life may be theirs. But the Alainn do not possess the ability the descendants of Samhradh's daughters hold--the ability for their souls to transmigrate."

Bran's scowl accompanied his, "What the hell does that mean?"

"Transmigration is the soul's ability to join with a new host following the death of the previous one. Some call it reincarnation. A rebirth, if you will."

Bran's scowl deepened, twitching at the thought. "I always

assumed the stories referring to rebirth meant precisely what the word implies. Being reborn as an infant."

"So it was," Del acknowledged. "At least in the beginning when we had no control over the paths our souls took following the death of the body. How many times can one return as a babe, however, before they weary of the process of passing from infancy through childhood while possessing memories of past lives? There were other issues, as well. Would you, for instance, want one of us turning up in the physical housing of the fetus of your child? People expect their children to be...well...their children. And so they should. Over the centuries, we discovered a means of controlling the paths of our souls.

Caer shared Brandon's blanching response. With a shake of his head, Bran ventured, "So. If I have this straight, the Alainn possess magic, live very long lives, but live only once. Witches possess magic, and can live many lifetimes, thanks to this...this...transmigration thing. People like me...the...what'd you call us? Tanee? We hold no magic, and are afforded only one, very short lifetime." His lip curled. "Somehow, I feel cheated."

Del chuckled. "Don't sell yourself short, Mr. Jase. You are among a very rare breed of Tanai. You have the ability to sense anyone who possesses magic, even when their gift is so minor that they, themselves, are unaware of it. Dana's and Roisin's lines valued and protected Sensitives like yourself, learning from some among them who of the Tanai might hold just enough magic to draw Nemhain's unwelcome attention. Always, the Dark Heart and her descendants seek to eliminate such individuals, fearing that they might lead to a new line of Witches. Dana's and Roisin's descendants, however, have watched over these few Tanai, removing them to places of safety when necessary. As for you, who's to say how long you will live? Stick with us, and we might be able to guarantee you a good many years."

Bran cocked a dubious brow at her. "Or end me all too soon."

"Not if you give us no reason to do so."

"And you're sure that we...the Tanee...don't have this other ability? We can't do this...transmigration thing?"

"Let me just say that we have never perceived any Tanai to be older than what is suggested by their bodies, nor do they possess the mark of a returned soul."

Brandon sat a little straighter. "Just how is a returned soul perceived?"

"Old, older, or older still, depending on how many times their soul has returned." Del dismissed his annoyed snort with, "Truthfully. I don't know how else to put it. One who has lived before carries an unmistakable sense of age that goes beyond their body's count of years."

"And the mark?" Brandon pressed. "What's that?"

"A burning deep within the eyes."

"You mean like the way everyone's eyes glowed during that fight on that damnable hillside? And like the way they glowed last night while everyone was focused on healing this Lord Stoirm?"

Del nodded, sipping more delicately at her again replenished wine.

"So... Why aren't your eyes glowing, now? And why is it that Caer's don't glow? They have never glowed, so far as I'm aware."

Venting a long exhale, Del wandered to the dais steps and sat. "My, but you are full of questions. Caer's eyes don't glow for the same reason she lacks any sense of profound age. Apparently, she is an Uair Amhain. And before you ask, that means she is a Witch in her very first lifetime. The deep burning only begins to appear after the soul's first transmigration. Becomes more prominent the more transmigrations one experiences. As for why my eyes aren't glowing, now..." Del shrugged before adding with a sigh, "Like all Witches, I suppress it. Very unhealthy for us, if the Tanai learn who we are."

"So, you didn't suppress this...this mark during the battle on that hill or last night."

"Can't. Don't ask me why, because I don't know. All I can say is that it is impossible for us to maintain the suppression of the glow at the same time we are employing other forms of magic, though employing multiples of other spells simultaneously poses little to no difficulty."

Taking another sip, she conceded, "Not that it would make any difference, concealing the mark when we are working magic, since the very act of employing our gifts tends to give us away. Which, if done in the presence of non-Witches, tends not to end well for us. Hence our great care not to demonstrate our abilities openly. The evolution of Sensitives, however, made the task of keeping our secret more challenging. Through the ages, some few among them sought us out, allied with us." An edge cut across her tone. "Most, however, chose to point us out for persecution and execution, granting Nemhain all the justification she wished for seeking them out and slaughtering them."

"I have never..." Bran's fleeting hesitation caught Caer's attention, as it did Del's, the woman's scrutiny of him intensifying. "...never pointed anyone out for persecution or execution."

Caer assumed from the anxious glance Bran flashed her that he was feeling no small degree of unease over the information forced from him by those who murdered his sister and her family. His glance darted to his hands, which he briskly swiped over the knees of his pants. Quick to his rescue, she shifted the topic back to the Alainn. "I don't understand. How can they live so long? Stoirm's people, I mean. Judging from what happened to Stoirm they are as vulnerable to physical harm as any human."

Del set her glass aside. "The Alainn possess even greater regenerative and recuperative abilities than Witches, and that's saying quite a lot. If we lacked such skill, we would not be able to prolong the life span of our various hosts to upwards of a few hundred years. In truth, we'd not be able to repair or regenerate damaged or diseased bodies in order to occupy them in the first place. Which would set us a serious problem." She ran her finger around the lip of her glass, apparently lost in thought for some time.

"Legend says," she continued at last, "that many attempts were made on Tar On Tine's life in the years after he first appeared on Earth. The strength of his magic was far beyond that of the Witches of the time and left many fearing him the way Tanai fear us. Thus, they employed a combination of spells and poisons sufficient to wipe out several clans of their own kind. And still, years passed before they succeeded even in subduing that one ancient Alainn. Once subdued, however, they quickly beheaded him. Suffice it to say, that's enough to kill any living creature."

Gesturing in the direction of the back rooms, Del pointed out, "Lord Stoirm still retains his head, in case you hadn't noticed. Even so..." Her features clouded. "Given the number and degree of his wounds and the strength of magic behind the toxins used in the attack, I have to admit that his survival long enough to be brought here seems nothing short of miraculous."

Del's lips pursed. "Never could I have imagined how great Nemhain's powers would become. The extent of her ability to enhance the venoms of beasts such as the Coran'ian is...is beyond formidable. Had I realized how much I was asking of Emer, even as gifted as I know her to be, I would not have requested she attempt to keep Lord Stoirm from the grave."

"Seems a bit curious, don't you think?" Dylan's voice snapped Caer's attention to the doorway at the back of the dais, where the man stood eyeing his mother. "The attack on the Alainn being called off as soon as Nemhain recognized him."

Caer realized that she had, in fact, felt the charge of his return teleportation just moments ago. Where had he been off to, this time?

Striding down from the dais, he stopped at the table only long enough to take up a glass and fill it with wine, before making his way across to Caer. He halted a few paces from her, pulling a pair of floppy black items from his back pocket. "You call these shoes?"

Caer caught them as he tossed them to her, one at a time. Shoes, indeed! And they were hers. Sturdy cloth, flexible soles. What other type of shoe did one need within the confines of ships or domes? Tucked inside one of them was a pair of socks. Also hers. Caer raised her eyes to thank Dylan, but his back was to her as he returned to the table, Del rumbling at him from her perch on the steps.

"That's the second time you've cast your suspicions on Lord Stoirm," the woman thundered. "If you'd ever studied your family history, you would know better. Nemhain is deeply in love with her half-brother. Always has been. She'd no more willingly harm him than she would herself."

"So the stories say," Dylan snorted, seating himself on the table's vacant end. "Even assuming that Nemhain's unrequited love is truth, the mere fact that this Alainn bears the name of another from the past is no guarantee that he is, in fact, that same person. Forgive me if I want more proof."

"What proof would you ask?"

The shock of seeing Stoirm step out onto the dais had Caer bobbing to her feet so quickly that stars swam before her. Del, too, was on her feet, looking equally stunned. Even allowing for what Del claimed to be the Alainn's recuperative abilities, it didn't seem possible that Stoirm could be walking about so soon. Yet, here he stood, tall and proudly erect, the gashes on his face already fading to fine, silvery lines, the clear topaz of his eyes skimming across the group. Still, when he moved again, he did so with a cautious gait, his open shirt exposing the fresh bandages wound across his shoulders and around his chest, their thickness on his arms straining the long sleeves.

Granting Del a courteous, albeit shallow bow, he moved gingerly to the steps, descending them with care before making his way to the bench. A faint bead of sweat showed on his brow as he eased down.

"My son deserves no proof, my lord," Del apologized, her heated glower locked on Dylan. "He's a..."

"Fat-headed fool," Dylan finished with a snarl. "So you've told me often enough."

"No," Stoirm countered softly. "He is wise to be suspicious." Glancing to Dylan, he said, "Let me make this offer. You are a Dream Reader, if I understand Lord Amhranai Fearalite correctly."

"Don't know who that is or how he would know," Dylan retorted.

"That would be me." Adrian's long, deliberate tread swept him across the dais, down the steps, and across to stand at Stoirm's side.

Caer gaped. Adrian? A lord? Lord of what?

Dylan spared him a disconcerted scrutiny before returning his attention to the Alainn. "I see. And the offer?"

"That you look into my dreams when next I sleep. It should answer at least a few of your doubts."

Dylan's brow shot up. "You would invite my intrusion?"

"Do you impose yourself without invitation?"

"Only when it seems necessary for the safety of..."

His words cut off abruptly, the air suddenly frigid as a brooding, malevolent blackness crept across the great hall.

"Nemhain," hissed between Dylan's teeth. "How did she..."

The oppressive darkness lifted as quickly as it had come.

Running footsteps announced the two Healers as they burst from the corridor onto the dais. "My lords," Ian panted, relief flooding his face as he spotted both Adrian and Stoirm. "We feared.... We feared she might be here!"

Falling breathless against the wall, her hand to her breast, Blath's expression was also one of tremendous relief.

"That took less time than I had hoped," Adrian spat.

Dylan shot an outraged glare at the man. "You've betrayed us! You've led..."

Adrian rounded on him. "Hardly. Did you think you could take Caer and the key without Croi Breag searching for them? It was Caer she traced to the estate; Caer that she hoped to take when she trapped Stoirm and me. It appears she believes her powers to be strong enough for her to take the key forcibly and without consequences. She'll not stop searching until she finds what she seeks."

Bran rose from his pile of blankets, demanding, "Who the hell is this Cree Bray-ugh?"

Del waived him silent, "Nemhain. The Dark Heart. They are

one and the same. She's one of the three daughters I spoke of earlier. Croi Breag means Dark Heart. An apt enough epitaph, if the bitch would just die and stay dead."

Adrian gave a humorless huff. "Stoirm and I have been attempting that outcome for centuries. As have a host of others. We see how far that's gotten us. It was my hope that the spells employed to conceal this place, and ultimately Caer's presence, might succeed as well with Croi Breag as they did with me. For the moment, at least, it appears to be the case. Otherwise, we would be under attack by now."

His gaze hardened, fixed on Dylan. "We cannot, however, count on your efforts sufficing for long. Now that she is on the full hunt, she will begin to isolate those locations where the sense of anything more than ambient magic is the strongest. That's where she will send her beasts. Given the strength of magic imposed around your manor house, Master Dream Reader, it is likely to place it near the top of her list."

Del's eyes darted to every shadow, every corner, as though expecting to see the beasts of hell emerging at that very instant. "Lord Whatshisname is right. We need to teleport Caer out of here. Now. Emer and Mr. Jase, as well."

Stoirm shook his head. "I suspect it may be too late for that. We are not yet under attack, but Croi Breag has likely laid her trap. She will be doing so over every site she skims, hoping sooner or later to snare her prey in the same manner she snared Lord Amhranai and myself."

"I knew it would be wiser to take Caer and Ms. Kyot to you," Adrian moaned. "Rather than bringing you here."

Stoirm minced a shrug. "No doubt you brought me because Caer refused to leave. Am I not right, Amhranai? You must trust her choices."

Caer shivered as Stoirm glanced her direction. She was certain that, in that brief instant, he had looked straight through to her core, studying whatever lay there. If that were so, he had confirmed it was her decision to stay, if for no other reason than to convince Bran to do likewise. Swallowing, she declared, "Nor am I leaving, now." Though her words sounded half strangled, they were filled with resolve. "Not unless everyone goes. I'll not have anyone left behind to fight while I run away. I won't let anyone else die on my account."

Stoirm rose slowly, pressing a hand to his chest, pain evident on his face. "You have little to say in who chooses to protect you, Caer DaDhrga. Nor do you bear any blame for the deaths that have followed in your shadow. I believe, however, that you are correct to assert that all of us must remain together. Surely, there is another way for us to leave this place. One that does not require magic."

Anguished, Dylan closed his eyes, his brow creasing in concentration. "I can't tell," he groaned at last. "My shielding seems untouched, but I can't tell what lies above it. The way might be clear."

The amber in the depth of his eyes burned brightly as he leveled a brief scrutiny on Caer. Turning sharply from her, he addressed Adrian. "I've had no difficulty with my last teleportations away from here, or with returning. I will teleport out first. If there is a trap, I will spring it, clearing the way for the rest of you."

Adrian shook his head. "A wasted sacrifice on your part, I fear. The setting of a single trap, as they did with the one around the estate that ensnared Stoirm and myself, is an oversight that won't be repeated. I'm guessing someone in Croi Breag's ranks lost both their head and their soul as a result of their failure to lay their traps in series. There is sure to be a succession employed from here on."

Dylan turned to Stoirm, who nodded his agreement. "Trust us in this, Master Dream Reader. For so far as it is knowable, we know the mind of Croi Breag better than any other."

Defeated, Dylan groaned. "I won't risk sending Caer into a trap. But neither can I have her sitting here awaiting Nemhain's assault." With a contemptuous glare back to Adrian, he asked, "You know of a better place to take her? You swear that your purpose is to protect her?"

"I swear it. Do you read the truth of my words?"

Dylan affirmed with a reluctant nod. "Very well. Mother can lead you out, then. Once she gets you to the secret passages, she can guide you through. I'll give you time to be well into their depths, then I will do what I can to draw Nemhain's attention straight to the manor house."

Adrian tipped his head toward Dylan. "I'll give you credit for guts, Dream Reader. But you are no match of those she'll send. Not alone."

"Maybe not. But I can keep them occupied for a while. Just... just promise me that you will keep Caer and Emer and Mother safe."

Del stiffened. "You truly are a fat-headed fool! I don't remember the way out of here. And even if I could stumble my way to your hidden entrance, I couldn't navigate those passages. You're the one with them etched into your skull."

"And I've told you," Caer huffed defiantly. "I'm not leaving anyone behind. Either you come with us, or I stay."

38

The whistle of wind through the closed shutter slats provided an arrhythmic counterpoint to the nervous thumping of Caer's dangling legs against the face of the dais. Her eyes darted from the rattling windows to the lone door near the back of the hall's outside wall. Her first glimpse of it came while standing over Dylan, trying to maintain pressure on his wounds, though the door's presence scarcely registered at the time. Other concerns had weighed on her attention, since. Now that they were about to leave, the door seemed a menacing portal. The manor house may not be the most comfortable of accommodations, but it at least provided some degree of warmth and shelter from... Her uneasy glance shot to the shutters as they banged, again.

Brandon shuffled past, pulling her fidgety gaze away from the windows. Turning, he shuffled past again. Caer's annoyance grew with each pass he made, which, in turn, added to her anxieties. Biting back the urge to snap at him, she set to plucking at the top blanket on the pile next to her.

A sharper whine blew through the shutters, their slats setting up a series of loud clatters. Caer jerked around with a deepening grimmace. Her Earth studies often mentioned the world's weather patterns, though they rarely dwelled on them. What was the need to do so when domes protected the planet's inhabitants?

"We shouldn't leave," Bran hissed, echoing her distress as he passed her again. Thumbing toward the back of the hall where

Adrian and Dylan gestured in a muted but intense dialog, he persisted with, "If those two are right about this Cree...Cree Brayugh or whatever her name is. then we're going to be attacked sooner or later, no matter where we go. At least here, we have shelter. Maybe this building protects us from the toxins in the atmosphere the way domes do. Or maybe it does so magically. What if we can't breathe out there? If we can't beat back an attack, here, maybe we can at least hold out against it."

Caer swallowed, fighting down the tremor in her voice. "I don't want to leave, either. But how can we hold out? If there are traps laid for anyone who tries to teleport away, then no one can get out to replenish our food...or the pellets for the fire. Emer and Stoirm aren't likely to be capable of much, magic-wise, for some time. They won't be much use if those pursuing us attack with magic. And who knows what sort of battle skills the Healers possess. That leaves Adrian, Dylan, and Del to do the fighting." She took a ragged breath. "Not that a battle would be necessary if we run out of food or a means to keep warm. They could choose to simply starve us or freeze us out." Another edgy glance in the direction of the windows prefaced, "As for being able to breathe...out there. We managed well enough on that hill. No dome. No manor house. Just open sky."

"Yeah," Bran snorted. "Open sky and some frigid rain. Not this...this bloody howling of the elements. You think these old blankets are going to protect us from being blown away?"

Caer flattened her hand against the pile, offering a weary shrug. "I don't think Dylan sent us to collect them for the purpose of rooting us to the ground. They'll keep us warmer than going without them, though." Her gaze drifted back to where Dylan and Adrian remained in animated discussion. "I just wish they'd stop arguing, or whatever it is they're doing. If they want us to leave, why don't we just get on with it?"

Brandon turned to retrace his path yet again. "So far as I'm concerned, they can take all the time they want." Nodding toward the fireplace, he mumbled, "That Healer lady doesn't look any too happy about going, either."

Caer followed the direction of Bran's gesture. Standing a few paces in front of the low-burning fire, the beautiful onyx-skinned wisp of a woman called Blath held her ground in Stoirm's looming shadow, outrage clear on her face, her whispered words as muted and as animated as those of Adrian and Dylan. Ian, likewise, held a persistent, angry frown, his arms folded as he leaned against the wall a wary distance from Blath and the Alainn, his scrutiny on Emer. Sitting silently on the bench, Emer's shoulders were slumped, her face drawn, her dark-rimmed eyes closed. In truth, neither she nor Stoirm were fit to be traveling anywhere, which was likely the cause of Blath's ire.

"It's time," Dylan announced.

Caer jumped at the proximity of his voice, unaware that he and Adrian had ended their discussion. Both men strode past her to the long table, each taking up one of the two dilapidated backpacks Dylan scrounged from who-knew-where. Caer assumed the packs contained food since the table's abundance was greatly diminished when she and Bran returned to the hall with the blankets. She shot another troubled grimace at the rattling windows, wondering how long they expected to have their little company on the move, if such stores were necessary.

"This is insane!" Blath blurted, her words directed as much at Adrian as at Stoirm.

Stoirm lifted her hands and kissed them, then leaned to kiss her forehead. "Insane or not," he said, "this is the way of our path." Turning from her, he made his way to Emer and laid a hand on her shoulder.

Emer's eyes fluttered open, her glazed stare momentarily blank. When awareness at last gained a foothold, she waived aside the Alainn's offer of assistance. Pushing to her feet, she wobbled briefly, then steadied.

Caer's mouth opened to add her agreement with the Healer

woman's assessment, but a warning glance from Adrian silenced her. It did not, however, prevent her from attempting to bore holes through him with the fury of her glare.

Bran moved to Caer's side, his hand on her elbow as she slipped from the dais. "There's no dome out there," he repeated. "They're taking us outside, and there's no protection from anything."

Caer acknowledged with a stiff, "No dome." What else could she say?

Striding away from her, Bran squared off in front of Dylan. "Explain to me just what it is that protects us if there's no dome. Toxins. Raging weather. An attack. What does it matter what we do if we're going to end up dead, anyway?"

No toxins. Caer was certain of that much. They didn't die on the hill. She didn't expect they would die, here. Not from any poisons they might breathe in, at least. Her fretful glance went yet again to the banging shutters, eyeing the moisture that dripped from them, running a stream down the wall to pool on the floor. It wasn't the toxins that worried her. Earth's weather, however...that was a different matter.

An unexpected surge of excitement burst through Caer's dark apprehensions. For the fraction of a heartbeat, she imagined a wash of fresh rain on her face and a gentle breeze through her hair, its breath carrying a heady salt scent. As the wooden slats clattered and clacked, the image dissipated, replaced by the more familiar churn of queasy trepidation.

The brief lapse in Caer's attention left her to catch only the last of Dylan's response to Bran's query. "...explanation really necessary, Mr. Jase?"

Bran hesitated, then accused, "Either you expect me to believe that we've been protected, here, by some of your hocus pocus, or everything we've been taught regarding Earth's atmosphere is a lie. How you might keep such a secret from the population of an entire planet, however, is beyond me."

A murmur rose to press against the back of Caer's mind. *When breath comes clear and the barren is blessed, the way may be opened and our souls at last rest.* It was an old rhyme. Sidra taught it to her. Or...or had it been her mother? The words played through her mind again. When breath comes clear. Earth's breath. The rhyme was speaking of Earth's cleansed atmosphere.

Dylan turned an appraising eye to her. *"I suspected you understood...on some level."*

Caer returned his scrutiny with a heated scowl. "I'll thank you very much to stay out of my head! If you want to know something, ask me. If you have something to say to me, say it aloud."

Dylan dismissed her with a cocked brow, turning back to Bran. "Lies aren't that difficult to sell. It helps, of course, that we have Family strategically placed in the political and scientific communities, ready to cast the truth from the minds of any who come too close to discovering it."

Bran blinked at him, stunned to silence for a moment. Finding his voice again, he ventured, "So, the domes here are nothing more than a huge hoax? I suppose you'll zap the truth from my mind, now."

"You are welcome to the truth for so long as you remain stuck with us, Mr. Jase--which, at this point, is likely to be till the end of your days. Keeping the truth from others, however, is a necessity."

Bran took a slow breath. "Why?"

"Why are you likely be stuck with us for the rest of your days, or why the need to conceal the truth?"

"According to you, I'm stuck with you for my own bloody protection," Bran snorted.

Dylan nodded. "Emer and Mother have declared that to be the case, yes. And I trust them on that score. In answer to the other question, Earth's recovery from all that was wrought by civilization gone amuck has been long and difficult. Many have dedicated multiples of lifetimes assisting in the process. Our success can be seen in the re-establishment of a few pockets of sustainable ecosystems. Should the truth of this become known, there would likely be a mass migration out of the domes. Our world is yet too fragile to survive such a strain.

...and the barren is blessed... Caer's eyes widened as the second piece of the phrase echoed through her skull. That, too, seemed a reality. At least parts of the barren Earth have been blessed with the ability to sustain life once more. She'd seen proof of it on that hill.

Again, Dylan shot her an appraising glance. Caer ignored him, rolling the whole of the rhyme through her mind once again. *When breath comes clear and the barren is blessed, the way may be opened and our souls at last rest.* She understood the first two pieces, now, but what did the last part mean? Whose souls needed to rest?

Adrian broke her train of thought with a bang of his fist on the table. "We're wasting time!" Cinching up the backpack's strap across his sternum, he declared, "Something I assure you Croi Breag is not doing."

Dylan huffed his reluctant assent and adjusted his pack, turning to scan the group. "Where the hell is Mother?"

"Here," Del returned, fiddling with a cloth sling that draped from her right shoulder to her left hip as she trotted in from the kitchen. Caer caught a glimpse of a lumpy cloth sack cradled within the sling.

"You're not," Dylan groaned, "bringing that bloody cat, are you? Why that animal isn't dead, already, I'll never know."

"Believe me, it wasn't easy keeping her alive," Del sniffed. "And I am not leaving her here to be tortured or killed by Nemhain's ugly brood." With a gentle stroke to the lump, she added, "Don't worry. She's sedated. She'll be no trouble."

Dylan stumped across to the dais with a disgusted snort. Grabbing a blanket from the pile, he tossed it around his pack and tied its corners to the sternum strap. "Everyone is to take one of these. Wrap yourselves securely and make sure you hang onto it." Heading for the door, he finished with, "The wind is in a fearsome mood, today."

Caer took the next blanket, throwing it around her shoulders.

Bran sidled up next to her, securing his wrap with a knot tied under his chin. "You're absolutely sure you trust these people?"

"Yeah," she nodded. The truth of her confirmation surprised her. She trusted them. They saved her life—twice. But the trust ran deeper than that. Why?

Behind them, one of the shutters banged open. Caer spun around to find a heavy, swirling mist blowing in. Setting off for the far door, she breathed a wary, "It's not the people. It's the conditions that give me pause."

Dylan waited for the whole of their group to join him. Then, bracing his palms against the door's dense wood, he commanded, "Release."

White sparks flicked along the length and breadth of the door's frame, splinters along its edge igniting and extinguishing in puffs of smoke. So, too, sparks licked at the thick, metal hinges, setting them aglow with a silvery sheen. A sudden crackle followed, tendrils of blue fire sweeping towards Caer as tiny charges spiraled along her flesh. Horrified, she cast about at the others, watching tendrils sweeping toward and momentarily wrapping each of them before withdrawing.

Again, Bran leaned close, his voice low. "I considered breaking out of here. Before the weather turned bad. Might have done so anyway, had I known for a certainty that I could survive whatever lay outside. I should have guessed that door would be booby trapped."

"The spell would have thrown you half the length of the hall like a lump of rag," Dylan stated. "And you'd likely not have regained your senses for a week."

Bran's mouth fell open. With a shake of his head, he grumbled, "And you didn't think to warn us of that?"

"Doing so would likely have guaranteed your testing my statement," Dylan returned. "Saying nothing removed that temptation." His brow cocked at Bran's flinched reaction. As the last of the fiery tendrils dissipated, the door swung inward with a thick whoosh that ushered in an icy gale of dancing vapors. "You first, Mr.

Jase. Wait at the end of the building until the rest of us have joined you. I will trust you to stay close to Caer after that."

Brandon shot Caer a resigned grimace. "I don't need him telling me to stay close. You're the nearest thing to family I have left. And you need someone sane looking after you." Squaring his shoulders, he moved past Dylan and out.

Caer followed, pulling her blanket up over her head and gripping it snuggly beneath her chin. She only just cleared the threshold when a howling gust slammed her sideways, billowing her wrap out like the sail on some ancient maritime vessel. Driving mists stung her eyes and whipped her hair from its loose braid. Long strands slapped across her face as she struggled to keep her feet beneath her. An even greater effort was required to grapple her wrap back around her head and shoulders. The winds were, indeed, in a fearsome mood!

A shudder of crashes and low thunder rolled an undertone through the bluster, shaking the ground beneath her. As suddenly as the delight in her earlier vision of soft rain and gentle breezes had taken her, a new rapture emerged, this one with a flashing image of a vast sea. The beauty of it hung in Caer's mind, the blue of its immense surface rolling with fringed caps of white, the scent of salt thick on the tumbling spray. Another slamming from the gale sent the vision skittering away. Some small voice deep inside, however, rejoiced at the vast waters that lay there...just off to her left...so short a distance away. Fighting for a couple of steps toward the thunder and crash, Caer blinked against the stinging needles of mist on her face in search of some glimpse of shoreline, some fleeting view of a rushing surf.

She saw only a world dissolved within the dense and perpetually moving vapors, with no clear demarcation of land from air or from sea...if such a body of water truly existed where the voice indicated. Still, the scent of salt was strong in the frigid spray. Salt from an ocean. Salt... Caer was stunned by the thought. Never had she considered that salt might have a scent. Yet she recognized it... associated it with the sea. A memory?

"Keep moving," Del cried above the din, nudging Caer from behind.

With one more glance in the direction of the roar, Caer renewed her grip on the blanket and turned into the blow, pushing to where Bran waited for her.

"What'd you stop for?" he bellowed as she approached.

"The sea."

"What'd you see?"

Emer trudged around the two of them irritably waving off not only Stoirm, but Dylan and Adrian and the Healers, as well. "I'm fine!" she snapped, her words swimming in the surrounding noise. "Leave me alone!"

Dylan threw a hand up in vexation, striding past, barking, "This way," as he led them off at an angle to their initial path.

Caer adjusted her direction, in no mood to try and clarify 'sea' from 'see'. Bran promptly fell into step behind her. They covered less than a dozen meters, however, when she was once again tempest-tossed, this time backward and seriously off balance.

"The air may be safe to breathe," Bran rumbled, catching her. "But it can still blow us away."

Caer stared bleakly ahead at Emer. Though she, too, was bent and struggling, the woman remained resolute in ignoring Adrian, who marched practically on her heels. Caer set her jaw. No tycoon, typhoon, or whatever this bit of nastiness was called, was going to get the better of her! If Emer could manage this, then so could she!

Footfall by footfall, she battled against the incessant battering, dripping as much beneath the blanket as on its outside. Her toes squished inside her soggy shoes as she fought her way through the cold muck underfoot. The gray world around her made it impossible to guess what time of day it might be, save that it had not yet turned black with night. It seemed like an age since they left the comfort of the manor house, though Caer feared it may have been no more than minutes gone by. So, too, it was impossible to know what distance they had covered. She could see no landmarks save the ghosts of boulders and the scrub underfoot. With the bite of the cold gnawing at her bones and the growing fatigue in her muscles, Caer's one miserable certainty was that she would never be able to maintain Dylan's pace.

Panting and staggering, she slowed and glanced over her shoulder. Brandon remained ever at her back, thank the heavens. The others, little more than silhouettes in the churning, drizzling fog, straggled out in two groups--Stoirm and the Healers to one side of her, Del, Emer, and Adrian to the other. Shivering, Caer found a certain guilty reassurance in noting that neither trio was progressing any faster than she could manage.

The ubiquitous gray continued to wear on her, disorienting her as she trudged on. Bad enough not knowing where their destination might lie; worse not seeing what progress they were...or were not... making. Only the occasional ghost glimmer of Dylan in the shrouded distance gave reassurance that she had not strayed from his path.

Caer's stumble prompted a blinking glance at her feet where the sparse brush and scrub was now dotted with marsh grasses and reeds. The sight offered up a startling giddiness. Life returning. Just as Dylan had said. As she slogged on, the grasses grew longer and denser, the blades slapping wetly at her legs while the occasional ragged sedge snagged and tore her clothing. Occasionally, a thorny twig or branch scratched at bare skin through the rips in her pant legs. Dark impressions of things scuttling along wildly dancing leaves or skittering across a rippling mire left her to wonder what sorts of creatures they might be. Her thrill at the discovery of their existence, however, was soon overshadowed as a series of barbed twigs scraped along her shins, granting her a growing accumulation of cuts and abrasions.

With the momentary giddiness dashed, Caer's exhaustion began to take its toll. The soft soles of her shoes slipped on moss and lichen-covered rocks that lay hidden in the grasses, slowing her pace still further. Bran matched her stride, sticking to her like a shadow. After a few more unsteady paces, a foot slid again, dropping her to her right knee, the sharp edge of a rock stabbing hard against it and torqueing her weight sharply to one side.

Bran immediately wrapped his arm around her waist, lifting her to her feet as he called above the persistent wail of the wind, "Where'd that Dylan guy get to?"

Wincing at the pain of standing, Caer anxiously scanned the area, realizing she could no longer make out the haze of his silhouette in the thickening gloom. Yet she was aware, somehow, of his presence ahead of them. "That way," she yelled, pointing; praying her sense of Dylan's whereabouts was accurate. If not...

"Trust yourself, Caer. And trust me. I'm never more than a hundred meters away. Just keep the sound of the ocean to your left, the hills to your right, and keep moving."

Hills? She didn't want hills...assuming she could even see them. She just wanted Dylan to remain within sight, and to... "Stay out of my head!"

Bran pressed closer to her. "What?"

"Uh. Hills," she grumbled, looking to her right and straining her eyes, the undulating shadows of darker gray vaguely discernable in the distance. "Over there."

"Yeah. I see them." There was an uneasy pause, leaving Caer to worry that Bran might set out for them. "Doesn't look like we're going that way." Frustration edged his booming tone.

Caer gave a ragged sigh and swiped at her runny nose with the end of her sodden blanket. No. They weren't. Why not that way? The hills might offer some cave or crevice in which to shelter. No such possibility was visible in the direction Dylan was leading them.

Her knee throbbed, and, now that she was standing still, she couldn't stop shivering. She flexed her stiff fingers, first of one hand, then the other, before tugging her wrap forward, trying to cover more of her head. Not that it did any good. She was soaked to the bone. Her hair was lashing out from under the blanket like the images of writhing snakes she'd seen in holographs depicting an ancient mythological creature. Her shoes were worse than useless. And her toes, fingers, and nose were rapidly going from icy to numb.

Gingerly testing her knee, Caer moaned, "Just give me a dome. A nice, warm, dry..." Her complaint instantly stilled as the unmistakable prickle of a teleportation ignited and knotted her nerves. Coran'ian? If another of the beasts materialized here...now... how could she and Bran possibly fight it?

For several petrified seconds, she stood braced, waiting, while her heart slammed against her ribs. Nothing. Caer took a measured breath. Whoever had come through, she concluded, had done so a fair distance away.

Her relief evaporated as, *"Maura! Keep moving!"* jarred through her head.

As if to emphasize the warning, the air exploded in the electrified charge of multiple teleportations. Grabbing urgently at Bran's arm, Caer pulled him along with her, moving as fast as her injured knee would permit. How many had come? How closely did they follow?

Brown eyes set in a shadowed face on a sinewy body--searching!

The vision spawned renewed panic. Blood drummed in Caer's ears as she drove forward, the sense of pursuit hounding her every tortured step. A burning ache had long ago conquered her legs and lungs, and her knee screamed its protest, but she refused to stop. Bran, bless him, remained constantly at her side, reaching to support her at each stumble.

Struggling to breathe and fighting to keep to her feet, Caer at last spotted Dylan standing near the crumbling remains of a stone tower.

"Here!" Gesturing to the jagged edge of a craggy opening, he shouted, "Hurry!"

Risking one more backward glance, she half expected the figure from her vision to burst upon them. Instead, the distant haze flared with a blur of an orange glow. Dylan's manor house! Had they set it ablaze?

"Inside!" Dylan charged.

The tower's high walls, broken though they were, provided a reprieve from the greatest fury of the wind. Stray gusts, however, continued to swirl in the confines, and the mist remained as thick, the light as dim and gray as outside. Caer blinked up into the fine water droplets that continued to drizzle down. Only the scant remains of flooring from a couple of the upper stories stood as shield against the weeping skies. Bran grasped her shoulders and guided her to stand beneath the largest overhang. Teeth chattering and body trembling, Caer leaned, exhausted, against him. Adrian ducked in shortly afterward, carrying Emer.

The woman looked utterly drowned, her black hair clumped in soggy strands across her pale face. Her voice sounded more strangled than commanding as her blue lips formed around, "Put me down!"

Ignoring her, Adrian turned, first to watch the rest of their companions trudge into the confines of the tower, and then to acknowledge Dylan. "This is the place?"

Dylan nodded, drawing off his blanket and thrusting it at Caer. "Take it and use it. The blankets are wool. They will still help against the cold, even wet." Bran retrieved it, adding it over the top of the one already hanging heavily around Caer's shoulders. Pulling off his backpack, Dylan set it against one of the broken walls, then splashed through the puddles to the center of the enclosure. There, he stomped out a radiating pattern across a roughly four-meter area, all the while seemingly listening for something. When the splat of his footfalls echoed with an underlying dull thud, he dropped to his knees and began scooping aside great handfuls of mud. Caer stared at him, certain he'd lost his mind.

Adrian appeared to understand the man's efforts. Setting Emer gently on her feet next to Caer, he removed his blanket and draped it over Emer's, then stripped off his pack, leaving it next to Dylan's.

"Stoirm," he called, indicating the opening in the tower wall with a jerk of his head as he joined Dylan. "Better keep watch."

Flicking nervous glances between the two men flinging arms full of mud and the opening from which Stoirm stood watch, Caer edged closer to Emer, stammering, "The mmmanor house. Emmer, is it bbburning?"

Emer shot a glance in the direction from which they'd come, though the tower wall now stood in their way. "I ddon't think so. Mmaura is trying to bbreak through Dylan's pprotections. The glow is probably from the heat of her ssspells ccclashing against his."

It was beginning to rain in earnest, now, the water running unbroken rivulets off the jagged sections above them and washing muck back into the depression almost as fast as Dylan and Adrian could scoop it out. After considerable effort, Dylan reached into the sludge and, with the accompaniment of a thick squelch, yanked a metal hatch up and out of the way, a gush of mud and water cascading down the dark hole.

"How far?" Adrian asked, leaning to peer in.

Dylan considered. "About four meters, if memory serves. I've not used this passage for several centuries."

With a nod, Adrian sat and pushed off, disappearing down the abyss. A short time later, the hollow echo of his voice called, "Hand the packs and the ladies down to me."

39

Caer clung to Adrian's arms despite his firm grasp of her waist. A river of muck gushed around her ankles and over the tops of her shoes, making it difficult to find a solid purchase. When at last her footing seemed secure, she eased from Adrian's grasp. Taking her full weight, Caer's right knee buckled with a sharp stab of pain and a burning throb.

Adrian's grip tightened once more. "You all right?"

Her face flushed with agitation. Madmen pursued her. Her knee was on fire. She was soaked to the very marrow of her bones. Her jaw ached all the way into her ears from clenching it against the constant chatter of her teeth. And she was currently without her blankets, having given them over to Ian while Dylan lowered her into this...this pit. Dylan was right. As sodden as they were, they provided more warmth than the flimsy jumpsuit that clung to her like a soppy skin. Was she all right?

"Ffine," she stuttered through her teeth, her intended snap lost in the effort just to get the word out.

"Truth," Adrian demanded.

Caer blinked up at him through the rain and the splattering of mud that cascaded over the edges of the opening, ashamed. He looked like shit. His shirt, once black, hung from him in more of a sludge gray, the saturated fabric rising and falling with the tension of his breathing. His dark hair was plastered to his head, limp strands trailing down his forehead and running rivulets along his haggard face. Still, his gaze pierced her.

Struggling to keep most of her weight shifted to her good side, she managed a curt nod, hoping, this time, that he did take the time to read her thoughts, as it was easier than getting her lips to form words. *"As all right as any of the rest of our little company. Including you. Just let me get out of your way."*

Adrian's eyes narrowed and he looked about to say something more. Instead, he released her, shouting up to Dylan. "Pass down Caer's wraps." A heavy torrent poured from their corners as Dylan lowered the blankets. Adrian did what he could to squeeze the moisture from them before laying them across Caer's head, handing her the edges to clutch beneath her chin. Gesturing to his left, he instructed, "Move downslope if you can. Just don't go far. And mind the grade once you clear this landing. It's steep."

Biting at her lip to try and still the clatter of her teeth, Caer stared in the direction Adrian indicated, seeing only a wall of black. Her first hesitant step found a clump of slime that sent her skidding. Only Adrian's quick catch kept her from falling. She tried to avoid meeting his darkening scrutiny as she straightened, pushing his hands aside, all the while working to bite back a cry from the pain that flared anew.

It was near impossible not to hobble as she turned and ducked past the curtain of sludge. Even more so, thanks to the angle of the decline, which added considerably to the strain on her knee. Nor did it help that mud continued to run ankle deep, keeping the footing treacherous. Lip still clamped in her teeth, she edged her way down, her eyes gradually adjusting to the thin light from the opening above. It was, for the moment, enough to make out perhaps a couple of meters ahead.

Her attempt to ease forward dispelled any notion of attempting to hide her limp. Reaching out, she found the wet and slimy wall and used it to keep her moving in a straight line. Mercifully, the mud began to spread out to a thin sheen, granting her somewhat easier going for several more paces. At last, she paused, dropping the blankets from her head to listen to the drip and trickle of water and the whistle of the biting downdraft. Where in all the heavens were they? Was this some sort of tunnel, or just a big hole in the ground?

Follow.

"Follow what?" she muttered, squinting into the darkness. There came no response. Shivering uncontrollably, she shuffled one foot after the other, one hand clutching her blankets, the other maintaining contact with the wall. Even as her eyes continued to adjust, the blackness was too dense to penetrate far.

Muttered irritation accompanied each tentative step. She wanted no more voices in her head. Not Adrian's. Not Dylan's. Not the one telling her to follow, whomever it belonged to. Definitely female, the voice carried something of an ethereal thinness, as though it came from the depths of a dream. Disturbingly, it was the same voice as had spoken to her when she first gazed out of the high windows of the manner house at blue sky and clouds. So, too, she recognized it from the warning to prevent Adrian and Dylan from fighting. Who could speak to her of such things, unless someone in their party? Yet it didn't match Emer's voice, nor Del's...nor Blath's, for that matter.

Caer's mincing steps hit an unexpected hole, her knee shooting flames of agony up and down her leg. Bracing her back to the wall, she slid down, sitting with a soggy plop, sucking in at the stars in her head. Once they cleared, she squinted again at the brooding darkness, making out that she now sat to one side of a broad passage, its width roughly equivalent to its height--about four meters, if Dylan had it right. Massive stone supports along the sides braced a barrel-vaulted ceiling that dripped water. The wet walls consisted of stone blocks, tightly fitted, many splotched with lichen. Beneath her, the uneven footing was the result of crumbling stone slabs which descended beyond her range of vision. Mud still ran narrow rivulets between the broken pieces. Unyielding blackness swallowed everything that extended more than perhaps a dozen paces in front of her.

Follow.

Caer shook her head, muttering through her chattering teeth, "I ddon't know who you are. So, stop mmuddling in my head and show yourself."

Follow.

Lips pinched, and cringing from the pain, she hissed, "You fffollow! I was ttold not to go far." More to the point, she doubted she could stand again. Closing her eyes, she tried to will the pain away.

Wraiths.

The word held a sad acknowledgment rather than a warning. Still, Caer's eyes snapped open, the hair on the back of her neck standing on end as a thin series of wailing moans rose from the depths. Breath held, she fixed her anxious gaze on the blackness, bracing a hand to the wall, prepared to gain her feet, if flight was required. Would she be able to do so quickly enough? Could she make it back up the slope to the others if an enemy beset them from below?

No more wails rose. The only sounds sifting to her, now, consisted of those of her companions, underscored by the steady drip of moisture and the incessant whine of the draft. Caer buried herself within the blankets, leaving only her eyes uncovered.

For a handful of seconds, she remained staring into the obsidian abyss, mumbling reassurances that the wail had been nothing more than the distant echo of the downdraft. And then she saw the few tiny gray swirls of mist in the obsidian depths. They drifted, at first, then seemed to collect. She rubbed her eyes, blinked, and stared again. Below her, the gray vapors continued to coalesce, twisting and writhing, then swooping like something alive. Caer's breath froze, choking off any cry of alarm as the formless mass moved toward her, growing denser and larger as it came. Just as abruptly, and scarcely a meter from where she sat, it stopped. Caer managed a tremulous inhale, her eyes riveted as the shifting haze slowly separated out again, a dozen or more amorphous specters gaining vague definition, their vacant eyes regarding her.

Her blankets fell from her hands as she reached reflexively to grasp her necklace. The instant her fingers touched the charm and chain, a sigh fluttered, so delicately that she wasn't entirely sure she'd heard it. "You are here. At long last." As the sigh faded, so, too, did the phantoms.

"How bad is it?"

Caer jumped, her hand darting back to her covers, her startled jerk of them landing a punch to her mouth.

Emer grimaced. "Sorry. I didn't mean to scare you." The midnight luminosity of the woman's eyes held more than a hint of disquiet as she flicked a glance to the depths. "This is a disturbing place, I know; even for someone who's been here before."

Licking her lips, Caer rasped, "You...you know wwwhere we are?"

Emer nodded, her words tight. "I was here, once. A very long time ago."

Caer wanted to press her with a 'why', but Emer had turned her attention upslope, apparently drawn by the loud splash and the unmistakable tone of Brandon's grumbling as he cleared the still cascading curtain of mud. Del stood to one side, waiting for him. Dylan was last down, retrieving his pack from where he'd tossed it ahead of himself. At a nod from Adrian, Dylan strode across to join him, the two men settling into another muffled discussion.

Bran stopped a couple of paces down from the two, though his grumbling continued. After fumbling with a long, thin rod, his triumphant, "Hah!" accompanied the abrupt flare of green light. Sweeping the rod around, he spotted Del, who cocked her head questioningly.

"Chemical light," he said.

"I know what it is," Del returned. "Where'd you find it?"

"That Dylan fellow had it in his pack. Said I would need it down here." Holding the light aloft, he caught sight of the two Healers, now busy with their own quiet dialogue a few meters above and across from where Caer sat. At last, he spotted Caer and Emer. "How

361

come he didn't give you ladies one of these?" he asked as he and Del joined them.

Emer shrugged. "Maybe he only had one of them in his stores."

"Then why didn't he give it to Caer? She was the first down. How'd you manage to get this far in the dark, anyway?" Without waiting for a reply, he thrust the light aloft again, frowning into the descending blackness. "And where the hell are we?"

Those who come must know the way. Must not linger; they cannot stay.

"Sanctuary," Caer breathed, echoing what next whispered in her mind. "A place of hiding. We led them through, Family and Tanai alike...any who dared defy Nemhain." Stiffening, she clamped her lips shut. What was she saying? Those weren't her words.

Bran lowered the rod, shining the light in her face, frowning. "I thought you said you've never been to Earth before."

"I...I haven't." Again, her mouth clamped shut. How was she to explain that the words came from a voice in her head? They would think she'd lost her mind entirely.

"But you just said..."

Bran jerked around as Del placed a hand on his arm, interrupting him. Passing a troubled scrutiny over Caer, she suggested, "She's just quoting a...well-known story. I think we should take the few minutes available to us, Mr. Jase, and rest."

"But..."

"This path is long and difficult," Del persisted, nudging him away from Caer. "You don't want to be lagging behind, down here. The passage is a maze with multiple branches that go nowhere. Stay with us and you'll be safe. Stray behind and you'll be lost. Lost, you will die. So, take my advice. Rest your breath as well as your body."

"I ask again," Emer repeated, regarding Caer with guarded curiosity. "How bad is it?"

Caer blinked, her mind still grappling with the certainty that someone was using her as a mouthpiece. "How..." She blinked again, realizing Emer was still hovering over her. "What?"

"Your knee, dear. How bad is your injury?"

The mention impressed the pain back on Caer's awareness. "It's not a problem," she lied, the chattering of her teeth finally minimal enough to allow her to speak without so much stuttering. "I just... just slipped a little out there."

Emer sighed. "Everyone was aware when you went down, dear. Your pain telepathed sufficiently to cause us each some degree of empathic misery. Well, most of us, anyway. So, you can forgo offering anything but the truth."

Caer groaned, shooting a demoralized glance upslope, expecting disgruntled confirmation from everyone but Brandon. Dylan, Ian, and Stoirm, however, were tucked off to one side in earnest conversation while Adrian and Blath now stood somewhat below them, faced off in what was obviously another argument.

"It's a minor thing," she grumbled to Emer. "I'm no worse off than you are. Adrian had to carry you into the ruins."

Emer shook her head, contesting with considerable volume. "Mr. Starn had to do no such thing. I was just fine without his bloody interference." Toning her voice down with a belligerent huff, she added, "I can't help it if that man has an impossible stride to match. I may be slow, but I'd have made it here without his help. Now. Let's see that knee."

Slumping beneath her waterlogged wraps, Caer gave an equally belligerent snort. "I don't need a nursemaid, either."

"Let Ms. Kyot see to you!" barked in her head. There was no doubt that the sending was Adrian's.

"Mind your own bloody business!" she returned.

"You are my business. I should have come to you the moment I saw you fall and felt the stab to your knee."

"Business?" Caer tried, unsuccessfully, to turn a glower on him. *"Is that what I am to you? Your business? Who hired you to be my nanny?"*

She could feel Adrian's anguish in his brief silence. *"It isn't like that. You know it isn't."*

"I don't know what I know, anymore. I don't...I..." Subtly, the edges of Caer's anger and exasperation slipped away, yielding to a rising passion, the heat of it melting away the cold in her bones.

"I know that you are always here for me when I need you, Amhranai."

While the words skimmed softly off Caer's tongue, they came from the same source that had tormented her thoughts all those other times...the same one that urged her to follow, and that spoke to her of the phantoms before she saw them. The same source that called this place 'sanctuary'.

"Amhranai," it whispered.

He stood before her, young and tall and confident, with wild, raven-dark hair that framed a pale brow, strong cheekbones, and a proudly set jaw. His gaze of winter blue saw through to her soul.

"Sing for me, my love...my lord."

Caer gasped, trying to dislodge the image. It refused to fade, the most delicate of songs hovering in her mind with it. Though she couldn't make out the words, the melody was clear and sweet and rich, the voice carrying it so very familiar. So, too, was the young man who sang. The image revealed a far younger Adrian, but the voice, the confident stance, the penetrating eyes with the heat of molten turquoise deep within--all unmistakably his.

The music evaporated as Adrian's stricken face peered down at Caer. The sight of him rolled an achingly sad melancholy through her...melancholy and a deep yearning for another time...a time when...

The smell of wood smoke hanging on crisp air. The soft caress of furs beneath her. Amhranai's weight pressing down, hot against her bare skin. Bodies joined. Burning desire.

Heat flushed Caer's face as she struggled once again to shove the image from her head. Like the voice that repeatedly spoke to her, this vision did not belong to her. True enough, she and Adrian had been occasional lovers. But not...never like that. Never with such... The return swell of passion scorched her.

Shaking, she made to rise, wanting to flee from the sight of the others. What if they knew what had just filled her head like they seemed to know everything else? This was something to which they should never be privy. Nor should she.

Her awkward movements reignited the agony of her knee, depositing her jarringly back to the ground.

Ian gave an embarrassed clearing of his throat as he and Blath threaded their way past the others to stand behind Emer. "That leg needs attention," he declared.

"It doesn't," Caer moaned, aware of the hint of distressed surprise flicking across Emer's face.

Emer forced her countenance to a firm scowl. "Yes, it does. So, stop arguing."

Heat again flushed Caer's face. Emer and Ian, at least, had seen. As had Adrian. Their expressions gave proof. She bowed her head, unable to face anyone, and yanked her pant leg up. "Fine. Take a look and then let me be."

Brandon gave a low whistle. "Why didn't you tell me? I..."

"What?" Caer snapped. "You'd have carried me? I managed just fine, thank you very much!"

Emer's short huff accompanied her fingers' gentle investigation of the discolored and severely swollen area surrounding Caer's knee. "I'll give you credit for being thorough," she said. "If every tendon and ligament isn't torn, it's a wonder." She rocked back, weary lines creasing her brow. "In my current state, though, I don't know that I can help much."

"We're each of us worn and frazzled," Blath agreed, squatting beside Emer and patting her hand. "Ian and I spent ourselves trying to save Lord Stoirm before we were aware of your skills. I would that we had known of you sooner, Ms. Kyot. Had our efforts been jointly made at the outset, likely none of us would be in such a sorry state, now. Still, I'm better rested than you, I think."

After completing her own careful examination of Caer's injury, Blath laid a hand over the damaged area, her lips moving in silent chant. The pain diminished to a dull throb.

"This is the best any of us can manage, for now, I'm afraid. While my spell should help the healing process some, it will likely take a few days before all of the damage can thoroughly mend. Perhaps one of us will recover the strength to do more before then. Just be forewarned. Take it easy with that leg."

"Didn't take Stoirm that long to recover," Caer pouted. "And his wounds were far graver."

Blath rose. "You're not an Alainn, child."

"Didn't take Dylan that long, either."

The Healer leaned to brush Caer's face lightly with the backs of her fingers. "You are Witch, dear. There is no doubt of it. You should, therefore, possess some degree of the Family's recuperative powers. Sadly, you must know how to focus them before you can affect a quick mending. Lacking that, you must be patient and keep weight off that leg for a while."

Caer glared at her knee, venting a long and ragged sigh. "And how am I supposed to get where we're going? Sit and scoot?"

Hearing Bran's opening, "I", she snapped him off.

"No way! You are not going to carry me!" She couldn't bear letting him close enough to look her in the eyes. Not after that vision. He may not have seen it as the others had, but he might guess more than she wished from her countenance."

Murmurs rolled through the group. Eyes still downcast and lips pinched thin, she fidgeted with her necklace. She didn't need to hear their words to know they were discussing her. Injured. Utterly useless. She posed a grave risk for everyone. She needed those recuperative powers, assuming she was as they said, one of the Family. Damn Adrian! Damn anyone who had messed with her memories, concealing them from her! She needed to know who she was; needed to know what her capabilities were.

The subtle pulse of her charm grew a little stronger, its touch a little warmer as her hand closed on it. Slowly, a distant chant rose, thrumming in rhythmic cadence in her head.

Abred. Gwynfyd. Ceugant.

Always, these words came to her. There should be others, though. Not always the same ones, she realized. The words depended on the circumstances. Closing her eyes, she ran through the three, again, hoping they would stir other memories.

Abred. Gwynfyd. Ceugant. Abred Gwynfyd. Ceugant.

The chant lingered, the warmth of the charm growing; radiating through her fingers, her hand, her arm; coursing down through her body, bathing her.

Abred. Gwynfyd. Ceugant.

A new outbreak of visions began to chase through her mind. Hundreds of them. Some offered glimpses of villagers from Lillith II, their injuries or illnesses tended by Sidra. Others...others she saw as if through a long tunnel, distant and vague until...

The flash of a book. Two books. Each scrawled with flaming letters. Book of Secrets. A face hovered over each. Mother. Aunt. Two books overlap. Two faces merge. Book covers fly open, pages upon pages fanning past. Spells. Incantations. Recipes for tinctures and ointments and... Hundreds...thousands of spells, incantations, enchantments, recipes passed down through long ages. New ones added by the hand of Mother... the hand of Aunt. Two books. Different and the same. All of it there...in her head...flashing past...going backward in time from Aunt to Mother to Grandmother to...Back and back and back to...

Fear and pain. Blood rushes from around the arrow shaft protruding from her stomach. Fierce flames encircle them, creeping close.

The music of his tone soothes. "I am with you."

The bark of Adrian's, "No! Don't! Let it go!" cut through the vision. Caer blinked, seeing his face darkened by anguish, his eyes flashing hot. She took a deep breath. If this way lay the secret to unlocking the appropriate spells of healing...spells laid down by her mother and her aunt...spells committed to their books through generations that came before them...then so be it. Closing her eyes once more, she sought for the vision again. It rose with difficulty as she felt Dylan in her head, trying to shut her down. Strength of determination shoved him aside, her concentration focused on that one hazy scene.

He grasps the arrow shaft; jerks it free. Dizziness. Nausea. Agony.

His hand lays on the wound, pressing. "You know the words. Find the words."

The world spins wildly.

"Stay with me! Find the words! I will speak them with you."

Two voices joined, the music of his quiet, the tightness of hers tortured.

Abred. Struggle to know the way.

Gwynfyd. In purity speak the healing.

Ceugant. Infinite be the power.

Abred. Struggle to know the way. See the injury. Know its degree.

Gwynfyd. In purity speak the healing. Guide its path. Let it flow.

Ceugant. Infinite be the power. Hold it within. Breathe it...

"Caer! Release the image! Let it go!" The command was urgent.

A stir of hot breath on her face brought Caer's eyes open. For a moment, she didn't know who was bent so near, or why she was lying down. She knew only that she was not the one in the vision. She could still hear the echo of Adrian's voice, encouraging, buoying the sweet, suffering murmur of the woman's. The woman whose voice was the same as the one that kept speaking inside her skull. The one whose passion for Adrian was...

Sluggishly, Caer's mind cleared, and she saw Dylan's unreadable expression as he knelt beside her. He helped her to sit, holding her hands, keeping them from...from reaching for her necklace.

Emer's tight voice sounded close beside her. "Are you aware of the power she just called up? She has the skills of a Master Healer to put behind her spells! I felt her assisting with Stoirm, but her chant was limited. Now...now she's called a full sequence. She's done it before, I'll wager."

Pushing to her feet, Emer spun on Adrian. "How could you let such memories stay hidden from her all this time? Why didn't you return that knowledge to her when you gave her back the memories of her childhood? She possesses the strength of a Master Healer! Had Caer tended the Alainn... He might have died needlessly at my hands! You kept Caer's magic of healing from her, and it could have cost the Alainn his life!"

Adrian returned Emer's heated fury with an icy glare as he pushed past her. "There are some things that are not hers to know; some things that must not be disturbed." Extending a hand to Dylan, he pulled the Dream Reader to his feet, then offered his hand to Caer.

She ignored him. "I'm a Master...? What?"

Emer indicated Caer's knee with a nod. "You healed yourself. You called up the words and the magic...tremendous magic. More than was necessary for such an injury. Focused...directed...you could..."

Adrian silenced her with a sharp hiss.

Healed. No. Caer turned a confused scrutiny to her knee. The swelling and discoloration were completely gone. So, too, was the pain. How could she do that? Even if she recalled every spell from the books of her mother and her aunt, she couldn't accomplish such a feat. The magic came from elsewhere. From...from the woman whose voice spoke in her head. Or...or from Adrian.

"You're not to do anything of that sort again! Do you understand? You must leave those images to the darkness!" Adrian's admonition held far more pleading than harshness.

At last, Caer accepted his hand, pulling to her feet and tentatively settling her weight onto her leg. The knee held without so much as a twinge.

"I trust you can manage on your own, now," Adrian rumbled. Without waiting for her response, he rounded on Dylan. "And I'm trusting you to keep your word."

"I gave it, didn't I? It's increasingly difficult, but I pulled her from this latest vision." Dylan scowled at Caer, his expression a wash of agitation. "I will do everything in my power to continue doing so."

Caer glared at both men, ready to erupt, but was cut off by Adrian's drained, "It's time, then." Trudging back upslope, he retrieved his backpack, handing it to Ian as he returned to Caer, his face more drawn than before. To Dylan, he said, "Once you reach the chamber, make sure everyone takes some food and gets some rest."

Dylan nodded, shouldering his pack and fastening the straps. "We will wait for you."

"Don't wait long. Blath can see you the rest of the way if need be."

Blath looked about to explode in mutiny, but Adrian hushed her with a volcanic glare. Turning his narrowed gaze on Caer, he commanded, "You are not to stray from the group. Do I make myself clear? And stop digging in your head!"

Withdrawing a small, antiquated gun from his pocket, Adrian approached Brandon. "I believe this belongs to you. I trust you know how to use it."

Caer gaped. Where would Bran come up with a gun? And why?

"It's not mine," Brandon objected. "I found it next to..." Caer could see that he fought to keep his eyes from Del. "...next to Brenna's body," he finished. "But, yes. I know how to use it."

"How well?"

"Well enough to shoot an Andromedin skelter rat from forty-five meters."

Adrian pressed the weapon into Brandon's reluctant hand. "Good. I was afraid your having threatened us with an empty chamber might indicate a lack of proficiency. Here." He produced a small box from the same pocket. "A friend scrounged up some ammunition when Fedel'ma and I went for Stoirm."

Brandon glanced at the box, looking about to reject both gun and ammunition. Then, shrugging, he took them.

"Stay with her," Adrian grunted, jerking a thumb at Caer. "Protect her."

"With this? Against the likes of you people?"

"Magic has its weaknesses."

Bran stuffed the gun in his belt and pocketed the box. "I have no intention of leaving her side."

"Thought as much." Adrian offered a curt nod to Dylan. "Master Dream Reader."

"I've told you before. The name's Dylan."

"Dylan, then. They are in your hands. Lead them in."

Stiffening, Caer planted her feet and folded her arms in defiance. "Adrian Starn! If you think you're sending me away while you stay here to cover my ass, you can just think again! I told you already, I'm not leaving anyone behind to fight my battles for me. If you're staying, then so am I!"

Adrian ran a hand down his face. "By all that is merciful, why are the women in this family so damnably difficult?"

"I believe I've expressed that sentiment more than once, recently," Dylan harrumphed. Grabbing Caer's shoulder, he turned her firmly toward the descending passage, pressing her forward with his grip. "The man can take care of himself. Now shut up and get moving. Unless you prefer that I use the butt of Jase's gun on your stubborn head and carry you across the top of my pack."

40

Ne'r fear for me,
Only flee, my love, flee.
Here shall I stand.
My oath have I taken,
For love ne'r forsaken.
Here shall I stand.
Beyond death and time,
Against our foes' crime,
Here shall I stand.
And when thou dost need me,
Always I'll find thee.
And again shall I stand.

Though it was Caer who cast one last, belligerent glare back at him, it was another's softer glance Adrian saw shimmering ghostly in her eyes. The impression lingered in his mind long after Caer disappeared and the faint light of Jase's chemical wand was swallowed by the darkness.

"The stirring is strong, down here, Amhranai. This place draws things out for you as well as for Caer that are best left undisturbed."

Adrian refused to meet Stoirm's scrutiny, turning his glower, instead, to search for the metal rod he spotted when he first dropped down the hole. Collecting it, he ducked back through the gushing mud and water. Using the rod, Adrian caught the edge of the hatch above them and maneuvered it back into place, sealing off the entrance. Swiping muck from his face, he contended, "Do not meddle in my thoughts."

"I would never do so. You sang the song aloud. Are you aware of that?"

An uncomfortable silence fell as the two men remained in place, waiting for their eyes to adapt. With the thin light from outside extinguished, the walls and ceiling of the tunnel provided the faintest of shimmers. Not sufficient for a Tanai to navigate by, but certainly enough for an Alainn or one of the Family.

"You believe it is Roisin whom Caer harbors," Stoirm prompted, a note of unease to his tone.

"You saw the vision as clearly as I. You know it is." Adrian shook his head. "I wish this burden had never fallen to Caer."

"I like it no more than you. But to whom should it fall?"

Adrian's jaw tensed. "Any number of others would shoulder this task."

"Caer is the last remaining survivor of the triple line," Stoirm countered. "The task lies where it was foretold."

"Caer is too vulnerable. I made her so. Not only in keeping her identity from her, but in denying her the training required for the proper use of her gifts."

"It was out of necessity that you did so."

"Was it?" Adrian growled.

"Her ignorance protected her from a series of traumas no child should have to endure. And it kept her safe from discovery for far longer than any of us dared hope."

"Yes. Well, she's been discovered, now." Stripping from his shirt, Adrian wrung it out and used it to wipe the rest of the mud from his face. As he donned it once more, he set out along the tunnel, studying each deeper shadow, watching for branching or crossing passages.

Stoirm kept pace beside him, casting an edgy glance back toward the covered entrance. "Not only discovered but is being hunted.

Could you sense the whereabouts of our current pursuer before you closed us in?"

"Lurking just beyond the ruins, though I doubt he'll remain there for long. Once he's certain that the tower is clear he'll begin nosing about. Shouldn't take him long to find the hatch. Even in the downpour above, the mire won't completely obscure the depression."

For several minutes they slogged downward with only the sound of dripping and trickling water and their own soggy footfalls accompanying them. At length, Adrian ventured a dismal, "You said I sang aloud."

"You did."

"I should never have agreed to bring Caer to this place."

There was a hesitation before Stoirm submitted, "You knew its nature before we came, then."

"Master Dream Reader informed me. Not in so many words. His description, however, left no doubt. I knew it would be risky, subjecting Caer to these passages. Still, if this place can draw the song from me...aloud and without my awareness of that fact...what will it draw from her? Too much is already seeping through to her awareness. And with her in the company of the Dream Reader..."

"Caer is stronger than you think, my friend."

"It's not the measure of her strength that troubles me. It's her bullheadedness," Adrian huffed. "I should never have concealed the truth from her. Now, however, is not the time for her to be digging for it. I worry that the Dream Reader may not be capable of keeping her in check." Heaving an anguished exhale, Adrian rumbled, "Perhaps I should have encouraged his threat to knock her out."

He fell silent, training his eyes on the steep grade, ticking off each intersecting passage, making a turn here; another there. His mind, however, could not shake the image of Roisin. He longed for her waking presence; longed for her to acquire a physical form that was no longer shared with another. She was so close. So close. It was difficult. After so many centuries, believing Stoirm to be the one with the power to spell the Awakening; believing and refraining from begging him to work the magic. Adrian bit back his groan. He'd never asked, just as Stoirm would never comply, even had the power been his. Nemhain would know the moment either sister's soul woke. Alone, neither Roisin nor Dana stood a chance against the Dark Heart. They must be awakened together. And to accomplish that, the one hosting Dana's soul must be found.

"As you said," Adrian muttered. "Caer is the last of the triple line, which begs the question, where does Dana's soul slumber? In one of her own line, perhaps? Or is she long perished? Assuming she lives and we can find her, where do we find the individual responsible for the sisters' slumber? Without knowledge of their spell, any waking is dangerous."

The weight of Adrian's concern carried in his slump-shouldered sigh. "While we cast about in the dark for answers, hoping Nemhain does not find them first, the Dark Heart's strength continues to grow. The increasing violence of her attacks suggests she believes her power to be great enough, now, for her to take the key by force and without consequence. If she succeeds…"

"The magic that guards the key will hold, Amhranai. As it has always done."

"That does little to help Caer," Adrian snarled.

"You cannot assume guilt for everything that may happen to the girl. She would hold neither the soul nor the key had she not willingly accepted them."

"It's hardly willing when done in ignorance. She was a child. Is still a child."

"You did not consider her a child when first you bedded her."

Adrian stumbled, his moan weighting the silence around them.

"Caer was a woman in Tanai terms, Amhranai," Stoirm persisted. "Do not forget, she desired you long before you relented."

"Hers was a child's infatuation. It has never been more."

"Perhaps. It is true that she does not love you in the same manner as she cares for the Dream Reader. There are many kinds, many degrees of love, Amhranai. You cannot have failed to grasp that in the long course of your life. Yet, of all those whom you've taken to your bed, it is only with Caer that you feel guilt. Because you see Roisin in her. Roisin would never begrudge you your love for this girl."

"Do I? Love her? Or is it the ghost I see in her eyes?"

"Both, if I am any judge. Now, leave such distractions. Turn your mind to the needs of the moment, or you risk the lives of both Caer and Roisin. Nemhain must be kept from Caer, not only for sake of keeping the key from the Dark Heart's hands. She must not be allowed to discover that Caer is also the host to one of her sisters' souls. We do not know what strength remains to the one Caer harbors. If Roisin is weak, if her soul is captured, the Dark Heart's threats to the whole of humankind might persuade her to give over her secrets for opening the way, even without Dana."

Aware of Stoirm's slowing stride, Adrian turned a questioning glance to his friend, who was rubbing his temples. "They are a curse as much as a blessing, the ancient spells worked in these passages," Stoirm grumbled. "While they prevent Ailill from detecting our precise location, they likewise prevent us from knowing his. He may well be within the tunnels. Let us hope he has not alerted Maura."

"He won't. He teleported to the site of the Dream Reader's manor house a few seconds before his half-sister and her troops, and well behind their line. I suspect he came with no intention of making his presence known to them."

Stoirm vented a disgusted snarl. "I am not quite myself, yet. I did not pick up on the difference in the time of their arrivals, or the difference in their locations. You think Ailill was sent to spy on his sister?"

"Not an unwarranted assumption. Nemhain does not trust her daughter. Maura is too much of her own mind and holds ample ambition to go with it. Ailill is far easier to manipulate. His arrival to spy on Maura, however, must have placed him close enough to us to sense our flight, and, I fear, to discern Caer's presence among us. She's too great a prize for him to let slip again. I'm betting he's decided on a bit of freelance treachery, thinking to take Caer and the key before Maura finds them."

"If such is the case," Stoirm sighed, "he must also know that we are with her. Ailill is not his mother. He lacks her strength and her abilities. Surely, he does not think to take Caer from both of us."

"When have you known Ailill to act with anything resembling reasonable judgment?"

"Never," Stoirm admitted. "Perhaps it is fortunate for us that he failed to inherit any of his father's intelligence."

Adrian's jaw twitched. Even after so many ages, the memory of Lamh Laidir brought sorrow. In truth, Ailill had inherited nothing at all from his father. Lamh was a thoughtful man; slow to anger; a man of justice. Sadly, his gifts in magic, though numerous, were greatly inferior to Nemhain's. His expertise as a warrior resulted from his keen strategic mind and his tremendous physical prowess. Had his magic been stronger, he might have defended himself against his wife...maybe even defeated her. Often, Adrian wondered if Ailill had witnessed the twisting and breaking of his father's mind at the hands of his mother. Was that what accounted for the son's madness? Or...or was some degree of insanity the price paid by every Witch for their magic?

Adrian's bleak thoughts were interrupted as the whistling draft carried the scent of sweat and fear down to him. The ancient spells might block one's ability to sense the precise whereabouts of others, but they did not hide Ailill's stench. Obviously, the fool had found the hatch and come down the hole. Thanks to another aspect of the magic worked down here, there would be no trail left for him to follow, making the chance that their stalker could find his way through the tunnels without getting irrevocably lost a very slim one. Still, it was a risk Adrian was unwilling to take. Ailill had, after all, made it this far. He might, in truth, be able to follow them, now, simply by listening. Though it would be exceedingly difficult to isolate from which tunnel the sound of Adrian's and Stoirm's conversation echoed, it wasn't impossible. So, who was the real fool? Ailill for his insanity and incompetence, or himself for carrying on an audible dialogue with his companion?

With a gesture to Stoirm, the two men picked up their pace, stopping when they reached the next intersecting passages. Separating, they slipped soundlessly into the shadows of the branching corridors, keeping close to the walls. At length, a silhouetted figure appeared in the middle of the crossroads, Ailill's semi-crouched profile a darker shade of black against the oppressive cloak of the underworld. The murky brown glow of his eyes darted warily between the tunnels.

Flattening against the wall, his face averted to prevent Ailill from detecting the smolder within his own eyes, Adrian waited, not daring to breathe. Slowly, Ailill turned, giving lengthier scrutiny to each passage, his head cocked to listen, thus supporting Adrian's hypothesis and increasing his irritation. Still, he waited in perfect stillness until, from the periphery of his vision, he could tell that Ailill's back was to him. His leap away from the wall was nearly equaled by Ailill's return spin. The men's hands rose almost simultaneously. Adrian's spell shot out only a fraction of an instant before Ailill could cast his. Stoirm's spell hit their quarry in the same fraction of a heartbeat as Adrian's. With a sharp squeal, Ailill went rigid.

Adrian stormed toward their captive. That was entirely too close. Either he was slowing down in his old age, or his foe had been practicing--something Ailill had not been known for in the past.

"Looking for someone?" Adrian spat, though he knew there could be no reply. Only the man's eyes moved, their brown burning with hatred.

Before Adrian could consider precisely what to do with their captive, the scent of char and ash and singed fabric wafted down, along with the charge of a spell bearing Maura's unmistakable signature. Apparently, she was attempting to fry anything that might occupy the passages for a good distance in front of her. Adrian bit back his heated expletives. He'd hoped her attack on the manor house would keep her busy for a good deal longer. Either Ailill had alerted her to the fact that her prey was no longer within, or she'd detected her half-brother's presence and opted to leave the destruction of the house to others while she hunted him.

"Brother!" The distant throatiness of Maura's call drained the inert man of all color and replaced the hatred in his eyes with panic.

"Where are you? What are you up to, skulking around behind my back?" The soft splat of wet shoes against slimy stone indicated she was already much closer than Adrian initially anticipated. Bending Ailill over his shoulder, he nodded down the passage they'd been traversing. The correct one from this point was the branch that led to the left. They needed to lead Maura the wrong direction. Adrian gritted his teeth. He also needed to warn Caer, as the repercussions of any serious assault from Maura would likely be felt throughout the maze. And he could almost guarantee Caer's reaction. Drawing his earlier song back to mind, he focused, singing it silently. If he could just make Caer...or make the one she harbored...hear it; make them understand that they were not to come back for him.

The charge of magic flared again, illuminating each of the corridors for several meters, while the sweep of the accompanying stun ricocheted from the very spot where he and Stoirm had ambushed Ailill. Adrian drove forward, the sizzle of the charge on his back muted by Ailill's inert presence. As it died away, he realized that Stoirm had turned back, returning to the crossroads while motioning Adrian to remain beyond the reach of Maura's assaults.

"You, Uncle!" Maura squawked, her ire thundering in echo. Adrian judged from the sound that she was still a fair distance above where Stoirm stood. "It's you down here? Who goes with you?"

"None who are of any concern to you," Stoirm shot back.

"You have my brother. I'd say that's my concern."

The charge and heat of slamming spells as Stoirm's met Maura's blasted through the passages like ringing metal hammered on a giant forge, the surge of the clash rolling out like a mighty storm. Maura's rage mixed with the still echoing rumble. "I am not my mother!" she screeched. "I've no compunction about eliminating you, Uncle!" Another crash of spells exploded through the passages. More thunder. The crack of stone. Adrian heaved his burden sideways into another intersecting corridor, and dove after him as earth and stone crashed to the floor.

41

Caer poured as much belligerence into her expression as her frigid face and clamped teeth allowed. Even in the dim light and from downslope of Adrian, even though his eyes followed her, she could tell he looked through her.

"What?" she rumbled. "Am I invisible, now?"

An indignant stamp of her foot landed on an uneven piece of slimy stone, sending her skidding. Dylan caught her before she ended in a butt plant, the indignity adding to her growing list of snarled emotions. Yanking free of his supporting hands, she turned her back on the group, muttering under her breath as she picked her way down the rubble and mud that covered the floor, listening to the splat and shuffle of their feet as the others trailed her. Dylan remained uncomfortably close, the sense of his presence like a hot breath on her neck. The others dropped back enough for the thin green light of Bran's chemical wand to extend barely a couple of meters beyond her. The constant bob and sway of it proved far more annoying than helpful. She preferred the faint shimmer of the walls and ceiling to the sickly cast of Bran's light, but refrained from demanding he douse it. The shimmer, she'd discovered, seemed enough for her to navigate the passage, but she was certain Bran would be utterly blind without the wand.

They covered little more than a dozen meters when Adrian's beautiful tenor lifted faintly above the whistle of the downdraft and the tread of so many feet. Though the music rose delicate and sweet, most of the lyrics were lost in the steady drip, trickle, and footfalls that echoed around her. Only "flee my love, flee" and "shall I stand" claimed discernable notice. Jaw set, she jerked one more glower upslope.

Dylan's fingers clamped on her shoulders, turning her face forward once more. "Don't even think about turning back," he warned. "They want you far from the entrance before your pursuers realize you're here."

Caer wrenched free, muttering, "I'm well aware of that!" Shooting a scathing backward glance, she added, "You can sing until the moon melts, Adrian Starn. But no sweet melody is going to make up for sending me off while you martyr yourself."

"They are trying to keep you safe," Dylan returned flatly. "We all are."

Keep her safe, indeed! As if any of them actually gave a damn about what happens to her. Stoirm, after all, abandoned her and Sidra on Lillith II all those years ago. Adrian's lies, his persistence in hiding so much of her life from her—that was proof against his caring. Okay. So he rescued her from the pyre. So he took her to the Healers. He did so only because Sidra cried out for a guardian. Caer never asked him to remain in her life afterward, pretending to be her friend.

She swallowed the sudden, pained whimper that threatened. At the very least, he might have been honest with her about that other woman—the one whose passion for him still singed her nerves. Caer's face grew hot as she recalled the vision. Never once, in all the years of their friendship, had he mentioned her. Now, this woman's voice kept finding its way into her head. "Wherever you are," she whispered. "Get out of my mind! You want to talk to Adrian? Telepath to him and leave me out of it!"

Tugging the blankets up around her ears, Caer shrugged deeper into them, her lower lip shoved forward in a pout. And what of her heart? Stolen by Dr. Hugh Jorn. Had things been different...had Hugh Jorn not died on Ahira...she would have told Adrian how she felt about the man. Turns out, there was never any such person as Dr. Hugh Jorn. His very existence was a lie. His kisses were lies. His death on Ahira...that was a lie, as well. And when he turned up wearing a new...a new...persona, he lied to her all over again.

Caer's hand sought the familiarity of her necklace as solace in her misery, then jerked from its touch. These people didn't care about her. Their concern was for this bloody piece of jewelry they called a key--a key that would never have become a key had Jorn...Dylan... not given the charm to her. And it didn't even belong to him. It was his sister's. A ragged sigh accompanied her hand's reach, once more, for the necklace, her fingers tentatively, tracing the charm's pattern. Warm against the hollow of her neck, the faint pulse of the stone set within the trinity knot matched the weary slug of her heart. For the hundredth time, she wondered what sort of key this thing could possibly be. Why did it have to come to her? Why was it sought with such deadly violence? Her lips pinched tight. And why she couldn't throw the cursed thing away. The fact that she could no more part with it than she could willingly part with an arm or a leg terrified her almost as much as the people who wanted to take it from her. How long would she have to carry this...this key?

Adrian knew. Probably. Just one more secret he kept from her. And what about the others in their little party? What did they know? Undoubtedly, far more than she did. Why should she be left in the dark? She was the one stuck carrying the bloody thing. Her pinched lips shifted to a determined thin line. Somewhere, buried in the depths of her blocked memories, she likely already knew the answers to her questions. If she could just find a little privacy to go deep-brain diving again. Her promise to Adrian that she wouldn't was of little consequence. Those who lie have no right to demand honesty from others.

Sucking in, Caer ventured an apprehensive glance over her shoulder, worrying that Dylan might be eavesdropping on her thoughts, again! If so, he would make sure she never got a single heartbeat's worth of privacy. Jaw set, she forced her attention away from the matter. If she didn't think on it, no one could read it in her thoughts.

The shift of her attention allowed a glimpse of two dark voids on either side of their passage. There were others, though the only note of them she'd taken was when Dylan's hand to her shoulder directed her to turn down one.

Pointing, Caer grumbled, "Do we turn at one of those, or go straight?"

"Straight," Dylan replied.

"Where do the crossing ones go?"

"No place we want to be."

"Why?"

"Death dwells within those ways. Those who go there never come out."

Shivering took Caer. She was an idiot for not paying attention earlier! How many openings had they passed? How many turns had they made, and were they right or left? What if she should have to retrace her steps?

"I don't advise trying it," Dylan put in.

Caer barely contained her ire at his having intruded in her thoughts again, shooting back, "If the maze is so deadly, why aren't you leading?"

"I can do so easily enough from where I am. I'll not risk your falling behind, down here."

Dylan kept them to the same path for what seemed an eternity, ignoring numerous side passages. Claustrophobia crowded in on Caer. So, too, the ever-present drip of water, the whistling draft, and the scuffling of feet ate at her nerves. Moreover, her hips and ankles ached from forever moving downward, as well as from the cold. And her knees had long since gone wobbly.

Dylan, at last, pointed them toward a passage that branched to their right, where the degree of descent increased sharply. Caer could scarcely remain upright. Hugging more tightly to the wall, she shifted her blankets so that she could keep one hand pressed to the stonework for support. A dull headache had joined the ache and throb of her joints, no doubt due, in some measure, to the constant bob of Bran's light from behind her. The dancing shadows swayed ever more erratically with his increasing slips and skids, indicating that he was as bone weary as she.

Bran's light took a sudden, sharp, upward lurch, followed by a loud splunk and the rattling of expletives that rolled harshly all around. Stopping, Caer braced her back against the wall and peered back in time to see Del move to Bran's side, a hand to his elbow to help him regain his feet. Once Del assured everyone, including Bran, that he was uninjured, Dylan urged Caer forward once more. But she couldn't make her feet move. If she lifted one foot to take a step, she feared the standing leg would refuse to hold her up any longer. She needed to sit; needed to rest.

Dylan grasped her arms, preventing her from sliding down the wall to the floor. "We must stay on our feet. Lean on me, if you need to. Just keep moving."

Caer stared dismally into the blackness, about to ask how much further they had to go. The question died in a startled gasp at the swirls of gray mist stirring in the depths. They swooped at her notice of them, just as the ones near the entrance had done. Rising against the downdraft, they stopped to flutter a hair's breadth beyond the reach of Brandon's light. Behind her, his sharp inhale suggested he saw them, as well. Caer's anxious breath stuck painfully in her lungs when six distinctly separate swirls glided forward to hover near her. Elongating and thickening, they slowly coalesced in hazy masses of vaguely human form, again much like the previous apparitions. Darting a glance at the swirls that remained in the depths, she realized that they, too, had separated, morphing into semblances of the human form. Her attempt to count them failed as their vapors shifted constantly, sometimes overlapping the shapes of neighboring specters.

"They'll do us no harm," Dylan encouraged, trying to nudge Caer forward. "We have to keep moving."

Still, Caer balked. What if he was wrong? What if the wraiths wrapped her in their mists? Would they suffocate her?

"Caer," Dylan snapped. "Move." How her feet managed to obey, she couldn't say. She knew only that each step came with reluctance, pain, and mind-numbing dread. The apparitions moved with her, skimming along to match her unwilling tread. The obsidian holes that served as their eyes seemed to penetrate through her, not with the vacancy of those who'd materialized near the entrance, but with a blackness more intense than that of the pit from which they'd risen. A faint murmur stirred among them, sounding, at first, like an echo of the drip and trickle of water. Gradually, the sound shaped into words.

"Is it true?" the nearest vapor murmured. "Are you the one?"

Ne'r fear for me,
Only flee, my love, flee.
Here shall I stand.

The song broke through the rasping slush of vaporous sound, the lyrics coming sharp and clear to Caer's mind. The suddenness of the imposition brought her to a stumbling halt. Phantom stares turned instantly from her, lifting to the upper passages as if they, too, heard the music and sought to identify the source.

My oath have I taken,
For love ne'r forsaken.
Here shall I stand.

Adrian. Why was he singing again?

Dylan's hands were again on her shoulders, twisting her around to prod her forward. Caer set her heels, straining to listen.

"I told you," Dylan pressed, "These spirits mean us no harm."

Caer waived him off with a sharp shush.

Beyond death and time,
Against our foes' crime,
Here shall I stand.

Dylan hesitated. "What?" he asked, casting a quick glance in the direction the apparitions now darted.

And when thou dost need me,
Always I'll find thee.

"The song. Don't you hear it?"

He listened intently for a second, his brow furrowing. "All I hear is the water, the draft, and our breathing."

How could he not hear it? It was so clear, the music flowing with such bittersweet melancholy.

And again shall I stand.

The refrain died away. Filling the silence, however, came the familiar, delicate lilt of that unknown woman's voice, insinuating itself like thin veins of quicksilver through Caer's mind.

"Always you are there for me, Amhranai. Always you give me courage to do what I must. Sing for me again, my love...my lord."

Amhranai. Caer sucked in on her lip. Stoirm had called Adrian by that name back at the manor house. Lord Amhranai Fearalite, he'd said. It was the same name whispered to the young Adrian in that embarrassingly heated vision.

Dylan pushed her, his patience gone. "You're hearing things. That can happen down here."

Caer acquiesced, clinging to the wall, her brain too busy trying to recall the lyrics to focus on resisting. It was real, that song. Not imagined. Adrian had sung it many times. Many times. But not for her. Never for her. Before Caer could sort through how or why she knew that, the thread of her concentration slipped, replaced by a swell of panic. As the knot of dread and terror rose to her throat, the specters suddenly reappeared, surrounding her for a fraction of an instant before evaporating like so many lights blinking out.

"We know you," they fluttered. "You've returned at last. But you cannot stay. Not here. Hurry."

The sense of alarm was suddenly so overwhelming that Caer could practically smell it; so electric that it raised every hair on her body. Once more, she wrested free of Dylan's hands, clutching at the wall, turning her terrified gaze back upslope. Something was wrong...or was about to be. There was a time when she'd scoffed at

Brandon's assertions that she seemed to know things before they happened. No more. Not with her flesh raised and the charm on her necklace duplicating the racing pace of her heart.

Dylan attempted to aim her toward the depths again. "There's no singing, Caer. And you're not going back just to try and prove me wrong."

No. She couldn't go back. Every fiber of her screamed as much. Adrian's song. It told her he would find her. Her way was down. Adrian would come. Come for the sake of the one who spoke inside her head, at least. Still, she held her ground. Not yet. They couldn't go, yet. Adrian and Stoirm might be following, even now. They had to be if she could hear Adrian's song. How far back were they? Just out of sight, perhaps? Just around that last change of passages? She listened again, praying for the echo of approaching footfalls.

"Where are you?" she sent, trying to stretch the thought; trying to push it as far through the passages as possible. *"What are you doing? Why aren't you here?"*

Dylan gripped her arm, forcefully shoving her forward. Again, she yanked free. "Look" he groaned. His exhaustion was plain in the tight lines of his face. "I've done my best to honor your wish to stay out of your head, difficult as it often is. If you want me to put more distance between us, fine. You can follow behind me. But I warn you, if you try anything foolish, like attempting to run back the way we came..."

"You'll knock me in the head," Caer muttered, leveling a withering glower on him and almost daring him to try. For a moment, she feared he just might, so angrily pinched was his countenance. Instead, he moved past her with a guttural smattering of expletives that concluded with something unseemly about the Family's women. Hearing nothing else, sensing nothing more, Caer forced herself around to follow him. Her way was down. Adrian would find her.

Brandon cautiously worked his way to her side, frowning as he stumbled over the uneven stone and rubble. "Did you really hear someone singing?"

Caer nodded. "You didn't?"

"No. Are you sure our friend Dylan doesn't have it right? That your mind isn't just playing tricks? This place is weird enough to pull all sorts of bizarre things from mine."

She harbored no doubt. She knew what she heard. There seemed little point in arguing, though. Instead, Caer focused on the business of watching her footing as her sense of urgency motivated her to move with increasing haste. A crunch beneath her feet drew her up short, her breath cut off with a choke. Scatterings of decaying bones splotched with gray and brown dust or mold now lay underfoot. The need to keep moving...to reach their destination...pressed her on, her eyes seeking ways to avoid the grizzly remains, praying that they were animal and not human. A glimpse of several skulls proved otherwise.

"Folks who made it this far, but lacked the strength or courage to continue on," Emer offered softly. "Sad souls. Likely, they were fleeing some of Nemhain's ilk when they stumbled on the maze. Without a guide, though, there was no way for them to reach sanctuary at the heart of this place, or to find their way back."

Bran nervously cleared his throat, asking, "Is it their ghosts we saw?"

"No. I can't say what happened to these souls. The spirits who...."

Blast of heat. Crush of stone.

Caer cried out, stumbling and dropping to her knees in the midst of the bones, her blankets falling from her grasp as she jerked her arms up to protect her head from the tumble of rocks. Beside her, Brandon yanked his gun from his belt, sweeping his waning light frantically from side to side and squinting into the shadows.

"What is it? What?" he demanded. Dylan charged back to join them, while Del, Emer, and the Healers closed ranks just above them. Caer tried to warn them; tried to scream out that the passage was crumbling. The words lodged in the back of her throat. Nothing fell. Nothing crumbled.

Cavern. Flames leaping. Menacing eyes seeking.

Thunder rolled and echoed in the distance above. A heartbeat later, the ground all around them convulsed, jarring damp earth from the walls and ceiling. Then came silence. Wide-eyed, Caer extended a trembling hand, catching small bits of the detritus that rained down. Just bits of debris. Nothing more. She tugged her blankets back to her shoulders, unable to shake the foreboding that gnawed at her. Realization hit like the sickening slam of a mat-trans arrival. Adrian and Stoirm! They were the ones in trouble! They were the ones caught beneath collapsing stone. Or were about to be.

Blath's plaintive, "We have to go back!" proved the Healer sensed it, as well.

"That's the one thing we can't do," Dylan growled.

"Tell me the way," Blath implored. "Please! I'll go alone!"

Cavern. Fire. Seeking.

"No." Caer sucked in, stunned by the authority asserted in her denial. "The chamber. That's where we must go. That's where you can help them." Though the declaration breathed out through her lips, it had not been by her will. She knew of no chamber.

Blath spun on her. "What would you know of such things?"

"I..." There was no explanation she could give. Yet she knew her words to be true. Giving in to the conviction that drove her, Caer proclaimed, "I know that you will know what to do when we get there."

Fear and doubt shrouded the Healer woman's face as she shot tremulous glances both up and down the way. "How far is it?"

"Another hour," Dylan advised. "If we hurry."

"Can't we do that...that..." Brandon licked his lips, his face pale, his eyes darting. "Do that popping in and out of places thing?"

Dylan gave a quick shake of his head. "Not possible down here. The passages are protected against the use of teleportation. The only way to the chamber is by foot."

Another thunderous boom reverberated from above, shaking them even more violently. This time, several large stones dislodged from the center of the ceiling, sending everyone in a dash to plaster themselves against the walls.

"Better if this place was protected against falling in on itself!" Brandon yelped.

Dylan grabbed Caer's arm once again. "We're wasting time. We need to..." His command was lost in the frenzied hammer of her heart and the roar of blood throbbing in her ears. Too long, Caer knew. An hour was too long. Standing rooted, her fingers clutching her necklace in a vise grip, certainty tracing an icy rivulet down her spine, she prepared. The magic in this place could not hold against her. She could do this. If she could just 'see' the chamber, she could get them there. She needed only to concentrate.

Fire. Cavern. Deep.

The world lurched into a spin, impressions of the passage melding with a sense of endlessly whirling darkness. Caer closed her eyes against the rush of vertigo. Focus. She had to focus. Had to see...

Fire and light. Shadows on patterned stone high overhead.

Dylan's frantic, "Caer! Stop!" edged through. Caer forced him out; tried to call the flitting image to clarity. The floor dropped away as the vision firmed and held.

A cavernous space carved from the bedrock of the earth. Granite veined in grays, whites, and reds. Shallow niches dotting a polished stone wall. A single narrow arch the only entry. Patterns--serpentine lines, knots, whorls--etched in glistening wall and high ceiling. At the chamber's heart, embers burn within an enormous pit.

42

Cold, unyielding ground slammed against her feet, the impact nearly doubling Caer over. Catching herself, she staggered, then dropped to her hands and knees, her lungs screaming for air, her head spinning with nauseating pain.

"Lay her down!" Emer barked.

Someone shifted her around, laying her back. Struggling for her breath, Caer fought to sit.

"Caer!" Dylan snapped. "Be still!"

She couldn't. She had to find...someone. Had to find someone.

"Damn it, Caer! Stop fighting me. Just lay still and breathe."

One halting, shallow breath. A second. The burn in her lungs subsided with a third. The fourth and fifth brought a slow stop to the whirling world, revealing Dylan's face hovering in front of her, his fury and dismay obvious, even through the haze that still clouded her vision.

"I thought," Bran wheezed, sounding from somewhere off to Caer's right. "I thought you said that couldn't be done down here."

Emer's pale face appeared next to Dylan's, her glowing midnight eyes wide as she stared down at Caer. "It should be impossible."

"Only the..." Dylan swallowed whatever he'd intended to say. His features hardened, his voice ringing with rage. "You could have killed yourself, pulling such a stunt. Could have killed us all."

"Caer did this?" Bran's still shaky inhalation whistled between his teeth. "She got us here?"

Stripping off his backpack, Dylan sought Caer's frigid hands within the tangle of her wet blankets, rubbing them vigorously.

"Blath," she whimpered, pulling her hands free and struggling to sit. She remembered that Blath would know what to do, once they got here--assuming this was the chamber she'd envisioned. "Where's...?"

Dylan nodded across the low-glowing embers of the pit that filled the center of the room. "She's here. Now be still."

"I can help her," Caer persisted. "I can..."

Dylan's brow cut down menacingly. "Not after what you just did! No one attempts magic of that magnitude without lifetimes of practice. And not even the best among us dares attempt it here. Try something like that again and I'll do more than knock you in the head."

Caer winced, half expecting a blow to be immediately forthcoming. The wince triggered a new round of hammering in her skull. As gingerly as she could manage, she turned her head, averting her attention from Dylan's harsh scrutiny. For a moment, the motion sent a new roll of nausea through her. Fighting it, she fixed her gaze on a single point, waiting for the queasiness to settle and the last of the fog to lift from her sight. The fixed point proved to be a section of a highly polished stone wall. Daring the subtlest shift of her position, she noted the wall enclosed a circular chamber. Etched into the stone and running a continuity of patterns up and across the ceiling were the designs from the vision that delivered them this place.

Another shift allowed her scan to seek out the others. Ian was striding to a section of wall near the single arched entrance to the chamber, Dylan's pack in hand. Propping it against the wall next to the one Adrian left with him, he turned his glance her way, his countenance a mix of curiosity and concern. Fedel'ma was busy using sparks from her fingertips to light lanterns that occupied small, evenly spaced niches carved into the wall, observing Caer obliquely as she went. And then there was Bran, who stood half crouched between her and an arched opening, seemingly uncertain as to whether he should spring back into the black passages, or leap to her side to protect her from...from...who-knew-what. That left Blath, whom Caer had yet to locate. Her repeated attempt to sit and turn was greeted with yet another wash of nausea, forcing her back down, again waiting, watching only that which was in her line of sight.

Having completed her task of lamp-lighting, Del joined Ian near the arch, removing the sling from across her shoulder. Within the sling's bundle a lump thrashed about. Del peeled back the covering, whispering a few soft shushes as she withdrew a woefully bedraggled and protesting Merripen. The agitated animal spit and hissed, taking a swipe at Del with claws extended before wriggling free and darting on wobbly legs to a stretch of wall furthest from the humans.

"Guess I deserve that," Del sighed.

"She going to be all right?" Bran's edgy query drew Caer's sluggish attention back to him. His face was filled with as much anxiety as his voice, though the fact that he was concerned about the cat surprised her.

"Yeah," Dylan rumbled, snugging Caer's blankets around her once more. "I'll throttle her, though, the next time she looks to pull such a stupid stunt."

Caer blinked, realizing Bran's attention was on her, not the cat.

Emer pushed to her feet. "So," she mumbled, brushing her damp hair from her face as she continued to study Caer, her features suggesting a dumbfounded understanding. "She's a host..."

"Don't!" Dylan warned.

Truth rang through Emer's words. But what truth? Caer's head was too scrambled to think. The others could cast magic without their brains turning to mush. Why couldn't she?

The subtle warming of the chamber returned Caer's fragmented contemplations to Blath. Daring another attempt to sit, she squirmed around, at last spotting the woman on the far side of the pit. The Healer's arms were lifted toward the distant, unseen heavens, the dampness of her white hair glistening in the growing dance of sparks rising from the bed of embers within the pit. Though the woman's lips moved, her words were too hushed to be heard. Still, Caer recognized the content of the invocation from the cadence of Blath's murmurs and the feel of the magic that charged the air. This was the spell her aunt used to call Stoirm through their cooking fire in the middle of their small hut; the same that Sidra used to call Adrian through the flames of the great pyre.

The sputtering blaze responded to the Healer's efforts erratically at first, dying back and flaring again and again. At last, spikes of flame leapt to life, flicking from yellow and red to white-tinged blue as they thrust upwards. Their brightness reflected off the pattern-etched wall and ceiling, leaving Caer teary-eyed and squinting. Along with the intense light, heat spilled out in waves. Blath never faltered; her chant never ceased. It was just as Sidra had done.

"What's she doing?" Bran asked, his hand raised to shield his eyes.

"Summoning," Emer replied, awe in her tone, even as she blinked against the brightness.

Bran cleared his throat, darting uneasy glances around. "Summoning who...or what?"

Emer waved him silent. "The Alainn possess the ability to travel within the flames," she said quietly. "Or, so the ancient stories claim. Samhradh was said to possess a bit of the magic, as well. The first human to do so. Her gift allowed her to use fire to call out to others who were too far away for their early evolving telepathic abilities to connect with directly. It's said that she could even use the flames to speak to those without the gift of telepathy. Legend would have us believe that Samhradh could speak to anyone using her magic with fire. That's how she first encountered the mind of the Alainn, Tar On Tine. What she lacked was the ability to travel between blazes to go to him. So, Tar On Tine came to her--an incredible jump from one world to another, if the story is true.

"Legend further declares that their daughters inherited the full gift from their Alainn father, possessing the ability to communicate, to summon, and to travel. Pyro-mages, they were called. If there are others of their descendants who've inherited all three aspects, we've not found them." She nodded toward Blath. "At best, some of the women inherited the ability to communicate. Never before were we aware that they might also be capable of summoning, since humans can't pass through the flames, and we thought the Alainn either myth or long gone from our world."

Pausing, Emer chewed her lip, staring with cocked brow into the fitful play of shadow and light. "Stoirm is Alainn, though. Seems reasonable to assume he should, therefore, be able to accomplish all three aspects." Sucking in, she added a stunned. "And Starn!"

"What about him?" Bran asked.

"I don't know which of the sisters he's descended from, but if what I saw of Caer's vision from Lillith II was wholly true and not some amalgam of…then…then Adrian Starn also possesses the gift to travel from fire to fire. Not only does that make him the only human capable of doing so, he's the only male to possess any of the abilities of a Pyro-mage."

Brandon regarded her with a dubious cock of his head. "You aren't suggesting that the Healer, here, is summoning those two to show up in the middle of that bloody inferno! Why don't they do what we just did? It was a bit of a rough ride, but it obviously worked."

Emer gave a soft huff. "The precise lay of one's destination must be known before attempting to teleport. Otherwise, we risk turning up in some very unhealthy places, like inside solid walls or large pieces of furniture, or teetering off the edge of a cliff…or worse. Neither Stoirm nor Starn can possibly know how this chamber is laid out. And then there's the magic within the confines of the tunnels. The spells counteract any attempt to teleport." Her brow drew down as she again eyed Caer. "Or, at least they did so once upon a time. Still, the feel of those old powers remains strong, here. How Caer…"

Dylan shot her a warning glare. Emer responded with an almost imperceptible nod, resuming the discussion of the Healer woman. "To answer your question, yes. I believe Blath intends to summon Starn and Stoirm through the flames. Trouble is, assuming I understand the stories correctly, a fire is required on both ends. The summoner manipulates the flames of one fire, the summoned the other, each shifting the patterns of the flames until they match. Only then can someone be brought safely through the blazes. I don't know that Starn or Stoirm have access to anything that will burn, though. They can ignite sparks at their fingertips, certainly. But that can't be sufficient for them to pass through."

Brandon's troubled gaze flicked back to Caer. "You need to know a place before you can make this teleportation work, you said. The teleportation without the fire, that is. So, how did Caer make it work? She says she's never been here before."

Emer shrugged, her suspicious scrutiny causing Caer to squirm. "That, my friend, is the question, isn't it?"

Bran renewed his study of Blath. "You think she can do it?"

"Hmm?"

"The Healer. Do you think she can really bring those two men here? Through that?" he finished, pointing toward the blaze.

Emer shook her head. "I don't know. Until now, I believed the only way to arrive was by foot. Perhaps the magic in this ancient place has changed. Perhaps..." Drawing a slow breath, she muttered, "All I can say for certain, Mr. Jase..."

"Brandon," he corrected.

"Brandon. All I can say is that something has changed. I don't know what, or how. In truth, I no longer know what is or isn't possible."

Bran snorted a harrumph. "Now you know how I feel."

"Yes. Well, let's just hope that no undesirables manage to duplicate Caer's success, or to hitch a ride through Blath's summoning. We don't want Maura turning up here."

In front of them, the fire suddenly exploded, spewing ash and embers along with a burst of glaring light and scorching heat. Caer choked on her sharp inhale as, across the pit, Blath was tossed forcefully backward with an anguished screech, spasms jerking her body. Within the pit, the blaze fell instantly back to a mere glow.

Dylan's lunge around the chamber carried him to the Healer at the same instant as Ian. Between them, they lifted and supported the woman, escorting her toward the wall. Despite the pain and panic that glazed Blath's face, she appeared unharmed. Fighting the men's efforts to seat her, she pushed back to her feet, trembling, her features drawn in anguish.

"I've lost him!" she cried. "I had him...for a moment. But..." Wrestling away from them, Blath stumbled forward, palms toward the embers once more. As her arms rose again, so, fitfully, rose the hot, yellow-red tongues. "Attend to me, Tine Fearalite!" The strength of her command rang around them like a clarion call.

The pit continued to hold no more than a sparking smolder beneath a handful of ragged, flicking tongues for a long second before erupting once more, this time with ribbons of a blue-white inferno that streaked upward, blood red curls lacing through them. Within the conflagration the indistinct outline of a face appeared, too thinly translucent to make out any details.

"I hear...not find..." The voice was faint and broken.

"You must come, Tine!" Blath pled.

Still, the image faltered.

"Tine!"

The face, and then the whole of a young man, dark-skinned and looking to be barely eighteen, gradually took form. Within minutes, he stepped from the fire, tall and sturdy, a flowing brown cloak draped around his broad shoulders.

Blath moved forward, tentatively reaching a hand to him as though to verify that he was truly there. Then, slumping to her knees, her shoulders shook with her weeping.

"Mother," the young man soothed, stooping to her. "What purpose is so great that you call me from the urgency of our hunt?" The delicate point of his ears and his indisputably elegant features proclaimed him Alainn, though his skin shone with the same rich onyx as his human mother's. Thick curls of black hair framed his fine face, giving startling contrast to the piercing blue glow of his eyes as he scanned the small group. "These people are surely no threat to you."

"It's your father and grandfather," Blath managed, choking back her sobs.

The young man's features tensed, his expression pained with grief as he wrapped his arms around her. "Father is dead, then. I did not sense it. Nor did I sense that Grandfather had perished. My mind has been too keenly tuned to the hunt, I fear."

"No... No." Blath pushed back from him and gained her feet once more, slowly squaring her shoulders as she swallowed. "They both live. Or at least they did so moments ago." She gave a small nod toward Emer. "This woman is a Master Healer like no other I have ever witnessed. She saved him; returned my husband, your father, to us. But now... Now, your father is in grave peril and I cannot find him. I was able to reach your grandfather, but the image is weak. Too weak. You must help me find him again. Go to him. Perhaps he can tell you where your father is. Bring them back, Tine. Both of them."

"I will try. Show me."

Blath returned her gaze to the pit, her small frame still shaking as she again raised the flames. Tine stood close as his mother's tremulous voice gained strength in the molding of her chant.

"I hear Grandfather speaking," he acknowledged. "But his sight is too limited for me to see more than vague shapes of broken boulders and shattered rock."

Husband. Grandfather. Caer stared, dazed and dumbstruck. It was one thing to recognize that Blath's husband, this young man's father was Stoirm. But...but Adrian? His grandfather? The concept was almost impossible to grasp. For uncounted long seconds, she continued to watch Blath and her son struggle; waited for them to announce they'd found him...found Adrian. Growing ever more anxious, Caer braced herself with a measured breath. There was someone else who might be able to help.

"He needs you. Can you find him? I don't know where you are, or if you can, at this moment hear me. If you can, can you tell us where Adrian is? Where Amhranai is?" Every bit of concentration Caer could muster was thrown into that plea, pushing it outward, feeling it drawn inward.

"When your need is great, Amhranai, I will find you, as you have ever done for me."

The promise swept through Caer, overriding all else. Sitting straight and tossing off her blankets, she waited just long enough for the renewed reeling of the room to slow, then rose to her feet, swaying. Dylan dashed around the pit, again, reaching to push her back. Caer edged away from him, her hands raised to keep him at a distance. "I can help." Her voice was as shaky as her legs, but she held no doubts. She could do this. She had to do this. The woman who spoke within her head would show her the way.

"Caer!" Dylan growled.

This time it was Caer who leveled a threatening glare. "Don't!" she hissed.

For a moment, it looked like he would press the issue. Grudgingly, miserably, he yielded.

With a slow breath, Caer made her way around the pit on unsteady legs, thankful that she at least remained upright. Her head swam as she reached Blath's side, and not just from dizziness. Images flitted past, none identifiable, all blinking in and out as though she were flipping through some enormous file. Struggling to calm her thoughts, she worked to focus. After several deep breaths, she raised another silent plea, stretching it outward.

"Adrian! Where are you?" Threaded through the thought was a companion entreaty, muted as in a dream, but strong. *"Show me, Amhranai. Let me see. Let me help."*

Heavy shadows of tumbled stone blocks...a feeling of confinement... Caer could sense it, but could see nothing firm, nothing that could be used to hold a vision of his location firmly in her head.

"You need a flame, my love."

For worrisome moments, darkness remained. Then, faintly, the hint of a spark grew to a small blaze.

"Yes," Tine said. "I see it."

The young man stepped back into the blazing pit. "Hold to the pattern, Mother," he called. And then he was gone.

Caer and Blath clung to one another, their eyes holding firm to the sweep and curl of the flames before them. Sparks hissed and skittered as long seconds dragged by.

"We're here," came the young man's voice, at last. "I need your help to get us through."

Straining to keep to her feet, Caer drew herself up, Blath straightening with her.

"I hold the pattern that you will know the way. Through the flames I summon thee."

One final burst of heat and light shot out, containing a dance of scarlet tongues. Within the blaze, images rippled...then solidified. Tine stepped out, supporting his father. Behind him staggered Adrian, shirtless, covered in caked mud and soot, and half carrying, half dragging another man.

No more strength. No more will. Caer's legs crumpled beneath her. As her magic died, so, too, did the flames within the pit, the heat and light collapsing inward until all that remained once more was the glow and the flickering light and shadow from the lanterns.

43

Adrian stumbled half a dozen steps before dropping his hostage and thudding to a knee, his eyes clamped shut against the lurch of the chamber. His head rang like a bloody gong, the throbbing in his temples sharply hammering the counterpoint, while every nerve in his body reverberated like a bodhran in high jig-time. Bracing, he opened his eyes to the reeling room. Much as it disgusted him to admit it, the consequences of overtaxing his magic affected him as much as any Witch. His endurance might be greater than most, but even he had his limits. And Maura pushed him damnably close to them when she brought the world down on top of him.

Forcing a steadying breath, he fought down the queasiness and shoved the throb in his head to the background. He needed his wits; needed to ascertain the severity of Stoirm's injuries; needed to determine everyone else's state. As the pitch and roll of the chamber slowly eased, his focus settled on those nearest him. Jase and the Dream Reader knelt opposite one another, perhaps two meters in front of him. Between them lay Caer, curled and unmoving. Skin gray as ash, her breathing rose and fell in a series of shallow, tattered rasps. Adrian erupted in a guttural round of expletives. She'd drawn on her magic, again. He remembered feeling the flare of it; sensing her signature in it.

Heaving unsteadily to his feet, Adrian hissed a low snarl at the Dream Reader. "You gave your word. You promised to keep her from calling on her powers again!"

Dylan shot him a heated glower but gave no reply. Instead, he finished brushing several long, tangled strands of hair from Caer's face, then pressed his fingers to her temples, his gaze intent on her as he whispered a brief chant. Straightening, he waited as color crept back into her flesh and the rasp of her breathing relaxed to a quiet and even rhythm. When at last he seemed satisfied, he rose, his features a contorted mix of contempt and resignation-dulled anger. *"Perhaps you could do a better job stopping her,"* he challenged, stalking past. *"But I very much doubt it. You're aware, I trust, that you owe the fact that you are still with us to her."*

Adrian jerked his scowl back to Caer. The events, from the moment Maura brought the passage down to Tine's appearance in the flames, hovered as a surrealistic wash in his head. He recalled the singe of Caer's magic. Yet it was Roisin he heard calling out to him. He shuddered. The slumbering soul should not be capable of interjecting more than fragments of memory from her dreams into Caer's. Had the two become so entangled that Caer now tapped more deeply into Roisin's mind?

Caer's whimpered stir and the glint of her earthen green eyes from beneath her fluttering lids brought an audible sigh of relief from Jase. The Tanai stroked her hands for several seconds before she struggled to sit, her voice a thick crackle. "Where's...?"

"Everyone is here," Jase cut in, pressing her back. "Now, stay still. I can't afford to lose you, too. You're all I have left, Caer. No more funny business or I'll...I'll..." He took a deep breath, his shoulders slumping. "To be honest, I don't know what the hell I can do with the likes of you. Just stop it with the weird stuff. Okay? Are you hungry? We have food. Don't move. I'll bring you a bite or two and some water."

She tried to wave him off, but couldn't control the shake in her raised hand. "Don't," she managed. "Please, Bran. I don't want anything."

"You really do need to eat something, dear," Fedel'ma pressed, pointing Jase to the backpacks. Her soggy blanket hung from her

403

shoulders, leaving her damp hair in short, muddied twists around her solemn face. The sincerity of the woman's concern did not escape Adrian. Neither did the pointedly speculative glance she turned to him.

"I'm not hungry," Caer insisted, pushing up enough to brace herself shakily on an elbow. "Just tell me if Adrian and Stoirm are safe."

Striding around her, Adrian squatted, gripping her shoulders to prevent her from moving any further. "You'll eat," he growled. "And there will be no more magic from you. If I catch so much as a wisp of a spell rising, I'll knock you out and immobilize you for a month!"

The briefest flash of relief shot through Caer's eyes as she stared up at him. A faint and tremulous frown promptly doused it. "You wouldn't dare!"

"I'll do whatever it takes to stop you from throwing magic around so witlessly."

Caer's jaw set, her frown deepening. *"I didn't do anything. The magic came from...from her."* The thought held a frightened hesitance. *"She's inside me, isn't she?"*

For several agonizing seconds, Adrian sought for some hint of doubt in Caer's eyes.

"You knew," she accused. *"Why didn't you tell me? You had no right to keep this from me."*

Stifling his moan, Adrian shot back, *"I told you not to dig for any more memories. I'll banish the Dream Reader's soul for allowing you to..."*

"I did no digging. Not this time. When Blath couldn't hold her contact with you, not even with her son's assistance, I realized that the one who keeps speaking in my head might know a way to help. So, I sent out my plea, hoping she would hear. Then I opened my mind to her response expecting some message, some fuzzy imagery or vague statement that would suggest how we might rescue you."

Caer shook off Adrian's grasp, her lips pinched. *"For a while, now, I suspected that this woman telepathing images and thoughts to me is someone who loves you. What purpose lay behind her telepathing to me, though, I couldn't guess. Always, it's flitting things, often oddly disjointed. Usually, the images or the words make little sense. But sometimes...sometimes they're clear and immediate. Sometimes even urgent."*

She fixed him with an intense and searching gaze. *"But it isn't telepathy, is it? Not in the sense of thoughts being sent out from one autonomous person to another. The woman who speaks to me does so from within me. Because that's where she resides, isn't it? Once I opened my mind to her, I could feel her presence. How dare you keep such a thing from me!"*

Adrian slumped down beside her, speaking aloud, though his voice was low and tight. "Long before I promised to protect you, I swore to protect the secrets of the one you harbor. I could not tell you. For the sake of your safety and hers. The spells employed in setting her soul in its slumber should have been sufficient to conceal her from you. I could not...would not go against that magic." Running a hand over his face, he muttered, "The spells I employed to keep you from knowing your past were to protect you, as well. Both of you. Digging for your memories risked drawing hers out. Risked entangling the two. And still, you dug. You've endangered yourself and the soul you carry."

Adrian closed his eyes, swallowing against the knot in his throat as his mind spun back to those long, terrible moments huddled beneath the crush of earth and stone in the passage above. Caer was wrong. Her magic worked with Blath's to hold the way open. He sensed it at the same moment Roisin's gentle-sweet voice sought for him; urging him to strike a fire that she may find him. The delicate brush of that voice in his head gave him hope. Diverting as much of his energy as he dared from the shielding that held back the tons of earth, he managed to strip Ailill of his cloak and to remove his own shirt. He coaxed a few small sparks to smolder and at last ignite the wet fabric. He maintained his shielding, even as he held the pattern of the flames in his mind because Roisin asked it of him. And all the while, Caer's magic helped to hold the way open.

Exhaling a ragged and despairing groan, he accepted this new truth. Even in slumber, Roisin understood Caer's plea and responded. Even in slumber, she reached out to him; touched his mind; brought him through. Their souls--Roisin's and Caer's--were so entangled, now, that the two acted as one. And they'd acted to save his life.

"Who is she, Adrian?"

There was no answer he could give. Roisin's identity had to be kept hidden if they were to have any hope of defending her.

"You love her," Caer pressed. *"As much as she loves you. She's why you came for me when I was a child. It was to save her."*

The note of anguish in Caer's thoughts sliced through him. *"No,"* he returned. *"I came for you. I did not know that you bore any soul but your own."*

May she accept his words and not read the half-truth in them. What he claimed held truth at the time he was called. He answered Sidra's cry to save the child. As he emerged within the flames, however, there came the faintest impression of an achingly familiar signature. Though it brushed his mind for less than a fraction of a heartbeat, he sensed that Roisin's soul had passed from the old woman to Caer. Roisin. After so many centuries of hiding, suddenly, he believed she was close...so very close.

"...Starn?"

The warmth of a hand on his bare shoulder at last registered, along with the realization that it had been there for some while.

"Mr. Starn. I ask again. Are you injured?"

"No," he growled, rising and spinning so abruptly that Emer stumbled backward. The rush of his movement left Adrian momentarily swaying. Only as the vertigo settled did he glimpse Emer's surprised and defensive look. "No," he repeated dully, running his hand over his face again. "Forgive me. I'm tired and on edge. Nothing more serious than that."

"Good," the Dream Reader declared, kicking at another body

that lay sprawled on the floor. "Then you'll feel up to explaining why you brought this retrograde piece of protoplasm along with you. I thought the plan was to eliminate our stalker, should the opportunity present itself. Not save his worthless hide."

Ailill. Adrian breathed out a long and exasperated exhale. He'd forgotten about his nephew. "I didn't drag him here for the sake of saving his life. This 'retrograde piece of protoplasm', as you put it, has always managed to snuffle out aspects of his mother's and sister's schemes. That's information that might well help us keep Caer out of their hands. Given that Maura just tried to destroy her brother, perhaps he'll prove eager to share his knowledge."

"Those two have never been clandestine about their hatred of one another," Blath observed tersely. "I'm only surprised that it's taken Maura this long to attempt her brother's murder. For her to act as she did, though, she must not have realized who stood with him."

Adrian glanced around for his daughter. Blath stood next to her seated husband, her back propped against the wall, arms folded, a look of profound disdain on her face. Ian and Tine sat just beyond Stoirm, quietly talking amongst themselves. Again, Adrian wondered at Tine's presence.

"I summoned him." Blath's simple proclamation reflected the intensity of her emotions. *"I will not lose my husband after just having him returned to me. Nor am I in the mood to lose my father."*

Adrian gave a faint nod as he regarded Stoirm. The Alainn looked somewhat battered, but conscious and intact, a fact for which Adrian was beyond grateful. He saw his friend go down just as the top of the passage gave way, and instantly extended his shielding to encompass the Alainn. Whether the action was for a living or a dead man, however, he'd lacked the reserves to ascertain.

Returning his attention to his nephew, Adrian moved around to stand over him, rolling the prone form over with the toe of his boot. The spells he and Stoirm had cast to immobilize their stalker had long since lifted. So too, he guessed, had Ailill's state of unconsciousness. The extension of Adrian's shielding had, of course, gone first to Stoirm. Ailill had already taken a blow to the head from falling stones before Adrian included his enemy in his protection. Still, the man hadn't taken that great a blow.

"Maura knew full well that both Stoirm and I accompanied her brother," he said. "No doubt, Nemhain's camp would celebrate my removal from the universe had her daughter succeeded." The faintest tick of a smile at the corner of Ailill's mouth gave him away. He was listening. Good.

Adrian continued. "Seems, however, that Maura wasn't content with simply slaying me and banishing my soul. She went so far as to attach a banishing spell to her attack on Stoirm, as well. Overkill, if you ask me, since the Alainn are not known to possess the ability for their souls to transmigrate."

"Surely Maura's actions were reckless rather than intentional," Fedel'ma asserted. "No offense, Mr. Starn, but it seems far more likely that you, and perhaps even that idiot at your feet, were her targets. In her eagerness to eliminate the two of you, her kill and banishing attacks went wide."

Adrian shook his head. "Maura made her intent quite clear. She holds no love of Stoirm, and has only contempt for her mother's affections."

Blath shot her husband a stunned glance before turning a cocked brow back to her father. "Nemhain's orders have always been that Stoirm be taken alive and unharmed. Why would Maura risk ignoring her mother's dictates?"

"Ask her for her reasons, not me," Adrian huffed. "I doubt she has much fear of retribution, though. Nemhain will never hear what her daughter attempted unless one of us is willing to tell her."

Fedel'ma scowled. "We may, none of us, live long enough to tell anything to anyone if Maura survived the calamity she just wrought. It may take her a while to dig through the debris, but she will seek for us again."

"Indeed." Adrian took a moment to scan the disheveled group.

Bone weary, the lot of them. They couldn't risk resting for long, though. "We need to be well away from here as quickly as possible."

"And how do you propose we do that?" Jase put in. "Seems to me that our escape is blocked. Even if we can get past it, that bitch is still up there."

"This chamber provides its own exit," Fedel'ma replied, fixing Adrian with a pointed scrutiny. "I'll wager you knew that at the outset, Mr. Starn. It occurs to me that you harbored no doubts regarding your ability to negotiate the passages, with or without Dylan's assistance. Very curious for someone who isn't a Keeper. And even they are granted knowledge only of the lay of the maze for which they are responsible." Her smile remained friendly enough, though wariness shone in her eyes. "Perhaps you'd explain that confidence."

Jase darted a glance from Fedel'ma to Adrian. "What's a Keeper?"

"One who maintains, protects, and can find the way through a labyrinth," Fedel'ma returned.

"And what makes you think Starn isn't one?"

"There were nine, originally. Nine labyrinths and nine Keepers. Each Keeper held the responsibility of guarding the secrets of a single labyrinth—the location of the entrance and the single safe passage through it. Theirs was the task of delivering any who fled Nemhain's murderous hunts to the safety of the chamber at the heart of their maze. Most of the hunted were Tanai, of course. People whose families served or were loyal to one of Nemhain's two sisters, or who..." Fedel'ma cocked her head at Jase. "Who, like yourself, were suspected of being Sensitives. That's not to say that there weren't also a few Witches fleeing her wrath. But the Tanai had the greater disadvantage, possessing no magic, and therefore holding little means of protecting themselves. Unfortunately, with centuries at her disposal, the Dark Heart long ago succeeded in finding and destroying eight of the great labyrinths. This one is the last; Dylan the last remaining Keeper."

Her lips pursed as she considered Adrian again. "So, how is it,

Mr. Starn, that you could be so certain of finding your way through, unmolested by the spirits or the magic that dwell here?"

"They are mine," he answered with a long sigh.

Fedel'ma frowned. "Excuse me?"

"I am the architect; the grand designer for each of the nine ways; each one different, each unique. The signature of my magic is imprinted in this place. By that, the guardians recognize me. The specters will always allow me to pass."

"How can they recognize you?" Emer objected. "Your magic holds no signature."

"Every Witch has a signature. Mine is subtler than most. I can assure you, however, that the guardians sense me by it. They know me for who I am." He might confess more, were he of a mind to. More than architect, his was also the magic that constructed the nine ways. A grave and grueling challenge; by far the most demanding task of any Adrian had ever undertaken for Dana and Roisin. For more than a half-dozen lifetimes after their completion, he remained depleted of all but the most rudimentary of his powers.

Dana intended to conceal all knowledge of Adrian's accomplishments from him, but Roisin interceded, arguing that, for the sake of what his efforts had cost him, he had earned the right to remember. Instead, only the knowledge of their locations was hidden from him--that and the design of each entrance. He could make his way through any of them...if he could find them.

"Architect of the ways!" Fedel'ma muttered, shaking her head. "That makes you older than me by a good, long span. Didn't think anyone save for the three sisters dated that far back." Her narrowed eyes went from Adrian to her son. "Architect and Keeper. Together in the last of the great mazes. Very curious."

More ominous than curious. From the moment the Dream Reader described this place, Adrian recognized the man as the last Keeper. And for that Adrian accorded him a fair degree of respect. Neither Dana nor Roisin chose their Keepers lightly. His respect, however, was gravely tempered by the man's disquieting abilities as a Dream Reader. For, therein, lay a gift that held both threat and promise. There was no question of the man's having touched and interpreted some pieces of Caer's dreams. In doing so, had he also touched Roisin's mind and discovered her for who she is? A man with such an ability might also hold the capacity to call forth the Awakening. Adrian could not deny that he longed for the release of Roisin's soul, that she might once again transmigrate into an unshared host. But he understood the dangers of accomplishing that feat until she and Dana could be awakened together. His foreboding doubled at the acknowledgment of this new complication—the intricate entanglement of Roisin's soul with Caer's. Difficult enough for a shared host to lose the alien soul without damage to its own. With the two now wrapped together...

The Dream Reader seemed to sense Adrian's growing concerns. *"You still do not trust me,"* he sent.

"Nor you, me, I'm guessing."

Darting a glance at Caer, the Reader pressed with, *"I will always do what is necessary to protect Caer. Trust that."*

"Is it something you swore, Master Dream Reader?"

"I need no swearing for this task."

"But you took oaths. Your role as a Keeper bears that out. Did you not, I wonder, also swear to something larger?"

"Such as?"

"Was it accident only that drew you to Caer on Ahira, or were you seeking for the Sleepers?"

"She came to me of her own accord," thundered back. *"I long ago withdrew from all matters pertaining to the sisters beyond the vow I gave as a Keeper."* Conviction thrummed in the intensity of the Reader's response. But doubt also flickered. Adrian sensed it at the back of the man's mind.

The Reader thrust back at Adrian with, *"And what of you? What oaths did you swear? Has it always been your intent to deliver Caer like a lamb to slaughter? Do you intend to strip her of the soul she harbors, regardless of what it may do to her?"*

411

Adrian sucked in. The man just nailed the very heart of his own private hell. His soul was tormented by his conflict. He promised to protect Caer. But that was not his oath. He swore to protect Dana and Roisin; to fight for the fulfillment of their quest. If all the centuries of waiting, of keeping the two sisters safe from Nemhain, of hoping to see any semblance of what once thrived on this dismal planet returned to it--if they were to be successful, he must continue to defend the sisters; must fight for them until their own oaths were fulfilled or they were dead—no matter the cost.

44

A frigid ripple stirred the crisping air, dragging Adrian's agonized introspection back to the present. The chill, he realized, was not solely the result of the dying flames. Rather, it swept in from the mists that were forming in the passage just beyond the chamber's arched entry. Amid the swirling fog, portions of the vapors began to coalesce, forming distorted and fluctuating human shapes, the suggestion of human faces turned toward the chamber.

Adrian's breath caught at the sense of their anticipation...their relief. The protectors of the labyrinth knew that one of the sisters had returned. He could hear the subtle murmur of *'you've come'* in their minds--if these ancient and bodiless specters could be said to possess minds. More kept coming, until they filled the passage as far back as he could discern. They came, drawn by their awareness of Roisin. Why? They should hold their stations in the upper tunnels until Dana, too, made herself known to them. Had the centuries dulled their memory of the oaths they had taken to both sisters?

Adrian heard Jase gasp; saw him jerk the gun from his belt and level it at the undulating apparitions. "What are those things?"

"Those," Adrian submitted with solemn respect, "are the guardians. Once human, they voluntarily shed their bodies, pledging their souls to the protection of this chamber. For centuries, guardians dwelt in the dark spaces of every maze, harassing and leading astray any who found the entrance and sought the chamber without a Keeper to guide them." Whatever else Adrian might have added was cut off as the chamber rocked in time to the distant rumble far above them.

"Maura!" he spat. "She's working her way through the rubble." Moving to Caer, Adrian reached down, drawing her to her unsteady feet. "We must leave. Before she gets through."

"She doesn't know the way through the maze," Emer interjected. "We need to give Caer and Stoirm more time to rest."

Adrian jerked a nod toward the apparitions, some of which now drifted well into the chamber, though they hung back from the living. "Somehow, the magic of this place has been broken. I fear that the strength of our combined magic might lead Maura straight to us."

Turning to Stoirm, he asked, "Are you strong enough to help?"

"He isn't!" Blath declared.

Stoirm braced against the wall, taking his son's extended hand to gain his feet. "It's only a minor wound," he assured her. "And the fault for that is my own. I reacted to Maura's attack too slowly." Poking gingerly at the purplish discoloration that ran from his forehead, down over his right eye, and across the bridge of his nose, he huffed, "Next time, I think I will let Amhranai battle up close with that one while I hold up the earth in the aftermath." Heaving another huff at his wife's continued scowl, he offered, "When we are away from here, I will concentrate on mending. For now, I agree with Amhranai."

Jase waved his gun nervously at the vaporous shades. "Yeah. Well, if there's a way out of here that doesn't take us through those things, or straight into the path of that bloody bitch..." His eyes narrowed as he set a worried gaze on Adrian. "You're not thinking of asking Caer to perform another bit of abracadabra to get us out of here, are you? Just look at her. She's in no condition to do anything."

"Agreed." Adrian snorted, stepping toward the great pit.

Jase's brow shot up. "Oh no! If you're looking to take us into blazing glory, you can forget me! Just let me fight it out right here. Or, better yet, let me shoot myself and be done with it."

Fedel'ma grabbed the barrel of Jase's weapon, shoving it down. "Put that damned thing away before you hurt someone," she grumbled. "We aren't about to leave you to face Maura, or to shoot yourself. And we don't need to go into the flames. The chamber may block all attempts to gain entry by any means other than walking... or did so until Caer broke through that particular piece of magic... but it won't block our ability to teleport out."

Adrian turned a stunned grimace to Caer. So, that was the flare of magic he'd felt from her just after Maura's attack. He moaned. Roisin. Such magic had to initiate from her, with Caer building on it. Only the combination of their powers could break the ancient spells.

"We can take our little group to wherever seems best," Fedel'ma continued. "I suggest..."

"Slieve na Calliagh." Caer's pronouncement was clear, despite the trembling of her hand as it clasped tightly around the charm on her necklace. Adrian watched the color drain from her face at her decision; noted that she fought the threat of her knees to drop her to the floor once more. The Dream Reader was instantly at her back, his hands gently bracing her. Worrying her lip, she repeated, "Slieve na Calliagh. I must go there."

Adrian's growing dismay slithered to a deeper level of damnation. On top of recognizing the presence of Roisin's soul and apparently drawing on Roisin's magic, had she also managed to glean the gateway's location from Roisin's memories?

"No," he growled. "Not directly. Remember what happened when you turned up on her slopes before? Nemhain holds the grounds of Slieve na Calliagh. And by now there is likely an army of beasts at her side. Trust me, Caer. You can't fight the Dark Heart. Not yet. You'll need our support. And there isn't one of us in a fit state to engage her in battle, right now."

A second rumble shook the chamber. "There is but one choice, one way out; only one haven left to us." Adrian nodded toward the pit. "We need to leave. Now. The flames are our only escape."

"I agree," Fedel'ma put in. "Slieve na Calliagh is out of the question. I do not agree, however, that we must become people crisps to escape from here. A simple teleportation will suffice. If it's a trap you're worried about, Mr. Starn, there hasn't been time for Nemhain to lay one here. Not yet. Not without knowing the exact underground position of the chamber. Even assuming Maura telepathed the location of the entrance to her mother, neither of them know the coordinates of the chamber. Nor can they sense it from above. So, they can set no trap above it. But you know that, already."

Adrian's glower indicated his evaporating patience. "Maura is aware, by now, of the signatures of everyone who sheltered in the manor house. If she's worked it out, you can be sure her mother knows, as well. Nemhain's kin will be scanning everywhere for the arrival of each and every one of us. Our destination will be surrounded within seconds of our materializing, no matter where we emerge."

He gestured toward the pit. "They can't detect us if we use the flames. A Watcher waits to deliver us to place neither Maura nor Nemhain can yet penetrate. Blath was to summon the Alainn for aid in taking you there if Stoirm and I failed to rejoin you."

Emer stepped back, fear igniting in her widened eyes, her hands running anxiously up and down along her pants. "But those of us who aren't Alainn...or who aren't...whatever you happen to be, Mr. Starn...we can't simply step into a blazing fire."

"We will protect you. Stoirm, Tine, and myself."

"How?"

"Did I not come through the fire to reach this chamber while dragging Ailill with me?"

"Yes, but...he's just one, and we're..." Emer swallowed. "Why didn't you mention this ability before? Why didn't you offer to take us from the manor house using the flames, if you are so confident in it?"

"I offered to teleport you to sanctuary," he rumbled. "At that time, the flames were not necessary. Master Dream Reader, however, refused to allow anyone but his mother to leave the manor house with me."

Doubt shadowed the amber of the Dream Reader's gaze as he swept it to his mother. "Just where, precisely, did you go?"

A third rumble sounded from above, louder than the others, and followed by the distant, ululating echo of howls. "Maura is through," Adrian contended urgently. "And from the sounds of things, she's brought some of her creatures with her. Given the likelihood of her keying on our magic, we have, at best, perhaps half an hour before she reaches us, much less time for her beasts to do so. I ask you..." He leveled his attention on the Dream Reader. "Trust me for once."

Stooping, he grasped Ailill's arm, jerking the limp form up and bracing him. The man gave a low groan as he leaned against his uncle.

Ian moved to take the burden from Adrian. Tugging Ailill's arm around his neck to support the man, the Healer asked, "Are you sure about this, my lord? About taking this son of a monstrosity with us?"

Making no direct reply to Ian, Adrian bent his head, instead, to Ailill, speaking low. "I know you are conscious, nephew. If you value your life, you will give us no grief."

Ailill peered at his uncle through narrowly slit lids, disdain in his sneer.

"If not..." Malice now sounded in sharp discord through the music of Adrian's voice. "I will be happy to pick up where your sister failed, relieving you of your life, present, and future."

Ailill's tongue ran a slow circuit of his lips, his reply coming in a hushed snarl. "That's one ability you can't claim, Uncle, even if you wished to go against the precious code of my two dear aunties. You can't banish my soul, or any other."

"Don't believe for a second that those of your mother's line are the only Witches willing to sear themselves by learning an art as black as banishing. I assure you, the skill is mine. Give me the slightest provocation and I will destroy you. I'm no stranger to breaking the code."

The sudden wash of horror on Ailill's face proved his recognition of the truth in Adrian's words. Straightening, Adrian turned to the Dream Reader. "I'll not set my power against yours to command that you come with us. I merely ask you for your trust, as I trust your word that you will do whatever is necessary to protect Caer."

The man nodded. "Fine. We'll do it your way."

"Are you ready?" Adrian asked of Stoirm.

"Of course," his friend affirmed, despite Blath's muttered objections.

Adrian's scowl was no less disapproving than the Dream Reader's when Fedel'ma cornered and scooped up her cat, tossing the cloth she'd earlier used as a sling over the hissing animal's head and bundling Merripen loosely. "I'm not leaving her behind!" she snapped.

The Dream Reader turned from his mother with a contentious growl. Sweeping the unsuspecting Caer into his arms, he stifled her struggling protestations with a commanding, "You will do absolutely nothing for this little endeavor. Got that?"

Adrian tensed. Caer should travel removed from the Dream Reader. It would be too easy for the man to cast his own teleportation at the last minute, taking her with him.

"You want my trust," the Reader sent sharply. *"Yet it appears you still fail to trust me. I agreed to come with you. I do not go back on my word."*

Adrian acknowledged with a faint nod, his glance skimming to Emer, who stood close at Dylan's side, growing terror sharp on her face. On the other side of Emer, Fedel'ma was busy trying to hang onto her wriggling wrapping of cat. If the beast panicked and broke free once they entered the fire..."

"Merri won't be a problem," Fedel'ma assured him as the animal went limp. Cradling her bundle in the fold of her arms, she added, "All it takes is a little coaxing, with a pinch of magic."

"Remember when I came for you on Lillith?" Adrian sent to Caer.

The slight bob of her head gave affirmation.

"Sidra's call came too late. I could do nothing for her, and found you already within the flames. I could only protect you from suffering any more grievous harm than you had already sustained. This time I am with you from the beginning. You will not feel the flames, Caer. I promise you."

Stoirm and Tine began a hushed chant, unbroken by the icy breeze that abruptly chased around the room, triggering a display of brightly sparking embers within the rising blaze. The guardians had come to the fire's edge, ringing the pit. Again, Adrian could only wonder why. Perhaps they sensed through Roisin that Dana would soon be found, as well. The thought provided a glimmer of hope.

Summoning what strength remained to him, Adrian reached out, seeking for the familiar and welcoming mind of his Watcher.

"My Lord Amhranai. Grant me but a moment to enhance the flames and hold to the pattern, that you may come through."

"Make it as quickly as possible, Maired."

The press of the amorphous phantoms still lurked at the edge of his awareness, their faint murmur of, *"We have served well. Take us,"* pressing through Adrian's mind.

"Prepare, as well, to hold the way open beyond our arrival. Guardians of the last of the ways wish to follow us. They believe their oaths fulfilled. Let them pass through to their freedom."

45

Caer shrank against Dylan, the chamber now thrumming with the alien words of Stoirm's and Tine's chant, their intonation carrying on the steady, even cadence of seven beats and a hold, seven beats and a hold. With each repetition, the flames danced higher and brighter, scorching Caer's mind with tormented memories--the blood-russet inferno engulfing her; the agony of the savage blaze eating at her; the stench of blood and burning flesh mingled with the choking chemicals used to ignite the pyre; the terror in Sidra's eyes when she realized Caer was with her; Sidra's final scream for a guardian.

Adrian's sending brushed her mind once more, the feel of it tinged with ice. *"Sidra's death and your suffering have been partially avenged. The debt will be paid in full before I am done."*

Revenge. The swell of it overwhelmed all else. Caer wanted retribution; wanted payment with interest. It was not sufficient for providence to exact its toll, sending the plague to wipe out the village responsible for Sidra's death. Such an end was not enough. Not for the man who tore Caer from her aunt's side; forced her to witness her aunt's burning. Not enough to atone for the hatred in the villagers' chant of 'witch', and their cry for blood. The intensity of that hatred would never be erased from her soul.

Caer's breath caught painfully in her lungs as a new visage burst unbidden upon her. Within it, a great swirl of flames and smoke swept upward from the pyre, rushing toward the high curve of their village dome, gathering and focusing energy in a roiling black, tempest-driven, and thunderous tumult. The pulse of its deep and crackling rumble jarred along her nerves before the massive, churning storm held in abrupt and malevolent silence. For the space of a heartbeat, it hung in the heights. Then, with an explosive downward thrust, the fiery gale rushed outward, blasting to ash all who stood within the village square.

Pain slashed behind Caer's eyes and hammered through her temples as Adrian wrenched shut the flood of his own dark memories. *"That was never meant for you to see!"*

Fighting for her breath in short, sharp gasps, Caer gaped at Adrian. He accomplished the very thing Caer sought! The plague did not kill those people. Burning everything within their dome was not for the sake of destroying diseased corpses, as the public records indicated. The horrific tempest of flames was wrought by Adrian's magic. The villagers saw his rage manifest. They knew the same torture they inflicted on Sidra; the same torture Caer experienced. And then they were no more.

Bile rose in her throat. Here was her payment with interest! Her retribution! Her soul choked on it. How many dead? How many had been innocents caught up and swept along in the madness? How did such violence, whether wished for as she had just done or executed as Adrian carried out...how did that make them any different from those who murdered Sidra? And Adrian wasn't done. He just proclaimed as much.

Why? What could he hope to gain? It wouldn't bring Sidra back. Nor was there anyone left to pay the price he demanded. No one could have escaped his wrath on that day.

Doubt gnawed its way into Caer's sickened thoughts. With it came the impression of a man. The mayor. The one person she and Sidra most trusted. By his command, Sidra was beaten and dragged away. By his bruising grip, Caer was shoved through the square and forced to stand at the foot of the pyre, there to watch her aunt burn. The image of the man's face clarified. Though for no more than a fleeting second, the flash was enough to note the mayor's broad features stricken with the horror of his deeds. His horror evaporated as quickly as it rose, replaced by a gloating leer and a madness of laughter.

Caer swallowed a strangled cry. The leer...the laughter...neither belonged to the Tanai she and her aunt knew as friend. They belonged to someone else. The belonged to that man on the shuttle; the same man who attacked Emer's pod; the same man who stood with Maura and Ailill on the hillside of Slieve na Calliagh.

"Madadh Mire."

The foreboding whisper at the back of her skull ushered forth a haze of misted imagery. Each provided a jarring glimmer of a life Caer knew was not hers--each life woven through with the violence it suffered. So many lifetimes belonging to so many different individuals! So much pain and anguish! All of it wrought by the vile corruption of an alien soul that forced its way into a still living body, laying claim to it, twisting its mind to madness.

This was Madadh Mire's doing. He forced his soul into the mayor's body; twisted his mind; forced him to Madadh's bidding. Why? Why should Sidra have been his target? Why had their community been so eager to believe his lies and turn on a woman who spent years healing their injuries and illnesses? Caer had no answer. That it was so, however, was clear. Nor did she doubt that it was on Madadh Mire that Adrian intended to exact the last of his vengeance.

"Leave it!" Adrian commanded. *"It is not your concern."*

His warning ignited in his molten eyes, holding there for scarcely a breath before his gaze returned to the flames. Long, jagged spikes of blue-white lightning darted and danced around him. Then came the song. Adrian lifted it silently, yet it filled Caer's head and rushed her nerves with the sense of his power. The flow of the song altered the cadence of Stoirm's and Tine's background chant, adding two sets of three beats and a hold to the end of every set of sevens. One, two, three, four, five, six, seven. One, two, three. One, two, three.

So familiar the rhythm, though never before had it held such a strength of purpose.

Open the path for our weary souls.
Call us home. Bring us home.
Hear our plea and know our names.
See the way. Let us come.
Lift the flames and mark the dance.
Hold the door. Hold the door.
Grant us peace and bring us forth.
Keep us safe. Bring us home.

The words hung in Caer's mind, though the song had stopped with Adrian's audible pronouncement, "My Watcher is ready." The sound was a harsh dissonance set against the thrumming of Stoirm and Tine's continued chant.

Mesmerized, Caer's attention fixed on the sparking blue of the charged air that now encompassed Adrian. Undulating, the pale electric aura spread, extending outward. So, too, a similar aura encompassed and stretched out from Stoirm and from Tine, each field touching the other with a series of crackling flashes that died away as they united to become one. The single, larger aura stabilized for an instant, then stretched outward yet again, until the whole of their company was enclosed in a cool and faintly pulsating cocoon.

"Now," Adrian declared, giving a short nod toward where the flames rippled in steady measure with the cadence of the chant.

Caer's momentary fascination evaporated as she felt Dylan step forward. Her head whipped around, her attention snapping back to the eerily dancing inferno, her arms tightening around Dylan's neck. Another step. And another. Her breath caught as Dylan crossed the threshold of the pit and moved into the rising blaze. The agony she anticipated, however, did not accompany the flames that surrounded them. The enchantment of the cocoon protected them, just as Adrian promised. All about them, bright with the intensity of its heat, the fiercely blazing dance went on unabated, but they felt none of its torment.

Caer had no sense of how long the fire and shadow danced on, only that the chamber slowly vanished into blackness, the rhythm of Stoirm's and Tine's chant running through the stillness within their cocoon. Then came a pinprick of pale light in the black abyss.

"Deosil turns the circle." The words drifted from a great distance, spoken by a female voice that cracked with the impression of tremendous age, the cadence of her phrasing set to match the rhythm of the sevens. The impact of her simple statement hit Caer with a vertiginous sense of spinning wildly about. The fire blurred, and beyond it, the pinprick of light swept past again...and again...and again...growing steadily larger.

"Return the rounding Widdershins."

Once more, the phrasing synchronized with the sevens. And again came the rush of vertigo, this time with the sense of spinning in the opposite direction. Through the rise and fall of a glowing haze of flame played the impression of a room whirling around them. Round and round, until the sensation slowed...slowed...and at last ceased. Still, the chant continued while the conflagration burned on.

"Move out," Adrian urged. "Just be cautious that you do not interfere with my Watcher."

Dylan shifted abruptly to the right to avoid the woman who sat erect on a low stool squarely in front of the blaze, her hands folded and resting on her lap. Her attention never wavered, her sight locked on the flames through which they'd just passed. As Dylan turned back to check on the others, Caer spotted Bran, Blath, Emer, and Del, all moving off to the Watcher's left. Ian followed them, his hands firmly gripping Ailill's shoulders, directing his captive forward and well past the others. With Adrian, Stoirm, and Tine still within, Caer at last took note of the behemoth size of the gaping fireplace from which most of their company had already emerged. The massive opening rose well above Adrian's towering height and extended to a width that could have accommodated twice the number of their group.

At last, the three remaining strode out, the blue-tinged

enchantment that had protected the company falling away. The dissipation brought a close and near smothering warmth weighing down on Caer. Her awareness of the discomfort was fleeting, however, so stunned was she by the strange giddiness of homecoming.

Her lips pinched. The feeling must belong to the soul she harbored. For this was no home of hers.

"Put me down," she mumbled.

Dylan hesitated before reluctantly setting her feet to the earthen floor. "Just don't try anything foolish," he admonished. "No magic. Understand?"

Much to her dismay, Caer's legs proved wobblier than anticipated. Automatically grabbing for Dylan's arm, she steadied herself and cast a curious glance around. Shadows jigged along what appeared to be walls of solid marble that formed a trapezoidal room. The two parallel walls each possessed a slight curve, suggesting that the chamber must be part of some enormous wheel.

None of the walls held any window and there was but one lone door, a narrow thing that looked to be roughly hewn from wood. Where it might lead, Caer couldn't guess, as it stood closed near the far corner of the shorter, outwardly curved concave wall. As for furnishings, they were scant, at best. A rumpled cot and a small square table also stood along the shorter wall. On the table, a silver pitcher glistened. Next to it was an empty glass and a silver plate with some nibbled pieces of bread and a few shriveled grapes. Aside from those few items, there was only the stool upon which the Watcher still sat.

Caer willed her legs to hold her unassisted, venturing a step closer to the unmoving woman, careful not to come between the Watcher and the fire upon which she remained so intent. Still as stone the woman sat, her brown, loose-fitting gown falling in folds across her lap and pooling around her ankles, the fabric fluttering in the disturbances of the air. Beneath her tightly knotted coil of thick, gray hair, her pale and blotchy face sagged in a series of wrinkles, softening what had once been proud, high cheekbones. Deep creases fanned out from the corners of the woman's eyes, while finer creases formed small puckers around her thin lips. Despite the profound appearance of withered antiquity, a surprising sense of strength emanated from her.

The Watcher took no notice of Caer's scrutiny. Her position remained rigidly set, her gaze ever fixed on the flames as they continued their unerring jig. To each side of her, Stoirm and Tine stood waiting, the chant still playing across their lips.

Adrian frowned as he glanced from the woman to the table and back again. "When she has finished, someone needs to escort Maired to her quarters and make certain she eats more than a mouthful of stale bread before she rests."

From the fireplace came a fitful hiss, followed by a wind--not of heat, but of biting cold--that burst suddenly out, tossing a glitter of embers into the room on a rushing hum of ghostly murmurs. Then, with a low howl, the door of the room whipped open and the wind vanished. The chant ceased. The flames died.

"What the hell was that?" Brandon choked, fanning down a cloud of ash and dust.

"The guardians," Adrian returned.

"And welcome they are." The old woman's shoulders drooped as she relaxed and turned from her completed duty. There was a startling contrast between the aged crackle of her voice and the crisp blue eyes with which she briefly regarded Caer. Even more startling was the familiar shimmer of brightly burning turquoise deep within them.

Tine honored her with a bow before moving away. Stoirm, however, remained at the woman's side, affection obvious in the quietness of his smile. With a faint wince, the Watcher reached for his offered arm.

"You needn't waste your worries on me, Grandfather," she huffed, setting an indignant glower on Adrian. With Stoirm's support, she rose to her feet, adding, "The sight of my lords safely returned is all the feast I need. And I am fully capable of seeing myself to my rooms. My time at watch has not been so long nor the burden of this body's age become so great that I can't remember the way." She patted Stoirm's hand. "Though I'd be a silly old goose, indeed, to refuse such an escort."

Blath stepped from the edge of the room, slipping between Stoirm and the Watcher. "Allow me to go with you, Dear One." To Stoirm she grumbled, "The two of you will have one another telling tales well into the wee hours of tomorrow if I allow you to go off together. I shouldn't have to remind you, husband, that you are as much in need of rest as Maired. I will have a proper meal sent to Maired's quarters and will make certain she eats. You, husband, will be sleeping soundly when I join you or suffer my wrath."

The old woman leaned into Blath's arm, shrugging. "Very well. I will eat and rest, as well." She passed another glance Caer's direction, then gave a long-toothed grin to her new companion. "But only if you will sing me the tale of recent events."

As Blath ushered Maired past, Tine nodded respectfully. "Keep Mother occupied for a good while, Cousin. Perhaps if you keep her singing, it will prevent her smothering Father with her worry."

The Watcher's chuckle brought a chagrinned sigh from Blath and a broad smile to Tine. When his mother and cousin had gone, however, he asserted, "I must take my leave. I need to report back to my men."

Adrian stiffened. "You should remain here."

One corner of Tine's mouth ticked up in mild annoyance. "You can leave off worrying after me as well, Grandfather. Send for me if you have need. Otherwise, allow me to go where I am most useful." There was neither the conjuring of a spell nor any glowing cocoon when he returned to the now low-burning fire. He merely focused on and raised the flames, stepped within, turned to salute Adrian and Stoirm with a hand to his forehead, and was gone.

"What about this one?" Ian asked, marching Ailill forward. The captive's scrawny, mud-caked frame, the loosely hanging shirt and pants, and the nervously darting eyes, gave him a demented and feral appearance.

"Show our 'guest' to the appropriate quarters," Adrian returned with a curl to his lips. "Should he prove troublesome, do whatever you deem necessary to resolve the matter."

Ian's face brightened as he shoved Ailill toward the door. "With pleasure."

"Wait." Ailill drew back, crouching slightly as he cast an anxious glance at Adrian. "There is something I can offer you in exchange for my freedom?"

"Not bloody likely," Ian snapped.

"Information?" Ailill whined. "You said you wanted information from me, Uncle. I heard you say it there in the chamber." He inclined his head toward Del. "That one. She's a spy, like Aifa Eliz. They worked together. Sent information to my mother."

The unified gasp and loud protestations from both Emer and Del brought an ugly grin to his thin lips. "News to you, isn't it? This one thinks to deny it, of course. But now you know that I can pay for my freedom with something valuable."

Adrian's jaw set. "I'll determine what's valuable. What proof do you have of your accusations?"

Ailill hesitated.

"Thought as much," Adrian snarled. "You think you can buy me off with fabrications? Show the fool to the..."

"No! No. Wait. It was Aifa Eliz who arranged the attack on Gwynlyn Berring. Gwynlyn had grown suspicious of Aifa. After their last meeting, Aifa feared Gwynlyn would return to Ahira to raise the warning and stop the transfer of Caer DaDhrga. When she failed to murder Gwynlyn, Aifa changed her approach. She used the threat of annihilating the whole of the Scion complex and every Witch and Tanai within it, should Gwynlyn dare to speak of what she knew."

Nodding again toward Del, Ailill spat, "And that one...Ms. Cowl. She was the one who sabotaged the pod of that meddlesome old hag called Fedel'ma." His mouth twisted into a sneer. "The Tanai bitch you now have traveling in your company thought too highly of herself after her meager success, though. Got greedy. Wanted guarantees that she would be granted the gift of transmigration for her soul, or she would go to the authorities; tell them that Aifa sabotaged the pod and killed the old woman."

Snorting his disgust, he proclaimed, "Returning granted for a Tanai! Can't happen, can it?" With a finger pointed at Del, he added, "Maura was supposed to kill you. Obviously, she met with no more success at murder than did Aifa. Impotent bitches, both!"

Del drew herself up, her hand taking a purposeful aim at the man's head, sparks igniting from both her palm and her fingertips. With a bewildered yelp, Ailill staggered back, slinking behind Ian, his eyes wide. "You're not her! You're not the Tanai!"

Del's brow cocked. "How very observant of you."

Adrian waved Del off with a brusque, "Save your energy. He's not worth the expenditure." To Ailill, he scorned, "You still haven't mastered the most basic of skills. Missed the fact that the one you claim to be the greedy Tanai is no longer that person, but now the very Witch you say she murdered. Were you, at least, aware that Stoirm and I were among those you followed from the manor house, or were you blind to that, as well? Were you drawn only by the key? Even you couldn't miss sensing its power, now that it is whole. Eager to take it for yourself, no doubt. I'm sure your mother will be pleased to learn of your ambition."

Ailill shrank further behind Ian. "No! Not for me! It was for Mother. Maura wouldn't have done that! You know she wouldn't. Even Mother doesn't trust her."

"Your mother doesn't trust her own shadow," Adrian scoffed.

Ailill straightened a little. "She trusts me."

Tipping his head toward the door, Adrian rumbled, "Get this imbecile out of my sight. I'll deal with him, later."

"I'm no imbecile!" Ailill shouted. "I know many things you'll find of interest." His darting gaze skimmed back to Caer. "Took

Mother many a century to track one of the pieces of the key to your family, didn't it? She thought she could take it by killing your parents. Thought the piece would be easy to identify by the signature of its power. But there was no sign of it in the ashes of the lab on that Perimeter Ship.

"The Tanai were, of course, convinced the child died with her parents. But Mother never believed you dead. She sought for you, certain the piece of key held by the mother must have passed into your hands. And she found you. Found you with your aunt. How easily Madadh Mire deranged the people in that little village; how easily he took control of the simple-minded mayor. Kill Sidra. Take the child. Force from her mind the form imposed on the piece of key she held. Then relieve her of both the key and her life. That was the plan. But you..."

He jerked a sneering nod, first toward Caer and then Adrian. "The child managed the unthinkable, breaking away, charging into the flames. And you, Uncle. You turned up and managed to whisk her away." His demented countenance squared on Caer. "Took another while to find you again. Were it not for Aifa's suspicions as to your identity, you might have remained hidden." A dark frown wormed across his drawn face. "Yet you escaped even the Coran'ian. Escaped again during that little mat-trans venture, and again from the attack in New Haven. Curious, don't you think? You're prescient, I was guessing. Or..." His eyes glinted maliciously. "Or perhaps Mother has guessed correctly. She has long suspected that you host another and that it is she who warns you of danger."

Caer blanched at his words.

"Ah. You know Mother's suspicion is true, then." Ailill nodded, looking pleased with the confirmation. "No doubt, your guest soul was the one who led you to the second piece of the key and allowed for the two to be joined. Of course, now that the key is whole, it can only be parted from you, Caer DaDhrga, when it accomplishes what it was designed to do. Or when you are dead." There was a chilling trill of delighted anticipation in his last proclamation.

Adrian's spell struck Ailill, sending him sprawling before Caer could register what had happened.

Ailill's lips curled in a pained grin, blood trickling at one corner of his mouth. "The girl doesn't know who it is she carries." His grin broadened. "It's good you stick with your friends, Caer DaDhrga. Good that they hide you while you coddle one of Mother's weak sisters within you. You'd not fare well on your own. Mother's creatures stand poised to breach and attack every Earth dome, every off-world colony, in search of you. Once she gives the command, they will leave no Tanai, nor any Witch of her sisters' lines alive. It's blood thirst she has throbbing through her. She will have war, and she will have victory, and she will have Slievgall'ion."

Wincing to his feet, his voice dropped to a conspiratorial undertone as he eyed Adrian warily. "They are ready to slaughter the whole of your line, as well, Uncle. All you need do is give the girl and the key over to me. Return me, along with this gift, to my mother. She will repay you by sparing you and any Witches of your choosing. Not her sisters, of course. She dares not spare them."

"Your mother intends to spare no one beyond a handful of her own close kin, regardless of what I do," Adrian spat. "She has always intended the annihilation of the rest. You know that as well as I."

Lurching, Caer grabbed for the Watcher's stool and, with Dylan's quick assistance, dropped heavily onto it. This is what they were fighting against? A Witch who was not only willing but apparently capable of decimating virtually the whole of humankind?

With a glance toward Ian, Adrian hissed, "I repeat. Get this filth out of my sight."

"Gladly." Grabbing Ailill by his neck, Ian pushed him again toward the door.

"She may not be able to reach you...for now. But I'm betting Mother will soon enough discover where you are." Ailill was half chortling, half sniveling as he was shoved out of the room. For several minutes, his mix of whimper and laughter carried back to them, until, at last, it was cut off by the echoing sound of another door opening and slamming.

Fatigue stooping his shoulders and with a stretched tone to the musical lilt of his voice, Adrian said simply, "Come with me."

46

Ailill's claim of impending war hung menacingly in Caer's mind as she struggled to her feet, her fingers twisting the chain of her necklace back and forth. Were there truly enough Witches to wage a war across the colonies?

"Not by themselves. With their alien beasts fighting for them, however..." Adrian's words trailed off in anxious confirmation.

How could ordinary humans survive such an impending disaster? How could they even prepare? But that was the point, wasn't it? That was this Nemhain's intent. Decimate humanity. Leave only her kin and their beasts to control everything.

The weight of Caer's growing hopelessness coupled with her exhaustion bore down on her, her body slumping under the burden. Dylan's proximity as he stepped up beside her, taking her arm, was overshadowed by the creeping terror eating at her insides. What prayer did she have of stopping this Dark Heart? Even if she managed to slip through the guards and beasts and who-knew-what-else that apparently lurked on the slopes of Slieve na Calliagh...even if she managed to confront this vile Witch...what then? She had no idea what magic she might possess, much less how to use it. She didn't even have Bran's skill with a firearm. Swallowing, she acknowledged the likelihood that she was going to die. She and anyone foolish enough to stand with her.

The fact that Adrian offered nothing more drew her ragged breath as she closed the last few shuffling steps to the doorway.

Hesitating, she turned to skim the faces of the others. Despite her frustrations, anger, and expressed suspicions, this small group of individuals had, in a very short time, become the nearest to family and friends she had. All of them, including the all-too-often hovering bane of her existence, Adrian. Each had saved her life; was trying to protect her, still. Beyond any understanding or reason, she trusted them. More than that, she cared for them. She couldn't allow any of them to take part in...in any mad effort to assault the unassailable.

From beyond the door, Adrian sent, *"Enough worry. What you need is to eat and to sleep. What will come will come. When it is time."*

Caer stared past the threshold and into the dim light, searching for a glimpse of him. *"Suppose I...we...succeed. Suppose this...this Dark Heart is eliminated. What good is that? Sooner or later, Maura or this Madadh creature or some other demented Witch will surely take her place."*

"One problem at a time, Caer. We will face the rest..."

"When it is time," she finished for him with a perturbed sigh. *"You keep saying that."* Slipping her arm from Dylan's support, she stepped from the relatively bright light of the Watcher's chamber into dense shadow. The instant she cleared the threshold an overwhelming press of sorrow drove away all previous woes, bearing her back, stunned, against cold rock. Dylan closed the distance to her once more, waving Emer and Del past, the two women exchanging troubled glances. Bran came next, stopping a couple of paces just beyond her. Though he did not turn to show his face, she sensed his ill ease.

"This place feels wrong," hissed through his low growl. "We shouldn't be..."

Dylan nudged him on. "Go to Mother and Emer. Stay with them, and stay close to the wall. They'll see that you don't fall on your face."

Grudgingly, Bran edged off after the women.

The last to join them was Stoirm, his manner somber, though relief and joy lit his eyes. "Grief is not the sole dweller in this fastness. Beyond this chamber, you will find much to soothe a weary soul.

You will see." Behind him, the door to the Watcher's room swung shut with a muffled thump, shutting off the warmth from the embers that yet glowed on the hearth, and leaving their company to a hollow, torch-lit grayness.

The chill of the dead air bit through Caer, raising a new ripple of shivers. What was it about Witches that drew them so often to dank, dark places? Reaching for her blankets to snug them around her shoulders, her fingers closed only on her clammy shirt. The blankets had been left behind, though whether in the chamber at the heart of the labyrinth or in the Watcher's room, she couldn't recall.

Dylan's movement next to her suggested he intended to strip out of his own shirt, probably to wrap around her, unless she denied him the opportunity. Though every joint and muscle protested, she forced her legs to move away from him. Doing as he'd indicated for Bran, she stayed close to the wall, her hand braced to it for support while making such a need as inconspicuous as possible. She wanted no one hovering to see to her. The others made their way on their own. She could do no less. With her bleary gaze sagging to her soggy, grime-encrusted shoes, she focused on lifting first one leaden foot and setting it down, and then the other.

The slow progression drug on and on, her aching body protesting every move, her head threatening to drop her into unconsciousness with each step. When at last she ventured a look around, praying their destination was near, and found only more shadowy gray space before her, she could not suppress the involuntary whimper.

"You all right?" Dylan's hand was at her elbow again.

Her nod was so slight she wasn't sure she'd made it. Nor did she realize her feet had come to a halt as she passed a dull scan over the massive, circular space. She almost giggled. Not only did these people seem to like dark, dank places, they also seemed to have an affinity for round spaces. The cairn on the top of Slieve na Calliagh. The chamber at the center of the labyrinth. Now this. Not that she cared about the shape, or that the feeble illumination came from a now familiar pattern of wall-mounted torches scattered around the grand perimeter. Now, if a chair was at hand, or better, a bed... Her near giggle deteriorated into another whimper when she spotted the only other exits. The total of three doors appeared equally spaced, the distances between them daunting.

The pressure of Dylan's increasing support prompted her trudging shuffle to pick up once more. No one else was whimpering... or complaining...or... Hand still braced to the stone wall, she set her attention to a study of it rather than staring across the dim void. Dark gray with a flecking of white veins glistened in the wan light. Across its surface, twitching shadows played off pale etchings that resembled the ones in the labyrinth's chamber. The great whorls, loops, and intricate knots flowed across the stone, the whole of the pattern running a single, seemingly unbroken master design that covered wall and doors alike. Were it not for the change from stone to wood, and the thin blue glow that spilled beneath them, the doors would have been near impossible to detect. The outlines of two—the one from which they'd come and the one to her right—were so fine as to barely delineate them from the encircling wall. The third door was made more obvious by the thin blue glow emanating from it.

Blinking, Caer attempted to take in the chamber's entire design. The effort proved dizzying, the undulating pattern almost appearing to writhe as she stared at its scrawling serpentine flow from ceiling to floor. Barely averting a stumble, she pulled her gaze away, choosing the openness of the chamber while the vertigo dissipated. No smoldering embers within a pit marked the center, here. Instead, a single, large, horizontally rectangular block of white marble stood at its heart, the same etched design from the walls flowing out from beneath it and crossing the floor. All one, she realized. The entire pattern, beginning beneath the marble block, traversing the floor, and continuing up the walls at the location of the three doors.

This time there was no avoiding the stumble, so suddenly did a shudder take her. Teetering, Caer stopped and leaned against the wall, her heart pounding as she took in the marble block once more.

Death dwelled here. That was the source of the sorrow. This chamber was a crypt containing a solitary sarcophagus.

Adrian stood, now, before the coffin, straight-backed, his hands at his sides. Stoirm, likewise, hovered near, his head bent, a hand pressed solemnly to the marble tomb's smooth lid. Caer ventured another glance around, eerily fascinated. Why so great a crypt for a single burial? And why all the etchings?

Again, she studied the design, beginning where the three initial serpentine patterns emerged from beneath the sarcophagus, tracing them to where they swept upward over the doors like twisting tendrils of some strange plant. From the top of the doorsills, each of the three tendrils wound their way ever round and up, filling the entire wall with overlapping undulations until they rejoined in a single tendril at junctures where the wall met the ceiling. From there, it continued to snake in a dizzying spiral. At last, the massive tendril flowed into an enormous trinity knot, the ceiling's apex and the knot's center marked with a stone the color of dark blood.

Caer's hand shot to her necklace, her fingers closing on the charm, its delicate pulse as thin and rapid as her own. As her fingers made contact with the stone at the center of the charm, the stone above shimmered faintly with the same fluttering throb.

"This is the source." Adrian's words, though hushed, lifted clearly through the vast emptiness. "Beneath our feet lies the root of three veins of magic that flow through this world. Each of the three loops of the trinity knot above point in the outward direction of their flow, the stone at the center marking their nexus. The magic in each vein gradually dissipates as it flows outward. Here, however, the strength of magic is greatest."

Nodding toward Caer, he added, "The key you hold was made as a reflection of the power that is centered here, and works in harmony with it. The stone of your charm is imbued with spells that grant the key its ability to unlock what we must find."

Bran's nervous throat clearing accompanied his wagging a finger at the marble block where the light reflected from the subtly pulsing stone high above to give the impression of some phantom heart beating. "Tell me," he managed. "Tell me that...that thing isn't alive."

"Stone does not live," Stoirm replied. "Nor do those who lie here. This is the resting place of Tar On Tine and Samhradh. The chamber still resonates with the grief of their daughters and the whole of the Alainn people."

Back peddling, Bran sucked in, his intake whistling. "That's... that's a coffin? With the bodies of the ones who started the whole bloody business of Witches? There's no way for them to rise up out of that thing, is there?"

Adrian responded with an amused huff as he turned and strode toward the faintly illuminated door. "You need fear nothing from the corpses, Mr. Jase. Their slumber is the eternal sort. They are, perhaps, fortunate in that." Only the sound of footfalls followed his pronouncement, each person left to their own weary thoughts.

Adrian and Stoirm reached the door first, waiting until the others joined them before Adrian turned to Brandon. "Neither Samhradh nor Tar On Tine started the line of Witches. Magic arose within Samhradh's family many generations prior to her time. For those who continued to live in the proximity of this place, the magic remained and grew stronger within them. Know this, too, Mr. Jase. None within the lines of the Witches are solely to blame for the insanity, mayhem, and bloodshed that continues to follow us. Tanai hold their share of guilt in that."

"Not arguing," Bran conceded tightly, clearing his throat again. "So. What happened to those earlier Witches? The ones who preceded Sour-oo and Tar on Chinee?"

"Sowrooh," Del enunciated with a sigh, emphasizing the smoothness of the syllables as they ran together. "And Tar Owin Chinee. Witches numbered perhaps a hundred, all told, during Samhradh's time, counting her brothers and their families and a few cousins, as well as Samhradh and Tar On Tine and their daughters. All murdered." With a somber shake of her head, Del concluded with, "Dana, Nemhain, and Roisin were the only ones to survive the massacre, thanks to the curse they cast—that they and their descendants would always return to seek vengeance on those who did them harm. Their lines are the only ones that exist, today."

"Not entirely true," Adrian countered quietly. "Madadh survived."

Something about the lines at the corners of his mouth, about the fleeting pinch of pain that crossed his face, suggested to Caer that he might say more. She was both disappointed and relieved that he did not. The story might be worthwhile, but only after she slept.

Emer's dubious, "Madadh? Madadh Mire?" seemed to match Del's questioning glance. Even Dylan gave a disbelieving snort.

"The archives list him as one of Nemhain's descendants," Emer declared.

"Indeed," Adrian returned. "Archiving the lines of the Family, however, was begun generations after the slaughter. Those chosen for the task had nothing to go by save what was remembered by the sisters of those earlier times. Suffice it to say that it suited Nemhain's perversity to have Madadh listed as one of her kin, though he certainly does not descend from her."

"Why didn't Dana or Roisin correct the record? And if not Nemhain's line, if not of any of the sisters' lines, what's his origin?" Emer pressed.

Adrian shrugged. "Let's just say it seemed best to Dana and Roisin to let certain things alone. And for now, that remains the case."

"I thought," Bran put in, scratching his head. "I thought this Madadh jerk was Nemhain's husband. Why would she want him listed as one of her descendants? That's like telling the universe that she's married one of her own children. Or grandchildren. Or. Why would she want everyone to think her so degenerate?"

"What the universe thinks of her matters not at all to Nemhain," Adrian growled. "Never has. As for inbreeding, early human history is full of it. It's been an accepted reality for Witches from the beginning. A matter of self-preservation, given the Tanai's fear of us. Nemhain, I admit, took it a step further, decreeing inbreeding as law for those of her line, boasting that it prevented them from being tainted with the blood of traitors or sub-humans."

"I take the latter as meaning those of us who aren't Witch," Bran muttered.

Adrian nodded. "Nemhain has gone so far as to enforce her edict by murdering and banishing the souls of any of her descendants who wed outside of her line. Nor does she allow the offspring of such unions to survive."

He inclined his head toward Stoirm. "She would, however, be willing to make one exception for herself."

Stoirm cringed. "An exception she will never see come to pass."

"That's one messed up bitch," Bran snorted in disgust. A brief hesitation prefaced, "You said we will be safe from her by coming here. But that insane fellow you sent off with the doc. He said that his mother--that being this same Nemhain, if I understand correctly--knows where we are."

"Ailill may be correct, after a fashion," Adrian confessed. "We can assume that Nemhain has been informed that her prey was found in the company of Stoirm and myself. She may well suspect that we've brought Caer and the rest of you to this sanctuary. That doesn't mean, however, that our foe knows where the sanctuary lies."

"Emer cocked her head. "And it lies..."

"Directly beneath Slieve na Calliagh."

"Beneath!" Bran's mouth worked in sputtering consternation, his voice squeaking in an anxious whisper. "I...I thought you were trying to keep Caer away from this place! I thought you said it was guarded. What's to stop that bloody gorgon from figuring out that we're trotting around right under her nose? She could bring her entire horde down on us!"

"You needn't concern yourself with whispering," Adrian harrumphed. "We are far below her encampment. There is no possibility of our being heard. And the currents of magic that are the very essence of this place will prevent Nemhain's being able to detect the presence of our magic."

Turning, he at last pushed the door to, light piercing a shaft into the gloom. "Now, if you please. Welcome to my home."

47

After so long in dark places, moving into the bright light brought a flood of tears. Shielding her eyes with one hand, Caer used the other to dab at them with her grimy shirtsleeve. The mutterings from Del, Emer, and Bran indicated they suffered the same issue. Precisely where they stood, though, she could only guess. Nor did she know that it was Dylan who gently nudged her aside until his grumbled, "Turn the damned lights down!" came from right next to her. The lights, however, remained undimmed.

When at last, the shock of the brightness eased and the tears subsided, Caer stumbled a turn-about, gaping at the broad hallway that stretched out on both sides of their little group. Underfoot, the floor glistened with polished jade tile, while the high, white walls swept away in a grand curve that obviously followed the perimeter of the crypt. Vivid medieval tapestries draped large sections of the wall on both sides, their colors enhanced by the even, blue-white radiance that emanated from the ceiling.

Across the corridor and a little to her left, a wide, arched doorway broke one of the expanses of wall. Through it, Caer could see rows of long tables butted end to end with benches tucked beneath. Several people bustled around, some scrubbing tabletops, some sweeping or mopping the floor. Everyone, men and women alike, was similarly dressed in an assortment of vibrantly colored and belted tunics, along with matching britches. The billow and sweep of their garments offered almost as dazzling a display as Del's vast array of flowers

442

bobbing in the stir of her dome's circulating air. The clothing lacked only the flowers' heady perfume. Instead, the air smelled of soup.

From behind her, the door to the crypt closed with a resounding thud, drawing the startled attention of several workers. A short, stocky man with a frizzled mane of unruly black hair dropped his cleaning brush to the table he was scouring and scurried toward them. The rolled sleeves of his magenta tunic flapped out over his elbows, his britches fluttering over the tops of his brown knee-high boots as he approached, bobbing a series of bows.

To one side, Emer shuffled closer to Del, whispering, "What's that all about?"

"M'lord Amhranai!" the man declared, straightening. Deep-set green eyes stared out from a striking, albeit age-worn face. "Lady Maired sent word that you'd returned. Welcome!"

Another bow was promptly offered as the man's skimming gaze took in the Alainn. "M'lord Stoirm! We feared you were lost to us! How glad I am to see that was not the case. Welcome, welcome." Quickly scanning the rest of the assemblage with interest, he submitted, "Welcome to you all."

"Thank you, Colm," Adrian returned.

The man frowned as he checked all the faces again. "But, where is Lord Tine? We were told he was with you."

"Gone back to his men."

"And Lady Blath?"

Stoirm grinned. "My wife is with Maired. She will join us once she's certain that our beloved Watcher is properly attended and updated; a task that I am guessing may take a while."

Colm returned the grin with a conspiratorial nod. "It's good to know that your lady wife is in the company of Lady Maired. Brigid has tried for several days to get our Watcher to eat more than a few nibbles. No doubt, Lady Blath will succeed where Brigid failed." Twitching his head back in the direction of the large room, he apologized. "We've cleared away this evening's meal, I'm afraid. And the dining hall is being cleaned. But food for your company is being taken to the common room of the east quarters. I hope that will suffice?"

"My thanks," Adrian nodded. "I owe you and Brigid much."

Colm shook his head. "Hardly, m'lord. You honor us with your return. Now, if you will excuse me. The chores aren't inclined to do themselves."

As the man trotted back toward the dining hall, Brandon noted with hushed voice, "He's not one of you. He's not Witch. At least, he didn't feel like one."

Gesturing for the others to follow, Adrian set off down the corridor with the bearing of a man just returned to a greatly missed and much-beloved home. Though he walked at a leisurely pace, his long stride meant Caer had to scuttle after him. Her will to keep moving, however was fast ebbing away.

"There are currently but a few Witches within these halls," Adrian was saying. "Most of the residents are Tanai. Among them, you will find the occasional Sensitive, such as yourself."

Brandon cast a stunned backward glance. "More like me? I thought I was the last."

"So I thought," Del put in.

"Your kind has always been rare," Adrian acknowledged. "Rarer, still, these days." Glancing back with a raised brow, he suggested, "Perhaps we should give you over to Nemhain and let her think she truly has succeeded in eliminating the very last. It might make it safer for the few here, should they decide to leave."

Bran pulled up short, sucking in before he noted the glint of amusement on Adrian's face. Falling back into step with the others, he muttered, "Not many Witches. Mostly Tanai. I just might like this place. Maybe I'll stay."

Adrian shrugged. "You may feel otherwise in the not too distant future. The ratio of Tanai to Witch appears to be on the cusp of changing. Most of these families have lived in these halls for many multiples of generations, now, and they are beginning to see subtle variants in a few of their children. Some minor skill with magic is beginning to emerge in the youngest of them. Long-term exposure to this place may well be giving rise to a new line of Witches, just as it must have done for our ancestors whose people lived on or near the grounds above us."

"You mean, if I stay here long enough, I might develop a bit of magic, myself?"

Adrian shook his head. "Not likely, unless you find the means of living far beyond the normal span of years for Tanai. And even then, it is more likely to be your great, great, great grandchildren who experience the changes."

Huffing his disappointment, Bran proceeded with another question. "How many people live down here, if you don't mind my asking?"

"Varies. The last time I bothered to take a count was several years ago. I believe the number was a little shy of three hundred, then. How many are here now, I can't say. Depends on how many babes were born and how many young people coming of age have made the decision to leave."

"The rest live their whole lives here? Why?"

"Most are people whose families worked with or served the lines of Nemhain's sisters, or who did so for me for generations out of mind. If they leave, they risk being found out. If found, they are likely to be slaughtered. They are safe, here. Those who stay maintain our sanctuary for others in need."

"Until Nemhain learned of the nine labyrinths," Stoirm put in. "Learned and began destroying them, people could seek a Keeper who would lead them through to a chamber like the one we left. After the destruction of the eighth and the loss of the lives of those who were caught within, people stopped looking for the Keeper of the last labyrinth. Now, Amhranai searches for those fleeing Croi Breag's hunts, delivering the weakest and most grievously injured here to recover. The majority choose to leave, once healed. A few remain."

Bran's face creased with his puzzlement. "If this Cree..uh... Nemhain is such a threat, why don't they all stay?"

"We can't house everyone," Adrian replied. "Nor do most wish to stay hidden underground. Not when they've known the world above. Even living within the confines of domes, they can still recognize the suns and the moons of their worlds; know night from day. Humans weren't meant to live as moles."

"As mo...as what?"

"Small, furry animals," Del chuckled. "They dug tunnels and lived in the ground, though they, too, periodically poked their heads out. They've been extinct for more than a thousand years, now."

Bran considered in silence. "So," he ventured. "We are underground...in this sanctuary. And Nemhain can't get us, here. I suppose Starn designed this place, as well as the labyrinths."

"He did," Stoirm replied. "His design. The labor was provided by some among Dana and Roisin's lines and a few of my people. The crypt, of course, already existed. In their first returning, the three sisters sought for and found the remains of their parents and established their tomb, hidden in the depths to protect them from further atrocities, whether at the hands of Tanai or Witch. A handful of generations later, after Nemhain dishonored her parents and her sisters by attempting the murder of her younger sister, Dana, Roisin, Lord Amhranai, and I joined forces, working spells preventing the Dark Heart from ever again gaining entry to Samhradh's and Tar On Tine's resting place. She could wander above, but never cross below. As a result, she and her kin declared war on all other Witches.

"That was when plans were first made for the labyrinths and for this sanctuary. For those who dedicated their efforts to the construction, the sanctuary was the most difficult and dangerous of undertakings, smuggling in individuals with sufficient skill to expand out from the tomb. We could not have succeeded, were it not for the strength of magic permeating this place, as it concealed our presence and our activity."

Emer shook her head. "And Nemhain never suspected?"

"She's always held an inflated sense of her own abilities," Adrian huffed. "That we would have the intelligence and the strength to attempt such a feat without alerting her never occurred to her."

At last, he halted at an ornately wrought and very heavy looking metal door. Passing his hand lightly across its surface, the door slipped aside with a faint swoosh, disappearing into a wall pocket. Adrian cleared the slightly raised threshold, indicating with a nod that the others should follow.

Caer's struggle to keep up had dropped her to the back of the group, Dylan persistently falling back with her. Mind numb and body aching, she watched the others step through. Then, with a deep breath, she forced each knee to lift enough for her feet to clear the rise. It was all she could manage. Dylan caught her as she teetered on trembling legs just inside the doorway.

"Over there," he said, glancing toward a grouping of armchairs and a couple of sofas. "I'll carry you if you can't..."

She cut him off with as much of a glare as she could muster, though she didn't decline his support. The short trek took them across the warmth of a thick, sapphire blue rug laid over glistening white tiles, the rug's softness easing the jar to her joints. Still, it was only Dylan's grip that kept Caer upright. Reaching the nearest of the chairs, she collapsed on it, dizzy with relief. For several seconds she simply sat, her eyes closed, hoping she might be allowed to remain where she was, sunk in the comfort of the chair's cushions, for hours, or maybe even days.

The buzz of conversations, however, at last brought Caer's eyes open again. Dylan stood with Adrian and Stoirm some distance away, while Del, Emer, and Bran remained a couple of meters from her, staring about and commenting with a distinct note of awe. Straightening a little, Caer followed the line of their attention, drawing a stunned breath.

In shape, this...common room, she thought the man from the dining hall had called it...was like the Watcher's room, the curvature and angle of walls making the room resemble a section of a great wheel. In size, however, there was no comparison. Where the Watcher's room was small, this space was sufficient to serve as an auditorium or lecture hall. No blank concrete walls or tiered rows of seats, here, though. Rather, massive beams of dark wood braced the high ceiling from which the same blue-white brilliance emanated as had done within the corridor. More rich tapestries along with elegantly framed paintings of landscapes and portraits adorned some of the sections of smooth, glossy, pale blue walls. Floor-to-ceiling shelves accommodating a tremendous library, the books all leather bound, filled other sections. Even from where she sat, Caer could tell that the spines of the books were scrawled with ornate lettering.

The room's furnishings were no less impressive. In front of the shelves, chairs stood about, each with a small table next to it. Beneath a cluster of paintings in one of the inside corners, a trio of pianos waited for their musicians. The other inside and tapestry-draped corner bore a cluster of game tables. Some held boards for games like chess and backgammon. Decks of cards awaited players on other tables, and odd sets of dice on still others. At least half a dozen seating areas like the one where she now sat were scattered across the interior of the room. Each area was arranged for conversing in small groups, each with a low table in front of a pair of sofas and small tables next to the well-cushioned chairs.

Turning, Caer's gaze fell on the elegant dark wood and silver inlaid table that occupied the enormous space of one of the broad-angled corners. Set round it was no less than twenty matching, high-backed chairs. Three women quietly bustled around the table, setting out plates and goblets and silverware, as well as several large covered dishes--all of which they took from hovering carts that followed along after them.

Each woman was attired in the same sort of clothing as the people in the dining hall, their colors equally striking. The youngest was dressed in bright pink that highlighted her fair complexion and youthfully flushed cheeks. Another was dressed in a shimmering deep rose, her dark braid trimmed with a ribbon to match. The last and eldest was a woman of somewhat rounded stature and possessing a tumble of bright copper hair that fell in near eye-crossing contrast down the back of her iridescent purple tunic and britches. Her age was hard to guess beyond the fact that she was somewhere north of forty-ish. Apparently finished with her work, she tapped her hovering cart to stillness and advanced with a broad smile.

"Welcome!" she proclaimed, poking a strand of hair behind her ear, her soft brown eyes brightening as they swept across Stoirm. "M'lord!" she exclaimed, dipping a curtsy, the delicacy of the gesture oddly incongruent with the boldness of her clothing. "What a relief and honor it is to see you! We had so feared for you!"

Stoirm acknowledged her with a bow, which set her to blushing.

"M'lord Amhranai," she added, offering another curtsy before straightening with matronly concern. "The both of you look worn to a fare-thee-well."

Granting a tisked scrutiny at the muddied condition of the whole of their company, she gestured toward the back of the huge room, where three open archways stood. "No doubt you will all wish to bathe before you dine. Ladies quarters are to the left, the gentlemen's to the right. There are quarters through the center, should any among you be couples. You'll find fresh cloths and towels in the baths and clean garments laid out in the sleeping quarters. Lady Blath was good enough to provide us with an estimation of your sizes. The food we've laid out will remain warm for so long as you need. If there is anything else you desire, anything at all..."

Adrian raised his hand, his smile warm. "Our thanks, Brigid. I'm sure you've more than covered every possibility of our needs."

Another flush reddened the woman's face and she dipped an additional curtsy. Turning with a clap of her hands, she gained the attention of the two women who yet lingered at the table venturing curious glances at the newcomers. A dismissing flip of Brigid's hand set them to collecting their carts and making a quiet retreat. Brigid was about to join them when she hesitated. Turning back to the group once more, her interested scan of faces settled on Bran's, her brow furrowing.

"Excuse me," she ventured. "You have come through Havenhall before, sir?"

"Havenhall?"

"This place."

"Uh. No. Never been to Earth until..." He shot a disconcerted glance at Caer. "How long have I been on this world, anyway? I've lost track of whether it's been days or weeks or months."

"An off-world stranger," the woman mused. "Yet you look so familiar." Her intensified scrutiny left Brandon fidgeting. Finally, she waved the matter aside with, "Well, never mind." Still, her eyes lingered on him as she gave one more parting curtsy, then trotted from the room with a look of bafflement still perched on her brow.

48

"Are you awake?"

Caer lifted her arm from its drape across her eyes, blinking into the room's soft light. Rolling her head to the side, she found Emer perched on the far edge of the bed next to hers tucking her pant legs into a pair of boots.

"Barely," she confessed. "After the hot shower, clean clothes, and now the warmth of the room, I feel like a puddle of warm butter."

"Yes, well..." Emer pulled a dark tunic over her head and hung the empty hanger in the wardrobe adjacent to a small bedside table. "You know, if you don't trot back to the common room soon, someone will come looking for you."

"Tell them not to bother," Caer sniffed. "Leaves that much more food for everyone else."

"Won't work. You're expected to be there." Rounding her bed, Emer snatched the empty hanger from the end of Caer's, depositing it in the wardrobe that went with Caer's chosen sleeping space. "At least you're dressed. Mostly," she amended, glancing down at the boots and stockings still on the floor. Extending a hand, she offered, "Here. Let me help you up."

Caer accepted with a grudging groan, swinging her legs around to dangle over the bed's side, her loose black britches catching mid-calf. Mumbling, she pushed the ends of them back down to her ankles, then sat staring blearily at nothing in particular. Catching sight of the slightly rumpled bed on the other side of Emer's, she managed a yawned, "Where's Del?"

"Auntie was bathed, dressed, and off to rejoin the others while you were still sitting cross-legged on the floor of your shower stall, letting the hot water pour over your head."

Caer's mouth puckered at recalling that the stall doors were translucent. Even in a place without security cams, she had no privacy. She passed a more focused scan around the room to verify the lack of cameras. The walls, the same pale blue as the ones in the common room, were completely unadorned, providing no place to conceal such mechanisms. Yawning again, she cast one more scrutiny about the room, taking in the three long rows of beds, each neatly covered with blankets matching the pale cream color of the carpet; each separated by a single wardrobe and a bedside table.

Tying a braided cord belt over her tunic, Emer also glanced around. "Nice dorm. A bit stark for my liking, but comfortable enough, so long as you don't mind living in a hole in the ground. I would go crazy after a while, though."

Caer slipped forward, stretching her legs to the floor and wriggling her toes in the deep pile of the carpet as she eyed the stockings and boots. It would require effort to put those on. "Can't I just stay here?"

"I told you." A faint tension underscored Emer's words. "You're expected."

"Why should anyone care? No one will miss me."

Emer bent to pick up the stockings and tossed them onto Caer's lap. "Believe me, dear. You would be missed."

With a resigned sigh, Caer pulled on the stockings and reached for the boots. They were almost as soft as the fabric of her tunic and pants. Once the pant legs were tucked inside, the boots hugged her ankles and calves comfortably. Straightening, she adjusted the belt at the waist of her tunic, the fullness of the garment's sleeves falling across the backs of her hands. It came as no surprise that the clothing left for them resembled that of Havenhall's residents.

"I'm glad they granted us something a bit less dizzying in hue than the garments worn by the people we've seen, here."

"Mmm," Emer agreed, smoothing the front of her dark blue shirt. Were it not for its juxtaposition against her black pants, the color would be nearly undetectable. Matched her eyes, Caer noted.

"Wish they'd forgone this nonsense, too," Emer complained, batting at the fullness of the fabric billowing around her arms. "Sleeves should be roomy enough for ease of movement. There is enough excess, here, to make sails for a galleon."

Caer suspected it was something other than the style of the shirt that was eating at her companion but hesitated to pry. Emer seemed to catch Caer's perplexed glance. "Are you aware," Emer asked, managing the glint of a softened smile. "Of just how well the deep jade green of your shirt suits you?"

Caer couldn't tell whether the question required a reply. Shrugging, she submitted, "I like green. Especially the darker shades." Her lips pursed for a moment. "Curious, though, isn't it?"

"What is?"

"That everyone we've seen so far looks like a mix of Del's bright garden flowers, while we look...uhm...subdued, I guess. Even counting for the iridescence of our shirts. Not that I'm complaining, mind you."

"Black pants are basic enough," Emer nodded. "The tunics are the jewel tones of the Orders. At least, that's what you and I now wear. I'll wager the same holds true for the rest of our troop."

"The jewel...what?"

"The Orders. We're required to wear the color of our Order when called to Council. Seems that's what the people here assume we've come for." Getting only a look of bafflement from Caer, Emer gave her nose a thoughtful scratch and plopped down on the nearer edge of her bed, musing, "I wonder how much of this is lost in your head and how much you never learned in the first place." Venting a minor huff, she explained, "A Witch's primary...their strongest gift determines the Order to which they are aligned. At times of Council, everyone called is required to don the color indicative of that Order. It allows the heads of Council to identify those with the strength of skills necessary for resolving whatever crisis is at hand. For instance, garnet, the color I'm sure Del is wearing, represents House Garnet, the Order of Witches who possess the ability to...communicate with animals, shall we say."

The odd tenor to that last statement suggested that Emer was hedging the explanation to some degree. Caer's abrupt understanding jerked her straighter. "Communicate with animals. Del can...can communicate with her cat. She can...can talk to Merri?"

"Not exactly. Del has the ability to...well...join with Merri, for lack of a better term. She connects with Merri's mind, allowing her to see the world as her cat does, while Merri, in turn, senses what it is that Del wants of her and usually accommodates. Del recognized where to find you and Mr. Jase when you disappeared from the estate because Merri was transported with you."

Caer was still blinking, dumbfounded, trying to process that little piece of information as Emer continued. "Joining with an animal is a very useful skill for some types of reconnaissance. Councils place tremendous value on House Garnett for that very reason."

Nodding at Caer's tunic, she added, "House Jade is the Order of the Healers. The shade of your tunic designates the highest of its rank. What you accomplished, both in assisting me with Stoirm and what you did for yourself in the labyrinth, even without any training or experience, suggests Master status. I'm guessing Blath or Ian provided that information to those who came up with our garments. Like I said, the color suits you."

"Why aren't you wearing jade, then?" Caer asked. "Your healing skills are far superior to mine."

"Only because of my training and many lifetimes of practice. Healing, however, isn't my primary gift." For a moment, Emer fell silent, staring at the floor. "Mine," she said at last, "is the ability to identify the specific nature of a Witch's attributes, as well as their relative strength. Handy, should someone wish, for whatever reason, to conceal their primary gift by wearing the color of one of their lesser skills." She tapped a sleeve. "Puts me in House Onyx."

Caer tensed. "You...you knew, then. You knew all along. That I am Witch and that I possess the...the 'attributes' of a Healer. Why didn't you tell me? Why didn't you explain to me how to call on it? I might have been of assistance with Dylan and...and greater assistance with Stoirm. And I'd have mended my knee when I first injured it, instead of hobbling around in pain, making myself a burden to the rest of you."

Nervous agitation creased Emer's features. "I didn't know. I can't detect anything more about your abilities, Caer, than the overall sense of their tremendous power. It took your acting overtly before I realized your ability with healing. I can't begin to fathom how or why, but by some means or other, the nature of your skills are as well concealed from me as from you." Shooting a speculative glance toward the door at the far end of the room, Emer mumbled, "If intentionally hidden, it took some exceptionally serious magic to mask your gifts, especially from me. Hard to believe that even a Witch of the House of Black Mist could accomplish such a feat."

"Black Mist?"

"Starn's Order, I'm betting. Their ability to alter or conceal another's memories made them prime targets for assassination. Their order was wiped out ages ago. We had no idea any among them survived."

Emer's brow drew down with doubt and worry. "But Black Mist is just a guess." Swallowing, she breathed out, "I think I may be losing my abilities. You're not the only one I've been unable to get a solid read on, lately. Your friend Adrian Starn...or Lord Amhranai... or whoever he claims to be...is an equal mystery." Standing, she swiped absently at the front of her shirt, again. "Not only am I guessing that he's Black Mist, what other skills he might possess I can't begin to fathom."

"Is that really possible?" Caer posed. "I mean, that a Witch can lose their abilities?"

Bracing herself with a measured breath, Emer faced Caer squarely. "Truthfully? I don't know. I'm not aware of its ever occurring before. At least not permanently. A Witch's magic can be damaged for a time if they overextend their powers, or if they sustain a serious enough injury. I pushed my healing ability near to the breaking point, but that shouldn't be sufficient for damaging my primary gift. Plus, I was unable to get a read on you…and on Starn…before I had to call on my Healer's abilities. And I certainly haven't sustained any serious injury. But…"

No wonder the woman was agitated and edgy, Caer concluded. She was afraid her magic, or at least some part of it, had abandoned her. "If there is no record of any Witch losing their abilities before, then I wouldn't think it likely, now. More likely that this is Adrian's doing…somehow."

Emer flicked a half-hearted grin. "More likely," she agreed, though doubt still hung in her assent. "That man is like a bloody black hole. The more I try to penetrate who he is, the more I feel my gift sucked into a void."

"Suits him," Caer sniffed. "Adrian and black. If he belongs to any order, it would have to be something like 'Black Mist.'"

"Indeed."

"So…" Caer dropped her gaze to her lap, fidgeting with the folds of her sleeves. "What of Dylan? What's his Order?"

"House Silver, the Order of the Dream Readers. That's his strongest gift. Like all of us, he holds any number of attributes."

"What about Bran," Caer put in. "He doesn't have any magic. I hope they don't try to dress him in anything so shockingly bright as super-charged orange or luminescent purple or some such."

Some of the strain went out of Emer's voice as she responded with a bemused, "They'll probably grant him something in bronze. It's the color that designates the Sensitives. Not that they have an Order, really. But those who served Dana's or Roisn's lines were granted status in the Councils, and thus given bronze as their honor color."

"Do Orders extend to the Alainn?"

"No question they share in our ability with magic, but... Who's to say? I don't know anything about them. My mother used to tell me wonderful stories of ancient times when the Alainn were said to roam among the Witches. And Del always believed they were real. I failed to share that belief until Stoirm popped up."

"What would you guess him to be, if you were to assign him to an Order?"

Emer shrugged. "He's a Fire Manipulator. The stories always spoke of their abilities in that regard, though I never believed in those, either, until now. Beyond that, I have no more idea about Stoirm's capabilities than about Starn's. As for Orders, if the Alainn have such, I have no way of knowing what colors they might assign for various attributes." Emer's brow nudged into another anxious curl. "Now that I think about it, I don't recall detecting Madadh Mire's gifts when we confronted him on Slieve na Calliagh."

"Just how is it you determine someone's gifts? Can you tell just by looking at them?"

Emer considered for several seconds. "More a...a whiff...a taste...a flash of colors, some sharper, others subdued...all mixed together in a single sensation. The sum of the impression tells me which attributes are present within any given individual. With sufficient time in the presence of another Witch, I can key on which of their attributes are their strongest, which their weakest."

"Did you detect anything about the other two--Maura and Ailill--while we were on that hill?"

"With both of those two, brutality and hatred glare through all else. Even with the extra time I had around Ailill in the labyrinth's chamber and the Watcher's room, most of what I detected was a muddle of twisted impressions, like the man isn't capable of focusing on any specific gift long enough to perfect it. That's not to say he doesn't possess tremendous strength. It just doesn't seem to lie with any specific set of attributes."

"Yes, well," Caer harrumphed. "Look what you're dealing with. The man's brain is a twisted muddle of insanity. And you had a lot going on with the battle on that hill. Have you ever tried to figure out someone's abilities and strengths in the middle of a fight, before? Shouldn't be a surprise you couldn't focus on them long enough to detect anything specific, I would think. And Stoirm is an alien. Maybe that accounts for your inability to read him. As for Adrian." Heaving a huge groan, she concluded with, "Adrian is just Adrian. He's like a solid tungsten wall. Nobody gets through to figure out anything about him."

"Black hole," Emer corrected. "It's certainly added to Dylan's lack of trust for the man that I can't read him."

"Is that why he's so antagonistic toward Adrian?"

Emer shrugged. "It's a mutual antagonism, in case you hadn't noticed."

"Oh, I've noticed."

"Too much testosterone," Emer snipped before shrugging again.. "Truthfully, most Witches tend to be distrustful of any we don't know personally. Nemhain has her spies everywhere. Too often, we've been betrayed by people we thought to be our allies. As for Starn's and Dylan's animosity toward one another..." Emer darted a sidelong glance at Caer. "It doesn't help that both have a vested interest in protecting you, and neither of them are willing to relinquish that task to the other."

"I get that Adrian thinks he has to protect me. To protect the soul I carry, more to the point. But Dylan has no cause to..."

Emer cut her off with a snort. "Seriously?"

"Seriously what?"

Emer shook her head. "I'll leave you to figure it out."

Caer sat purse-lipped for a moment. "Do you trust Adrian?" Getting no immediate response, she added, "I do. He's a pain in the backside. And…and I know it isn't for me that he's concerned. Well, not primarily for me, anyway. But I trust him."

Emer nodded. "That's good enough for me."

"So…" Caer cocked her head. "So, you trust me, then."

"Initially, I didn't know what to make of you. When Dylan vouched for you, though, I was satisfied. And once I met you, I had no doubts. Del, on the other hand, took a little longer to come around. After the number of times you've been attacked by one of Nemhain's clan or her creatures, however, Auntie finally concluded that you at least were not part of their cadre."

Caer was about to press the matter but the rumbling of her stomach matched that of Emer's when the aromas of roasted meats, fresh bread, and a mix of herbs and spices wafted into the room on the circulating air.

"Smells like someone has uncovered the dishes laid out in the common room," Emer sighed. "Telling us to hurry, no doubt. I'm starving. How about you?"

Caer balked. Though hunger gnawed behind her ribs, she had no desire to venture back to the rest of their group. The press of a whisper lurked at the back of her mind, suggesting someone was attempting to get into her head, again. Not the Sleeper, this time. The feel of it suggested some external source, which meant it had to be either Adrian or Dylan. She was only just beginning to learn to block their intrusions—a difficult enough task when she was fully rested. Her current state of exhaustion made it all the more challenging. They had no right to poke about in her thoughts. Worse, Adrian's most recent intrusions seemed to stir up either painfully uncomfortable, downright embarrassing, or utterly horrifying images.

"I really would prefer to stay here. Can't you simply 'abracadabra' something back here for me to eat, later?"

Emer shook her head. "I told you. Council. We are expected to show up. Anything less is unacceptable."

"Nobody asked me about making such rules," Caer grumbled, pushing off from the bed. "Maybe if I…" Her comment cut short with a gasp. Dropping back, her eyes darted about the room anxiously as the whisper pressing at her mind became a distinct whimper, its impact carrying the tinge of familiarity, though not that of Adrian or Dylan.

"Something wrong, dear?"

"I, uh..." She held her breath, 'listening'. There was nothing save a gathering sense of unease. "Just feeling...unsettled."

"There," Emer sniffed. "That's what comes of hunger. Tell you what. I'll teleport us to the common room and save you all the plodding footsteps."

"You're sure I can't just stay here?"

"I'm sure." Emer regarded Caer a little more closely. "Who are you trying to avoid, if you don't mind my asking?"

"Adrian." The name popped out before Caer could censor it.

Emer plopped back onto the edge of her bed, her features unreadable. "Quite the love-hate relationship you have with Mr. Starn."

Caer's face went instantly hot. "If you're referring to that stupid vision back in the maze, that wasn't meant to be shared," she rumbled. "Not even with me. It didn't belong to me."

The statement seemed to catch Emer off guard, her brow creasing with confusion. "What didn't belong to you?"

"The vision. The memory. It belongs to this other soul. The one I'm apparently carting around. I won't deny the fact that Adrian is my friend, despite the fact that he makes me crazy. We've even been lovers on occasion. But neither of us ever felt...well...nothing like that! Not for each other." Her lips pushed into a pout. "Whomever it is I carry; she's the reason he's watched over me all this time. I'm sure of it." He'd told her otherwise, of course. But his reassurance felt hollow.

Emer's demoralized face caught her attention. If the woman hadn't fallen entirely for Adrian, she was at the very least mightily smitten with him! That explained the strain she'd sensed in Emer, ever since that damned revelation of Adrian's steamy passion.

460

The notion so stunned Caer that she blurted out, "It's Dylan who loves you."

Emer blinked at her. "Look, Caer," she began softly. "What Dylan and I feel for each other isn't what you think. We mistook our love for the 'better or worse 'til the end of our days' sort once...a very long time ago. Didn't take us long to figure out our mistake. Still, we tried to make our marriage work, each of us afraid of hurting the other if we bowed out. Kept trying until..."

Caer waited, wanting to know 'until' what, but afraid to ask.

At length, Emer volunteered, "Until Dylan disappeared."

This was the first time Caer had seen Emer looking so flustered and tormented. Even so, she couldn't resist pressing, "Disappeared?"

"I was pregnant at the time. Our first child. Our...our only child. I was less than a month from my due date. The baby was in trouble from the start. Nothing unusual for Witches. We have considerable difficulty conceiving, and when we do, the babe often fails to go to term. Even when they survive that long, our infant mortality rate is exceedingly high. We don't understand the reason. The price we pay for our eternal run of lifetimes, some believe." Emer studied her lap for several long moments. "Just as well, I suppose. Otherwise, humanity would long since have been overrun with us."

Caer gaped at her, dumbfounded. "And Dylan left you. Just like that." She could scarcely grasp his doing anything of the sort.

Emer's shoulders slumped. "So it seemed at the time. When he turned up more than a year later and couldn't account for where he'd been, it made it all the easier for both Del and me to think the worst of him. Like Del, I believed he couldn't admit that he'd abandoned us because he couldn't stand to watch our baby die. Believed he was lying about his lack of memory. It took me a long time to accept that he truly didn't remember anything about where he'd been or why."

There was a pause as Emer raised her eyes to Caer and then lowered them again. "The not knowing proved to be as hard on him as it was on me. Harder, perhaps. It was only when he returned, after all, that he realized his absence had spanned so many months.

Realized that our daughter was dead. He never saw her. Never held her in his arms before she died. Was not there to share in my grief. He had no explanation he could give himself, much less give to anyone else. Dylan has carried the guilt of that absence ever since. Del and I weren't any help to him, either. But...I...I understand, now. I'm fairly certain of it."

"Understand!" Caer blinked at her. What was to understand? How could any man just vanish like that, knowing beforehand what his wife and child faced?

Emer nodded. "Yes. Understand. His leaving, you see, coincided with the time that we began to realize Dana and Roisin had gone missing. Rumors slowly surfaced that the two had been spelled into hiding. I never made the connection to Dylan until..."

Again, Caer waited.

"Well, like you said, dear. You carry another's soul. One of the two sisters, without a doubt. While bodiless spirits can consciously force their way into a vessel already containing another essence, to my knowledge, there are no other cases of slumbering souls. Both Dana and Roisin have been sleeping for many centuries, now, each passed on to another host as need dictates Or, at least, that is the belief. At some point, Caer, you accepted the burden of hosting one of the sisters. You can only do so by swearing an oath to protect her." Emer gave a long, weary sigh. "Each of us gave oaths to Dana or to Roisin at some juncture in our lives. You. Your friend Starn, from all appearances. Del. Myself...Dylan."

"I don't follow," Caer objected. "What's any of that got to do with Dylan's disappearance?"

"Dana and Roisin were forced into hiding when Nemhain's constant assaults left them severely weakened. They needed time to recover--a lot of time. Waking, there was no safe place to hide that Nemhain couldn't sense them. A spell of deep sleep, however, might haze their identities; mask them from her.

"Once I realized that you carry one of the sisters, it made sense. It had to be Dylan who'd cast the sisters into their long sleep all those ages ago. It's why he was called away from me. Why he had to go. Why...somehow, he and you were drawn together."

She fell silent again for several long heartbeats before reflecting aloud. "I had always assumed, of course, that the one who worked the original spells to hide the sisters had to come from House Amethyst--the Sleep Casters. And that they would, in turn be the ones called upon for the Awakening. Dylan possesses tremendous skill as a Sleep Caster, there's no denying it. It is the attribute that most strongly rivals his ability as Dream Reader, perhaps even equals it, now. I've not paid that close attention, lately, to make that determination. Dylan would certainly know if he'd improved his skills to that extent. Still, to be capable of casting two such demanding spells of slumber in close succession--spells that would hold for centuries... Such a Master could not merely be from House Amethyst. They would have to hold one the highest positions in the Order. They would wear the Council color of deepest purple. If Dylan holds that position, I would know. I think."

Her lips pinched as she shook her head. "The sisters didn't call on House Amethyst, though. I'm sure of it, now. I can't imagine why they opted to call on one solitary individual. But they did. They called on Dylan. It was stupid of me not to see it sooner. I thought that the faint signature of Dylan's magic surrounding you was merely the remnants of the spell of protection he worked before sending you from Ahira. He did, you know...work a spell of protection. But the spell dissipated before your arrival into our keeping. I just...ignored that fact, I guess. Now, though, considering it, along with everything else." Emer let out another sigh. "Dylan's lingering signature has to be connected to the spell surrounding the Sleeper, not directly to you."

Her expression increasingly pained, she continued. "Little wonder he was so weakened when he finally turned up again. All his attributes had suffered tremendous damage. He was hardly able to move a salt shaker across a table. Took him a couple of lifetimes just to begin rebuilding his strength. I allowed myself to believe, as

Del did, that his guilt was responsible. His disappearance just when Dana and Roisin were rumored missing...his weakened magic upon his return... Combined, the evidence should have been more than sufficient for me to guess what had happened. I'm such an idiot!"

Leaning forward, Emer braced her elbows on her knees and rested her chin on her hands. "Dylan was telling the truth. Deep down, I knew it. It was just easier to blame him for my pain." Her quiet moan was as remorseful as her expression. "His memories would, of course, be shaken and clouded by the enormous strain of his task. Perhaps the sisters had further suppressed them with some spell activated by his actions. On some level, I think he understood; recognized it was the sisters' demands that took him away. He not only withdrew from Del and me--our fault for not trusting in him--he also rebelled against Dana and Roisin, resenting even the mention of their...and our...ultimate goal."

"Why didn't he wait? Go to them after your baby was born?"

"It isn't ours to decide when our oaths come due, Caer. Chance is as much at play as anything. All we can do is to decide whether to honor our oaths when we are called to fulfill them. There are consequences, of course, should we fail to act. Had Dylan broken his oath and not gone when called, the torment in his mind would drive him mad. And not just for that lifetime. The insanity would endure, even as his soul transmigrated through multiples of lifetimes."

Caer tensed, her eyes wide. "How could anyone ask so much of someone, cursing them with eternal insanity because they fail to keep a promise?"

"No one casts any curse, dear. This is part of who...of what we are. When a Witch gives their word, the magic inherent in them binds them to it. Not that we can't break ordinary promises. We can, and often do, every bit as readily as any Tanai. The consequences are minor. A short-term irritating rash, perhaps. Or the inability to use one of our minor spells for a while. Taking an oath, though. That's a different matter." Flicking an apprehensive glance toward the door, Emer stated an anxious, "I'm sure Dylan and Starn would both free my soul from my current accommodations if they knew I was telling you all of this. But I think you deserve to know."

Eyes lowered, she stared dully at her boots. "When a Witch swears an oath, Caer, their very soul is bound to it. Most never utter such pledges. Those of us who do never undertake the swearing lightly. Our bond is given with our deepest conviction and our willingness to risk our very essence for what we believe.

"Likely, even Nemhain believed in what she swore when she pledged to stand with and protect her sisters. Assuming that to be the case, though, Nemhain's conviction didn't last. It's very much what accounts for her madness, I think. Not just that she failed to fulfill her sworn oath to her sisters, but that she willfully refused to honor it, making repeated attempts to destroy them."

Swallowing, Caer reached for her charm. She was no more than a child when she swore to protect the piece of the key she carried; to deliver it into the rightful hands. The promise, long forgotten, now loomed clearly in her mind. While she still had no clear recollection of any promise to the alien soul within her, she felt the truth of having done so in her bones. She would not go back on her word. But how could she keep promises she didn't remember?

Emer rose and shuffled across to sit at Caer's side, laying her hand on Caer's arm. "You're projecting your thoughts again, dear. You really do need to learn how to control that. Perhaps I can ease your mind, though. You've already delivered the key to the rightful person. It is, after all, in the hands of one of the sisters. As for whatever oath you gave that soul, have a little faith. It likely had something to do with protecting whichever sister you harbor. And you are, after all, allowing her to hide within you, are you not?"

Caer fiddled again with her sleeves. "Faith. Fine." There was a long silence before she pressed with, "But why are the sisters doing this? Why did they set so much violence in motion? Why destroy so many lives."

Emer braced her arms behind her, leaning back with a weary exhale. "What the sisters set in motion was two-fold. First was the curse that allows our souls to return lifetime after lifetime—a curse sworn by three terrified children as a means of seeking vengeance on those who murdered their parents and who were about to murder the little girls, as well. Second, and in a different lifetime, they set in motion a means of offering another chance for a future to a blighted world. Some of us remember what Earth was like...before the devastation...before humankind's stupidity and the resulting Great Wars."

"And you think this..." Caer brushed the necklace. "You think this is the key to accomplishing that? How?"

"Ask the soul you carry, if you can. None of us understands how magic in general works. Never mind how something so complex as what the sisters set in motion operates. It is said that the sisters were far more gifted than any Witch before or after them; that they learned to access far more of their magic than any other. Roisin was certainly the greatest Seer ever to walk our world. It was through her ability that Earth's eventual devastation was foreseen; through her that a means to save much of the life here was found. With their magic, the sisters forged a gateway, Caer. They opened a corridor to a world where life from Earth might take root, safe from the destruction that the hand of man would eventually bring about.

"In the generations before the gateway was sealed and hidden, many volunteered to go to Slievgall'ion to help oversee and protect the abundance of life forms that the three sent with them. Dana and Roisin...even Nemhain, before she turned on her sisters. Each made frequent trips to the world. Slievgall'ion is where Shannon went."

"Shannon," Caer repeated. "Dylan's sister?"

"Yes. Del still grieves the loss of her daughter, though she's never lost faith in Dana and Roisin's vision for the rebirth of this world." Emer breathed out a softly murmured, "I trust in the word brought back by the sisters many centuries ago--that life, indeed, took hold on Slievgall'ion. That it flourishes. I have to. Believing is what sustains me, just as it sustains Del. And I will give my last breath to accomplish what I believe we must do to see that abundance brought home, once more.

"For nearly three millennia Witches have waited for the time to come. In the beginning, it was anticipated with great hope and joy. Unfortunately, as great as her gift of Seeing was, Roisin never foresaw Nemhain's betrayal. When it came, hope for this world darkened; became woven through with fear. Nemhain intends to take Slievgall'ion for herself; intends to destroy much of humanity in the process. Yet we've no choice but to push forward. In order to protect humanity, you see, the gateway must be broken. But to do that, it must first be opened. Our prayer is to allow abundance to flow once again back into our world before we destroy the gate. Assuming we can figure out how to do so."

Rising, Emer pulled Caer up with her. "That's a task for another day, though. For now, we need to eat, take council--if Starn or the Alainn or anyone else has any to give--and rest. When the time comes, when the still missing sister is found and both Dana and Roisin are awakened and drawn out from their hosts, we will fight to give this world the renewal it was promised. And we will help them destroy the gateway so that Nemhain cannot use it to undo everything."

Shooting one more nervous glance at the door, she finished with, "Just...just don't tell the others what I've told you. I would like to survive long enough to see this battle through to its end."

"Was that your oath? To fight with them--Dana and Roisin?"

Emer smiled faintly. "Something like that."

49

The richness of the meal was more than Caer's constitution was prepared to handle, leaving her to nibble at it while the drone of conversation buzzed in her head. Around her sat the hazy wash of jewel-toned presences. There was Del in a long, garnet gown, Blath in a similar one of Jade. The tunic styled shirts of the others included Emer's deep onyx with the faintest hint of blue, another jade for Ian, bronze for Bran, Dylan's crisp silver shot through with threads of dark amethyst, Adrian's silvered obsidian, and Stoirm's rich topaz. The wash of colors mesmerized her; flowed together...

"For the love of all that's sacred, Caer, if you aren't going to pay attention to the discussion, at least eat."

Adrian's abrupt command brought her head up just before she nodded, face first, into her plate. Too weary to snap at his dictate, she instead blinked at him several times before muttering indignantly, "I'm going to bed." Pushing from the table, she offered a half-hearted glower, adding, "I didn't want to come out here in the first place. I can't follow most of what you're talking about, and I don't know anything to add to your...your 'counsel'." Not the rebuff she wanted to throw back at him, lacking as it was in wit and edge. Even her departure lacked the impact she wished, her tread a cross between a shuffle and a trudge as she made her way back to the women's sleeping quarters. Too tired to hang her clothes in the wardrobe, she dropped them across the end of the bed, donning the simple nightgown that had been left for her.

So, why was it that, the moment she collapsed into bed with the lights called down, her brain immediately bubbled over with waking? The aggravatingly renewed mental activity submitted nothing useful; nothing even intelligible. Rather, it tumbled with disjointed murmurs that twisted together pieces from everything Emer had earlier confided with bits of Ailill's mad rantings in the Watcher's room. Each attempt to shut out the mental noise succeeded only in redoubling the anarchy of her thoughts.

For how long the chaos inside her skull continued, she couldn't begin to guess. It felt like hours. As it stretched on and on, a whisper began to ripple in its depths. At first, it was little more than a faint hiss. Slowly, it took on a sound more like a cry, gaining prominence over the rest of the mental bedlam. A cry. Not from the Sleeper. Nor was it from any of her companions. While it bore a faint familiarity, the voice matched none of theirs, and it seemed to assail her from a great distance.

She tried again to silence her brain, pulling the pillow over her head and squeezing it against her ears. The sound came again, this time as a wailing and frantic plea. *"Help! Help me! Please! Someone!"*

Caer shot upright, her gaze darting across the heavily shadowed rows of empty beds. The plaintive voice vanished, leaving only the sound of her own fretful breathing, the drumming of her pulse, and the muffled thrum of voices drifting in from the common room. Muttering, she slipped back beneath the covers. Help indeed! The culmination of all the stress, fear, and exhaustion, was making pudding of her sanity. The Sleeper within might be resting peacefully, but for her, slumber had staggered off to some other realm. In its wake, her nerves tingled with her growing sense of unease. Even her necklace seemed agitated, the charm's subtle pulse throbbing the anxious tattoo of her heart.

Again, Caer sat up, her mounting disquiet reminding her darkly of those other times. The moments just prior to her narrow escape from the collapse of a section of the university's library; the moments before she discovered Mirra's decapitated body in her apartment;

the seconds before that Coran'ian beast sprung from the very air in Adrian's quarters on Bestor. Brooding tension lurked at the fringes of her awareness and seeped along her nerves just before each of those events, erupting at last in horrific visions heralding murder or mayhem.

Pressing herself into the corner that backed her bed, Caer called, "Lights full up." The brightened glow, however, did nothing to dispel her unease. White-knuckled, her fists drew her blankets up, snugging them around her like a shield. At any moment, now...at any moment, visions of gore would explode through her head. There would be screams and death and...

There was nothing. Only the anxious drumming of her heart in sync with the pulsing charm on her necklace. That and the faint murmur of distant conversation. Seconds drug by. Minutes. Still, she sat pressed into the corner, staring out at the empty room, wishing, now, that she'd not left the company of the others. At last, tossing aside the blankets, Caer rose, tugged off the nightgown, and scrambled back into her clothes.

Bran's voice was the first to be heard clearly as she padded barefoot down the hall. "My great, great...grandfather?"

"I thought you were going to sleep." Adrian's frustration jarred through Caer's mind well before she reached the archway to the common room. She stiffened but continued on.

At the same time as his sending, the music of Adrian's voice commented reflectively, "You need at least one more 'great', I believe."

Bran moved into Caer's line of sight as she approached; disappeared briefly; returned and disappeared again. Pacing, apparently. As she entered the common room, she saw him come to rest at the end of the grouping of chairs and sofas nearest the dining area. The rolled-up sleeves of his bronze shirt puffed out over his elbows as his intense scrutiny fixed on an age-discolored square of paper in his hands. A boy of maybe twelve stood before him, studying Bran with profound curiosity. The youth's unruly red curls, his gangly limbs, and the rumpled bright yellow of his britches and leather-belted tunic gave him a comically petulant look. Bran offered the paper to him.

"Mother says you should keep it," the boy replied, the softness of his tone at odds with the boldness of his appearance.

"Go back to bed!" snapped at Caer as she edged a few steps further into the room.

Turning, her fists shoved to her hips, she glanced around in search of Adrian, struggling to compose a nasty retort. As usual, words failed her, leaving her with no more than an agitated frown as she spotted him.

Adrian didn't bother to meet her gaze. Half-seated on the nearer end of the dining table, one leg crooked over its corner, he stared with a well-practiced lack of expression into the mug in his hands. That, combined with the misty shimmer of his silver-frosted black shirt, emphasized his air of detachment, ticking Caer's belligerent mood up a notch.

Noting Caer's entrance, Del gave a backward gesture toward the table. "Hunger bring you back? There's still plenty of food, dear." Just down from the corner Adrian occupied, Del's dining chair was turned to face the nearest seating arrangement and the path Bran was now pacing, again. Emer, who'd snuggled into the corner of one of the sofa's, sat with an open book on her lap. Stoirm, Blath, and Ian seemed to be missing. Probably sleeping.

The airy sleeves of the long gown Del wore fluttered delicately around her arms as her fingers tapped on the rim of her wine goblet. Her fascinated gaze, however, remained on Bran and the boy. Emer was likewise watching the twosome with interest.

"How long have you known?" Bran asked.

Shrugging, Adrian tucked a thumb into the wide, black belt that cinched his long shirt. "Caer mentioned you as a friend some time ago, but only referred to you by your first name. So, I didn't initially make the connection. When I saw you for the first time, there on the upper slopes of Slieve na Calliagh, I thought you looked familiar. I was too preoccupied to work out why. Wasn't until you turned up at the ladies' estate that I realized who you were. The remnants of your injuries matched those described by the man who found you on Andromeda and got you to safety."

Bran cast Adrian a puzzled glance. "You knew about what happened on Andromeda? Who was it pulled me from the flames? I woke up in the hospital, not knowing how I got there."

"The man is one of our own."

"A Witch?"

Adrian nodded. "He contacted me to say some of Nemhain's men were asking about a family of Sensitives. By the time he tracked them to the farmstead, all save one young man were dead. He managed to pull the young man from the destruction before the flames could finish what the beatings had begun. Once safely clear, he recognized the survivor as the brother of the murdered woman. He was aware that the young man went away some years prior, and was surprised to find him returned. When he told me the name-- one Brandon Jase--and that the victim had been on Ahira before returning to his home, I suspected he might be the Brandon Caer spoke of."

Adrian gave a disgruntled snort. "More proof of your identity came when you turned up toting that gun." With an ironic cock to his brow, he explained, "Not only do you bear a striking resemblance to Branuff--the gentleman in the picture you hold--it seems you also share something of his nature. Branuff never missed an opportunity to pick up a gun. Any gun, if it was left unattended. An excellent marksman, Branuff."

Adrian turned a look of undisguised annoyance to Caer. *"I thought you were desperate to go to bed. Why are you now back out here?"*

Caer shoved her jaw forward and stomped across the room to stand behind the sofa where Emer sat. *"I was! Only now I can't sleep!"* she returned hotly. *"Command away, but I'm betting even you can't shut down the tumbling chaos in my head."*

Dylan paused long enough in his silent stalking around the

periphery to scowl at Adrian. "You say the man who found Mr. Jase was Witch. Given the remoteness of the Andromeda colony, it would seem to suggest that he was among those forced into hiding out of fear for his soul. Witches who've fled under such circumstances tend not to broadcast their whereabouts. Yet he contacted you."

Adrian took up a near pitcher of ale and refilled his mug. "Not all who flee cut all ties with us. You may be content, Master Dream Reader, in withdrawing from our cause and sitting idly by. Others, despite the risk to themselves, choose to assist us in laying spy networks."

Dylan tensed, his jaw twitching. It was Emer, however, who twisted around to glare at Adrian, her anger rumbling as she declared, "You have no idea what Dylan has accomplished, Mr. Starn. Nor what it cost him!" Her sudden defensive outburst brought everyone but Bran's attention to her, Dylan ashen as he stared at her.

"You are correct," Adrian confessed icily. "I don't. We each carry our battles in our own way, I suppose. This much I do know. There appears to be a task that yet remains for our resident Dream Reader."

"A task that, if I understand correctly, can be accomplished only if we get the appropriate cooperation," he sent sharply to Caer. *"If you aren't going to fortify yourself with food, then go back to bed."*

Caer stifled a growl. *"First you expect me to participate in your little meeting, this evening. And now you demand that I sleep. If you want me to do that, then have 'Master Dream Reader' spell me to my slumber!"*

"Can't be done that way," Dylan interjected.

"Why didn't you tell me before?" Bran muttered, his attention still fixed on the aged photo.

"What do you mean, 'not for this'?" Caer snapped at Dylan.

Adrian took a long draught from his mug, directing his comments once more to Brandon. "Not much in the way of opportunity for the telling until now. Nor was I inclined, after that little episode at the estate, to offer information to someone so intent on threatening the ladies' lives, not to mention my own."

Caer's ire snagged. Bran had threatened Adrian, Del, and Emer? When the hell had he done that? And why? He must have been completely out of his mind to challenge any one of those three, never mind all of them!

"I thought you people were responsible for Brenna's death," Bran snarled back. "And for Jenna's and...my family's and...and all of Ahira and..." He hesitated, glancing down at the boy who still studied him. Forcing several measured breaths, he managed, "Then Brenna showed up...or..." Casting a distressed glance at Del, he corrected, "Or who I thought was Brenna." His shoulders slumped. "Besides. The gun had no ammunition."

A humorless smile played across Adrian's lips. "Of course it didn't. You'd not be standing here, now, had I taken your threat seriously."

"I'm sorry," Del offered, setting aside her goblet as she rose and crossed to Brandon. "For all the distress I caused. I didn't intend to scare you half out of your existence that night. In truth, I hadn't yet realized whose body I occupied. I was in rather a hurry when I found it." Her lips pursed for a moment as she considered him. "You must have cared quite a lot for Ms. Cowl."

"Cared for?" Bran blinked in confusion. Running a hand through his hair, he huffed, "I can't say that I particularly disliked her. Nor was I attracted to her, if that's what you're suggesting. She offered the possibility of answers. That's all."

Taking another measured breath, he went on. "Shortly after I arrived on Earth, after I'd made something of a pest of myself at the university, Brenna seemed to take an interest in my plight. She told me she knew what was happening. Said that the same people who wiped out Ahira were trying to take Caer hostage. Said you and Emer were behind it and that she was afraid of you. I promised to do everything in my power to protect her, if she would tell me everything. She said she needed to meet with me in private; that she'd let me know when and where.

"I got her call after you collected us from that bloody business on that damned hillside...after Del took me back to my hotel. Brenna was hysterical, screaming something about being wrong to trust 'them', that 'they'd' lied, though she never specified who 'they' might be. Said she accomplished what they demanded of her, but that they weren't going to reward her like they'd promised. Said they were coming for her; were planning to kill her. She begged me to help her. By the time I arrived, there was nothing I could do, except watch her bleed out." He took another long breath. "I thought one of you was responsible for her murder."

"I wish you'd told us all of this earlier," Del muttered, shaking her head. "Perhaps I could have disavowed you of such notions." Glancing down, she tapped the picture in Bran's hand. "You do, you know. Look like him."

Caer stared from Del to Brandon, their exchange making precious little sense. Inside her skull, Adrian's heated impatience throbbed. *"What must I do to get you to follow a simple command? Find someplace, any place out of the way, and go to sleep!"*

Brandon glanced sheepishly at Caer. "I should have trusted her instincts. Caer said she liked you and Emer, and that Brenna made her uncomfortable. I just...I really thought Brenna could give me the answers I needed." His gaze settled back on the photo. "So," he sniffed. "Could someone at least explain to me how a picture of this great, great...great grandfather of mine came to be here?"

Adrian set his mug to the table with another shrug. "Your ancestors, Mr. Jase, were among those who served me loyally for many generations. Sensitives all. Branuff was, unquestionably, the most gifted of them. Unfortunately, both his gift and his loyalties to me brought him afoul of Nemhain. He sustained a mortal injury while defending his family against those sent to slaughter them. Had he not been able to raise the alarm in time, they would all have died. My people reached them quickly enough to save his wife and children, at least.

"They were brought here, afterward. New identities were

established for his wife and one of his two children. The wife and son were then relocated off-world, to the Andromeda colony."

Bran cocked a speculative brow at the boy who still lingered before him. "That would be my great, great...whatever grandmother...and my great grandfather, I'm guessing." What of Branuff's other child?"

"His daughter chose to remain here. To continue her family's service to me."

"Sadbh," the boy murmured.

"Sadbh," Adrian agreed. "Distant grandmother to Niall, here."

Bran returned a dull stare to the photograph. "We fought. A lot. Father and me. About my leaving Andromeda. He said I would bring woe to my family if I left. He never explained. And I refused to stay. Mede sent me a letter after father's death, saying she'd discovered some strange pieces of family history among his belongings, and that she was beginning to understand why certain people gave us the sense of standing on the edge of an electrical field. There were only a handful...five or six, maybe...on Andromeda who made us feel that way. They kept to themselves, and we were content to let them. But when I got to Ahira..."

He shook his head again. "I should have listened to father. Should never have left. Mede and Traxton and their baby would still be alive if I'd listened."

"You don't know that," Del submitted. "While many of us thought Sensitives had already been hunted to extinction, the huntress, herself – Nemhain - remained unconvinced. Her pursuit won't stop until she's guaranteed that every one of your kind has been utterly exterminated."

"All of that because some Sensitives served Mr. Starn?"

"Or her sisters," Del added.

"Not solely for those offenses." Adrian lifted his mug again, staring into it as he continued. "In case it hasn't sunk in for you yet, from the beginning it was the Sensitives who were most instrumental in naming Witches, and naming as Witch any Tanai they disliked, to whatever authorities happened to be seeking our extermination. Sensitives hunted us, and helped to torture and kill our kind."

Bran frowned, his gaze taking in Adrian for several pained seconds. "But you don't die. At least your souls don't."

"Torture is torture, Mr. Jase, whether you survive it or not. And many a Witch did die. In the beginning, there were few of us whose souls carried the sisters' curse--that they and their line should live eternally, to seek vengeance on the lines of those who murdered our kind. While it was their curse that led to the ability of our souls to return time and again, transmigration is not visited on every Witch. There are some who are born with but one life to live. None knows until their first returning whether they inherited that particular aspect of magic."

"This Nemhain," Bran growled. "She holds the travesties of some of our ancestors against all of us for all time?"

"As Stoirm has pointed out previously, she is not a forgiving soul."

Bran's face pinched with uncertainty. "You, though. The rest of you. You just magnanimously forgave those sins?"

"Hardly," Adrian admitted. "For far too long, we also regarded all Sensitives with contempt and hatred. It was Roisin who insisted that the cycle of vengeance and malice had to stop. Over many generations, her gentleness, her understanding of the fears on both sides, persuaded Dana and most of those in their two lines to protect rather than destroy. Roisin even won over some among the Sensitives, including those who went on to serve us."

"Sir," Niall ventured, tapping at Bran's arm. "Am I to understand that you don't have family, anymore?" Bran's lack of response seemed all the answer necessary. "You do," the boy stated. "You have us. Mother and..."

The remainder of Niall's statement was lost to the raised flesh that chased down the back of Caer's neck as a moaning, *"No... Please..."* seeped dimly into her head. Distant and detached, the sending felt like something inadvertently overheard, something intended for someone else.

"Help me..."

Del gasped, taking an unsteady step away from Brandon. Surprise shot to a grimace of dismay and shifted instantly to a spread of horror across her face. Her eyes snapped shut, her hands raised as though to ward off some great blow. Her eyes fluttered open again, her features overrun with bewilderment and doubt.

"Wha...Gwyn!" The sharpness of Emer's strangled cry echoed around the common room, bringing Dylan's agitated meandering to a startled halt.

"Em?"

"She's..." Emer's midnight eyes went wide with shock, and for a long moment, she held her breath. When at last she released it, she did so in an unbroken stream of, "She's alive Gwyn's alive and we have to help her!"

Del nearly tripped as she bolted toward her niece. "No! Don't!"

"Help me! Please!" now hammered through Caer's skull, carrying with it an exploding vision of dark, splattering blood and a rush of terror so great as to buckle her knees. Only Adrian's sudden appearance at her side kept her from falling.

"Where?" Emer called to the air. "Where are you? Gwyn, how can I help?"

Frigid blackness ate into Caer's marrow as a sickly sweet, menacing laughter trickled through. Something vile had come into Havenhall.

"Ah, but you already have!"

The thundering pulse in Caer's ears all but drowned Emer's mortified wail. "No! Not through me! Not through me!" Bounding from where she sat, her eyes wild, she screeched, "I've let her in! I've opened the way for Nemhain!"

Adrian's towering frame was still as death next to Caer, his mounting fury leveled on Emer. "You've..."

"Not her fault!" Del shouted. "It was Gwyn! Nemhain must

have tortured her, knowing that in her terror, Gwyn would be able to reach through to one of us. Emer merely..."

Adrian waved her silent, his expressions shifting from fury to a tensed waiting, as though he was searching for something. "It's not Nemhain who's come through," he hissed. "She's sent Madadh Mire. Slain his foul vessel so that she could send his soul here. He'll need another host." Adrian's jaw clenched. "Ailill. He'll seek for and join with Ailill. With the magic breached, if he succeeds, their joining might allow them to teleport others through. Niall, get to your mother! She's preparing Ailill's meal. Tell her to stay clear of his cell!"

Gripping Caer's arm, Adrian forcibly directed her to a chair, shoving her down. "We have no more time, Dream Reader. For the sake of us all, if it is in your power, then do the waking now! Before Nemhain can claim her!"

"I told you," Dylan bellowed. "Caer must be sleeping. And the sisters should only be awakened together!"

"We can't locate the missing sister if we don't wake this one. And we've just run out of time. Do it! The rest of you, rearrange the furniture. Throw up barriers! And..." Adrian stabbed a finger at Caer. "Whatever happens, protect her!"

With a rush of charged air, he disappeared. An instant later, the door to the common room was shoved into its wall pocket, slamming shut again in Niall's wake as he raced out.

50

Frozen, Del stared at the door, her heart thundering its anguish before her outrage erupted in a long stream of expletives. How could she be so stupid? She gave Emer no warning.

Aiming spell after spell at chairs and tables, she whipped them from their positions; overturned them; slammed some back-to-back or in groups of two and three deep; stacked others in tall, unstable piles. With a furious flourish, books shot from their cases, spines splitting and pages fluttering. Another sweeping gesture ripped now empty cases from the walls, scattering splintered fragments and dumping them with jagged edges exposed.

Emer sidestepped several times, tears tracking a glistening trail down her cheeks as she gave way before Del's violent outburst. At last, catching sight of her niece's mortified face, Del sucked a shallow breath and shouted, "If Starn wants barriers, let's give him barriers! Move some of the furnishings to block the door. Turn the rest into obstacles."

Emer managed a faint nod and set to work, the air taking on an increasingly electrified buzz as her magic joined her aunt's. More tables and chairs went sailing. Shelving units stacked with soaps, bottles, and jars were summoned from the ladies' bath and tossed into the mayhem, containers shattering, the contents spilling out in sticky puddles over broken furniture and patches of exposed carpet.

"What the..." Brandon ducked as a wardrobe appeared in the air and sailed past his head.

"Jase! Over here!" Del shouted, indicating Caer with a jerk of her head while she slammed the wardrobe near a pile of chair remains. "And stay put unless you want your head knocked off!"

It occurred to her, suddenly, that Dylan was not in her range of sight. Spinning, she spotted her son still hovering on the far side of the dining area, his agonized gaze fixed on Caer. The resignation that days ago began seeping into his countenance was now a look of haunted defeat. Del shuddered, remembering that look from only once before--when Dylan returned from the absence that left Emer to face alone the ordeal of birthing a child destined to die in her arms.

After all this time, Del at last grasped her son's plight. In her haste to believe the worst of him, she never once gave credence to his claim that he didn't remember where he'd been or what had transpired in the time he was gone.

"Stop standing about, fool!" she bellowed. "Work your craft, or we're all lost!" She recoiled instantly, ashamed. After denying her son any sense of understanding or comfort in all this time, she now labeled him a fool, when the epitaph belonged to her. Yet she had to break him free of his inaction. Someday. Someday she would tell him of her remorse. Just not this day.

Dylan responded with a violent flip of his hand, sending a sofa tumbling end-over-end through the air to land in a crunched heap, mere meters from his mother. In the next instant, he and one of the dining chairs vanished, popping back into existence directly in front of the chair Caer now stood behind. Her eyes were closed, and Del suspected she was seeking for spells...any spells that might be useful.

"Caer!" Dylan made no effort to conceal his sending, the impact of it reverberating through Del. *"Stop!"* he demanded. *"We have something more important to accomplish. I need you here. I need you seated."*

Caer glanced at him but remained where she was. "I know spells. They're in my head. They were in the Books of Secrets. My mother's book. My aunt's book. But they're in my head, now. Every spell they ever showed me from their books. I can find them. I can…"

"Not now. Caer, listen to me. That's not our job. Please." Dylan's voice was flat, but he seemed to connect with her as she cast him another glance. Confused, she still hesitated. Then, slowly, she acquiesced.

Del watched as her son raised a rippling fog, surrounding the two of them, cutting them off from the chaos. She could still see them, though she could no longer hear what either said. It was Emer's choked sobs that cut through.

"I'm sssorry, Del! I didn't know. I…I just wanted to help Gwyn."

The bile of Del's inability to console her son coupled with her failure to warn and thereby protect Emer…and Caer…seared an acid hollow in her stomach. "The fault is mine," she moaned. Unable to face her niece, Del summoned first one bed, then another from the ladies' sleeping quarters and sent them spiraling wildly toward the front of the common room, there to land with a shattering vengeance behind the already accumulated piles of debris.

"I w…was the one who reached out to Gwyn," Emer stammered through her sobs.

Del closed her eyes and forced a long, slow breath before turning. "I was the first Gwyn called out to. Not you, child. I sensed something was not right. So, I shut her out, then allowed doubt to cloud my judgment instead of warning you." Guilt strangled whatever else she might say, her mind going back over her failure. One bloody instant of doubt. Fear that by shutting her mind to Gwyn, she had consigned her oldest and dearest friend to death and a banished soul rather than jumping to her aid. And in that hesitation, when she might have warned her niece, Nemhain found the more compassionate recipient for Gwyn's plea.

Burning with contempt at her inexhaustible shortcomings, Del sent another flurry of tomes sailing without regard to her aim. Brandon barely managed to duck in time.

"What the bloody hell are you doing?" he yelped, scrambling at last to close the distance between himself and the faintly sparking fog that now completely engulfed Caer and Dylan. "And what are they doing?" he demanded, jerking a thumb toward them. "I thought you wanted me to protect Caer. Can't do it if I can't get near her!"

Del shot him the briefest of glances as she finished stripping the walls of more bookshelves, tossing them into new piles. "It was a forced take-over," she spat, waving a hand in the direction of the dining table. Its remaining complement of chairs spun away as the table turned ninety degrees, lifted into the air, and thudded onto its side. Baskets, pitchers, plates, platters, mugs, food, and drink skittered and sloshed across the carpeted floor. "Gwyn would never cooperate with Nemhain. Not to save herself."

"A forced... A what?" Brandon glowered at her "Someone talk to me, damn it! Stop leaving me in the dark!"

Del spared him another glance. "Look, Mr. Jase. Brandon." Summoning another bed from the women's quarters, she dropped it in an open space. "I don't expect you to understand this, but Nemhain must have forced her will on Gwyn's mind. Forced her to..."

Brandon's face whitened with an unexpected depth of comprehension, taking Del so by surprise that the wardrobe she'd just summoned split apart, raining fragments down on her and Emer.

Brandon's mouth pressed to a thin, tight line, his jaw twitching with his tension. "Andromeda." The word came as a mournful exhale. "When I went home." Licking his lips, he proceeded haltingly. "One...one of the men who was waiting for me. He got into my head. Asked questions. Demanded...demanded answers. I couldn't stop him. I..."

Del sucked in. Jase had mentioned something of this before, but without providing much in the way of detail. Near her, she sensed Emer's rigid attention.

"He wanted information. About anyone...anyone from whom I'd sensed...sensed this power...this magic, or whatever it is that makes you people feel like...feel like an electrified tempest in the making. He got names from me. Caer's and...and others. And when he was done...when they took all they wanted from me..." Swallowing, Brandon's voice lowered to a coarse rasp. "They made me watch. They set the fires and...and made me stand there as my family burned. Then they beat me. Left me there. Expected me to die in the flames, too."

Del shuddered. She, too, once endured another's force of will on her mind. Sinead sensed the attack and came to her rescue...and paid the ultimate price. How often Del wished the assault had gone undetected. Del lost her beloved sister on that day. Emer, an Uair Amhain, a child scarcely turned two, at the time, lost her mother.

"Know this," Del offered dully. "Though we may be capable of enduring much more, than any Tanai, even a Witch may not be able, alone, to overcome such an intrusion. And you are no Witch. What was done to you is unconscionable. What you gave up was through no fault of yours. Nor do I believe it made any difference in matters. They likely already knew all that you could offer."

For a long breath, there was silence, Del wiping her hands up and down on her gown, her eyes staring into the ether, seeing again Sinead's death...sensing the banishment of her sister's soul. She knew only too well the torture Brandon experienced; the greater torture Gwyn endured. Might still be enduring.

"What they did to you, multiply that many times over and you'll begin to understand what has been done to Gwyn. They've pressed her mind to the breaking point, and not solely in search of information. They enjoy watching the minds of their foes shatter. Still, for all that they might take from her, nothing is so damaging as their discovery of Gwyn's connection to us...to Emer and me. Gwynlyn Berring is our sister through an ancient blood ceremony. It is rarely done any longer, because it binds the participants so tightly. Gwyn and I initiated it. Emer was far too young, at the time, to object. After Emer's mother was killed, we felt the best way to protect her was to guarantee that either of us could reach through to her, and her to either of us, at any time and in any place.

"Nemhain was able to wrench that piece of information from Gwyn's mind. Was able to use that connection, applying such power to force the plea from Gwyn that there was no doubt of her reaching out to us. I sensed a malignance behind the plea, and shut my mind to Gwyn. But I did not give warning in time. When Emer opened her mind to Gwyn, the Dark Heart was able to create a rift in the magic that protects this place. It was too small, apparently, for a physical body to pass through, but sufficient for her to send Madadh Mire's soul. The fault is mine. I initiated the blood ceremony. I failed to warn Emer."

Brandon chewed at the corner of his mouth, glancing from one woman to the other before gesturing to the room at large. "And all of this? This mayhem you're now creating helps us how?"

Del gave an anguished shrug. "In the brief time Nemhain was able to use Gwyn to break through to Emer, she likely glimpsed this area through Emer's eyes. Meaning, she detected the lay of this room and who was present in it. Nemhain has most certainly shared that information with Madadh. Once his soul finds physical housing and begins bringing in others, they'll try to teleport here, looking for Caer. That's why Starn called for us to throw up barriers. We've nowhere else to take Caer. Here is where we take a stand."

Swinging her hand in a stab of motion aimed in the direction of the last bookshelf, she ripped it asunder, stirring its remains in the air and whisking pieces to plant themselves like spikes across any open space she could find. "If Madadh and his unholy henchmen try to break into the room, if they try to teleport here, they will not find it as Nemhain saw it. Hardly deadly, popping into a space occupied by something less than a solid wall, but we can certainly make it troublesome, and potentially damaging. Perhaps it will buy us time. Time for the others to get back to us." Her gaze shot nervously to her son. "Maybe, even, time for Dylan to accomplish his task. If the Sleeper's only hope of survival is to flee once she's awakened, we can at least grant her that chance, and pray she finds a better haven than I've allowed this to be."

From the corridor beyond came the muffled sounds of shouts and running feet. Brandon lunged forward, grabbing his gun from his belt as he braced himself in front of the fog surrounding Dylan and Caer just as the door was thrown back into its pocket. Stumbling up against a pile of debris and narrowly missing being skewered by one of the spikes, her bloody arms flailing, Maired fought to free herself from the combined grips of Stoirm and Niall. Blath followed close behind, slamming the door shut on the echoing screams and cries. Blinking out from where they'd entered, the foursome reappeared in a less hazardous location.

"Maired, stop it!" Blath yelled. "You can't keep fighting them! You need time to recover!"

The Watcher straightened as much as her aged frame would permit, her fury sparking all around her. Her flailing ceased, however, allowing Blath to focus on Niall, who was also covered in the dark stains of murderous battle. "Where are you hurt, child?"

The boy's eyes flashed from Blath to the trio of open archways at the back of the common room. "Not!" he rasped.

"Let me take a look. Quickly. Before..."

"I'm not!" he repeated, twisting away from her and dodging his way through the debris-strewn room toward the arches. Seconds later, he disappeared into the hallway leading to the men's quarters.

Blath started after him, but was restrained by Stoirm. "Let him be. He knows the way to Amhranai's private quarters. He'll be safer there than out here."

Emer turned on Stoirm, demanding, "What's happening? Where's Starn?"

He gestured toward the door. "Amhranai is teleporting as many children and their mothers away as he can. There are Alainn waiting in secret places off-world, ready to receive them. Many of the women, though, are refusing to leave. They insist on fighting alongside their husbands."

"Sending the children away," Brandon blurted, spinning to face the archway through which Niall had fled. "He's missing one."

486

The rage that moments before defined Maired's bearing now vanished, her frame sagging. "Niall," she groaned, staring at the blood on her arms as Blath continued to wipe at it with the ragged edges of her torn sleeves. The old one's injuries, however, appeared minor--no more than a few cuts and scrapes.

"He came to me when he couldn't find his mother," Maired murmured. "We were running down the corridor looking for her when some of Madadh's beasts, Caspians, judging from their appearance, came up from Ailill's cell, dragging the bodies of Brigid and Ian. Niall could have tried to battle his way to his mother, but it was obvious she was beyond help. Instead, he stayed at my side. Tried to defend me with nothing more than a carving knife from the kitchen. He managed to sink it into one of those ugly reptiles, I think. Tine turned up with some of his men just at that moment, though, or we'd not have survived the rest."

"Yet you wouldn't stop fighting," Blath accused. "You and Niall should have fled the very second Tine appeared. Your body is too old for this, no matter how much your soul may wish otherwise."

Maired's eyes smoldered. "Most of those beasts are without magic. I could take down a good many of them before they..."

"Tine," Del interrupted, almost fearing to hope. "With more Alainn?"

Blath nodded. "Father sent out the call. The gathering begins."

"And Madadh Mire?" Emer pressed. "Where is he?"

A sharp cry cut off any response. Whirling around, Del discovered that the foggy ripples of Dylan's spell no longer shrouded he and Caer. Slumped in his chair, her son sat ashen-faced, both hands clutching his chest.

Caer blinked at him, stunned, then shot forward, reaching to support him.

"Don't!" Dylan hissed between clenched teeth, his shaking hands raised for his own inspection. "No blood." He thrust both hands forward for Caer to see. "It's illusion. Banish it."

Doubt clouded her face. Glancing back at the others, her mouth formed around a plea for their assistance.

Again, Dylan barked, "Don't! Listen to me, Caer. The blood isn't real. Isn't there. Think of the past. Go back. Think of..." The rest was lost as he straightened, isolating them once more within a cloud of undulating fog.

"The Reader best complete the Awakening soon," Stoirm rumbled. "We were able to lure Madadh and several of his thugs into the crypt, but our spells sealing them within won't hold for long."

51

A flood of red blinded her as molten pain slashed through Caer's back and erupted in her chest, doubling her over. Mid gasp, the agony was gone. So, too, she realized, was the haze of Dylan's encompassing fog; vanished when he cried out. Teary-eyed, struggling for breath, she straightened, her tremulous inhale catching abruptly in her throat. Before her, Dylan sat slouched in his chair, his hands pressed firmly to his chest, blood coating his fingers and running between them to stain his lap.

"Don't!" The harshness of his command cut short her anxious reach for him. Grim acceptance darkened his features as he lifted his shaking hands to examine them. "No blood. Look." He thrust his hand before her. "It's illusion. Banish it."

The blood was there...soaking his shirt...pooling on the floor. Caer's gaze darted around, seeking the others. Why were they just standing there? Why weren't they rushing to help?

"Don't" he demanded again, killing her plea before she could voice it. "Listen to me, Caer. The blood isn't real. Isn't there. Think of the past. Go back. Think of dancing."

Dylan quickly recalled the haze to envelop them, a renewed and more potent charge running through it.

"Think of Sidra. Think of your childhood."

Caer rocked forward, snatching his hands. Her trembling made it difficult to hold onto them as she turned them this way and that.

They were frigid, but he was right. There was no blood. She blinked to make certain. No blood.

"It was nothing," he declared.

Shifting on her chair, she rubbed her arms against the chill of understanding that raised her flesh. It was a seeing--a premonition. The vision carried the same intensity, the same reverberations of truth as those that came before. In the library on Ahira, the vision was one of cracking, crumbling walls. On the way to her apartment on Ahira, it was Mirra's death in all its violence. Here, now, it was Dylan's pain and blood. Because their minds were linked, Dylan experienced the premonition with her.

"There is precious little time, Caer. Trust me. Forget the vision." The nudge of his mental presence pressed against her awareness once more. *"Return me to your thoughts. Seek for your dreams."*

She recoiled. It might be more than his blood that the next vision displayed. Might be his death. She couldn't bear that.

Leaning forward, Dylan grasped her arms, holding them securely. "This is not the time to discover how to shut me out. Please, Caer. I ask again. Trust me. We must do this."

Reluctantly, she willed her mind to lay open once more, exposing her fears--fears for him, fears for others...

"Don't waste your energy on us. We've a long history of taking care of ourselves. I ask you again, find a strand of your dreams. A strand from your childhood. A single thread of memory might lead me to the one who needs waking. Focus on the past. Dream of it."

With one long, fractured sigh, Caer closed her eyes. Splattering scarlet exploded in dark rivers bearing broken and dismembered bodies. Her eyes shot open again, her hand grabbing automatically for her necklace, feeling its racing pulse near double, even as her own did so. Rigid with terror, she stared past Dylan, her breath breaking in short bursts.

"Block it! Push it aside. I need your past. Your dreams. Not the Sleeper's. Think back. Focus. Since we cannot wait for you to sleep, you must seek for the memories of your dreams."

The charm bit into her palm as her fingers tightened around it. Block the vision. Shut it out. Forcing an extended inhale and release, the rapid pulse of the charm calmed and found a cadence, clear and persistent.

One, two, three, four, five, six, seven. One, two, three. One, two, three.

A distant melody wound through its repetitions, rising and falling with the rhythm, gaining strength with its progression. The music was bright with metered drumming and the sweet trill of flute and whistle. With it, too, came the sensation of movement, as in a cadence-driven circle moving round. Shadowed remembrances and tattered dreams drifted to the fore, shifting in the music's lively tempo. Sweet images from her childhood on the Perimeter Ship. Images from Bestor and from Ahira and Lillith. They jostled in disorderly riot, all lacking continuity of proper chronology. She traversed the dark maze; wandered through Del's estate; fell into the chamber at the maze's heart; stumbled around Dylan's manor house. Jenna's laughing eyes greeted her, superimposed over her family's quarters aboard the great ship. Sidra's gardens drifted through the lab where Caer's parents had worked. Underlying it all thrummed the quickening sequence of a dance...so familiar...so powerful.

Forward and back. Sidestep Deosil--one, two, three, four, five, six, seven. One, two, three. One, two, three. Heat and flame. Fires within fires. Return the rounding Widdershins--one, two, three, four, five, six, seven. One, two, three. One, two, three. Searing flesh. Child! You must away! I call upon the guardian! Protect her!

Soft light. Mingled smells of disinfectants and herbs. Adrian smiles and steps away. Others gaze down on her--Alainn and human. Delicately, they work the magic of their healing while Adrian weaves a song of forgetfulness, hiding the agony, hiding the memory.

From a place far beyond the images, Dylan's voice imposed, "Abred. Struggle and hold. Return to the flames. Return to the moments before the guardian's arrival. See for me."

Crushing waves of hatred and fear. Faces warped with rage.

491

Chanting. Witch! Witch! Witch! Nausea burns her gut, its bitterness a sharp acid in her mouth. Cackled mirth, dark and tormented, boils from the lungs of the man beside her. The mayor. Their friend. His features warp to a demented grin, his fingers locking in an iron grip of her shoulder, the filth of his laughter still bubbling from him. **It is done.**

Tears cloud her eyes as she searches for Sidra. For her aunt. Atop the pyre, flames curl hungry tongues around Sidra's writhing body. This cannot happen! They can't take her beloved aunt from her! Bruising struggle. Freedom from the grip. Running. Heat. Searing pain eating at flesh. Something glows that is not fire. Her small voice cries out, breaking...full of resolve. **To me! I shall protect you! I pledge it on my life! On my soul! On my magic!**

No! You do not know what you've taken upon yourself! Child! You must away! I call upon the guardian! Protect her!

Again, Dylan's distant voice breaks through. "Gwynfyd. Purity. I sense what I seek. I feel your presence, Daughter of The Gifting. I know where you reside. Know me. Hear my words. Slumber binds you. Passion sustains you. Heed, now, the spell of unbinding. By the..." White energy exploded through Caer's skull, obliterating her connection with Dylan and singeing every nerve in her body. Even through the blurred lurch of the room, she could tell that the haze surrounding them was gone. Before her, Dylan sat slumped, this time, his head to his knees. Blood soaked his back; ran from his chest, covering his pants; trickled down his unmoving arms to drip from his fingertips to the floor. Illusion. Caer rubbed her eyes to clear them. He would sit up. Would command that she dismiss this foul scene. All she need do is take his hands and...

Stoirm's grip of her shoulder and Blath's quietly spoken "stay still," snapped Caer's awareness to the proximity of the others. Stoirm and Blath hovered close on her left, while Niall and Maired stood silently to her right. Emer was on her knees next to Dylan's chair, devastation clear on her face, a large bruise spreading over her right brow. Beside Emer stood Del, with Brandon backing her.

"He used the banishing," Emer sobbed. "Ailill used the banishing spell."

Dylan's warm blood seeped beneath Caer's bare feet, conveying the reality and bringing the sudden weight of guilt crushing down on her. The vision told her this was coming. And she did nothing to prevent it.

"There is nothing you could have done, child." Del offered Caer a simple nod, though the focus of the woman's grief-stricken eyes was set on a brown reptilian Caspian, her hands aimed at the beast, ready for spell casting. The alien snarled from a wary distance, a scorched pistol in one hand. Its other arm dangled, burned and withered and useless at its side. Next to the creature squatted a second Caspian, green ooze bleeding from near its neck. A large, bulky firearm lay almost within its reach.

"Go ahead," Bran growled. "Lucky for you that the ladies' spells merely incapacitated you for a moment. Move and my next bullets won't miss your ugly faces."

Niall choked a forlorn, "I'm sorry." The sword in his hands dripped a sickly purple. On the floor behind him lay the blue mass of a Renthorian. The alien's severed head, along with one of its six arms and a bladed weapon, rested in a dark violet puddle.

"I'm sorry," the boy repeated. "I couldn't find Lord Amhranai's sword fast enough. I thought I knew where he kept it. I thought..." His voice trailed off and he turned to kick hard at the Renthorian's body, sending a splatter of gore up his pant leg.

"You did well," Maired consoled softly, wrapping an arm around him. "The beast never saw you coming."

"You did, indeed." It was only at the constrained music of Adrian's comment that Caer realized he was standing a short distance beyond Dylan's chair. Like Del, Adrian's hands were poised for spell casting. His target, however, was a wild-eyed Ailill, who sat hunched on top of an upended sofa, rubbing his shins. Adrian flicked the briefest of glances back at Niall. "Time for you to leave. Let Blath send you to one of the waiting Alainn."

"No." The boy moved closer to Caer. "They took my ancestors. They took my mother and likely my father. They took the Dream Reader. I'm not leaving so long as I can help protect the lady."

"Foolish words for a powerless Tanai brat." Ailill's face twitched from indignant fury to manic exhilaration and back again. With the return of the rage came a ranting outburst, borne on a heavier, more malicious tone than Ailill's previous proclamation, though it uttered from the same mouth. "Foolish idiot to cast the banishing! If you'd killed only his body, his soul's flight might be tracked and captured as he merged with a new host. No telling what information about our foes he held."

"Yours the worry, Uncle!" sniveled back, again from the same mouth. "I'll tell Mother it was you who did it."

Niall sucked in. "Lord...Lord Amhranai was right. The two have joined. Ailill and Madadh Mire share the same body!" Tensing, the boy lifted the point of the sword toward the figure bearing the two. "I'll kill you both!"

Ailill's voice squeaked at the beginning of a retort, only to dribble to a tortured whine as Madadh Mire took control. "Not a chance, boy." The dual-souled body jerked clumsily out of its hunch to sit with legs dangling over the sofa's end. Through the shattered doorway behind him came the echoing cries and clashes of ongoing battle. The distant screams returned a manic grin to the face.

"Put down your toy, boy," Madadh grunted. Awkwardly he gestured two men forward from their flanking positions several meters back of him. "Or my wife's kin will snap you in half."

Adrian shifted his hands in the direction of the two. "Power so much as flickers from them and they'll burn within their own spells."

"You can't take them on and still defeat me."

One of Adrian's hands readjusted slightly. "Wish to wager on that?"

The grin disappeared, a gruesome series of contortions warping the face into a distorted representation of the man Caer remembered from the shuttle to Bestor; the same man who had appeared on the rooftop in New Haven and again on the hillside of Slieve na Calliagh. His eyes narrowed to slits for a moment, doubt slithering through them before they settled in a shallow bravado. "That one," he proclaimed, making a more controlled sweep of a hand toward Caer. "The girl. Give her to me, brother. And I'll spare the rest."

Adrian's response was harsh and discordant. "I disavowed you as brother centuries ago, Madadh."

"Dog, you still name me?"

"And Mire. Though mad is too gentle a label. The very worst of rabid canines pale by your standards."

"Ah. Yes. Well, I accept your label as dog, brother. Hound of death seems fair enough." Madadh patted himself on the head, grinning. "But our dear nephew, my stepson, here, is the one who's truly crazed. The more so, now that I've sealed him, helpless, inside his own skull and skin. Not a particularly pleasant atmosphere for me to endure, either, I assure you. Perhaps I should have dispensed with this useless mass and taken that kitchen servant who delivered his meal. I dare say, that woman would have provided more sport and less sniveling."

All color drained from Niall, though the aim of his sword remained fixed on the monstrosity whose body was now contorting as much as the face had done, shifting away from Ailill's characteristics in an attempt to make the controlling soul and the body housing it match. The bone structure and muscle, however, proved too thin to take on the obscene girth of stretching and sagging flesh. The result was a grotesquely misshapen and only vaguely human form.

"You remain as repulsive as ever," Adrian sneered. "Outside as well as in."

The laughter that broke from the madman sent needles of ice through Caer's marrow. Like his face, she knew that laugh. It was the same as had come from Lilith's mayor while Sidra burned.

"All the better to cause revulsion from my narcissistic wife," chortled back.

Niall tried to break forward, raising the sword toward the

abomination's face as he yelled, "If you detest her so, then let me relieve you of your need to serve her!"

Maired instantly tightened her grip, struggling to hold the boy back.

Madadh dropped from his perch, struggling briefly to stand upright, snarling, "Ailill! Stop fighting me! The body is mine, now!" At last he wrenched his mass into something more or less erect, leveling one hand at Adrian, the other at Niall. "I'll use your bones to pick that boy's flesh from my teeth. And I will still take the girl. I wonder. How long do you suppose she will be able to stand against my 'beloved' wife's torment?"

"You should be more concerned with your own torment." Adrian jerked his head toward Dylan. "Clever, really, battering away at his shielding just enough for a single bullet to slip through. Too bad you didn't stop to consider whom it was you just directed your lizard friends to kill. With this man dead, his soul banished, Nemhain has no chance of waking either of her sisters, much less finding or opening the gateway. I'm sure she will be very pleased."

Unable to choke back her sobs, Caer sank to the floor beside Emer, burying her face in Dylan's bloodied lap.

"My wife," Madadh thundered, "has Dream Readers of her own line. They will serve well enough."

"There is no one who can serve as well as Dylan," Emer hissed, her voice trembling. "He was more than a Master Dream Reader. You murdered the Master Sleep Caster whose enchantments sealed Dana and Roisin in their slumber. Do you really think there is any other who can undo the entwined spells of both of his master skills without destroying the very thing you seek?"

"You lie!"

Adrian's gaze flicked almost imperceptibly to Emer before returning to Madadh. "You know she speaks the truth."

Madadh's face contorted again, his eyes widening as if seeing for the first time the shell from which he'd stolen both life and soul. "Take the body from them!" he boomed, gesturing at pair of men who hung uneasily behind him. "There may still be a spark of life in that bloody Reader. The banishing can't work so long as..."

Raised to her feet by the tempest of her rage, Caer screamed, "No! You will not touch him!"

"Take her, as well!" Madadh roared. Caer heard the pop, and guessed that Adrian had disappeared. Beside her, Emer shot to her feet, shoving past as Adrian materialized directly in front of Caer. The air erupted with light as the force of Emer's spell joined Del's and Blath's, throwing the two advancing men across the room and slamming them to the floor in twisted heaps.

"Get Caer to the back. To my quarters!" Adrian barked.

Brandon hesitated only a fraction of a heartbeat before thrusting his gun back in his belt. Darting forward, he wrapped an arm tightly around Caer's waist, lifting her as he swooped around and set out for the appropriate arch. Still defiant, Caer wriggled until her feet touched the floor. Finding her footing, she braced against Bran's momentum, her sudden resistance bringing him to a stumbling halt. Bran had only an instant to grapple with her before inhaling sharply as two of Nemhain's kinsmen vanished from near the shattered door, reappearing astride where he and Caer would have been, had she not stopped him. Stoirm's spell caught one of the assailants full in the chest, erupting in flames and incinerating the man's body. Lunging, Niall caught the other with the edge of his blade, slicing a deep gash in the man's chest. There followed a gurgling scream, but the man did not topple. His wound closed even as he whirled on the boy, a hand poised for the kill.

In the fraction of an eye blink, Maired disappeared and reappeared, shoving Niall to the floor, her shielding barely deflecting the attack. As she staggered backward, Madadh and Adrian launched their own attacks at each other. The clash as the their massive works of magic violently collided lit the room like a miniature sun, with the ear-rending blast of a bomb. The electrified force of it threw Madadh tumbling backward, debris bursting into flames all around him.

"I said," Adrian bellowed, yanking Niall to his feet. "Get Caer out of here!" Niall glanced between Adrian and the fallen Maired, his pale features streaked with blood and grime. Nodding, he clambered across the littered floor to where Bran still fought to hold Caer. For her part, Caer only half noticed the boy, her attention more on the small blaze that marked where Madadh had been. She wished fervently that Adrian's blast had destroyed the demon, though she knew otherwise. She could sense him, dazed, but unharmed and lurking somewhere behind the sputtering flames.

"Help me!" Emer cried.

Caer glanced back to where Dylan's body still sat slumped on the chair. Emer was trying to lift the corpse. Jaw stiffening, Caer struggled harder to break free of Brandon's hold, desperate to aid Emer.

"No," Brandon rumbled, partially lifting her from her feet again. "You're coming with me. I need to get you..."

The last of his proclamation was lost in the clang and clatter just beyond the door, announcing more of Madadh's troops. Caspian, Renthorian, Witch...they pushed and shoved their way into the common room in clusters. Caer felt the last of hope drain from her as a trio of Coran'ian lumbered through the mangled doorway.

Stoirm jerked Brandon and Caer toward him. "Over here!" he commanded, shoving them both in the direction of the arches once more. "Niall, show them the way!"

Brandon did his best to comply, but Caer was in no mood to obey, fighting his every step. She refused to flee while others stayed to fight. No one else was going to die trying to protect her while she did nothing.

Blath charged past her to hold off a number of beasts that were closing on Del. "Go!" she ordered, grabbing and flinging Del back toward Caer and Brandon.

Del cried out as she staggered to gain her balance. "Emer! Leave him! We can do nothing for him, now!"

Behind Emer, rising from the glowing ash and rubble, Ailill's manic laughter rippled an erratic undertone to the murderous snarl that was surely Madadh's. It wasn't the threat from the dual-souled abomination, however, that suddenly set Caer's mind reeling. It was the subtle, fluttering feel of an unexpected presence. Dylan was alive!

No. He couldn't be. She was right there, felt the last of Dylan's breath leave his body, felt the utter lack of a heartbeat as she knelt next to him, his bloodied chest so near. The thing that Emer was dragging was as lifeless as stone. Yet...yet the sense of him, frighteningly thin and weak as it was, brushed again through her mind. His soul. That's what lingered. Caer's resolve doubled. She had to help Emer; had to protect his body. Maybe...just maybe his soul could find its way back.

Brandon's grip tightened again, but her will was stronger. Closing her eyes, Caer held firm, blotting out Bran's eruptions of swearing; blotting out all the chaos surrounding her. Desperately, she turned her focus inward. *Whomever I bear, I beg you hear me. Do not let the Dream Reader be taken. Do not let my friends die here. They've sacrificed so much for you. There must be a way out. Show me what to do.*

A flash of vertigo staggered her as images swept her mind. Like slivers of nightmares spliced end-to-end, they flooded past, dark with malice, red with blood and fire. Through them raced a chant, the words gushing beyond awareness the way individual droplets of water are lost to a white-water rush.

Caer's eyes came open again, watching with a strange detachment as her hands stretched upwards in a gesture of supplication. The action was not by her bidding. Nor had she willed the chant that raced through her head and past her lips.

"From beginning to ending, the circle moves round, repeating until what was hidden is found."

A small breeze stirred, lifting ash, cinders, and splinters of wood in a delicate swirl around Caer's ankles. Madadh's stunned attention snapped around, and for a moment, his gaze locked on hers. In the next instant, he was battling his way toward her. Caer's heart slammed against her ribs with the same pace as the internal chant that still outran her thoughts, even as the words continued to pour across her tongue and lips. At last, she began to grasp them. "I claim the hidden as the wheel spins on. Return the rounding to whe..."

Stoirm shoved her sideways, knocking her breathless and thudding her to her knees, a wave of heat flashing over her head and singeing her hair. Blath sprinted past, firing spells, though at whom...or what, Caer didn't wait to find out. Whether the Sleeper had shown her the only means of escape, or was leading her and those she wished to protect to their doom, the simple fact was that they could not stay here.

Scrambling to her feet, she called the words back, and found that they came readily. "...to...to where it began," she finished. Then she spoke the chant again. "From beginning to ending, the circle moves round, repeating until what was hidden is found. I claim the hidden as the wheel spins on. Return the rounding to where it began."

The words were little more than a whisper at first, growing slowly to echo across the debris-strewn and scorched common room as Caer recited the chant over and over. They were her words, now. For better or worse, the Sleeper's dreams had passed the chant to her. With each repetition, the gusting breeze around her ankles gained strength, until at last, a great wind whipped the loose fabric of Caer's tunic and pants. Long tangles of her hair danced across her face in the bluster that spiraled upward around her, the sweep of the winds expanding ever outward, picking up a whine that swelled to a wail. Madadh/Ailill braced against the tempest. Caer watched with grim satisfaction as he failed to hold fast. Buffeted and dodging the airborne debris, he screeched obscenities as he blasted one more furious, though misaimed attack, then dove for cover amongst the piles of shattered furnishings.

52

The growing toxic taint within the ambient magic spoke all too clearly of the strength of Ailill/Madadh's banishing spells. Most charged with no specific target, set adrift within the confines of Havenhall to attach to any soul torn free by the death of its vessel. The abomination had no care as to whose souls he destroyed. Adrian knew Madadh would not rely on that alone, though. Some few of the Dog's black spells sought him, specifically.

As if in confirmation of Adrian's assessment, Madadh rose from behind his sheltering pile and launched such a powerful blast that the flash of it as it surged past scorched his nerves, the full impact missing him by less than a hair's breadth. Before he recovered from the glancing blow, a sudden flash of agony sliced through his mind, the searing of it carrying Maired's scream. Spinning on his heels, Adrian saw her driven to her knees by Madadh's attack. Her eyes met his as she fell. Instinct launched him. Extending his shielding as protection, Adrian landed spread eagle across Maired's body, willing that she make some movement beneath him. Some exhale. Anything to let him know she still lived. There was nothing. No movement. No struggle. No breath. The void left by the lack of any sense of her presence carved into Adrian's soul.

Stunned and empty, he lay there, knowing Madadh had chosen a target whose strength was too age- and battle-worn to withstand his assault. Worse, he chose his target knowing precisely who she was. Maired. Adrian's beloved granddaughter. Daughter of his first-born daughter, Rowan. The memory of Rowan's long-ago entreaty, as sharp with her urgency as it had been in those dark hours of that black morning, raised Adrian to his knees, images painful in their clarity. Snapped awake by his sudden awareness of his daughter's panic, her desperate plea shot through his head. In the next heartbeat, he held Rowan's baby, the newborn still white from birthing. Attacked in the midst of labor, Rowan was defenseless, her husband and household falling to Nemhain's slaughter. Her child's only hope of survival lay in Rowan's ability to teleport her tiny daughter halfway across the globe and into her father's arms. Whether his daughter ever 'heard' his promise to protect her child, he never knew.

"I'm sorry," he whispered, his voice choked as he leaned to kiss his granddaughter one last time.

A sharp sting welted a bloodied trail across his back as airborne debris sailed past, alerting him to the dangerous thinning of his shielding. With weary effort, he drew upon his magic, silently singing new strength into his protections, even as his scan swept the room in search of his opponent. Once more he swore the oath sworn so many times before. Madadh Mire and Nemhain would pay.

Scooping the lifeless body into his arms and stumbling to his feet, Adrian located the massive, overturned table and sprinted for it. Failing, in the end, to protect his granddaughter's soul, he refused to leave this, the last vessel to hold her bright spirit, to be mutilated at the hands of the madman or his beasts, or to be dashed by Caer's rising maelstrom. Skidding around the table's end, he dropped to his knees, his weighted grief plunged to an even darker hell. For there, he also found Stoirm. The Alainn glanced up from where he knelt, his lips drawn tight, his eyes dull. Beside him lay Blath, as silent and empty as the shell Adrian held in his arms. Stoirm's gaze flicked to Maired, then returned to his wife, his hand gently caressing her face.

"They...they should not have come to this, Amhranai."

For a long, sickening moment, Adrian remained unmoving, unable to breathe, unable to take his eyes from his daughter. She couldn't be dead. He would know. Numb, he lay Maired next to Blath, then slumped down, his back against the table, his face buried in his hands.

"I would that I had saved her, Amhranai," Stoirm murmured, his words hushed and ragged. "She bolted past me as I was protecting Caer. Threw herself between Madadh/Ailill and their attack on Emer, I...I could not react swiftly enough." A fractured inhale preceded, "There was nothing left for me but to honor my promise to her...a promise she begged of me long ago. That I shield you from her torture, should the madness of this ancient battle claim her. Her wish, Amhranai, was to spare you the experience of her banished soul."

Rage and resentment flared. Stoirm had no right to conceal the moment of Blath's death from him! No right! But the emotions snuffed out as quickly as they'd ignited. His friend had honored his promise to his wife—to Adrian's daughter.

"How many more?" Adrian moaned. "How many must we sacrifice before this is done?"

Stoirm made no reply. When at last he spoke, it was not an answer, but a question edged with ice. "Where is the Dog, now?"

Adrian's jaw clenched as he closed his eyes, searching for some sense of the vile toxicity that was the man. Everywhere stank of him, his odor carried on the gale that continued to swirl about Caer. "Still cowering," he spat. "He dove behind a debris pile when Caer raised her storm, though he may well have crept off to some other mound by now. I cannot tell his precise location in this chaos."

Slumping further, he sat listening to the whine of Caer's tempest and the banging and shattering of debris as it was tossed about. Adrian's anguished exhale filled with bitterness and self-recrimination prefaced a muttered, "She has succeeded in calling up her magic, but she lacks the knowledge and skill to control it. I should never have hidden her powers from her. She deserved to be schooled in their use. Had I done so, Blath and Maired might yet be alive."

Stoirm gave a faint shake of his head, his own torment reflected in the worn creases of his face. "Without concealing the child's magic, you could not keep her hidden. The Dark Heart would surely have found and murdered her long before now, and perhaps taken hostage the soul of the one Caer harbors."

Lifting Blath's hands, Stoirm kissed them and folded them across her breast. Then he kissed his fingers and leaned to press them to Maired's brow. "We shall mourn their deaths properly, in time. For now, our grieving must be put aside. It is the living who need us. The storm of Caer's unruly magic may protect her for the present, but if she tires before she discovers how to control it, Madadh will find his chance to take her. We must get to her, first." Shifting around, he raised up just enough to peer over the table's edge. "Let us hope Caer's raging does not bring Havenhall down on our heads in the meantime. No one's soul is safe, Amhranai. Not with the dozens of banishing spells Madadh has loosed to the ether." Dropping back, Stoirm returned his troubled gaze to Adrian. "Does she truly mean to take us above? To the slopes of Slieve na Calliagh?"

"Her chant suggests as much." Hammering his fist against the floor, Adrian growled, "What good will it do for us to confront Nemhain if Caer drags Madadh and his beasts right behind us? If she doesn't rein in her magic, the very strength of it will see that she accomplishes precisely that. Assuming, of course, that her lack of familiarity with the hill does not, instead, grind us into the stones of the great cairn."

Stoirm lowered his gaze again to the body beside him before shaking his head. "No amount of training, nor the strength of Caer's magic can equal the centuries upon centuries of experience that have granted Croi Breag her devious cunning. The presence of the Dream Reader was our real hope. Now he is lost. Still..." Stoirm's features hardened. "We are here, Amhranai. I will not simply sit here, now, and await my demise. Blath would never forgive that."

Adrian bit back his surprise. Stoirm didn't know. The sense of it was faint, yet Caer had detected it. Her stunned recognition had reverberated through him like the shock of a high voltage charge. Cast out from his body, the Reader's shielding managed to repel Madadh's banishing and, though it struggled, still protected his soul. If Stoirm remained unaware of its faint presence, perhaps Madadh did, as well. So long as Madadh/Ailill remained convinced of the Reader's demise, their attention might remain diverted. Assuming Caer's maelstrom did not wipe away that remaining flicker of the Reader's existence, they might buy sufficient time for the damaged soul to recover. Cautiously, Adrian wove a spell of concealment and protection around the Reader's struggling soul. Let him recover quickly. Let him return to his body. Hope yet remained.

"Amhranai!" Stoirm's low hiss pressed through. "Tine has sent to me that he and his men have pursued most of Madadh's beasts out of Havenhall. They are above, and in the midst of a war that has spread down Slieve na Calliagh's flanks and across the surrounding valleys and hills. Your call to arms was heard. Nemhain's armies are being challenged.

"I've advised Tine of Caer's desire to take us out onto the slopes. He warns against it. Croi Breag, it seems, stands alone on Slieve na Calliagh's crest, isolated for the moment by a ring of ancient spirits. What specific magic these phantoms wield, Tine cannot tell. But no living thing seems capable of breaking through them. The Dark Heart can neither draw her armies to her, nor can she go to them. If we allow Caer to teleport us, we risk her dropping us into the middle of the raging battle, or possibly into the midst of the ring of wraiths. What the latter would do to us, I cannot say."

"Nor can I dissuade Caer," Adrian rumbled. "Since it began, Caer's chant has not once deviated. Her will is not only set but is locked on this course. All that prevents her from taking us above at this very instant is her lack of understanding of her magic's fundamentals."

Stoirm considered for less than a heartbeat. "Give me a moment to confer." It was some seconds, however, before he announced, "Tine says one among the wraiths has approached him with an offer.

If we use fire to teleport, the wraiths will allow us through. Tine is laying fire to a small section of ground immediately before the ring, and the wraiths are moving to encompass it." A fraction of hesitation was followed by, "My son is not so gifted a Watcher as Maired, but he believes that, if we gather the remainder of our group, he can hold and send me the pattern of the flames. It should provide us passage to an area that, for now, the battle cannot touch, and should provide us with some degree of cover against the Dark Heart."

Drawing a long breath, he finished with, "If it's to Slieve na Calliagh Caer is determined to take us, this is our best chance of avoiding slaughter the moment of our arrival. If we can raise the flames around us here, if we can reach Caer, I will use the pattern Tine sends to direct her teleportation. If she will allow it."

Adrian liked the idea of teleporting above no more now than he did before. Allowing Caer to deliver them straight to Nemhain, whether the bitch was isolated or not, was a path he preferred not to risk. Caer, however, was giving him little choice. Grudgingly, he agreed. "I will try to break through to her."

Glancing over the table's edge, he verified that Caer remained only a few paces from the overturned chairs where she and Dylan had been sitting. Her hands were still lifted skyward, her clothes billowing as her frustrated attempts to control her magic continued to rage around her. The winds whipped the long strands of her hair, giving her the appearance of the mythical Medusa with her head of writhing snakes as she stood over her prey. It was no cowering victim, however, that lay sprawled at her feet. It was the Dream Reader's body.

Emer was there, as well, hunched protectively over the corpse, her flapping clothes as coated in dark, wet stains as Caer's feet and legs. Though her face was hidden, Emer did nothing to keep the depth of her pain and anguish from filling her mind. Like Stoirm, she believed the Reader lost. She shielded his body for no more reason than that which had driven Adrian to carry Maired's to the shelter of the table. He would ease her sorrow; would send to her that the man was not gone. But Adrian needed her ignorance for a while longer.

"Caer!" His sending met with the resistance of dashing headlong into a solid wall. Shaking off the mental impact, Adrian forced again, *"Caer, hear me! I need for you to listen and to trust me! Make no further attempt to teleport until we are with you. Wait for us!"*

She gave no sign of hearing. Nor could he wait for any. Raising up, he took stock, both of the locations of the remaining members of their company and the locations of Madadh's minions. Most of their assailants had taken cover at the periphery of the room, preferring to stay tucked away from the turbulence of furniture fragments and shards of broken glass that were carried in the sheering winds. A small cluster of Renthorians, however, were braving the battering to threaten Fedel'ma and Jase. The beasts were crouched, the gale at their backs, the barrage from their charged weapons pinning the two against the wall between two of the three archways. Fedel'ma's shielding held off the attack, but she was tiring, each round of the Renthorian's continuous salvo penetrating a little deeper into her magic.

Vaulting from the cover of the table, Adrian aimed. The destructive force of his assault seared a blast straight through the tight rank of the beasts, sending weapon fragments, alien body parts, and the blue mist of their blood into the swirling winds. Stoirm ran close on Adrian's heels, one of the Alainn's spells hissing past and sizzling into a reptilian torso as the Caspian moved from behind a jumble of broken chairs. The creature's wail screeched around the chamber on the wings of the storm, its body in the throes of violent spasms as it was whipped sideways.

Gesturing urgently, Adrian shouted to Fedel'ma, "Get Jase and get to Caer!" In answer, the woman grabbed Jase's arm and bolted, running as straight a path across the littered floor as the broken, splintered, and blasted remains of the room permitted.

That left Niall to locate. Adrian glanced anxiously around, finally catching sight of the boy a fair distance to the other side of Caer, his feet planted as he ducked various clouds of airborne shrapnel. The lad still bore Adrian's sword, the blade's edge dripping from its encounters. Near him lay the tattered bodies of a Renthorian and two Caspians.

Stoirm, his fiery spells protecting Fedel'ma and Jase from the weapon fire that rang out from several debris piles, shouted to Adrian. "Come! Now!"

"A moment more!" Adrian yelled back, sprinting for the boy.

Off to Adrian's right, Madadh/Ailill rose from behind the remains of one of the shattered bookshelves. The mixed magic of the two souls within the single body shot wildly about as the abomination attempted to charge Adrian, each of the dwellers within the hulk obviously vying for control. Adrian blasted a spell at the demonic duo without bothering to verify his accuracy. Grabbing Niall, he extended his shielding to protect the boy from some of the wind's fury, as well as from flying debris. Together, they raced to join the others.

Niall skidded through Dylan's blood before dropping to his backside in front of Caer. His clothes and hair whipped in the winds as he pushed to his knees and again raised the blade, gripping it in both hands and pointing it defiantly outward. Satisfied that the boy could hold steady, Adrian turned and aimed a full series of molten spells at various shambles of furnishings that were already smoldering from multiple strikes of both magic and weapon fire. They ignited in a conflagration that encircled the bedraggled group, sealing out Madadh and his men and beasts.

Protected, at least momentarily, behind the wall of flame, Adrian forced another impassioned plea. *"By everything you hold sacred, Caer, listen to me! The trick for magic is to calm your senses and focus on your intent. You must know your destination. Hold it in your head. Let Stoirm assist! He will show you the safest way to Slieve na Calliagh. Unless you wish to destroy us all, you must open your mind to him and focus on the vision he sends to you. And you must let me bind your efforts to those of us whose living souls stand with you. Do you understand? For the sake of us all, Caer, pull in your damned emotions and concentrate!"*

Again, he had no time to wait for any hint of understanding or acceptance. The shadows of several of Madadh's beasts were surging out from their places of shelter. Already, those bearing firearms were discharging them through the blaze.

Adrian felt Fedel'ma's magic flare as she threw renewed strength into another layer of protection around their small party. Her efforts freed him to sing out new spells, these defining the limits for Caer's teleportation. If Caer would just hear and heed him! Otherwise, the ever-growing power of her raw magic might well blast them all to a fine mist before Stoirm could get the image of their destination through to her. If destruction was to be their end, at least let them take Nemhain with them!

From somewhere beyond the deafening hell, Madadh's frenzied anger and frustration rose in a crazed bellow. And then there was silence---deep and long--smothered by the cool cocoon of Adrian's making. Not even the firestorm that now engulfed them gave a whisper. In the heavy stillness, the winds gradually receded and the great blaze retreated, diminishing until, at last, all that remained was a hazy swirl of gray smoke and thick mist.

53

Adrian braced for the eruption of sound as the last of the magic from the fire passage dissipated, the spell of his cocoon releasing. Still, the din that rang out--filled with the echoing crash of metal on metal, the discharge of firearms, explosive bursts, and the screams of the wounded and dying--stumbled him back a pace. So, too, came the reek of carnage, thick on the smoky mists that, for several seconds, shrouded them.

When the smoke cleared, the thin light of partially cloud-veiled stars and a high, slivered crescent moon lit the blackened and scorched trail that led to a translucent blue band as it retreated downslope from them. A quick glance suggested that the band ringed the whole of the great hill. Within it stirred the amorphous forms of wraiths. And just beyond them stretched a great battle, the leading edge pushing up against their undulating haze.

Aside from the patch of scorched ground upon which their small company had emerged, their surroundings were dotted with the scattered remains of burial mounds, clusters of sedges, and patches of reedy grasses. Adrian had no need to turn to know what lay behind and above him. For there, rose the ancient cairn. There, peril lurked. He sensed her eyes on them, the heat of her malice gnawing at his nerves. Nemhain.

The raw tension of her malevolent hatred did not surprise him. Her restraint did. The air buzzed with it. So eager, was she, for a kill.

Yet she waited. For what? Caer, the sister she harbors, and the key were precisely where Nemhain wanted them.

Taking advantage of Nemhain's reticence to attack, Adrian cast an anxious scan over the others with him. Emer remained on her knees, Dylan's head cradled in her lap. Sorrow etched across her grime and blood encrusted face. Much as he desired to erase her grief, he dared not, as yet.

Fedel'ma and Niall stood just beyond Emer, their wary attention fixed on the massive battle playing out beyond the ring of spirits. Niall still gripped the hilt of Adrian's sword, though its point now rested on the ground. Tired and fearful as the boy was, there remained an unwavering determination about him.

Stoirm appeared equally intent on what lay below. Caer, however, had wandered away from the others, Jase her somber shadow. Though she was up and moving rather than sprawled on the ground and comatose, as Adrian half expected to find her, her bedraggled, hunched, and dazed appearance did little to put his mind at ease. Ashen and hollow-eyed, she trembled in the drizzle, her confused gaze set on the muck that squished between her bare toes.

Jase reached a hand to her shoulder, urging her to sit. Instead, she stumbled a few more paces, wobbling to a halt near a tumble of stones that marked the remnants of one of the low burial mounds, regarding them as blankly as she had the mud. Finally, turning, her eyes followed the slope upward, to the great cairn.

"We're...we're here. We're on..." Her stammering trilled thin as water.

"Yeah," Jase grumbled. "We're back. Satisfied? Now sit down before you fall on your face."

Straightening slightly, she shifted enough to glance back at Adrian and Stoirm. "I was afraid," she murmured, her cheeks flushing beneath their gray cast as she met Stoirm's gaze. "Afraid that you might direct me to deliver us to...to some other place. Thank you. For guiding me here. It's where I'm meant to be."

Stoirm's scowl indicated he shared Adrian's gloomy misgivings.

With a resigned shrug, the Alainn replied, "You can thank Tine, should the opportunity ever present itself." Pointing, he added, "And those specters."

Adrian again glanced down at the bright ring. Magic swirled within their lapis light, raising series after series of eddies, the buzz and thrum of the spells cast by the phantoms mixing with the incessant thundering echo of the battle that battered against them.

"They allowed us passage clear of the fighting," Adrian acknowledged, turning at last to face the cairn. "But we are not without threat." For a moment, a thick patch of clouds moved across the slivered moon, blotting out its pale light. Yet she stood out--a darker silhouette against the night sky. As the clouds passed, the waning moon's light reflected off the long cloak that draped her, shimmering silver-violet. Though her features were hidden, her eyes studied him. Her heated and hostile scrutiny throbbed along his nerves, her rage that they had come through when her minions could not and the manner of their arrival was clear in his mind.

Nemhain's lack of ability with fire galled her. The more so when Adrian had, from his earliest childhood, shown tremendous talent with many of its attributes, including the ability to use the fire passage. It was nothing short of blasphemous, to her mind. She, a daughter of Tar On Tine and Samhradh, should possess the gift. She, the daughter of the Alainn whose gift with fire was extraordinary, even among his own people. She, the daughter of Samhradh, the first human ever to display more skill than the ability to make the flames dance. Dana and Roisin each held some part of their parent's fire gifts, yet she was blessed with none. The greatest sin, however, was that he, a mere cousin, possessed such a significant degree of the magic. It was a sin for which Nemhain would never forgive him.

The sense of her probing edged along his mind, cautious and shallow. If she pressed too deeply, she risked revealing her own thoughts and strengths...as well as her weaknesses. Her efforts lasted but a second. Concerned that she had turned her mental scrutiny on others of their company, Adrian raised a silent song, strengthening and adjusting a spell of shielding to protect Jase and the three women. Stoirm was capable of warding off any probe the Dark Heart might attempt of him. The others, exhausted by their unending tribulations, were vulnerable.

"Amhranai." Stoirm nodded toward the massive clash below. Adrian turned to follow the line of his friend's gesture, noting for the first time how the chaotic shadows of frenzied fighting stretched out well beyond Slieve na Calliagh and the near valley to cover the whole of the night-shrouded landscape, bursts of magic and weapon fire illuminating the darkness like fireworks. Down into the valleys and up and over the heavily fog-tendrilled shoulders of neighboring hills, the battle rang, flashes of light offering brief glimpses of the crimsoned earth beneath the creeping sprawl of combatants. Everywhere there was fighting and blood and dying.

"Croi Breag must believe she is about to win all. Why marshal her legions if she did not consider this to be the time of reckoning?"

Even as Stoirm's anxious words touched Adrian's mind, a terrible itch crept over him, his body thrumming with surges of fear, doubt, hope, determination...and purpose. The emotions driving his descendants into action carried to him, their thoughts telling him the masses, Witch and Tanai alike, were answering Tine's call to arms.

Adrian's fists clenched. Stoirm was right. Though Nemhain seemed, for the moment, reluctant to strike on her own, she appeared confident that victory would be hers. For the voices of his descendants also told him that her battle lay not just here, but her command had gone out, declaring war within every Earth dome, upon every major ship, and in every off-world colony. The whole of humanity's realm was besieged.

Adrian's weighted silence, at last, attracted Jase to his side. With a nervous jerk of his head toward the bright ring, the Tanai ventured an uneasy, "Just what the hell is that? How is it keeping the bloodbath from overtaking us, and how long do you think it will stand?"

Time and again, the battle swarmed and broke violently against the bright barrier, its light fluctuating with each thunderous blow. Within it, the wraiths continued their ever-skittering dance of spell casting, setting new eddies in motion to replace those that faded and died. Stunned realization jolted Adrian as the faded and ragged signatures of the apparitions slowly impinged on his awareness. "They are the guardians!" he breathed. "These are the souls who followed us out of the maze."

They should not be here. A grievous, gnawing hunger for the solidity of flesh, for the ability to move again within the warm, pulsing, breathing realm of the living drove every bodiless spirit. To deny the sating of that hunger, to bind themselves as cold and fleshless guardians to the labyrinth, had been a terrible sacrifice; one carried out only by those Witches with the greatest magic and the gravest hatred for Nemhain, and held only by means of Dana's spells binding them to their cause. Their release from that last of the ancient passageways should have scattered them in tortured and ravenous pursuit of the freshly deceased bodies so long denied them.

Adrian shook his head. "I don't understand why they are here."

In answer, a single voice, delicate as a wisp of silken thread, slipped quietly through his consciousness.

"Our oaths were spoken to the Two, Lord Amhranai Fearalite. Nor shall we abandon Them in the hour of Their return. We sensed the Dark Heart's gathering forces; knew there was no time to seek new flesh, no matter our craving. Though without solid form we can lift no weapon, nor focus any spell directly against our ancient foe, our magic is yet sufficient to keep Croi Breag's demons from Their backs...for a time. But know this, my lord. Our strength will hold for only a small while longer. You must call out the Two. Call out the Sleepers that they may fight to defeat the Mistress of Calamity while she yet stands alone."

The subtle paling of their light was already noticeable. The ring was weakening. Adrian was sure Nemhain was aware, as well. It was their will alone that held these fading spirits to this last cause, though the incessant battle that crashed against them diminished their strength with every blow.

More incredible than the persistence of these wraiths, however, was the suggestion of the presence of both sisters. 'Nor shall we abandon Them in the hour of Their return." The specters had sensed Roisin's presence within the labyrinth. But Dana's as well? If Dana was, indeed, here, who...

Adrian sucked in, fighting the urge to spin and stare, forcing to silence the stream of expletives that raced to his tongue. A million times an imbecile he was for not figuring it out from the first! How better to guarantee that the two sisters would reunite before their waking but to hide one of them within the family of the man who set them in their slumber--the very man who would also be required to release them from it?

Adrian shook himself. The time of reckoning was, indeed, at hand. There was no question that Earth was ready. Once again, she possessed a life-sustaining breath. Once again, life was being coaxed from seeds set within her soils. Wiping the drizzle from his face, he shot a glance skyward. Even the night was right--from the fog that crept across the land, to the mist, to the angled tip of the high, crescent moon. Aside from the current war being waged around them, everything was as it had been on the night of the gateway's creation, just as Roisin had foreseen it would be. This was the night that abundance might be restored to their world.

Might. Abundance might be returned. Roisin had proclaimed it with that very word in her long-ago foreseeing, though on the night the three had joined their powers together to set the possibility in motion, neither she nor her sisters...nor he...paid heed to the chance of failure. Not until Nemhain's jealousies and delusions of grandeur led to her treachery, did any of them consider the potential for a darker outcome. Now, the vile prospect hung like a black abyss around them. There was but one chance for success. It had to happen this night; had to be accomplished just as the wraiths said--while the Dark Heart stood alone.

"Dream Reader!" Adrian pressed through his spell of concealment, driving at the wounded soul within it. *"You must fulfill your oath! Wake the two who sleep!"* There followed, however, not the faintest glimmer of a stir. The soul required more time to recover--time that stood to benefit Nemhain, not them.

The sense of motion and the clatter of tumbling stones snapped Adrian's attention back to the dark cairn. Nemhain had at last begun edging her way down the steep curve, the shimmer of her cloak moving eerily against the heavy gray of earth and rock and the blackness of shadow. Though the footing was both damp and loose, she moved with grace, finally coming to rest on the stone lintel above the tomb's narrow, gaping entrance.

Hidden within the folds and the deep hood of her silver-violet wrap, she seemed as much specter as the wraiths below. Adrian knew her vanity and narcissism well, though. She would not remain concealed for long. True to his estimation, and with a grand flourish, Nemhain flipped the front edges of her cloak back, the gusting breezes catching and flaring them to present a glittering backdrop to her dark gossamer gown. So deep a purple was it that it verged on bruised black, the sheen glistening against the subtle olive tones of her bare arms and the swell of her ample breasts where they threatened to burst from the scooped neckline. A silver cord cinched her narrow waist, the delicate drape of her gown highlighting the curve of her hips. Below the hips, the fabric fluttered seductively between and around her long legs, skimming the tops of her slippered feet. Here, stood an almost perfectly crafted duplicate of Nemhain's original body.

"What a sorry lot you make," brushed through Adrian's skull, carrying with it the impression of mixed wariness and impatient bloodlust.

"Less sorry than you, if you think to entice anyone to your cause with your vain display."

Nemhain threw back her hood with a growl. Her elegantly slim face and proud cheekbones, the v-shaped mouth, the thin and delicately upturned nose and almond-shaped eyes bore a striking resemblance to her sisters. But there remained equally striking differences. Where Dana and Roisin had been pale of skin, Nemhain's glistened with darker tones. Where her sisters had inherited their mother's diminutive frame, Nemhain inherited the tall and stately stature of their Alainn father. So, too, her raven black hair set her apart, coming from Samhradh's father's line, while Dana and Roisin's had the deep, golden red of their maternal grandmother.

Nemhain prided herself on every feature that distinguished her from her sisters. The one thing she begrudge them was the fact that they inherited their father's pointed ears, while she inherited her mother's merely human ones.

"I have no need to entice you, cousin! Nor any among the rabble who stand with you."

Any retort Adrian might consider was lost; his startled gaze caught suddenly by Nemhain's eyes. They should be sapphire. At first glance, their new color seemed no more than a trick of the thin light. Only now, as he met her gaze full on, did he realize there was not the faintest suggestion of blue to their glow. Rather, they shone with the same iced silver-violet iridescence as her cloak.

Such a change should not be possible. Though altering eye color was not a tremendous feat, it required the existence of the desired hue within the genes of the host. This...this was wholly unnatural.

The sodden gusts teased at Nemhain's long, dark hair, flicking it across her face as she regarded him, contempt thinning her silver-painted lips to a chill smile. *"Ah, my dear Amhranai. You see only one small sampling of my most recently acquired gift."*

For less than an instant, her eyes flicked to jet, their shape flowing from almond to abnormally large and triangular. In that same fraction of a heartbeat, her flesh reddened to the deepest fuchsia, her tall frame stooping and further elongating into something feline. The changes both occurred and returned to Nemhain's all too familiar and disturbingly radiant visage, in the span of Adrian's gasp. *"I am become shape-shifter,"* rippled gleefully across his scrambled thoughts.

That no one else reacted left Adrian momentarily doubting what he'd witnessed. Perhaps it was a trick of the mind--a projected image rather than a physical change. Not that it mattered in the end. If she could make him see her as she wished, she could do the same to others. What terror might she strike, simply by assuming or projecting the image of some grotesque beast? Whose trust might she gain by taking on the appearance of a loved one?

With a languorous sweep of her hand, Nemhain gestured toward Slieve na Calliagh's lower slopes and all that stretched out around them. "Welcome, cousin," she proclaimed, the thick sweetness of her tone rising like honey to coat the battle din. "Welcome to Hell."

"Only to its first level." Giving a curt nod toward the circle of blue light, Adrian derided, "The same level as has sealed you here, unable to call your hounds to your side."

The feel of Nemhain's fury flared anew, yet she failed to act on the taunt. Dismissing him with a snarl, she shifted her attention pointedly to the others, her saccharine voice lifting once more as her eyes settled on Caer. "Ah. And here is your little pet, I believe. Barely a waif of a thing, is she not? Little wonder that you enjoyed bedding her, cousin. She is the very image of your beloved."

The truth of her words bit deep. Tensing, Adrian glanced anxiously to Caer, but the dig seemed not to register with her. Instead, Caer's recognition of Nemhain's cloying tones rang through her mind.

The sweetness thinned as Nemhain eyed Caer with irritation. "You certainly are a troublesome waif, succeeding for too long in escaping my hunts and hiding from me. Succeeded, as well, in concealing the fact that you carried more than just a piece of the key. That much, at least, I suspected from the moment my fool spies failed to find the piece among your parents' remains and further failed to discover any indication that you had perished with them. It was not difficult to surmise that your parents managed to send you away at the last instant, and the piece of the key with you. Very cunning of them, and annoyingly time-consuming for me, trying to find you again."

Her words took on an ever-darker pique as she continued. "The fact that you also host one of my sisters...that came as a bit of news I'd not anticipated. That one of them would be insane enough to trust her soul to a mere Uair Amhain..." Disgust shook her.

Flicking a molten glare at Adrian, she asserted, "The child could never have led Madadh or Maura such a prolonged chase had she not had help. Still, my Dog and my daughter's perseverance paid off. Even you cannot prevail against my efforts indefinitely."

Her frigid gaze hardened as she returned it to Caer. "Imagine my shock when I detected your mat-trans flight from Bestor and reached out to you, seeking to obtain information concerning the piece of key you held. Reached out and sensed a most familiar presence. Sadly, so brief was the occurrence that I could not be certain which of my dear sisters I detected; nor even whether you were, in fact, the bearer. It was possible that some other Witch near to the path of your travel had recently shed her body, thereby exposing the Sleeper they had borne."

Her tone further soured as she jabbed a finger toward Adrian. "The girl's soul was mine for the taking. Hers and, as it turns out, whichever of my siblings is bound to her, along with the piece of key she held. Mine for the taking, had it not been for your constant meddling interference, driving me back!" Her face screwed into a mask of deadly intent as she swung her hands forward, aiming her palms at Adrian.

Having anticipated her, Adrian was already poised to meet her attack; Stoirm and Fedel'ma leaped to his side, likewise set with palms aimed. Nemhain froze, holding her position for several long heartbeats as she studied Fedel'ma. Gradually, her stance relaxed her voice going smooth and sugared once more. "No matter," she purred, lowering her arms. "No matter. The girl is here, now, along with her Sleeper and the whole of the key."

With a disdainful huff, she submitted, "You are a weakling and a fool, Amhranai, letting this child drag you here, knowing what she possesses. I can almost feel the phantoms of uneasy dreams stirring through the sister that lies within her. For I'm sure my sweet sibling feels my presence. I'll see that her dreams are nightmares in earnest before she wakes."

Passing a glance once more at Fedel'ma, Nemhain turned to Emer, sullenly musing, "What I am left to ponder is the question of which of the two of you hides my remaining sister."

Adrian stiffened. Insane the bitch might be, but she was not stupid; certainly not as slow-witted as he'd been. He could only wonder when she realized that one of these women was the second host, though she seemed, as yet, undecided as to which it might be. For their part, both Fedel'ma and Emer were stunned by the supposition. Dana, it appeared, was better at keeping her dreams buried.

Of the two, Fedel'ma seemed the most likely in Adrian's first moments of understanding. The pod explosion, however, would have exposed Dana's soul as it and Fedel'ma's were ripped from the body. Fleeting as that exposure might be, both he and Nemhain would have sensed it.

Feeling the Dark Heart's eyes on him yet again, Adrian returned the scrutiny with a dissembling shrug and empty scowl. She likely knew nothing of the incident with Fedel'ma's pod. And she'd learn nothing from him.

"A pity," Nemhain sighed. "You're as useless as ever, though you're not such a moron as to fail to discover what this wretched, unschooled child holds. A shame you let the waif lead you around by the nose, Amhranai. Otherwise, you might have prevented her dragging you here before waking my half-witted sisters."

Her brow creased as she regarded him more intensely "Or, perhaps the problem isn't a matter of your foolishness so much as a matter of your failing powers. After all these centuries, after all the effort poured into protecting humanity's pitiful and powerless, perhaps, dear cousin, your magic is stretched too thin; has become too weak for you to control your little ward."

Adrian's hands raised, his palms leveled at Nemhain for a second time. "Shall we test that theory--cousin?"

Again, Stoirm and Fedel'ma reacted with him, their hands taking aim. Nemhain, however, refused to meet their challenge. At least now, Adrian understood why. She dared not kill her sisters' hosts. Not until she worked out a way of capturing the Sleepers' souls.

Stoirm sizzled a spell off Nemhain's shielding, his way of determining the degree to which she was protected. The loud, hissing zing indicated her shielding was undertaken with great care and strength. The attack, however, drew hungry eyes to the Alainn, the honey of her voice growing husky. "Looking for my attention, my love? I am sorry I've paid you so little heed. Pests do tend to get in the way of pleasure. I've not failed to read your pain and deep sorrow, though. Has your wife abandoned you, then, here in the final hour?"

"She's dead, her soul banished!" Emer growled. "But you know that, already, I'll wager."

Adrian started at Emer's sudden outburst. Venturing a darted glance her way, he found the Healer's head down-turned, her hand resting gently on Dylan's bloodied chest.

"Truly?" The violet within Nemhain's eyes deepened with her mirth. "Oh my. I am sorry for your loss, of course, my sweet Stoirm. But it does eliminate my competition. And who do we thank for this turn of events?"

Emer raised her head, the blue-black depths of her eyes glowing with the heat of her loathing.

"Ah!" Nemhain grinned. "Yes. Of course. It was the work of my son and my husband, I believe."

"You can thank them, as well," Emer spat, "for destroying the only chance of properly waking either of your sisters. Your dear husband and son, you see, murdered the Master Dream Reader, as well, and banished his soul. You've lost, hag, and you don't even know it."

"Hag!" Nemhain hissed. "Hag! I'll..." Glancing between Emer and Fedel'ma, her tone took on disdain as she offered an oddly lilting nod toward Dylan's body. "This sorry excuse of a Witch for whom you grieve is nothing! I might have made use of him, of course. I never waste a decent talent when it falls into my lap. But aggrieved by the folly of my Dog and my son in this loss, I'm not. I have Masters of my own."

"Indeed!" Adrian snorted. "And which of them is the equal to the one who cast the original spells, setting your sisters in their long sleep? Call forth your experts, if you can. Even if you manage to draw them past the ring, you'll find their magic insufficient to your cause. There is none within your lineage with the capacity to reach through the incantations woven by this man. As the lady stated, the ability to wake your sisters is lost, along with the secret for opening the gateway. Your most dearly and desperately held aspirations are no longer possible."

How much truth lay within his words, Adrian didn't know, though he suspected Emer's claims to be accurate enough. Waking her sisters, however, was not the Dark Heart's only option for victory. If she murdered the hosts and captured both the slumbering souls, she might find a way to force what she needed from them by way of torturing their dreams. Short of that, she could bind them as bodiless prisoners until their tormented spirits faded and vanished. Perhaps the gateway would survive their deaths. Perhaps not. His only option, however, was to keep the bitch off balance; buy more time for the Dream Reader to recover.

"You're at quite the disadvantage," he declared. "You cannot wake your sisters. Cannot set yourself at the gateway's center, as you planned to do the moment they revealed and opened the way. Therefore, you cannot use the way to destroy them and all they hoped to accomplish. Nor can you claim the gateway's powers for yourself. You can try to take their souls, of course. But you can't take them both at the same time. Wait for the battle to overwhelm us, and you risk at least one of them escaping or being destroyed before you get what you want from her. Try to take either of them now, and you have to fight us, again risking the loss of at least one of your sisters."

That Nemhain flinched gave Adrian some small measure of hope. Still, once the wraiths' no longer cut her off, Nemhain could telepath to those at the forefront of the battle that the three women must be taken alive and removed from the battlefield.

"Dream Reader!" Adrian pressed once more. *"The Sleepers are both with us! You must wake them, now! Wake them together!"*

Nemhain stared at Dylan's lifeless body for several long moments, her countenance darkening as she grasped what his death had cost her. At last, her outrage exploded, the air all about the hill's crest lurching, stirring the strands of fog and clouds in blackening whorls as she screeched, "Idiots! Ailill! Madadh! Attend me! Now!"

In answer, great sparks ignited along the lapis ring and arched far up over the cairn. The wraiths were resisting Nemhain's attempts to command her husband and son to her side.

"Dream Reader," Adrian pressed for a third time. *"You must act!"* And for a third time, he went unanswered.

Nemhain's still mounting rage poured into a blinding flash that crashed against the glimmering wraiths. At the point of contact, the light distorted and thinned. Yet it held--for now.

With increasing desperation, Adrian persisted. *"Dream Reader! You must execute the Awakening! There is no time left for us. Do it! Now!"*

Faintly, it came.

Slumber binds you. Passion sustains you. Heed, now, the spell of unbinding.

A quick glance at the body indicated no movement. No sign of life. Emer, however, fell back, shock and desperate hope widening her eyes. Weak as he was, the Reader had responded, drawing from Slieve na Calliagh's deep-running magic to strengthen his own. And Emer had detected it. Adrian would offer further strength to the struggling soul, but dared not relinquish his concealment of it to do so. He had to keep Nemhain ignorant of the Reader's state for as long as possible.

Still standing on the lintel, the Dark Heart was summoning

power for another strike at the ring of light, her efforts drawing together and thickening the clouds overhead until they blotted out the stars and moon. All the while, the bloody mayhem below them continued to batter at the fading specters.

Stoirm and Fedel'ma, determined to block Nemhain's efforts, hurled attack after attack, their spells shattering in charged sparks against the Dark Heart's shielding. They needed Adrian's attack as well. He, however, maintained his concealment of the Dream Reader, allowing the man to shape his spell.

A swirl of mist stirred around Caer, Emer, and the Reader's body.

By the air that breathes life within thee, heed my summons.

The air crackled. Nemhain, so intent on breaking the ring of wraiths, either took no notice or assumed it to be the result of her own efforts. Adrian prayed the spell of Awakening would complete while Nemhain remained preoccupied.

By the water of the blood that gives thee passion, heed my summons.

By the fires of strength born unto thee, heed my summons.

By power bright in deep of night, I set thee in thy sleep.

The force of Nemhain's fury hammered the ring again. A large section of the blue light blinked out, sending tumultuous spasms through the remainder of the circle. Then other sections blinked out. The wraiths were breached.

So now to break, with strength to take,

I bid thee wake.

The surge of the Dream Reader's spell rushed the whole of Slieve na Calliagh's upper slope in an outward expanding tidal wave of energy, for a moment driving back the battle that threatened to erupt through the fractured ring of light.

Nemhain's wild eyes snapped back to Emer, her enraged scream all but drowning out the sounds of the surrounding war. "You lied! He lives!"

54

It was too much too fast--all the visions that had long haunted Caer's dreams, all the half-recalled memories clinging to the darkest corners of her unconsciousness, a thousand-fold flashes of places and events she could not name--all bursting over her like a great wave over a crumbling seawall. She would surely drown in such a rush! The visions churned together, every aspect of her past tangling with the myriad lifetimes that belonged to the soul newly awakened.

Fighting for her breath, Caer sought for a single focus, a familiar moment to act as a lifeline. But the image that frothed to the surface threatened to drown her anew. Sidra's death. It stood more prominent, now, than it had ever done, either in her dreams or her unsettled day visions. Never again would she forget the jolting touch of her fingers against her aunt's burning flesh or the shock of sensing two separate souls contained within her aunt's body. Pain seared through her mind as, once more, the tortured and rapidly fading glow of her aunt's soul seized her mind, this time accompanied with the icy rending of the banishing as it attached to Sidra, slowly shredding her very essence with merciless brutality.

Through the agony and anguish, Caer recalled the flash of foreboding that overwhelmed even her grief and terror on that horrific night. The very spell devouring Sidra would soon destroy the second essence that thrummed wildly within the confines of her aunt's writhing body. Sidra was beyond her help, but she might yet save this other spirit.

Crying out, Caer called it to her, swearing to hide and protect it. And for a brief instant, in the binding of the soul to her, Caer glimpsed the identity of the spirit she'd rescued. Dana, it named itself, eldest of the three ancient sisters, the flood of her dreams sweeping Caer with the soul's long and disturbing history. From the joys and promise of childhood to the grievous injuries that dictated her need for long concealment, and every moment between- -centuries upon centuries washed through Caer's mind before, in that distant moment, being swept away by some enchantment. Now, however, every memory of this soul's long life held strong.

Caer's gasp strangled in her shallow, halting breath. Their souls. Every memory of their souls. The identities...the memories of two alien spirits battered against her own. Dana. Hard. Angry. Filled with deadly purpose. And...

"Shhhh, my sister. I am here, as well. Calm yourself lest you panic our sweet host."

This was the presence Caer expected, the voice soft and sorrowful. Caer's every fiber thrummed with its energy, calming...soothing the fury of the other. Two distinct energies. She hosted both the sisters. But how and when...

Fighting past the overload of imagery and sensations, back through her past, she searched. Dana's soul she took from her aunt. But when did she obtain the other?

Back and back she pressed until she discovered a moment that held no visual construct. Yet the impressions were clear - the touch, the warmth, the sorrow tinged with hope. This was the bright spirit she'd encountered while still in her mother's womb. This was Roisin's soul. Her presence had stirred within Caer the first glimmer of the gift of foresight. Caer's gift. And through that emerging prescience came the conviction that this gentle soul who lay in uneasy slumber next to her mother's was not safe where it rested. As she had done later, drawing Dana's soul from her aunt, so she did with Roisin's, calling to it her with the innocence of her heart, taking it within, swearing to protect it. So, too, on that occasion, came the rush of Roisin's memories, only to vanish within a heartbeat.

"We are sorry." Roisin's silent words came, heavily weighted with testament to their truth. *"It was never our desire that you should bear the full brunt of our lives. Nor was it our intent that you know what you must face, now. You were to sleep at the time of our Awakening, letting our lives wash over your dreams, coloring them, perhaps, but nothing more. Separating ourselves from you would have been easier, had you slept. Your death would be quick and painless. As only by your death can we depart your body. We would have cushioned your soul's departure, freeing you to seek another vessel, just as we must do."*

The voice of Dana pushed forward, tense and urgent. *"It grieves us much to bring you such death while you are so young, child. But it must be so. If we do not act now, Nemhain will take us. By your death, at least, you may find a better life."*

The charged energy of magic flared within her. The nature of the spell she recognized from Sidra's Book of Secrets, though her aunt had never drawn up on it. Here stirred a kill spell. Rare was the Witch willing to turn such destructive power inward on the vessel that hosted them, as the likelihood of success without damaging their own psyche was tremendous. This, Caer glimpsed from the still thundering breakers of memories crashing against her mind. Dana and Roisin, however, in their desperation, were about to attempt that very delicate balance. The spell was near its full potential when the shock of another truth lifted abruptly from the underlying tumult.

"But you need a physical form!" Caer pressed at them. *"For you to open the way and to defeat Nemhain, you need to be contained within a physical vessel. Otherwise, your powers are too diffuse. They cannot be properly focused."*

Thinned by the firming of the spell, Roisin's response sounded faint and reedy. *"Indeed. But that is no longer your burden to bear. There is another here who long ago committed to such a task for this time and place. Once your soul is free, flee as far and fast as you can manage."*

"Amhranai. Adrian." The naming of the oath-giver leaped to

Caer's mind. His was the body they intended to use. Instantly, Caer sought for him; realized he stood behind her, his supporting hands at her waist, Emer standing at his side.

"Amhranai." The dual souls acknowledged. *"We need his strength."*

Caer did not doubt Adrian's willing acceptance of this sacrifice. The prickling of her prescience, though, warned her it would mean his death. Would mean the banishment of his soul.

"My powers may not be as great as his, but they are yours to use. Work through me," Caer returned, not as a command, but as a plea.

"You still do not know yourself, child," Roisin whispered through her sorrow. *"Your strength is great. But we can ask no more of you. Your oaths are fulfilled. Death will allow you to seek a new host; will give you new life. Let us do this while Nemhain remains uncertain as to where her second sister hides. Once she understands where we both reside, she will cast a spell to ensnare our souls, even as she destroys yours. Let us free you, child. Live again. Learn what you are capable of. Use your gifts for others."*

The last syllables of Nemhain's, "You lied! He lives!" reverberated through Roisin's quiet offering, granting to Caer the stunned realization that everything, from the moment of the Awakening to this very instant, had occurred in the time taken by Nemhain's outraged scream.

The sense of urgency from the souls she harbored redoubled. Still, Caer balked, fighting to hold the intensity of their spell at bay. There was no guarantee her soul would survive. Many Uair Amhain failed to return following the death of their body. The memories entwined with hers confirmed as much. She understood, too, that unless Dana and Roisin were successful, the survival of her soul would mean nothing. Nemhain would seek her out; would destroy her, just as she would destroy all who stood in her way.

Setting her jaw, Caer persisted. *"If whatever powers I possess are sufficient to your cause, I pledge them to you. Act through me. Tell me what I must do."*

Dana's reply was instantaneous. *"Withdraw. If you mean to do this. You must grant us command of your body."*

Terror raked Caer. What had she just promised? To relinquish her essence to their command?

"Not yourself," Roisin soothed. *"We will not rule your soul, only the ability of your body to act. If it is truly your wish to assist us in Amhranai's stead, then you must relax your mind. Let your senses meld with ours. You must do this, now, or you must let us complete our spell."*

Breathing in deeply, Caer attempted to calm and quiet her thoughts. For Adrian's sake. For the sake of all the others who sacrificed and would continue to sacrifice themselves to keep her safe. Her fingers twitched as she fought the doubt that skimmed beneath her resolve. One, two, three short breaths. Her shoulders slumped as she worked to turn her focus inward, relaxing her senses, giving her will for action over to the souls that were not her own.

The sensation that washed through her was a sort of diminishing while the sisters' presence strengthened. Impressions of her surroundings hazed, taking on the aspect of a dream. Someone else's dream. Words were spoken. They flowed past her lips, but not with her voice. It was Roisin's that lifted above the battle din.

"You wanted us, Sister. We are here."

From behind her, came Adrian's stunned gasp. *"You were to flee. They were to use me!"*

Bewilderment flicked across Nemhain's face before shock set her back a pace, her fury struck dumb. Eyes narrowed, she leaned forward, appearing almost reptilian as she tested the air for a scent. "It's true!" she gaped. "Both of you! Contained in this..."

Her gaze darted to Dylan, who sat, now, leaning weakly against Fedel'ma. "I'll admit," Nemhain sneered. "Your act was well done, Dream Reader. How you managed to conceal your living essence from me I'll not pretend to guess. It's obvious, however, that your soul is stretched quite thin by your efforts. My warriors will soon enough snuff it out in earnest." A malicious smile lifted the corners of her lips. "Though I thank you for delivering my sisters waking souls to me."

Straightening, she cast a reappraising eye over Caer. "I assumed you would not suffer too much distance to come between you, Sisters. I did not think you would be so stupid as to trust both your souls to a single host." Her brow pinched in a disdain matched by her too-sweet tone. "And an Uair Amhain, at that. A first born! How broken your powers must be to attract no stronger aid than an ineffectual child."

The battle closed more tightly around their clustered group, the tumult of screams and clanging, the smell of blood and death growing ever more pressing. So close was Adrian, now that the anxious beating of his heart drummed against Caer's back as the warmth of his tensed breathing fluttered her damp hair. For but a second her gaze scanned to the others who were near. Though he remained pale as death, Dylan was now on his feet, he and Del flanking Niall; mother and son braced, arms outstretched, palms aimed toward the steadily encroaching mêlée. So, too, Niall stood, Adrian's sword still in his hands, its point once more raised and held steady. In front of Caer, Bran nervously swept his gun back and forth while Stoirm moved into position on the opposite side of Adrian from Emer.

Tine was also near. The crisp call of his voice carried through the tumult. Occasional bursts of firearms erupted in the distance, the tightness of battle now leaving swords to rule where there was room to swing them, knife and hand-to-hand combat prevailing where sword thrust and sweep grew impossible. Even those wielding magic dared not to do so in such confined quarters, lest the clash of magic off of magic blast every caster apart.

Nemhain's face brightened as she watched from the safety of her lintel roost. "The protection afforded you by your friends is crumbling, Sisters. You cannot hold against the whole of my armies. Show me the gateway. Open it and perhaps I'll call them off. Maybe even let your friends live. Perhaps I will feel magnanimous enough to direct my armies to turn from their slaughter to the taking of slaves."

"Deceitful as ever," rumbled from Caer, its originator Dana. "You have no intention of letting any of us survive this. Not even your beloved Stoirm."

Nemhain hissed, passing the Alainn a final lustful glance. "Him I would save if he chooses to stand at my side."

If Stoirm gave reply, Caer did not hear, her senses overwhelmed by a flush of heat that began at the base of her stomach. Power was again being drawn inward, the heat rising as the power grew. No kill spell, this, though its purpose was unclear. Around her, mists changed to a steady drizzle, lifting faint curls of steam from her body. In the chill and the wet, even with the frigid mud coating her feet, she felt only the burning of the power inside her.

Again, her gaze cast about, this time seeking beyond the tight ranks of her protectors. In hazy detachment, she watched the encompassing battle, unable to guess how many thousands of warriors clashed. Nearer, Tine and a small contingent of Alainn at last burst through the front of the chaos, bracing themselves at the outer edge of the shielding magic maintained by Stoirm, Emer, Del, and Dylan. There they hacked with sword and spell at any enemy who attempted to breach the shielding, while Adrian kept vigilant watch over their nemesis on the cairn.

And still the heat grew.

Perhaps Nemhain had become aware of the rising power. Holding to her perch, her eyes anxiously scoured the front curve of the great mound. Finding nothing, she cast further afield, seeking eagerly among the clusters of blood-drenched boulders around and over which human and alien alike were fighting and dying.

A vague satisfaction brushed Caer's mind. Nemhain would not find what she sought until Dana revealed it. The gateway would manifest wherever Dana willed it, so long as it remained in the confines of the uniquely potent magical field that encompassed Slieve na Calliagh. Nemhain never understood that. She believed the gateway required a solid surface, like that of the great cairn, or perhaps one of the standing rock faces. There was another aspect Nemhain failed to grasp, as well. While Dana held the power to determine the location of the gateway and Roisin the power to open it, the two were not sufficient to initiate the task.

"You must speak the spell, Sister," Roisin called. "The key is rejoined. You must offer the chant to call up its purpose."

Confusion flashed once more across Nemhain's face. "Me?" Her eyes widened. "Me! I created the spell to bind the gateway to its purpose. For all your 'great and wonderful' skills, you cannot act without me."

Weary resentment colored Dana's retort. "Nor you without us. We are grateful to Amhranai's song for concealing knowledge of the requirements from you until this moment."

Murderous contempt flooded Nemhain's countenance as she darted her outraged glare back to Adrian. "You! That was why you wooed me all those long ages ago? Why you agreed, at last, to come to my bed and sing your sweet songs? To weave concealments in my head? Was your bedding me no more than illusion then? Did you merely make me believe you lay with me while you wove your treacherous spells?"

"The bedding," Adrian snarled, "was real enough, though it burned like venom in my veins. Courting you, bedding you...they were the only way to get close enough to sing you my spells. As for treacherous, do not speak to me of treacherous. You were the one to break oath; to attempt the murder of your own sisters."

"Venom!" Nemhain's face went florid with her rage. "Let me show you venom!"

With a sweeping flourish of her hands, thunder rolled across the sky, Nemhain's command booming with it. "Maura! Ailill! Madadh! To me! See what glory I hold! At last I can bring an end to our foes!"

Maura responded at once, the wraiths no longer barring her way. Her sudden materialization on the great mound just above her mother, however, came with less grandiosity than she might have wished, her booted feet slipping in the wet grasses and mud, thereby requiring an awkward scramble to gain a solid footing. The cowering and grotesque form of Madadh/Ailill joined mother and daughter only reluctantly, finding a reasonable purchase on the sloping mound near Maura. Their cowering gave way to seething as the abomination's gaze came to rest on Dylan. Straightening, the misshapen hulk pointed with a fury-trembling hand at the Dream Reader. "Take the key from them," the dual-souls growled to Nemhain. "Kill them all save that one! Let us shrivel him to dust!"

Adrian's arms tightened around Caer's waist. *"This was not yours to take on, Caer. Know this. I am with you. I will do all in my power to see that you survive."*

"May my magic be sufficient to my oath," Emer murmured. "For I swore to protect the bearer of the key."

Del gave a faint nod. "As did I."

Nemhain's palms leveled on the group, the glow of her eyes turned to sapphire and reflecting the intensity of her hatred and malice. "With the key here, in my presence, I've no more need of you."

Satisfaction brushed Caer again as Roisin acknowledged, "Yours is the power of the chant of the gateway's purpose. But you cannot set it firmly upon our world or demand its opening. For that you need our spells, our strength, and Amhranai's song to bind them. You know the truth of my words, Sister. Together, the four of us created the way. And though Dana, Amhranai, and I hid it, we require the four powers to open it again."

Somewhere through the distance of rolling hills emerged the echo of pipes and drums, the cadence distinct, though the melody remained buried in the clash and tortured screams of war. One, two, three, four, five, six, seven. One, two, three. One, two, three. Whether the sound was real or borne on the ghosts of age-old memories, Caer couldn't say--until Adrian's hushed song also brushed her mind.

Come join together, pow'rs old,
Fix the spells as they told.
Heath and dance with magic fold,
Pow'r gained, now must hold.
Fairy realm of magic mists
To Slievgall'ion life affix.
Take us, show us, let us see
Abundant beauty, ever be.

The song repeated, aloud, this time. From deep within Caer's mind, a vision arose, revealing a great blaze lifting skyward on a burial mound-strewn hillside. In the shadows to one side hung the tall, dark silhouette of a man, bodhran in hand, the lyrics flowing from him, while around the fire danced three sky-clad women. The rhythm drove them, the song stirring the flames ever higher.

The subtle suggestion of yet another chant began to weave subtly in and out of the song, the indistinguishable words seeming to come from only one of the dancing women, her dark hair swirling round her as she lifted her voice in time with her measured tread. As the chant's rhythm melded into the music, a diffuse glow throbbed from the two silent dancers. The illumination emanating from the pair brightened, their dance coming to a halt before the faint, crystalline outline of an arched doorway that appeared against the wall of the great cairn behind them.

This, Caer realized, was the original forging of the bridge that lay between worlds--the gateway between Earth and a place the sisters named Slievgall'ion. It required the compelling force of Adrian's song and the sisters' dance to unite their energies and their purpose for that first opening. But open the way, they did, and through it the sisters went, to this new place to witness the burgeoning life being created from the very essence of Earth. Through the gateway, too, they returned, hopeful that Earth's abundance would remain safe, protected in that other world from the scourge of centuries to come.

As the vision flashed and disappeared, the heat of the magic within Caer roiled like a seething volcano seeking release.

Dana's stern voice proclaimed, "We await your chant, Sister!"

Internally, Roisin offered, *"Nemhain's chant will not accomplish what she believes, child. You must be prepared, for the moment she understands, her fury will be horrible. She will strike us with as much torture as she can bring to bear before she seeks to kill."*

Nemhain's eyes flicked down across the curve of the great mound again, still searching for the doorway between worlds, her chant beginning softly, then rising in mingled cadence with Adrian's continued song--the lyricism of each set against that of the other.

Come join together, pow'rs old.	Bring thunder and fire to dance upon us.
Fix the spells as they told.	Bring gale to speak of our lives.
Heat and dance with magic fold,	Join strength upon strength to foster our purpose.
Pow'r now gained, now must hold.	Grant us the power, grant us the prize.
Fairy realm of magic mists,	Bring thunder and fire to dance upon us.
To Slievgall'ion life affix.	Bring gale to speak of our lives.
Take us, show us, let us see,	Join strength upon strength to foster our purpose.
Abundant beauty ever be.	Grant us the power, grant us the prize.

Overhead, jagged tongues of lightning emblazoned the dark and churning purple sky. Another mighty flash heralded an explosion of light, its intense brilliance engulfing Caer. Her eyes snapped shut, and yet the illumination near blinded her--not a light exterior to her, she realized, but emanating from her. The songs had served to unite the full measure of Dana and Roisin's powers; uniting them, too, with whatever strength and magic Caer possessed. She prayed it would be enough for whatever the two souls planned next.

A sudden intense snap abruptly returned control of her body to Caer. With it came Dana's guarded, *"Nemhain will sense it immediately, should I set the way's location. She'll not read the signature of your magic as readily, especially since she has already deemed you to be no threat."*

Roisin added softly, *"I am holding the gateway closed until your will determines its placement. You possess the strength. Set the way quickly, before she understands what is being done. If we enter the gateway without her, we may yet keep both worlds safe."*

Caer's decision was instinctive, the pale, flicking outline of a crystalline canopy arching above her and their small company. In another explosion of light, the canopy firmed, supported by two crystalline pillars. Within the glistening opening, tiny tendrils of green sprouted from the ground, writhing upwards as they grew. In less than a single exhale, the tendrils spread outward in every direction, blanketing the summit and upper slope in rich green.

Emer gasped. "We are within the way! The sisters have set it around us!"

The hiss of Nemhain's shocked inhale was followed by her screech. "No! Not possible!" Cloak and gown billowing, she leaped from her lintel perch, her glowing eyes fixed with murderous intent on Caer. "The child cannot make the gateway!"

Tine charged and whirled to meet her, swinging his sword in a broad, ringing, upward curve, catching Nemhain as she swept down from the great cairn. Abrupt, strangled silence stole the air from her lungs. And then gurgling death took her, her body crumpling to the ground with a thud. The chill of Nemhain's soundless scream as her soul was ripped from its vessel might have frozen Caer's heart, had the throbbing power within her not held such intense heat.

Adrian, she sensed, longed to use the sundering of Nemhain's soul from her body to cast the curse of banishment, but he was bound to the singing of his song, unable to release it until death took him, or until Dana and Roisin closed or shattered the gateway.

"You cannot win! You haven't the strength to keep me out. Not while you hold the gate's position!"

Agony exploded as Nemhain's fury smote Caer's every molecule. Terror rolled through Dana and Roisin while Caer fought to see through the searing pain. Within her now roiled another consciousness, virulent, vile, and vengeful. Nemhain had joined with them, her outrage focused, her energy feeding on the powers of her sisters. In the night's thickening mists, Caer watched with alarm as a faint blue charge extended out from her, guided by Nemhain's murderous intent, reaching for Adrian. If the Dark Heart destroyed Adrian and controlled her sisters, she might force them to hold the way open. Too long open, and the strength of magic flowing from Slievgall'ion would pulse with too much power. Instead of breathing life back into Earth, it would sweep around the globe, destroying everything it touched.

"Brandon!" Struggling to overcome the vice of the Dark Heart's hold, Caer pulled together her fragmenting consciousness, cautiously setting up what barrier she could manage between her mind and Nemhain's torture of her sisters. *"Brandon!"* she beseeched.

Jumping, he spun on her, eyes wild.

"The gun! Bran, use the gun!"

Confused and frantic, his gaze darted around, seeking for a clear target in the mayhem pressing against the ring of Alainn who fought for control in their diminishing circle.

"On me, Bran! Use the gun on me! A clean shot. Quick. Straight into my heart."

Horrified, his eyes locked on Caer's, his hand fumbling with and nearly dropping his weapon.

"Please, Bran. Nemhain has joined with us. She is inside me! She will destroy us all! The only way to stop her is to force her from my body. Remember what was said--that death tears the soul from the body. We must tear Nemhain's from mine."

Still, he hesitated. Grasses and seedlings were cropping up all across the landscape, growing at an alarming rate. Clashing warriors dropped their battle, scrambling to jump away from shrubs and trees that were shooting upwards.

"Now, Bran! If we are to save Earth, if we are to save most of humanity, you must do as I ask."

"I am with you," Adrian whispered.

Brandon took reluctant aim. Grim-faced, he fired.

Through the rending torture swelled a cacophony of voices, their shouted words a storm of unintelligible sound. Only the pain registered. A torment that lasted forever, tearing...scorching... rending. And then there was nothing. No light. No sensations. Only silence in a black abyss.

"Caer!"

Sound? Was there sound in death, then?

"Caer! You must go back!"

Not sound. More a disturbance. It rippled, urgent in its insistence. Dimly, a shape appeared. A body. From a great height, Caer looked down on it, near translucent pale in its stillness. It bore a strange familiarity, though she couldn't think why.

"You can do this! If you can see your body, reach out. Touch it. Do this. For me."

Another ripple joined the urging. *"You must act now, and with purpose, child. There will be no more chances after this. We cannot hold back Nemhain's banishment spell for long."*

A thin, faint shimmer stretched out from where she hovered. As it grew in intensity, it coiled downward, a blue-white filament, pulsing, irrepressible desire guiding it. A hunger as Caer had never known pushed the delicate strand toward the distant body. As they touched, there came a shock of biting ice that lasted but a fraction of an instant, followed by a bird's breath of a breeze that supplanted the cold with gnawing heat. Throbbing red, now, the filament expanded, dragging her down...down...down...

"Stay awake, Caer. Stay with us. Concentrate. Call on your gift. Begin the healing."

55

Consciousness came as a gossamer thing. Wispy snatches of voices occasionally sifted through, as did impressions of warmth. Sometimes, the gentle touch of a hand lifted her head as cool liquid trickled across her lips. Fleeting moments filled with fuzzy puzzlement followed. Did death allow the senses to continue?

The dark emptiness that wrapped such moments gave way, at last, to the prolonged thrum of quiet voices, their murmured discussion seeming more substantial than before. So, too, did the weight of soft blankets. Caer's fingers closed weakly on their thickness. Blankets. In the afterlife? An uncertain flutter of her eyelids did nothing to resolve the question, inviting only a thin suggestion of illumination beneath them. Still, the faint light sent a roll of throbbing ache across her forehead and deep into her temples.

"I didn't expect death to hurt." The rasping croak startled her, the sound too strange to be her own voice. Yet the dry scratch it left in her throat suggested that it must be. Pain and the ability to speak... "Am I not dead?"

"Not at last check, though you have given us ample cause for concern."

Tentatively, Caer blinked into the light, a more potent throbbing her reward. Mercifully, it remained at a less-than-nauseating level. The unaccustomed brightness, however, left her eyes tear-filled, her vision blurred, and her brain struggling to make sense of the wash of indigo in front of her face. As the haze cleared, she ventured a hesitant upward scan.

Emer smiled. "Welcome back."

"Not dead," Caer rasped again. It took some time for the truth of the statement to work through the aching sludge in her head. She required several more seconds of murky considerations before realizing she lay on a bed in a room that smelled of woodfire and herbs.

Her brow dared a minor furrow, her tongue seeking fruitlessly to moisten her parched mouth as she struggled to sit. Not the wisest of moves, sitting. The effort slammed her head with a more serious hammering and added a searing stab to her chest for good measure.

A glint of silver edged into her watery view. Dylan's crisp command of, "Lie still!" was punctuated by his grip of her shoulders as he eased her back.

She made no attempt to fight him, staying utterly motionless for several uncomfortable breaths before trying to speak again. "I remember a...a fight. A battle." The surge of imagery sucked Caer's shallow breath from her. Glinting weapons; warriors pressed in tight combat; cries of challenge and screams of dying; bodies crumpled in thick pools of gore. So, too, came the flash of Brandon's mortified face, his anguished acceptance, and... The pain in her chest seared more sharply.

"He shot me." The words strangled out in a winded rasp. "Brandon. I told him to. Didn't I tell him to?"

"You pretty much broadcast the request," Emer sniffed. "Good thing Nemhain remained preoccupied with her sisters. Good thing, too, that Brandon didn't hesitate any longer. In the end, he saved all our skins with that one bullet. Thankfully, he was at point blank range. The poor man was shaking so hard, I doubt he could have hit the broad side of a Perimeter Ship, otherwise."

"Why..." Caer tried to lick her lips again, her tongue as dry as her mouth. "Why am I not dead?"

"You were," Dylan answered "You transmigrated."

She died. Death claimed her but did not keep her. The disjointed concepts rattled through Caer's pounding skull for what seemed an age before understanding clicked into place. Her soul found another body. Whose? She prayed it belonged to no one she knew."

Commanding her hands to rise from the bedcovers, she gave them a worried scrutiny, the effort proving more laborious than expected. "Whose...whose body did I take?" The scraping of her question across her throat added to the continued hammering of her head; her tentative breaths contributing to the burn in her chest. "I should have looked for one that hurts less."

Emer offered an apologetic shrug. "Goes with the territory, I'm afraid. It can be as agonizing for a soul to settle in a new vessel as it is to be ripped from the old one. The acquired body, after all, generally suffered some serious damage. Otherwise, its previous occupant would still be within." A grin stole across her face as she turned and slipped from Caer's sight. Caer shifted her head just enough to find Emer taking up a cup from a small table in the center of the room.

"Dylan," she continued, "insisted on coaxing you back into your original housing, given that it was available. Not that it would matter all that much to him. I believe he would flirt with you, even if you wore an alien's body. Well, maybe not if you wore Nemhain's."

A shudder took Caer at the thought of finding herself 'wearing' Nemhain's corpse.

Returning to the bedside, Emer held out the cup. "Here, dear. Drink this. It will help."

Dylan lifted Caer's shoulders, sitting behind her and propping her against him as she took the offering. The liquid was warm, the herbal aroma pleasant, though it tasted of minerals and alcohol.

"A good decision, I'd say," Emer went on. "Having you back in your familiar haunt, so to speak. The damage to your body amounted to that single gunshot. Allowed for a concentration of efforts to heal that one area. You're mending well, too. It'll just take your brain a little while to recognize that fact and cut off the confused misfiring of pain signals." She nodded at the cup as Caer finished with it and handed it back. "That little concoction is my favorite for speeding the process along. Give yourself a minute or two and you'll feel almost good as new." She hesitated, passing a scowl from Caer to Dylan and back again. "That doesn't mean, however, that you should bound from bed and go charging around the premises. You'll need to take it easy for a few days while you regain your strength."

Emer was right about the brew. The pain was lifting and her head clearing. At least it cleared enough for her to become aware of the lace tickling the backs of her hands. The lace, Caer discovered, was attached to the long sleeves of a soft, ivory-colored dressing gown.

"Uhm... Where did this come from?"

"Compliments of our hosts."

A second 'uhm' followed as Caer fumbled with the gown's scooped neckline. Pulling it out, she peered down her front for some indication of the fatal wound. She found nothing. Not even so much as a scar. "Why isn't there a hole...or a set of stitches...or something?"

"Like I said, dear, you're healing remarkably well. You can thank yourself for part of that. Once you were breathing again, Dylan kept you conscious long enough for you to begin the process from within. Only for a handful of minutes, mind you. Still, it provided a decent start for the Healers. They really are excellent."

"Don't let her play humble," Dylan interjected, one hand gesturing out from behind Caer toward a blanket-draped chaise along the wall between a closed door and a pot-bellied stove that occupied one corner. "Em invested more time and effort with you than all the other Healers combined. She hasn't been out of this room for more than a few minutes at a time since we arrived here."

"Thanks. I..." Caer's lips pursed. "What Healers? Where are Ian and Blath?"

Emer drew a measured breath. "They...died in the battle, Caer. The Healers Dylan refers to are the ones who responded to Tine's call for aid. They appeared almost the instant we arrived."

Caer's mind stumbled. Blath and Ian. Gone. She had little recollection of what had taken place around her once Dylan used his gift to awaken the sisters.

Emer glanced away, her voice soft with sorrow. "Blath and Ian fought with every spell they could conjure. Their shielding, though, was weakened by their fatigue and further strained by the barrage of attacks. They had no reserves left to deflect Madadh's banishing when his kill spells broke through. Maired is also gone."

Falling silent for several seconds, Emer at last shook herself and shifted the topic. "As soon we were confident that you would live, the Healers, here, saw to your comfort, as well as to your continued mending. You'll meet them soon enough, I'm sure. So." She paused again. "How's the pain? All gone, yet?"

Caer blinked. Yes. The pain was gone. If only the weight of grief would go with it. Sucking on her lower lip, she nodded.

"Good. Shall we try sitting all the way up, then?"

The lightheadedness that accompanied the motion was blessedly short-lived, and after a few halting breaths, Caer dared a more extensive survey of the room, noting that the illumination came from perhaps a dozen wall-mounted sconces, each holding a very fat candle. Nor was there more to the room's furnishings than she already noted, beyond two straight-backed chairs at the table.

"What is this place? How long have I been here? Is the battle over?"

No answer was immediately forthcoming. With Dylan still sitting behind her, Caer couldn't see his expression, but suspected from his silence that it was likely as guarded as Emer's.

"It's been six days since the battle," Emer said, at last, taking her time to stroll back to the table, there depositing the cup next to a stoppered bottle. "When you began snoring last night, I expected you might wake today. I sent to the others moments ago that you've done so."

"Snoring!"

"Very daintily," Dylan chuckled. Relinquishing his support of her, he rose, moving around to face her. His amusement, expressed in that oh-so-familiar half-smile, did nothing to assuage her indignation.

Leaning against the wall with his arm's folded, Dylan's one-sided grin broadened when a soft tap at the room's door was followed by a meekly queried, "My ladies? My lord?"

"Ugh," Emer groaned. "That didn't take long. Word travels fast around here. Just brace yourself, dear. These people will reverence you all the way into next week and back." Sighing, she called, "Come."

Come they did--a small flock of women fluttering like so many anxious birds, their long gowns of creamy yellows sweeping about them as they produced a flurry of curtsies, then scuttled to business. One carried a tray with a large silver decanter and three silver goblets. Setting them on the table, she collected the bottle and cup, then dipped another series of curtsies as she shuffled aside to allow a second woman forward. This one deposited a tray bearing a domed cover, also of silver. Removal of the cover revealed a steaming bowl of stew and a small loaf of bread, the aromas of which hit Caer with near faint-worthy hunger. Cover in hand, the second woman promptly joined the first, their heads bowed as they again dipped their obeisance several times, each shuffling back to hover near the door. Neither appeared to be in any hurry to leave, however, peeking surreptitious glimpses of Caer.

A third woman had, in the meantime, flitted to the chaise, plucking up the blankets and replacing them with fresh, while a fourth laid a pair of boots and a neatly folded stack of clothing on the seat. Finally, a fifth and older woman bobbed her way forward, discomfort showing in the creases of her face at the curtsies she attempted. "Lord Stoirm asked that I bring these." Her eyes darted a nervous and awed scan of Caer before she turned to Emer, extending a trio of black cloaks. Emer accepted them, shooting a glower at Dylan as she laid them over the end of Caer's bed.

"Do my ladies or my lord..." The woman executed an additional round of curtsies to each of them. "...require our assistance for anything further?"

Emer shook her head. "Nothing more is needed, Aster. And please! Do stand up! How many times must I tell you, all this bowing is ridiculous?"

Looking a little nonplused, Aster straightened, only to add a final slight dip as she concluded, "If you need nothing more..."

"Nothing," Emer repeated. "You are most considerate. Thank you, Aster."

With a short, dismissive wave of her hand, Aster gestured the others away, joining them as they flocked back through the door with as much bobbing up and down as had accompanied their entrance.

Caer gaped after the women. "What in the name of eternity was that all about?"

"Royalty," Emer huffed. "They're treating us like royalty. Very annoying, really."

Dylan shook his head, chuckling again. "You know you're wasting your breath. They aren't going to stop the nonsense just because you ask them to."

"Why?" Caer turned a bewildered glance between the two. "Who are they?"

"Explanations later, dear." Emer pointed to the table. "Right now, you need some nourishment."

Dylan also waved aside her questions, insisting, instead, on helping Caer to the nearest of the chairs and taking the time to wrap a blanket around her shoulders. Seeing that she was comfortably situated, he poured a goblet of wine, holding it slightly aloft as he made a grandly mocking flourish of a deep bow. Drink in hand, he headed for the door. "I will leave you in Em's good company, for now. I'll return to collect you shortly. In the meantime, eat and dress."

Despite the magnitude of her initial hunger, the stew and bread proved far more than Caer's stomach could handle in one sitting.

A minor battle of wills, however, was required to convince Emer of the fact.

"Very well," Emer conceded at last. "Perhaps a little at a time is best. If you're certain you can't manage another bite, then come, let's get you dressed."

The clothes were thicker and a different style than Havenhall had provided upon their arrival. Their comfort, however, was unquestionable, the linen shirt and brocade over jacket loosely form-fitting and falling to mid-calf. The linen-lined wool leggings fit snuggly and tucked neatly into the soft black boots.

Emer cast an appraising eye over Caer. "The clothiers worked night and day, getting these ready for us, and were amused at your measurements. They haven't, as yet, seen you, and think you must be a very skinny young child. A few of the excellent meals, here, should help resolve the skinny issue, I think. Assuming, of course, that you lay off any serious exertions for a while. Like the use of magic. That's off limits until you're stronger. And then you're going to need a lot of basic instruction."

Not use her magic, indeed! Caer had every intention of calling it up and at the earliest opportunity. How else could she sort out her capabilities? Nor did she want anyone hovering over her to instruct her like she was ten years old. She could work it all out for herself. Biting her lip, she darted a glance at Emer, hoping the thought was not inadvertently broadcast. If Emer picked up on it, however, she gave no indication.

"I said it before," Em smiled. "And I'll say it again. That color truly suits you."

Caer blinked down at her attire. The rich brocade of her jacket was the deepest jade she'd ever seen and was woven through with gold, adding far more depth and elegance than the shirt she'd been given when they first arrived. Still, she wondered if the people of Havenhall were going to insist she wear something in green all the time. Lips pursed, she reconsidered, taking in the intense blue-black indigo and silver of Emer's jacket. Dylan's, she recalled, was silver and a dark purple amethyst.

"I'm assuming," she sighed. "That we're expected at another Council or something. Or we wouldn't be so extravagantly dressed. Adrian and the others will be there, won't they?" A sudden hollow opened in Caer's insides. "They're all right, aren't they? I mean..."

Emer's brow creased. "No Council, dear. At least not today, though one is being planned, I'm told. And yes. Adrian and the others are fine." The crease of her brow deepened a little. "We're just taking you on a little outing, this afternoon. Against my better judgment, I might add. I think we should wait a day or two before trotting you outside. Stoirm, however, insisted that you...well...see things for yourself as soon as possible. And Dylan's no help. He's siding with the Alainn."

"See what things?"

Emer dodged the query with, "Del, Jase, and Niall will meet us there. Starn..." Her words cut off. When she continued several heartbeats later, it was with a subtle mix of anxiety and disappointment. "Starn isn't here. He went away two days after we arrived. No one's seen him since."

"Went away? Where? When's he coming back?"

Emer shrugged, which only added to Caer's dismay. Why would he leave? He didn't even stay to make sure she would wake.

Seeking to cover her distress with a short, quick gesture at Emer, she posed, "So, if we're not being summoned to a Council, why are we wearing...what did you call these before? The colors of the Orders?"

"They want everyone to understand our rank and importance, I suppose."

"Who wants everyone to know? Who's everyone? And what sort of importance?"

Once again Emer sidestepped Caer's question, nodding at her clothes. "Hope those are warm enough. At least they're better than what they wanted to put us in. They seem to think we should be wearing long, luxurious gowns. That's all very well for Del. She tends to fancy that sort of thing. You wouldn't believe how much effort it took for me to argue them into allowing the two of us to wear pants and boots, though."

Caer's exasperation was mounting by the second. Who expected and why did they expect it?

"Hey!" Dylan called, rapping on the door. "Aren't you ladies done, yet? Mother just sent to me that they're waiting."

"She's dressed," Emer returned with an edge. "But you know damn well I don't think she's ready to be prancing around in the cold."

Dylan cracked the door and peered in. Assured that Caer was, indeed, dressed, he pushed the door to and regarded her with a shake of his head. "You've gone from being the size of a sparrow to that of a half-starved wren."

Caer felt her face flush and shoved her lower lip out. "I'm not half starved! And my size is just fine, thank you."

"Well," he grinned, "Mother and everyone else around here is going to be stuffing you with no end of edibles to flesh you out a little, regardless. In the meantime, I'll see what I can do to keep you from blowing away in a stiff breeze." Fetching the cloaks from the bed, he handed one across to Emer and draped another around Caer before donning the last.

Caer slumped, surprised by the weight of the wrap. Sensing Emer's concerned scrutiny, she straightened. "So. Where are we off to?"

Emer's fists went to her hips, her glare leveled on Dylan. "I hope you know, you're doing this without my approval."

Dylan lifted the hood of Caer's cloak to cover her head. "It's been duly noted--more than once." The next moment, the room blinked out.

The shock of the thin sunlight did nothing to warm the frigid air against Caer's face. Its icy bite knifed into her lungs with her gasp, her immediate exhale producing a swirl of pale mist. Underfoot, the deep, crusty snow crunched as she staggered in her surprise.

Dylan's arm was instantly around her, righting her. "Steady, there."

"Where..." It was all she could verbalize as she squinted into the late afternoon light to take in the large, circular plateau where they stood. A good hundred meters away, at its center, blazed a large bonfire, sparks dancing merrily in the gusty air currents. Wooden benches ringed it. Only a few, however, were occupied. Instead, a large number of people were gathered in several clusters between the benches and the fire, talking and laughing. The rise and fall of their conversations on the sharp air suddenly stilled as everyone turned curious glances to the newly arrived threesome. Uncomfortable under their scrutiny, Caer sidled closer to Dylan, grateful when the buzz of chatter resumed once more, despite the continued glances from the strangers.

Still braced within the reassurance of Dylan's supporting arm, Caer steadied her breathing and made a more thorough scan of the plateau, noting the curve of a massive stone bench that ran an unbroken circumference around the plateau's edge. Fully backing the bench was a wall just high enough to serve as support for sitting without blocking one's view of what Caer guessed was a precipitous drop to a valley floor, while all around rose the white peaks of great and jagged mountains. She didn't recall this being part of Slieve na Calliagh's landscape. Even the hill's night mists couldn't disguise something like this!

"You'll find it warmer over here," Del called, rising from her perch on one of the benches nearest the fire. Sunlight glinted off a patch of the rich garnet and white brocade gown that peeked out from between the edges of her dark cloak as she glided across to meet them, her blond ringlets fluttering around her face. The hair color and fair complexion were all that remained of Brenna Cowl's appearance, the features having settled in Fedel'ma's distinct high cheekbones and finely defined nose. The combination was most striking.

"I'm delighted to see you up and about, child," Del proclaimed, hugging Caer. "Come back to the bench with me. We shouldn't keep you standing."

Before Caer managed another step, however, Brandon swooped across, grabbing her up in a back-popping squeeze. "You're alive!" he whooped. "They said you were, but they wouldn't let me see you. You really are, though!"

"Not for long if you don't let me breathe," Caer wheezed.

"Oh." Chagrin chased across his face as he gingerly set her feet back to the ground, grasping her shoulders until he was certain she wouldn't topple. "Sorry. I didn't mean to..."

"It's all right, Bran," she beamed, giddy with relief at seeing him. "You're all right, then? You weren't injured or anything?"

"Bit of a scrape and a knock to the head was all. The Healers had me fit again in a heartbeat."

Niall crept up to stand beside him. Like Bran, the boy wore the bronze of the Sensitives beneath his cloak. The color was far less garish set against his unruly red curls than the shocking yellow he'd worn before. Fidgeting, he folded in an awkward bow.

Caer moaned. "Emer's right. Please don't do that, Niall. No one needs to do that."

The boy straightened uncertainly, venturing a nervous, "I can't believe what you accomplished, my lady! Everyone's talking about it, still."

"What? My dying and returning?" Her eyes flicked to Dylan. "I'm not the only one ever to do it, you know. Nor did I manage it by myself. I vaguely recall a fair amount of guidance."

"You accomplished far more than your soul's transmigration, Caer." There was wonderfully familiar musical lilt to the statement.

Shooting an expectant survey in the direction of the fire, Caer spotted Adrian, Stoirm, and Tine striding toward her, their cloaks tossed back from their shoulders. The sun's waning light shimmered off Tine's topaz shirt and skittered across Stoirm's ornately woven waistcoat of topaz and gold. Adrian, too, wore an elegant waistcoat, the silver threads embroidered through its onyx silk reflecting like glistening strands of a spider's web.

With a squeal of delight, Caer dove at Adrian, throwing her arms up around his neck. "I was told you'd gone away! I was afraid I might not see you anytime soon. Where did you go? Why didn't you stay here with the rest of us?"

The subtle hint of sorrow cast a long shadow about her friend, sending a momentary chill over her enthusiasm. His smile, however, was warmer than she could ever remember as he lifted her in a gentle embrace. "I left you in excellent hands," he said with a nod at Emer. The compliment sent a crimson flush across the woman's cheeks. Depositing Caer back to the ground, he contended, "And there were things needing to be done."

"My lady," Stoirm acknowledge as her gaze sought him out.

Her jaw shot forward when she realized the Alainn was about to offer a bow. "Don't you dare!" she rumbled, wrapping him in a hug. "Didn't I say I didn't want anyone doing that?"

"Ah!" he huffed. "I guess we will save the decorum for later, then."

"How about never!" Cocking her head at Tine, she emphasized the point with, "And don't you even think about it, either!"

A grin brightened the young man's countenance, adding an extra depth to the allure of his bright blue eyes. His Alainn features set off by his rich, dark skin was turning a number of ladies' heads, though he seemed to take no notice.

"I'm glad to see you recovered, my lady. We feared for you, at first, that you might not have the strength left for your transmigration to hold. I'm only sorry that I cannot stay. I should like the opportunity to get to know you better. It will have to keep for another time, however, as I must take my leave for a while." Turning, Tine granted a crisp nod to his father and grandfather. "I will get word to you as soon as we know something." With an additional nod toward Del, he added, "And as soon as I locate your great granddaughter, I will send her to you." Then, with his hand gripping his sword hilt, he was gone.

Stoirm gestured toward the benches near the fire. "Please, Caer. Fedel'ma is correct. You should come and sit."

She held her ground, staring uneasily at the spot where Tine had been. "What word does he need to get back to you? We won, didn't we?"

"Come and sit down, first," Dylan insisted.

Grudgingly, she acquiesced. Once seated, she fixed her friends with a determined frown. Between their apparent reticence to answer her earlier questions and Tine's abrupt departure, along with the constant curious stares from the strangers all around, she was feeling more and more that something was profoundly amiss.

"Alright," she said. "I'm sitting. Now I want some explanations." With a vague gesture toward the various knots of individuals whose gazes seemed drawn to her like matter to a black hole, and fearful that if she didn't get everything asked at once, someone would stop her, she blurted, "Who are all these people? Why do some of them keep bowing to us like spring-loaded dolls? We're obviously not at Slieve na Calliagh, and I don't think we're anywhere near Havenhall, so where, exactly, are we? I didn't know Del had a great granddaughter. Why does she need locating? Why is Tine still wearing a sword, and why was he in such a hurry to leave? Something's gone wrong, hasn't it? The gateway didn't close in time. Nemhain got away, or..."

Stoirm raised a hand, his gaze taking in the curious stares from the gathered throng. "Give us a moment's reprieve, Caer. Some of these people are the Healers who've taken such care of you. They want to assure themselves that you are fully recovered. Some are, well, for lack of a better term, priestesses. They are our current hosts. Others are dignitaries who've been called for an upcoming Council. Grant them some indication of your good health and your appreciation for their hospitality."

Caer hesitated, uncertain how she might accomplish the deed.

Rising, she stepped in front of Dylan, using her cloak to mask the fact that she braced against him. Feeling stable, she offered a deep curtsy, her gesture accepted with delighted cheers.

"Nicely done," Dylan offered, covertly assisting as she straightened.

"Alright," she repeated, returning her scrutiny to Stoirm and Adrian. "I assume from the landscape that Earth has recovered to a fair degree. What damage did we do? And where did Tine go?"

Stoirm's hesitation was fleeting, albeit heavily weighted. "You saw for yourself the eruption of life at our feet as we stood on Slieve na Calliagh."

"I saw," she acknowledged.

"Earth's regeneration was begun."

There was a universe full of things left unsaid in that statement. Darting a confused glimpse at the surrounding slopes, she murmured, "Was begun?"

Adrian indicated the nearest section of the low, encircling wall. "If you're up to walking a little more, come tell me what you see."

"Mountains," Caer replied. Shivering set in as she moved away from the great blaze, though whether it was due to leaving the fire's warmth or the prickling anticipation of some ominous revelation, she couldn't say. Pulling her cloak tighter, she gave silent thanks that Dylan followed so close behind, blocking some of the brisk gusts as she trudged after Adrian. The icy crunch beneath her feet prompted, "And a lot of snow."

Reaching the wall-backed bench, Adrian gestured to what lay below the plateau's edge. "And there. What do you see?"

The lengthening shadows of fading daylight did not hide the dense vegetation covering the lower flanks of the plateau's steep grade. Nor did it conceal the vegetation that extended across the valley floor and up the lower mountain slopes. She sucked in. "Trees! A whole jungle!"

"Forests," Adrian corrected with quiet amusement. "Wrong climate, here, for a jungle. There are some immense ones, though, further to the south." Pointing to an appendage of land that jutted out about midway down the slope behind which the sun was setting, he asked, "Can you see, just over there?"

Caer squinted at the shadows overtaking the outcrop. A building of pale gray stone was all but lost in the darkening drifts surrounding it.

"That's the hall from which you just came. A courtyard sets on the other side. Spring is only beginning to call up a few blossoms through the snow, there." Adrian nodded again at the valley. "The season's change is a little more evident below. In daylight, you can see the pale green indicating the new leaf sprouts on the deciduous trees."

Caer turned her gaze from the building to the thickening darkness of the valley, trying to make everything compute properly in her head. Spring. She understood the concept of Earth's seasons from her studies of the planet and its ancient civilizations. Spring was the time of rebirth that followed a period of cold dormancy in the planet's age-old migration around its sun. The seasons were all but forgotten by contemporary Earthers. So desolate had their world become that few ventured beyond the safety of the domes. Here, now, the cycle of rebirth could once again be witnessed.

"Is it like this everywhere?" she breathed, settling at last on the bench, her eyes still scanning the panorama. "Trees and the beginning of blossoms and...and you said there are even jungles!"

Adrian nodded. "Life is everywhere, Caer. Even in the deepest deserts."

"And...and all of this was brought about, just by opening the gateway?" She swallowed, shaking her head. "I'll have to admit, I didn't understand what to expect. But this... For all of Earth to recover so much so quickly!"

Adrian shifted, pointing toward a section of the sky above the slopes opposite the last glimmers of sunglow. "Look there."

At first, Caer thought he meant for her to observe the faint suggestions of stars, the fading light allowing their distant shimmer to peek out now and again from behind a fluff of gathering clouds.

"A little higher," he directed.

Her breath snagged mid inhale. Hazed by some of the thin, higher clouds, were clustered three moons. Caer watched, transfixed, as the clouds separated enough to reveal them in their full glory, clearly defined against the encroaching twilight. The first and largest was a pale and glistening blue-white. The second, smallest, but riding highest in the sky, held a soft cast of rose. The last, lowest in the sky and partially occluded by the shadow of the larger moon, was a deep blood red.

"I thought... I thought Earth had only one moon."

"Only one." Seating himself beside her, Dylan took her hand, his grip firm. "This isn't Earth, Caer. This is Slievgall'ion."

For several long seconds, Caer sat quite still, her mouth open, her mind reeling. Why would they come here? It was Earth she needed to see--Earth where Stoirm said life was returning.

Dylan's hands squeezed hers, though his hold couldn't stop her sudden trembling. "Just before the gateway was destroyed, those of us within it were blasted through to this side. We can't go back, Caer. This is where we are."

"And..." She could barely get the words out, so tight was her chest. "And Earth? What's become of ...?"

"We don't know with any certainty," Dylan admitted. "Thanks to you, the magic of this world was able to flush through her. We all witnessed as much when life took sudden hold beneath our feet."

A sickening twist strangled Caer's throat and stomach. Withdrawing her hand from Dylan's, she fidgeted with the edge of her cloak, struggling to catch her breath. "Thanks to me." She was shaking her head. She couldn't seem to stop shaking her head. "I allowed the way to open. But..." She bit anxiously at her lip, trying to force her brain to consider the possibilities. "But, what if I didn't protect the two sisters long enough for them to close it in time? Thanks to me, Earth and everyone on it could well be dead. Everything...everyone...destroyed."

"If that were so," Stoirm said, "I believe the backlash of the destructive energy would have carried through the gateway. I doubt we'd have survived long enough to escape to this side. In truth, I believe Slievgall'ion might well have been destroyed, as well."

"You believe. You doubt." Caer managed a long, shuddered inhale, breathing it out with, "But you don't know." It was an automatic reaction, reaching for her necklace. Perhaps its magic held the answers she sought; perhaps it would come to life and whisk them all back to where they belonged. Instead, the charm fell cold and lifeless in her hand. The shock of its emptiness was redoubled by another stark realization. The souls of the sisters no longer whispered within her.

The impact was as overwhelming as the question of Earth's fate. Despite the fact that, for most of her life, Caer had been unaware of the two souls she harbored, their absence now left a profound and frightening void. She was alone; alone with the responsibility for having opened the way one last time; alone with the fear that she'd failed Dana and Roisin, and with them, the whole of humanity that existed on the other side of the gateway. What if...because of her... everything had gone horribly wrong?

"Caer." Stoirm's reassuring tone drew her eyes to him. "It took tremendous strength of will for you to accept the only means of casting the sisters from you. But you managed it. We are still alive. No repercussions swept Slievgall'ion. Trust that Earth survives, as well."

"I need to know." Her voice choked, her eyes filling with tears. "I need to know that I didn't destroy an entire world. That I didn't destroy everything else with it."

"Such absolute knowledge is beyond us. And regardless of what has befallen, the fault is not yours."

"What of Roisin's prescience? She would have foreseen such a calamity." Frantically, Caer sought for some fragment of dream left over from Roisin's presence.

"Roisin's gift was exceptional," Stoirm agreed. "That she foresaw such a distant future as to both forewarn her of Earth's demise, and to find the potential for its rebirth attests to that. Unlike other gifts, however, where lifetimes of practice impart the bearer with varying degrees of control, prescience cannot be commanded at will. Not by anyone. A seer never knows what they will be shown or when. Roisin never foresaw the final outcome of our efforts, only the possibility of our success."

Fixing her with his steady gaze, he added, "We experienced the beginning of the renewal as we stood on Slieve na Calliagh. That much knowledge is ours. If the rate remained as we witnessed, it undoubtedly caused panic and chaos to sweep around the globe. It could be no more devastating, however, than the mayhem created by Nemhain's invading armies. Primarily Tanai populations, ignorant of the existence of magic—how were they to cope with such attacks? How were they to cope with the realization that magic was also being employed to protect them? It will take generations for humanity to come to terms with such events. Less time, I think, to grasp the new reality of their world, whether it be reborn or otherwise."

Adrian lifted a booted foot to the bench, leaning to rest his arms on his raised knee as he surveyed the distant, silhouetted slopes. "None of us ever expected circumstances to turn out as they have. I make no apologies, though. What Roisin foresaw was a terrible wrong wrought upon an undeserving world, a wrong for which she also brought the hope of redemption. And we acted on that. It would have been a great and vile sin, I think, for us to have done nothing. Whatever the consequences, whether we wish it or not, Caer, Earth's fate no longer lies with us. That does not mean, however, that we are left with no difficulties, no responsibilities to address."

"Among those difficulties," Emer remarked, "is trying to keep these people from fawning all over us."

"Yeah." Bran muttered from the periphery where he stood with

Del and Niall. "About that. We pop into existence, here, bringing with us the remnants of a raging bloody war and destroying the only means for any of us to return to the other side of the gateway, and these people treat us as though we've just done something magnificent. They should be damned furious. I mean...they have no more way of getting back to their places of origin, now, than we do."

Adrian gave a quiet huff. "The last group of people to migrate through the gateway to Slievgall'ion was more than a thousand years ago. From all I've learned in the past few days, less than a handful of those from that last migration still live. For those who dwell here, now, this is the only home they know."

Brandon's brow shot up. "I thought Witches could live forever, compliments of this...this returning business that you do."

"Not all of those who came were Witches, Mr. Jase. Nor does the curse that bound our souls to transmigration appear to hold in this realm. I suspected it might be so, almost from the beginning, though Nemhain refused to believe it. My visits to various locations these last few days, appear to bear out my suspicions. Even among the Tanai, here, life can be long. But none, Witch or otherwise, carry any indication of their souls transmigrating. The only connection remaining between the people of Slievgall'ion and Earth, now, is one of myth, legend, and superstition. Mingled within the stories and cultures of these peoples, are reflections of some of the practices and beliefs brought over by their ancestors." Adrian gestured at his waistcoat. "Like the designation of colors to certain Orders of magic. And they still practice many of the same rituals for certain types of holidays, though the reasons behind most of the practices are lost, replaced by new sets of mythologies."

His face clouded. "Part of those myths involves the conversion of the three sisters to goddesses. It's nonsense, of course. You'll find it impossible to convince anyone here of that, though. The belief that we delivered their 'goddesses' back to this world is the reason they hold us in such high esteem. Caer, especially. There is among the priestesses, here, one whose gift is similar to our Master Dream

Reader's. She lacks his strength. Still, her gift is sufficient for her to read from Caer's fevered dreams the fact that each of the sisters resided within her for a time. Such knowledge the priestess was eager to share with the others."

He was silent for a while. "A peculiar place, Slievgall'ion," he said at last. "What was once magically drawn here from Earth has since been enhanced. The world has become more beautiful over the ages. And perhaps more dangerous."

Emer cocked her head, regarding Adrian. "This isn't your first trip to this world, is it?"

Caer gaped at him, her mind once again reeling as the truth practically battered her over the head. Of course, Adrian had been here before. "You were here at the beginning," she breathed. "You were with the sisters each of the times they came." She held not the slightest doubt that it was so. The sisters might be gone from her, but their memories, she realized, remained, imprinted in the depths of her mind. That's what the priestess had glimpsed in her dreams. It was a frightening revelation. But it was also intriguing.

"The sisters couldn't hold the way open without you," Caer persisted. "Yours was the song...the power that bound their dance. They needed you for both coming and returning to Earth." Her shoulders squared, daring him to deny it. Adrian's lack of response provided all the affirmation she needed.

Emer considered in silence for several seconds, not quite daring to fix Adrian with her stare. "I figured it might be something like that. That you are as old as they."

"Older by a little," Adrian sighed. "Their mother was my aunt, youngest sister to my father."

Sinking onto the bench, Emer's words were barely audible. "Explains a lot. Why I was never able to discern a signature in your magic. It isn't just Madadh who came from a line other than the sisters'. It was you, as well. You're brothers, you and the Mad Dog. I heard you both say it, though I didn't take it as literal at the time.

Neither of you descended from Samhradh and Tar on Tine. Your gifts aren't marked by their lineage."

"The underlying structure of our magic is but a slight variant. Like yours, our magic carries the signature of our line combined with our individual characteristics. Since our lineage is from the brother of Samhradh and from his wife, who descended from one of Samhradh's cousins, our signature is more difficult for you to detect."

"I thought..." Brandon scratched his head. "I thought it was just the sisters' lines that had the ability to transmigrate. How..."

Adrian shrugged. "Roisin's doing. She wove into the curse an attachment to me, knowing that if I returned, I would seek her out. Madadh happened to be with me at the time. Somehow, the spell attached to him, as well."

The wind blowing down from the slopes had stiffened since the sun disappeared, and now carried a sharper bite. Caer pulled the hood of her cloak closer about her face, fearing the bluster might somehow blow her thoughts away. There were so many of them--thoughts--and she wished not to relinquish a single one. How many of the gaps in her life could the sisters' memories fill? How much of her understanding of Adrian and of everything that led to this moment?

"You're shivering," Adrian noted. "Perhaps we should return to the building."

"No," she declared. "Not yet." For a long while, she sat staring between the now night-shrouded mountains and the sky. The stars and the three rising moons blinked from behind the thickening clouds less often, now, though when they did, they took Caer's breath away anew.

It occurred to her gradually that Adrian was singing. Softly. It was a familiar song with the familiar rhythm of sevens and threes. It was the song he wove for the sisters, the one to which they set their dance beneath Slieve na Calliagh's great cairn all those long centuries ago. They stepped the rhythm in a dance of peculiar pattern to open the way between worlds. Stepped it again in varied pattern to hide it from Nemhain. Had Nemhain not betrayed Dana and Roisin, the three sisters and Adrian might have opened the way, here at the last, granting Earth her rebirth without the centuries of bloodshed and death. Instead, the Dark Heart sought to take everything for herself.

"You prevented that," Dylan sent.

Caer nodded. Her fear remained, though--the fear that Earth was destroyed, and that the responsibility lay with her.

"I, too, believe we were successful, Caer."

Again, Caer nodded, her sigh long and deep. At length, she turned to Adrian, cocking her head at him, her question hesitant. "Are you really?"

Adrian's song fell away. "Am I really what?"

"My grandfather. Nemhain said you're my grandfather."

For a moment, she didn't think he would answer.'

"You need several 'greats' ahead of the title," he said at last. "And not from this flesh, certainly But from one of my earliest vessels. My soul, however, does indeed hold that connection. Does it trouble you?"

'Trouble' wasn't the right term. Still, the notion was going to take some getting used to. Adrian. Her friend. Her guardian. Her occasional lover. The singer of magic. The soul of her great, great... whatever...grandfather. She couldn't help wondering if her line lay through his and Roisin, perhaps. They were definitely lovers. But he also bedded Nemhain. The thought of that connection sent a shiver through her. Who knew how many others Adrian had bedded in his unimaginably long existence. The answer to her lineage might well lay within her mind, buried in the memories 'bequeathed' to her by the sisters.

She considered pressing those memories, but deferred the effort for some other time, fearing the flood from three sets of multiple lifetimes. And, yes, Nemhain's memories dwelled there, alongside Dana's and Roisin's. Despite the brevity of her stay within Caer, it was still sufficient to impress the Dark Heart's lifetimes into the back of Caer's awareness. What she needed was a place of privacy and a lot of time before she delved into all those centuries of accumulated thoughts and experiences.

"Where did they go, Adrian?"

His eyes narrowed questioningly.

"The sisters. You said the people here think we brought them back. Did we?"

"In a manner of speaking. Their souls came through with us. As I said before, though, there is no transmigration here. What became of their souls once we reached Slievgall'ion, I can't say. It is the belief of the priestesses, here, that the three sisters are now united with the spirit of this world."

"You keep saying souls can't return, here," Caer frowned. "But I managed it."

Adrian shook his head. "You died within the gateway, Caer. And you returned to your body before we were shunted to this side."

She considered for some time. "They could have lived again, too," she whispered, rubbing her arms, the sense of her emptiness seeping into her very marrow. "Dana and Roisin could have reunited with me. It wasn't so bad."

"Nemhain tried. Dana was able to prevent her accomplishing it--barely." Adrian straightened, rubbing the back of his neck. "Neither Dana nor Roisin, however, would ask that you grant them hosting for all the remaining days of your life." His eyes skimmed once more out across the ghosted nightscape. "Perhaps I'm as much a fool as the priestesses, but I, too, believe that the sisters are joined with this world. Sometimes, even, I think I can sense their awareness."

Caer's fingers curled tightly around her necklace, hoping for some sign, some faint glimmer of them. Again, there was nothing.

"At least..." She licked her lips and vented a nervous sigh. "At least Nemhain can no longer wreak havoc on Earth...or anywhere else."

"Nemhain can't. But that doesn't mean we're without serious concerns." Adrian turned, casting a glance back at the festivities around the fire--laughing, drinking, conversations with curious gazes flashing their direction. "We aren't the only ones who came through, Caer. Anyone within at least fifty meters of us when Jase shot you was sucked into the gateway."

He gestured toward the peak behind which the sun had disappeared. No more light glistened from its crest or along its shoulders, not even that of the stars or moons, the moisture-laden clouds having sealed the night in an ever-deepening gray. "The gateway deposited us up there at the summit. Deposited us, Tine and some of his fellow Alainn, along with Madadh/Ailill, Maura, and a number of their kin and beasts. Fortunately, the Watchers of Slievgall'ion heard my song of opening and recognized it from their legends. They were already preparing to come to us when Tine sent to them that there was a battle and wounded. Madadh/Ailill and Maura and those with them panicked at the sight of so many teleporting to us and scattered down the slopes to the forests.

"Once I was certain you would survive, I set out to pick up their trail. They've gone off in too many directions, though, with no indication of which might lead to Madadh/Ailill or Maura. Tine and his men have been tracking some of their beasts, but have yet to pick up any sign of our real prey." With a weary shake of his head, Adrian finished with, "I spent the past several days traveling from village to village, talking with the Watchers, warning of the danger and advising of the need for a Council."

Fat flakes of snow were beginning to fall. Caer stretched out a hand, allowing several to drift to her palm and melt. Adrian smiled. "Beautiful, isn't it? So is every aspect of Slievgall'ion. So much life, here. Maura and Madadh/Ailill, however, now pose a tremendous threat to this world. All they need is one small stronghold, and they can inflict untold damage." Running a hand over his hair, he breathed in, exhaling a faint groan. "It seems it is our fate--Stoirm's, Tine's and mine--to do as we've always done. We must once again pursue their kind; defend all that we can against their evil."

Caer stiffened. It was because of her that such evil came into this world. She was the one whose actions dragged so many of their enemies into the gateway with her. If there was to be a pursuit, she would be part of it.

Dylan's hand closed on hers again, squeezing it. Emer rose and moved to stand at Adrian's side. "You're not leaving me out of the hunt."

"It's for all of us to do," Dylan confirmed. "Together."

Pronunciation Guide

Aifa – Eef-a

Ailill – Eye-lill

Alainn – Aalin

Amhranai Fearalite – Oerann Faerallchi

Blath Trathonona – Blaa Truhnoonuh

Caer DaDhrga – Kyair Daa Derga

Croi Ag Damsa – Kree Eg Dowsu

Croi Breag – Kree Braeug

Croi Ciuin – Kree Kyooin

Dana – Danna

Fedel'ma – Fe-Dell-maa

Lahm Laidir – Laaoo Laajir

MacFaolan – MacFweelan

Madadh Mire – Madoo Mirri

Nemhain – Noo-wann

Roisin – Roe-ish-Een

Sadbh - Syve

Samhradh – Sow-rooh

Sidra Eirene – Sidrah Ih-Ray-nee

Sinead – Shin-Aid

Slieve Na Calliagh – Slyabh na Calli

Slievgall'ion – Sly-eev-gallion

Stoirm – Sterim

Tanai –Tanee

Tar On Tine – Tar Owin Chinee

Uair Amhain – Ooir u-wann